Agatha Christie is known throughout [illegible]
Her books have sold over a billion copies in English with another billion in foreign languages. She is the most widely published author of all time and in any language, outsold only by the Bible and Shakespeare. She is the author of 80 crime novels and short story collections, 19 plays, and six novels written under the name of Mary Westmacott.

Agatha Christie's first novel, *The Mysterious Affair at Styles*, was written towards the end of the First World War, in which she served as a VAD. In it she created Hercule Poirot, the little Belgian detective who was destined to become the most popular detective in crime fiction since Sherlock Holmes. It was eventually published by The Bodley Head in 1920.

In 1926, after averaging a book a year, Agatha Christie wrote her masterpiece. *The Murder of Roger Ackroyd* was the first of her books to be published by Collins and marked the beginning of an author-publisher relationship which lasted for 50 years and well over 70 books. *The Murder of Roger Ackroyd* was also the first of Agatha Christie's books to be dramatised – under the name *Alibi* – and to have a successful run in London's West End. *The Mousetrap*, her most famous play of all, opened in 1952 and is the longest-running play in history.

Agatha Christie was made a Dame in 1971. She died in 1976, since when a number of books have been published posthumously: the bestselling novel *Sleeping Murder* appeared later that year, followed by her autobiography and the short story collections *Miss Marple's Final Cases*, *Problem at Pollensa Bay* and *While the Light Lasts*. In 1998 *Black Coffee* was the first of her plays to be novelised by another author, Charles Osborne.

THE AGATHA CHRISTIE COLLECTION

The Man in the Brown Suit
The Secret of Chimneys
The Seven Dials Mystery
The Mysterious Mr Quin
The Sittaford Mystery
The Hound of Death
The Listerdale Mystery
Why Didn't They Ask Evans?
Parker Pyne Investigates
Murder is Easy
And Then There Were None
Towards Zero
Death Comes as the End
Sparkling Cyanide
Crooked House
They Came to Baghdad
Destination Unknown
Ordeal by Innocence
The Pale Horse
Endless Night
Passenger to Frankfurt
Problem at Pollensa Bay
While the Light Lasts

Poirot
The Mysterious Affair at Styles
The Murder on the Links
Poirot Investigates
The Murder of Roger Ackroyd
The Big Four
The Mystery of the Blue Train
Peril at End House
Lord Edgware Dies
Murder on the Orient Express
Three-Act Tragedy
Death in the Clouds
The ABC Murders
Murder in Mesopotamia
Cards on the Table
Murder in the Mews
Dumb Witness
Death on the Nile
Appointment With Death
Hercule Poirot's Christmas
Sad Cypress
One, Two, Buckle My Shoe
Evil Under the Sun
Five Little Pigs
The Hollow
The Labours of Hercules
Taken at the Flood
Mrs McGinty's Dead
After the Funeral
Hickory Dickory Dock
Dead Man's Folly
Cat Among the Pigeons
The Adventure of the Christmas Pudding
The Clocks
Third Girl
Hallowe'en Party
Elephants Can Remember
Poirot's Early Cases
Curtain: Poirot's Last Case

Marple
The Murder at the Vicarage
The Thirteen Problems
The Body in the Library
The Moving Finger
A Murder is Announced
They Do It With Mirrors
A Pocket Full of Rye
4.50 from Paddington
The Mirror Crack'd from Side to Side
A Caribbean Mystery
At Bertram's Hotel
Nemesis
Sleeping Murder
Miss Marple's Final Cases

Tommy & Tuppence
The Secret Adversary
Partners in Crime
N or M?
By the Pricking of My Thumbs
Postern of Fate

Published as Mary Westmacott
Giant's Bread
Unfinished Portrait
Absent in the Spring
The Rose and the Yew Tree
A Daughter's a Daughter
The Burden

Memoirs
An Autobiography
Come, Tell Me How You Live

Play Collections
The Mousetrap and Selected Plays
Witness for the Prosecution
and Selected Plays

Play Adaptations by Charles Osborne
Black Coffee (Poirot)
Spider's Web
The Unexpected Guest

Agatha Christie

POIROT

THE PERFECT MURDERS

•

THE MURDER OF ROGER ACKROYD

•

MURDER ON THE ORIENT EXPRESS

•

MURDER IN THE MEWS

•

HERCULE POIROT'S CHRISTMAS

•

HarperCollins*Publishers*

HarperCollins*Publishers*
77–85 Fulham Palace Road,
Hammersmith, London W6 8JB
www.harpercollins.co.uk

This edition first published 2004
1

ISBN 0 00 719064 6

Typeset in Plantin Light and Gill Sans by
Palimpsest Book Production Limited,
Polmont, Stirlingshire

Printed and bound in Great Britain by
Clays Ltd, St Ives plc

CONTENTS

THE MURDER OF ROGER ACKROYD

To Punkie

who likes an orthodox detective story, murder, inquest, and suspicion falling on everyone in turn!

CONTENTS

CHAPTER 1

DR SHEPPARD AT THE BREAKFAST TABLE

Mrs Ferrars died on the night of the 16th–17th September – a Thursday. I was sent for at eight o'clock on the morning of Friday the 17th. There was nothing to be done. She had been dead some hours.

It was just a few minutes after nine when I reached home once more. I opened the front door with my latchkey, and purposely delayed a few moments in the hall, hanging up my hat and the light overcoat that I had deemed a wise precaution against the chill of an early autumn morning. To tell the truth, I was considerably upset and worried. I am not going to pretend that at that moment I foresaw the events of the next few weeks. I emphatically did not do so. But my instinct told me that there were stirring times ahead.

From the dining-room on my left there came the rattle of tea-cups and the short, dry cough of my sister Caroline.

'Is that you, James?' she called.

An unnecessary question, since who else could it be? To tell the truth, it was precisely my sister Caroline who was the cause of my few minutes' delay. The motto of the mongoose family, so Mr Kipling tells us, is: 'Go and find out.' If Caroline ever adopts a crest, I should certainly suggest a mongoose rampant. One might omit the first part of the motto. Caroline can do any amount of finding out by sitting placidly at home. I don't know how she manages it, but there it is. I suspect that the servants and the tradesmen constitute her Intelligence Corps. When she goes out, it is not to gather in information, but to spread it. At that, too, she is amazingly expert.

It was really this last named trait of hers which was causing me these pangs of indecision. Whatever I told Caroline now concerning the demise of Mrs Ferrars would be common knowledge all over the village within the space of an hour and a half. As a professional man, I naturally aim at discretion. Therefore I have got into the habit of continually withholding all information possible from my sister. She usually finds out just the same, but I have the moral satisfaction of knowing that I am in no way to blame.

Mrs Ferrars's husband died just over a year ago, and Caroline has constantly asserted, without the least foundation for the assertion, that his wife poisoned him.

She scorns my invariable rejoinder that Mr Ferrars died of acute gastritis, helped on by habitual overindulgence in alcoholic beverages. The symptoms of gastritis and arsenical poisoning are not, I agree, unlike, but Caroline bases her accusation on quite different lines.

'You've only got to look at her,' I have heard her say.

Mrs Ferrars, though not in her first youth, was a very attractive woman, and her clothes, though simple, always seemed to fit her very well, but all the same, lots of women buy their clothes in Paris, and have not, on that account, necessarily poisoned their husbands.

As I stood hesitating in the hall, with all this passing through my mind, Caroline's voice came again, with a sharper note in it.

'What on earth are you doing out there, James? Why don't you come and get your breakfast?'

'Just coming, my dear,' I said hastily. 'I've been hanging up my overcoat.'

'You could have hung up half a dozen overcoats in this time.'

She was quite right. I could have.

I walked into the dining-room, gave Caroline the accustomed peck on the cheek, and sat down to eggs and bacon. The bacon was rather cold.

'You've had an early call,' remarked Caroline.

'Yes,' I said. 'King's Paddock. Mrs Ferrars.'

'I know,' said my sister.

'How did you know?'

'Annie told me.'

Annie is the house parlourmaid. A nice girl, but an inveterate talker.

There was a pause. I continued to eat eggs and bacon. My sister's nose, which is long and thin, quivered a little at the tip, as it always does when she is interested or excited over anything.

'Well?' she demanded.

'A sad business. Nothing to be done. Must have died in her sleep.'

'I know,' said my sister again.

This time I was annoyed.

'You can't know,' I snapped. 'I didn't know myself until I got there, and haven't mentioned it to a soul yet. If that girl Annie knows, she must be a clairvoyant.'

'It wasn't Annie who told me. It was the milkman. He had it from the Ferrarses' cook.'

As I say, there is no need for Caroline to go out to get information. She sits at home and it comes to her.

My sister continued:

'What did she die of? Heart failure?'

'Didn't the milkman tell you that?' I inquired sarcastically.

Sarcasm is wasted on Caroline. She takes it seriously and answers accordingly.

'He didn't know,' she explained.

After all, Caroline was bound to hear sooner or later. She might as well hear from me.

'She died of an overdose of veronal. She's been taking it lately for sleeplessness. Must have taken too much.'

'Nonsense,' said Caroline immediately. 'She took it on purpose. Don't tell me!'

It is odd, when you have a secret belief of your own which you do not wish to acknowledge, the voicing of it by someone else will rouse you to a fury of denial. I burst immediately into indignant speech.

'There you go again,' I said. 'Rushing along without rhyme or reason. Why on earth should Mrs Ferrars wish to commit suicide? A widow, fairly young still, very well off, good health, and nothing to do but enjoy life. It's absurd.'

'Not at all. Even you must have noticed how different she has been looking lately. It's been coming on for the last six months. She's looked positively hag-ridden. And you have just admitted that she hasn't been able to sleep.'

'What is your diagnosis?' I demanded coldly. 'An unfortunate love affair, I suppose?'

My sister shook her head.

'*Remorse*,' she said, with great gusto.

'Remorse?'

'Yes. You never would believe me when I told you she poisoned her husband. I'm more than ever convinced of it now.'

'I don't think you're very logical,' I objected. 'Surely if a woman committed a crime like murder, she'd be sufficiently cold-blooded to enjoy the fruits of it without any weak-minded sentimentality such as repentance.'

Caroline shook her head.

'There probably are women like that – but Mrs Ferrars wasn't one of them. She was a mass of nerves. An overmastering impulse drove her on to get rid of her husband because she was the sort of person who simply can't endure suffering of any kind, and there's no doubt that the wife of a man like Ashley Ferrars must have had to suffer a good deal –'

I nodded.

'And ever since she's been haunted by what she did. I can't help feeling sorry for her.'

I don't think Caroline ever felt sorry for Mrs Ferrars whilst she was alive. Now that she has gone where (presumably) Paris frocks can no longer be worn, Caroline is prepared to indulge in the softer emotions of pity and comprehension.

I told her firmly that her whole idea was nonsense. I was all the more firm because I secretly agreed with some part, at least, of what she had said. But it is all wrong that Caroline should arrive at the truth simply by a kind of inspired guesswork. I wasn't going to encourage that sort of thing. She will go round the village airing her views, and everyone will think that she is doing so on medical data supplied by me. Life is very trying.

'Nonsense,' said Caroline, in reply to my strictures. 'You'll see. Ten to one she's left a letter confessing everything.'

'She didn't leave a letter of any kind,' I said sharply, and not seeing where the admission was going to land me.

'Oh!' said Caroline. 'So you *did* inquire about that, did you? I believe, James, that in your heart of hearts, you think very much as I do. You're a precious old humbug.'

'One always has to take the possibility of suicide into consideration,' I said impressively.

'Will there be an inquest?'

'There may be. It all depends. If I am able to declare myself absolutely satisfied that the overdose was taken accidentally, an inquest might be dispensed with.'

'And are you absolutely satisfied?' asked my sister shrewdly.

I did not answer, but got up from the table.

CHAPTER 2

WHO'S WHO IN KING'S ABBOT

Before I proceed further with what I said to Caroline and what Caroline said to me, it might be as well to give some idea of what I should describe as our local geography. Our village, King's Abbot, is, I imagine, very much like any other village. Our big town is Cranchester, nine miles away. We have a large railway station, a small post office, and two rival 'General Stores'. Able-bodied men are apt to leave the place early in life, but we are rich in unmarried ladies and retired military officers. Our hobbies and recreations can be summed up in the one word, 'gossip'.

There are only two houses of any importance in King's Abbot. One is King's Paddock, left to Mrs Ferrars by her late husband. The other, Fernly Park, is owned by Roger Ackroyd. Ackroyd has always interested me by being a man more impossibly like a country squire than any country squire could really be. He reminds one of the red-faced sportsmen who always appeared early in the first act of an old-fashioned musical comedy, the setting being the village green. They usually sang a song about going up to London. Nowadays we have revues, and the country squire has died out of musical fashion.

Of course, Ackroyd is not really a country squire. He is an immensely successful manufacturer of (I think) wagon wheels. He is a man of nearly fifty years of age, rubicund of face and genial of manner. He is hand in glove with the vicar, subscribes liberally to parish funds (though rumour has it that he is extremely mean in personal expenditure), encourages cricket matches, Lads' Clubs, and Disabled Soldiers' Institutes. He is, in fact, the life and soul of our peaceful village of King's Abbot.

Now when Roger Ackroyd was a lad of twenty-one, he fell in love with, and married, a beautiful woman some five or six years his senior. Her name was Paton, and she was a widow with one child. The history of the marriage was short and painful. To put it bluntly, Mrs Ackroyd was a dipsomaniac. She succeeded in drinking herself into her grave four years after her marriage.

In the years that followed, Ackroyd showed no disposition to make a second matrimonial adventure. His wife's child by her first marriage was only seven years old when his mother died. He is now twenty-five. Ackroyd has always regarded him as his own son, and has brought him up accordingly, but he has been a wild lad and a continual source of worry and trouble to his stepfather. Nevertheless we are all very fond of Ralph Paton in King's Abbot. He is such a good-looking youngster for one thing.

As I said before, we are ready enough to gossip in our village. Everybody noticed from the first that Ackroyd and Mrs Ferrars got on very well together. After her husband's death, the intimacy became more marked. They were always seen about together, and it was freely conjectured that at the end of her period of mourning, Mrs Ferrars would become Mrs Roger Ackroyd. It was felt, indeed, that there was a certain fitness in the thing. Roger Ackroyd's wife had admittedly died of drink. Ashley Ferrars had been a drunkard for many years before his death. It was only fitting that these two victims of alcoholic excess should make up to each other for all that they had previously endured at the hands of their former spouses.

The Ferrarses only came to live here just over a year ago, but a halo of gossip has surrounded Ackroyd for many years past. All the time that Ralph Paton was growing up to manhood a series of lady housekeepers presided over Ackroyd's establishment, and each in turn was regarded with lively suspicion by Caroline and her cronies. It is not too much to say that for at least fifteen years the whole village has confidently expected Ackroyd to marry one of his housekeepers. The last of them, a redoubtable lady called Miss Russell, has reigned undisputed for five years, twice as long as any of her predecessors. It is felt that but for the advent of Mrs Ferrars, Ackroyd could hardly have escaped. That – and one other factor – the unexpected arrival of a widowed sister-in-law with her daughter from Canada. Mrs Cecil Ackroyd, widow of Ackroyd's ne'er-do-well younger brother, has taken up her residence at Fernly Park, and has succeeded, according to Caroline, in putting Miss Russell in her proper place.

I don't know exactly what a 'proper place' constitutes – it sounds chilly and unpleasant – but I know that Miss Russell goes about with pinched lips, and what I can only describe as an acid smile, and that she professes the utmost sympathy for 'poor Mrs Ackroyd – dependent on the charity of her husband's brother. The bread of charity is so bitter, is it not? *I* should be quite miserable if I did not work for my living.'

I don't know what Mrs Cecil Ackroyd thought of the Ferrars affair when it came on the tapis. It was clearly to her advantage that Ackroyd should remain unmarried. She was always very charming – not to say gushing – to Mrs Ferrars when they met. Caroline says that proves less than nothing.

Such have been our preoccupations in King's Abbot for the last few years. We have discussed Ackroyd and his affairs from every standpoint. Mrs Ferrars has fitted into her place in the scheme.

Now there has been a rearrangement of the kaleidoscope. From a mild discussion of probable wedding presents, we had been jerked into the midst of tragedy.

Revolving these and sundry other matters in my mind, I went mechanically on my round. I had no cases of special interest to attend, which was, perhaps, as well, for my thoughts returned again and again to the mystery of Mrs Ferrars's death. Had she taken her own life? Surely, if she had done so, she would have left some word behind to say what she contemplated doing? Women, in my experience, if they once reach the determination to commit suicide, usually wish to reveal the state of mind that led to the fatal action. They covet the limelight.

When had I last seen her? Not for over a week. Her manner then had been normal enough considering – well – considering everything.

Then I suddenly remembered that I had seen her, though not to speak to, only yesterday. She had been walking with Ralph Paton, and I had been surprised because I had had no idea that he was likely to be in King's Abbot. I thought, indeed, that he had quarrelled finally with his stepfather. Nothing had been seen of him down here for nearly six months. They had been walking along, side by side, their heads close together, and she had been talking very earnestly.

I think I can safely say that it was at this moment that a foreboding of the future first swept over me. Nothing tangible as yet – but a vague premonition of the way things were setting. That earnest *tête-à-tête* between Ralph Paton and Mrs Ferrars the day before struck me disagreeably.

I was still thinking of it when I came face to face with Roger Ackroyd.

'Sheppard!' he exclaimed. 'Just the man I wanted to get hold of. This is a terrible business.'

'You've heard then?'

He nodded. He had felt the blow keenly, I could see. His big red cheeks seemed to have fallen in, and he looked a positive wreck of his usual jolly, healthy self.

'It's worse than you know,' he said quietly. 'Look here, Sheppard, I've got to talk to you. Can you come back with me now?'

'Hardly. I've got three patients to see still, and I must be back by twelve to see my surgery patients.'

'Then this afternoon – no, better still, dine tonight. At 7.30. Will that suit you?'

'Yes, I can manage that all right. What's wrong? Is it Ralph?'

I hardly knew why I said that – except, perhaps, that it had so often been Ralph.

Ackroyd stared blankly at me as though he hardly understood. I began to realize that there must be something very wrong indeed somewhere. I had never seen Ackroyd so upset before.

'Ralph?' he said vaguely. 'Oh! no, it's not Ralph. Ralph's in London – Damn! Here's old Miss Gannett coming. I don't want to have to talk to her about this ghastly business. See you tonight, Sheppard. Seven-thirty.'

I nodded, and he hurried away, leaving me wondering. Ralph in London? But he had certainly been in King's Abbot the preceding afternoon. He must have gone back to town last night or early this morning, and yet Ackroyd's manner had conveyed quite a different impression. He had spoken as though Ralph had not been near the place for months.

I had no time to puzzle the matter out further. Miss Gannett was upon me, thirsting for information. Miss Gannett has all the characteristics of my sister Caroline, but she lacks that unerring aim in jumping to conclusions which lends a touch of greatness to Caroline's manoeuvres. Miss Gannett was breathless and interrogatory.

Wasn't it sad about poor dear Mrs Ferrars? A lot of people were saying she had been a confirmed drug-taker for years. So wicked the way people went about saying things. And yet, the worst of it was, there was usually a grain of truth somewhere in these wild statements. No smoke without fire! They were saying too that Mr Ackroyd had found out about it, and had broken off the engagement – because there *was* an engagement. She, Miss Gannett, had proof positive of that. Of course *I* must know all about it – doctors always did – but they never tell?

And all this with a sharp beady eye on me to see how I reacted to these suggestions. Fortunately, long association with Caroline has led me to preserve an impassive countenance, and to be ready with small non-committal remarks.

On this occasion I congratulated Miss Gannett on not joining in ill-natured gossip. Rather a neat counter-attack, I thought. It left her in difficulties, and before she could pull herself together, I had passed on.

I went home thoughtful, to find several patients waiting for me in the surgery.

I had dismissed the last of them, as I thought, and was just contemplating a few minutes in the garden before lunch when I perceived one more patient waiting for me. She rose and came towards me as I stood somewhat surprised.

I don't know why I should have been, except that there is a suggestion of cast iron about Miss Russell, a something that is above the ills of the flesh.

Ackroyd's housekeeper is a tall woman, handsome but forbidding in appearance. She has a stern eye, and lips that shut tightly, and I feel that if I were an under housemaid or a kitchenmaid I should run for my life whenever I heard her coming.

'Good morning, Dr Sheppard,' said Miss Russell. 'I should be much obliged if you would take a look at my knee.'

I took a look, but, truth to tell, I was very little wiser when I had done so. Miss Russell's account of vague pains was so unconvincing that with a woman of less integrity of character I should have suspected a trumped-up tale. It did cross my mind for one moment that Miss Russell might have deliberately invented this affliction of the knee in order to pump me on the subject of Mrs Ferrars's death, but I soon saw that there, at least, I had misjudged her. She made a brief reference to the tragedy, nothing more. Yet she certainly seemed disposed to linger and chat.

'Well, thank you very much for this bottle of liniment, doctor,' she said at last. 'Not that I believe it will do the least good.'

I didn't think it would either, but I protested in duty bound. After all, it couldn't do any harm, and one must stick up for the tools of one's trade.

'I don't believe in all these drugs,' said Miss Russell, her eyes sweeping over my array of bottles disparagingly. 'Drugs do a lot of harm. Look at the cocaine habit.'

'Well, as far as that goes –'

'It's very prevalent in high society.'

I'm sure Miss Russell knows far more about high society than I do. I didn't attempt to argue with her.

'Just tell me this, doctor,' said Miss Russell. 'Suppose you are really a slave of the drug habit, is there any cure?'

One cannot answer a question like that off-hand. I gave her a short lecture on the subject, and she listened with close attention. I still suspected her of seeking information about Mrs Ferrars.

'Now, veronal, for instance –' I proceeded.

But, strangely enough, she didn't seem interested in veronal. Instead she changed the subject, and asked me if it was true that there were certain poisons so rare as to baffle detection.

'Ah!' I said. 'You've been reading detective stories.'

She admitted that she had.

'The essence of a detective story,' I said, 'is to have a rare poison – if possible something from South America, that nobody has ever heard of – something that one obscure tribe of savages use to poison their arrows with. Death is instantaneous, and Western science is powerless to detect it. Is that the kind of thing you mean?'

'Yes. Is there really such a thing?'

I shook my head regretfully.

'I'm afraid there isn't. There's *curare*, of course.'

I told her a good deal about curare, but she seemed to have lost interest once more. She asked me if I had any in my poison cupboard, and when I replied in the negative I fancy I fell in her estimation.

She said she must be getting back, and I saw her out at the surgery door just as the luncheon gong went.

I should never have suspected Miss Russell of a fondness for detective stories. It pleases me very much to think of her stepping out of the housekeeper's room to rebuke a delinquent housemaid, and then returning to a comfortable perusal of *The Mystery of the Seventh Death*, or something of the kind.

CHAPTER 3

THE MAN WHO GREW VEGETABLE MARROWS

I told Caroline at lunch that I should be dining at Fernly. She expressed no objection – on the contrary.

'Excellent,' she said. 'You'll hear all about it. By the way, what is the trouble with Ralph?'

'With Ralph?' I said, surprised; 'there isn't any.'

'Then why is he staying at the Three Boars instead of at Fernly Park?'

I did not for a minute question Caroline's statement that Ralph Paton was staying at the local inn. That Caroline said so was enough for me.

'Ackroyd told me he was in London,' I said. In the surprise of the moment I departed from my valuable rule of never parting with information.

'Oh!' said Caroline. I could see her nose twitching as she worked on this.

'He arrived at the Three Boars yesterday morning,' she said. 'And he's still there. Last night he was out with a girl.'

That did not surprise me in the least. Ralph, I should say, is out with a girl most nights of his life. But I did rather wonder that he chose to indulge in the pastime in King's Abbot instead of in the gay Metropolis.

'One of the barmaids?' I asked.

'No. That's just it. He went out to meet her. I don't know who she is.'

(Bitter for Caroline to have to admit such a thing.)

'But I can guess,' continued my indefatigable sister.

I waited patiently.

'His cousin.'

'Flora Ackroyd?' I exclaimed in surprise.

Flora Ackroyd is, of course, no relation whatever really to Ralph Paton but Ralph has been looked upon for so long as practically Ackroyd's own son, that cousinship is taken for granted.

'Flora Ackroyd,' said my sister.

'But why not go to Fernly if he wanted to see her?'

'Secretly engaged,' said Caroline, with immense enjoyment. 'Old Ackroyd won't hear of it, and they have to meet this way.'

I saw a good many flaws in Caroline's theory, but I forebore to point them out to her. An innocent remark about our new neighbour created a diversion.

The house next door, The Larches, has recently been taken by a stranger. To Caroline's extreme annoyance, she has not been able to find out anything about him, except that he is a foreigner. The Intelligence Corps has proved a broken reed. Presumably the man has milk and vegetables and joints of meat and occasional whitings just like everybody else, but none of the people who make it their business to supply these things seem to have acquired any information. His name, apparently, is Mr Porrott – a name which conveys an odd feeling of unreality. The one thing we do know about him is that he is interested in the growing of vegetable marrows.

But that is certainly not the sort of information that Caroline is after. She wants to know where he comes from, what he does, whether he is married, what his wife was, or is, like, whether he has children, what his mother's maiden name was – and so on. Somebody very like Caroline must have invented the questions on passports, I think.

'My dear Caroline,' I said. 'There's no doubt at all about what the man's profession has been. He's a retired hairdresser. Look at that moustache of his.'

Caroline dissented. She said that if the man was a hairdresser, he would have wavy hair – not straight. All hairdressers did.

I cited several hairdressers personally known to me who had straight hair, but Caroline refused to be convinced.

'I can't make him out at all,' she said in an aggrieved voice. 'I borrowed some garden tools the other day, and he was most polite, but I couldn't get anything out of him. I asked him point blank at last whether he was a Frenchman, and he said he wasn't – and, somehow, I didn't like to ask him any more.'

I began to be more interested in our mysterious neighbour. A man who is capable of shutting up Caroline and sending her, like the Queen of Sheba, empty away, must be something of a personality.

'I believe,' said Caroline, 'that he's got one of those new vacuum cleaners –'

I saw a meditated loan and the opportunity of further questioning gleaming from her eye. I saw the chance to escape into the garden. I am rather fond of gardening. I was busily exterminating dandelion roots when a shout of warning sounded from close by and a heavy body whizzed by my ears and fell at my feet with a repellent squelch. It was a vegetable marrow!

I looked up angrily. Over the wall, to my left, there appeared a face. An egg-shaped head, partially covered with suspiciously black hair, two immense moustaches, and a pair of watchful eyes. It was our mysterious neighbour, Mr Porrott.

He broke at once into fluent apologies.

'I demand of you a thousand pardons, monsieur. I am without defence. For some months now I cultivate the marrows. This morning suddenly I enrage myself with these marrows. I send them to promenade themselves – alas! not only mentally but physically. I seize the biggest. I hurl him over the wall. Monsieur, I am ashamed. I prostrate myself.'

Before such profuse apologies, my anger was forced to melt. After all, the wretched vegetable hadn't hit me. But I sincerely hoped that throwing large vegetables over walls was not our new friend's hobby. Such a habit could hardly endear him to us as a neighbour.

The strange little man seemed to read my thoughts.

'Ah! no,' he exclaimed. 'Do not disquiet yourself. It is not with me a habit. But you can figure to yourself, monsieur, that a man may work towards a certain object, may labour and toil to attain a certain kind of leisure and occupation, and then find that, after all, he yearns for the old busy days, and the old occupations that he thought himself so glad to leave?'

'Yes,' I said slowly. 'I fancy that that is a common enough occurrence. I myself am perhaps an instance. A year ago I came into a legacy – enough to enable me to realize a dream. I have always wanted to travel, to see the world. Well, that was a year ago, as I said, and – I am still here.'

My little neighbour nodded.

'The chains of habit. We work to attain an object, and the object gained, we find that what we miss is the daily toil. And mark you, monsieur, my work was interesting work. The most interesting work there is in the world.'

'Yes?' I said encouragingly. For the moment the spirit of Caroline was strong within me.

'The study of human nature, monsieur!'

'Just so,' I said kindly.

Clearly a retired hairdresser. Who knows the secrets of human nature better than a hairdresser?

'Also, I had a friend – a friend who for many years never left my side. Occasionally of an imbecility to make one afraid, nevertheless he was very dear to me. Figure to yourself that I miss even his stupidity. His *naïveté*, his honest outlook, the pleasure of delighting and surprising him by my superior gifts – all these I miss more than I can tell you.'

'He died?' I asked sympathetically.

'Not so. He lives and flourishes – but on the other side of the world. He is now in the Argentine.'

'In the Argentine,' I said enviously.

I have always wanted to go to South America. I sighed, and then looked up to find Mr Porrott eyeing me sympathetically. He seemed an understanding little man.

'Will you go there, yes?' he asked.

I shook my head with a sigh.

'I could have gone,' I said. 'A year ago. But I was foolish – and worse than foolish – greedy. I risked the substance for the shadow.'

'I comprehend,' said Mr Porrott. 'You speculated?'

I nodded mournfully, but in spite of myself I felt secretly entertained. This ridiculous little man was so portentously solemn.

'Not the Porcupine Oilfields?' he asked suddenly.

I stared.

'I thought of them, as a matter of fact, but in the end I plumped for a gold mine in Western Australia.'

My neighbour was regarding me with a strange expression which I could not fathom.

'It is Fate,' he said at last.

'What is Fate?' I asked irritably.

'That I should live next to a man who seriously considers Porcupine Oilfields, and also West Australian Gold Mines. Tell me, have you also a penchant for auburn hair?'

I stared at him open-mouthed, and he burst out laughing.

'No, no, it is not the insanity that I suffer from. Make your mind easy. It was a foolish question that I put to you there, for, you see, my friend of whom I spoke was a young man, a man who thought all women good, and most of them beautiful. But you are a man of middle age, a doctor, a man who knows the folly and the vanity of most things in this life of ours. Well, well, we are neighbours. I beg of you to accept and present to your excellent sister my best marrow.'

He stooped, and with a flourish produced an immense specimen of the tribe, which I duly accepted in the spirit in which it was offered.

'Indeed,' said the little man cheerfully, 'this has not been a wasted morning. I have made the acquaintance of a man who in some ways resembles my far-off friend. By the way, I should like to ask you a question. You doubtless know everyone in this tiny village. Who is the young man with the very dark hair and eyes, and the handsome face. He walks with his head flung back, and an easy smile on his lips?'

The description left me in no doubt.

'That must be Captain Ralph Paton,' I said slowly.

'I have not seen him about here before?'

'No, he has not been here for some time. But he is the son – adopted son, rather – of Mr Ackroyd of Fernly Park.'

My neighbour made a slight gesture of impatience.

'Of course, I should have guessed. Mr Ackroyd spoke of him many times.'

'You know Mr Ackroyd?' I said, slightly surprised.

'Mr Ackroyd knew me in London – when I was at work there. I have asked him to say nothing of my profession down here.'

'I see,' I said, rather amused by this patent snobbery, as I thought it.

But the little man went on with an almost grandiloquent smirk.

'One prefers to remain incognito. I am not anxious for notoriety. I have not even troubled to correct the local version of my name.'

'Indeed,' I said, not knowing quite what to say.

'Captain Ralph Paton,' mused Mr Porrott. 'And so he is engaged to Mr Ackroyd's niece, the charming Miss Flora.'

'Who told you so?' I asked, very much surprised.

'Mr Ackroyd. About a week ago. He is very pleased about it – has long desired that such a thing should come to pass, or so I understood from him. I even believe that he brought some pressure to bear upon the young man. That is never wise. A young man should marry to please himself – not to please a stepfather from whom he has expectations.'

My ideas were completely upset. I could not see Ackroyd taking a hairdresser into his confidence, and discussing the marriage of his niece and stepson with him. Ackroyd extends a genial patronage to the lower orders, but he has a very great sense of his own dignity. I began to think that Porrott couldn't be a hairdresser after all.

To hide my confusion, I said the first thing that came into my head.

'What made you notice Ralph Paton? His good looks?'

'No, not that alone – though he is unusually good-looking for an Englishman – what your lady novelists would call a Greek God. No, there was something about that young man that I did not understand.'

He said the last sentence in a musing tone of voice which made an indefinable impression upon me. It was as though he was summing up the boy by the light of some inner knowledge that I did not share. It was that impression that was left with me, for at that moment my sister's voice called me from the house.

I went in. Caroline had her hat on, and had evidently just come in from the village. She began without preamble.

'I met Mr Ackroyd.'

'Yes?' I said.

'I stopped him, of course, but he seemed in a great hurry, and anxious to get away.'

I have no doubt but that that was the case. He would feel towards Caroline much as he had felt towards Miss Gannett earlier in the day – perhaps more so. Caroline is less easy to shake off.

'I asked him at once about Ralph. He was absolutely astonished. Had no idea the boy was down here. He actually said he thought I must have made a mistake. I! A mistake!'

'Ridiculous,' I said. 'He ought to have known you better.'

'Then he went on to tell me that Ralph and Flora are engaged.'

'I knew that, too,' I interrupted, with modest pride.

'Who told you?'

'Our new neighbour.'

Caroline visibly wavered for a second or two, much as if a roulette ball might coyly hover between two numbers. Then she declined the tempting red herring.

'I told Mr Ackroyd that Ralph was staying at the Three Boars.'

'Caroline,' I said, 'do you never reflect that you might do a lot of harm with this habit of yours of repeating everything indiscriminately?'

'Nonsense,' said my sister. 'People ought to know things. I consider it my duty to tell them. Mr Ackroyd was very grateful to me.'

'Well,' I said, for there was clearly more to come.

'I think he went straight off to the Three Boars, but if so he didn't find Ralph there.'

'No?'

'No. Because as I was coming back through the wood –'

'Coming back through the wood?' I interrupted.

Caroline had the grace to blush.

'It was such a lovely day,' she exclaimed. 'I thought I would make a little round. The woods with their autumnal tints are so perfect at this time of year.'

Caroline does not care a hang for woods at any time of year. Normally she regards them as places where you get your feet damp, and where all kinds of unpleasant things may drop on your head. No, it was good sound mongoose instinct which took her to our local wood. It is the only place adjacent to the village of King's Abbot where you can talk with a young woman unseen by the whole of the village. It adjoins the Park of Fernly.

'Well,' I said, 'go on.'

'As I say, I was just coming back through the wood when I heard voices.'

Caroline paused.

'Yes?'

'One was Ralph Paton's – I knew it at once. The other was a girl's. Of course I didn't mean to listen –'

'Of course not,' I interjected, with patent sarcasm – which was, however, wasted on Caroline.

'But I simply couldn't help overhearing. The girl said something – I didn't quite catch what it was, and Ralph answered. He sounded very angry. "My dear girl," he said. "Don't you realize that it is quite on the cards the old man will cut me off without a shilling? He's been pretty fed up with me for the last few years. A little more would do it. And we need the dibs, my dear. I shall be a very rich man when the old fellow pops off. He's mean as they make 'em, but he's rolling in money really. I don't want him to go altering his will. You leave it to me, and don't worry." Those were his exact words. I remember them perfectly. Unfortunately, just then I stepped on a dry twig or something, and they lowered their voices and moved away. I couldn't, of course, go rushing after them, so wasn't able to see who the girl was.'

'That must have been most vexing,' I said. 'I suppose, though, you hurried on to the Three Boars, felt faint, and went into the bar for a glass of brandy, and so were able to see if both the barmaids were on duty?'

'It wasn't a barmaid,' said Caroline unhesitatingly. 'In fact, I'm almost sure that it was Flora Ackroyd, only –'

'Only it doesn't seem to make sense,' I agreed.

'But if it wasn't Flora, who could it have been?'

Rapidly my sister ran over a list of maidens living in the neighbourhood, with profuse reasons for and against.

When she paused for breath, I murmured something about a patient, and slipped out.

I proposed to make my way to the Three Boars. It seemed likely that Ralph Paton would have returned there by now.

I knew Ralph very well – better, perhaps, than anyone else in King's Abbot, for I had known his mother before him, and therefore I understood much in him that puzzled others. He was, to a certain extent, the victim of heredity. He had not inherited his mother's fatal propensity for drink, but nevertheless he had in him a strain of weakness. As my new friend of this morning had declared, he was extraordinarily handsome. Just on six feet, perfectly proportioned, with the easy grace of an athlete, he was dark, like his mother, with a handsome, sunburnt face always ready to break into a smile. Ralph Paton was of those born to charm easily and without effort. He was self-indulgent and extravagant, with no veneration for anything on earth, but he was lovable nevertheless, and his friends were all devoted to him.

Could I do anything with the boy? I thought I could.

On inquiry at the Three Boars I found that Captain Paton had just come in. I went up to his room and entered unannounced.

For a moment, remembering what I had heard and seen, I was doubtful of my reception, but I need have had no misgivings.

'Why, it's Sheppard! Glad to see you.'

He came forward to meet me, hand outstretched, a sunny smile lighting up his face.

'The one person I am glad to see in this infernal place.'

I raised my eyebrows.

'What's the place been doing?'

He gave a vexed laugh.

'It's a long story. Things haven't been going well with me, doctor. But have a drink, won't you?'

'Thanks,' I said, 'I will.'

He pressed the bell, then coming back threw himself into a chair.

'Not to mince matters,' he said gloomily, 'I'm in the devil of a mess. In fact, I haven't the least idea what to do next.'

'What's the matter?' I asked sympathetically.

'It's my confounded stepfather.'

'What has he done?'

'It isn't what he's done yet, but what he's likely to do.'

The bell was answered, and Ralph ordered the drinks. When the man had gone again, he sat hunched in the armchair, frowning to himself.

'Is it really – serious?' I asked.

He nodded.

'I'm fairly up against it this time,' he said soberly.

The unusual ring of gravity in his voice told me that he spoke the truth. It took a good deal to make Ralph grave.

'In fact,' he continued, 'I can't see my way ahead . . . I'm damned if I can.'

'If I could help –' I suggested diffidently.

But he shook his head very decidedly.

'Good of you, doctor. But I can't let you in on this. I've got to play a lone hand.'

He was silent a minute and then repeated in a slightly different tone of voice:

'Yes – I've got to play a lone hand . . .'

CHAPTER 4

DINNER AT FERNLY

I

It was just a few minutes before half-past seven when I rang the front-door bell of Fernly Park. The door was opened with admirable promptitude by Parker, the butler.

The night was such a fine one that I had preferred to come on foot. I stepped into the big square hall and Parker relieved me of my overcoat. Just then Ackroyd's secretary, a pleasant young fellow by the name of Raymond, passed through the hall on his way to Ackroyd's study, his hands full of papers.

'Good evening, doctor. Coming to dine? Or is this a professional call?'

The last was in allusion to my black bag which I had laid down on the oak chest.

I explained that I expected a summons to a confinement case

at any moment, and so had come out prepared for an emergency call. Raymond nodded, and went on his way, calling over his shoulder:

'Go into the drawing-room. You know the way. The ladies will be down in a minute. I must just take these papers to Mr Ackroyd, and I'll tell him you're here.'

On Raymond's appearance Parker had withdrawn, so I was alone in the hall. I settled my tie, glanced in a large mirror which hung there, and crossed to the door directly facing me, which was, as I knew, the door of the drawing-room.

I noticed, just as I was turning the handle, a sound from within – the shutting down of a window, I took it to be. I noticed it, I may say, quite mechanically, without attaching any importance to it at the time.

I opened the door and walked in. As I did so I almost collided with Miss Russell who was just coming out. We both apologized.

For the first time I found myself appraising the housekeeper and thinking what a handsome woman she must once have been – indeed, as far as that goes, still was. Her dark hair was unstreaked with grey, and when she had a colour, as she had at this minute, the stern quality of her looks was not so apparent.

Quite subconsciously I wondered whether she had been out, for she was breathing hard, as though she had been running.

'I'm afraid I'm a few minutes early,' I said.

'Oh! I don't think so. It's gone half-past seven, Dr Sheppard.' She paused a minute before saying, 'I – didn't know you were expected to dinner tonight. Mr Ackroyd didn't mention it.'

I received a vague impression that my dining there displeased her in some way, but I couldn't imagine why.

'How's the knee?' I inquired.

'Much the same, thank you, doctor. I must be going now. Mrs Ackroyd will be down in a moment. I – I only came in here to see if the flowers were all right.'

She passed quickly out of the room. I strolled to the window, wondering at her evident desire to justify her presence in the room. As I did so, I saw what, of course, I might have known all the time had I troubled to give my mind to it, namely, that the windows were long french ones opening on the terrace. The sound I had heard, therefore, could not have been that of a window being shut down.

Quite idly, and more to distract my mind from painful thoughts than for any other reason, I amused myself by trying to guess what could have caused the sound in question.

Coals on the fire? No, that was not the kind of noise at all. A drawer of a bureau pushed in? No, not that.

Then my eye was caught by what, I believe, is called a silver table, the lid of which lifts, and through the glass of which you can see the contents. I crossed over to it, studying the contents. There were one or two pieces of old silver, a baby shoe belonging to King Charles I, some Chinese jade figures, and quite a number of African implements and curios. Wanting to examine one of the jade figures more closely, I lifted the lid. It slipped through my fingers and fell.

At once I recognized the sound I had heard. It was this same table lid being shut down gently and carefully. I repeated the action once or twice for my own satisfaction. Then I lifted the lid to scrutinize the contents more closely.

I was still bending over the open silver table when Flora Ackroyd came into the room.

Quite a lot of people do not like Flora Ackroyd, but nobody can help admiring her. And to her friends she can be very charming. The first thing that strikes you about her is her extraordinary fairness. She has the real Scandinavian pale gold hair. Her eyes are blue – blue as the waters of a Norwegian fiord, and her skin is cream and roses. She has square, boyish shoulders and slight hips. And to a jaded medical man it is very refreshing to come across such perfect health.

A simple straightforward English girl – I may be old-fashioned, but I think the genuine article takes a lot of beating.

Flora joined me by the silver table, and expressed heretical doubts as to King Charles I ever having worn the baby shoe.

'And anyway,' continued Miss Flora, 'all this making a fuss about things because someone wore or used them seems to me all nonsense. They're not wearing or using them now. That pen that George Eliot wrote *The Mill on the Floss* with – that sort of thing – well, it's only just a pen after all. If you're really keen on

George Eliot, why not get *The Mill on the Floss* in a cheap edition and read it.'

'I suppose you never read such old out-of-date stuff, Miss Flora?'

'You're wrong, Dr Sheppard. I love *The Mill on the Floss*.'

I was rather pleased to hear it. The things young women read nowadays and profess to enjoy positively frighten me.

'You haven't congratulated me yet, Dr Sheppard,' said Flora. 'Haven't you heard?'

She held out her left hand. On the third finger of it was an exquisitely set single pearl.

'I'm going to marry Ralph, you know,' she went on. 'Uncle is very pleased. It keeps me in the family, you see.'

I took both her hands in mine.

My dear,' I said, 'I hope you'll be very happy.'

'We've been engaged for about a month,' continued Flora in her cool voice, 'but it was only announced yesterday. Uncle is going to do up Cross-stones, and give it to us to live in, and we're going to pretend to farm. Really, we shall hunt all the winter, town for the season, and then go yachting. I love the sea. And, of course, I shall take a great interest in the parish affairs, and attend all the Mothers' Meetings.'

Just then Mrs Ackroyd rustled in, full of apologies for being late.

I am sorry to say I detest Mrs Ackroyd. She is all chains and teeth and bones. A most unpleasant woman. She has small pale flinty blue eyes, and however gushing her words may be, those eyes of hers always remain coldly speculative.

I went across to her, leaving Flora by the window. She gave me a handful of assorted knuckles and rings to squeeze, and began talking volubly.

Had I heard about Flora's engagement? So suitable in every way. The dear young things had fallen in love at first sight. Such a perfect pair, he so dark and she so fair.

'I can't tell you, my dear Dr Sheppard, the relief to a mother's heart.'

Mrs Ackroyd sighed – a tribute to her mother's heart, whilst her eyes remained shrewdly observant of me.

'I was wondering. You are such an old friend of dear Roger's.

We know how much he trusts to your judgment. So difficult for me – in my position as poor Cecil's widow. But there are so many tiresome things – settlements, you know – all that. I fully believe that Roger intends to make settlements upon dear Flora, but, as you know, he is just a *leetle* peculiar about money. Very usual, I've heard, amongst men who are captains of industry. I wondered, you know, if you could just *sound* him on the subject? Flora is so fond of you. We feel you are quite an old friend, although we have only really known you just over two years.'

Mrs Ackroyd's eloquence was cut short as the drawing-room door opened once more. I was pleased at the interruption. I hate interfering in other people's affairs, and I had not the least intention of tackling Ackroyd on the subject of Flora's settlements. In another moment I should have been forced to tell Mrs Ackroyd as much.

'You know Major Blunt, don't you, doctor?'

'Yes, indeed,' I said.

A lot of people know Hector Blunt – at least by repute. He has shot more wild animals in unlikely places than any man living, I suppose. When you mention him, people say: 'Blunt – you don't mean the big-game man, do you?'

His friendship with Ackroyd has always puzzled me a little. The two men are so totally dissimilar. Hector Blunt is perhaps five years Ackroyd's junior. They made friends early in life, and though their ways have diverged, the friendship still holds. About once in two years Blunt spends a fortnight at Fernly, and an immense animal's head, with an amazing number of horns which fixes you with a glazed stare as soon as you come inside the front door, is a permanent reminder of the friendship.

Blunt had entered the room now with his own peculiar, deliberate, yet soft-footed tread. He is a man of medium height, sturdily and rather stockily built. His face is almost mahogany coloured, and is peculiarly expressionless. He has grey eyes that give the impression of always watching something that is happening very far away. He talks little, and what he does say is said jerkily, as though the words were forced out of him unwillingly.

He said now: 'How are you, Sheppard?' in his usual abrupt fashion, and then stood squarely in front of the fireplace looking over our heads as though he saw something very interesting happening in Timbuctoo.

'Major Blunt,' said Flora, 'I wish you'd tell me about these African things. I'm sure you know what they all are.'

I have heard Hector Blunt described as a woman hater, but I noticed that he joined Flora at the silver table with what might be described as alacrity. They bent over it together.

I was afraid Mrs Ackroyd would begin talking about settlements again, so I made a few hurried remarks about the new sweet pea. I knew there was a new sweet pea because the *Daily Mail* had told me so that morning. Mrs Ackroyd knows nothing about horticulture, but she is the kind of woman who likes to appear well-informed about the topics of the day, and she, too, reads the *Daily Mail*. We were able to converse quite intelligently until Ackroyd and his secretary joined us, and immediately afterwards Parker announced dinner.

My place at table was between Mrs Ackroyd and Flora. Blunt was on Mrs Ackroyd's other side, and Geoffrey Raymond next to him.

Dinner was not a cheerful affair. Ackroyd was visibly preoccupied. He looked wretched, and ate next to nothing. Mrs Ackroyd, Raymond, and I kept the conversation going. Flora seemed affected by her uncle's depression, and Blunt relapsed into his usual taciturnity.

II

Immediately after dinner Ackroyd slipped his arm through mine and led me off to his study.

'Once we've had coffee, we shan't be disturbed again,' he explained. 'I told Raymond to see to it that we shouldn't be interrupted.'

I studied him quietly without appearing to do so. He was clearly under the influence of some strong excitement. For a minute or two he paced up and down the room, then, as Parker entered with the coffee tray, he sank into an arm-chair in front of the fire.

The study was a comfortable apartment. Bookshelves lined one wall of it. The chairs were big and covered in dark blue leather. A large desk stood by the window and was covered with papers neatly docketed and filed. On a round table were various magazines and sporting papers.

'I've had a return of that pain after food lately,' remarked Ackroyd calmly, as he helped himself to coffee. 'You must give me some more of those tablets of yours.'

It struck me that he was anxious to convey the impression that our conference was a medical one. I played up accordingly.

'I thought as much. I brought some up with me.'

'Good man. Hand them over now.'

'They're in my bag in the hall. I'll get them.'

Ackroyd arrested me.

'Don't you trouble. Parker will get them. Bring in the doctor's bag, will you, Parker?'

'Very good, sir.'

Parker withdrew. As I was about to speak, Ackroyd threw up his hand.

'Not yet. Wait. Don't you see I'm in such a state of nerves that I can hardly contain myself?'

I saw that plainly enough. And I was very uneasy. All sorts of forebodings assailed me.

Ackroyd spoke again almost immediately.

'Make certain that window's closed, will you,' he asked.

Somewhat surprised, I got up and went to it. It was not a french window, but one of the ordinary sash type. The heavy blue velvet curtains were drawn in front of it, but the window itself was open at the top.

Parker re-entered the room with my bag while I was still at the window.

'That's all right,' I said, emerging again into the room.

'You've put the latch across?'

'Yes, yes. What's the matter with you, Ackroyd?'

The door had just closed behind Parker, or I would not have put the question.

Ackroyd waited just a minute before replying.

'I'm in hell,' he said slowly, after a minute. 'No, don't bother with those damn tablets. I only said that for Parker. Servants are so curious. Come here and sit down. The door's closed too, isn't it?'

'Yes. Nobody can overhear; don't be uneasy.'

'Sheppard, nobody knows what I've gone through in the last twenty-four hours. If a man's house ever fell in ruin about him, mine has about me. This business of Ralph's is the last straw. But we won't talk about that now. It's the other – the other –! I don't know what to do about it. And I've got to make up my mind soon.'

'What's the trouble?'

Ackroyd remained silent for a minute or two. He seemed curiously averse to begin. When he did speak, the question he asked came as a complete surprise. It was the last thing I expected.

'Sheppard, you attended Ashley Ferrars in his last illness, didn't you?'

'Yes, I did.'

He seemed to find even greater difficulty in framing his next question.

'Did you ever suspect – did it ever enter your head – that – well, that he might have been poisoned?'

I was silent for a minute or two. Then I made up my mind what to say. Roger Ackroyd was not Caroline.

'I'll tell you the truth,' I said. 'At the time I had no suspicion whatever, but since – well, it was mere idle talk on my sister's part that first put the idea into my head. Since then I haven't been able to get it out again. But, mind you, I've no foundation whatever for that suspicion.'

'He *was* poisoned,' said Ackroyd.

He spoke in a dull heavy voice.

'Who by?' I asked sharply.

'His wife.'

'How do you know that?'

'She told me so herself.'

'When?'

'Yesterday! My God! yesterday! It seems ten years ago.'

I waited a minute, then he went on.

'You understand, Sheppard, I'm telling you this in confidence. It's to go no further. I want your advice – I can't carry the whole weight by myself. As I said just now, I don't know what to do.'

'Can you tell me the whole story?' I said. 'I'm still in the dark. How did Mrs Ferrars come to make this confession to you?'

'It's like this. Three months ago I asked Mrs Ferrars to marry me. She refused. I asked her again and she consented, but she refused to allow me to make the engagement public until her year of mourning was up. Yesterday I called upon her, pointed out that a year and three weeks had now elapsed since her husband's death, and that there could be no further objection to making the engagement public property. I had noticed that she had been very strange in her manner for some days. Now, suddenly, without the least warning, she broke down completely. She – she told me everything. Her hatred of her brute of a husband, her growing love for me, and the – the dreadful means she had taken. Poison! My God! It was murder in cold blood.'

I saw the repulsion, the horror, in Ackroyd's face. So Mrs Ferrars must have seen it. Ackroyd's is not the type of the great lover who can forgive all for love's sake. He is fundamentally a good citizen. All that was sound and wholesome and law-abiding in him must have turned from her utterly in that moment of revelation.

'Yes,' he went on, in a low, monotonous voice, 'she confessed everything. It seems that there is one person who has known all along – who has been blackmailing her for huge sums. It was the strain of that that drove her nearly mad.'

'Who was the man?'

Suddenly before my eyes there arose the picture of Ralph Paton and Mrs Ferrars side by side. Their heads so close together. I felt a momentary throb of anxiety. Supposing – oh! but surely that was impossible. I remembered the frankness of Ralph's greeting that very afternoon. Absurd!

'She wouldn't tell me his name,' said Ackroyd slowly. 'As a matter of fact, she didn't actually say that it was a man. But of course –'

'Of course,' I agreed. 'It must have been a man. And you've no suspicion at all?'

For answer Ackroyd groaned and dropped his head into his hands.

'It can't be,' he said. 'I'm mad even to think of such a thing. No, I won't even admit to you the wild suspicion that crossed my mind. I'll tell you this much, though. Something she said made me think that the person in question might be actually among my household – but that can't be so. I must have misunderstood her.'

'What did you say to her?' I asked.

'What could I say? She saw, of course, the awful shock it had been to me. And then there was the question, what was my duty in the matter? She had made me, you see, an accessory after the fact. She saw all that, I think, quicker than I did. I was stunned, you know. She asked me for twenty-four hours – made me promise to do nothing till the end of that time. And she steadfastly refused to give me the name of the scoundrel who had been blackmailing her. I suppose she was afraid that I might go straight off and hammer him, and then the fat would have been in the fire as far as she was concerned. She told me that I should hear from her before twenty-four hours had passed. My God! I swear to you, Sheppard, that it never entered my head what she meant to do. Suicide! And I drove her to it.'

'No, no,' I said. 'Don't take an exaggerated view of things. The responsibility for her death doesn't lie at your door.'

'The question is, what am I to do now? The poor lady is dead. Why rake up past trouble?'

'I rather agree with you,' I said.

'But there's another point. How am I to get hold of that scoundrel who drove her to death as surely as if he'd killed her? He knew of the first crime, and he fastened on to it like some obscene vulture. She's paid the penalty. Is he to go scot free?'

'I see,' I said slowly. 'You want to hunt him down? It will mean a lot of publicity, you know.'

'Yes, I've thought of that. I've zigzagged to and fro in my mind.'

'I agree with you that the villain ought to be punished, but the cost has got to be reckoned.'

Ackroyd rose and walked up and down. Presently he sank into the chair again.

'Look here, Sheppard, suppose we leave it like this. If no word comes from her, we'll let the dead things lie.'

'What do you mean by word coming from her?' I asked curiously.

'I have the strongest impression that somewhere or somehow she must have left a message for me – before she went. I can't argue about it, but there it is.'

I shook my head.

'She left no letter or word of any kind?' I asked.

'Sheppard, I'm convinced that she did. And more, I've a feeling that by deliberately choosing death, she wanted the whole thing to come out, if only to be revenged on the man who drove her to desperation. I believe that if I could have seen her then, she would have told me his name and bid me go for him for all I was worth.'

He looked at me.

'You don't believe in impressions?'

'Oh, yes, I do, in a sense. If, as you put it, word should come from her –'

I broke off. The door opened noiselessly and Parker entered with a salver on which were some letters.

'The evening post, sir,' he said, handing the salver to Ackroyd.

Then he collected the coffee cups and withdrew.

My attention, diverted for a moment, came back to Ackroyd. He was staring like a man turned to stone at a long blue envelope. The other letters he had let drop to the ground.

'*Her writing*,' he said in a whisper. 'She must have gone out and posted it last night, just before – before –'

He ripped open the envelope and drew out a thick enclosure. Then he looked up sharply.

'You're sure you shut the window?' he said.

'Quite sure,' I said, surprised. 'Why?'

'All this evening I've had a queer feeling of being watched, spied upon. What's that –'

He turned sharply. So did I. We both had the impression of hearing the latch of the door give ever so slightly. I went across to it and opened it. There was no one there.

'Nerves,' murmured Ackroyd to himself.

He unfolded the thick sheets of paper, and read aloud in a low voice.

'My dear, my very dear Roger, – A life calls for a life. I see that – I saw it in your face this afternoon. So I am taking the only road open to me. I leave to you the punishment of the person who has made my life a hell upon earth for the last year. I would not tell you the name, this afternoon, but I propose to write it to you

now. I have no children or near relations to be spared, so do not fear publicity. If you can, Roger, my very dear Roger, forgive me the wrong I meant to do you, since when the time came, I could not do it after all . . .'

Ackroyd, his finger on the sheet to turn it over, paused.

'Sheppard, forgive me, but I must read this alone,' he said unsteadily. 'It was meant for my eyes, and my eyes only.'

He put the letter in the envelope and laid it on the table.

'Later, when I am alone.'

'No,' I cried impulsively, 'read it now.'

Ackroyd stared at me in some surprise.

'I beg your pardon,' I said, reddening. 'I do not mean read it aloud to me. But read it through whilst I am still here.'

Ackroyd shook his head.

'No, I'd rather wait.'

But for some reason, obscure to myself, I continued to urge him.

'At least, read the name of the man,' I said.

Now Ackroyd is essentially pig-headed. The more you urge him to do a thing, the more determined he is not to do it. All my arguments were in vain.

The letter had been brought in at twenty minutes to nine. It was just on ten minutes to nine when I left him, the letter still unread. I hesitated with my hand on the door handle, looking back and wondering if there was anything I had left undone. I could think of nothing. With a shake of the head I passed out and closed the door behind me.

I was startled by seeing the figure of Parker close at hand. He looked embarrassed, and it occurred to me that he might have been listening at the door.

What a fat, smug, oily face the man had, and surely there was something decidedly shifty in his eye.

'Mr Ackroyd particularly does not want to be disturbed,' I said coldly. 'He told me to tell you so.'

'Quite so, sir. I – I fancied I heard the bell ring.'

This was such a palpable untruth that I did not trouble to reply. Preceding me to the hall, Parker helped me on with my overcoat, and I stepped out into the night. The moon was overcast, and everything seemed very dark and still.

The village church clock chimed nine o'clock as I passed through the lodge gates. I turned to the left towards the village, and almost cannoned into a man coming in the opposite direction.

'This the way to Fernly Park, mister?' asked the stranger in a hoarse voice.

I looked at him. He was wearing a hat pulled down over his eyes, and his coat collar turned up. I could see little or nothing of his face, but he seemed a young fellow. The voice was rough and uneducated.

'These are the lodge gates here,' I said.

'Thank you, mister.' He paused, and then added, quite unnecessarily, 'I'm a stranger in these parts, you see.'

He went on, passing through the gates as I turned to look after him.

The odd thing was that his voice reminded me of someone's voice that I knew, but whose it was I could not think.

Ten minutes later I was at home once more. Caroline was full of curiosity to know why I had returned so early. I had to make up a slightly fictitious account of the evening in order to satisfy her, and I had an uneasy feeling that she saw through the transparent device.

At ten o'clock I rose, yawned, and suggested bed. Caroline acquiesced.

It was Friday night, and on Friday night I wind the clocks. I did it as usual, whilst Caroline satisfied herself that the servants had locked up the kitchen properly.

It was a quarter past ten as we went up the stairs. I had just reached the top when the telephone rang in the hall below.

'Mrs Bates,' said Caroline immediately.

'I'm afraid so,' I said ruefully.

I ran down the stairs and took up the receiver.

'What?' I said. '*What?* Certainly, I'll come at once.'

I ran upstairs, caught up my bag, and stuffed a few extra dressings into it.

'Parker telephoning,' I shouted to Caroline, 'from Fernly. They've just found Roger Ackroyd murdered.'

CHAPTER 5

MURDER

I got out the car in next to no time, and drove rapidly to Fernly. Jumping out, I pulled the bell impatiently. There was some delay in answering, and I rang again.

Then I heard the rattle of the chain and Parker, his impassivity of countenance quite unmoved, stood in the open doorway.

I pushed past him into the hall.

'Where is he?' I demanded sharply.

'I beg your pardon, sir?'

'Your master. Mr Ackroyd. Don't stand there staring at me, man. Have you notified the police?'

'The police, sir? Did you say the police?' Parker stared at me as though I were a ghost.

'What's the matter with you, Parker? If, as you say, your master has been murdered –'

A gasp broke from Parker.

'The master? Murdered? Impossible, sir!'

It was my turn to stare.

'Didn't you telephone to me, not five minutes ago, and tell me that Mr Ackroyd had been found murdered?'

'Me, sir? Oh! no indeed, sir. I wouldn't dream of doing such a thing.'

'Do you mean to say it's all a hoax? That there's nothing the matter with Mr Ackroyd?'

'Excuse me, sir, did the person telephoning use my name?'

'I'll give you the exact words I heard. "*Is that Dr Sheppard? Parker, the butler at Fernly, speaking. Will you please come at once, sir. Mr Ackroyd has been murdered.*"'

Parker and I stared at each other blankly.

'A very wicked joke to play, sir,' he said at last, in a shocked tone. 'Fancy saying a thing like that.'

'Where is Mr Ackroyd?' I asked suddenly.

'Still in the study, I fancy, sir. The ladies have gone to bed, and Major Blunt and Mr Raymond are in the billiard room.'

'I think I'll just look in and see him for a minute,' I said. 'I know he didn't want to be disturbed again, but this odd practical joke has made me uneasy. I'd just like to satisfy myself that he's all right.'

'Quite so, sir. It makes me feel quite uneasy myself. If you don't object to my accompanying you as far as the door, sir –?'

'Not at all,' I said. 'Come along.'

I passed through the door on the right, Parker on my heels, traversed the little lobby where a small flight of stairs led upstairs to Ackroyd's bedroom, and tapped on the study door.

There was no answer. I turned the handle, but the door was locked.

'Allow me, sir,' said Parker.

Very nimbly, for a man of his build, he dropped on one knee and applied his eye to the keyhole.

'Key is in the lock all right, sir,' he said, rising. 'On the inside. Mr Ackroyd must have locked himself in and possibly just dropped off to sleep.'

I bent down and verified Parker's statement.

'It seems all right,' I said, 'but, all the same, Parker, I'm going to wake your master up. I shouldn't be satisfied to go home without hearing from his own lips that he's quite all right.'

So saying, I rattled the handle and called out, 'Ackroyd, Ackroyd, just a minute.'

But still there was no answer. I glanced over my shoulder.

'I don't want to alarm the household,' I said hesitatingly.

Parker went across and shut the door from the big hall through which we had come.

'I think that will be all right now, sir. The billiard room is at the other side of the house, and so are the kitchen quarters and the ladies' bedrooms.'

I nodded comprehendingly. Then I banged once more frantically on the door, and stooping down, fairly bawled through the keyhole:

'Ackroyd, Ackroyd! It's Sheppard. Let me in.'

And still – silence. Not a sign of life from within the locked room. Parker and I glanced at each other.

'Look here, Parker,' I said, 'I'm going to break this door in – or rather, we are. I'll take the responsibility.'

'If you say so, sir,' said Parker, rather doubtfully.

'I do say so. I'm seriously alarmed about Mr Ackroyd.'

I looked round the small lobby and picked up a heavy oak chair. Parker and I held it between us and advanced to the assault. Once, twice, and three times we hurled it against the lock. At the third blow it gave, and we staggered into the room.

Ackroyd was sitting as I had left him in the arm-chair before the fire. His head had fallen sideways, and clearly visible, just below the collar of his coat, was a shining piece of twisted metalwork.

Parker and I advanced till we stood over the recumbent figure. I heard the butler draw in his breath with a sharp hiss.

'Stabbed from be'ind,' he murmured. ''Orrible!'

He wiped his moist brow with his handkerchief, then stretched out a gingerly hand towards the hilt of the dagger.

'You mustn't touch that,' I said sharply. 'Go at once to the telephone and ring up the police station. Inform them of what has happened. Then tell Mr Raymond and Major Blunt.'

'Very good, sir.'

Parker hurried away, still wiping his perspiring brow.

I did what little had to be done. I was careful not to disturb the position of the body, and not to handle the dagger at all. No object was to be attained by moving it. Ackroyd had clearly been dead some little time.

Then I heard young Raymond's voice, horror-stricken and incredulous, outside.

'What do you say? Oh! impossible! Where's the doctor?'

He appeared impetuously in the doorway, then stopped dead, his face very white. A hand put him aside, and Hector Blunt came past him into the room.

'My God!' said Raymond from behind him; 'it's true, then.'

Blunt came straight on till he reached the chair. He bent over the body, and I thought that, like Parker, he was going to lay hold of the dagger hilt. I drew him back with one hand.

'Nothing must be moved,' I explained. 'The police must see him exactly as he is now.'

Blunt nodded in instant comprehension. His face was expressionless as ever, but I thought I detected signs of emotion beneath the stolid mask. Geoffrey Raymond had joined us now, and stood peering over Blunt's shoulder at the body.

'This is terrible,' he said in a low voice.

He had regained his composure, but as he took off the pince-nez he habitually wore and polished them I observed that his hand was shaking.

'Robbery, I suppose,' he said. 'How did the fellow get in? Through the window? Has anything been taken?'

He went towards the desk.

'You think it's burglary?' I said slowly.

'What else could it be? There's no question of suicide, I suppose?'

'No man could stab himself in such a way,' I said confidently. 'It's murder right enough. But with what motive?'

'Roger hadn't an enemy in the world,' said Blunt quietly. 'Must have been burglars. But what was the thief after? Nothing seems to be disarranged?'

He looked round the room. Raymond was still sorting the papers on the desk.

'There seems nothing missing, and none of the drawers show signs of having been tampered with,' the secretary observed at last. 'It's very mysterious.'

Blunt made a slight motion with his head.

'There are some letters on the floor here,' he said.

I looked down. Three or four letters still lay where Ackroyd had dropped them earlier in the evening.

But the blue envelope containing Mrs Ferrars's letter had disappeared. I half opened my mouth to speak, but at that moment the sound of a bell pealed through the house. There was a confused murmur of voices in the hall, and then Parker appeared with our local inspector and a police constable.

'Good evening, gentlemen,' said the inspector. 'I'm terribly sorry for this! A good kind gentleman like Mr Ackroyd. The butler says it's murder. No possibility of accident or suicide, doctor?'

'None whatever,' I said.

'Ah! A bad business.'

He came and stood over the body.

'Been moved at all?' he asked sharply.

'Beyond making certain that life was extinct – an easy matter – I have not disturbed the body in any way.'

'Ah! And everything points to the murderer having got clear away – for the moment, that is. Now then, let me hear all about it. Who found the body?'

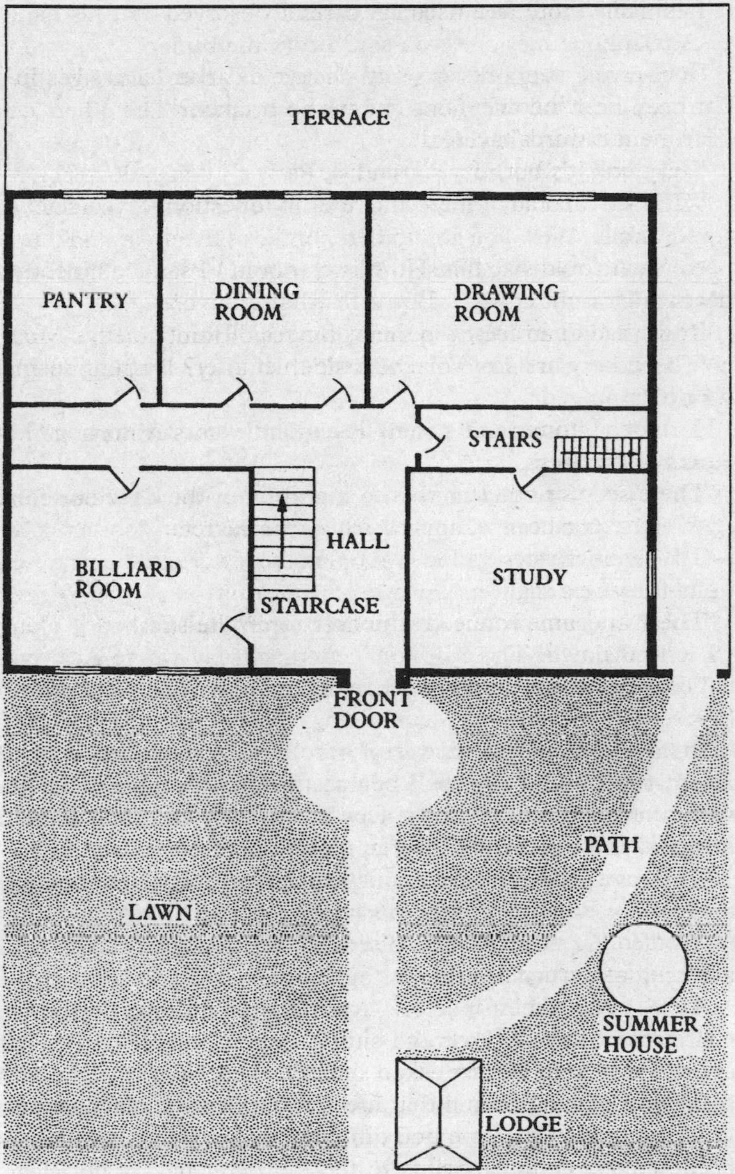
TERRACE
PANTRY
DINING ROOM
DRAWING ROOM
STAIRS
HALL
BILLIARD ROOM
STAIRCASE
STUDY
FRONT DOOR
PATH
LAWN
SUMMER HOUSE
LODGE

I explained the circumstances carefully.

'A telephone message, you say? From the butler?'

'A message that I never sent,' declared Parker earnestly. 'I've not been near the telephone the whole evening. The others can bear me out that I haven't.'

'Very odd, that. Did it sound like Parker's voice, doctor?'

'Well – I can't say I noticed. I took it for granted, you see.'

'Naturally. Well, you got up here, broke in the door, and found poor Mr Ackroyd like this. How long should you say he had been dead, doctor?'

'Half an hour at least – perhaps longer,' I said.

'The door was locked on the inside, you say? What about the window?'

'I myself closed and bolted it earlier in the evening at Mr Ackroyd's request.'

The inspector strode across to it and threw back the curtains.

'Well, it's open now, anyway,' he remarked.

True enough, the window was open, the lower sash being raised to its fullest extent.

The inspector produced a pocket torch and flashed it along the sill outside.

'This is the way he went all right,' he remarked, '*and* got in. See here.'

In the light of the powerful torch, several clearly defined footmarks could be seen. They seemed to be those of shoes with rubber studs in the soles. One particularly clear one pointed inwards, another, slightly overlapping it, pointed outwards.

'Plain as a pikestaff,' said the inspector. 'Any valuables missing?'

Geoffrey Raymond shook his head.

'Not so far that we can discover. Mr Ackroyd never kept anything of particular value in this room.'

'H'm,' said the inspector. 'Man found an open window. Climbed in, saw Mr Ackroyd sitting there – maybe he'd fallen asleep. Man stabbed him from behind, then lost his nerve and made off. But he's left his tracks pretty clearly. We ought to get hold of *him* without much difficulty. No suspicious strangers been hanging about anywhere?'

'Oh!' I said suddenly.

'What is it, doctor?'

'I met a man this evening – just as I was turning out of the gate. He asked me the way to Fernly Park.'

'What time would that be?'

'Just nine o'clock. I heard it chime the hour as I was turning out of the gate.'

'Can you describe him?'

I did so to the best of my ability.

The inspector turned to the butler.

'Anyone answering that description come to the front door?'

'No, sir. No one has been to the house at all this evening.'

'What about the back?'

'I don't think so, sir, but I'll make inquiries.'

He moved towards the door, but the inspector held up a large hand.

'No, thanks. I'll do my own inquiring. But first of all I want to fix the times a little more clearly. When was Mr Ackroyd last seen alive?'

'Probably by me,' I said, 'when I left at – let me see – about ten minutes to nine. He told me that he didn't wish to be disturbed, and I repeated the order to Parker.'

'Just so, sir,' said Parker respectfully.

'Mr Ackroyd was certainly alive at half-past nine,' put in Raymond, 'for I heard his voice in here talking.'

'Who was he talking to?'

'That I don't know. Of course, at the time I took it for granted that it was Dr Sheppard who was with him. I wanted to ask him a question about some papers I was engaged upon, but when I heard the voices I remembered that he had said he wanted to talk to Dr Sheppard without being disturbed, and I went away again. But now it seems that the doctor had already left?'

I nodded.

'I was at home by a quarter past nine,' I said. 'I didn't go out again until I received the telephone call.'

'Who could have been with him at half-past nine?' queried the inspector. 'It wasn't you, Mr – er –'

'Major Blunt,' I said.

'Major Hector Blunt?' asked the inspector, a respectful tone creeping into his voice.

Blunt merely jerked his head affirmatively.

'I think we've seen you down here before, sir,' said the inspector. 'I didn't recognize you for the moment, but you were staying with Mr Ackroyd a year ago last May.'

'June,' corrected Blunt.

'Just so, June it was. Now, as I was saying, it wasn't you with Mr Ackroyd at nine-thirty this evening?'

Blunt shook his head.

'Never saw him after dinner,' he volunteered.

The inspector turned once more to Raymond.

'You didn't overhear any of the conversation going on, did you, sir?'

'I did catch just a fragment of it,' said the secretary, 'and, supposing as I did that it was Dr Sheppard who was with Mr Ackroyd, that fragment struck me as distinctly odd. As far as I can remember, the exact words were these. Mr Ackroyd was speaking. "The calls on my purse have been so frequent of late" – that is what he was saying – "of late, that I fear it is impossible for me to accede to your request . . ." I went away again at once, of course, so I did not hear any more. But I rather wondered because Dr Sheppard –'

'– Does not ask for loans for himself or subscriptions for others,' I finished.

'A demand for money,' said the inspector musingly. 'It may be that here we have a very important clue.' He turned to the butler. 'You say, Parker, that nobody was admitted by the front door this evening?'

'That's what I say, sir.'

'Then it seems almost certain that Mr Ackroyd himself must have admitted this stranger. But I don't quite see –'

The inspector went into a kind of day-dream for some minutes.

'One thing's clear,' he said at length, rousing himself from his absorption. 'Mr Ackroyd was alive and well at nine-thirty. That is the last moment at which he is known to have been alive.'

Parker gave vent to an apologetic cough which brought the inspector's eyes on him at once.

'Well?' he said sharply.

'If you'll excuse me, sir, Miss Flora saw him after that.'

'Miss Flora?'

'Yes, sir. About a quarter to ten that would be. It was after that that she told me Mr Ackroyd wasn't to be disturbed again tonight.'

'Did he send her to you with that message?'

'Not exactly, sir. I was bringing a tray with soda and whisky when Miss Flora, who was just coming out of this room, stopped me and said her uncle didn't want to be disturbed.'

The inspector looked at the butler with rather closer attention than he had bestowed on him up to now.

'You'd already been told that Mr Ackroyd didn't want to be disturbed, hadn't you?'

Parker began to stammer. His hands shook.

'Yes, sir. Yes, sir. Quite so, sir.'

'And yet you were proposing to do so?'

'I'd forgotten, sir. At least I mean, I always bring the whisky and soda about that time, sir, and ask if there's anything more, and I thought – well, I was doing as usual without thinking.'

It was at this moment that it began to dawn upon me that Parker was most suspiciously flustered. The man was shaking and twitching all over.

'H'm,' said the inspector. 'I must see Miss Ackroyd at once. For the moment we'll leave this room exactly as it is. I can return here after I've heard what Miss Ackroyd has to tell me. I shall just take the precaution of shutting and bolting the window.'

This precaution accomplished, he led the way into the hall and we followed him. He paused a moment, as he glanced up at the little staircase, then spoke over his shoulder to the constable.

'Jones, you'd better stay here. Don't let anyone go into that room.'

Parker interposed deferentially.

'If you'll excuse me, sir. If you were to lock the door into the main hall, nobody could gain access to this part. That staircase leads only to Mr Ackroyd's bedroom and bathroom. There is no communication with the other part of the house. There once was a door through, but Mr Ackroyd had it blocked up. He liked to feel that his suite was entirely private.'

To make things clear and explain the position, I have appended a rough sketch of the right-hand wing of the house. The small staircase leads, as Parker explained, to a big bedroom made by two being knocked into one, and an adjoining bathroom and lavatory.

The inspector took in the position at a glance. We went through into the large hall and he locked the door behind him, slipping the key into his pocket. Then he gave the constable some low-voiced instructions, and the latter prepared to depart.

'We must get busy on those shoe tracks,' explained the inspector. 'But first of all, I must have a word with Miss Ackroyd. She was the last person to see her uncle alive. Does she know yet?'

Raymond shook his head.

'Well, no need to tell her for another five minutes. She can answer my questions better without being upset by knowing the truth about her uncle. Tell her there's been a burglary, and ask her if she would mind dressing and coming down to answer a few questions.'

It was Raymond who went upstairs on this errand.

'Miss Ackroyd will be down in a minute,' he said, when he returned. 'I told her just what you suggested.'

In less than five minutes Flora descended the staircase. She was wrapped in a pale pink silk kimono. She looked anxious and excited.

The inspector stepped forward.

'Good evening, Miss Ackroyd,' he said civilly. 'We're afraid there's been an attempt at robbery, and we want you to help us. What's this room – the billiard room? Come in here and sit down.'

Flora sat down composedly on the wide divan which ran the length of the wall, and looked up at the inspector.

'I don't quite understand. What has been stolen? What do you want me to tell you?'

'It's just this, Miss Ackroyd. Parker here says you came out of your uncle's study at about a quarter to ten. Is that right?'

'Quite right. I had been to say goodnight to him.'

'And the time is correct?'

'Well, it must have been about then. I can't say exactly. It might have been later.'

'Was your uncle alone, or was there anyone with him?'

'He was alone. Dr Sheppard had gone.'

'Did you happen to notice whether the window was open or shut?'

Flora shook her head.

'I can't say. The curtains were drawn.'

'Exactly. And your uncle seemed quite as usual?'

'I think so.'

'Do you mind telling us exactly what passed between you?'

Flora paused a minute, as though to collect her recollections.

'I went in and said, "Goodnight, Uncle, I'm going to bed now. I'm tired tonight." He gave a sort of grunt, and – I went over and kissed him, and he said something about my looking nice in the frock I had on, and then he told me to run away as he was busy. So I went.'

'Did he ask specially not to be disturbed?'

'Oh! yes, I forgot. He said: "Tell Parker I don't want anything more tonight, and that he's not to disturb me." I met Parker just outside the door and gave him Uncle's message.'

'Just so,' said the inspector.

'Won't you tell me what it is that has been stolen?'

'We're not quite – certain,' said the inspector hesitatingly.

A wide look of alarm came into the girl's eyes. She started up.

'What is it? You're hiding something from me?'

Moving in his usual unobtrusive manner, Hector Blunt came between her and the inspector. She half stretched out her hand, and he took it in both of his, patting it as though she were a very small child, and she turned to him as though something in his stolid, rocklike demeanour promised comfort and safety.

'It's bad news, Flora,' he said quietly. 'Bad news for all of us. Your Uncle Roger –'

'Yes?'

'It will be a shock to you. Bound to be. Poor Roger's dead.'

Flora drew away from him, her eyes dilating with horror.

'When?' she whispered. 'When?'

'Very soon after you left him, I'm afraid,' said Blunt gravely.

Flora raised her hand to her throat, gave a little cry, and I hurried to catch her as she fell. She had fainted, and Blunt and I carried her upstairs and laid her on her bed. Then I got him to wake Mrs Ackroyd and tell her the news. Flora soon revived, and I brought her mother to her, telling her what to do for the girl. Then I hurried downstairs again.

CHAPTER 6

THE TUNISIAN DAGGER

I met the inspector just coming from the door which led into the kitchen quarters.

'How's the young lady, doctor?'

'Coming round nicely. Her mother's with her.'

'That's good. I've been questioning the servants. They all declare that no one has been to the back door tonight. Your description of that stranger was rather vague. Can't you give us something more definite to go upon?'

'I'm afraid not,' I said regretfully. 'It was a dark night, you see, and the fellow had his coat collar well pulled up and his hat squashed down over his eyes.'

'H'm,' said the inspector. 'Looked as though he wanted to conceal his face. Sure it was no one you know?'

I replied in the negative, but not as decidedly as I might have done. I remembered my impression that the stranger's voice was not unfamiliar to me. I explained this rather haltingly to the inspector.

'It was a rough, uneducated voice, you say?'

I agreed, but it occurred to me that the roughness had been of an almost exaggerated quality. If, as the inspector thought, the man had wished to hide his face, he might equally well have tried to disguise his voice.

'Do you mind coming into the study with me again, doctor? There are one or two things I want to ask you.'

I acquiesced. Inspector Davis unlocked the door of the lobby, we passed through, and he locked the door again behind him.

'We don't want to be disturbed,' he said grimly. 'And we don't want any eavesdropping either. What's all this about blackmail?'

'Blackmail!' I exclaimed, very much startled.

'Is it an effort of Parker's imagination? Or is there something in it?'

'If Parker heard anything about blackmail,' I said slowly, 'he must have been listening outside this door with his ear glued against the keyhole.'

Davis nodded.

'Nothing more likely. You see, I've been instituting a few inquiries as to what Parker has been doing with himself this evening. To tell the truth, I didn't like his manner. The man knows something. When I began to question him, he got the wind up, and plumped out some garbled story of blackmail.'

I took an instant decision.

'I'm rather glad you've brought the matter up,' I said. 'I've been trying to decide whether to make a clean breast of things or not. I'd already practically decided to tell you everything, but I was going to wait for a favourable opportunity. You might as well have it now.'

And then and there I narrated the whole events of the evening as I have set them down here. The inspector listened keenly, occasionally interjecting a question.

'Most extraordinary story I ever heard,' he said, when I had finished. 'And you say that letter has completely disappeared? It looks bad – it looks very bad indeed. It gives us what we've been looking for – a motive for the murder.'

I nodded.

'I realize that.'

'You say that Mr Ackroyd hinted at a suspicion he had that some member of his household was involved? Household's rather an elastic term.'

'You don't think that Parker himself might be the man we're after?' I suggested.

'It looks very like it. He was obviously listening at the door when you came out. Then Miss Ackroyd came across him later bent on entering the study. Say he tried again when she was safely out of the way. He stabbed Ackroyd, locked the door on the inside, opened the window, and got out that way, and went round to a side door which he had previously left open. How's that?'

'There's only one thing against it,' I said slowly. 'If Ackroyd went on reading that letter as soon as I left, as he intended to do, I don't see him continuing to sit on here and turn things over in his mind for another hour. He'd have had Parker in at once, accused him then and there, and there would have been a fine old uproar. Remember, Ackroyd was a man of choleric temper.'

'Mightn't have had time to go on with the letter just then,' suggested the inspector. 'We know someone was with him at half-past nine. If that visitor turned up as soon as you left, and after he went, Miss Ackroyd came in to say goodnight – well, he wouldn't be able to go on with the letter until close upon ten o'clock.'

'And the telephone call?'

'Parker sent that all right – perhaps before he thought of the locked door and open window. Then he changed his mind – or got in a panic – and decided to deny all knowledge of it. That was it, depend upon it.'

'Ye – es,' I said rather doubtfully.

'Anyway, we can find out the truth about the telephone call from the exchange. If it was put through from here, I don't see how anyone else but Parker could have sent it. Depend upon it, he's our man. But keep it dark – we don't want to alarm him just yet, till we've got all the evidence. I'll see to it he doesn't give us the slip. To all appearances we'll be concentrating on your mysterious stranger.'

He rose from where he had been sitting astride the chair belonging to the desk, and crossed over to the still form in the arm-chair.

'The weapon ought to give us a clue,' he remarked, looking up. 'It's something quite unique – a curio, I should think, by the look of it.'

He bent down, surveying the handle attentively, and I heard him give a grunt of satisfaction. Then, very gingerly, he pressed his hands down below the hilt and drew the blade out from the wound. Still carrying it so as not to touch the handle, he placed it in a wide china mug which adorned the mantelpiece.

'Yes,' he said, nodding at it. 'Quite a work of art. There can't be many of them about.'

It was indeed a beautiful object. A narrow, tapering blade, and a hilt of elaborately intertwined metals of curious and careful workmanship. He touched the blade gingerly with his finger, testing its sharpness, and made an appreciative grimace.

'Lord, what an edge,' he exclaimed. 'A child could drive that into a man – as easy as cutting butter. A dangerous sort of toy to have about.'

'May I examine the body properly now?' I asked.

He nodded.

'Go ahead.'

I made a thorough examination.

'Well?' said the inspector, when I had finished.

'I'll spare you the technical language,' I said. 'We'll keep that for the inquest. The blow was delivered by a right-handed man standing behind him, and death must have been instantaneous. By the expression on the dead man's face, I should say that the blow was quite unexpected. He may have died without knowing who his assailant was.'

'Butlers can creep about as soft-footed as cats,' said Inspector Davis. 'There's not going to be much mystery about this crime. Take a look at the hilt of that dagger.'

I took the look.

'I dare say they're not apparent to you, but *I* can see them clearly enough.' He lowered his voice. '*Fingerprints!*'

He stood off a few steps to judge of his effect.

'Yes,' I said mildly. 'I guessed that.'

I do not see why I should be supposed to be totally devoid of intelligence. After all, I read detective stories, and the newspapers, and am a man of quite average ability. If there had been toe marks on the dagger handle, now, that would have been quite a different thing. I would then have registered any amount of surprise and awe.

I think the inspector was annoyed with me for declining to get thrilled. He picked up the china mug and invited me to accompany him to the billiard room.

'I want to see if Mr Raymond can tell us anything about this dagger,' he explained.

Locking the outer door behind us again, we made our way to the billiard room, where we found Geoffrey Raymond. The inspector held up his exhibit.

'Ever seen this before, Mr Raymond?'

'Why – I believe – I'm almost sure that is a curio given to Mr Ackroyd by Major Blunt. It comes from Morocco – no, Tunis. So the crime was committed with that? What an extraordinary thing. It seems almost impossible, and yet there could hardly be two daggers the same. May I fetch Major Blunt?'

Without waiting for an answer, he hurried off.

'Nice young fellow that,' said the inspector. 'Something honest and ingenuous about him.'

I agreed. In the two years that Geoffrey Raymond has been secretary to Ackroyd, I have never seen him ruffled or out of temper. And he has been, I know, a most efficient secretary.

In a minute or two Raymond returned, accompanied by Blunt.

'I was right,' said Raymond excitedly. 'It *is* the Tunisian dagger.'

'Major Blunt hasn't looked at it yet,' objected the inspector.

'Saw it the moment I came into the study,' said the quiet man.

'You recognized it, then?'

Blunt nodded.

'You said nothing about it,' said the inspector suspiciously.

'Wrong moment,' said Blunt. 'Lot of harm done by blurting out things at the wrong time.'

He returned the inspector's stare placidly enough.

The latter grunted at last and turned away. He brought the dagger over to Blunt.

'You're quite sure about it, sir. You identify it positively?'

'Absolutely. No doubt whatever.'

'Where was this – er – curio usually kept? Can you tell me that, sir?'

It was the secretary who answered.

'In the silver table in the drawing-room.'

'What?' I exclaimed.

The others looked at me.

'Yes, doctor?' said the inspector encouragingly.

'It's nothing,' said the inspector again, still encouragingly.

'It's so trivial,' I explained apologetically. 'Only that when I arrived last night for dinner I heard the lid of the silver table being shut down in the drawing-room.'

I saw profound scepticism and a trace of suspicion on the inspector's countenance.

'How did you know it was the silver table lid?'

I was forced to explain in detail – a long, tedious explanation which I would infinitely rather not have had to make.

The inspector heard me to the end.

'Was the dagger in its place when you were looking over the contents?' he asked.

'I don't know,' I said. 'I can't say I remember noticing it – but, of course, it may have been there all the time.'

'We'd better get hold of the housekeeper,' remarked the inspector, and pulled the bell.

A few minutes later Miss Russell, summoned by Parker, entered the room.

'I don't think I went near the silver table,' she said, when the inspector had posed his question. 'I was looking to see that all the flowers were fresh. Oh! yes, I remember now. The silver table was open – which it had no business to be, and I shut the lid down as I passed.'

She looked at him aggressively.

'I see,' said the inspector. 'Can you tell me if this dagger was in its place then?'

Miss Russell looked at the weapon composedly.

'I can't say I'm sure,' she replied. 'I didn't stop to look. I knew the family would be down any minute, and I wanted to get away.'

'Thank you,' said the inspector.

There was just a trace of hesitation in his manner, as though he would have liked to question her further, but Miss Russell clearly accepted the words as a dismissal, and glided from the room.

'Rather a Tartar, I should fancy, eh?' said the inspector, looking after her. 'Let me see. This silver table is in front of one of the windows, I think you said, doctor?'

Raymond answered for me.

'Yes, the left-hand window.'

'And the window was open?'

'They were both ajar.'

'Well, I don't think we need go into the question much further. Somebody – I'll just say somebody – could get that dagger any time he liked, and exactly when he got it doesn't matter in the least. I'll be coming up in the morning with the chief constable, Mr Raymond. Until then, I'll keep the key of that door. I want Colonel Melrose to see everything exactly as it is. I happen to know that he's dining out the other side of the county, and, I believe, staying the night . . .'

We watched the inspector take up the jar.

'I shall have to pack this carefully,' he observed. 'It's going to be an important piece of evidence in more ways than one.'

A few minutes later as I came out of the billiard room with Raymond, the latter gave a low chuckle of amusement.

I felt the pressure of his hand on my arm, and followed the direction of his eyes. Inspector Davis seemed to be inviting Parker's opinion of a small pocket diary.

'A little obvious,' murmured my companion. 'So Parker is the suspect, is he? Shall we oblige Inspector Davis with a set of our fingerprints also?'

He took two cards from the card tray, wiped them with his silk handkerchief, then handed one to me and took the other himself. Then, with a grin, he handed them to the police inspector.

'Souvenirs,' he said. 'No. 1. Dr Sheppard; No. 2, my humble self. One from Major Blunt will be forthcoming in the morning.'

Youth is very buoyant. Even the brutal murder of his friend and employer could not dim Geoffrey Raymond's spirits for long. Perhaps that is as it should be. I do not know. I have lost the quality of resilience long since myself.

It was very late when I got back, and I hoped that Caroline would have gone to bed. I might have known better.

She had hot cocoa waiting for me, and whilst I drank it, she extracted the whole history of the evening from me. I said nothing of the blackmailing business, but contented myself with giving her the facts of the murder.

'The police suspect Parker,' I said, as I rose to my feet and prepared to ascend to bed. 'There seems a fairly clear case against him.'

'Parker!' said my sister. 'Fiddlesticks! That inspector must be a perfect fool. Parker indeed! Don't tell me.'

With which obscure pronouncement we went up to bed.

CHAPTER 7

I LEARN MY NEIGHBOUR'S PROFESSION

On the following morning I hurried unforgivably over my round. My excuse can be that I had no very serious cases to attend. On my return Caroline came into the hall to greet me.

'Flora Ackroyd is here,' she announced in an excited whisper.

'What?'

I concealed my surprise as best as I could.

'She's very anxious to see you. She's been here half an hour.'

Caroline led the way into our small sitting-room, and I followed.

Flora was sitting on the sofa by the window. She was in black and she sat nervously twisting her hands together. I was shocked by the sight of her face. All the colour had faded away from it. But when she spoke her manner was as composed and resolute as possible.

'Dr Sheppard, I have come to ask you to help me?'

'Of course he'll help you, my dear,' said Caroline.

I don't think Flora really wished Caroline to be present at the interview. She would, I am sure, have infinitely preferred to speak to me privately. But she also wanted to waste no time, so she made the best of it.

'I want you to come to The Larches with me.'

'The Larches?' I queried, surprised.

'To see that funny little man?' exclaimed Caroline.

'Yes. You know who he is, don't you?'

'We fancied,' I said, 'that he might be a retired hairdresser.'

Flora's blue eyes opened very wide.

'Why, he's Hercule Poirot! You know who I mean – the private detective. They say he's done the most wonderful things – just like detectives do in books. A year ago he retired and came to live down here. Uncle knew who he was, but he promised not to tell anyone, because M. Poirot wanted to live quietly without being bothered by people.'

'So that's who he is,' I said slowly.

'You've heard of him, of course?'

'I'm rather an old fogey, as Caroline tells me,' I said, 'but I *have* just heard of him.'

'Extraordinary!' commented Caroline.

I don't know what she was referring to – possibly her own failure to discover the truth.

'You want to go and see him?' I asked slowly. 'Now why?'

'To get him to investigate this murder, of course,' said Caroline sharply. 'Don't be so stupid, James.'

I was not really being stupid. Caroline does not always understand what I am driving at.

'You haven't got confidence in Inspector Davis?' I went on.

'Of course she hasn't,' said Caroline. 'I haven't either.'

Anyone would have thought it was Caroline's uncle who had been murdered.

'And how do you know he would take up the case?' I asked. 'Remember he has retired from active work.'

'That's just it,' said Flora simply. 'I've got to persuade him.'

'You are sure you are doing wisely?' I asked gravely.

'Of course she is,' said Caroline. 'I'll go with her myself if she likes.'

'I'd rather the doctor came with me, if you don't mind, Miss Sheppard,' said Flora.

She knows the value of being direct on certain occasions. Any hints would certainly have been wasted on Caroline.

'You see,' she explained, following directness with tact, 'Dr Sheppard being the doctor, and having found the body, he would be able to give all the details to M. Poirot.'

'Yes,' said Caroline grudgingly, 'I see that.'

I took a turn or two up and down the room.

'Flora,' I said gravely, 'be guided by me. I advise you not to drag this detective into the case.'

Flora sprang to her feet. The colour rushed into her cheeks.

'I know why you say that,' she cried. 'But it's exactly for that reason I'm so anxious to go. You're afraid! But I'm not. I know Ralph better than you do.'

'Ralph!' said Caroline. 'What has Ralph got to do with it?'

Neither of us heeded her.

'Ralph may be weak,' continued Flora. 'He may have done foolish things in the past – wicked things even – but he wouldn't murder anyone.'

'No, no,' I exclaimed. 'I never thought it of him.'

'Then why did you go to the Three Boars last night?' demanded Flora. 'On your way home – after Uncle's body was found?'

I was momentarily silenced. I had hoped that that visit of mine would remain unnoticed.

'How did you know about that?' I countered.

'I went there this morning,' said Flora. 'I heard from the servants that Ralph was staying there –'

I interrupted her.

'You had no idea that he was in King's Abbot?'

'No. I was astounded. I couldn't understand it. I went there and asked for him. They told me, what I suppose they told you last night, that he went out at about nine o'clock yesterday evening – and – and never came back.'

Her eyes met mine defiantly, and as though answering something in my look, she burst out:

'Well, why shouldn't he? He might have gone – anywhere. He may even have gone back to London.'

'Leaving his luggage behind?' I asked gently.

Flora stamped her foot.

'I don't care. There must be a simple explanation.'

'And that's why you want to go to Hercule Poirot? Isn't it better to leave things as they are? The police don't suspect Ralph in the least, remember. They're working on quite another tack.'

'But that's just *it*,' cried the girl. 'They *do* suspect him. A man from Cranchester turned up this morning – Inspector Raglan, a horrid, weaselly little man. I found he had been to the Three Boars this morning before me. They told me all about his having been there, and the questions he had asked. He must think Ralph did it.'

'That's a change of mind from last night, if so,' I said slowly. 'He doesn't believe in Davis's theory that it was Parker then?'

'Parker indeed,' said my sister, and snorted.

Flora came forward and laid her hand on my arm.

'Oh! Dr Sheppard, let us go at once to this M. Poirot. He will find out the truth.'

'My dear Flora,' I said gently, laying my hand on hers. 'Are you quite sure it is the truth we want?'

She looked at me, nodding her head gravely.

'You're not sure,' she said. 'I am. I know Ralph better than you do.'

'Of course he didn't do it,' said Caroline, who had been keeping silent with great difficulty. 'Ralph may be extravagant, but he's a dear boy, and has the nicest manners.'

I wanted to tell Caroline that large numbers of murderers have had nice manners, but the presence of Flora restrained me. Since the girl was determined, I was forced to give in to her and we started at once, getting away before my sister was able to fire off any more pronouncements beginning with her favourite words, 'Of course'.

An old woman with an immense Breton cap opened the door of The Larches to us. M. Poirot was at home, it seemed.

We were ushered into a little sitting-room arranged with formal precision, and there, after a lapse of a minute or so, my friend of yesterday came to us.

'Monsieur le docteur,' he said, smiling. 'Mademoiselle.'

He bowed to Flora.

'Perhaps,' I began, 'you have heard of the tragedy which occurred last night.'

His face grew grave.

'But certainly I have heard. It is horrible. I offer mademoiselle all my sympathy. In what way can I serve you?'

'Miss Ackroyd,' I said, 'wants you to – to –'

'To find the murderer,' said Flora in a clear voice.

'I see,' said the little man. 'But the police will do that, will they not?'

'They might make a mistake,' said Flora. 'They are on their way to make a mistake now, I think. Please, M. Poirot, won't you help us? If – if it is a question of money –'

Poirot held up his hand.

'Not that, I beg of you, mademoiselle. Not that I do not care for money.' His eyes showed a momentary twinkle. 'Money, it means much to me and always has done. No, if I go into this, you must understand one thing clearly. *I shall go through with it to the end.* The good dog, he does not leave the scent, remember! You may wish that, after all, you had left it to the local police.'

'I want the truth,' said Flora, looking him straight in the eyes.

'All the truth?'

'All the truth.'

'Then I accept,' said the little man quietly. 'And I hope you will not regret those words. Now, tell me all the circumstances.'

'Dr Sheppard had better tell you,' said Flora. 'He knows more than I do.'

Thus enjoined, I plunged into a careful narrative, embodying all the facts I have previously set down. Poirot listened carefully, inserting a question here and there, but for the most part sitting in silence, his eyes on the ceiling.

I brought my story to a close with the departure of the inspector and myself from Fernly Park the previous night.

'And now,' said Flora, as I finished, 'tell him all about Ralph.'

I hesitated, but her imperious glance drove me on.

'You went to this inn – this Three Boars – last night on your way home?' asked Poirot, as I brought my tale to a close. 'Now exactly why was that?'

I paused a moment to choose my words carefully.

'I thought someone ought to inform the young man of his uncle's death. It occurred to me after I had left Fernly that possibly no one but myself and Mr Ackroyd were aware that he was staying in the village.'

Poirot nodded.

'Quite so. That was your only motive in going there, eh?'

'That was my only motive,' I said stiffly.

'It was not to – shall we say – reassure yourself about *ce jeune homme*?'

'Reassure myself?'

'I think, M. le docteur, that you know very well what I mean, though you pretend not to do so. I suggest that it would have been a relief to you if you had found that Captain Paton had been at home all the evening.'

'Not at all,' I said sharply.

The little detective shook his head at me gravely.

'You have not the trust in me of Miss Flora,' he said. 'But no matter. What we have to look at is this – Captain Paton is missing, under circumstances which call for an explanation. I will not hide from you that the matter looks grave. Still, it may admit of a perfectly simple explanation.'

'That's just what I keep saying,' cried Flora eagerly.

Poirot touched no more upon that theme. Instead he suggested an immediate visit to the local police. He thought it better for Flora to return home, and for me to be the one to accompany him there and introduce him to the officer in charge of the case.

We carried out this plan forthwith. We found Inspector Davis outside the police station looking very glum indeed. With him was Colonel Melrose, the chief constable, and another man whom, from Flora's description of 'weaselly', I had no difficulty in recognizing as Inspector Raglan from Cranchester.

I know Melrose fairly well, and I introduced Poirot to him and explained the situation. The chief constable was clearly vexed, and Inspector Raglan looked as black as thunder. Davis, however, seemed slightly exhilarated by the sight of his superior officer's annoyance.

'The case is going to be plain as a pikestaff,' said Raglan. 'Not the least need for amateurs to come butting in. You'd think any fool would have seen the way things were last night, and then we shouldn't have lost twelve hours.'

He directed a vengeful glance at poor Davis, who received it with perfect stolidity.

'Mr Ackroyd's family must, of course, do what they see fit,' said Colonel Melrose. 'But we cannot have the official investigation hampered in any way. I know M. Poirot's great reputation, of course,' he added courteously.

'The police can't advertise themselves, worse luck,' said Raglan.

It was Poirot who saved the situation.

'It is true that I have retired from the world,' he said. 'I never intended to take up a case again. Above all things, I have a horror of publicity. I must beg, that in the case of my being able to contribute something to the solution of the mystery, my name may not be mentioned.'

Inspector Raglan's face lightened a little.

'I've heard of some very remarkable successes of yours,' observed the colonel, thawing.

'I have had much experience,' said Poirot quietly. 'But most of my successes have been obtained by the aid of the police. I admire enormously your English police. If Inspector Raglan permits me to assist him, I shall be both honoured and flattered.'

The inspector's countenance became still more gracious.

Colonel Melrose drew me aside.

'From all I hear, this little fellow's done some really remarkable things,' he murmured. 'We're naturally anxious not to have to call in Scotland Yard. Raglan seems very sure of himself, but I'm not quite certain that I agree with him. You see, I – er – know the parties concerned better than he does. This fellow doesn't seem out after kudos, does he? Would work in with us unobtrusively, eh?'

'To the greater glory of Inspector Raglan,' I said solemnly.

'Well, well,' said Colonel Melrose breezily in a louder voice, 'we must put you wise to the latest developments, M. Poirot.'

'I thank you,' said Poirot. 'My friend, Doctor Sheppard, said something of the butler being suspected?'

'That's all bunkum,' said Raglan instantly. 'These high-class servants get in such a funk that they act suspiciously for nothing at all.'

'The fingerprints?' I hinted.

'Nothing like Parker's.' He gave a faint smile, and added: 'And yours and Mr Raymond's don't fit either, doctor.'

'What about those of Captain Ralph Paton?' asked Poirot quietly.

I felt a secret admiration of the way he took the bull by the horns. I saw a look of respect creep into the inspector's eye.

'I see you don't let the grass grow under your feet, Mr Poirot. It will be a pleasure to work with you, I'm sure. We're going to take that young gentleman's fingerprints as soon as we can lay hands upon him.'

'I can't help thinking you're mistaken, Inspector,' said Colonel Melrose warmly. 'I've known Ralph Paton from a boy upward. He'd never stoop to murder.'

'Maybe not,' said the inspector tonelessly.

'What have you got against him?' I asked.

'Went out just on nine o'clock last night. Was seen in the neighbourhood of Fernly Park somewhere about nine-thirty. Not been seen since. Believed to be in serious money difficulties. I've got a pair of his shoes here – shoes with rubber studs in them. He had two pairs, almost exactly alike. I'm going up now to compare them with those footmarks. The constable is up there seeing that no one tampers with them.'

'We'll go at once,' said Colonel Melrose. 'You and M. Poirot will accompany us, will you not?'

We assented, and all drove up in the colonel's car. The inspector was anxious to get at once to the footmarks, and asked to be put down at the lodge. About half-way up the drive, on the right, a path branched off which led round to the terrace and the window of Ackroyd's study.

'Would you like to go with the inspector, M. Poirot,' asked the chief constable, 'or would you prefer to examine the study?'

Poirot chose the latter alternative. Parker opened the door to us. His manner was smug and deferential, and he seemed to have recovered from his panic of the night before.

Colonel Melrose took a key from his pocket, and unlocking the door which let into the lobby, he ushered us through into the study.

'Except for the removal of the body, M. Poirot, this room is exactly as it was last night.'

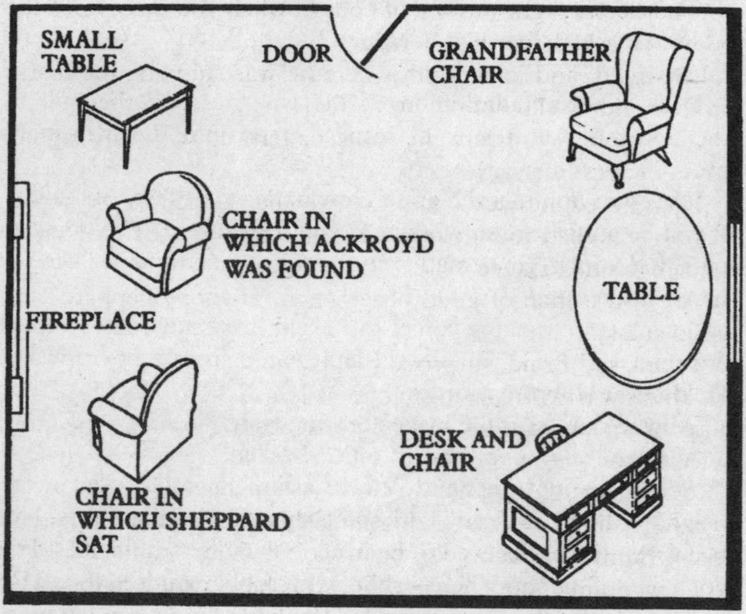

'And the body was found – where?'

As precisely as possible, I described Ackroyd's position. The arm-chair still stood in front of the fire.

Poirot went and sat down in it.

'The blue letter you speak of, where was it when you left the room?'

'Mr Ackroyd had laid it down on this little table at his right hand.'

Poirot nodded.

'Except for that, everything was in its place?'

'Yes, I think so.'

'Colonel Melrose, would you be so extremely obliging as to sit down in this chair a minute. I thank you. Now M. le docteur, will you kindly indicate to me the exact position of the dagger?'

I did so, whilst the little man stood in the doorway.

'The hilt of the dagger was plainly visible from the door then. Both you and Parker could see it at once?'

'Yes.'

Poirot went next to the window.

'The electric light was on, of course, when you discovered the body?' he asked over his shoulder.

I assented, and joined him where he was studying the marks on the window-sill.

'The rubber studs are the same pattern as those in Captain Paton's shoes,' he said quietly.

Then he came back once more to the middle of the room. His eye travelled round, searching everything in the room with a quick, trained glance.

'Are you a man of good observation, Doctor Sheppard?' he asked at last.

'I think so,' I said, surprised.

'There was a fire in the grate, I see. When you broke the door down and found Mr Ackroyd dead, how was the fire? Was it low?'

I gave a vexed laugh.

'I – I really can't say. I didn't notice. Perhaps Mr Raymond or Major Blunt –'

The little man opposite me shook his head with a faint smile.

'One must always proceed with method. I made an error of judgment in asking you that question. To each man his own knowledge. You could tell me the details of the patient's appearance – nothing there would escape you. If I wanted information about the papers on that desk, Mr Raymond would have noticed anything there was to see. To find out about the fire, I must ask the man whose business it is to observe such things. You permit –'

He moved swiftly to the fireplace and rang the bell.

After a lapse of a minute or two Parker appeared.

'The bell rang, sir,' he said hesitatingly.

'Come in, Parker,' said Colonel Melrose. 'This gentleman wants to ask you something.'

Parker transferred a respectful attention to Poirot.

'Parker,' said the little man, 'when you broke down the door with Dr Sheppard last night, and found your master dead, what was the state of the fire?'

Parker replied without a pause.

'It had burned very low, sir. It was almost out.'

'Ah!' said Poirot. The exclamation sounded almost triumphant. He went on:

'Look round you, my good Parker. Is this room exactly as it was then?'

The butler's eye swept round. It came to rest on the windows.

'The curtains were drawn, sir, and the electric light was on.'

Poirot nodded approval.

'Anything else?'

'Yes, sir, this chair was drawn out a little more.'

He indicated a big grandfather chair to the left of the door between it and the window. I append a plan of the room with the chair in question marked with an X.

'Just show me,' said Poirot.

The butler drew the chair in question out a good two feet from the wall, turning it so that the seat faced the door.

'*Voilà ce qui est curieux*,' murmured Poirot. 'No one would want to sit in a chair in such a position, I fancy. Now who pushed it back into place again, I wonder? Did you, my friend?'

'No, sir,' said Parker. 'I was too upset with seeing the master and all.'

Poirot looked across at me.

'Did you, doctor?'

I shook my head.

'It was back in position when I arrived with the police, sir,' put in Parker. 'I'm sure of that.'

'Curious,' said Poirot again.

'Raymond or Blunt must have pushed it back,' I suggested. 'Surely it isn't important?'

'It is completely unimportant,' said Poirot. 'That is why it is so interesting,' he added softly.

'Excuse me a minute,' said Colonel Melrose. He left the room with Parker.

'Do you think Parker is speaking the truth?' I asked.

'About the chair, yes. Otherwise I do not know. You will find, M. le docteur, if you have much to do with cases of this kind, that they all resemble each other in one thing.'

'What is that?' I asked curiously.

'Everyone concerned in them has something to hide.'

'Have I?' I asked, smiling.

Poirot looked at me attentively.

'I think you have,' he said quietly.

'But –'

'Have you told me everything known to you about this young man Paton?' He smiled as I grew red. 'Oh! do not fear. I will not press you. I shall learn it in good time.'

'I wish you'd tell me something of your methods,' I said hastily, to cover my confusion. 'The point about the fire, for instance?'

'Oh! that was very simple. You leave Mr Ackroyd at – ten minutes to nine, was it not?'

'Yes, exactly, I should say.'

'The window is then closed and bolted and the door unlocked. At a quarter past ten when the body is discovered, the door is locked and the window is open. Who opened it? Clearly only Mr Ackroyd himself could have done so, and for one of two reasons. Either because the room became unbearably hot, but since the fire was nearly out and there was a sharp drop in temperature last night, that cannot be the reason, or because he admitted someone that way. And if he admitted someone that way, it must have been someone well known to him, since he had previously shown himself uneasy on the subject of that same window.'

'It sounds very simple,' I said.

'Everything is simple, if you arrange the facts methodically. We are concerned now with the personality of the person who was with him at nine-thirty last night. Everything goes to show that that was the individual admitted by the window, and though Mr Ackroyd was seen alive later by Miss Flora, we cannot approach a solution of the mystery until we know who that visitor was. The window may have been left open after his departure and so afforded entrance to the murderer, or the same person may have returned a second time. Ah! here is the colonel who returns.'

Colonel Melrose entered with an animated manner.

'That telephone call has been traced at last,' he said. 'It did not come from here. It was put through to Dr Sheppard at 10.15 last night from a public call office at King's Abbot station. And at 10.23 the night mail leaves for Liverpool.'

CHAPTER 8

INSPECTOR RAGLAN IS CONFIDENT

We looked at each other.

'You'll have inquiries made at the station, of course?' I said.

'Naturally, but I'm not over sanguine as to the result. You know what that station is like.'

I did. King's Abbot is a mere village, but its station happens to be an important junction. Most of the big expresses stop there, and trains are shunted, re-sorted, and made up. It has two or three public telephone boxes. At that time of night, three local trains come in close upon each other, to catch the connection with the express for the north which comes in at 10.19 and leaves at 10.23. The whole place is in a bustle, and the chances of one particular person being noticed telephoning or getting into the express are very small indeed.

'But why telephone at all?' demanded Melrose. 'That is what I find so extraordinary. There seems no rhyme or reason in the thing.'

Poirot carefully straightened a china ornament on one of the bookcases.

'Be sure there was a reason,' he said over his shoulder.

'But what reason could it be?'

'When we know that, we shall know everything. This case is very curious and very interesting.'

There was something almost indescribable in the way he said those last words. I felt that he was looking at the case from some peculiar angle of his own, and what he saw I could not tell.

He went to the window and stood there, looking out.

'You say it was nine o'clock, Dr Sheppard, when you met this stranger outside the gate?'

He asked the question without turning round.

'Yes,' I replied. 'I heard the church clock chime the hour.'

'How long would it take him to reach the house – to reach this window, for instance?'

'Five minutes at the outside. Two or three minutes only if he took the path at the right of the drive and came straight here.'

'But to do that he would have to know the way. How can I explain myself? – it would mean that he had been here before – that he knew his surroundings.'

'That is true,' replied Colonel Melrose.

'We could find out, doubtless, if Mr Ackroyd had received any strangers during the past week?'

'Young Raymond could tell us that,' I said.

'Or Parker,' suggested Colonel Melrose.

'*Ou tous les deux*,' suggested Poirot, smiling.

Colonel Melrose went in search of Raymond, and I rang the bell once more for Parker.

Colonel Melrose returned almost immediately, accompanied by the young secretary, whom he introduced to Poirot. Geoffrey Raymond was fresh and debonair as ever. He seemed surprised and delighted to make Poirot's acquaintance.

'No idea you'd been living among us incognito, M. Poirot,' he said. 'It will be a great privilege to watch you at work – Hallo, what's this?'

Poirot had been standing just to the left of the door. Now he moved aside suddenly, and I saw that while my back was turned he must have swiftly drawn out the arm-chair till it stood in the position Parker had indicated.

'Want me to sit in the chair whilst you take a blood test?' asked Raymond good-humouredly. 'What's the idea?'

'M. Raymond, this chair was pulled out – so – last night when Mr Ackroyd was found killed. Someone moved it back again into place. Did you do so?'

The secretary's reply came without a second's hesitation.

'No, indeed I didn't. I don't even remember that it was in that position, but it must have been if you say so. Anyway, somebody else must have moved it back to its proper place. Have they destroyed a clue in doing so? Too bad!'

'It is of no consequence,' said the detective. 'Of no consequence whatever. What I really want to ask you is this, M. Raymond: Did any stranger come to see Mr Ackroyd during this past week?'

The secretary reflected for a minute or two, knitting his brows, and during the pause Parker appeared in answer to the bell.

'No,' said Raymond at last. 'I can't remember anyone. Can you, Parker?'

'I beg your pardon, sir?'

'Any stranger coming to see Mr Ackroyd this week?'

The butler reflected for a minute or two.

'There was the young man who came on Wednesday, sir,' he said at last. 'From Curtis and Troute, I understood he was.'

Raymond moved this aside with an impatient hand.

'Oh! yes, I remember, but that is not the kind of stranger this gentleman means.' He turned to Poirot. 'Mr Ackroyd had some idea of purchasing a dictaphone,' he explained. 'It would have enabled us to get through a lot more work in a limited time. The firm in question sent down their representative, but nothing came of it. Mr Ackroyd did not make up his mind to purchase.'

Poirot turned to the butler.

'Can you describe this young man to me, my good Parker?'

'He was fair-haired, sir, and short. Very neatly dressed in a blue serge suit. A very presentable young man, sir, for his station in life.'

Poirot turned to me.

'The man you met outside the gate, doctor, was tall, was he not?'

'Yes,' I said. 'Somewhere about six feet, I should say.'

'There is nothing in that, then,' declared the Belgian. 'I thank you, Parker.'

The butler spoke to Raymond.

'Mr Hammond has just arrived, sir,' he said. 'He is anxious to know if he can be of any service, and he would be glad to have a word with you.'

'I'll come at once,' said the young man. He hurried out. Poirot looked inquiringly at the chief constable.

'The family solicitor, M. Poirot,' said the latter.

'It is a busy time for this young M. Raymond,' murmured M. Poirot. 'He has the air efficient, that one.'

'I believe Mr Ackroyd considered him a most able secretary.'

'He has been here – how long?'

'Just on two years, I fancy.'

'His duties he fulfils punctiliously. Of that I am sure. In what manner does he amuse himself? Does he go in for *le sport*?'

'Private secretaries haven't much time for that sort of thing,' said Colonel Melrose, smiling. 'Raymond plays golf, I believe. And tennis in the summer time.'

'He does not attend the courses – I should say the running of the horses?'

'Race meetings? No, I don't think he's interested in racing.'

Poirot nodded and seemed to lose interest. He glanced slowly round the study.

'I have seen, I think, all that there is to be seen here.'

I, too, looked round.

'If those walls could speak,' I murmured.

Poirot shook his head.

'A tongue is not enough,' he said. 'They would have to have also eyes and ears. But do not be too sure that these dead things' – he touched the top of the bookcase as he spoke – 'are always dumb. To me they speak sometimes – chairs, tables – they have their message!'

He turned away towards the door.

'What message?' I cried. 'What have they said to you today?'

He looked over his shoulder and raised one eyebrow quizzically.

'An opened window,' he said. 'A locked door. A chair that apparently moved itself. To all three I say "Why?" and I find no answer.'

He shook his head, puffed out his chest, and stood blinking at us. He looked ridiculously full of his own importance. It crossed my mind to wonder whether he was really any good as a detective. Had his big reputation been built up on a series of lucky chances?

I think the same thought must have occurred to Colonel Melrose, for he frowned.

'Anything more you want to see, M. Poirot?' he inquired brusquely.

'You would perhaps be so kind as to show me the silver table from which the weapon was taken? After that, I will trespass on your kindness no longer.'

We went to the drawing-room, but on the way the constable waylaid the colonel, and after a muttered conversation the latter excused himself and left us together. I showed Poirot the silver table, and after raising the lid once or twice and letting it fall, he pushed open the window and stepped out on the terrace. I followed him.

Inspector Raglan had just turned the corner of the house, and was coming towards us. His face looked grim and satisfied.

'So there you are, M. Poirot,' he said. 'Well, this isn't going to be much of a case. I'm sorry, too. A nice enough young fellow gone wrong.'

Poirot's face fell, and he spoke very mildly.

'I'm afraid I shall not be able to be of much aid to you, then?'

'Next time, perhaps,' said the inspector soothingly. 'Though we don't have murders every day in this quiet little corner of the world.'

Poirot's gaze took on an admiring quality.

'You have been of a marvellous promptness,' he observed. 'How exactly did you go to work, if I may ask?'

'Certainly,' said the inspector. 'To begin with – method. That's what I always say – method!'

'Ah!' cried the other. 'That, too, is my watchword. Method, order, and the little grey cells.'

'The cells?' said the inspector, staring.

'The little grey cells of the brain,' explained the Belgian.

'Oh, of course; well, we all use them, I suppose.'

'In a greater or lesser degree,' murmured Poirot. 'And there are, too, differences in quality. Then there is the psychology of a crime. One must study that.'

'Ah!' said the inspector, 'you've been bitten with all this psycho-analysis stuff? Now, I'm a plain man –'

'Mrs Raglan would not agree, I am sure, to that,' said Poirot, making him a little bow.

Inspector Raglan, a little taken aback, bowed.

'You don't understand,' he said, grinning broadly. 'Lord, what a lot of difference language makes. I'm telling you how I set to work. First of all, method. Mr Ackroyd was last seen alive at a quarter to ten by his niece, Miss Flora Ackroyd. That's fact number one, isn't it?'

'If you say so.'

'Well, it is. At half-past ten, the doctor here says that Mr Ackroyd had been dead at least half an hour. You stick to that, doctor?'

'Certainly,' I said. 'Half an hour or longer.'

'Very good. That gives us exactly a quarter of an hour in which the crime must have been committed. I make a list of everyone in the house, and work through it, setting down opposite their names where they were and what they were doing between the hour of 9.45 and 10 p.m.'

He handed a sheet of paper to Poirot. I read it over his shoulder. It ran as follows, written in a neat script:

Major Blunt In billiard room with Mr Raymond. (Latter confirms.)

Mr Raymond Billiard room. (See above.)

Mrs Ackroyd 9.45 watching billiard match. Went up to bed 9.55. (Raymond and Blunt watched her up staircase.)

Miss Ackroyd Went straight from her uncle's room upstairs. (Confirmed by Parker, also housemaid, Elsie Dale.)

Servants:

Parker Went straight to butler's pantry. (Confirmed by housekeeper, Miss Russell, who came down to speak to him about something at 9.47, and remained at least ten minutes.)

Miss Russell As above. Spoke to housemaid, Elsie Dale, upstairs at 9.45.

Ursula Bourne (parlourmaid) In her own room until 9.55. Then in Servants' Hall.

Mrs Cooper (cook) In Servants' Hall.

Gladys Jones (second housemaid) In Servants' Hall.

Elsie Dale Upstairs in bedroom. Seen there by Miss Russell and Miss Flora Ackroyd.

Mary Thripp (kitchenmaid) Servants' Hall.

'The cook has been here seven years, the parlourmaid eighteen months, and Parker just over a year. The others are new. Except for something fishy about Parker, they all seem quite all right.'

'A very complete list,' said Poirot, handing it back to him. 'I am quite sure that Parker did not do the murder,' he added gravely.

'So is my sister,' I struck in. 'And she's usually right.' Nobody paid any attention to my interpolation.

'That disposes pretty effectually of the household,' continued the inspector. 'Now we come to a very grave point. The woman at the lodge – Mary Black – was pulling the curtains last night when she saw Ralph Paton turn in at the gate and go up towards the house.'

'She is sure of that?' I asked sharply.

'Quite sure. She knows him well by sight. He went past very quickly and turned off by the path to the right, which is a short cut to the terrace.'

'And what time was that?' asked Poirot, who had sat with an immovable face.

'Exactly twenty-five minutes past nine,' said the inspector gravely.

There was a silence. Then the inspector spoke again.

'It's all clear enough. It fits in without a flaw. At twenty-five minutes past nine, Captain Paton is seen passing the lodge; at nine-thirty or thereabouts, Mr Geoffrey Raymond hears someone in here asking for money and Mr Ackroyd refusing. What happens next? Captain Paton leaves the same way – through the window. He walks along the terrace, angry and baffled. He comes to the open drawing-room window. Say it's now a quarter to ten. Miss Flora Ackroyd is saying goodnight to her uncle. Major Blunt, Mr Raymond, and Mrs Ackroyd are in the billiard room. The drawing-room is empty. He steals in, takes the dagger from the silver table, and returns to the study window. He slips off his shoes, climbs in, and – well, I don't need to go into details. Then he slips out again and goes off. Hadn't the nerve to go back to the inn. He makes for the station, rings up from there –'

'Why?' said Poirot softly.

I jumped at the interruption. The little man was leaning forward. His eyes shone with a queer green light.

For a moment Inspector Raglan was taken aback by the question.

'It's difficult to say exactly why he did that,' he said at last. 'But murderers do funny things. You'd know that if you were in the police force. The cleverest of them make stupid mistakes sometimes. But come along and I'll show you those footprints.'

We followed him round the corner of the terrace to the study window. At a word from Raglan a police constable produced the shoes which had been obtained from the local inn.

The inspector laid them over the marks.

'They're the same,' he said confidently. 'That is to say, they're not the same pair that actually made these prints. He went away in those. This is a pair just like them, but older – see how the studs are worn down?'

'Surely a great many people wear shoes with rubber studs in them?' asked Poirot.

'That's so, of course,' said the inspector. 'I shouldn't put so much stress on the footmarks if it wasn't for everything else.'

'A very foolish young man, Captain Ralph Paton,' said Poirot thoughtfully. 'To leave so much evidence of his presence.'

'Ah! well,' said the inspector, 'it was a dry, fine night, you know. He left no prints on the terrace or on the gravelled path. But, unluckily for him, a spring must have welled up just lately at the end of the path from the drive. See here.'

A small gravelled path joined the terrace a few feet away. In one spot, a few yards from its termination, the ground was wet and boggy. Crossing this wet place there were again the marks of footsteps, and amongst them the shoes with rubber studs.

Poirot followed the path on a little way, the inspector by his side.

'You noticed the women's footprints?' he said suddenly.

The inspector laughed.

'Naturally. But several different women have walked this way – and men as well. It's a regular short cut to the house, you see. It would be impossible to sort out all the footsteps. After all, it's the ones on the window-sill that are really important.'

Poirot nodded.

'It's no good going farther,' said the inspector, as we came in view of the drive. 'It's all gravelled again here, and hard as it can be.'

Again Poirot nodded, but his eyes were fixed on a small garden house – a kind of superior summer-house. It was a little to the left of the path ahead of us, and a gravelled walk ran up to it.

Poirot lingered about until the inspector had gone back towards the house. Then he looked at me.

'You must have indeed been sent from the good God to replace my friend Hastings,' he said, with a twinkle. 'I observe that you do not quit my side. How say you, Doctor Sheppard, shall we investigate that summer-house? It interests me.'

He went up to the door and opened it. Inside, the place was almost dark. There were one or two rustic seats, a croquet set, and some folded deck-chairs.

I was startled to observe my new friend. He had dropped to his hands and knees and was crawling about the floor. Every now and then he shook his head as though not satisfied. Finally, he sat back on his heels.

'Nothing,' he murmured. 'Well, perhaps it was not to be expected. But it would have meant so much –'

He broke off, stiffening all over. Then he stretched out his hand to one of the rustic chairs. He detached something from one side of it.

'What is it?' I cried. 'What have you found?'

He smiled, unclosing his hand so that I should see what lay in the palm of it. A scrap of stiff white cambric.

I took it from him, looked at it curiously, and then handed it back.

'What do you make of it, eh, my friend?' he asked, eyeing me keenly.

'A scrap torn from a handkerchief,' I suggested, shrugging my shoulders.

He made another dart and picked up a small quill – a goose quill by the look of it.

'And that?' he cried triumphantly. 'What do you make of that?'

I only stared.

He slipped the quill into his pocket, and looked again at the scrap of white stuff.

'A fragment of a handkerchief?' he mused. 'Perhaps you are

right. But remember this – *a good laundry does not starch a handkerchief.*'

He nodded at me triumphantly, then he put away the scrap carefully in his pocket-book.

CHAPTER 9

THE GOLDFISH POND

We walked back to the house together. There was no sign of the inspector. Poirot paused on the terrace and stood with his back to the house, slowly turning his head from side to side.

'*Une belle propriété*,' he said at last appreciatively. 'Who inherits it?'

His words gave me almost a shock. It is an odd thing, but until that moment the question of inheritance had never come into my head. Poirot watched me keenly.

'It is a new idea to you, that,' he said at last. 'You had not thought of it before – eh?'

'No,' I said truthfully. 'I wish I had.'

He looked at me again curiously.

'I wonder just what you mean by that,' he said thoughtfully. 'Oh! no,' as I was about to speak. '*Inutile!* You would not tell me your real thought.'

'Everyone has something to hide,' I quoted, smiling.

'Exactly.'

'You still believe that?'

'More than ever, my friend. But it is not easy to hide things from Hercule Poirot. He has a knack of finding out.'

He descended the steps of the Dutch garden as he spoke.

'Let us walk a little,' he said over his shoulder. 'The air is pleasant today.'

I followed him. He led me down a path to the left enclosed in yew hedges. A walk led down the middle, bordered each side with formal flower beds, and at the end was a round paved recess with a seat and a pond of goldfish. Instead of pursuing the path to the end, Poirot took another which wound up the side of a wooded slope. In one spot the trees had been cleared away, and a seat had been put. Sitting there one had a splendid view over the countryside, and one looked right down on the paved recess and the goldfish pond.

'England is very beautiful,' said Poirot, his eyes straying over the prospect. Then he smiled. 'And so are English girls,' he said in a lower voice. 'Hush, my friend, and look at the pretty picture below us.'

It was then that I saw Flora. She was moving along the path we had just left and she was humming a little snatch of song. Her step was more dancing than walking, and, in spite of her black dress, there was nothing but joy in her whole attitude. She gave a sudden pirouette on her toes, and her black draperies swung out. At the same time she flung her head back and laughed outright.

As she did so a man stepped out from the trees. It was Hector Blunt.

The girl started. Her expression changed a little.

'How you startled me – I didn't see you.'

Blunt said nothing, but stood looking at her for a minute or two in silence.

'What I like about you,' said Flora, with a touch of malice, 'is your cheery conversation.'

I fancy that at that Blunt reddened under his tan. His voice, when he spoke, sounded different – it had a curious sort of humility in it.

'Never was much of a fellow for talking. Not even when I was young.'

'That was a very long time ago, I suppose,' said Flora gravely.

I caught the undercurrent of laughter in her voice, but I don't think Blunt did.

'Yes,' he said simply, 'it was.'

'How does it feel to be Methuselah?' asked Flora.

This time the laughter was more apparent, but Blunt was following out an idea of his own.

'Remember the johnny who sold his soul to the devil? In return for being made young again? There's an opera about it.'

'Faust, you mean?'

'That's the beggar. Rum story. Some of us would do it if we could.'

'Anyone would think you were creaking at the joints to hear you talk,' cried Flora, half vexed, half amused.

Blunt said nothing for a minute or two. Then he looked away from Flora into the middle distance and observed to an adjacent tree trunk that it was about time he got back to Africa.

'Are you going on another expedition – shooting things?'

'Expect so. Usually do, you know – shoot things, I mean.'

'You shot that head in the hall, didn't you?'

Blunt nodded. Then he jerked out, going rather red as he did so:

'Care for some decent skins any time? If so, I could get 'em for you.'

'Oh! please do,' cried Flora. 'Will you really? You won't forget?'

'I shan't forget,' said Hector Blunt.

He added, in a sudden burst of communicativeness:

'Time I went. I'm no good in this sort of life. Haven't got the manners for it. I'm a rough fellow, no use in society. Never remember the things one's expected to say. Yes, time I went.'

'But you're not going at once,' cried Flora. 'No – not while we're in all this trouble. Oh! please. If you go –'

She turned away a little.

'You want me to stay?' asked Blunt.

He spoke deliberately but quite simply.

'We all –'

'I meant you personally,' said Blunt, with directness.

Flora turned slowly back again and met his eyes.

'I want you to stay,' she said, 'if – if that makes any difference.'

'It makes all the difference,' said Blunt.

There was a moment's silence. They sat down on the stone seat by the goldfish pond. It seemed as though neither of them knew quite what to say next.

'It – it's such a lovely morning,' said Flora at last. 'You know, I can't help feeling happy, in spite – in spite of everything. That's awful, I suppose?'

'Quite natural,' said Blunt. 'Never saw your uncle until two years ago, did you? Can't be expected to grieve very much. Much better to have no humbug about it.'

'There's something awfully consoling about you,' said Flora. 'You make things seem so simple.'

'Things are simple as a rule,' said the big-game hunter.

'Not always,' said Flora.

Her voice had lowered itself, and I saw Blunt turn and look at her, bringing his eyes back from (apparently) the coast of Africa to do so. He evidently put his own construction on her change of tone, for he said, after a minute or two, in rather an abrupt manner:

'I say, you know, you mustn't worry. About that young chap, I mean. Inspector's an ass. Everybody knows – utterly absurd to think he could have done it. Man from outside. Burglar chap. That's the only possible solution.'

Flora turned to look at him.

'You really think so?'

'Don't you?' said Blunt quickly.

'I – oh, yes, of course.'

Another silence, and then Flora burst out:

'I'm – I'll tell you why I felt so happy this morning. However heartless you think me, I'd rather tell you. It's because the lawyer has been – Mr Hammond. He told us about the will. Uncle Roger has left me twenty thousand pounds. Think of it – twenty thousand beautiful pounds.'

Blunt looked surprised.

'Does it mean so much to you?'

'Mean much to me? Why, it's everything. Freedom – life – no more scheming and scraping and lying –'

'Lying?' said Blunt, sharply interrupting.

Flora seemed taken aback for a minute.

'You know what I mean,' she said uncertainly. 'Pretending to be thankful for all the nasty cast-off things rich relations give you. Last year's coat and skirts and hats.'

'Don't know much about ladies' clothes; should have said you were always very well turned out.'

'It cost me something, though,' said Flora in a low voice. 'Don't let's talk of horrid things. I'm so happy. I'm free. Free to do what I like. Free not to –'

She stopped suddenly.

'Not to what?' asked Blunt quickly.

'I forget now. Nothing important.'

Blunt had a stick in his hand, and he thrust it into the pond, poking at something.

'What are you doing, Major Blunt?'

'There's something bright down there. Wondered what it was – looks like a gold brooch. Now I've stirred up the mud and it's gone.'

'Perhaps it's a crown,' suggested Flora. 'Like the one Melisande saw in the water.'

'Melisande,' said Blunt reflectively – 'she's in an opera, isn't she?'

'Yes, you seem to know a lot about operas.'

'People take me sometimes,' said Blunt sadly. 'Funny idea of pleasure – worse racket than the natives make with their tom-toms.'

Flora laughed.

'I remember Melisande,' continued Blunt, 'married an old chap old enough to be her father.'

He threw a small piece of flint into the goldfish pond. Then, with a change of manner, he turned to Flora.

'Miss Ackroyd, can I do anything? About Paton, I mean. I know how dreadfully anxious you must be.'

'Thank you,' said Flora in a cold voice. 'There is really nothing to be done. Ralph will be all right. I've got hold of the most wonderful detective in the world, and he's going to find out all about it.'

For some time I had felt uneasy as to our position. We were not exactly eavesdropping, since the two in the garden below had only to lift their heads to see us. Nevertheless, I should have drawn attention to our presence before now, had not my companion put a warning pressure on my arm. Clearly he wished me to remain silent. Now, however, he acted briskly.

He rose quickly to his feet, clearing his throat.

'I demand pardon,' he cried. 'I cannot allow mademoiselle thus extravagantly to compliment me, and not draw attention to my presence. They say the listener hears no good of himself, but that is not the case this time. To spare my blushes, I must join you and apologize.'

He hurried down the path with me close behind him, and joined the others by the pond.

'This is M. Hercule Poirot,' said Flora. 'I expect you've heard of him.'

Poirot bowed.

'I know Major Blunt by reputation,' he said politely. 'I am glad to have encountered you, monsieur. I am in need of some information that you can give me.'

Blunt looked at him inquiringly.

'When did you last see M. Ackroyd alive?'

'At dinner.'

'And you neither saw nor heard anything of him after that?'

'Didn't see him. Heard his voice.'

'How was that?'

'I strolled out on the terrace –'

'Pardon me, what time was that?'

'About half-past nine. I was walking up and down smoking in front of the drawing-room window. I heard Ackroyd talking in his study –'

Poirot stopped and removed a microscopic weed.

'Surely you couldn't hear voices in the study from that part of the terrace,' he murmured.

He was not looking at Blunt, but I was, and to my intense surprise, I saw the latter flush.

'Went as far as the corner,' he explained unwillingly.

'Ah! indeed?' said Poirot.

In the mildest manner he conveyed an impression that more was wanted.

'Thought I saw – a woman disappearing into the bushes. Just a gleam of white, you know. Must have been mistaken. It was while I was standing at the corner of the terrace that I heard Ackroyd's voice speaking to that secretary of his.'

'Speaking to Mr Geoffrey Raymond?'

'Yes – that's what I supposed at the time. Seems I was wrong.'

'Mr Ackroyd didn't address him by name?'

'Oh, no.'

'Then, if I may ask, why did you think –?'

Blunt explained laboriously.

'Took it for granted that it *would* be Raymond, because he had said just before I came out that he was taking some papers to Ackroyd. Never thought of it being anybody else.'

'Can you remember what the words you heard were?'

'Afraid I can't. Something quite ordinary and unimportant. Only caught a scrap of it. I was thinking of something else at the time.'

'It is of no importance,' murmured Poirot. 'Did you move a chair back against the wall when you went into the study after the body was discovered?'

'Chair? No, why should I?'

Poirot shrugged his shoulders but did not answer. He turned to Flora.

'There is one thing I should like to know from you, mademoiselle. When you were examining the things in the silver table with Dr Sheppard, was the dagger in its place, or was it not?'

Flora's chin shot up.

'Inspector Raglan has been asking me that,' she said resentfully. 'I've told him, and I'll tell you. I'm perfectly certain the dagger was *not* there. He thinks it was and that Ralph sneaked it later in the evening. And – and he doesn't believe me. He thinks I'm saying it so – to shield Ralph.'

'And aren't you?' I asked gravely.

Flora stamped her foot.

'You, too, Dr Sheppard! Oh! it's too bad.'

Poirot tactfully made a diversion.

'It is true what I heard you say, Major Blunt. There is something that glitters in this pond. Let us see if I can reach it.'

He knelt down by the pond, baring his arm to the elbow, and lowered it in very slowly, so as not to disturb the bottom of the pond. But in spite of all his precautions the mud eddied and swirled, and he was forced to draw his arm out again empty-handed.

He gazed ruefully at the mud upon his arm. I offered him my handkerchief, which he accepted with fervent protestations of thanks. Blunt looked at his watch.

'Nearly lunch time,' he said. 'We'd better be getting back to the house.'

'You will lunch with us, M. Poirot?' asked Flora. 'I should like you to meet my mother. She is – very fond of Ralph.'

The little man bowed.

'I shall be delighted, mademoiselle.'

'And you will stay, too, won't you, Dr Sheppard?'

I hesitated.

'Oh, do!'

I wanted to, so I accepted the invitation without further ceremony.

We set out towards the house, Flora and Blunt walking ahead.

'What hair,' said Poirot to me in a low tone, nodding towards Flora. 'The real gold! They will make a pretty couple. She and the dark, handsome Captain Paton. Will they not?'

I looked at him inquiringly, but he began to fuss about a few microscopic drops of water on his coat sleeve. The man reminded me in some ways of a cat. His green eyes and his finicking habits.

'And all for nothing, too,' I said sympathetically. 'I wonder what it was in the pond?'

'Would you like to see?' asked Poirot.

I stared at him. He nodded.

'My good friend,' he said gently and reproachfully, 'Hercule Poirot does not run the risk of disarranging his costume without being sure of attaining his object. To do so would be ridiculous and absurd. I am never ridiculous.'

'But you brought your hand out empty,' I objected.

'There are times when it is necessary to have discretion. Do you tell your patients everything – but everything, doctor? I think not. Nor do you tell your excellent sister everything either, is it not so? Before showing my empty hand, I dropped what it contained into my other hand. You shall see what that was.'

He held out his left hand, palm open. On it lay a little circlet of gold. A woman's wedding ring.

I took it from him.

'Look inside,' commanded Poirot.

I did so. Inside was an inscription in fine writing:

From R., March 13th.

I looked at Poirot, but he was busy inspecting his appearance in a tiny pocket glass. He paid particular attention to his moustaches, and none at all to me. I saw that he did not intend to be communicative.

CHAPTER 10

THE PARLOURMAID

We found Mrs Ackroyd in the hall. With her was a small dried-up little man, with an aggressive chin and sharp grey eyes, and 'lawyer' written all over him.

'Mr Hammond is staying to lunch with us,' said Mrs Ackroyd. 'You know Major Blunt, Mr Hammond? And dear Doctor Sheppard – also a close friend of poor Roger's. And, let me see –'

She paused, surveying Hercule Poirot in some perplexity.

'This is M. Poirot, Mother,' said Flora. 'I told you about him this morning.'

'Oh! yes,' said Mrs Ackroyd vaguely. 'Of course, my dear, of course. He is to find Ralph, is he not?'

'He is to find out who killed Uncle,' said Flora.

'Oh! my dear,' cried her mother. 'Please! My poor nerves. I am a wreck this morning, a positive wreck. Such a dreadful thing to happen. I can't help feeling that it must have been an accident of some kind. Roger was so fond of handling queer curios. His hand must have slipped, or something.'

This theory was received in polite silence. I saw Poirot edge up to the lawyer, and speak to him in a confidential undertone. They moved aside into the embrasure of the window. I joined them – then hesitated.

'Perhaps I'm intruding,' I said.

'Not at all,' cried Poirot heartily. 'You and I, M. le docteur, we investigate this affair side by side. Without you I should be lost. I desire a little information from the good Mr Hammond.'

'You are acting on behalf of Captain Ralph Paton, I understand,' said the lawyer cautiously.

Poirot shook his head.

'Not so. I am acting in the interests of justice. Miss Ackroyd has asked me to investigate the death of her uncle.'

Mr Hammond seemed slightly taken aback.

'I cannot seriously believe that Captain Paton can be concerned in this crime,' he said, 'however strong the circumstantial evidence against him may be. The mere fact that he was hard pressed for money –'

'Was he hard pressed for money?' interpolated Poirot quickly.

The lawyer shrugged his shoulders.

'It was a chronic condition with Ralph Paton,' he said drily. 'Money went through his hands like water. He was always applying to his stepfather.'

'Had he done so of late? During the last year, for instance?'

'I cannot say. Mr Ackroyd did not mention the fact to me.'

'I comprehend. Mr Hammond, I take it that you are acquainted with the provisions of Mr Ackroyd's will?'

'Certainly. That is my principal business here today.'

'Then, seeing that I am acting for Miss Ackroyd, you will not object to telling me the terms of that will?'

'They are quite simple. Shorn of legal phraseology, and after paying certain legacies and bequests –'

'Such as –?' interrupted Poirot.

Mr Hammond seemed a little surprised.

'A thousand pounds to his housekeeper, Miss Russell; fifty pounds to the cook, Emma Cooper; five hundred pounds to his secretary, Mr Geoffrey Raymond. Then to various hospitals –'

Poirot held up his hand.

'Ah! the charitable bequests, they interest me not.'

'Quite so. The income on ten thousand pounds' worth of shares to be paid to Mrs Cecil Ackroyd during her lifetime. Miss Flora Ackroyd inherits twenty thousand pounds outright. The residue – including this property, and the shares in Ackroyd and Son – to his adopted son, Ralph Paton.'

'Mr Ackroyd possessed a large fortune?'

'A very large fortune. Captain Paton will be an exceedingly wealthy young man.'

There was a silence. Poirot and the lawyer looked at each other.

'Mr Hammond,' came Mrs Ackroyd's voice plaintively from the fireplace.

The lawyer answered the summons. Poirot took my arm and drew me right into the window.

'Regard the irises,' he remarked in a rather loud voice. 'Magnificent, are they not? A straight and pleasing effect.'

At the same time I felt the pressure of his hand on my arm, and he added in a low tone:

'Do you really wish to aid me? To take part in this investigation?'

'Yes, indeed,' I said eagerly. 'There's nothing I should like better. You don't know what a dull old fogey's life I lead. Never anything out of the ordinary.'

'Good, we will be colleagues then. In a minute or two I fancy Major Blunt will join us. He is not happy with the good mamma. Now there are some things I want to know – but I do not wish to seem to want to know them. You comprehend? So it will be your part to ask the questions.'

'What questions do you want me to ask?' I asked apprehensively.

'I want you to introduce the name of Mrs Ferrars.'

'Yes?'

'Speak of her in a natural fashion. Ask him if he was down here when her husband died. You understand the kind of thing I mean. And while he replies, watch his face without seeming to watch it. *C'est compris?*'

There was no time for more, for at that minute, as Poirot had prophesied, Blunt left the others in his abrupt fashion and came over to us.

I suggested strolling on the terrace, and he acquiesced. Poirot stayed behind.

I stopped to examine a late rose.

'How things change in the course of a day or two,' I observed. 'I was up here last Wednesday, I remember, walking up and down this same terrace. Ackroyd was with me – full of spirits. And now – three days later – Ackroyd's dead, poor fellow. Mrs Ferrars dead – you knew her, didn't you? But of course you did.'

Blunt nodded his head.

'Had you seen her since you'd been down this time?'

'Went with Ackroyd to call. Last Tuesday, think it was. Fascinating woman – but something queer about her. Deep – one would never know what she was up to.'

I looked into his steady grey eyes. Nothing there surely. I went on:

'I suppose you'd met her before?'

'Last time I was here – she and her husband had just come

here to live.' He paused a minute and then added: 'Rum thing, she had changed a lot between then and now.'

'How – changed?' I asked.

'Looked ten years older.'

'Were you down here when her husband died?' I asked, trying to make the question sound as casual as possible.

'No. From all I heard it would be good riddance. Uncharitable, perhaps, but the truth.'

I agreed.

'Ashley Ferrars was by no means a pattern husband,' I said cautiously.

'Blackguard, I thought,' said Blunt.

'No,' I said, 'only a man with more money than was good for him.'

'Oh! money! All the troubles in the world can be put down to money – or the lack of it.'

'Which has been your particular trouble?' I asked.

'Enough for what I want. I'm one of the lucky ones.'

'Indeed.'

'I'm not too flush just now, as a matter of fact. Came into a legacy a year ago, and like a fool let myself be persuaded into putting it into some wild-cat scheme.'

I sympathized, and narrated my own similar trouble.

Then the gong pealed out, and we all went in to lunch. Poirot drew me back a little.

'*Eh bien?*'

'He's all right,' I said. 'I'm sure of it.'

'Nothing – disturbing?'

'He had a legacy just a year ago,' I said. 'But why not? Why shouldn't he? I'll swear the man is perfectly square and above board.'

'Without doubt, without doubt,' said Poirot soothingly. 'Do not upset yourself.'

He spoke as though to a fractious child.

We all trooped into the dining-room. It seemed incredible that less than twenty-four hours had passed since I last sat at that table.

Afterwards, Mrs Ackroyd took me aside and sat down with me on a sofa.

'I can't help feeling a little hurt,' she murmured, producing a handkerchief of the kind obviously not meant to be cried into. 'Hurt, I mean, by Roger's lack of confidence in me. That twenty thousand pounds ought to have been left to *me* – not to Flora. A mother could be trusted to safeguard the interests of her child. A lack of trust, I call it.'

'You forget, Mrs Ackroyd,' I said, 'Flora was Ackroyd's own niece, a blood relation. It would have been different had you been his sister instead of his sister-in-law.'

'As poor Cecil's widow, I think my feelings ought to have been considered,' said the lady, touching her eyelashes gingerly with the handkerchief. 'But Roger was always most peculiar – not to say *mean* – about money matters. It has been a most difficult position for both Flora and myself. He did not even give the poor child an allowance. He would pay her bills, you know, and even that with a good deal of reluctance and asking what she wanted all those fal-lals for – so like a man – but – now I've forgotten what it was I was going to say! Oh, yes, not a penny we could call our own, you know. Flora resented it – yes, I must say she resented it – very strongly. Though devoted to her uncle, of course. But any girl would have resented it. Yes, I must say Roger had very strange ideas about money. He wouldn't even buy new face towels, though I told him the old ones were in holes. And then,' proceeded Mrs Ackroyd, with a sudden leap highly characteristic of her conversation, 'to leave all that money – a thousand pounds, fancy, a thousand pounds! – to that woman.'

'What woman?'

'That Russell woman. Something very queer about her, and so I've always said. But Roger wouldn't hear a word against her. Said she was a woman of great force of character, and that he admired and respected her. He was always going on about her rectitude and independence and moral worth. *I* think there's something fishy about her. She was certainly doing her best to marry Roger. But I soon put a stop to that. She always hated me. Naturally. *I* saw through her.'

I began to wonder if there was any chance of stemming Mrs Ackroyd's eloquence, and getting away.

Mr Hammond provided the necessary diversion by coming up to say goodbye. I seized my chance and rose also.

'About the inquest,' I said. 'Where would you prefer it to be held? Here, or at the Three Boars?'

Mrs Ackroyd stared at me with a dropped jaw.

'The inquest?' she asked, the picture of consternation. 'But surely there won't have to be an inquest?'

Mr Hammond gave a dry little cough and murmured, 'Inevitable. Under the circumstances,' in two short little barks.

'But surely Dr Sheppard can arrange –'

'There are limits to my powers of arrangement,' I said drily.

'If his death was an accident –'

'He was murdered, Mrs Ackroyd,' I said brutally.

She gave a little cry.

'No theory of accident will hold water for a minute.'

Mrs Ackroyd looked at me in distress. I had no patience with what I thought was her silly fear of unpleasantness.

'If there's an inquest, I – I shan't have to answer questions and all that, shall I?' she asked.

'I don't know what will be necessary,' I answered. 'I imagine Mr Raymond will take the brunt of it off you. He knows all the circumstances, and can give formal evidence of identification.'

The lawyer assented with a little bow.

'I really don't think there is anything to dread, Mrs Ackroyd,' he said. 'You will be spared all the unpleasantness. Now, as to the question of money, have you all you need for the present? I mean,' he added, as she looked at him inquiringly, 'ready money. Cash, you know. If not, I can arrange to let you have whatever you require.'

'That ought to be all right,' said Raymond, who was standing by. 'Mr Ackroyd cashed a cheque for a hundred pounds yesterday.'

'A hundred pounds?'

'Yes. For wages and other expenses due today. At the moment it is still intact.'

'Where is this money? In his desk?'

'No, he always kept his cash in his bedroom. In an old collar-box, to be accurate. Funny idea, wasn't it?'

'I think,' said the lawyer, 'we ought to make sure the money is there before I leave.'

'Certainly,' agreed the secretary. 'I'll take you up now . . . Oh! I forgot. The door's locked.'

Inquiry from Parker elicited the information that Inspector Raglan was in the housekeeper's room asking a few supplementary questions. A few minutes later the inspector joined the party in the hall, bringing the key with him. He unlocked the door and we passed into the lobby and up the small staircase. At the top of the stairs the door into Ackroyd's bedroom stood open. Inside the room it was dark, the curtains were drawn, and the bed was turned down just as it had been last night. The inspector drew the curtains, letting in the sunlight, and Geoffrey Raymond went to the top drawer of a rosewood bureau.

'He kept his money like that, in an unlocked drawer. Just fancy,' commented the inspector.

The secretary flushed a little.

'Mr Ackroyd had perfect faith in the honesty of all the servants,' he said hotly.

'Oh! quite so,' said the inspector hastily.

Raymond opened the drawer, took out a round leather collar-box from the back of it, and opening it, drew out a thick wallet.

'Here is the money,' he said, taking out a fat roll of notes. 'You will find the hundred intact, I know, for Mr Ackroyd put it in the collar-box in my presence last night when he was dressing for dinner, and of course it has not been touched since.'

Mr Hammond took the roll from him and counted it. He looked up sharply.

'A hundred pounds, you said. But there is only sixty here.'

Raymond stared at him.

'Impossible,' he cried, springing forward. Taking the notes from the other's hand, he counted them aloud.

Mr Hammond had been right. The total amounted to sixty pounds.

'But – I can't understand it,' cried the secretary, bewildered.

Poirot asked a question.

'You saw Mr Ackroyd put this money away last night when he was dressing for dinner? You are sure he had not paid away any of it already?'

'I'm sure he hadn't. He even said, "I don't want to take a hundred pounds down to dinner with me. Too bulgy."'

'Then the affair is very simple,' remarked Poirot. 'Either he paid out that forty pounds some time last evening, or else it has been stolen.'

'That's the matter in a nutshell,' agreed the inspector. He turned to Mrs Ackroyd. 'Which of the servants would come in here yesterday evening?'

'I suppose the housemaid would turn down the bed.'

'Who is she? What do you know about her?'

'She's not been here very long,' said Mrs Ackroyd. 'But she's a nice ordinary country girl.'

'I think we ought to clear this matter up,' said the inspector. 'If Mr Ackroyd paid that money away himself, it may have a bearing on the mystery of the crime. The other servants all right, as far as you know?'

'Oh, I think so.'

'Not missed anything before?'

'No.'

'None of them leaving, or anything like that?'

'The parlourmaid is leaving.'

'When?'

'She gave notice yesterday, I believe.'

'To you?'

'Oh, no. *I* have nothing to do with the servants. Miss Russell attends to the household matters.'

The inspector remained lost in thought for a minute or two. Then he nodded his head and remarked, 'I think I'd better have a word with Miss Russell, and I'll see the girl Dale as well.'

Poirot and I accompanied him to the housekeeper's room. Miss Russell received us with her usual sang-froid.

Elsie Dale had been at Fernly five months. A nice girl, quick at her duties, and most respectable. Good references. The last girl in the world to take anything not belonging to her.

What about the parlourmaid?

'She, too, was a most superior girl. Very quiet and ladylike. An excellent worker.'

'Then why is she leaving?' asked the inspector.

Miss Russell pursed up her lips.

'It was none of my doing. I understand Mr Ackroyd found fault with her yesterday afternoon. It was her duty to do the study, and she disarranged some of the papers on his desk, I believe. He was very annoyed about it, and she gave notice. At least, that is what I understood from her, but perhaps you'd like to see her yourselves?'

The inspector assented. I had already noticed the girl when she was waiting on us at lunch. A tall girl, with a lot of brown hair rolled tightly away at the back of her neck, and very steady grey eyes. She came in answer to the housekeeper's summons, and stood very straight with those same grey eyes fixed on us.

'You are Ursula Bourne?' asked the inspector.

'Yes, sir.'

'I understand you are leaving?'

'Yes, sir.'

'Why is that?'

'I disarranged some papers on Mr Ackroyd's desk. He was very angry about it, and I said I had better leave. He told me to go as soon as possible.'

'Were you in Mr Ackroyd's bedroom at all last night? Tidying up or anything?'

'No, sir. That is Elsie's work. I never went near that part of the house.'

'I must tell you, my girl, that a large sum of money is missing from Mr Ackroyd's room.'

At last I saw her roused. A wave of colour swept over her face.

'I know nothing about any money. If you think I took it, and that that is why Mr Ackroyd dismissed me, you are wrong.'

'I'm not accusing you of taking it, my girl,' said the inspector. 'Don't flare up so.'

The girl looked at him coldly.

'You can search my things if you like,' she said disdainfully. 'But you won't find anything.'

Poirot suddenly interposed.

'It was yesterday afternoon that Mr Ackroyd dismissed you – or you dismissed yourself, was it not?' he asked.

The girl nodded.

'How long did the interview last?'

'The interview?'

'Yes, the interview between you and Mr Ackroyd in the study?'

'I – I don't know.'

'Twenty minutes? Half an hour?'

'Something like that.'

'Not longer?'

'Not longer than half an hour, certainly.'

'Thank you, mademoiselle.'

I looked curiously at him. He was rearranging a few objects on the table, setting them straight with precise fingers. His eyes were shining.

'That'll do,' said the inspector.

Ursula Bourne disappeared. The inspector turned to Miss Russell.

'How long has she been here? Have you got a copy of the reference you had with her?'

Without answering the first question, Miss Russell moved to an adjacent bureau, opened one of the drawers, and took out a handful of letters clipped together with a patent fastener. She selected one and handed it to the inspector.

'H'm,' said he. 'Reads all right. Mrs Richard Folliott, Marby Grange, Marby. Who's this woman?'

'Quite good country people,' said Miss Russell.

'Well,' said the inspector, handing it back, 'let's have a look at the other one, Elsie Dale.'

Elsie Dale was a big fair girl, with a pleasant but slightly stupid face. She answered our questions readily enough, and showed much distress and concern at the loss of the money.

'I don't think there's anything wrong with her,' observed the inspector, after he had dismissed her. 'What about Parker?'

Miss Russell pursed her lips together and made no reply.

'I've a feeling there's something wrong about that man,' the inspector continued thoughtfully. 'The trouble is that I don't quite see when he got his opportunity. He'd be busy with his duties immediately after dinner, and he'd got a pretty good alibi all through the evening. I know, for I've been devoting particular attention to it. Well, thank you very much, Miss Russell. We'll leave things as they are for the present. It's highly probable Mr Ackroyd paid that money away himself.'

The housekeeper bade us a dry good afternoon, and we took our leave.

I left the house with Poirot.

'I wonder,' I said, breaking the silence, 'what the papers the girl disarranged could have been for Ackroyd to have got into such a state about them? I wonder if there is any clue there to the mystery.'

'The secretary said there were no papers of particular importance on the desk,' said Poirot quietly.

'Yes, but –' I paused.

'It strikes you as odd that Ackroyd should have flown into a rage about so trivial a matter?'

'Yes, it does rather.'

'But was it a trivial matter?'

'Of course,' I admitted, 'we don't know what those papers may have been. But Raymond certainly said –'

'Leave M. Raymond out of it for a minute. What did you think of that girl?'

'Which girl? The parlourmaid?'

'Yes, the parlourmaid. Ursula Bourne.'

'She seemed a nice girl,' I said hesitatingly.

Poirot repeated my words, but whereas I had laid a slight stress on the fourth word, he put it on the second.

'She *seemed* a nice girl – yes.'

Then, after a minute's silence, he took something from his pocket and handed it to me.

'See, my friend, I will show you something. Look there.'

The paper he had handed me was that compiled by the inspector and given by him to Poirot that morning. Following the pointing finger, I saw a small cross marked in pencil opposite the name Ursula Bourne.

'You may not have noticed it at the time, my good friend, but there was one person on this list whose alibi had no kind of confirmation. Ursula Bourne.'

'You don't think –?'

'Dr Sheppard, I dare to think anything. Ursula Bourne may have killed Mr Ackroyd, but I confess I can see no motive for her doing so. Can you?'

He looked at me very hard – so hard that I felt uncomfortable.

'Can you?' he repeated.

'No motive whatsoever,' I said firmly.

His gaze relaxed. He frowned and murmured to himself:

'Since the blackmailer was a man, it follows that she cannot be the blackmailer, then –'

I coughed.

'As far as that goes –' I began doubtfully.

He spun round on me.

'What? What are you going to say?'

'Nothing, Nothing. Only that, strictly speaking, Mrs Ferrars in her letter mentioned a *person* – she didn't actually specify a man. But we took it for granted, Ackroyd and I, that it *was* a man.'

Poirot did not seem to be listening to me. He was muttering to himself again.

'But then it is possible after all – yes, certainly it is possible – but then – ah! I must rearrange my ideas. Method, order, never have I needed them more. Everything must fit in – in its appointed place – otherwise I am on the wrong track.'

He broke off, and whirled round upon me again.

'Where is Marby?'

'It's on the other side of Cranchester.'

'How far away?'

'Oh! – fourteen miles, perhaps.'

'Would it be possible for you to go there? Tomorrow, say?'

'Tomorrow? Let me see, that's Sunday. Yes, I could arrange it. What do you want me to do there?'

'See this Mrs Folliott. Find out all you can about Ursula Bourne.'

'Very well. But – I don't much care for the job.'

'It is not the time to make difficulties. A man's life may hang on this.'

'Poor Ralph,' I said with a sigh. 'You believe him to be innocent, though?'

Poirot looked at me very gravely.

'Do you want to know the truth?'

'Of course.'

'Then you shall have it. My friend, everything points to the assumption that he is guilty.'

'What!' I exclaimed.

Poirot nodded.

'Yes, that stupid inspector – for he is stupid – has everything pointing his way. I seek for the truth – and the truth leads me every time to Ralph Paton. Motive, opportunity, means. But I will leave no stone unturned. I promised Mademoiselle Flora. And she was very sure, that little one. But very sure indeed.'

CHAPTER 11

POIROT PAYS A CALL

I was slightly nervous when I rang the bell at Marby Grange the following afternoon. I wondered very much what Poirot expected to find out. He had entrusted the job to me. Why? Was it because, as in the case of questioning Major Blunt, he wished to remain in the background? The wish, intelligible in the first case, seemed to me quite meaningless here.

My meditations were interrupted by the advent of a smart parlourmaid.

Yes, Mrs Folliott was at home. I was ushered into a big drawing-room, and looked round me curiously as I waited for the mistress of the house. A large bare room, some good bits of old china, and some beautiful etchings, shabby covers and curtains. A lady's room in every sense of the term.

I turned from the inspection of a Bartolozzi on the wall as Mrs Folliott came into the room. She was a tall woman, with untidy brown hair, and a very winning smile.

'Dr Sheppard,' she said hesitatingly.

'That is my name,' I replied. 'I must apologize for calling upon you like this, but I wanted some information about a parlourmaid previously employed by you, Ursula Bourne.'

With the utterance of the name the smile vanished from her face, and all the cordiality froze out of her manner. She looked uncomfortable and ill at ease.

'Ursula Bourne?' she said hesitatingly.

'Yes,' I said. 'Perhaps you don't remember the name?'

'Oh, yes, of course. I – I remember perfectly.'

'She left you just over a year ago, I understand?'

'Yes. Yes, she did. That is quite right.'

'And you were satisfied with her whilst she was with you? How long was she with you, by the way?'

'Oh! a year or two – I can't remember exactly how long. She – she is very capable. I'm sure you will find her quite satisfactory. I didn't know she was leaving Fernly. I hadn't the least idea of it.'

'Can you tell me anything about her?' I asked.

'Anything about her?'

'Yes, where she comes from, who her people are – that sort of thing?'

Mrs Folliott's face wore more than ever its frozen look.

'I don't know at all.'

'Who was she with before she came to you?'

'I'm afraid I don't remember.'

There was a spark of anger now underlying her nervousness. She flung up her head in a gesture that was vaguely familiar.

'Is it really necessary to ask all these questions?'

'Not at all,' I said, with an air of surprise and a tinge of apology in my manner. 'I had no idea you would mind answering them. I am very sorry.'

Her anger left her and she became confused again.

'Oh! I don't mind answering them. I assure you I don't. Why should I? It – it just seemed a little odd, you know. That's all. A little odd.'

One advantage of being a medical practitioner is that you can usually tell when people are lying to you. I should have known from Mrs Folliott's manner, if from nothing else, that she did mind answering my questions – minded intensely. She was thoroughly uncomfortable and upset, and there was plainly some mystery in the background. I judged her to be a woman quite unused to deception of any kind, and consequently rendered acutely uneasy when forced to practise it. A child could have seen through her.

But it was also clear the she had no intention of telling me anything further. Whatever the mystery centring round Ursula Bourne might be, I was not going to learn it through Mrs Folliott.

Defeated, I apologized once more for disturbing her, took my hat and departed.

I went to see a couple of patients and arrived home about six o'clock. Caroline was sitting beside the wreck of tea things. She had that look of suppressed exultation on her face which I know only too well. It is a sure sign with her of either the getting or the giving of information. I wondered which it had been.

'I've had a very interesting afternoon,' began Caroline, as I dropped into my own particular easy-chair and stretched out my feet to the inviting blaze in the fireplace.

'Have you?' I said. 'Miss Gannett drop in to tea?'

Miss Gannett is one of the chief of our newsmongers.

'Guess again,' said Caroline, with intense complacency.

I guessed several times, working slowly through all the members of Caroline's Intelligence Corps. My sister received each guess with a triumphant shake of the head. In the end she volunteered the information herself.

'M. Poirot!' she said. 'Now, what do you think of that?'

I thought a good many things of it, but I was careful not to say them to Caroline.

'Why did he come?' I asked.

'To see me, of course. He said that, knowing my brother so well, he hoped he might be permitted to make the acquaintance of his charming sister – your charming sister, I've got mixed up – but you know what I mean.'

'What did he talk about?' I asked.

'He told me a lot about himself and his cases. You know that Prince Paul of Mauretania – the one who's just married a dancer?'

'Yes?'

'I saw a most intriguing paragraph about her in *Society Snippets* the other day, hinting that she was really a Russian Grand Duchess – one of the Czar's daughters who managed to escape from the Bolsheviks. Well, it seems that M. Poirot solved a baffling murder mystery that threatened to involve them both. Prince Paul was beside himself with gratitude.'

'Did he give him an emerald tie pin the size of a plover's egg?' I inquired sarcastically.

'He didn't mention it. Why?'

'Nothing,' I said. 'I thought it was always done. It is in detective fiction anyway. The super-detective always has his rooms littered with rubies and pearls and emeralds from grateful Royal clients.'

'It's very interesting to hear about these things from the inside,' said my sister complacently.

It would be – to Caroline. I could not but admire the ingenuity of M. Hercule Poirot, who had selected unerringly the case of all others that would most appeal to an elderly lady living in a small village.

'Did he tell you if the dancer was really a Grand Duchess?' I inquired.

'He was not at liberty to speak,' said Caroline importantly.

I wondered how far Poirot had strained the truth in talking to Caroline – probably not at all. He had conveyed his innuendoes by means of his eyebrows and his shoulders.

'And after all this,' I remarked, 'I suppose you were ready to eat out of his hand?'

'Don't be coarse, James. I don't know where you get these vulgar expressions from.'

'Probably from my only link with the outside world – my patients. Unfortunately, my practice does not lie amongst Royal princes and interesting Russian *émigrés*.'

Caroline pushed her spectacles up and looked at me.

'You seem very grumpy, James. It must be your liver. A blue pill, I think, tonight.'

To see me in my own home, you would never imagine that I was a doctor of medicine. Caroline does the home prescribing both for herself and me.

'Damn my liver,' I said irritably. 'Did you talk about the murder at all?'

'Well, naturally, James. What else is there to talk about locally? I was able to set M. Poirot straight upon several points. He was very grateful to me. He said I had the makings of a born detective in me – and a wonderful psychological insight into human nature.'

Caroline was exactly like a cat that is full to overflowing with rich cream. She was positively purring.

'He talked a lot about the little grey cells of the brain, and of their functions. His own, he says, are of the first quality.'

'He would say so,' I remarked bitterly. 'Modesty is certainly not his middle name.'

'I wish you wouldn't be so horribly American, James. He thought it very important that Ralph should be found as soon as possible, and induced to come forward and give an account of himself. He says that his disappearance will produce a very unfortunate impression at the inquest.'

'And what did you say to that?'

'I agreed with him,' said Caroline importantly. 'And I was able to tell him the way people were talking already about it.'

'Caroline,' I said sharply, 'did you tell M. Poirot what you overheard in the wood that day?'

'I did,' said Caroline complacently.

I got up and began to walk about.

'You realize what you're doing, I hope,' I jerked out. 'You're putting a halter round Ralph Paton's neck as surely as you're sitting in that chair.'

'Not at all,' said Caroline, quite unruffled. 'I was surprised *you* hadn't told him.'

'I took very good care not to,' I said. 'I'm fond of that boy.'

'So am I. That's why I say you're talking nonsense. I don't believe Ralph did it, and so the truth can't hurt him, and we ought to give M. Poirot all the help we can. Why, think, very likely Ralph was out with that identical girl on the night of the murder, and if so, he's got a perfect alibi.'

'If he's got a perfect alibi,' I retorted, 'why doesn't he come forward and say so?'

'Might get the girl into trouble,' said Caroline sapiently. 'But if M. Poirot gets hold of her, and puts it to her as her duty, she'll come forward of her own accord and clear Ralph.'

'You seem to have invented a romantic fairy story of your own,' I said. 'You read too many trashy novels, Caroline. I've always told you so.'

I dropped into my chair again.

'Did Poirot ask you any more questions?' I inquired.

'Only about the patients you had that morning.'

'The patients?' I demanded, unbelievingly.

'Yes, your surgery patients. How many and who they were.'

'Do you mean to say you were able to tell him that?' I demanded.

Caroline is really amazing.

'Why not?' asked my sister triumphantly. 'I can see the path up to the surgery door perfectly from this window. And I've got an excellent memory, James. Much better than yours, let me tell you.'

'I'm sure you have,' I murmured mechanically.

My sister went on, checking the names on her fingers.

'There was old Mrs Bennett, and that boy from the farm with the bad finger, Dolly Grice to have a needle out of her finger; that American steward off the liner. Let me see – that's four. Yes, and old George Evans with his ulcer. And lastly –'

She paused significantly.

'Well?'

Caroline brought out her climax triumphantly. She hissed it in the most approved style – aided by the fortunate number of s's at her disposal.

'*Miss Russell!*'

She sat back in her chair and looked at me meaningly, and when Caroline looks at you meaningly, it is impossible to miss it.

'I don't know what you mean,' I said, quite untruthfully. 'Why shouldn't Miss Russell consult me about her bad knee?'

'Bad knee,' said Caroline. 'Fiddlesticks! No more bad knee than you and I. She was after something else.'

'What?' I asked.

Caroline had to admit that she didn't know.

'But depend upon it, that was what he was trying to get at – M. Poirot, I mean. There's something fishy about that woman, and he knows it.'

'Precisely the remark Mrs Ackroyd made to me yesterday,' I said. 'That there was something fishy about Miss Russell.'

'Ah!' said Caroline darkly, 'Mrs Ackroyd! There's another!'

'Another what?'

Caroline refused to explain her remarks. She merely nodded her head several times, rolling up her knitting, and went upstairs to don the high mauve silk blouse and the gold locket which she calls dressing for dinner.

I stayed there staring into the fire and thinking over Caroline's words. Had Poirot really come to gain information about Miss Russell, or was it only Caroline's tortuous mind that interpreted everything according to her own ideas?

There had certainly been nothing in Miss Russell's manner that morning to arouse suspicion. At least –

I remembered her persistent conversation on the subject of drug-taking – and from that she had led the conversation to poisons and poisoning. But there was nothing in that. Ackroyd had not been poisoned. Still, it was odd . . .

I heard Caroline's voice, rather acid in tone, calling from the top of the stairs.

'James, you will be late for dinner.'

I put some coal on the fire and went upstairs obediently.

It is well at any price to have peace in the home.

CHAPTER 12

ROUND THE TABLE

A joint inquest was held on Monday.

I do not propose to give the proceedings in detail. To do so would only be to go over the same ground again and again. By arrangement with the police, very little was allowed to come out. I gave evidence as to the cause of Ackroyd's death and the probable time. The absence of Ralph Paton was commented on by the coroner, but not unduly stressed.

Afterwards, Poirot and I had a few words with Inspector Raglan. The inspector was very grave.

'It looks bad, M. Poirot,' he said. 'I'm trying to judge the thing fair and square. I'm a local man, and I've seen Captain Paton many times in Cranchester. I'm not wanting him to be the guilty one – but it's bad whichever way you look at it. If he's innocent, why doesn't he come forward? We've got evidence against him, but it's just possible that the evidence could be explained away. Then why doesn't he give an explanation?'

A lot more lay behind the inspector's words than I knew at the time. Ralph's description had been wired to every port and railway station in England. The police everywhere were on the alert. His rooms in town were watched, and any houses he had been known to be in the habit of frequenting. With such a *cordon* it seemed impossible that Ralph should be able to evade detection. He had no luggage, and, as far as anyone knew, no money.

'I can't find anyone who saw him at the station that night,' continued the inspector. 'And yet he's well known down here, and you'd think somebody would have noticed him. There's no news from Liverpool either.'

'You think he went to Liverpool?' queried Poirot.

'Well, it's on the cards. That telephone message from the station, just three minutes before the Liverpool express left – there ought to be something in that.'

'Unless it was deliberately intended to throw you off the scent. That might just possibly be the point of the telephone message.'

'That's an idea,' said the inspector eagerly. 'Do you really think that's the explanation of the telephone call?'

'My friend,' said Poirot gravely, 'I do not know. But I will tell you this: I believe that when we find the explanation of that telephone call we shall find the explanation of the murder.'

'You said something like that before, I remember,' I observed, looking at him curiously.

Poirot nodded.

'I always come back to it,' he said seriously.

'It seems to me utterly irrelevant,' I declared.

'I wouldn't say that,' demurred the inspector. 'But I must confess I think Mr Poirot here harps on it a little too much. We've better clues than that. The fingerprints on the dagger, for instance.'

Poirot became suddenly very foreign in manner, as he often did when excited over anything.

'M. l'Inspecteur,' he said, 'beware of the blind – the blind – *comment dire*? – the little street that has no end to it.'

Inspector Raglan stared, but I was quicker.

'You mean a blind alley?' I said.

'That is it – the blind street that leads nowhere. So it may be with those fingerprints – they may lead you nowhere.'

'I don't see how that can well be,' said the police officer. 'I suppose you're hinting that they're faked? I've read of such things being done, though I can't say I've ever come across it in my experience. But fake or true – they're bound to lead *somewhere*.'

Poirot merely shrugged his shoulders, flinging out his arms wide.

The inspector then showed us various enlarged photographs

of the fingerprints, and proceeded to become technical on the subject of loops and whorls.

'Come now,' he said at last, annoyed by Poirot's detached manner, 'you've got to admit that those prints were made by someone who was in the house that night?'

'*Bien entendu*,' said Poirot, nodding his head.

'Well, I've taken the prints of every member of the household, everyone, mind you, from the old lady down to the kitchenmaid.'

I don't think Mrs Ackroyd would enjoy being referred to as the old lady. She must spend a considerable amount on cosmetics.

'Everyone's,' repeated the inspector fussily.

'Including mine,' I said drily.

'Very well. None of them correspond. That leaves us two alternatives. Ralph Paton, or the mysterious stranger the doctor here tells us about. When we get hold of those two –'

'Much valuable time may have been lost,' broke in Poirot.

'I don't quite get you, Mr Poirot.'

'You have taken the prints of everyone in the house, you say,' murmured Poirot. 'Is that the exact truth you are telling me there, M. l'Inspecteur?'

'Certainly.'

'Without overlooking anyone?'

'Without overlooking anyone.'

'The quick or the dead?'

For a moment the inspector looked bewildered at what he took to be a religious observation. Then he reacted slowly.

'You mean –?'

'The dead, M. l'Inspecteur.'

The inspector still took a minute or two to understand.

'I am suggesting,' said Poirot placidly, 'that the fingerprints on the dagger handle are those of Mr Ackroyd himself. It is an easy matter to verify. His body is still available.'

'But why? What would be the point of it? You're surely not suggesting suicide, Mr Poirot?'

'Ah! no. My theory is that the murderer wore gloves or wrapped something round his hand. After the blow was struck, he picked up the victim's hand and closed it round the dagger handle.'

'But why?'

Poirot shrugged his shoulders again.

'To make a confusing case even more confusing.'

'Well,' said the inspector. 'I'll look into it. What gave you the idea in the first place?'

'When you were so kind as to show me the dagger and draw attention to the fingerprints. I know very little of loops and whorls – see, I confess my ignorance frankly. But it did occur to me that the position of the prints was somewhat awkward. Not so would I have held a dagger in order to strike. Naturally, with the right hand brought up over the shoulder backwards, it would have been difficult to put it in exactly the right position.'

Inspector Raglan stared at the little man. Poirot, with an air of great unconcern, flecked a speck of dust from his coat sleeve.

'Well,' said the inspector. 'It's an idea. I'll look into it all right, but don't you be disappointed if nothing comes of it.'

He endeavoured to make his tone kindly and patronizing. Poirot watched him go off. Then he turned to me with twinkling eyes.

'Another time,' he observed, 'I must be more careful of his *amour propre*. And now that we are left to our own devices, what do you think, my good friend, of a little reunion of the family?'

The 'little reunion', as Poirot called it, took place about half an hour later. We sat round the table in the dining-room at Fernly. Poirot at the head of the table, like the chairman of some ghastly board meeting. The servants were not present, so we were six in all. Mrs Ackroyd, Flora, Major Blunt, young Raymond, Poirot and myself.

When everyone was assembled, Poirot rose and bowed.

'Messieurs, mesdames, I have called you together for a certain purpose.' He paused. 'To begin with, I want to make a very special plea to mademoiselle.'

'To me?' said Flora.

'Mademoiselle, you are engaged to Captain Ralph Paton. If anyone is in his confidence, you are. I beg you, most earnestly, if you know of his whereabouts, to persuade him to come forward. One little minute' – as Flora raised her head to speak – 'say nothing till you have well reflected. Mademoiselle, his position grows daily more dangerous. If he had come forward at once, no matter how damning the facts, he might have had a chance of explaining them away. But this silence – this flight – what can it mean? Surely only one thing, knowledge of guilt. Mademoiselle, if you really believe in his innocence, persuade him to come forward before it is too late.'

Flora's face had gone very white.

'Too late!' she repeated, very low.

Poirot leant forward, looking at her.

'See now, mademoiselle,' he said very gently, 'it is Papa Poirot who asks you this. The old Papa Poirot who has much knowledge and much experience. I would not seek to entrap you, mademoiselle. Will you not trust me – and tell me where Ralph Paton is hiding?'

The girl rose and stood facing him.

'M. Poirot,' she said in a clear voice, 'I swear to you – swear solemnly – that I have no idea where Ralph is, and that I have neither seen him nor heard from him either on the day of – of the murder, or since.'

She sat down again. Poirot gazed at her in silence for a minute or two, then he brought his hand down on the table with a sharp rap.

'*Bien!* That is that,' he said. His face hardened. 'Now I appeal to these others who sit round this table, Mrs Ackroyd, Major Blunt, Dr Sheppard, Mr Raymond. You are all friends and intimates of the missing man. If you know where Ralph Paton is hiding, speak out.'

There was a long silence. Poirot looked to each in turn.

'I beg of you,' he said in a low voice, 'speak out.'

But still there was silence, broken at last by Mrs Ackroyd.

'I must say,' she observed in a plaintive voice, 'that Ralph's absence is most peculiar – most peculiar indeed. Not to come forward at such a time. It looks, you know, as though there were something *behind* it. I can't help thinking, Flora dear, that it was a very fortunate thing your engagement was never formally announced.'

'Mother!' cried Flora angrily.

'Providence,' declared Mrs Ackroyd. 'I have a devout belief in Providence – a divinity that shapes our ends, as Shakespeare's beautiful line runs.'

'Surely you don't make the Almighty directly responsible for thick ankles, Mrs Ackroyd, do you?' asked Geoffrey Raymond, his irresponsible laugh ringing out.

His idea was, I think, to loosen the tension, but Mrs Ackroyd threw him a glance of reproach and took out her handkerchief.

'Flora has been saved a terrible amount of notoriety and unpleasantness. Not for a moment that I think dear Ralph had anything to do with poor Roger's death. I *don't* think so. But then I have a trusting heart – I always have had, ever since a child. I am loath to believe the worst of anyone. But, of course, one must remember that Ralph was in several air raids as a young boy. The results are apparent long after, sometimes, they say. People are not responsible for their actions in the least. They lose control, you know, without being able to help it.'

'Mother,' cried Flora, 'you don't think Ralph did it?'

'Come, Mrs Ackroyd,' said Blunt.

'I don't know what to think,' said Mrs Ackroyd tearfully. 'It's all very upsetting. What would happen to the estate, I wonder, if Ralph were found guilty?'

Raymond pushed his chair away from the table violently. Major Blunt remained very quiet, looking thoughtfully at her.

'Like shell-shock, you know,' said Mrs Ackroyd obstinately, 'and I dare say Roger kept him very short of money – with the best intentions, of course. I can see you are all against me, but I do think it is very odd that Ralph has not come forward, and I must say I am thankful Flora's engagement was never announced formally.'

'It will be tomorrow,' said Flora in a clear voice.

'Flora!' cried her mother, aghast.

Flora had turned to the secretary.

'Will you send the announcement to the *Morning Post*. And *The Times*, please, Mr Raymond.'

'If you are sure that it is wise, Miss Ackroyd,' he replied gravely.

She turned impulsively to Blunt.

'You understand,' she said. 'What else can I do? As things are, I must stand by Ralph. Don't you see that I must?'

She looked very searchingly at him, and after a long pause he nodded abruptly.

Mrs Ackroyd burst out into shrill protests. Flora remained unmoved. Then Raymond spoke.

'I appreciate your motives, Miss Ackroyd. But don't you think you're being rather precipitate? Wait a day or two.'

'Tomorrow,' said Flora in a clear voice. 'It's no good, Mother, going on like this. Whatever else I am, I'm not disloyal to my friends.'

'M. Poirot,' Mrs Ackroyd appealed tearfully. 'Can't you say anything at all?'

'Nothing to be said,' interpolated Blunt. 'She's doing the right thing. I'll stand by her through thick and thin.'

Flora held out her hand to him.

'Thank you, Major Blunt,' she said.

'Mademoiselle,' said Poirot, 'will you let an old man congratulate you on your courage and your loyalty? And will you not misunderstand me if I ask you – ask you most solemnly – to postpone the announcement you speak of for at least two days more?'

Flora hesitated.

'I ask it in Ralph Paton's interests as much as in yours, mademoiselle. You frown. You do not see how that can be. But I assure you that it is so. *Pas de blagues*. You put the case into my hands – you must not hamper me now.'

Flora paused a few minutes before replying.

'I do not like it,' she said at last, 'but I will do what you say.'

She sat down again at the table.

'And now, messieurs et mesdames,' said Poirot rapidly, 'I will continue with what I was about to say. Understand this, I mean to arrive at the truth. The truth, however ugly in itself, is always curious and beautiful to the seeker after it. I am much aged, my powers may not be what they were.' Here he clearly expected a contradiction. 'In all probability this is the last case I shall ever investigate. But Hercule Poirot does not end with a failure. Messieurs et mesdames, I tell you, I mean to *know*. And I shall know – in spite of you all.'

He brought out the last words provocatively, hurling them in our face as it were. I think we all flinched back a little, excepting Geoffrey Raymond, who remained good-humoured and imperturbable as usual.

'How do you mean – in spite of us all?' he asked, with slightly raised eyebrows.

'But – just that, monsieur. Every one of you in this room is concealing something from me.' He raised his hand as a faint murmur of protest arose. 'Yes, yes, I know what I am saying. It may be something unimportant – trivial – which is supposed to have no bearing on the case, but there it is. *Each one of you has something to hide.* Come now, am I right?'

His glance, challenging and accusing, swept round the table. And every pair of eyes dropped before his. Yes, mine as well.

'I am answered,' said Poirot, with a curious laugh. He got up from his seat. 'I appeal to you all. Tell me the truth – the whole truth.' There was a silence. 'Will no one speak?'

He gave the same short laugh again.

'*C'est dommage*,' he said, and went out.

CHAPTER 13

THE GOOSE QUILL

That evening, at Poirot's request, I went over to his house after dinner. Caroline saw me depart with visible reluctance. I think she would have liked to have accompanied me.

Poirot greeted me hospitably. He had placed a bottle of Irish whiskey (which I detest) on a small table, with a soda water siphon and a glass. He himself was engaged in brewing hot chocolate. It was a favourite beverage of his, I discovered later.

He inquired politely after my sister, whom he declared to be a most interesting woman.

'I'm afraid you've been giving her a swelled head,' I said drily. 'What about Sunday afternoon?'

He laughed and twinkled.

'I always like to employ the expert,' he remarked obscurely, but he refused to explain the remark.

'You got all the local gossip anyway,' I remarked. 'True, and untrue.'

'And a great deal of valuable information,' he added quietly.

'Such as –'

He shook his head.

'Why not have told me the truth?' he countered. 'In a place like this, all Ralph Paton's doings were bound to be known. If your sister had not happened to pass through the wood that day somebody else would have done so.'

'I suppose they would,' I said grumpily. 'What about this interest of yours in my patients?'

Again he twinkled.

'Only one of them, doctor. Only one of them.'

'The last?' I hazarded.

'I find Miss Russell a study of the most interesting,' he said evasively.

'Do you agree with my sister and Mrs Ackroyd that there is something fishy about her?' I asked.

'Eh? What do you say – fishy?'

I explained to the best of my ability.

'And they say that, do they?'

'Didn't my sister convey as much to you yesterday afternoon?'

'*C'est possible.*'

'For no reason whatever,' I declared.

'*Les femmes*,' generalized Poirot. 'They are marvellous! They invent haphazard – and by miracle they are right. Not that it is that, really. Women observe subconsciously a thousand little details, without knowing that they are doing so. Their subconscious mind adds these little things together – and they call the result intuition. Me, I am very skilled in psychology. I know these things.'

He swelled his chest out importantly, looking so ridiculous that I found it difficult not to burst out laughing. Then he took a small sip of his chocolate, and carefully wiped his moustache.

'I wish you'd tell me,' I burst out, 'what you really think of it all?'

He put down his cup.

'You wish that?'

'I do.'

'You have seen what I have seen. Should not our ideas be the same?'

'I'm afraid you're laughing at me,' I said stiffly. 'Of course, I've no experience of matters of this kind.'

Poirot smiled at me indulgently.

'You are like the little child who wants to know the way the engine works. You wish to see the affair, not as the family doctor sees it, but with the eye of a detective who knows and cares for no one – to whom they are all strangers and all equally liable to suspicion.'

'You put it very well,' I said.

'So I give you, then, a little lecture. The first thing is to get a clear history of what happened that evening – always bearing in mind that the person who speaks may be lying.'

I raised my eyebrows.

'Rather a suspicious attitude.'

'But necessary – I assure you, necessary. Now first – Dr Sheppard leaves the house at ten minutes to nine. How do I know that?'

'Because I told you so.'

'But you might not be speaking the truth – or the watch you went by might be wrong. But Parker also says that you left the house at ten minutes to nine. So we accept that statement and pass on. At nine o'clock you run into a man – and here we come to what we will call the Romance of the Mysterious Stranger – just outside the Park gates. How do I know that that is so?'

'I told you so,' I began again, but Poirot interrupted me with a gesture of impatience.

'Ah! but it is that you are a little stupid tonight, my friend. *You* know that it is so – but how am *I* to know? *Eh bien*, I am able to tell you that the Mysterious Stranger was not a hallucination on your part, because the maid of a Miss Gannett met him a few minutes before you did, and of her too he inquired the way to Fernly Park. We accept his presence, therefore, and we can be fairly sure of two things about him – that he was a stranger to the neighbourhood, and that whatever his object in going to Fernly, there was no great secrecy about it, since he twice asked the way there.'

'Yes,' I said, 'I see that.'

'Now I have made it my business to find out more about this man. He had a drink at the Three Boars, I learn, and the barmaid there says that he spoke with an American accent and mentioned having just come over from the States. Did it strike you that he had an American accent?'

'Yes, I think he had,' I said, after a minute or two, during which I cast my mind back; 'but a very slight one.'

'*Précisément*. There is also this, which, you will remember, I picked up in the summer-house.'

He held out to me the little quill. I looked at it curiously. Then a memory of something I had read stirred in me.

Poirot, who had been watching my face, nodded.

'Ycs, heroin, "snow". Drug-takers carry it like this, and sniff it up the nose.'

'Diamorphine hydrochloride,' I murmured mechanically.

'This method of taking the drug is very common on the other side. Another proof, if we wanted one, that the man came from Canada or the States.'

'What first attracted your attention to that summer-house?' I asked curiously.

'My friend the inspector took it for granted that anyone using that path did so as a short cut to the house, but as soon as I saw the summer-house, I realized that the same path would be taken by anyone using the summer-house as a rendezvous. Now it seems fairly certain that the stranger came neither to the front nor to the back door. Then did someone from the house go out and meet him? If so, what could be a more convenient place than that little summer-house? I searched it with the hope that I might find some clue inside. I found two, the scrap of cambric and the quill.'

'And the scrap of cambric?' I asked curiously. 'What about that?'

Poirot raised his eyebrows.

'You do not use your little grey cells,' he remarked drily. 'The scrap of starched cambric should be obvious.'

'Not very obvious to me.' I changed the subject. 'Anyway,' I said, 'this man went to the summer-house to meet somebody. Who was that somebody?'

'Exactly the question,' said Poirot. 'You will remember that Mrs Ackroyd and her daughter came over from Canada to live here?'

'Is that what you meant today when you accused them of hiding the truth?'

'Perhaps. Now another point. What did you think of the parlourmaid's story?'

'What story?'

'The story of her dismissal. Does it take half an hour to dismiss a servant? Was the story of those important papers a likely one? And remember, though she says she was in her bedroom from nine-thirty until ten o'clock, there is no one to confirm her statement.'

'You bewilder me,' I said.

'To me it grows clearer. But tell me now your own ideas and theories.'

I drew a piece of paper from my pocket.

'I just scribbled down a few suggestions,' I said apologetically.

'But excellent – you have method. Let us hear them.'

I read out in a somewhat embarrassed voice.

'To begin with, one must look at the thing logically –'

'Just what my poor Hastings used to say,' interrupted Poirot, 'but alas! he never did so.'

'*Point No. 1.* – Mr Ackroyd was heard talking to someone at half-past nine.

'*Point No. 2.* – At some time during the evening Ralph Paton must have come in through the window, as evidenced by the prints of his shoes.

'*Point No. 3.* – Mr Ackroyd was nervous that evening, and would only have admitted someone he knew.

'*Point No. 4.* – The person with Mr Ackroyd at nine-thirty was asking for money. We know Ralph Paton was in a scrape.

'*These four points go to show that the person with Mr Ackroyd at nine-thirty was Ralph Paton. But we know that Mr Ackroyd was alive at a quarter to ten, therefore it was not Ralph who killed him. Ralph left the window open. Afterwards the murderer came in that way.*'

'And who was the murderer?' inquired Poirot.

'The American stranger. He may have been in league with Parker, and possibly in Parker we have the man who blackmailed Mrs Ferrars. If so, Parker may have heard enough to realize the game was up, have told his accomplice so, and the latter did the crime with the dagger which Parker gave him.'

'It is a theory that,' admitted Poirot. 'Decidedly you have cells of a kind. But it leaves a good deal unaccounted for.'

'Such as –'

'The telephone call, the pushed-out chair –'

'Do you really think that latter important?' I interrupted.

'Perhaps not,' admitted my friend. 'It may have been pulled out by accident, and Raymond or Blunt may have shoved it into place unconsciously under the stress of emotion. Then there is the missing forty pounds.'

'Given by Ackroyd to Ralph,' I suggested. 'He may have reconsidered his first refusal.'

'That still leaves one thing unexplained.'

'What?'

'Why was Blunt so certain in his own mind that it was Raymond with Mr Ackroyd at nine-thirty?'

'He explained that,' I said.

'You think so? I will not press the point. Tell me, instead, what were Ralph Paton's reasons for disappearing?'

'That's rather more difficult,' I said slowly. 'I shall have to speak as a medical man. Ralph's nerves must have gone phut! If he suddenly found out that his uncle had been murdered within a few minutes of his leaving him – after, perhaps, a rather stormy interview – well, he might get the wind up and clear right out. Men have been known to do that – act guiltily when they're perfectly innocent.'

'Yes, that is true,' said Poirot. 'But we must not lose sight of one thing.'

'I know what you're going to say,' I remarked: 'motive. Ralph Paton inherits a great fortune by his uncle's death.'

'That is one motive,' agreed Poirot.

'One?'

'*Mais oui*. Do you realize that there are three separate motives staring us in the face. Somebody certainly stole the blue envelope and its contents. That is one motive. Blackmail! Ralph Paton may have been the man who blackmailed Mrs Ferrars. Remember, as far as Hammond knew, Ralph Paton had not applied to his uncle for help of late. That looks as though he were being supplied with money elsewhere. Then there is the fact that he was in some – how do you say – scrape? – which he feared might get to his uncle's ears. And finally there is the one you have just mentioned.'

'Dear me,' I said, rather taken aback. 'The case does seem black against him.'

'Does it?' said Poirot. 'That is where we disagree, you and I.

Three motives – it is almost too much. I am inclined to believe that, after all, Ralph Paton is innocent.'

CHAPTER 14

MRS ACKROYD

After the evening talk I have just chronicled, the affair seemed to me to enter on a different phase. The whole thing can be divided into two parts, each clear and distinct from the other. Part I ranges from Ackroyd's death on the Friday evening to the following Monday night. It is the straightforward narrative of what occurred, as presented to Hercule Poirot. I was at Poirot's elbow the whole time. I saw what he saw. I tried my best to read his mind. As I know now, I failed in this latter task. Though Poirot showed me all his discoveries – as, for instance, the gold wedding ring – he held back the vital and yet logical impressions that he formed. As I came to know later, this secrecy was characteristic of him. He would throw out hints and suggestions, but beyond that he would not go.

As I say, up till the Monday evening, my narrative might have been that of Poirot himself. I played Watson to his Sherlock. But after Monday our ways diverged. Poirot was busy on his own account. I got to hear of what he was doing, because in King's Abbot you get to hear of everything, but he did not take me into his confidence beforehand. And I, too, had my own preoccupations.

On looking back, the thing that strikes me most is the piecemeal character of this period. Everyone had a hand in the elucidation of the mystery. It was rather like a jig-saw puzzle to which everyone contributed their own little piece of knowledge or discovery. But their task ended there. To Poirot alone belongs the renown of fitting those pieces into their correct place.

Some of the incidents seemed at the time irrelevant and unmeaning. There was, for instance, the question of the black boots. But that comes later . . . To take things strictly in chronological order, I must begin with the summons from Mrs Ackroyd.

She sent for me early on Tuesday morning, and since the

summons sounded an urgent one, I hastened there, expecting to find her *in extremis.*

The lady was in bed. So much did she concede to the etiquette of the situation. She gave me her bony hand, and indicated a chair drawn up to the bedside.

'Well, Mrs Ackroyd,' I said, 'and what's the matter with you?'

I spoke with that kind of spurious geniality which seems to be expected of general practitioners.

'I'm prostrated,' said Mrs Ackroyd in a faint voice. 'Absolutely prostrated. It's the shock of poor Roger's death. They say these things often aren't felt at the *time*, you know. It's the reaction afterwards.'

It is a pity that a doctor is precluded by his profession from being able sometimes to say what he really thinks.

I would have given anything to be able to answer 'Bunkum!'

Instead, I suggested a tonic. Mrs Ackroyd accepted the tonic. One move in the game seemed now to be concluded. Not for a moment did I imagine that I had been sent for because of the shock occasioned by Ackroyd's death. But Mrs Ackroyd is totally incapable of pursuing a straightforward course on any subject. She always approaches her object by tortuous means. I wondered very much why it was she had sent for me.

'And then that scene – yesterday,' continued my patient.

She paused as though expecting me to take up a cue.

'What scene?'

'Doctor, how can you? Have you forgotten? That dreadful little Frenchman – or Belgian – or whatever he is. Bullying us all like he did. It has quite upset me. Coming on the top of Roger's death.'

'I'm very sorry, Mrs Ackroyd,' I said.

'I don't know what he meant – shouting at us like he did. I should hope I know my duty too well to *dream* of concealing anything. I have given the police *every* assistance in my power.'

Mrs Ackroyd paused, and I said, 'Quite so.' I was beginning to have a glimmering of what all the trouble was about.

'No one can say that I have failed in my duty,' continued Mrs Ackroyd. 'I am sure Inspector Raglan is perfectly satisfied. Why should this little upstart of a foreigner make a fuss? A most ridiculous-looking creature he is too – just like a comic Frenchman in a revue. I can't think why Flora insisted on bringing him into the case. She never said a word to me about it. Just went off and did it on her own. Flora is too independent. I am a woman of the world and her mother. She should have come to me for advice first.'

I listened to all this in silence.

'What does he think? That's what I want to know. Does he actually imagine I'm hiding something? He – he – positively *accused* me yesterday.'

I shrugged my shoulders.

'It is surely of no consequence, Mrs Ackroyd,' I said. 'Since you are not concealing anything, any remarks he may have made do not apply to you.'

Mrs Ackroyd went off at a tangent, after her usual fashion.

'Servants are so tiresome,' she said. 'They gossip, and talk amongst themselves. And then it gets round – and all the time there's probably nothing in it at all.'

'Have the servants been talking?' I asked. 'What about?'

Mrs Ackroyd cast a very shrewd glance at me. It quite threw me off my balance.

'I was sure *you'd* know, doctor, if anyone did. You were with M. Poirot all the time, weren't you?'

'I was.'

'Then of course you know. It was that girl, Ursula Bourne, wasn't it? Naturally – she's leaving. She *would* want to make all the trouble she could. Spiteful, that's what they are. They're all alike. Now, you being there, doctor, you must know exactly what she did say? I'm most anxious that no wrong impression should get about. After all, you don't repeat every little detail to the police, do you? There are family matters sometimes – nothing to do with the question of the murder. But if the girl was spiteful, she may have made out all sorts of things.'

I was shrewd enough to see that a very real anxiety lay behind these outpourings. Poirot had been justified in his premises. Of the six people round the table yesterday, Mrs Ackroyd at least had had something to hide. It was for me to discover what that something might be.

'If I were you, Mrs Ackroyd,' I said brusquely, 'I should make a clean breast of things.'

She gave a little scream.

'Oh! doctor, how can you be so abrupt. It sounds as though – as though – And I can explain everything so simply.'

'Then why not do so?' I suggested.

Mrs Ackroyd took out a frilled handkerchief, and became tearful.

'I thought, doctor, that you might put it to M. Poirot – explain it, you know – because it's so difficult for a foreigner to see our point of view. And you don't know – nobody could know – what I've had to contend with. A martyrdom – a long martyrdom. That's what my life has been. I don't like to speak ill of the dead – but there it is. Not the smallest bill but it had all to be gone over – just as though Roger had had a few miserly hundreds a year instead of being (as Mr Hammond told me yesterday) one of the wealthiest men in these parts.'

Mrs Ackroyd paused to dab her eyes with the frilled handkerchief.

'Yes,' I said encouragingly. 'You were talking about bills?'

'Those dreadful bills. And some I didn't like to show Roger at all. They were things a man wouldn't understand. He would have said the things weren't necessary. And of course they mounted up, you know, and they kept coming in –'

She looked at me appealingly, as though asking me to condole with her on this striking peculiarity.

'It's a habit they have,' I agreed.

And the tone altered – became quite abusive. 'I assure you, doctor, I was becoming a nervous wreck. I couldn't sleep at nights. And a dreadful fluttering round the heart. And then I got a letter from a Scotch gentleman – as a matter of fact there were two letters – both Scotch gentlemen. Mr Bruce MacPherson was one, and the other was Colin MacDonald. Quite a coincidence.'

'Hardly that,' I said drily. 'They are usually Scotch gentlemen, but I suspect a Semitic strain in their ancestry.'

'Ten pounds to ten thousand on note of hand alone,' murmured Mrs Ackroyd reminiscently. 'I wrote to one of them, but it seemed there were difficulties.'

She paused.

I gathered that we were just coming to delicate ground. I have never known anyone more difficult to bring to the point.

'You see,' murmured Mrs Ackroyd, 'it's all a question of

expectations, isn't it? Testamentary expectations. And though, of course, I expected that Roger would provide for me, I didn't *know*. I thought that if only I could glance over a copy of his will – not in any sense of vulgar prying – but just so that I could make my own arrangements.'

She glanced sideways at me. The position was now very delicate indeed. Fortunately words, ingeniously used, will serve to mask the ugliness of naked facts.

'I could only tell this to you, dear Doctor Sheppard,' said Mrs Ackroyd rapidly. 'I can trust you not to misjudge me, and to represent the matter in the right light to M. Poirot. It was on Friday afternoon –'

She came to a stop and swallowed uncertainly.

'Yes,' I repeated encouragingly. 'On Friday afternoon. Well?'

'Everyone was out, or so I thought. And I went into Roger's study – I had some real reason for going there – I mean, there was nothing underhand about it. And as I saw all the papers heaped on the desk, it just came to me, like a flash: "I wonder if Roger keeps his will in one of the drawers of the desk." I'm so impulsive, always was, from a child. I do things on the spur of the moment. He'd left his keys – very careless of him – in the lock of the top drawer.'

'I see,' I said helpfully. 'So you searched the desk. Did you find the will?'

Mrs Ackroyd gave a little scream, and I realized that I had not been sufficiently diplomatic.

'How dreadful it sounds. But it wasn't at all like that really.'

'Of course it wasn't,' I said hastily. 'You must forgive my unfortunate way of putting things.'

'Of course, men are so peculiar. In dear Roger's place, I should have not objected to revealing the provisions of my will. But men are so secretive. One is forced to adopt little subterfuges in self-defence.'

'And the result of the little subterfuge?' I asked.

'That's just what I'm telling you. As I got to the bottom drawer, Bourne came in. Most awkward. Of course I shut the drawer and stood up, and I called her attention to a few specks of dust on the surface. But I didn't like the way she looked – quite respectful in manner, but a very nasty light in her eyes. Almost contemptuous, if you know what I mean. I never have liked that girl very much. She's a good servant, and she says Ma'am, and doesn't object to wearing caps and aprons (which I declare to you a lot of them do nowadays), and she can say "Not at home" without scruples if she has to answer the door instead of Parker, and she doesn't have those peculiar gurgling noises inside which so many parlourmaids seem to have when they wait at table – Let me see, where was I?'

'You were saying, that in spite of several valuable qualities, you never liked Bourne.'

'No more I do. She's – odd. There's something different about her from the others. Too well educated, that's my opinion. You can't tell who are ladies and who aren't nowadays.'

'And what happened next?' I asked.

'Nothing. At last, Roger came in. And I thought he was out for a walk. And he said: "What's all this?" and I said, "Nothing. I just came in to fetch *Punch*." And I took *Punch* and went out with it. Bourne stayed behind. I heard her asking Roger if she could speak to him for a minute. I went straight up to my room, to lie down. I was very upset.'

There was a pause.

'You will explain to M. Poirot, won't you? You can see for yourself what a trivial matter the whole thing was. But, of course, when he was so stern about concealing things, I thought of this at once. Bourne may have made some extraordinary story out of it, but you can explain, can't you?'

'That is all?' I said. 'You have told me everything?'

'Ye-es,' said Mrs Ackroyd. 'Oh! yes,' she added firmly.

But I had noted the momentary hesitation, and I knew that there was still something she was keeping back. It was nothing less than a flash of sheer genius that prompted me to ask the question I did.

'Mrs Ackroyd,' I said, 'was it you who left the silver table open?'

I had my answer in the blush of guilt that even rouge and powder could not conceal.

'How did you know?' she whispered.

'It was you, then?'

'Yes – I – you see – there were one or two pieces of old silver

– very interesting. I had been reading up the subject and there was an illustration of quite a small piece which had fetched an immense sum at Christies. It looked to be just the same as the one in the silver table. I thought I would take it up to London with me when I went – and – and have it valued. Then if it really was a valuable piece, just think what a charming surprise it would have been for Roger.'

I refrained from comments, accepting Mrs Ackroyd's story on its merits. I even forbore to ask her why it was necessary to abstract what she wanted in such a surreptitious manner.

'Why did you leave the lid open?' I asked. 'Did you forget?'

'I was startled,' said Mrs Ackroyd. 'I heard footsteps coming along the terrace outside. I hastened out of the room and just got up the stairs before Parker opened the front door to you.'

'That must have been Miss Russell,' I said thoughtfully. Mrs Ackroyd had revealed to me one fact that was extremely interesting. Whether her designs upon Ackroyd's silver had been strictly honourable I neither knew nor cared. What did interest me was the fact that Miss Russell must have entered the drawing-room by the window, and that I had not been wrong when I judged her to be out of breath with running. Where had she been? I thought of the summer-house and the scrap of cambric.

'I wonder if Miss Russell has had her handkerchiefs starched!' I exclaimed on the spur of the moment.

Mrs Ackroyd's start recalled me to myself, and I rose.

'You think you can explain to M. Poirot?' she asked anxiously.

'Oh, certainly. Absolutely.'

I got away at last, after being forced to listen to more justifications of her conduct.

The parlourmaid was in the hall, and it was she who helped me on with my overcoat. I observed her more closely than I had done heretofore. It was clear that she had been crying.

'How is it,' I asked, 'that you told us that Mr Ackroyd sent for you on Friday to his study? I hear now that it was *you* who asked to speak to *him*.'

For a minute the girl's eyes dropped before mine.

Then she spoke.

'I meant to leave in any case,' she said uncertainly.

I said no more. She opened the front door for me. Just as I was passing out, she said suddenly in a low voice:

'Excuse me, sir, is there any news of Captain Paton?'

I shook my head, looking at her inquiringly.

'He ought to come back,' she said. 'Indeed – indeed he ought to come back.'

She was looking at me with appealing eyes.

'Does no one know where he is?' she asked.

'Do you?' I said sharply.

She shook her head.

'No, indeed. I know nothing. But anyone who was a friend to him would tell him this: he ought to come back.'

I lingered, thinking that perhaps the girl would say more. Her next question surprised me.

'When do they think the murder was done? Just before ten o'clock?'

'That is the idea,' I said. 'Between a quarter to ten and the hour.'

'Not earlier? Not before a quarter to ten?'

I looked at her attentively. She was so clearly eager for a reply in the affirmative.

'That's out of the question,' I said. 'Miss Ackroyd saw her uncle alive at a quarter to ten.'

She turned away, and her whole figure seemed to droop.

'A handsome girl,' I said to myself as I drove off. 'An exceedingly handsome girl.'

Caroline was at home. She had had a visit from Poirot and was very pleased and important about it.

'I am helping him with the case,' she explained.

I felt rather uneasy. Caroline is bad enough as it is. What will she be like with her detective instincts encouraged?

'Are you going round the neighbourhood looking for Ralph Paton's mysterious girl?' I inquired.

'I might do that on my own account,' said Caroline. 'No, this is a special thing M. Poirot wants me to find out for him.'

'What is it?' I asked.

'He wants to know whether Ralph Paton's boots were black or brown,' said Caroline with tremendous solemnity.

I stared at her. I see now that I was unbelievably stupid about these boots. I failed altogether to grasp the point.

'They were brown shoes,' I said. 'I saw them.'

'Not shoes, James, boots. M. Poirot wants to know whether a pair of boots Ralph had with him at the hotel were brown or black. A lot hangs on it.'

Call me dense if you like. I didn't see.

'And how are you going to find out?' I asked.

Caroline said there would be no difficulty about that. Our Annie's dearest friend was Miss Gannett's maid, Clara. And Clara was walking out with the Boots at the Three Boars. The whole thing was simplicity itself, and by the aid of Miss Gannett, who co-operated loyally, at once giving Clara leave of absence, the matter was rushed through at express speed.

It was when we were sitting down to lunch that Caroline remarked, with would-be unconcern:

'About those boots of Ralph Paton's.'

'Well,' I said, 'what about them?'

'M. Poirot thought they were probably brown. He was wrong. They're black.'

And Caroline nodded her head several times. She evidently felt that she had scored a point over Poirot.

I did not answer. I was puzzling over what the colour of a pair of Ralph Paton's boots had to do with the case.

CHAPTER 15

GEOFFREY RAYMOND

I was to have a further proof that day of the success of Poirot's tactics. That challenge of his had been a subtle touch born of his knowledge of human nature. A mixture of fear and guilt had wrung the truth from Mrs Ackroyd. She was the first to react.

That afternoon when I returned from seeing my patients, Caroline told me that Geoffrey Raymond had just left.

'Did he want to see me?' I asked, as I hung up my coat in the hall.

Caroline was hovering by my elbow.

'It was M. Poirot he wanted to see,' she said. 'He'd just

come from The Larches. M. Poirot was out. Mr Raymond thought that he might be here, or that you might know where he was.'

'I haven't the least idea.'

'I tried to make him wait,' said Caroline, 'but he said he would call back at The Larches in half an hour, and went away down the village. A great pity, because M. Poirot came in practically the minute after he left.'

'Came in here?'

'No, to his own house.'

'How do you know?'

'The side window,' said Caroline briefly.

It seemed to me that we had now exhausted the topic. Caroline thought otherwise.

'Aren't you going across?'

'Across where?'

'To The Larches, of course.'

'My dear Caroline,' I said, 'what for?'

'Mr Raymond wanted to see him very particularly,' said Caroline. 'You might hear what it's all about.'

I raised my eyebrows.

'Curiosity is not my besetting sin,' I remarked coldly. 'I can exist comfortably without knowing exactly what my neighbours are doing and thinking.'

'Stuff and nonsense, James,' said my sister. 'You want to know just as much as I do. You're not so honest, that's all. You always have to pretend.'

'Really, Caroline,' I said, and retired into my surgery.

Ten minutes later Caroline tapped at the door and entered. In her hand she held what seemed to be a pot of jam.

'I wonder, James,' she said, 'if you would mind taking this pot of medlar jelly across to M. Poirot? I promised it to him. He has never tasted any home-made medlar jelly.'

'Why can't Annie go?' I asked coldly.

'She's doing some mending. I can't spare her.'

Caroline and I looked at each other.

'Very well,' I said, rising. 'But if I take the beastly thing, I shall just leave it at the door. You understand that?'

My sister raised her eyebrows.

'Naturally,' she said. 'Who suggested you should do anything else?'

The honours were with Caroline.

'If you *do* happen to see M. Poirot,' she said, as I opened the front door, 'you might tell him about the boots.'

It was a most subtle parting shot. I wanted dreadfully to understand the enigma of the boots. When the old lady with the Breton cap opened the door to me, I found myself asking if M. Poirot was in, quite automatically.

Poirot sprang up to meet me, with every appearance of pleasure.

'Sit down, my good friend,' he said. 'The big chair? This small one? The room is not too hot, no?'

I thought it was stifling, but refrained from saying so. The windows were closed, and a large fire burned in the grate.

'The English people, they have a mania for the fresh air,' declared Poirot. 'The big air, it is all very well outside, where it belongs. Why admit it to the house? But let us not discuss such banalities. You have something for me, yes?'

'Two things,' I said. 'First – this – from my sister.'

I handed over the pot of medlar jelly.

'How kind of Mademoiselle Caroline. She has remembered her promise. And the second thing?'

'Information – of a kind.'

And I told him of my interview with Mrs Ackroyd. He listened with interest, but not much excitement.

'It clears the ground,' he said thoughtfully. 'And it has a certain value as confirming the evidence of the housekeeper. She said, you remember, that she found the silver table lid open and closed it down in passing.'

'What about her statement that she went into the drawing-room to see if the flowers were fresh?'

'Ah! we never took that very seriously, did we, my friend? It was patently an excuse, trumped up in a hurry, by a woman who felt it urgent to explain her presence – which, by the way, you would probably never have thought of questioning. I considered it possible that her agitation might arise from the fact that she had been tampering with the silver table, but I think now that we must look for another cause.'

'Yes,' I said. 'Whom did she go out to meet? And why?'

'You think she went to meet someone?'

'I do.'

Poirot nodded.

'So do I,' he said thoughtfully.

There was a pause.

'By the way,' I said, 'I've got a message for you from my sister. Ralph Paton's boots were black, not brown.'

I was watching him closely as I gave the message, and I fancied that I saw a momentary flicker of discomposure. If so, it passed almost immediately.

'She is absolutely positive they are not brown?'

'Absolutely.'

'Ah!' said Poirot regretfully. 'That is a pity.'

And he seemed quite crestfallen.

He entered into no explanations, but at once started a new subject of conversation.

'The housekeeper, Miss Russell, who came to consult you on that Friday morning – is it indiscreet to ask what passed at the interview – apart from the medical details, I mean?'

'Not at all,' I said. 'When the professional part of the conversation was over, we talked for a few minutes about poisons, and the ease or difficulty of detecting them, and about drug-taking and drug-takers.'

'With special reference to cocaine?' asked Poirot.

'How did you know?' I asked, somewhat surprised.

For answer, the little man rose and crossed the room to where newspapers were filed. He brought me a copy of the *Daily Budget*, dated Friday, 16th September, and showed me an article dealing with the smuggling of cocaine. It was a somewhat lurid article, written with an eye to picturesque effect.

'That is what put cocaine into her head, my friend,' he said.

I would have catechized him further, for I did not quite understand his meaning, but at that moment the door opened and Geoffrey Raymond was announced.

He came in fresh and debonair as ever, and greeted us both.

'How are you, doctor? M. Poirot, this is the second time I've been here this morning. I was anxious to catch you.'

'Perhaps I'd better be off,' I suggested rather awkwardly.

'Not on my account, doctor. No, it's just this,' he went on, seating himself at a wave of invitation from Poirot, 'I've got a confession to make.'

'*En vérité?*' said Poirot, with an air of polite interest.

'Oh, it's of no consequence, really. But, as a matter of fact, my conscience has been pricking me ever since yesterday afternoon. You accused us all of keeping back something, M. Poirot. I plead guilty. I've had something up my sleeve.'

'And what is that, M. Raymond?'

'As I say, it's nothing of consequence – just this. I was in debt – badly, and that legacy came in the nick of time. Five hundred pounds puts me on my feet again with a little to spare.'

He smiled at us both with that engaging frankness that made him such a likeable youngster.

'You know how it is. Suspicious-looking policemen – don't like to admit you were hard up for money – think it will look bad to them. But I was a fool, really, because Blunt and I were in the billiard room from a quarter to ten onwards, so I've got a watertight alibi and nothing to fear. Still, when you thundered out that stuff about concealing things, I felt a nasty prick of conscience, and I thought I'd like to get it off my mind.'

He got up again and stood smiling at us.

'You are a very wise young man,' said Poirot, nodding at him with approval. 'See you, when I know that anyone is hiding things from me, I suspect that the thing hidden may be something very bad indeed. You have done well.'

'I'm glad I'm cleared from suspicion,' laughed Raymond. 'I'll be off now.'

'So that is that,' I remarked, as the door closed behind the young secretary.

'Yes,' agreed Poirot. 'A mere bagatelle – but if he had not been in the billiard room – who knows? After all, many crimes have been committed for the sake of less than five hundred pounds. It all depends on what sum is sufficient to break a man. A question of relativity, is it not so? Have you reflected, my friend, that many people in that house stood to benefit by Mr Ackroyd's death? Mrs Ackroyd, Miss Flora, young Mr Raymond, the housekeeper, Miss Russell. Only one, in fact, does not, Major Blunt.'

His tone in uttering that name was so peculiar that I looked up, puzzled.

'I don't understand you,' I said.

'Two of the people I accused have given me the truth.'

'You think Major Blunt has something to conceal also?'

'As for that,' remarked Poirot nonchalantly, 'there is a saying, is there not, that Englishmen conceal only one thing – their love? And Major Blunt, I should say, is not good at concealments.'

'Sometimes,' I said, 'I wonder if we haven't rather jumped to conclusions on one point.'

'What is that?'

'We've assumed that the blackmailer of Mrs Ferrars is necessarily the murderer of Mr Ackroyd. Mightn't we be mistaken?'

Poirot nodded energetically.

'Very good. Very good indeed. I wondered if that idea would come to you. Of course it is possible. But we must remember one point. The letter disappeared. Still, that, as you say, may not necessarily mean that the murderer took it. When you first found the body, Parker may have abstracted the letter unnoticed by you.'

'Parker?'

'Yes, Parker. I always come back to Parker – not as the murderer – no, he did not commit the murder; but who is more suitable than he as the mysterious scoundrel who terrorized Mrs Ferrars? He may have got his information about Mr Ferrars's death from one of the King's Paddock servants. At any rate, he is more likely to have come upon it than a casual guest such as Blunt, for instance.'

'Parker might have taken the letter,' I admitted. 'It wasn't till later that I noticed it was gone.'

'How much later? After Blunt and Raymond were in the room, or before?'

'I can't remember,' I said slowly. 'I think it was before – no, afterwards. Yes, I'm almost sure it was afterwards.'

'That widens the field to three,' said Poirot thoughtfully. 'But Parker is the most likely. It is in my mind to try a little experiment with Parker. How say you, my friend, will you accompany me to Fernly?'

I acquiesced, and we set out at once. Poirot asked to see Miss Ackroyd, and presently Flora came to us.

'Mademoiselle Flora,' said Poirot, 'I have to confide in you a little secret. I am not yet satisfied of the innocence of Parker. I propose to make a little experiment with your assistance. I want to reconstruct some of his actions on that night. But we must think of something to tell him – ah! I have it. I wish to satisfy myself as to whether voices in the little lobby could have been heard outside on the terrace. Now, ring for Parker, if you will be so good.'

I did so, and presently the butler appeared, suave as ever.

'You rang, sir?'

'Yes, my good Parker. I have in mind a little experiment. I have placed Major Blunt on the terrace outside the study window. I want to see if anyone there could have heard the voices of Miss Ackroyd and yourself in the lobby that night. I want to enact that little scene over again. Perhaps you would fetch the tray or whatever it was you were carrying?'

Parker vanished, and we repaired to the lobby outside the study door. Presently we heard a chink in the outer hall, and Parker appeared in the doorway carrying a tray with a siphon, a decanter of whisky, and two glasses on it.

'One moment,' cried Poirot, raising his hand and seemingly very excited. 'We must have everything in order. Just as it occurred. It is a little method of mine.'

'A foreign custom, sir,' said Parker. 'Reconstruction of the crime they call it, do they not?'

He was quite imperturbable as he stood there politely waiting on Poirot's orders.

'Ah! he knows something, the good Parker,' cried Poirot. 'He has read of these things. Now, I beg you, let us have everything of the most exact. You came from the outer hall – so. Mademoiselle was – where?'

'Here,' said Flora, taking up her stand just outside the study door.

'Quite right, sir,' said Parker.

'I had just closed the door,' continued Flora.

'Yes, miss,' agreed Parker. 'Your hand was still on the handle as it is now.'

'Then *allez*,' said Poirot. 'Play me the little comedy.'

Flora stood with her hand on the door handle, and Parker came stepping through the door from the hall, bearing the tray.

He stopped just inside the door. Flora spoke.

'Oh! Parker. Mr Ackroyd doesn't want to be disturbed again tonight.'

'Is that right?' she added in an undertone.

'To the best of my recollection, Miss Flora,' said Parker, 'but I fancy you used the word evening instead of night.' Then, raising his voice in a somewhat theatrical fashion: 'Very good, miss. Shall I lock up as usual?'

'Yes, please.'

Parker retired through the door, Flora followed him, and started to ascend the main staircase.

'Is that enough?' she asked over her shoulder.

'Admirable,' declared the little man, rubbing his hands. 'By the way, Parker, are you sure there were two glasses on the tray that evening? Who was the second one for?'

'I always bring two glasses, sir,' said Parker. 'Is there anything further?'

'Nothing. I thank you.'

Parker withdrew, dignified to the last.

Poirot stood in the middle of the hall frowning. Flora came down and joined us.

'Has your experiment been successful?' she asked. 'I don't quite understand, you know –'

Poirot smiled admiringly at her.

'It is not necessary that you should,' he said. 'But tell me, were there indeed two glasses on Parker's tray that night?'

Flora wrinkled her brows a minute.

'I really can't remember,' she said. 'I think there were. Is – is that the object of your experiment?'

Poirot took her hand and patted it.

'Put it this way,' he said. 'I am always interested to see if people will speak the truth.'

'And did Parker speak the truth?'

'I rather think he did,' said Poirot thoughtfully.

A few minutes later saw us retracing our steps to the village.

'What was the point of that question about the glasses?' I asked curiously.

Poirot shrugged his shoulders.

'One must say something,' he remarked. 'That particular question did as well as any other.'

I stared at him.

'At any rate, my friend,' he said seriously, 'I know now something I wanted to know. Let us leave it at that.'

CHAPTER 16

AN EVENING AT MAH JONG

That night we had a little Mah Jong party. This kind of simple entertainment is very popular in King's Abbot. The guests arrive in galoshes and waterproofs after dinner. They partake of coffee and later of cake, sandwiches and tea.

On this particular night our guests were Miss Gannett and Colonel Carter, who lives near the church. A good deal of gossip is handed round at these evenings, sometimes seriously interfering with the game in progress. We used to play bridge – chatty bridge of the worst description. We find Mah Jong much more peaceful. The irritated demand as to why on earth your partner did not lead a certain card is entirely done away with, and though we still express criticisms frankly, there is not the same acrimonious spirit.

'Very cold evening, eh, Sheppard?' said Colonel Carter, standing with his back to the fire. Caroline had taken Miss Gannett to her own room, and was there assisting her to disentangle herself from her many wraps. 'Reminds me of the Afghan passes.'

'Indeed?' I said politely.

'Very mysterious business this about poor Ackroyd,' continued the colonel, accepting a cup of coffee. 'A deuce of a lot behind it – that's what I say. Between you and me, Sheppard, I've heard the word blackmail mentioned!'

The colonel gave me the look which might be tabulated 'one man of the world to another'.

'A woman in it, no doubt,' he said. 'Depend upon it, a woman in it.'

Caroline and Miss Gannett joined us at this minute. Miss Gannett drank coffee whilst Caroline got out the Mah Jong box and poured out the tiles upon the table.

'Washing the tiles,' said the colonel facetiously. 'That's right – washing the tiles, as we used to say in the Shanghai Club.'

It is the private opinion of both Caroline and myself that Colonel Carter has never been in the Shanghai Club in his life. More, that he has never been farther east than India, where he juggled with tins of bully beef and plum and apple jam during the Great War. But the colonel is determinedly military, and in King's Abbot we permit people to indulge their little idiosyncrasies freely.

'Shall we begin?' said Caroline.

We sat round the table. For some five minutes there was complete silence, owing to the fact that there is tremendous secret competition amongst us as to who can build their wall quickest.

'Go on, James,' said Caroline at last. 'You're East Wind.'

I discarded a tile. A round or two proceeded, broken by the monotonous remarks of 'Three Bamboos', 'Two Circles', 'Pung', and frequently from Miss Gannett 'Unpung', owing to that lady's habit of too hastily claiming tiles to which she had no right.

'I saw Flora Ackroyd this morning,' said Miss Gannett. 'Pung – no – Unpung. I made a mistake.'

'Four Circles,' said Caroline. 'Where did you see her?'

'She didn't see *me*,' said Miss Gannett, with that tremendous significance only to be met with in small villages.

'Ah!' said Caroline interestedly. 'Chow.'

'I believe,' said Miss Gannett, temporarily diverted, 'that it's the right thing nowadays to say "Chee" not "Chow".'

'Nonsense,' said Caroline. 'I have always said "*Chow*".'

'In the Shanghai Club,' said Colonel Carter, 'they say "*Chow*".'

Miss Gannett retired, crushed.

'What were you saying about Flora Ackroyd?' asked Caroline, after a moment or two devoted to the game. 'Was she with anyone?'

'Very much so,' said Miss Gannett.

The eyes of the two ladies met, and seemed to exchange information.

'Really,' said Caroline interestedly. 'Is that it? Well, it doesn't surprise me in the least.'

'We're waiting for you to discard, Miss Caroline,' said the colonel. He sometimes affects the pose of the bluff male, intent on the game and indifferent to gossip. But nobody is deceived.

'If you ask me,' said Miss Gannett. ('Was that a Bamboo you discarded, dear? Oh! no, I see now – it was a Circle.) As I was saying, if you ask me, Flora's been exceedingly lucky. Exceedingly lucky she's been.'

'How's that, Miss Gannett?' asked the colonel. 'I'll Pung that Green Dragon. How do you make out that Miss Flora's been lucky? Very charming girl and all that, I know.'

'I mayn't know very much about crime,' said Miss Gannett, with the air of one who knows everything there is to know, 'but I can tell you one thing. The first question that's always asked is "Who last saw the deceased alive?" And the person who did is regarded with suspicion. Now, Flora Ackroyd last saw her uncle alive. It might have looked very nasty for her – very nasty indeed. It's my opinion – and I give it for what it's worth, that Ralph Paton is staying away on her account, to draw suspicion away from her.'

'Come, now,' I protested mildly, 'you surely can't suggest that a young girl like Flora Ackroyd is capable of stabbing her uncle in cold blood?'

'Well, I don't know,' said Miss Gannett. 'I've just been reading a book from the library about the underworld of Paris, and it says that some of the worst women criminals are young girls with the faces of angels.'

'That's in France,' said Caroline instantly.

'Just so,' said the colonel. 'Now, I'll tell you a very curious thing – a story that was going round the Bazaars in India . . .'

The colonel's story was one of interminable length, and of curiously little interest. A thing that happened in India many years ago cannot compare for a moment with an event that took place in King's Abbot the day before yesterday.

It was Caroline who brought the colonel's story to a close by fortunately going Mah Jong. After the slight unpleasantness always caused by my corrections of Caroline's somewhat faulty arithmetic, we started a new hand.

'East Wind passes,' said Caroline. 'I've got an idea of my

own about Ralph Paton. Three Characters. But I'm keeping it to myself for the present.'

'Are you, dear?' said Miss Gannett. 'Chow – I mean Pung.'

'Yes,' said Caroline firmly.

'Was it all right about the boots?' asked Miss Gannett. 'Their being black, I mean?'

'Quite all right,' said Caroline.

'What was the point, do you think?' asked Miss Gannett.

Caroline pursed up her lips, and shook her head with an air of knowing all about it.

'Pung,' said Miss Gannett. 'No – Unpung. I suppose that now the doctor's in with M. Poirot he knows all the secrets?'

'Far from it,' I said.

'James is so modest,' said Caroline. 'Ah! A concealed Kong.'

The colonel gave vent to a whistle. For the moment gossip was forgotten.

'Your own wind, too,' he said. '*And* you've got two Pungs of Dragons. We must be careful. Miss Caroline's out for a big hand.'

We played for some minutes with no irrelevant conversation.

'This M. Poirot now,' said Colonel Carter, 'is he really such a great detective?'

'The greatest the world has ever known,' said Caroline solemnly. 'He has to come here incognito to avoid publicity.'

'Chow,' said Miss Gannett. 'Quite wonderful for our little village, I'm sure. By the way, Clara – my maid, you know – is great friends with Elsie, the housemaid at Fernly, and what do you think Elsie told her? That there's been a lot of money stolen, and it's her opinion – Elsie's, I mean – that the parlourmaid had something to do with it. She's leaving at the month, and she's crying a good deal at night. If you ask me, the girl is very likely in league with a *gang*. She's always been a queer girl – she's not friends with any of the girls round here. She goes off by herself on her days out – very unnatural, I call it, and most suspicious. I asked her once to come to our Friendly Girls' Evenings, but she refused, and then I asked her a few questions about her home and her family – all that sort of thing, and I'm bound to say I considered her manner most impertinent. Outwardly very respectful – but she shut me up in the most barefaced way.'

Miss Gannett stopped for breath, and the colonel, who was totally uninterested in the servant question, remarked that in the Shanghai Club brisk play was the invariable rule.

We had a round of brisk play.

'That Miss Russell,' said Caroline. 'She came here pretending to consult James on Friday morning. It's my opinion she wanted to see where the poisons were kept. Five Characters.'

'Chow,' said Miss Gannett. 'What an extraordinary idea! I wonder if you can be right.'

'Talking of poisons,' said the colonel. 'Eh – what? Haven't I discarded? Oh! Eight Bamboos.'

'Mah Jong!' said Miss Gannett.

Caroline was very much annoyed.

'One Red Dragon,' she said regretfully, 'and I should have had a hand of three doubles.'

'I've had two Red Dragons all the time,' I mentioned.

'So exactly like you, James,' said Caroline reproachfully. 'You've no conception of the spirit of the game.'

I myself thought I had played rather cleverly. I should have had to pay Caroline an enormous amount if she had gone Mah Jong. Miss Gannett's Mah Jong was of the poorest variety possible, as Caroline did not fail to point out to her.

East Wind passed, and we started a new hand in silence.

'What I was going to tell you just now was this,' said Caroline.

'Yes?' said Miss Gannett encouragingly.

'My idea about Ralph Paton, I mean.'

'Yes, dear,' said Miss Gannett, still more encouragingly. 'Chow!'

'It's a sign of weakness to Chow so early,' said Caroline severely. 'You should go for a big hand.'

'I know,' said Miss Gannett. 'You were saying – about Ralph Paton, you know?'

'Yes. Well, I've a pretty shrewd idea where he is.'

We all stopped to stare at her.

'This is very interesting, Miss Caroline,' said Colonel Carter. 'All your own idea, eh?'

'Well, not exactly. I'll tell you about it. You know that big map of the county we have in the hall?'

We all said Yes.

'As M. Poirot was going out the other day, he stopped and

looked at it, and he made some remark – I can't remember exactly what it was. Something about Cranchester being the only big town anywhere near us – which is true, of course. But after he had gone – it came to me suddenly.'

'What came to you?'

'His meaning. Of course Ralph is in Cranchester.'

It was at that moment that I knocked down the rack that held my pieces. My sister immediately reproved me for clumsiness, but half-heartedly. She was intent on her theory.

'Cranchester, Miss Caroline?' said Colonel Carter. 'Surely not Cranchester! It's so near.'

'That's exactly it,' cried Caroline triumphantly. 'It seems quite clear by now that he didn't get away from here by train. He must simply have walked into Cranchester. And I believe he's there still. No one would dream of his being so near at hand.'

I pointed out several objections to the theory, but when once Caroline has got something firmly into her head, nothing dislodges it.

'And you think M. Poirot has the same idea,' said Miss Gannett thoughtfully. 'It's a curious coincidence, but I was out for a walk this afternoon on the Cranchester road, and he passed me in a car coming from that direction.'

We all looked at each other.

'Why, dear me,' said Miss Gannett suddenly, 'I'm Mah Jong all the time, and I never noticed it.'

Caroline's attention was distracted from her own inventive exercises. She pointed out to Miss Gannett that a hand consisting of mixed suits and too many Chows was hardly worth going Mah Jong on. Miss Gannett listened imperturbably and collected her counters.

'Yes, dear, I know what you mean,' she said. 'But it rather depends on what kind of a hand you have to start with, doesn't it?'

'You'll never get the big hands if you don't go for them,' urged Caroline.

'Well, we must all play our own way, mustn't we?' said Miss Gannett. She looked down at her counters. 'After all, I'm up, so far.'

Caroline, who was considerably down, said nothing.

East Wind passed, and we set to once more. Annie brought in the tea things. Caroline and Miss Gannett were both slightly ruffled as is often the case during one of these festive evenings.

'If you would only play a leetle quicker, dear,' said Caroline, as Miss Gannett hesitated over her discard. 'The Chinese put down the tiles so quickly it sounds like little birds pattering.'

For some minutes we played like the Chinese.

'You haven't contributed much to the sum of information, Sheppard,' said Colonel Carter genially. 'You're a sly dog. Hand in glove with the great detective, and not a hint as to the way things are going.'

'James is an extraordinary creature,' said Caroline. 'He can *not* bring himself to part with information.'

She looked at me with some disfavour.

'I assure you,' I said, 'that I don't know anything. Poirot keeps his own counsel.'

'Wise man,' said the colonel with a chuckle. 'He doesn't give himself away. But they're wonderful fellows, these foreign detectives. Up to all sorts of dodges, I believe.'

'Pung,' said Miss Gannett, in a tone of quiet triumph. 'And Mah Jong.'

The situation became more strained. It was annoyance at Miss Gannett's going Mah Jong for the third time running which prompted Caroline to say to me as we built a fresh wall:

'You are too tiresome, James. You sit there like a dead-head, and say nothing at all!'

'But, my dear,' I protested, 'I have really nothing to say – that is, of the kind you mean.'

'Nonsense,' said Caroline, as she sorted her hand. 'You *must* know something interesting.'

I did not answer for a moment. I was overwhelmed and intoxicated. I had read of there being such a thing as The Perfect Winning – going Mah Jong on one's original hand. I had never hoped to hold the hand myself.

With suppressed triumph I laid my hand face upwards on the table.

'As they say in the Shanghai Club,' I remarked – 'Tin-ho – the Perfect Winning!'

The colonel's eyes nearly bulged out of his head.

'Upon my soul,' he said. 'what an extraordinary thing. I never saw that happen before!'

It was then that I went on, goaded by Caroline's gibes, and rendered reckless by my triumph.

'And as to anything interesting,' I said. 'What about a gold wedding ring with a date and "From R." inside.'

I pass over the scene that followed. I was made to say exactly where this treasure was found. I was made to reveal the date.

'March 13th,' said Caroline. 'Just six months ago. Ah!'

Out of a babel of excited suggestions and suppositions three theories were evolved:

1. That of Colonel Carter: that Ralph was secretly married to Flora. The first or most simple solution.

2. That of Miss Gannett: that Roger Ackroyd had been secretly married to Mrs Ferrars.

3. That of my sister: that Roger Ackroyd had married his housekeeper, Miss Russell.

A fourth or super-theory was propounded by Caroline later as we went up to bed.

'Mark my words,' she said suddenly, 'I shouldn't be at all surprised if Geoffrey Raymond and Flora weren't married.'

'Surely it would be "From G.," not "From R." then,' I suggested.

'You never know. Some girls call men by their surnames. And you heard what Miss Gannett said this evening – about Flora's carryings on.'

Strictly speaking, I had not heard Miss Gannett say anything of the kind, but I respected Caroline's knowledge of innuendoes.

'How about Hector Blunt?' I hinted. 'If it's anybody –'

'Nonsense,' said Caroline. 'I dare say he admires her – may even be in love with her. But depend upon it a girl isn't going to fall in love with a man old enough to be her father when there's a good-looking secretary about. She may encourage Major Blunt just as a blind. Girls are very artful. But there's one thing I *do* tell you, James Sheppard. Flora Ackroyd does not care a penny piece for Ralph Paton, and never has. You can take it from me.'

I took it from her meekly.

CHAPTER 17

PARKER

It occurred to me the next morning that under the exhilaration produced by Tin-ho or the Perfect Winning, I might have been slightly indiscreet. True, Poirot had not asked me to keep the discovery of the ring to myself. On the other hand, he had said nothing about it whilst at Fernly, and as far as I knew, I was the only person aware that it had been found. I felt distinctly guilty. The fact was by now spreading through King's Abbot like wildfire. I was expecting wholesale reproaches from Poirot any minute.

The joint funeral of Mrs Ferrars and Roger Ackroyd was fixed for eleven o'clock. It was a melancholy and impressive ceremony. All the party from Fernly were there.

After it was over, Poirot, who had also been present, took me by the arm, and invited me to accompany him back to The Larches. He was looking very grave, and I feared that my indiscretion of the night before had got round to his ears. But it soon transpired that his thoughts were occupied by something of a totally different nature.

'See you,' he said. 'We must act. With your help I propose to examine a witness. We will question him, we will put such fear into him that the truth is bound to come out.'

'What witness are you talking about?' I asked, very much surprised.

'Parker!' said Poirot. 'I asked him to be at my house this morning at twelve o'clock. He should await us there at this very minute.'

'What do you think?' I ventured, glancing sideways at his face.

'I know this – that I am not satisfied.'

'You think that it was he who blackmailed Mrs Ferrars?'

'Either that, or –'

'Well?' I said, after waiting a minute or two.

'My friend, I will say this to you – I hope it was he.'

The gravity of his manner, and something indefinable that tinged it, reduced me to silence.

On arrival at The Larches, we were informed that Parker was already there awaiting our return. As we entered the room, the butler rose respectfully.

'Good morning, Parker,' said Poirot pleasantly. 'One instant, I pray of you.'

He removed his overcoat and gloves.

'Allow me, sir,' said Parker, and sprang forward to assist him. He deposited the articles neatly on a chair by the door. Poirot watched him with approval.

'Thank you, my good Parker,' he said. 'Take a seat, will you not? What I have to say may take some time.'

Parker seated himself with an apologetic bend of the head.

'Now what do you think I asked you to come here for this morning – eh?'

Parker coughed.

'I understood, sir, that you wished to ask me a few questions about my late master – private like.'

'*Précisément*,' said Poirot, beaming. 'Have you made many experiments in blackmail?'

'Sir!'

The butler sprang to his feet.

'Do not excite yourself,' said Poirot placidly. 'Do not play the farce of the honest, injured man. You know all there is to know about the blackmail, is it not so?'

'Sir, I – I've never – never been –'

'Insulted,' suggested Poirot, 'in such a way before. Then why, my excellent Parker, were you so anxious to overhear the conversation in Mr Ackroyd's study the other evening, after you had caught the word blackmail?'

'I wasn't – I –'

'Who was your last master?' rapped out Poirot suddenly.

'My last master?'

'Yes, the master you were with before you came to Mr Ackroyd.'

'A Major Ellerby, sir –'

Poirot took the words out of his mouth.

'Just so, Major Ellerby. Major Ellerby was addicted to drugs, was he not? You travelled about with him. When he was in Bermuda there was some trouble – a man was killed. Major

Ellerby was partly responsible. It was hushed up. But you knew about it. How much did Major Ellerby pay you to keep your mouth shut?'

Parker was staring at him open-mouthed. The man had gone to pieces, his cheeks shook flabbily.

'You see, me, I have made inquiries,' said Poirot pleasantly. 'It is as I say. You got a good sum then as blackmail, and Major Ellerby went on paying you until he died. Now I want to hear about your latest experiment.'

Parker still stared.

'It is useless to deny. Hercule Poirot *knows*. It is so, what I have said about Major Ellerby, is it not?'

As though against his will, Parker nodded reluctantly once. His face was ashen pale.

'But I never hurt a hair of Mr Ackroyd's head,' he moaned. 'Honest to God, sir, I didn't. I've been afraid of this coming all the time. And I tell you I didn't – I didn't kill him.'

His voice rose almost to a scream.

'I am inclined to believe you, my friend,' said Poirot. 'You have not the nerve – the courage. But I must have the truth.'

'I'll tell you anything, sir, anything you want to know. It's true that I tried to listen that night. A word or two I heard made me curious. And Mr Ackroyd's wanting not to be disturbed, and shutting himself up with the doctor the way he did. It's God's own truth what I told the police. I heard the word blackmail, sir, and well –'

He paused.

'You thought there might be something in it for you?' suggested Poirot smoothly.

'Well – well, yes, I did, sir. I thought that if Mr Ackroyd was being blackmailed, why shouldn't I have a share of the pickings?'

A very curious expression passed over Poirot's face. He leaned forward.

'Had you any reason to suppose before that night that Mr Ackroyd was being blackmailed?'

'No, indeed, sir. It was a great surprise to me. Such a regular gentleman in all his habits.'

'How much did you overhear?'

'Not very much, sir. There seemed what I might call a spite against me. Of course I had to attend to my duties in the pantry. And when I did creep along once or twice to the study it was no use. The first time Dr Sheppard came out and almost caught me in the act, and another time Mr Raymond passed me in the big hall and went that way, so I knew it was no use; and when I went with the tray, Miss Flora headed me off.'

Poirot stared for a long time at the man, as if to test his sincerity. Parker returned his gaze earnestly.

'I hope you believe me, sir. I've been afraid all along the police would rake up that old business with Major Ellerby and be suspicious of me in consequence.'

'*Eh bien,*' said Poirot at last. 'I am disposed to believe you. But there is one thing I must request of you – to show me your bank-book. You have a bank-book, I presume?'

'Yes, sir, as a matter of fact, I have it with me now.'

With no sign of confusion, he produced it from his pocket. Poirot took the slim, green-covered book and perused the entries.

'Ah! I perceive you have purchased £500 worth of National Savings Certificates this year?'

'Yes, sir. I have already over a thousand pounds saved – the result of my connection with – er – my late master, Major Ellerby. And I have had quite a little flutter on some horses this year – very successful. If you remember, sir, a rank outsider won the Jubilee. I was fortunate enough to back it – £20.'

Poirot handed him back the book.

'I will wish you good morning. I believe that you have told me the truth. If you have not – so much the worse for you, my friend.'

When Parker had departed, Poirot picked up his overcoat once more.

'Going out again?' I asked.

'Yes, we will pay a little visit to the good M. Hammond.'

'You believe Parker's story?'

'It is credible enough on the face of it. It seems clear that – unless he is a very good actor indeed – he genuinely believes it was Ackroyd himself who was the victim of blackmail. If so, he knows nothing at all about the Mrs Ferrars business.'

'Then in that case – who –?'

'*Précisément*! Who? But our visit to M. Hammond will accomplish one purpose. It will either clear Parker completely or else –'

'Well?'

'I fall into the bad habit of leaving my sentences unfinished this morning,' said Poirot apologetically. 'You must bear with me.'

'By the way,' I said, rather sheepishly, 'I've got a confession to make. I'm afraid I have inadvertently let out something about that ring.'

'What ring?'

'The ring you found in the goldfish pond.'

'Ah! yes,' said Poirot, smiling broadly.

'I hope you're not annoyed? It was very careless of me.'

'But not at all, my good friend, not at all. I laid no commands upon you. You were at liberty to speak of it if you so wished. She was interested, your sister?'

'She was indeed. It created a sensation. All sorts of theories are flying about.'

'Ah! And yet it is so simple. The true explanation leapt to the eye, did it not?'

'Did it?' I said drily.

Poirot laughed.

'The wise man does not commit himself,' he observed. 'Is not that so? But here we are at Mr Hammond's.'

The lawyer was in his office, and we were ushered in without any delay. He rose and greeted us in his dry, precise manner.

Poirot came at once to the point.

'Monsieur, I desire from you certain information, that is, if you will be so good as to give it to me. You acted, I understand, for the late Mrs Ferrars of King's Paddock?'

I noticed the swift gleam of surprise which showed in the lawyer's eyes, before his professional reserve came down once more like a mask over his face.

'Certainly. All her affairs passed through our hands.'

'Very good. Now, before I ask you to tell me anything, I should like you to listen to the story Dr Sheppard will relate to you. You have no objection, have you, my friend, to repeating the conversation you had with Mr Ackroyd last Friday night?'

'Not in the least,' I said, and straightaway began the recital of that strange evening.

Hammond listened with close attention.

'That is all,' I said, when I had finished.

'Blackmail,' said the lawyer thoughtfully.

'You are surprised?' asked Poirot.

The lawyer took off his pince-nez and polished them with his handkerchief.

'No,' he replied, 'I can hardly say that I am surprised. I have suspected something of the kind for some time.'

'That brings us,' said Poirot, 'to the information for which I am asking. If anyone can give us an idea of the actual sums paid, you are the man, monsieur.'

'I see no object in withholding the information,' said Hammond, after a moment or two. 'During the past year, Mrs Ferrars has sold out certain securities, and the money for them was paid into her account and not re-invested. As her income was a large one, and she lived very quietly after her husband's death, it seems certain that these sums of money were paid away for some special purpose. I once sounded her on the subject, and she said that she was obliged to support several of her husband's poor relations. I let the matter drop, of course. Until now, I have always imagined that the money was paid to some woman who had had a claim on Ashley Ferrars. I never dreamed that Mrs Ferrars herself was involved.'

'And the amount?' asked Poirot.

'In all, I should say the various sums totalled at least twenty thousand pounds.'

'Twenty thousand pounds!' I exclaimed. 'In one year!'

'Mrs Ferrars was a very wealthy woman,' said Poirot drily. 'And the penalty for murder is not a pleasant one.'

'Is there anything else that I can tell you?' inquired Mr Hammond.

'I thank you, no,' said Poirot, rising. 'All my excuses for having deranged you.'

'Not at all, not at all.'

'The word derange,' I remarked, when we were outside again, 'is applicable to mental disorder only.'

'Ah!' cried Poirot. 'Never will my English be quite perfect. A curious language. I should then have said disarranged, *n'est-ce pas*?'

'Disturbed is the word you had in mind.'

'I thank you, my friend. The word exact, you are zealous for it. *Eh bien*, what about our friend Parker now? With twenty thousand pounds in hand, would he have continued being a butler? *Je ne pense pas*. It is, of course, possible that he banked the money under another name, but I am disposed to believe he spoke the truth to us. If he is a scoundrel, he is a scoundrel on a mean scale. He has not the big ideas. That leaves us as a possibility, Raymond, or – well – Major Blunt.'

'Surely not Raymond,' I objected. 'Since we know that he was desperately hard up for a matter of five hundred pounds.'

'That is what he says, yes.'

'And as to Hector Blunt –'

'I will tell you something as to the good Major Blunt,' interrupted Poirot. 'It is my business to make inquiries. I make them. *Eh bien* – that legacy of which he speaks, I have discovered that the amount of it was close upon twenty thousand pounds. What do you think of that?'

I was so taken aback that I could hardly speak.

'It's impossible,' I said at last. 'A well-known man like Hector Blunt.'

Poirot shrugged his shoulders.

'Who knows? At least he is a man with big ideas. I confess that I hardly see him as a blackmailer, but there is another possibility that you have not even considered.'

'What is that?'

'The fire, my friend. Ackroyd himself may have destroyed that letter, blue envelope and all, after you left him.'

'I hardly think that likely,' I said slowly. 'And yet – of course, it may be so. He might have changed his mind.'

We had just arrived at my house, and on the spur of the moment I invited Poirot to come in and take pot luck.

I thought Caroline would be pleased with me, but it is hard to satisfy one's womenfolk. It appears that we were eating chops for lunch – the kitchen staff being regaled on tripe and onions. And two chops set before three people are productive of embarrassment.

But Caroline is seldom daunted for long. With magnificent mendacity, she explained to Poirot that although James laughed at her for doing so, she adhered strictly to a vegetarian diet. She descanted ecstatically on the delights of nut cutlets (which I am quite sure she has never tasted) and ate a Welsh rarebit with gusto and frequent cutting remarks as to the dangers of 'flesh' foods.

Afterwards, when we were sitting in front of the fire and smoking, Caroline attacked Poirot directly.

'Not found Ralph Paton yet?' she asked.

'Where should I find him, mademoiselle?'

'I thought, perhaps, you'd found him in Cranchester,' said Caroline, with intense meaning in her tone.

Poirot looked merely bewildered.

'In Cranchester? But why in Cranchester?'

I enlightened him with a touch of malice.

'One of our ample staff of private detectives happened to see you in a car on the Cranchester road yesterday,' I explained.

Poirot's bewilderment vanished. He laughed heartily.

'Ah, that! A simple visit to the dentist, *c'est tout*. My tooth, it aches. I go there. My tooth, it is at once better. I think to return quickly. The dentist, he says No. Better to have it out. I argue. He insists. He has his way! That particular tooth, it will never ache again.'

Caroline collapsed rather like a pricked balloon.

We fell to discussing Ralph Paton.

'A weak nature,' I insisted. 'But not a vicious one.'

'Ah!' said Poirot. 'But weakness, where does it end?'

'Exactly,' said Caroline. 'Take James here – weak as water, if I weren't about to look after him.'

'My dear Caroline,' I said irritably, 'can't you talk without dragging in personalities?'

'You *are* weak, James,' said Caroline, quite unmoved. 'I'm eight years older than you are – oh! I don't mind M. Poirot knowing that –'

'I should never have guessed it, mademoiselle,' said Poirot, with a gallant little bow.

'Eight years older. And I've always considered it my duty to look after you. With a bad bringing up, Heaven knows what mischief you might have got into by now.'

'I might have married a beautiful adventuress,' I murmured, gazing at the ceiling, and blowing smoke rings.

'Adventuress!' said Caroline, with a snort. 'If we're talking of adventuresses –'

She left the sentence unfinished.

'Well?' I said, with some curiosity.

'Nothing. But I can think of someone not a hundred miles away.'

Then she turned to Poirot suddenly.

'James sticks to it that you believe someone in the house committed the murder. All I can say is, you're wrong.'

'I should not like to be wrong,' said Poirot. 'It is not – how do you say – my *métier*?'

'I've got the facts pretty clearly,' continued Caroline, taking no notice of Poirot's remark, 'from James and others. As far as I can see, of the people in the house, only two *could* have had the chance of doing it. Ralph Paton and Flora Ackroyd.'

'My dear Caroline –'

'Now, James, don't interrupt me. I know what I'm talking about. Parker met her *outside* the door, didn't he? He didn't hear her uncle saying goodnight to her. She could have killed him then and there.'

'Caroline!'

'I'm not saying she *did*, James. I'm saying she *could* have done. As a matter of fact, though, Flora is like all these young girls nowadays, with no veneration for their betters and thinking they know best on every subject under the sun, I don't for a minute believe she'd kill even a chicken. But there it is. Mr Raymond and Major Blunt have alibis. Mrs Ackroyd's got an alibi. Even that Russell woman seems to have one – and a good job for her it is she has. Who is left? Only Ralph and Flora! And say what you will, I don't believe Ralph Paton is a murderer. A boy we've known all our lives.'

Poirot was silent for a minute, watching the curling smoke rise from his cigarette. When at last he spoke, it was in a gentle far-away voice that produced a curious impression. It was totally unlike his usual manner.

'Let us take a man – a very ordinary man. A man with no idea of murder in his heart. There is in him somewhere a strain of weakness – deep down. It has so far never been called into play. Perhaps it never will be – and if so he will go to his grave honoured and respected by everyone. But let us suppose that something occurs. He is in difficulties – or perhaps not that even. He may stumble by accident on a secret – a secret involving life or death to someone. And his first impulse will be to speak out – to do his duty as an honest citizen. And then the strain of weakness tells. Here is a chance of money – a great amount of money. He wants money – he desires it – and it is so easy. He has to do nothing for it – just keep silence. That is the beginning. The desire for money grows. He must have more – and more! He is intoxicated by the gold mine which has opened at his feet. He becomes greedy. And in his greed he overreaches himself. One can press a man as far as one likes – but with a woman one must not press too far. For a woman has at heart a great desire to speak the truth. How many husbands who have deceived their wives go comfortably to their graves, carrying their secret with them! How many wives who have deceived their husbands wreck their lives by throwing the fact in those same husbands' teeth! They have been pressed too far. In a reckless moment (which they will afterwards regret, *bien entendu*) they fling safety to the winds and turn at bay, proclaiming the truth with great momentary satisfaction to themselves. So it was, I think, in this case. The strain was too great. And so there came your proverb, the death of the goose that laid the golden eggs. But that is not the end. Exposure faced the man of whom we are speaking. And he is not the same man he was – say, a year ago. His moral fibre is blunted. He is desperate. He is fighting a losing battle, and he is prepared to take any means that come to his hand, for exposure means ruin to him. And so – the dagger strikes!'

He was silent for a moment. It was as though he had laid a spell upon the room. I cannot try to describe the impression his words produced. There was something in the merciless analysis, and the ruthless power of vision which struck fear into both of us.

'Afterwards,' he went on softly, 'the dagger removed, he will be himself again, normal, kindly. But if the need again arises, then once more he will strike.'

Caroline roused herself at last.

'You are speaking of Ralph Paton,' she said. 'You may be right, you may not, but you have no business to condemn a man unheard.'

The telephone bell rang sharply. I went out into the hall, and took off the receiver.

'What?' I said. 'Yes. Dr Sheppard speaking.'

I listened for a minute or two, then replied briefly. Replacing the receiver, I went back into the drawing-room.

'Poirot,' I said, 'they have detained a man at Liverpool. His name is Charles Kent, and he is believed to be the stranger who visited Fernly that night. They want me to go to Liverpool at once and identify him.'

CHAPTER 18

CHARLES KENT

Half an hour later saw Poirot, myself, and Inspector Raglan in the train on the way to Liverpool. The inspector was clearly very excited.

'We may get a line on the blackmailing part of the business, if on nothing else,' he declared jubilantly. 'He's a rough customer, this fellow, by what I heard over the phone. Takes dope, too. We ought to find it easy to get what we want out of him. If there was the shadow of a motive, nothing's more likely than that he killed Mr Ackroyd. But in that case, why is young Paton keeping out of the way. The whole thing's a muddle – that's what it is. By the way, M. Poirot, you were quite right about those fingerprints. They were Mr Ackroyd's own. I had rather the same idea myself, but I dismissed it as hardly feasible.'

I smiled to myself. Inspector Raglan was so very plainly saving his face.

'As regard this man,' said Poirot, 'he is not yet arrested, eh?'

'No, detained under suspicion.'

'And what account does he give of himself?'

'Precious little,' said the inspector, with a grin. 'He's a wary bird, I gather. A lot of abuse, but very little more.'

On arrival at Liverpool I was surprised to find that Poirot was welcomed with acclamation. Superintendent Hayes, who met us, had worked with Poirot over some case long ago, and had evidently an exaggerated opinion of his powers.

'Now we've got M. Poirot here we shan't be long,' he said cheerfully. 'I thought you'd retired, moosior?'

'So I had, my good Hayes, so I had. But how tedious is retirement! You cannot imagine to yourself the monotony with which day comes after day.'

'Very likely. So you've come to have a look at our own particular find? Is this Dr Sheppard? Think you'll be able to identify him, sir?'

'I'm not very sure,' I said doubtfully.

'How did you get hold of him?' inquired Poirot.

'Description was circulated, as you know. In the press and privately. Not much to go on, I admit. This fellow has an American accent all right, and he doesn't deny that he was near King's Abbot that night. Just asks what the hell it is to do with us, and that he'll see us in — before he answers any questions.'

'Is it permitted that I, too, see him?' asked Poirot.

The superintendent closed one eye knowingly.

'Very glad to have you, sir. You've got permission to do anything you please. Inspector Japp of Scotland Yard was asking after you the other day. Said he'd heard you were connected unofficially with this case. Where's Captain Paton hiding, sir, can you tell me that?'

'I doubt if it would be wise at the present juncture,' said Poirot primly, and I bit my lips to prevent a smile.

The little man really did it very well.

After some further parley, we were taken to interview the prisoner.

He was a young fellow, I should say not more than twenty-two or three. Tall, thin, with slightly shaking hands, and the evidences of considerable physical strength somewhat run to seed. His hair was dark, but his eyes were blue and shifty, seldom meeting a glance squarely. I had all along cherished the illusion that there was something familiar about the figure I had met that night, but if this were indeed he, I was completely mistaken. He did not remind me in the least of anyone I knew.

'Now then, Kent,' said the superintendent. 'Stand up. Here are some visitors come to see you. Recognize any of them?'

Kent glared at us sullenly, but did not reply. I saw his glance waver over the three of us, and come back to rest on me.

'Well, sir,' said the superintendent to me, 'what do you say?'

'The height's the same,' I said, 'and as far as general appearance goes it might well be the man in question. Beyond that, I couldn't go.'

'What the hell's the meaning of all this?' asked Kent. 'What have you got against me? Come on, out with it! What am I supposed to have done?'

I nodded my head.

'It's the man,' I said. 'I recognize the voice.'

'Recognize my voice, do you? Where do you think you heard it before?'

'On Friday evening last, outside the gates of Fernly Park. You asked me the way there.'

'I did, did I?'

'Do you admit it?' asked the inspector.

'I don't admit anything. Not till I know what you've got on me.'

'Have you not read the papers in the last few days?' asked Poirot, speaking for the first time.

The man's eyes narrowed.

'So that's it, is it? I saw an old gent had been croaked at Fernly. Trying to make out I did the job, are you?'

'You were there that night,' said Poirot quietly.

'How do you know, mister?'

'By this.' Poirot took something from his pocket and held it out.

It was the goose quill we had found in the summer-house.

At the sight of it the man's face changed. He half held out his hand.

'Snow,' said Poirot thoughtfully. 'No, my friend, it is empty. It lay where you dropped it in the summer-house that night.'

Charles Kent looked at him uncertainly.

'You seem to know a hell of a lot about everything, you little foreign cock duck. Perhaps you remember this: the papers say that the old gent was croaked between a quarter to ten and ten o'clock?'

'That is so,' agreed Poirot.

'Yes, but is it really so? That's what I'm getting at.'

'This gentleman will tell you,' said Poirot.

He indicated Inspector Raglan. The latter hesitated, glanced at Superintendent Hayes, then at Poirot, and finally, as though receiving sanction, he said:

'That's right. Between a quarter to ten and ten o'clock.'

'Then you've nothing to keep me here for,' said Kent. 'I was away from Fernly Park by twenty-five minutes past nine. You can ask at the Dog and Whistle. That's a saloon about a mile out of Fernly on the road to Cranchester. I kicked up a bit of a row there, I remember. As near as nothing to quarter to ten, it was. How about that?'

Inspector Raglan wrote down something in his note-book.

'Well?' demanded Kent.

'Inquiries will be made,' said the inspector. 'If you've spoken the truth, you won't have anything to complain about. What were you doing at Fernly Park anyway?'

'Went there to meet someone.'

'Who?'

'That's none of your business.'

'You'd better keep a civil tongue in your head, my man,' the superintendent warned him.

'To hell with a civil tongue. I went there on my own business, and that's all there is to it. If I was clear away before the murder was done, that's all that concerns the cops.'

'Your name, it is Charles Kent,' said Poirot. 'Where were you born?'

The man stared at him, then he grinned.

'I'm a full-blown Britisher all right,' he said.

'Yes,' said Poirot meditatively. 'I think you are. I fancy you were born in Kent.'

The man stared.

'Why's that? Because of my name? What's that to do with it? Is a man whose name is Kent bound to be born in that particular county?'

'Under certain circumstances, I can imagine he might be,' said Poirot very deliberately. 'Under certain circumstances, you comprehend.'

There was so much meaning in his voice as to surprise the two police officers. As for Charles Kent, he flushed a brick red, and for a moment I thought he was going to spring at Poirot.

He thought better of it, however, and turned away with a kind of laugh.

Poirot nodded as though satisfied, and made his way out through the door. He was joined presently by the two officers.

'We'll verify that statement,' remarked Raglan. 'I don't think he's lying, though. But he's got to come clean with a statement as to what he was doing at Fernly. It looks to me as though we'd got our blackmailer all right. On the other hand, granted his story's correct, he couldn't have had anything to do with the actual murder. He'd got ten pounds on him when he was arrested – rather a large sum. I fancy that forty pounds went to him – the numbers of the notes didn't correspond, but of course he'd have changed them first thing. Mr Ackroyd must have given him the money, and he made off with it as fast as possible. What was that about Kent being his birthplace? What's that got to do with it?'

'Nothing whatever,' said Poirot mildly. 'A little idea of mine, that was all. Me, I am famous for my little ideas.'

'Are you really?' said Raglan, studying him with a puzzled expression.

The superintendent went into a roar of laughter.

'Many's the time I've heard Inspector Japp say that. M. Poirot and his little ideas! Too fanciful for me, he'd say, but always something in them.'

'You mock yourself at me,' said Poirot, smiling; 'but never mind. The old ones they laugh last sometimes, when the young, clever ones do not laugh at all.'

And nodding his head at them in a sage manner he walked out into the street.

He and I lunched together at an hotel. I know now that the whole thing lay clearly unravelled before him. He had got the last thread he needed to lead him to the truth.

But at the time I had no suspicion of the fact. I over-estimated his general self-confidence, and I took it for granted that the things which puzzled me must be equally puzzling to him.

My chief puzzle was what the man Charles Kent could have been doing at Fernly. Again and again I put the question to myself and could get no satisfactory reply. At last I ventured a tentative query to Poirot. His reply was immediate.

'*Mon ami, I* do not think, I know.'

'Really?' I said incredulously.

'Yes, indeed. I suppose now that to you it would not make sense if I said that he went to Fernly that night because he was born in Kent?'

I stared at him.

'It certainly doesn't seem to make sense to me,' I said drily.

'Ah!' said Poirot pityingly. 'Well, no matter. I have still my little idea.'

CHAPTER 19

FLORA ACKROYD

As I was returning from my round the following morning, I was hailed by Inspector Raglan. I pulled up, and the inspector mounted on the step.

'Good morning, Dr Sheppard,' he said. 'Well, that alibi is all right enough.'

'Charles Kent's?'

'Charles Kent's. The barmaid at the Dog and Whistle, Sally Jones, she remembers him perfectly. Picked out his photograph from among five others. It was just a quarter to ten when he came into the bar, and the Dog and Whistle is well over a mile from Fernly Park. The girl mentions that he had a lot of money on him – she saw him take a handful of notes out of his pocket. Rather surprised her, it did, seeing the class of fellow he was, with a pair of boots clean dropping off him. That's where that forty pounds went right enough.'

'The man still refuses to give an account of his visit to Fernly?'

'Obstinate as a mule he is. I had a chat with Hayes at Liverpool over the wire this morning.'

'Hercule Poirot says he knows the reason the man went there that night,' I observed.

'Does he?' cried the inspector eagerly.

'Yes,' I said maliciously. 'He says he went there because he was born in Kent.'

I felt a distinct pleasure in passing on my own discomfiture.

Raglan stared at me for a moment or two uncomprehendingly.

Then a grin overspread his weaselly countenance and he tapped his forehead significantly.

'Bit gone here,' he said. 'I've thought so for some time. Poor old chap, so that's why he had to give up and come down here. In the family, very likely. He's got a nephew who's quite off his crumpet.'

'Poirot has?' I said, very surprised.

'Yes. Hasn't he ever mentioned him to you? Quite docile, I believe, and all that, but mad as a hatter, poor lad.'

'Who told you that?'

Again a grin showed itself on Inspector Raglan's face.

'Your sister, Miss Sheppard, she told me all about it.'

Really, Caroline is amazing. She never rests until she knows the last details of everybody's family secrets. Unfortunately, I have never been able to instil into her the decency of keeping them to herself.

'Jump in, Inspector,' I said, opening the door of the car. 'We'll go up to The Larches together, and acquaint our Belgian friend with the latest news.'

'Might as well, I suppose. After all, even if he is a bit barmy, it was a useful tip he gave me about those fingerprints. He's got a bee in his bonnet about the man Kent, but who knows – there may be something useful behind it.'

Poirot received us with his usual smiling courtesy.

He listened to the information we had brought him, nodding his head now and then.

'Seems quite O.K., doesn't it?' said the inspector rather gloomily. 'A chap can't be murdering someone in one place when he's drinking in the bar in another place a mile away.'

'Are you going to release him?'

'Don't see what else we can do. We can't very well hold him for obtaining money on false pretences. Can't prove a ruddy thing.'

The inspector tossed a match into the grate in a disgruntled fashion. Poirot retrieved it and put it neatly in a little receptacle designed for the purpose. His action was purely mechanical. I could see that his thoughts were on something very different.

'If I were you,' he said at last, 'I should not release the man Charles Kent yet.'

'What do you mean?'

Raglan stared at him.

'What I say. I should not release him yet.'

'You don't think he can have had anything to do with the murder, do you?'

'I think probably not – but one cannot be certain yet.'

'But haven't I just told you –?'

Poirot raised a hand protestingly.

'*Mais oui, mais oui.* I heard. I am not deaf – or stupid, thank the good God! But you see, you approach the matter from the wrong – the wrong – premises, is not that the word?'

The inspector stared at him heavily.

'I don't see how you make that out. Look here, we know Mr Ackroyd was alive at a quarter to ten. You admit that, don't you?'

Poirot looked at him for a moment, then shook his head with a quick smile.

'I admit nothing that is not – *proved*!'

'Well, we've got proof enough of that. We've got Miss Flora Ackroyd's evidence.'

'That she said goodnight to her uncle? But me – I do not always believe what a young lady tells me – no, not even when she is charming and beautiful.'

'But hang it all, man, Parker saw her coming out of the door.'

'No.' Poirot's voice rang out with sudden sharpness. 'That is just what he did not see. I satisfied myself of that by a little experiment the other day – you remember, doctor? Parker saw her *outside* the door, with her hand on the handle. He did not see her come out of the room.'

'But – where else could she have been?'

'Perhaps on the stairs.'

'The stairs?'

'That is my little idea – yes.'

'But those stairs only lead to Mr Ackroyd's bedroom.'

'Precisely.'

And still the inspector stared.

'You think she'd been up to her uncle's bedroom? Well, why not? Why should she lie about it?'

'Ah! that is just the question. It depends on what she was doing there, does it not?'

'You mean – the money? Hang it all, you don't suggest that it was Miss Ackroyd who took that forty pounds?'

'I suggest nothing,' said Poirot. 'But I will remind you of this. Life was not very easy for that mother and daughter. There were bills – there was constant trouble over small sums of money. Roger Ackroyd was a peculiar man over money matters. The girl might be at her wits' end for a comparatively small sum. Figure to yourself then what happens. She has taken the money, she descends the little staircase. When she is half-way down she hears the chink of glass from the hall. She has not a doubt of what it is – Parker coming to the study. At all costs she must not be found on the stairs – Parker will not forget it, he will think it odd. If the money is missed, Parker is sure to remember having seen her come down those stairs. She has just time to rush down to the study door – with her hand on the handle to show that she has just come out, when Parker appears in the doorway. She says the first thing that comes into her head, a repetition of Roger Ackroyd's orders earlier in the evening, and then goes upstairs to her own room.'

'Yes, but later,' persisted the inspector, 'she must have realized the vital importance of speaking the truth? Why, the whole case hinges on it!'

'Afterwards,' said Poirot drily, 'it was a little difficult for Mademoiselle Flora. She is told simply that the police are here and that there has been a robbery. Naturally she jumps to the conclusion that the theft of the money has been discovered. Her one idea is to stick to her story. When she learns that her uncle is dead she is panic-stricken. Young women do not faint nowadays, monsieur, without considerable provocation. *Eh bien!* There it is. She is bound to stick to her story, or else confess everything. And a young and pretty girl does not like to admit that she is a thief – especially before those whose esteem she is anxious to retain.'

Raglan brought his fist down with a thump on the table.

'I'll not believe it,' he said. 'It's – it's not credible. And you – you've known this all along?'

'The possibility has been in my mind from the first,' admitted Poirot. 'I was always convinced that Mademoiselle Flora was hiding something from us. To satisfy myself, I made the little experiment I told you of. Dr Sheppard accompanied me.'

'A test for Parker, you said it was,' I remarked bitterly.

'*Mon ami*,' said Poirot apologetically, 'as I told you at the time, one must say something.'

The inspector rose.

'There's only one thing for it,' he declared. 'We must tackle the young lady right away. You'll come up to Fernly with me, M. Poirot?'

'Certainly. Dr Sheppard will drive us up in his car.'

I acquiesced willingly.

On inquiry for Miss Ackroyd, we were shown into the billiard room. Flora and Major Hector Blunt were sitting on the long window seat.

'Good-morning, Miss Ackroyd,' said the inspector. 'Can we have a word or two alone with you?'

Blunt got up at once and moved to the door.

'What is it?' asked Flora nervously. 'Don't go, Major Blunt. He can stay, can't he?' she asked, turning to the inspector.

'That's as you like,' said the inspector drily. 'There's a question or two it's my duty to put to you, miss, but I'd prefer to do so privately, and I dare say you'd prefer it also.'

Flora looked keenly at him. I saw her face grow whiter. Then she turned and spoke to Blunt.

'I want you to stay – please – yes, I mean it. Whatever the inspector has to say to me, I'd rather you heard it.'

Raglan shrugged his shoulders.

'Well, if you will have it so, that's all there is to it. Now, Miss Ackroyd, M. Poirot here has made a certain suggestion to me. He suggests that you weren't in the study at all last Friday night, that you never saw Mr Ackroyd to say goodnight to him, that instead of being in the study you were on the stairs leading down from your uncle's bedroom when you heard Parker coming across the hall.'

Flora's gaze shifted to Poirot. He nodded back at her.

'Mademoiselle, the other day, when we sat round the table, I implored you to be frank with me. What one does not tell to Papa Poirot he finds out. It was that, was it not? See, I will make it easy for you. You took the money, did you not?'

'The money?' said Blunt sharply.

There was a silence which lasted for at least a minute.

Then Flora drew herself up and spoke.

'M. Poirot is right. I took that money. I stole. I am a thief – yes, a common, vulgar little thief. Now you know! I am glad it has come out. It's been a nightmare, these last few days!' She sat down suddenly and buried her face in her hands. She spoke huskily through her fingers. 'You don't know what my life has been since I came here. Wanting things, scheming for them, lying, cheating, running up bills, promising to pay – oh! I hate myself when I think of it all! That's what brought us together, Ralph and I. We were both weak! I understood him, and I was sorry – because I'm the same underneath. We're not strong enough to stand alone, either of us. We're weak, miserable, despicable things.'

She looked at Blunt and suddenly stamped her foot.

'Why do you look at me like that – as though you couldn't believe? I may be a thief – but at any rate I'm real now. I'm not lying any more. I'm not pretending to be the kind of girl you like, young and innocent and simple. I don't care if you never want to see me again. I hate myself, despise myself – but you've got to believe one thing, if speaking the truth would have made things better for Ralph, I would have spoken out. But I've seen all along that it wouldn't be better for Ralph – it makes the case against him blacker than ever. I was not doing him any harm by sticking to my lie.'

'Ralph,' said Blunt. 'I see – always Ralph.'

'You don't understand,' said Flora hopelessly. 'You never will.'

She turned to the inspector.

'I admit everything; I was at my wits' end for money. I never saw my uncle that evening after he left the dinner-table. As to the money, you can take what steps you please. Nothing could be worse than it is now!'

Suddenly she broke down again, hid her face in her hands, and rushed from the room.

'Well,' said the inspector in a flat tone, 'so that's that.'

He seemed rather at a loss what to do next.

Blunt came forward.

'Inspector Raglan,' he said quietly, 'that money was given to me by Mr Ackroyd for a special purpose. Miss Ackroyd never touched it. When she says she did, she is lying with the idea of shielding Captain Paton. The truth is as I said, and I am prepared to go into the witness-box and swear to it.'

He made a kind of jerky bow, then turning abruptly he left the room.

Poirot was after him in a flash. He caught the other up in the hall.

'Monsieur – a moment, I beg of you, if you will be so good.'

'Well, sir?'

Blunt was obviously impatient. He stood frowning down on Poirot.

'It is this,' said Poirot rapidly: 'I am not deceived by your little fantasy. No, indeed. It was truly Miss Flora who took the money. All the same it is well imagined what you say – it pleases me. It is very good what you have done there. You are a man quick to think and to act.'

'I'm not in the least anxious for your opinion, thank you,' said Blunt coldly.

He made once more as though to pass on, but Poirot, not at all offended, laid a detaining hand on his arm.

'Ah! but you are to listen to me. I have more to say. The other day I spoke of concealments. Very well, all along I have seen what you are concealing. Mademoiselle Flora, you love her with all your heart. From the first moment you saw her, is it not so? Oh! let us not mind saying these things – why must one in England think it necessary to mention love as though it were some disgraceful secret? You love Mademoiselle Flora. You seek to conceal that fact from all the world. That is very good – that is as it should be. But take the advice of Hercule Poirot – do not conceal it from mademoiselle herself.'

Blunt had shown several signs of restlessness whilst Poirot was speaking, but the closing words seemed to rivet his attention.

'What d'you mean by that?' he said sharply.

'You think that she loves the Capitaine Ralph Paton – but I, Hercule Poirot, tell you that that is not so. Mademoiselle Flora accepted Captain Paton to please her uncle, and because she saw in the marriage a way of escape from her life here which was becoming frankly insupportable to her. She liked him, and there was much sympathy and understanding between them. But love – no! It is not Captain Paton Mademoiselle Flora loves.'

'What the devil do you mean?' asked Blunt.

I saw the dark flush under his tan.

'You have been blind, monsieur. Blind! She is loyal, the little one. Ralph Paton is under a cloud, she is bound in honour to stick by him.'

I felt it was time I put in a word to help on the good work.

'My sister told me the other night,' I said encouragingly, 'that Flora had never cared a penny piece for Ralph Paton, and never would. My sister is always right about these things.'

Blunt ignored my well-meant offers. He spoke to Poirot.

'D'you really think –' he began, and stopped.

He is one of those inarticulate men who find it hard to put things into words.

Poirot knows no such disability.

'If you doubt me, ask her yourself, monsieur. But perhaps you no longer care to – the affair of the money –'

Blunt gave a sound like an angry laugh.

'Think I'd hold that against her? Roger was always a queer chap about money. She got in a mess and didn't dare tell him. Poor kid. Poor lonely kid.'

Poirot looked thoughtfully at the side door.

'Mademoiselle Flora went into the garden, I think,' he murmured.

'I've been every kind of a fool,' said Blunt abruptly. 'Rum conversation we've been having. Like one of those Danish plays. But you're a sound fellow, M. Poirot. Thank you.'

He took Poirot's hand and gave it a grip which caused the other to wince in anguish. Then he strode to the side door and passed out into the garden.

'Not every kind of a fool,' murmured Poirot, tenderly nursing the injured member. 'Only one kind – the fool in love.'

CHAPTER 20

MISS RUSSELL

Inspector Raglan had received a bad jolt. He was not deceived by Blunt's valiant lie any more than we had been. Our way back to the village was punctuated by his complaints.

'This alters everything, this does. I don't know whether you've realized it, Monsieur Poirot?'

'I think so, yes, I think so,' said Poirot. 'You see, me, I have been familiar with the idea for some time.'

Inspector Raglan, who had only had the idea presented to him a short half-hour ago, looked at Poirot unhappily, and went on with his discoveries.

'Those alibis now. Worthless! Absolutely worthless. Got to start again. Find out what everyone was doing from nine-thirty onwards. Nine-thirty – that's the time we've got to hang on to. You were quite right about the man Kent – we don't release *him* yet awhile. Let me see now – nine forty-five at the Dog and Whistle. He might have got there in a quarter of an hour if he ran. It's just possible that it was *his* voice Mr Raymond heard talking to Mr Ackroyd – asking for money which Mr Ackroyd refused. But one thing's clear – it wasn't he who sent the telephone message. The station is half a mile in the other direction – over a mile and a half from the Dog and Whistle, and he was at the Dog and Whistle until about ten minutes past ten. Dang that telephone call! We always come up against it.'

'We do indeed,' agreed Poirot. 'It is curious.'

'It's just possible that if Captain Paton climbed into his uncle's room and found him there murdered, *he* may have sent it. Got the wind up, thought he'd be accused, and cleared out. That's possible, isn't it?'

'Why should he have telephoned?'

'May have had doubts if the old man was really dead. Thought he'd get the doctor up there as soon as possible, but didn't want to give himself away. Yes, I say now, how's that for a theory? Something in that, I should say.'

The inspector swelled his chest out importantly. He was so

plainly delighted with himself that any words of ours would have been quite superfluous.

We arrived back at my house at this minute, and I hurried in to my surgery patients, who had all been waiting a considerable time, leaving Poirot to walk to the police station with the inspector.

Having dismissed the last patient, I strolled into the little room at the back of the house which I call my workshop – I am rather proud of the home-made wireless set I turned out. Caroline hates my workroom. I have kept my tools there, and Annie is not allowed to wreak havoc with a dustpan and brush. I was just adjusting the interior of an alarm clock which had been denounced as wholly unreliable by the household, when the door opened and Caroline put her head in.

'Oh! there you are, James,' she said, with deep disapproval. 'M. Poirot wants to see you.'

'Well,' I said, rather irritably, for her sudden entrance had startled me and I had let go of a piece of delicate mechanism. 'If he wants to see me, he can come in here.'

'In here?' said Caroline.

'That's what I said – in here.'

Caroline gave a sniff of disapproval and retired. She returned in a moment or two, ushering in Poirot, and then retired again, shutting the door with a bang.

'Aha! my friend,' said Poirot, coming forward and rubbing his hands. 'You have not got rid of me so easily, you see!'

'Finished with the inspector?' I asked.

'For the moment, yes. And you, you have seen all the patients?'

'Yes.'

Poirot sat down and looked at me, tilting his egg-shaped head on one side, with the air of one who savours a very delicious joke.

'You are in error,' he said at last. 'You have still one patient to see.'

'Not you?' I exclaimed in surprise.

'Ah, not me, *bien entendu*. Me, I have the health magnificent. No, to tell you the truth, it is a little *complot* of mine. There is someone I wish to see, you understand – and at the same time it is not necessary that the whole village should intrigue itself about the matter – which is what would happen if the lady were seen to come to my house – for it is a lady. But to you she has already come as a patient before.'

'Miss Russell!' I exclaimed.

'*Précisément*. I wish much to speak with her, so I send her the little note and make the appointment in your surgery. You are not annoyed with me?'

'On the contrary,' I said. 'That is, presuming I am allowed to be present at the interview?'

'But naturally! In your own surgery!'

'You know,' I said, throwing down the pincers I was holding, 'it's extraordinarily intriguing, the whole thing. Every new development that arises is like the shake you give to a kaleidoscope – the thing changes entirely in aspect. Now, why are you so anxious to see Miss Russell?'

Poirot raised his eyebrows.

'Surely it is obvious?' he murmured.

'There you go again,' I grumbled. 'According to you everything is obvious. But you leave me walking about in a fog.'

Poirot shook his head genially to me.

'You mock yourself at me. Take the matter of Mademoiselle Flora. The inspector was surprised – but you – you were not.'

'I never dreamed of her being the thief,' I expostulated.

'That – perhaps no. But I was watching your face and you were not – like Inspector Raglan – startled and incredulous.'

I thought for a minute or two.

'Perhaps you are right,' I said at last. 'All along I've felt that Flora was keeping back something – so the truth, when it came, was subconsciously expected. It upset Inspector Raglan very much indeed, poor man.'

'Ah! *pour ça oui*! The poor man must rearrange all his ideas. I profited by his state of mental chaos to induce him to grant me a little favour.'

'What was that?'

Poirot took a sheet of notepaper from his pocket. Some words were written on it, and he read them aloud.

'The police have, for some days, been seeking for Captain Ralph Paton, the nephew of Mr Ackroyd of Fernly Park, whose death occurred under such tragic circumstances last Friday.

Captain Paton has been found at Liverpool, where he was on the point of embarking for America.'

He folded up the piece of paper again.

'That, my friend, will be in the newspapers tomorrow morning.'

I stared at him, dumbfounded.

'But – but it isn't true! He's not at Liverpool!'

Poirot beamed on me.

'You have the intelligence so quick! No, he has not been found at Liverpool. Inspector Raglan was very loath to let me send this paragraph to the press, especially as I could not take him into my confidence. But I assured him most solemnly that very interesting results would follow its appearance in print, so he gave in, after stipulating that he was, on no account, to bear the responsibility.'

I stared at Poirot. He smiled back at me.

'It beats me,' I said at last, 'what you expect to get out of that.'

'You should employ your little grey cells,' said Poirot gravely.

He rose and came across to the bench.

'It is that you have really the love of the machinery,' he said, after inspecting the débris of my labours.

Every man has his hobby. I immediately drew Poirot's attention to my home-made wireless. Finding him sympathetic, I showed him one or two little inventions of my own – trifling things, but useful in the house.

'Decidedly,' said Poirot, 'you should be an inventor by trade, not a doctor. But I hear the bell – that is your patient. Let us go into the surgery.'

Once before I had been struck by the remnants of beauty in the housekeeper's face. This morning I was struck anew. Very simply dressed in black, tall, upright and independent as ever, with her big dark eyes and an unwonted flush of colour in her usually pale cheeks, I realized that as a girl she must have been startlingly handsome.

'Good-morning, mademoiselle,' said Poirot. 'Will you be seated? Dr Sheppard is so kind as to permit me the use of his surgery for a little conversation I am anxious to have with you.'

Miss Russell sat down with her usual composure. If she felt

any inward agitation, it did not display itself in any outward manifestation.

'It seems a queer way of doing things, if you'll allow me to say so,' she remarked.

'Miss Russell – I have news to give you.'

'Indeed!'

'Charles Kent has been arrested at Liverpool.'

Not a muscle of her face moved. She merely opened her eyes a trifle wider, and asked, with a tinge of defiance:

'Well, what of it?'

But at that moment it came to me – the resemblance that had haunted me all along, something familiar in the defiance of Charles Kent's manner. The two voices, one rough and coarse, the other painfully ladylike – were strangely the same in timbre. It was of Miss Russell that I had been reminded that night outside the gates of Fernly Park.

I looked at Poirot, full of my discovery, and he gave me an imperceptible nod.

In answer to Miss Russell's question, he threw out his hands in a thoroughly French gesture.

'I thought you might be interested, that is all,' he said mildly.

'Well, I'm not particularly,' said Miss Russell. 'Who is this Charles Kent anyway?'

'He is a man, mademoiselle, who was at Fernly on the night of the murder.'

'Really?'

'Fortunately for him, he has an alibi. At a quarter to ten he was at a public-house a mile from here.'

'Lucky for him,' commented Miss Russell.

'But we still do not know what he was doing at Fernly – who it was he went to meet, for instance.'

'I'm afraid I can't help you at all,' said the housekeeper politely. 'Nothing came to *my* ears. If that is all –'

She made a tentative movement as though to rise. Poirot stopped her.

'It is not quite all,' he said smoothly. 'This morning fresh developments have arisen. It seems now that Mr Ackroyd was murdered, not at a quarter to ten, but *before*. Between ten minutes to nine, when Dr Sheppard left, and a quarter to ten.'

I saw the colour drain from the housekeeper's face, leaving it dead white. She leaned forward, her figure swaying.

'But Miss Ackroyd said – Miss Ackroyd said –'

'Miss Ackroyd has admitted that she was lying. She was never in the study at all that evening.'

'Then –'

'Then it would seem that in this Charles Kent we have the man we are looking for. He came to Fernly, can give no account of what he was doing there –'

'I can tell you what he was doing there. He never touched a hair of old Ackroyd's head – he never went near the study. He didn't do it, I tell you.'

She was leaning forward. That iron self-control was broken through at last. Terror and desperation was in her face.

'M. Poirot! M. Poirot! Oh, do believe me.'

Poirot got up and came to her. He patted her reassuringly on the shoulder.

'But yes – but yes, I will believe. I had to make you speak, you know.'

For an instant suspicion flared up in her.

'Is what you said true?'

'That Charles Kent is suspected of the crime? Yes, that is true. You alone can save him, by telling the reason for his being at Fernly.'

'He came to see me.' She spoke in a low, hurried voice. 'I went out to meet him –'

'In the summer-house, yes, I know.'

'How do you know?'

'Mademoiselle, it is the business of Hercule Poirot to know things. I know that you went out earlier in the evening, that you left a message in the summer-house to say what time you would be there.'

'Yes, I did. I had heard from him – saying he was coming. I dared not let him come to the house. I wrote to the address he gave me and said I would meet him in the summer-house, and described it to him so that he would be able to find it. Then I was afraid he might not wait there patiently, and I ran out and left a piece of paper to say I would be there about ten minutes past nine. I didn't want the servants to see me, so I slipped out through the drawing-room window. As I came back, I met Dr Sheppard, and I fancied that he would think it queer. I was out of breath, for I had been running. I had no idea that he was expected to dinner that night.'

She paused.

'Go on,' said Poirot. 'You went out to meet him at ten minutes past nine. What did you say to each other?'

'It's difficult. You see –'

'Mademoiselle,' said Poirot, interrupting her, 'in this matter I must have the whole truth. What you tell us need never go beyond these four walls. Dr Sheppard will be discreet, and so shall I. See, I will help you. This Charles Kent, he is your son, is he not?'

She nodded. The colour had flamed into her cheeks.

'No one has ever known. It was long ago – long ago – down in Kent. I was not married . . .'

'So you took the name of the county as a surname for him. I understand.'

'I got work. I managed to pay for his board and lodging. I never told him that I was his mother. But he turned out badly, he drank, then took to drugs. I managed to pay his passage out to Canada. I didn't hear of him for a year or two. Then, somehow or other, he found out that I was his mother. He wrote asking me for money. Finally, I heard from him back in this country again. He was coming to see me at Fernly, he said. I dared not let him come to the house. I have always been considered so – so very respectable. If anyone got an inkling – it would have been all up with my post as housekeeper. So I wrote to him in the way I have just told you.'

'And in the morning you came to see Dr Sheppard?'

'Yes. I wondered if something could be done. He was not a bad boy – before he took to drugs.'

'I see,' said Poirot. 'Now let us go on with the story. He came that night to the summer-house?'

'Yes, he was waiting for me when I got there. He was very rough and abusive. I had brought with me all the money I had, and I gave it to him. We talked a little, and then he went away.'

'What time was that?'

'It must have been between twenty and twenty-five minutes past nine. It was not yet half-past when I got back to the house.'

'Which way did he go?'

'Straight out the same way he came, by the path that joined the drive just inside the lodge gates.'

Poirot nodded.

'And you, what did you do?'

'I went back to the house. Major Blunt was walking up and down the terrace smoking, so I made a detour to get round to the side door. It was just then on half-past nine, as I tell you.'

Poirot nodded again. He made a note or two in a microscopic pocket-book.

'I think that is all,' he said thoughtfully.

'Ought I –?' she hesitated. 'Ought I to tell all this to Inspector Raglan?'

'It may come to that. But let us not be in a hurry. Let us proceed slowly, with due order and method. Charles Kent is not yet formally charged with murder. Circumstances may arise which will render your story unnecessary.'

Miss Russell rose.

'Thank you very much, M. Poirot,' she said. 'You have been very kind – very kind indeed. You – you do believe me, don't you? That Charles had nothing to do with this wicked murder!'

'There seems no doubt that the man who was talking to Mr Ackroyd in the library at nine-thirty could not possibly have been your son. Be of good courage, mademoiselle. All will yet be well.'

Miss Russell departed. Poirot and I were left together.

'So that's that,' I said. 'Every time we come back to Ralph Paton. How did you manage to spot Miss Russell as the person Charles Kent came to meet? Did you notice the resemblance?'

'I had connected her with the unknown man long before we actually came face to face with him. As soon as we found that quill. The quill suggested dope, and I remembered your account of Miss Russell's visit to you. Then I found the article on cocaine in that morning's paper. It all seemed very clear. She had heard from someone that morning – someone addicted to drugs, she read the article in the paper, and she came to ask you a few tentative questions. She mentioned cocaine, since the article in question was on cocaine. Then, when you seemed too interested, she switched hurriedly to the subject of detective stories and untraceable poisons. I suspected a son or a brother, or some other undesirable male relation. Ah! but I must go. It is the time of the lunch.'

'Stay and lunch with us,' I suggested.

Poirot shook his head. A faint twinkle came into his eye.

'Not again today. I should not like to force Mademoiselle Caroline to adopt a vegetarian diet two days in succession.'

It occurred to me that there was not much which escaped Hercule Poirot.

CHAPTER 21

THE PARAGRAPH IN THE PAPER

Caroline, of course, had not failed to see Miss Russell come to the surgery door. I had anticipated this, and had ready an elaborate account of the lady's bad knee. But Caroline was not in a cross-questioning mood. Her point of view was that she knew what Miss Russell had really come for and that *I* didn't.

'Pumping you, James,' said Caroline. 'Pumping you in the most shameless manner, I've no doubt. It's no good interrupting. I dare say you hadn't the least idea she was doing it even. Men *are* so simple. She knows that you are in M. Poirot's confidence, and she wants to find out things. Do you know what I think, James?'

'I couldn't begin to imagine. You think so many extraordinary things.'

'It's no good being sarcastic. I think Miss Russell knows more about Mr Ackroyd's death than she is prepared to admit.'

Caroline leaned back triumphantly in her chair.

'Do you really think so?' I said absently.

'You are very dull today, James. No animation about you. It's that liver of yours.'

Our conversation then dealt with purely personal matters.

The paragraph inspired by Poirot duly appeared in our daily paper the next morning. I was in the dark as to its purpose, but its effect on Caroline was immense.

She began by stating, most untruly, that she had said as much all along. I raised my eyebrows, but did not argue. Caroline, however, must have felt a prick of conscience, for she went on:

'I mayn't have actually mentioned Liverpool, but I knew he'd try to get away to America. That's what Crippen did.'

'Without much success,' I reminded her.

'Poor boy, and so they've caught him. I consider, James, that it's your duty to see that he isn't hung.'

'What do you expect me to do?'

'Why, you're a medical man, aren't you? You've known him from a boy upwards. Not mentally responsible. That's the line to take, clearly. I read only the other day that they're very happy in Broadmoor – it's quite like a high-class club.'

But Caroline's words had reminded me of something.

'I never knew that Poirot had an imbecile nephew?' I said curiously.

'Didn't you? Oh, he told me all about it. Poor lad. It's a great grief to all the family. They've kept him at home so far, but it's getting to such a pitch that they're afraid he'll have to go into some kind of institution.'

'I suppose you know pretty well everything there is to know about Poirot's family by this time,' I said, exasperated.

'Pretty well,' said Caroline complacently. 'It's a great relief to people to be able to tell all their troubles to someone.'

'It might be,' I said, 'if they were ever allowed to do so spontaneously. Whether they enjoy having confidences screwed out of them by force is another matter.'

Caroline merely looked at me with an air of a Christian martyr enjoying martyrdom.

'You are so self-contained, James,' she said. 'You hate speaking out, or parting with any information yourself, and you think everybody else must be just like you. I should hope that I never screw confidences out of anybody. For instance, if M. Poirot comes in this afternoon, as he said he might do, I shall not dream of asking him who it was arrived at his house early this morning.'

'Early this morning?' I queried.

'Very early,' said Caroline. 'Before the milk came. I just happened to be looking out of the window – the blind was flapping. It was a man. He came in a closed car, and he was all muffled up. I couldn't get a glimpse of his face. But I will tell you *my* idea, and you'll see that I'm right.'

'What's your idea?'

Caroline dropped her voice mysteriously.

'A Home Office expert,' she breathed.

'A Home Office expert,' I said, amazed. 'My dear Caroline!'

'Mark my words, James, you'll see that I'm right. That Russell woman was here that morning after your poisons. Roger Ackroyd might easily have been poisoned in his food that night.'

I laughed out loud.

'Nonsense,' I cried. 'He was stabbed in the neck. You know that as well as I do.'

'After death, James,' said Caroline; 'to make a false clue.'

'My good woman,' I said, 'I examined the body, and I know what I'm talking about. That wound wasn't inflicted after death – it was the cause of death, and you need make no mistake about it.'

Caroline merely continued to look omniscient, which so annoyed me that I went on:

'Perhaps you will tell me, Caroline, if I have a medical degree or if I have not?'

'You have the medical degree, I dare say, James – at least, I mean I know you have. But you've no imagination whatever.'

'Having endowed you with a treble portion, there was none left over for me,' I said drily.

I was amused to see Caroline's manoeuvres that afternoon when Poirot duly arrived. My sister, without asking a direct question, skirted the subject of the mysterious guest in every way imaginable. By the twinkle in Poirot's eyes, I saw that he realized her object. He remained blandly impervious, and blocked her bowling so successfully that she herself was at a loss how to proceed.

Having, I suspect, enjoyed the little game, he rose to his feet and suggested a walk.

'It is that I need to reduce the figure a little,' he explained. 'You will come with me, doctor? And perhaps later, Miss Caroline will give us some tea.'

'Delighted,' said Caroline. 'Won't your – er – guest come in also?'

'You are too kind,' said Poirot. 'But no, my friend reposes himself. Soon you must make his acquaintance.'

'Quite an old friend of yours, so somebody told me,' said Caroline, making one last valiant effort.

'Did they?' murmured Poirot. 'Well, we must start.'

Our tramp took us in the direction of Fernly. I had guessed beforehand that it might do so. I was beginning to understand Poirot's methods. Every little irrelevancy had a bearing upon the whole.

'I have a commission for you, my friend,' he said at last. 'Tonight, at my house. I desire to have a little conference. You will attend, will you not?'

'Certainly,' I said.

'Good. I need also those in the house – that is to say: Mrs Ackroyd, Mademoiselle Flora, Major Blunt, Mr Raymond. I want you to be my ambassador. This little reunion is fixed for nine o'clock. You will ask them – yes?'

'With pleasure; but why not ask them yourself?'

'Because they will then put the questions: Why? What for? They will demand what my idea is. And, as you know, my friend, I much dislike to have to explain my little ideas until the time comes.'

I smiled a little.

'My friend Hastings, he of whom I told you, used to say of me that I was the human oyster. But he was unjust. Of facts, I keep nothing to myself. But to everyone his own interpretation of them.'

'When do you want me to do this?'

'Now, if you will. We are close to the house.'

'Aren't you coming in?'

'No, me, I will promenade myself in the grounds. I will rejoin you by the lodge gates in a quarter of an hour's time.'

I nodded, and set off on my task. The only member of the family at home proved to be Mrs Ackroyd, who was sipping an early cup of tea. She received me very graciously.

'So grateful to you, doctor,' she murmured, 'for clearing up that little matter with M. Poirot. But life is one trouble after another. You have heard about Flora, of course?'

'What exactly?' I asked cautiously.

'This new engagement. Flora and Hector Blunt. Of course not such a good match as Ralph would have been. But after all, happiness comes first. What dear Flora needs is an older man – someone steady and reliable, and then Hector is really a very distinguished man in his way. You saw the news of Ralph's arrest in the paper this morning?'

'Yes,' I said, 'I did.'

'Horrible.' Mrs Ackroyd closed her eyes and shuddered. 'Geoffrey Raymond was in a terrible way. Rang up Liverpool. But they wouldn't tell him anything at the police station there. In fact, they said they hadn't arrested Ralph at all. Mr Raymond insists that it's all a mistake – a – what do they call it? – *canard* of the newspaper's. I've forbidden it to be mentioned before the servants. Such a terrible disgrace. Fancy if Flora had actually been married to him.'

Mrs Ackroyd shut her eyes in anguish. I began to wonder how soon I should be able to deliver Poirot's invitation.

Before I had time to speak, Mrs Ackroyd was off again.

'You were here yesterday, weren't you, with that dreadful Inspector Raglan? Brute of a man – he terrified Flora into saying she took that money from poor Roger's room. And the matter was so simple, really. The dear child wanted to borrow a few pounds, didn't like to disturb her uncle since he'd given strict orders against it. But knowing where he kept his notes she went there and took what she needed.'

'Is that Flora's account of the matter?' I asked.

'My dear doctor, you know what girls are nowadays. So easily acted on by suggestion. You, of course, know all about hypnosis and that sort of thing. The inspector shouts at her, says the word "steal" over and over again, until the poor child gets an inhibition – or is it a complex? – I always mix up those two words – and actually thinks herself that she has stolen the money. I saw at once how it was. But I can't be too thankful for the whole misunderstanding in one way – it seems to have brought those two together – Hector and Flora, I mean. And I assure you that I have been very much worried about Flora in the past: why, at one time I actually thought there was going to be some kind of understanding between her and young Raymond. Just think of it!' Mrs Ackroyd's voice rose in shrill horror. 'A private secretary – with practically no means of his own.'

'It would have been a severe blow to you,' I said. 'Now,

Mrs Ackroyd, I've got a message for you from M. Hercule Poirot.'

'For me?'

Mrs Ackroyd looked quite alarmed.

I hastened to reassure her, and I explained what Poirot wanted.

'Certainly,' said Mrs Ackroyd rather doubtfully. 'I suppose we must come if M. Poirot says so. But what is it all about? I like to know beforehand.'

I assured the lady truthfully that I myself did not know any more than she did.

'Very well,' said Mrs Ackroyd at last, rather grudgingly, 'I will tell the others, and we will be there at nine o'clock.'

Thereupon I took my leave, and joined Poirot at the agreed meeting-place.

'I've been longer than a quarter of an hour, I'm afraid,' I remarked. 'But once that good lady starts talking it's a matter of the utmost difficulty to get a word in edgeways.'

'It is of no matter,' said Poirot. 'Me, I have been well amused. This park is magnificent.'

We set off homewards. When we arrived, to our great surprise Caroline, who had evidently been watching for us, herself opened the door.

She put her finger to her lips. Her face was full of importance and excitement.

'Ursula Bourne,' she said, 'the parlourmaid from Fernly. She's here! I've put her in the dining-room. She's in a terrible way, poor thing. Says she must see M. Poirot at once. I've done all I could. Taken her a cup of hot tea. It really goes to one's heart to see anyone in such a state.'

'In the dining-room?' asked Poirot.

'This way,' I said, and flung open the door.

Ursula Bourne was sitting by the table. Her arms were spread out in front of her, and she had evidently just lifted her head from where it had been buried. Her eyes were red with weeping.

'Ursula Bourne,' I murmured.

But Poirot went past me with outstretched hands.

'No,' he said, 'that is not quite right, I think. It is not Ursula Bourne, is it, my child – but Ursula Paton? Mrs Ralph Paton.'

CHAPTER 22

URSULA'S STORY

For a moment or two the girl looked mutely at Poirot. Then, her reserve breaking down completely, she nodded her head once, and burst into an outburst of sobs.

Caroline pushed past me, and putting her arm round the girl, patted her on the shoulder.

'There, there, my dear,' she said soothingly, 'it will be all right. You'll see – everything will be all right.'

Buried under curiosity and scandal-mongering there is a lot of kindness in Caroline. For the moment, even the interest of Poirot's revelation was lost in the sight of the girl's distress.

Presently Ursula sat up and wiped her eyes.

'This is very weak and silly of me,' she said.

'No, no, my child,' said Poirot kindly. 'We can all realize the strain of this last week.'

'It must have been a terrible ordeal,' I said.

'And then to find that you knew,' continued Ursula. 'How did you know? Was it Ralph who told you?'

Poirot shook his head.

'You know what brought me to you tonight,' went on the girl. '*This* –'

She held out a crumpled piece of newspaper, and I recognized the paragraph that Poirot had had inserted.

'It says that Ralph has been arrested. So everything is useless. I need not pretend any longer.'

'Newspaper paragraphs are not always true, mademoiselle,' murmured Poirot, having the grace to look ashamed of himself. 'All the same, I think you will do well to make a clean breast of things. The truth is what we need now.'

The girl hesitated, looking at him doubtfully.

'You do not trust me,' said Poirot gently. 'Yet all the same you came here to find me, did you not? Why was that?'

'Because I don't believe that Ralph did it,' said the girl in a very low voice. 'And I think that you are clever, and will find out the truth. And also –'

'Yes?'

'I think you are kind.'

Poirot nodded his head several times.

'It is very good that – yes, it is very good. Listen, I do in verity believe that this husband of yours in innocent – but the affair marches badly. If I am to save him, I must know all there is to know – even if it should seem to make the case against him blacker than before.'

'How well you understand,' said Ursula.

'So you will tell me the whole story, will you not? From the beginning.'

'You're not going to send *me* away, I hope,' said Caroline, settling herself comfortably in an arm-chair. 'What I want to know,' she continued, 'is why this child was masquerading as a parlourmaid?'

'Masquerading?' I queried.

'That's what I said. Why did you do it, child? For a wager?'

'For a living,' said Ursula drily.

And encouraged, she began the story which I reproduce here in my own words.

Ursula Bourne, it seemed, was one of a family of seven – impoverished Irish gentlefolk. On the death of her father, most of the girls were cast out into the world to earn their own living. Ursula's eldest sister was married to Captain Folliott. It was she whom I had seen that Sunday, and the cause of her embarrassment was clear enough now. Determined to earn her living and not attracted to the idea of being a nursery governess – the one profession open to an untrained girl – Ursula preferred the job of parlourmaid. She scorned to label herself a 'lady parlourmaid'. She would be the real thing, her reference being supplied by her sister. At Fernly, despite an aloofness which, as has been seen, caused some comment, she was a success at her job – quick, competent and thorough.

'I enjoyed the work,' she explained. 'And I had plenty of time to myself.'

And then came her meeting with Ralph Paton, and the love affair which culminated in a secret marriage. Ralph had persuaded her into that, somewhat against her will. He had declared that his stepfather would not hear of his marrying a penniless girl. Better to be married secretly, and break the news to him at some later and more favourable minute.

And so the deed was done, and Ursula Bourne became Ursula Paton. Ralph had declared that he meant to pay off his debts, find a job, and then, when he was in a position to support her, and independent of his adopted father, they would break the news to him.

But to people like Ralph Paton, turning over a new leaf is easier in theory than in practice. He hoped that his stepfather, whilst still in ignorance of the marriage, might be persuaded to pay his debts and put him on his feet again. But the revelation of the amount of Ralph's liabilities merely enraged Roger Ackroyd, and he refused to do anything at all. Some months passed, and then Ralph was bidden once more to Fernly. Roger Ackroyd did not beat about the bush. It was the desire of his heart that Ralph should marry Flora, and he put the matter plainly before the young man.

And here it was that the innate weakness of Ralph Paton showed itself. As always, he grasped at the easy, the immediate solution. As far as I could make out, neither Flora nor Ralph made any pretence of love. It was, on both sides, a business arrangement. Roger Ackroyd dictated his wishes – they agreed to them. Flora accepted a chance of liberty, money and an enlarged horizon, Ralph, of course, was playing a different game. But he was in a very awkward hole financially. He seized at the chance. His debts would be paid. He could start again with a clean sheet. His was not a nature to envisage the future, but I gather that he saw vaguely the engagement with Flora being broken off after a decent interval had elapsed. Both Flora and he stipulated that it should be kept a secret for the present. He was anxious to conceal it from Ursula. He felt instinctively that her nature, strong and resolute, with an inherent distaste for duplicity, was not one to welcome such a course.

Then came the crucial moment when Roger Ackroyd, always high-handed, decided to announce the engagement. He said no word of his intention to Ralph – only to Flora, and Flora, apathetic, raised no objection. On Ursula, the news fell like a bombshell. Summoned by her, Ralph came hurriedly down from town. They met in the wood, where part of their conversation was overheard by my sister. Ralph implored her to keep silent for a little while longer, Ursula was equally determined to have done with concealments. She would tell Mr Ackroyd the truth without any further delay. Husband and wife parted acrimoniously.

Ursula, steadfast in her purpose, sought an interview with Roger Ackroyd that very afternoon, and revealed the truth to him. Their interview was a stormy one – it might have been even more stormy had not Roger Ackroyd been already obsessed with his own troubles. It was bad enough, however. Ackroyd was not the kind of man to forgive the deceit that had been practised upon him. His rancour was mainly directed to Ralph, but Ursula came in for her share, since he regarded her as a girl who had deliberately tried to 'entrap' the adopted son of a very wealthy man. Unforgivable things were said on both sides.

That same evening Ursula met Ralph by appointment in the small summer-house, stealing out from the house by the side door in order to do so. Their interview was made up of reproaches on both sides. Ralph charged Ursula with having irretrievably ruined his prospects by her ill-timed revelation. Ursula reproached Ralph with his duplicity.

They parted at last. A little over half an hour later came the discovery of Roger Ackroyd's body. Since that night Ursula had neither seen nor heard from Ralph.

As the story unfolded itself, I realized more and more what a damning series of facts it was. Alive, Ackroyd could hardly have failed to alter his will – I knew him well enough to realize that to do so would be his first thought. His death came in the nick of time for Ralph and Ursula Paton. Small wonder the girl had held her tongue, and played her part so consistently.

My meditations were interrupted. It was Poirot's voice speaking, and I knew from the gravity of his tone that he, too, was fully alive to the implications of the position.

'Mademoiselle, I must ask you one question, and you must answer it truthfully, for on it everything may hang: What time was it when you parted from Captain Ralph Paton in the summer-house? Now, take a little minute so that your answer may be very exact.'

The girl gave a half laugh, bitter enough in all conscience.

'Do you think I haven't gone over that again and again in my own mind? It was just half-past nine when I went out to meet him.

Major Blunt was walking up and down the terrace, so I had to go round through the bushes to avoid him. It must have been about twenty-seven minutes to ten when I reached the summer-house. Ralph was waiting for me. I was with him ten minutes – not longer, for it was just a quarter to ten when I got back to the house.'

I saw now the insistence of her question the other day. If only Ackroyd could have been proved to have been killed before a quarter to ten, and not after.

I saw the reflection of that thought in Poirot's next question.

'Who left the summer-house first?'

'I did.'

'Leaving Ralph Paton in the summer-house?'

'Yes – but you don't think –'

'Mademoiselle, it is of no importance what I think. What did you do when you got back to the house?'

'I went up to my room.'

'And stayed there until when?'

'Until about ten o'clock.'

'Is there anyone who can prove that?'

'Prove? That I was in my room, you mean? Oh! no. But surely – oh! I see, they might think – they might think –'

I saw the dawning horror in her eyes.

Poirot finished the sentence for her.

'That it was *you* who entered by the window and stabbed Mr Ackroyd as he sat in his chair? Yes, they might think just that.'

'Nobody but a fool would think any such thing,' said Caroline indignantly.

She patted Ursula on the shoulder.

The girl had her face hidden in her hands.

'Horrible,' she was murmuring. 'Horrible.'

Caroline gave her a friendly shake.

'Don't worry, my dear,' she said. 'M. Poirot doesn't think that really. As for that husband of yours, I don't think much of him, and I tell you so candidly. Running away and leaving you to face the music.'

But Ursula shook her head energetically.

'Oh, no,' she cried. 'It wasn't like that at all. Ralph would not run away on his own account. I see now. If he heard of his stepfather's murder, he might think himself that I had done it.'

'He wouldn't think any such thing,' said Caroline.

'I was so cruel to him that night – so hard and bitter. I wouldn't listen to what he was trying to say – wouldn't believe that he really cared. I just stood there telling him what I thought of him, and saying the coldest, cruellest things that came into my mind – trying my best to hurt him.'

'Do him no harm,' said Caroline. 'Never worry about what you say to a man. They're so conceited that they never believe you mean it if it's unflattering.'

Ursual went on nervously twisting and untwisting her hands.

'When the murder was discovered and he didn't come forward, I was terribly upset. Just for a moment I wondered – but then I knew he couldn't – he couldn't . . . But I wished he would come forward and say openly that he'd had nothing to do with it. I knew that he was fond of Dr Sheppard, and I fancied that perhaps Dr Sheppard might know where he was hiding.'

She turned to me.

'That's why I said what I did to you that day. I thought, if you knew where he was, you might pass on the message to him.'

'I?' I exclaimed.

'Why should James know where he was?' demanded Caroline sharply.

'It was very unlikely, I know,' admitted Ursula, 'but Ralph had often spoken of Dr Sheppard, and I knew that he would be likely to consider him as his best friend in King's Abbot.'

'My dear child,' I said, 'I have not the least idea where Ralph Paton is at the present moment.'

'That is true enough,' said Poirot.

'But –' Ursula held out the newspaper cutting in a puzzled fashion.

'Ah! that,' said Poirot, slightly embarrassed; 'a *bagatelle*, mademoiselle. A *rien du tout*. Not for a moment do I believe that Ralph Paton has been arrested.'

'But then –' began the girl slowly.

Poirot went on quickly:

'There is one thing I should like to know – did Captain Paton wear shoes or boots that night?'

Ursula shook her head.

'I can't remember.'

'A pity! But how should you? Now, madame,' he smiled at her, his head on one side, his forefinger wagging eloquently, 'no questions. And do not torment yourself. Be of good courage, and place your faith in Hercule Poirot.'

CHAPTER 23

POIROT'S LITTLE REUNION

'And now,' said Caroline, rising, 'that child is coming upstairs to lie down. Don't you worry, my dear. M. Poirot will do everything he can for you – be sure of that.'

'I ought to go back to Fernly,' said Ursula uncertainly.

But Caroline silenced her protests with a firm hand.

'Nonsense. You're in my hands for the time being. You'll stay here for the present, anyway – eh, M. Poirot?'

'It will be the best plan,' agreed the little Belgian. 'This evening I shall want mademoiselle – I beg her pardon, madame – to attend my little reunion. Nine o'clock at my house. It is most necessary that she should be there.'

Caroline nodded, and went with Ursula out of the room. The door shut behind them. Poirot dropped down into a chair again.

'So far, so good,' he said. 'Things are straightening themselves out.'

'They're getting to look blacker and blacker against Ralph Paton,' I observed gloomily.

Poirot nodded.

'Yes, that is so. But it was to be expected, was it not?'

I looked at him, slightly puzzled by the remark. He was leaning back in the chair, his eyes half closed, the tips of his fingers just touching each other. Suddenly he sighed and shook his head.

'What is it?' I asked.

'It is that there are moments when a great longing for my friend Hastings comes over me. That is the friend of whom I spoke to you – the one who resides now in the Argentine. Always, when I have had a big case, he has been by my side. And he has helped me – yes, often he has helped me. For he had a knack, that one, of stumbling over the truth unawares – without noticing it himself, *bien entendu*. At times, he has said something particularly foolish, and behold that foolish remark has revealed the truth to me! And then, too, it was his practice to keep a written record of the cases that proved interesting.'

I gave a slightly embarrassed cough.

'As far as that goes,' I began, and then stopped.

Poirot sat upright in his chair. His eyes sparkled.

'But yes? What is it that you would say?'

'Well, as a matter of fact, I've read some of Captain Hasting's narratives, and I thought, why not try my hand at something of the same kind. Seemed a pity not to – unique opportunity – probably the only time I'll be mixed up with anything of this kind.'

I felt myself getting hotter and hotter, and more and more incoherent, as I floundered through the above speech.

Poirot sprang from his chair. I had a moment's terror that he was going to embrace me French fashion, but mercifully he refrained.

'But this is magnificent – you have then written down your impressions of the case as you went along?'

I nodded.

'*Epatant!*' cried Poirot. 'Let me see them – this instant.'

I was not quite prepared for such a sudden demand. I racked my brains to remember certain details.

'I hope you won't mind,' I stammered. 'I may have been a little – er – *personal* now and then.'

'Oh! I comprehend perfectly; you have referred to me as comic – as, perhaps, ridiculous now and then? It matters not at all. Hastings, he also was not always polite. Me, I have the mind above such trivialities.'

Still somewhat doubtful, I rummaged in the drawers of my desk and produced an untidy pile of manuscript which I handed over to him. With an eye on possible publication in the future, I had divided the work into chapters, and the night before I had brought it up to date with an account of Miss Russell's visit. Poirot had therefore twenty chapters.

I left him with them.

I was obliged to go out to a case at some distance away, and it was past eight o'clock when I got back, to be greeted with a plate of hot dinner on a tray, and the announcement that Poirot and my sister had supped together at half-past seven, and that the former had then gone to my workshop to finish his reading of the manuscript.

'I hope, James,' said my sister, 'that you've been careful in what you say about me in it?'

My jaw dropped. I had not been careful at all.

'Not that it matters very much,' said Caroline, reading my expression correctly. 'M. Poirot will know what to think. He understands me much better than you do.'

I went into the workshop. Poirot was sitting by the window. The manuscript lay neatly piled on a chair beside him. He laid his hand on it and spoke.

'*Eh bien*,' he said, 'I congratulate you – on your modesty!'

'Oh!' I said, rather taken aback.

'And on your reticence,' he added.

I said 'Oh!' again.

'Not so did Hastings write,' continued my friend. 'On every page, many, many times was the word "I". What *he* thought – what *he* did. But you – you have kept your personality in the background; only once or twice does it obtrude – in scenes of home life, shall we say?'

I blushed a little before the twinkle of his eye.

'What do you really think of the stuff?' I asked nervously.

'You want my candid opinion?'

'Yes.'

Poirot laid his jesting manner aside.

'A very meticulous and accurate account,' he said kindly. 'You have recorded all the facts faithfully and exactly – though you have shown yourself becomingly reticent as to your own share in them.'

'And it has helped you?'

'Yes. I may say that it has helped me considerably. Come, we must go over to my house and set the stage for my little performance.'

Caroline was in the hall. I think she hoped that she might be invited to accompany us. Poirot dealt with the situation tactfully.

'I should much like to have had you present, mademoiselle,'

he said regretfully, 'but at this juncture it would not be wise. See you, all these people tonight are suspects. Amongst them, I shall find the person who killed Mr Ackroyd.'

'You really believe that?' I said incredulously.

'I see that you do not,' said Poirot drily. 'Not yet do you appreciate Hercule Poirot at his true worth.'

At that minute Ursula came down the staircase.

'You are ready, my child?' said Poirot. 'That is good. We will go to my house together. Mademoiselle Caroline, believe me, I do everything possible to render you service. Good-evening.'

We went off, leaving Caroline rather like a dog who has been refused a walk, standing on the front door step gazing after us.

The sitting-room at The Larches had been got ready. On the table were various *siropes* and glasses. Also a plate of biscuits. Several chairs had been brought in from the other room.

Poirot ran to and fro rearranging things. Pulling out a chair here, altering the position of a lamp there, occasionally stooping to straighten one of the mats that covered the floor. He was specially fussing over the lighting. The lamps were arranged in such a way as to throw a clear light on the side of the room where the chairs were grouped, at the same time leaving the other end of the room, where I presumed Poirot himself would sit, in a dim twilight.

Ursula and I watched him. Presently a bell was heard.

'They arrive,' said Poirot. 'Good, all is in readiness.'

The door opened and the party from Fernly filed in. Poirot went forward and greeted Mrs Ackroyd and Flora.

'It is most good of you to come,' he said. 'And Major Blunt and Mr Raymond.'

The secretary was debonair as ever.

'What's the great idea?' he said, laughing. 'Some scientific machine? Do we have bands round our wrists which register guilty heart-beats? There is such an invention, isn't there?'

'I have read of it, yes,' admitted Poirot. 'But me, I am old-fashioned. I use the old methods. I work only with the little grey cells. Now let us begin – but first I have an announcement to make to you all.'

He took Ursula's hand and drew her forward.

'This lady is Mrs Ralph Paton. She was married to Captain Paton last March.'

A little shriek burst from Mrs Ackroyd.

'Ralph! Married! Last March! Oh! but it's absurd. How could he be?'

She stared at Ursula as though she had never seen her before.

'Married to Bourne?' she said. 'Really, M. Poirot, I don't believe you.'

Ursula flushed and began to speak, but Flora forestalled her.

Going quickly to the other girl's side, she passed her hand through her arm.

'You must not mind our being surprised,' she said. 'You see, we had no idea of such a thing. You and Ralph have kept your secret very well. I am – very glad about it.'

'You are very kind, Miss Ackroyd,' said Ursula in a low voice, 'and you have every right to be exceedingly angry. Ralph behaved very badly – especially to you.'

'You needn't worry about that,' said Flora, giving her arm a consoling little pat. 'Ralph was in a corner and took the only way out. I should probably have done the same in his place. I do think he might have trusted me with the secret, though. I wouldn't have let him down.'

Poirot rapped gently on a table and cleared his throat significantly.

'The board meeting's going to begin,' said Flora. 'M. Poirot hints that we mustn't talk. But just tell me one thing. Where is Ralph? You must know if anyone does.'

'But I don't,' cried Ursula, almost in a wail. 'That's just it, I don't.'

'Isn't he detained at Liverpool?' asked Raymond. 'It said so in the paper.'

'He is not at Liverpool,' said Poirot shortly.

'In fact,' I remarked, 'no one knows where he is.'

'Except Hercule Poirot, eh?' said Raymond.

Poirot replied seriously to the other's banter.

'Me, I know everything. Remember that.'

Geoffrey Raymond lifted his eyebrows.

'Everything?' He whistled. 'Whew! that's a tall order.'

'Do you mean to say you can really guess where Ralph Paton is hiding?' I asked incredulously.

'You call it guessing. I call it knowing, my friend.'

'In Cranchester?' I hazarded.

'No,' replied Poirot gravely, 'not in Cranchester.'

He said no more, but at a gesture from him the assembled party took their seats. As they did so, the door opened once more and two other people came in and sat down near the door. They were Parker and the housekeeper.

'The number is complete,' said Poirot. 'Everyone is here.'

There was a ring of satisfaction in his tone. And with the sound of it I saw a ripple of something like uneasiness pass over all those faces grouped at the other end of the room. There was a suggestion in all this as of a trap – a trap that had closed.

Poirot read from a list in an important manner.

'Mrs Ackroyd, Miss Flora Ackroyd, Major Blunt, Mr Geoffrey Raymond, Mrs Ralph Paton, John Parker, Elizabeth Russell.'

He laid the paper down on the table.

'What's the meaning of all this?' began Raymond.

'The list I have just read,' said Poirot, 'is a list of suspected persons. Every one of you present had the opportunity to kill Mr Ackroyd –'

With a cry Mrs Ackroyd sprang up, her throat working.

'I don't like it,' she wailed. 'I don't like it. I would much prefer to go home.'

'You cannot go home, madame,' said Poirot sternly, 'until you have heard what I have to say.'

He paused a moment, then cleared his throat.

'I will start at the beginning. When Miss Ackroyd asked me to investigate the case, I went up to Fernly Park with the good Doctor Sheppard. I walked with him along the terrace, where I was shown the footprints on the window-sill. From there Inspector Raglan took me along the path which leads to the drive. My eye was caught by a little summer-house, and I searched it thoroughly. I found two things – a scrap of starched cambric and an empty goose quill. The scrap of cambric immediately suggested to me a maid's apron. When Inspector Raglan showed me his list of the people in the house, I noticed at once that one of the maids – Ursula Bourne, the parlourmaid – had no real alibi. According to her own story, she was in her bedroom from nine-thirty until ten. But supposing that instead she was in the summer-house? If so, she must have gone there to meet someone. Now we know from Dr Sheppard that someone from outside *did* come to the house that night – the stranger whom he met just by the gate. At first glance it would seem that our problem was solved, and that the stranger went to the summer-house to meet Ursula Bourne. It was fairly certain that he *did* go to the summer-house because of the goose quill. That suggested at once to my mind a taker of drugs – and one who had acquired the habit on the other side of the Atlantic where sniffing "snow" is more common than in this country. The man whom Dr Sheppard met had an American accent, which fitted in with that supposition.

'But I was held up by one point. *The times did not fit.* Ursula Bourne could certainly not have gone to the summer-house before nine-thirty, whereas the man must have got there by a few minutes past nine. I could, of course, assume that he waited there for half an hour. The only alternative supposition was that there had been two separate meetings in the summer-house that night. *Eh bien*, as soon as I went into that alternative I found several significant facts. I discovered that Miss Russell, the housekeeper, had visited Dr Sheppard that morning, and had displayed a good deal of interest in cures for victims of the drug habit. Taking that in conjunction with the goose quill, I assumed that the man in question came to Fernly to meet the housekeeper, and not Ursula Bourne. Who, then, did Ursula Bourne come to the rendezvous to meet? I was not long in doubt. First I found a ring – a wedding ring – with "From R." and a date inside it. Then I learnt that Ralph Paton had been seen coming up the path which led to the summer-house at twenty-five minutes past nine, and I also heard of a certain conversation which had taken place in the wood near the village that very afternoon – a conversation between Ralph Paton and some unknown girl. So I had my facts succeeding each other in a neat and orderly manner. A secret marriage, an engagement announced on the day of the tragedy, the stormy interview in the wood, and the meeting arranged for the summer-house that night.

'Incidentally this proved to me one thing, that both Ralph Paton and Ursula Bourne (or Paton) had the strongest motives for wishing Mr Ackroyd out of the way. And it also made one other point unexpectedly clear. It could not have been Ralph Paton who was with Mr Ackroyd in the study at nine-thirty.

'So we come to another and most interesting aspect of the crime. Who was it in the room with Mr Ackroyd at nine-thirty? Not Ralph Paton, who was in the summer-house with his wife. Not Charles Kent, who had already left. Who, then? I posed my cleverest – my most audacious question: *Was anyone with him?*'

Poirot leaned forward and shot the last words triumphantly at us, drawing back afterwards with the air of one who has made a decided hit.

Raymond, however, did not seem impressed, and lodged a mild protest.

'I don't know if you're trying to make me out a liar, M. Poirot, but the matter does not rest on my evidence alone – except perhaps as to the exact words used. Remember, Major Blunt also heard Mr Ackroyd talking to someone. He was on the terrace outside, and couldn't catch the words clearly, but he distinctly heard the voices.'

Poirot nodded.

'I have not forgotten,' he said quietly. 'But Major Blunt was under the impression that it was *you* to whom Mr Ackroyd was speaking.'

For a moment Raymond seemed taken aback. Then he recovered himself.

'Blunt knows now that he was mistaken,' he said.

'Exactly,' agreed the other man.

'Yet there must have been some reason for his thinking so,' mused Poirot. 'Oh! no,' he held up his hand in protest, 'I know the reason you will give – but it is not enough. We must seek elsewhere. I will put it this way. From the beginning of the case I have been struck by one thing – the nature of those words which Mr Raymond overheard. It has been amazing to me that no one has commented on them – has seen anything odd about them.'

He paused a minute, and then quoted softly:

'. . . *the calls on my purse have been so frequent of late that I fear it is impossible for me to accede to your request*. Does nothing strike you as odd about that?'

'I don't think so,' said Raymond. 'He has frequently dictated letters to me, using almost exactly those same words.'

'Exactly,' cried Poirot. 'That is what I seek to arrive at. Would any man use such a phrase in *talking* to another? Impossible that

that should be part of a real conversation. Now, if he had been dictating a letter –'

'You mean he was reading a letter aloud,' said Raymond slowly. 'Even so, he must have been reading to someone.'

'But why? We have no evidence that there was anyone else in the room. No other voice but Mr Ackroyd's was heard, remember.'

'Surely a man wouldn't read letters of that type aloud to himself – not unless he was – well – going barmy.'

'You have all forgotten one thing,' said Poirot softly: 'the stranger who called at the house the preceding Wednesday.'

They all stared at him.

'But yes,' said Poirot, nodding encouragingly, 'on Wednesday. The young man was not of himself important. But the firm he represented interested me very much.'

'The Dictaphone Company,' gasped Raymond. 'I see it now. A dictaphone. That's what you think?'

Poirot nodded.

'Mr Ackroyd had promised to invest in a dictaphone, you remember. Me, I had the curiosity to inquire of the company in question. Their reply is that Mr Ackroyd *did* purchase a dictaphone from their representative. Why he concealed the matter from you, I do not know.'

'He must have meant to surprise me with it,' murmured Raymond. 'He had quite a childish love of surprising people. Meant to keep it up his sleeve for a day or so. Probably was playing with it like a new toy. Yes, it fits in. You're quite right – no one would use quite those words in casual conversation.'

'It explains, too,' said Poirot, 'why Major Blunt thought it was you who were in the study. Such scraps as came to him were fragments of dictation, and so his subconscious mind deduced that you were with him. His conscious mind was occupied with something quite different – the white figure he had caught a glimpse of. He fancied it was Miss Ackroyd. Really, of course, it was Ursula Bourne's white apron he saw as she was stealing down to the summer-house.'

Raymond had recovered from his first surprise.

'All the same,' he remarked, 'this discovery of yours, brilliant though it is (I'm quite sure I should never have thought of it), leaves the essential position unchanged. Mr Ackroyd was alive at nine-thirty, since he was speaking into the dictaphone. It seems clear that the man Charles Kent was really off the premises by then. As to Ralph Paton –?'

He hesitated, glancing at Ursula.

Her colour flared up, but she answered steadily enough.

'Ralph and I parted just before a quarter to ten. He never went near the house, I am sure of that. He had no intention of doing so. The last thing on earth he wanted was to face his stepfather. He would have funked it badly.'

'It isn't that I doubt your story for a moment,' explained Raymond. 'I've always been quite sure Captain Paton was innocent. But one has to think of a court of law – and the questions that would be asked. He is in a most unfortunate position, but if he were to come forward –'

Poirot interrupted.

'That is your advice, yes? That he should come forward?'

'Certainly. If you know where he is –'

'I perceive that you do not believe that I do know. And yet I have told you just now that I know everything. The truth of the telephone call, of the footprints on the window-sill, of the hiding-place of Ralph Paton –'

'Where is he?' said Blunt sharply.

'Not very far away,' said Poirot, smiling.

'In Cranchester?' I asked.

Poirot turned towards me.

'Always you ask me that. The idea of Cranchester, it is with you an *idée fixe*. No, he is not in Cranchester. He is – *there*!'

He pointed a dramatic forefinger. Everyone's head turned.

Ralph Paton was standing in the doorway.

CHAPTER 24

RALPH PATON'S STORY

It was a very uncomfortable minute for *me*. I hardly took in what happened next, but there were exclamations and cries of surprise! When I was sufficiently master of myself to be able to realize what was going on, Ralph Paton was standing by his wife, her hand in his, and he was smiling across the room at me.

Poirot, too, was smiling, and at the same time shaking an eloquent finger at me.

'Have I not told you at least thirty-six times that it is useless to conceal things from Hercule Poirot?' he demanded. 'That in such a case he finds out?'

He turned to the others.

'One day, you remember, we held a little séance about a table – just the six of us. I accused the other five persons present of concealing something from me. Four of them gave up their secret. Dr Sheppard did not give up his. But all along I have had my suspicions. Dr Sheppard went to the Three Boars that night hoping to find Ralph. He did not find him there; but supposing, I said to myself, that he met him in the street on his way home? Dr Sheppard was a friend of Captain Paton's, and he had come straight from the scene of the crime. He must know that things looked very black against him. Perhaps he knew more than the general public did –'

'I did,' I said ruefully. 'I suppose I might as well make a clean breast of things now. I went to see Ralph that afternoon. At first he refused to take me into his confidence, but later he told me about his marriage, and the hole he was in. As soon as the murder was discovered, I realized that once the facts were known, suspicion could not fail to attach to Ralph – or, if not to him, to the girl he loved. That night I put the facts plainly before him. The thought of having possibly to give evidence which might incriminate his wife made him resolve at all costs to – to –'

I hesitated, and Ralph filled up the gap.

'To do a bunk,' he said graphically. 'You see, Ursula left me to go back to the house. I thought it possible that she might have attempted to have another interview with my stepfather. He had already been very rude to her that afternoon. It occurred to me that he might have so insulted her – in such an unforgivable manner – that without knowing what she was doing –'

He stopped. Ursula released her hand from his, and stepped back.

'You thought that, Ralph! You actually thought that I might have done it?'

'Let us get back to the culpable conduct of Dr Sheppard,' said Poirot drily. 'Dr Sheppard consented to do what he could to help him. He was successful in hiding Captain Paton from the police.'

'Where?' asked Raymond. 'In his own house?'

'Ah, no, indeed,' said Poirot. 'You should ask yourself the question that I did. If the good doctor is concealing the young man, what place would he choose? It must necessarily be somewhere near at hand. I think of Cranchester. A hotel? No. Lodgings? Even more emphatically, no. Where, then? Ah! I have it. A nursing home. A home for the mentally unfit. I test my theory. I invent a nephew with mental trouble. I consult Mademoiselle Sheppard as to suitable homes. She gives me the names of two near Cranchester to which her brother has sent patients. I make inquiries. Yes, at one of them a patient was brought there by the doctor himself early on Saturday morning. That patient, though known by another name, I had no difficulty in identifying as Captain Paton. After certain necessary formalities, I was allowed to bring him away. He arrived at my house in the early hours of yesterday morning.'

I looked at him ruefully.

'Caroline's Home Office expert,' I murmured. 'And to think I never guessed!'

'You see now why I drew attention to the reticence of your manuscript,' murmured Poirot. 'It was strictly truthful as far as it went – but it did not go very far, eh, my friend?'

I was too abashed to argue.

'Dr Sheppard has been very loyal,' said Ralph. 'He has stood by me through thick and thin. He did what he thought was best. I see now, from what M. Poirot has told me, that it was not really the best. I should have come forward and faced the music. You see, in the home, we never saw a newspaper. I knew nothing of what was going on.'

'Dr Sheppard has been a model of discretion,' said Poirot drily. 'But me, I discover all the little secrets. It is my business.'

'Now we can have your story of what happened that night,' said Raymond impatiently.

'You know it already,' said Ralph. 'There's very little for me to tell. I left the summer-house about nine forty-five, and tramped about the lanes, trying to make up my mind as to what to do next – what line to take. I'm bound to admit that I've not the shadow of an alibi, but I give you my solemn word that I never went to the study, that I never saw my stepfather alive – or dead. Whatever the world thinks, I'd like all of you to believe me.'

'No alibi,' murmured Raymond. 'That's bad. I believe you, of course, but – it's a bad business.'

'It makes things very simple, though,' said Poirot, in a cheerful voice. 'Very simple indeed.'

We all stared at him.

'You see what I mean? No? Just this – to save Captain Paton the real criminal must confess.'

He beamed round at us all.

'But yes – I mean what I say. See now, I did not invite Inspector Raglan to be present. That was for a reason. I did not want to tell him all that I knew – at least I did not want to tell him tonight.'

He leaned forward, and suddenly his voice and his whole personality changed. He suddenly became dangerous.

'I who speak to you – I know the murderer of Mr Ackroyd is in this room now. It is to the murderer I speak. *Tomorrow the truth goes to Inspector Raglan.* You understand?'

There was a tense silence. Into the midst of it came the old Breton woman with a telegram on a salver. Poirot tore it open.

Blunt's voice rose abrupt and resonant.

'The murderer is amongst us, you say? You know – which?'

Poirot had read the message. He crumpled it up in his hand.

'I know – now.'

He tapped the crumpled ball of paper.

'What is that?' said Raymond sharply.

'A wireless message – from a steamer now on her way to the United States.'

There was a dead silence. Poirot rose to his feet bowing.

'Messieurs et mesdames, this reunion of mine is at an end. Remember – *the truth goes to Inspector Raglan in the morning*.'

CHAPTER 25

THE WHOLE TRUTH

A slight gesture from Poirot enjoined me to stay behind the rest. I obeyed, going over to the fire and thoughtfully stirring the big logs on it with the toe of my boot.

I was puzzled. For the first time I was absolutely at sea as to Poirot's meaning. For a moment I was inclined to think that the scene I had just witnessed was a gigantic piece of bombast – that he had been what he called 'playing the comedy' with a view to making himself interesting and important. But, in spite of myself, I was forced to believe in an underlying reality. There had been real menace in his words – a certain indisputable sincerity. But I still believed him to be on entirely the wrong tack.

When the door shut behind the last of the party he came over to the fire.

'Well, my friend,' he said quietly, 'and what do you think of it all?'

'I don't know what to think,' I said frankly. 'What was the point? Why not go straight to Inspector Raglan with the truth instead of giving the guilty person this elaborate warning?'

Poirot sat down and drew out his case of tiny Russian cigarettes. He smoked for a minute or two in silence. Then:

'Use your little grey cells,' he said. 'There is always a reason behind my actions.'

I hesitated for a moment, and then I said slowly:

'The first one that occurs to me is that you yourself do not know who the guilty person is, but that you are sure that he is to be found amongst the people here tonight. Therefore your words were intended to force a confession from the unknown murderer?'

Poirot nodded approvingly.

'A clever idea, but not the truth.'

'I thought, perhaps, that by making him believe you knew, you might force him out into the open – not necessarily by confession. He might try to silence you as he formerly silenced Mr Ackroyd – before you could act tomorrow morning.'

'A trap with myself as the bait! *Merci, mon ami*, but I am not sufficiently heroic for that.'

'Then I fail to understand you. Surely you are running the risk of letting the murderer escape by thus putting him on his guard?'

Poirot shook his head.

'He cannot escape,' he said gravely. 'There is only one way out – and that way does not lead to freedom.'

'You really believe that one of those people here tonight committed the murder?' I asked incredulously.

'Yes, my friend.'

'Which one?'

There was a silence for some minutes. Then Poirot tossed the stump of his cigarette into the grate and began to speak in a quiet, reflective tone.

'I will take you the way that I have travelled myself. Step by step you shall accompany me, and see for yourself that all the facts point indisputably to one person. Now, to begin with, there were two facts and a little discrepancy in time which especially attracted my attention. The first fact was the telephone call. If Ralph Paton were indeed the murderer, the telephone call became meaningless and absurd. Therefore, I said to myself, Ralph Paton is not the murderer.

'I satisfied myself that the call could not have been sent by anyone in the house, yet I was convinced that it was amongst those present on the fatal evening that I had to look for my criminal. Therefore I concluded that the telephone call must have been sent by an accomplice. I was not quite pleased with that deduction, but I let it stand for the minute.

'I next examined the *motive* for the call. That was difficult. I could only get at it by judging its *result*. Which was – that the murder was discovered that night instead of – in all probability – the following morning. You agree with that?'

'Ye-es,' I admitted. 'Yes. As you say, Mr Ackroyd, having given orders that he was not to be disturbed, nobody would have been likely to go to the study that night.'

'*Très bien*. The affair marches, does it not? But matters were still obscure. What was the advantage of having the crime discovered that night in preference to the following morning? The only idea I could get hold of was that the murderer, knowing the crime was to be discovered at a certain time, could make sure of being present when the door was broken in – or at any rate immediately afterwards. And now we come to the second fact – the chair pulled out from the wall. Inspector Raglan dismissed that as of no importance. I, on the contrary, have always regarded it as of supreme importance.

'In your manuscript you have drawn a neat little plan of the study. If you had it with you this minute you would see that – the chair being drawn out in the position indicated by Parker – it would stand in a direct line between the door and the window.'

'The window!' I said quickly.

'You, too, have my first idea. I imagined that the chair was drawn out so that something connected with the window should not be seen by anyone entering through the door. But I soon abandoned that supposition, for though the chair was a grandfather with a high back, it obscured very little of the window – only the part between the sash and the ground. No, *mon ami* – but remember that just in front of the window there stood a table with books and magazines upon it. Now that table *was* completely hidden by the drawn-out chair – and immediately I had my first shadowy suspicion of the truth.

'Supposing that there had been something on that table not intended to be seen? Something placed there by the murderer? As yet I had no inkling of what that something might be. But I knew certain very interesting facts about it. For instance, it was something that the murderer had not been able to take away with him at the time that he committed the crime. At the same time it was vital that it should be removed as soon as possible after the crime had been discovered. And so – the telephone message, and the opportunity for the murderer to be on the spot when the body was discovered.

'Now four people were on the scene before the police arrived. Yourself, Parker, Major Blunt, and Mr Raymond. Parker I eliminated at once, since at whatever time the crime was discovered, he was the one person certain to be on the spot. Also it was he who told me of the pulled-out chair. Parker, then, was cleared (of the murder, that is. I still thought it possible that he had been blackmailing Mrs Ferrars). Raymond and Blunt, however, remained under suspicion since, if the crime had been discovered in the early hours of the morning, it was quite possible that they might have arrived on the scene too late to prevent the object on the round table being discovered.

'Now what was that object? You heard my arguments tonight in reference to the scrap of conversation overheard? As soon as I learned that a representative of a dictaphone company had called, the idea of a dictaphone took root in my mind. You heard what I said in this room not half an hour ago? They all agreed with my theory – but one vital fact seems to have escaped them. Granted that a dictaphone was being used by Mr Ackroyd that night – why was no dictaphone found?'

'I never thought of that,' I said.

'We know that a dictaphone was supplied to Mr Ackroyd. But no dictaphone has been found amongst his effects. So, if something was taken from the table – why should not that something be the dictaphone? But there were certain difficulties in the way. The attention of everyone was, of course, focused on the murdered man. I think anyone could have gone to the table unnoticed by the other people in the room. But a dictaphone has a certain bulk – it cannot be slipped casually into a pocket. There must have been a receptacle of some kind capable of holding it.

'You see where I am arriving? The figure of the murderer is taking shape. A person who was on the scene straightaway, but who might not have been if the crime had been discovered the following morning. A person carrying a receptacle into which the dictaphone might be fitted –'

I interrupted.

'By why remove the dictaphone? What was the point?'

'You are like Mr Raymond. You take it for granted that what was heard at nine-thirty was Mr Ackroyd's voice speaking into a dictaphone. But consider this useful invention for a little minute. You dictate into it, do you not? And at some later time a secretary or a typist turns it on, and the voice speaks again.'

'You mean –?' I gasped.

Poirot nodded.

'Yes, I meant that. *At nine-thirty Mr Ackroyd was already dead.* It was the dictaphone speaking – not the man.'

'And the murderer switched it on. Then he must have been in the room at that minute?'

'Possibly. But we must not exclude the likelihood of some

mechanical device having been applied – something after the nature of a time lock, or even of a simple alarm clock. But in that case we must add two qualifications to our imaginary portrait of the murderer. It must be someone who knew of Mr Ackroyd's purchase of the dictaphone and also someone with the necessary mechanical knowledge.

'I had got thus far in my own mind when we came to the footprints on the window ledge. Here there were three conclusions open to me. (1) They might really have been made by Ralph Paton. He had been at Fernly that night, and might have climbed into the study and found his uncle dead there. That was one hypothesis. (2) There was the possibility that the footmarks might have been made by somebody else who happened to have the same kind of studs in his shoes. But the inmates of the house had shoes soled with crêpe rubber, and I declined to believe in the coincidence of someone from outside having the same kind of shoes as Ralph Paton wore. Charles Kent, as we know from the barmaid of the Dog and Whistle, had on a pair of boots "clean dropping off him". (3) Those prints were made by someone deliberately trying to throw suspicion on Ralph Paton. To test this last conclusion, it was necessary to ascertain certain facts. One pair of Ralph's shoes had been obtained from the Three Boars by the police. Neither Ralph nor anyone else could have worn them that evening, since they were downstairs being cleaned. According to the police theory, Ralph was wearing another pair of the same kind, and I found out that it was true that he had two pairs. Now for my theory to be proved correct it was necessary for the murderer to have worn Ralph's shoes that evening – in which case Ralph must have been wearing yet a *third* pair of footwear of some kind. I could hardly suppose that he would bring three pairs of shoes all alike – the third pair of footwear were more likely to be boots. I got your sister to make inquiries on this point – laying some stress on the colour, in order – I admit it frankly – to obscure the real reason for my asking.

'You know the result of her investigations. Ralph Paton *had* had a pair of boots with him. The first question I asked him when he came to my house yesterday morning was what he was wearing on his feet on the fatal night. He replied at once that he had worn *boots* – he was still wearing them, in fact – having nothing else to put on.

'So we get a step further in our description of the murderer – a person who had the opportunity to take these shoes of Ralph Paton's from the Three Boars that day.'

He paused, and then said, with a slightly raised voice:

'There is one further point. The murderer must have been a person who had the opportunity to purloin that dagger from the silver table. You might argue that anyone in the house might have done so, but I will recall to you that Flora Ackroyd was very positive that the dagger was not there when she examined the silver table.'

He paused again.

'Let us recapitulate – now that all is clear. A person who was at the Three Boars earlier that day, a person who knew Ackroyd well enough to know that he had purchased a dictaphone, a person who was of a mechanical turn of mind, who had the opportunity to take the dagger from the silver table before Miss Flora arrived, who had with him a receptacle suitable for hiding the dictaphone – such as a black bag – and who had the study to himself for a few minutes after the crime was discovered while Parker was telephoning for the police. In fact – *Dr Sheppard*!'

CHAPTER 26

AND NOTHING BUT THE TRUTH

There was a dead silence for a minute and a half.

Then I laughed.

'You're mad,' I said.

'No,' said Poirot placidly. 'I am not mad. It was the little discrepancy in time that first drew my attention to you – right at the beginning.'

'Discrepancy in time?' I queried, puzzled.

'But yes. You will remember that everyone agreed – you yourself included – that it took five minutes to walk from the lodge to the house – less if you took the short cut to the terrace. But you left the house at ten minutes to nine – both by your own statement and that of Parker, and yet it was nine o'clock when you passed through the lodge gates. It was a chilly night – not an evening a man would be inclined to dawdle; why had you taken ten minutes to do a five minutes' walk? All along I realized that we had only your statement for it that the study window was ever fastened. Ackroyd asked you if you had done so – he never looked to see. Supposing, then, that the study window was unfastened? Would there be time in that ten minutes for you to run round the outside of the house, change your shoes, climb in through the window, kill Ackroyd, and get to the gate by nine o'clock? I decided against that theory since in all probability a man as nervous as Ackroyd was that night would hear you climbing in, and then there would have been a struggle. But supposing that you killed Ackroyd *before* you left – as you were standing beside his chair? Then you go out of the front door, run round to the summer-house, take Ralph Paton's shoes out of the bag you brought up with you that night, slip them on, walk through the mud in them, and leave prints on the window ledge, you climb in, lock the study door on the inside, run back to the summer-house, change back into your own shoes, and race down to the gate. (I went through similar actions the other day, when you were with Mrs Ackroyd – it took ten minutes exactly.) Then home – and an alibi – since you had timed the dictaphone for half-past nine.'

'My dear Poirot,' I said in a voice that sounded strange and forced to my own ears, 'you've been brooding over this case too long. What on earth had I to gain by murdering Ackroyd?'

'Safety. It was you who blackmailed Mrs Ferrars. Who could have had a better knowledge of what killed Mr Ferrars than the doctor who was attending him? When you spoke to me that first day in the garden, you mentioned a legacy received about a year ago. I have been unable to discover any trace of a legacy. You had to invent some way of accounting for Mrs Ferrars's twenty thousand pounds. It has not done you much good. You lost most of it in speculation – then you put the screw on too hard, and Mrs Ferrars took a way out that you had not expected. If Ackroyd had learnt the truth he would have had no mercy on you – you were ruined for ever.'

'And the telephone call?' I asked, trying to rally. 'You have a plausible explanation of that also, I suppose?'

'I will confess to you that it was my greatest stumbling block when I found that a call had actually been put through to you from King's Abbot station. I at first believed that you had simply invented the story. It was a very clever touch, that. You must have some excuse for arriving at Fernly, finding the body, and so getting the chance to remove the dictaphone on which your alibi depended. I had a very vague notion of how it was worked when I came to see your sister that first day and inquired as to what patients you had seen on Friday morning. I had no thought of Miss Russell in my mind at that time. Her visit was a lucky coincidence, since it distracted your mind from the real object of my questions. I found what I was looking for. Among your patients that morning was the steward of an American liner. Who more suitable than he to be leaving for Liverpool by the train that evening? And afterwards he would be on the high seas, well out of the way. I noted that the *Orion* sailed on Saturday, and having obtained the name of the steward I sent him a wireless message asking a certain question. This is his reply you saw me receive just now.'

He held out the message to me. It ran as follows:

> 'Quite correct. Dr Sheppard asked me to leave a note at a patient's house. I was to ring him up from the station with the reply. Reply was "No answer."'

'It was a clever idea,' said Poirot. 'The call was genuine. Your sister saw you take it. But there was only one man's word as to what was actually said – your own!'

I yawned.

'All this,' I said, 'is very interesting – but hardly in the sphere of practical politics.'

'You think not? Remember what I said – the truth goes to Inspector Raglan in the morning. But, for the sake of your good sister, I am willing to give you the chance of another way out. There might be, for instance, an overdose of a sleeping draught. You comprehend me? But Captain Ralph Paton must be cleared – *ça va sans dire*. I should suggest that you finish that very interesting manuscript of yours – but abandoning your former reticence.'

'You seem to be very prolific of suggestions,' I remarked. 'Are you sure you've quite finished?'

'Now that you remind me of the fact, it is true that there is one thing more. It would be most unwise on your part to attempt to silence me as you silenced M. Ackroyd. That kind of business does not succeed against Hercule Poirot, you understand.'

'My dear Poirot,' I said, smiling a little, 'whatever else I may be, I am not a fool.'

I rose to my feet.

'Well, well,' I said, with a slight yawn, 'I must be off home. Thank you for a most interesting and instructive evening.'

Poirot also rose and bowed with his accustomed politeness as I passed out of the room.

CHAPTER 27

APOLOGIA

Five a.m. I am very tired – but I have finished my task. My arm aches from writing.

A strange end to my manuscript. I meant it to be published some day as the history of one of Poirot's failures! Odd, how things pan out.

All along I've had a premonition of disaster, from the moment I saw Ralph Paton and Mrs Ferrars with their heads together. I thought then that she was confiding in him; as it happened I was quite wrong there, but the idea persisted even after I went into the study with Ackroyd that night, until he told me the truth.

Poor old Ackroyd. I'm always glad that I gave him a chance. I urged him to read that letter before it was too late. Or let me be honest – didn't I subconsciously realize that with a pig-headed chap like him, it was my best chance of getting him *not* to read it? His nervousness that night was interesting psychologically. He knew danger was close at hand. And yet he never suspected *me*.

The dagger was an afterthought. I'd brought up a very handy little weapon of my own, but when I saw the dagger lying in the silver table, it occurred to me at once how much better it would be to use a weapon that couldn't be traced to me.

I suppose I must have meant to murder him all along. As soon as I heard of Mrs Ferrars's death, I felt convinced that she would have told him everything before she died. When I met him and he seemed so agitated, I thought that perhaps he knew the truth, but that he couldn't bring himself to believe it, and was going to give me the chance of refuting it.

So I went home and took my precautions. If the trouble were after all only something to do with Ralph – well, no harm would have been done. The dictaphone he had given me two days ago to adjust. Something had gone a little wrong with it, and I persuaded him to let me have a go at it, instead of sending it back. I did what I wanted to, and took it up with me in my bag that evening.

I am rather pleased with myself as a writer. What could be neater, for instance, than the following:

'The letters were brought in at twenty minutes to nine. It was just on ten minutes to nine when I left him, the letter still unread. I hesitated with my hand on the door handle, looking back and wondering if there was anything I had left undone.'

All true, you see. But suppose I had put a row of stars after the first sentence! Would somebody then have wondered what exactly happened in that blank ten minutes?

When I looked round the room from the door, I was quite satisfied. Nothing had been left undone. The dictaphone was on the table by the window, timed to go off at nine-thirty (the mechanism of that little device was rather clever – based on the principle of an alarm clock), and the armchair was pulled out so as to hide it from the door.

I must admit that it gave me rather a shock to run into Parker just outside the door. I have faithfully recorded that fact.

Then later, when the body was discovered, and I sent Parker to telephone for the police, what a judicious use of words: *'I did what little had to be done*!' It was quite little – just to shove the dictaphone into my bag and push back the chair against the wall in its proper place. I never dreamed that Parker would have noticed that chair. Logically, he ought to have been so agog over the body as to be blind to everything else. But I hadn't reckoned with the trained servant complex.

I wish I could have known beforehand that Flora was going to say she'd seen her uncle alive at a quarter to ten. That puzzled me more than I can say. In fact, all through the case there have been things that puzzled me hopelessly. Everyone seems to have taken a hand.

My greatest fear all through has been Caroline. I have fancied she might guess. Curious the way she spoke that day of my 'strain of weakness'.

Well, she will never know the truth. There is, as Poirot said, one way out . . .

I can trust him. He and Inspector Raglan will manage it between them. I should not like Caroline to know. She is fond of me, and then, too, she is proud . . . My death will be a grief to her, but grief passes . . .

When I have finished writing, I shall enclose this whole manuscript in an envelope and address it to Poirot.

And then – what shall it be? Veronal? There would be a kind of poetic justice. Not that I take any responsibility for Mrs Ferrars's death. It was the direct consequence of her own actions. I feel no pity for her.

I have no pity for myself either.

So let it be veronal.

But I wish Hercule Poirot had never retired from work and come here to grow vegetable marrows.

MURDER ON THE ORIENT EXPRESS

To M.E.L.M. Arpachiya, 1933

CONTENTS

PART 1 • THE FACTS

PART 2 • THE EVIDENCE

PART 3 • HERCULE POIROT SITS BACK AND THINKS

PART I • THE FACTS

CHAPTER I

AN IMPORTANT PASSENGER ON THE TAURUS EXPRESS

I

It was five o'clock on a winter's morning in Syria. Alongside the platform at Aleppo stood the train grandly designated in railway guides as the Taurus Express. It consisted of a kitchen and dining-car, a sleeping-car and two local coaches.

By the step leading up into the sleeping-car stood a young French lieutenant, resplendent in uniform, conversing with a small lean man, muffled up to the ears, of whom nothing was visible but a pink-tipped nose and the two points of an upward curled moustache.

It was freezingly cold, and this job of seeing off a distinguished stranger was not one to be envied, but Lieutenant Dubosc performed his part manfully. Graceful phrases fell from his lips in polished French. Not that he knew what it was all about. There had been rumours, of course, as there always were in such cases. The General – *his* General's – temper had grown worse and worse. And then there had come this Belgian stranger – all the way from England, it seemed. There had been a week – a week of curious tensity. And then certain things had happened. A very distinguished officer had committed suicide, another had resigned – anxious faces had suddenly lost their anxiety, certain military precautions were relaxed. And the General – Lieutenant Dubosc's own particular General – had suddenly looked ten years younger.

Dubosc had overheard part of a conversation between him and the stranger. 'You have saved us, *mon cher*,' said the General emotionally, his great white moustache trembling as he spoke. 'You have saved the honour of the French Army – you have averted much bloodshed! How can I thank you for acceding to my request? To have come so far –'

To which the stranger (by name M. Hercule Poirot) had made

a fitting reply including the phrase, 'But indeed do I not remember that once you saved my life?' And then the General had made another fitting reply to that disclaiming any merit for that past service, and with more mention of France, of Belgium, of glory, of honour and of such kindred things they had embraced each other heartily and the conversation had ended.

As to what it had all been about, Lieutenant Dubosc was still in the dark, but to him had been delegated the duty of seeing off M. Poirot by the Taurus Express, and he was carrying it out with all the zeal and ardour befitting a young officer with a promising career ahead of him.

'Today is Sunday,' said Lieutenant Dubosc. 'Tomorrow, Monday evening, you will be in Stamboul.'

It was not the first time he had made this observation. Conversations on the platform, before the departure of a train, are apt to be somewhat repetitive in character.

'That is so,' agreed M. Poirot.

'And you intend to remain there a few days, I think?'

'*Mais oui.* Stamboul, it is a city I have never visited. It would be a pity to pass through – *comme ça.*' He snapped his fingers descriptively. 'Nothing presses – I shall remain there as a tourist for a few days.'

'La Sainte Sophie, it is very fine,' said Lieutenant Dubosc, who had never seen it.

A cold wind came whistling down the platform. Both men shivered. Lieutenant Dubosc managed to cast a surreptitious glance at his watch. Five minutes to five – only five minutes more!

Fancying that the other man had noticed his surreptitious glance, he hastened once more into speech.

'There are few people travelling this time of year,' he said, glancing up at the windows of the sleeping-car above them.

'That is so,' agreed M. Poirot.

'Let us hope you will not be snowed up in the Taurus!'

'That happens?'

'It has occurred, yes. Not this year, as yet.'

'Let us hope, then,' said M. Poirot. 'The weather reports from Europe, they are bad.'

'Very bad. In the Balkans there is much snow.'

'In Germany too, I have heard.'

'*Eh bien*,' said Lieutenant Dubosc hastily as another pause seemed to be about to occur. 'Tomorrow evening at seven-forty you will be in Constantinople.'

'Yes,' said M. Poirot, and went on desperately, 'La Sainte Sophie, I have heard it is very fine.'

'Magnificent, I believe.'

Above their heads the blind of one of the sleeping-car compartments was pushed aside and a young woman looked out.

Mary Debenham had had little sleep since she left Baghdad on the preceding Thursday. Neither in the train to Kirkuk, nor in the Rest House at Mosul, nor last night on the train had she slept properly. Now, weary of lying wakeful in the hot stuffiness of her overheated compartment, she got up and peered out.

This must be Aleppo. Nothing to see, of course. Just a long, poor-lighted platform with loud furious altercations in Arabic going on somewhere. Two men below her window were talking French. One was a French officer, the other was a little man with enormous moustaches. She smiled faintly. She had never seen anyone quite so heavily muffled up. It must be very cold outside. That was why they heated the train so terribly. She tried to force the window down lower, but it would not go.

The Wagon Lit conductor had come up to the two men. The train was about to depart, he said. Monsieur had better mount. The little man removed his hat. What an egg-shaped head he had. In spite of her preoccupations Mary Debenham smiled. A ridiculous-looking little man. The sort of little man one could never take seriously.

Lieutenant Dubosc was saying his parting speech. He had thought it out beforehand and had kept it till the last minute. It was a very beautiful, polished speech.

Not to be outdone, M. Poirot replied in kind.

'*En voiture, Monsieur*,' said the Wagon Lit conductor.

With an air of infinite reluctance M. Poirot climbed aboard the train. The conductor climbed after him. M. Poirot waved his hand. Lieutenant Dubosc came to the salute. The train, with a terrific jerk, moved slowly forward.

'*Enfin*!' murmured M. Hercule Poirot.

'Brrrrr,' said Lieutenant Dubosc, realizing to the full how cold he was . . .

II

'*Voilà, Monsieur.*' The conductor displayed to Poirot with a dramatic gesture the beauty of his sleeping compartment and the neat arrangement of his luggage. 'The little valise of Monsieur, I have placed it *here*.'

His outstretched hand was suggestive. Hercule Poirot placed in it a folded note.

'*Merci, Monsieur.*' The conductor became brisk and business-like. 'I have the tickets of Monsieur. I will also take the passport, please. Monsieur breaks his journey in Stamboul, I understand?'

M. Poirot assented.

'There are not many people travelling, I imagine?' he said.

'No, Monsieur. I have only two other passengers – both English. A Colonel from India, and a young English lady from Baghdad. Monsieur requires anything?'

Monsieur demanded a small bottle of Perrier.

Five o'clock in the morning is an awkward time to board a train. There was still two hours before dawn. Conscious of an inadequate night's sleep, and of a delicate mission successfully accomplished, M. Poirot curled up in a corner and fell asleep.

When he awoke it was half-past nine, and he sallied forth to the restaurant-car in search of hot coffee.

There was only one occupant at the moment, obviously the young English lady referred to by the conductor. She was tall, slim and dark – perhaps twenty-eight years of age. There was a kind of cool efficiency in the way she was eating her breakfast and in the way she called to the attendant to bring her more coffee, which bespoke a knowledge of the world and of travelling. She wore a dark-coloured travelling dress of some thin material eminently suitable for the heated atmosphere of the train.

M. Hercule Poirot, having nothing better to do, amused himself by studying her without appearing to do so.

She was, he judged, the kind of young woman who could take care of herself with perfect ease wherever she went. She had poise and efficiency. He rather liked the severe regularity of her features and the delicate pallor of her skin. He liked the burnished black head with its neat waves of hair, and her eyes, cool, impersonal and grey. But she was, he decided, just a little too efficient to be what he called '*jolie femme*'.

Presently another person entered the restaurant-car. This was a tall man of between forty and fifty, lean of figure, brown of skin, with hair slightly grizzled round the temples.

'The Colonel from India,' said Poirot to himself.

The newcomer gave a little bow to the girl.

'Morning, Miss Debenham.'

'Good-morning, Colonel Arbuthnot.'

The Colonel was standing with a hand on the chair opposite her.

'Any objection?' he asked.

'Of course not. Sit down.'

'Well, you know, breakfast isn't always a chatty meal.'

'I should hope not. But I don't bite.'

The Colonel sat down.

'Boy,' he called in peremptory fashion.

He gave an order for eggs and coffee.

His eyes rested for a moment on Hercule Poirot, but they passed on indifferently. Poirot, reading the English mind correctly, knew that he had said to himself, 'Only some damned foreigner.'

True to their nationality, the two English people were not chatty. They exchanged a few brief remarks, and presently the girl rose and went back to her compartment.

At lunch time the other two again shared a table and again they both completely ignored the third passenger. Their conversation was more animated than at breakfast. Colonel Arbuthnot talked of the Punjab, and occasionally asked the girl a few questions about Baghdad where it became clear that she had been in a post as governess. In the course of conversation they discovered some mutual friends which had the immediate effect of making them more friendly and less stiff. They discussed old Tommy Somebody and Jerry Someone Else. The Colonel inquired whether she was going straight through to England or whether she was stopping in Stamboul.

'No, I'm going straight on.'

'Isn't that rather a pity?'

'I came out this way two years ago and spent three days in Stamboul then.'

'Oh, I see. Well, I may say I'm very glad you are going right through, because I am.'

He made a kind of clumsy little bow, flushing a little as he did so.

'He is susceptible, our Colonel,' thought Hercule Poirot to himself with some amusement. 'The train, it is as dangerous as a sea voyage!'

Miss Debenham said evenly that that would be very nice. Her manner was slightly repressive.

The Colonel, Hercule Poirot noticed, accompanied her back to her compartment. Later they passed through the magnificent scenery of the Taurus. As they looked down towards the Cilician Gates, standing in the corridor side by side, a sigh came suddenly from the girl. Poirot was standing near them and heard her murmur:

'It's so beautiful! I wish – I wish –'

'Yes?'

'I wish, I could enjoy it!'

Arbuthnot did not answer. The square line of his jaw seemed a little sterner and grimmer.

'I wish to Heaven you were out of all this,' he said.

'Hush, please. Hush.'

'Oh! it's all right.' He shot a slightly annoyed glance in Poirot's direction. Then he went on: 'But I don't like the idea of your being a governess – at the beck and call of tyrannical mothers and their tiresome brats.'

She laughed with just a hint of uncontrol in the sound.

'Oh! you mustn't think that. The downtrodden governess is quite an exploded myth. I can assure you that it's the parents who are afraid of being bullied by *me*.'

They said no more. Arbuthnot was, perhaps, ashamed of his outburst.

'Rather an odd little comedy that I watch here,' said Poirot to himself thoughtfully.

He was to remember that thought of his later.

They arrived at Konya that night about half-past eleven. The two English travellers got out to stretch their legs, pacing up and down the snowy platform.

M. Poirot was content to watch the teeming activity of the

station through a window pane. After about ten minutes, however, he decided that a breath of air would not perhaps be a bad thing, after all. He made careful preparations, wrapping himself in several coats and mufflers and encasing his neat boots in goloshes. Thus attired he descended gingerly to the platform and began to pace its length. He walked out beyond the engine.

It was the voices which gave him the clue to the two indistinct figures standing in the shadow of a traffic van. Arbuthnot was speaking.

'Mary –'

The girl interrupted him.

'Not now. Not now. When it's all over. When it's behind us – *then* –'

Discreetly M. Poirot turned away. He wondered.

He would hardly have recognized the cool, efficient voice of Miss Debenham . . .

'Curious,' he said to himself.

The next day he wondered whether, perhaps, they had quarrelled. They spoke little to each other. The girl, he thought, looked anxious. There were dark circles under her eyes.

It was about half-past two in the afternoon when the train came to a halt. Heads were poked out of windows. A little knot of men were clustered by the side of the line looking and pointing at something under the dining-car.

Poirot leaned out and spoke to the Wagon Lit conductor who was hurrying past. The man answered and Poirot drew back his head and, turning, almost collided with Mary Debenham who was standing just behind him.

'What is the matter?' she asked rather breathlessly in French. 'Why are we stopping?'

'It is nothing, Mademoiselle. It is something that has caught fire under the dining-car. Nothing serious. It is put out. They are now repairing the damage. There is no danger, I assure you.'

She made a little abrupt gesture, as though she were waving the idea of danger aside as something completely unimportant.

'Yes, yes, I understand that. But the *time*!'

'The time?'

'Yes, this will delay us.'

'It is possible – yes,' agreed Poirot.

'But we can't afford delay! The train is due in at 6.55 and one has to cross the Bosphorus and catch the Simplon Orient Express the other side at nine o'clock. If there is an hour or two of delay we shall miss the connection.'

'It is possible, yes,' he admitted.

He looked at her curiously. The hand that held the window bar was not quite steady, her lips too were trembling.

'Does it matter to you very much, Mademoiselle?' he asked.

'Yes. Yes, it does. I – I must catch that train.'

She turned away from him and went down the corridor to join Colonel Arbuthnot.

Her anxiety, however, was needless. Ten minutes later the train started again. It arrived at Haydapassar only five minutes late, having made up time on the journey.

The Bosphorus was rough and M. Poirot did not enjoy the crossing. He was separated from his travelling companions on the boat, and did not see them again.

On arrival at the Galata Bridge he drove straight to the Tokatlian Hotel.

CHAPTER 2

THE TOKATLIAN HOTEL

At the Tokatlian, Hercule Poirot asked for a room with bath. Then he stepped over to the concierge's desk and inquired for letters.

There were three waiting for him and a telegram. His eyebrows rose a little at the sight of the telegram. It was unexpected.

He opened it in his usual neat, unhurried fashion. The printed words stood out clearly.

'*Development you predicted in Kassner Case has come unexpectedly please return immediately.*'

'*Voilà ce qui est embêtant,*' murmured Poirot vexedly. He glanced up at the clock.

'I shall have to go on tonight,' he said to the concierge. 'At what time does the Simplon Orient leave?'

'At nine o'clock, Monsieur.'

'Can you get me a sleeper?'

'Assuredly, Monsieur. There is no difficulty this time of year. The trains are almost empty. First-class or second?'

'First.'

'*Très bien, Monsieur.* How far are you going?'

'To London.'

'*Bien, Monsieur.* I will get you a ticket to London and reserve your sleeping-car accommodation in the Stamboul-Calais coach.'

Poirot glanced at the clock again. It was ten minutes to eight.

'I have time to dine?'

'But assuredly, Monsieur.'

The little Belgian nodded. He went over and cancelled his room order and crossed the hall to the restaurant.

As he was giving his order to the waiter a hand was placed on his shoulder.

'Ah! *mon vieux*, but this is an unexpected pleasure,' said a voice behind him.

The speaker was a short, stout elderly man, his hair cut *en brosse*. He was smiling delightedly.

Poirot sprang up.

'M. Bouc.'

'M. Poirot.'

M. Bouc was a Belgian, a director of the Compagnie Internationale des Wagons Lits, and his acquaintance with the former star of the Belgian Police Force dated back many years.

'You find yourself far from home, *mon cher*,' said M. Bouc.

'A little affair in Syria.'

'Ah! And you return home – when?'

'Tonight.'

'Splendid! I, too. That is to say, I go as far as Lausanne, where I have affairs. You travel on the Simplon Orient, I presume?'

'Yes. I have just asked them to get me a sleeper. It was my intention to remain here some days, but I have received a telegram recalling me to England on important business.'

'Ah!' sighed M. Bouc. '*Les affaires – les affaires!* But you – you are at the top of the tree nowadays, *mon vieux*!'

'Some little success I have had, perhaps.' Hercule Poirot tried to look modest but failed signally.

Bouc laughed.

'We will meet later,' he said.

Hercule Poirot addressed himself to the task of keeping his moustaches out of the soup.

That difficult task accomplished, he glanced round him whilst waiting for the next course. There were only about half a dozen people in the restaurant, and of those half-dozen there were only two that interested Hercule Poirot.

These two sat at a table not far away. The younger was a likeable-looking man of thirty, clearly an American. It was, however, not he but his companion who had attracted the little detective's attention.

He was a man of between sixty and seventy. From a little distance he had the bland aspect of a philanthropist. His slightly bald head, his domed forehead, the smiling mouth that displayed a very white set of false teeth, all seemed to speak of a benevolent personality. Only the eyes belied this assumption. They were small, deep set and crafty. Not only that. As the man, making some remark to his young companion, glanced across the room, his gaze stopped on Poirot for a moment, and just for that second there was a strange malevolence, and unnatural tensity in the glance.

Then he rose.

'Pay the bill, Hector,' he said.

His voice was slightly husky in tone. It had a queer, soft, dangerous quality.

When Poirot rejoined his friend in the lounge, the other two men were just leaving the hotel. Their luggage was being brought down. The younger was supervising the process. Presently he opened the glass door and said:

'Quite ready now, Mr Ratchett.'

The elder man grunted an assent and passed out.

'*Eh bien*,' said Poirot. 'What do you think of those two?'

'They are Americans,' said M. Bouc.

'Assuredly they are Americans. I meant what did you think of their personalities?'

'The young man seemed quite agreeable.'

'And the other?'

'To tell you the truth, my friend, I did not care for him. He produced on me an unpleasant impression. And you?'

Hercule Poirot was a moment before replying.

'When he passed me in the restaurant,' he said at last, 'I had a curious impression. It was as though a wild animal – an animal savage, but savage! you understand – had passed me by.'

'And yet he looked altogether of the most respectable.'

'*Précisément!* The body – the cage – is everything of the most respectable – but through the bars, the wild animal looks out.'

'You are fanciful, *mon vieux*,' said M. Bouc.

'It may be so. But I could not rid myself of the impression that evil had passed me by very close.'

'That respectable American gentleman?'

'That respectable American gentleman.'

'Well,' said M. Bouc cheerfully. 'It may be so. There is much evil in the world.'

At that moment the door opened and the concierge came towards them. He looked concerned and apologetic.

'It is extraordinary, Monsieur,' he said to Poirot. 'There is not one first-class sleeping berth to be had on the train.'

'*Comment*?' cried M. Bouc. 'At this time of year? Ah, without doubt there is some party of journalists – of politicians –?'

'I don't know, sir,' said the concierge, turning to him respectfully. 'But that's how it is.'

'Well, well,' M. Bouc turned to Poirot. 'Have no fear, my friend. We will arrange something. There is always one compartment – the No. 16, which is not engaged. The conductor sees to that!' He smiled, then glanced up at the clock. 'Come,' he said, 'it is time we started.'

At the station M. Bouc was greeted with respectful empressement by the brown-uniformed Wagon Lit conductor.

'Good-evening, Monsieur. Your compartment is the No. 1.'

He called to the porters and they wheeled their load halfway along the carriage on which the tin plates proclaimed its destination:

ISTANBUL TRIESTE CALAIS

'You are full up tonight, I hear?'

'It is incredible, Monsieur. All the world elects to travel tonight!'

'All the same, you must find room for this gentleman here. He is a friend of mine. He can have the No. 16.'

'It is taken, Monsieur.'

'What? The No. 16?'

A glance of understanding passed between them, and the conductor smiled. He was a tall, sallow man of middle age.

'But yes, Monsieur. As I told you, we are full – full – everywhere.'

'But what passes itself?' demanded M. Bouc angrily. 'There is a conference somewhere? It is a party?'

'No, Monsieur. It is only chance. It just happens that many people have elected to travel tonight.'

M. Bouc made a clicking sound of annoyance.

'At Belgrade,' he said, 'there will be the slip coach from Athens. There will also be the Bucharest-Paris coach – but we do not reach Belgrade until tomorrow evening. The problem is for tonight. There is no second-class berth free?'

'There *is* a second-class berth, Monsieur –'

'Well, then –'

'But it is a lady's berth. There is already a German woman in the compartment – a lady's-maid.'

'*Là, là*, that is awkward,' said M. Bouc.

'Do not distress yourself, my friend,' said Poirot. 'I must travel in an ordinary carriage.'

'Not at all. Not at all.' He turned once more to the conductor. 'Everyone has arrived?'

'It is true,' said the man, 'that there is one passenger who has not yet arrived.'

He spoke slowly with hesitation.

'But speak then?'

'No. 7 berth – a second-class. The gentleman has not yet come, and it is four minutes to nine.'

'Who is it?'

'An Englishman,' the conductor consulted his list. 'A M. Harris.'

'A name of good omen,' said Poirot. 'I read my Dickens. M. Harris, he will not arrive.'

'Put Monsieur's luggage in No. 7,' said M. Bouc. 'If this M. Harris arrives we will tell him that he is too late – that berths cannot be retained so long – we will arrange the matter one way or another. What do I care for a M. Harris?'

'As Monsieur pleases,' said the conductor.

He spoke to Poirot's porter, directing him where to go.

Then he stood aside the steps to let Poirot enter the train. '*Tout à fait au bout, Monsieur,*' he called. 'The end compartment but one.'

Poirot passed along the corridor, a somewhat slow progress, as most of the people travelling were standing outside their carriages.

His polite '*Pardons*' were uttered with the regularity of clockwork. At last he reached the compartment indicated. Inside it, reaching up to a suitcase, was the tall young American of the Tokatlian.

He frowned as Poirot entered.

'Excuse me,' he said. 'I think you've made a mistake.' Then, laboriously in French, '*Je crois que vous avez un erreur.*'

Poirot replied in English.

'You are Mr Harris?'

'No, my name is MacQueen. I –'

But at that moment the voice of the Wagon Lit conductor spoke from over Poirot's shoulder. An apologetic, rather breathless voice.

'There is no other berth on the train, Monsieur. The gentleman has to come in here.'

He was hauling up the corridor window as he spoke and began to lift in Poirot's luggage.

Poirot noticed the apology in his tone with some amusement. Doubtless the man had been promised a good tip if he could keep the compartment for the sole use of the other traveller. However, even the most munificent of tips lose their effect when a director of the company is on board and issues his orders.

The conductor emerged from the compartment, having swung the suitcases up on to the racks.

'*Voilà Monsieur,*' he said. 'All is arranged. Yours is the upper berth, the number 7. We start in one minute.'

He hurried off down the corridor. Poirot re-entered the compartment.

'A phenomenon I have seldom seen,' he said cheerfully. 'A Wagon Lit conductor himself puts up the luggage! It is unheard of!'

His fellow traveller smiled. He had evidently got over his annoyance – had probably decided that it was no good to take the matter other than philosophically.

'The train's remarkably full,' he said.

A whistle blew, there was a long, melancholy cry from the engine. Both men stepped out into the corridor.

Outside a voice shouted.

'*En voiture.*'

'We're off,' said MacQueen.

But they were not quite off. The whistle blew again.

'I say, sir,' said the young man suddenly, 'if you'd rather have the lower berth – easier, and all that – well, that's all right by me.'

'No, no,' protested Poirot. 'I would not deprive you –'

'That's all right –'

'You are too amiable –'

Polite protests on both sides.

'It is for one night only,' explained Poirot. 'At Belgrade –'

'Oh, I see. You're getting out at Belgrade –'

'Not exactly. You see –'

There was a sudden jerk. Both men swung round to the window, looking out at the long, lighted platform as it slid slowly past them.

The Orient Express had started on its three-days' journey across Europe.

CHAPTER 3

POIROT REFUSES A CASE

M. Hercule Poirot was a little late in entering the luncheon-car on the following day. He had risen early, breakfasted almost alone, and had spent the morning going over the notes of the case that was recalling him to London. He had seen little of his travelling companion.

M. Bouc, who was already seated, gesticulated a greeting and summoned his friend to the empty place opposite him. Poirot sat down and soon found himself in the favoured position of the table which was served first and with the choicest morsels. The food, too, was unusually good.

It was not till they were eating a delicate cream cheese that M. Bouc allowed his attention to wander to matters other than nourishment. He was at the stage of a meal when one becomes philosophic.

'Ah!' he sighed. 'If I had but the pen of a Balzac! I would depict this scene.'

He waved his hand.

'It is an idea, that,' said Poirot.

'Ah, you agree? It has not been done, I think? And yet – it lends itself to romance, my friend. All around us are people, of all classes, of all nationalities, of all ages. For three days these people, these strangers to one another, are brought together. They sleep and eat under one roof, they cannot get away from each other. At the end of three days they part, they go their several ways, never, perhaps, to see each other again.'

'And yet,' said Poirot, 'suppose an accident –'

'Ah no, my friend –'

'From your point of view it would be regrettable, I agree. But nevertheless let us just for one moment suppose it. Then, perhaps, all these here are linked together – by death.'

'Some more wine,' said M. Bouc, hastily pouring it out. 'You are morbid, *mon cher*. It is, perhaps, the digestion.'

'It is true,' agreed Poirot, 'that the food in Syria was not, perhaps, quite suited to my stomach.'

He sipped his wine. Then, leaning back, he ran his eye thoughtfully round the dining-car. There were thirteen people seated there and, as M. Bouc had said, of all classes and nationalities. He began to study them.

At the table opposite them were three men. They were, he guessed, single travellers graded and placed there by the unerring judgment of the restaurant attendants. A big, swarthy Italian was picking his teeth with gusto. Opposite him a spare, neat Englishman had the expressionless disapproving face of the well-trained servant. Next to the Englishman was a big American in a loud suit – possibly a commercial traveller.

'You've got to put it over *big*,' he was saying in a loud nasal voice.

The Italian removed his toothpick to gesticulate with it freely.

'Sure,' he said. 'That whatta I say alla de time.'

The Englishman looked out of the window and coughed.

Poirot's eye passed on.

At a small table, sitting very upright, was one of the ugliest old ladies he had ever seen. It was an ugliness of distinction – it fascinated rather than repelled. She sat very upright. Round her neck was a collar of very large pearls which, improbable though it seemed, were real. Her hands were covered with rings. Her sable coat was pushed back on her shoulders. A very small expensive black toque was hideously unbecoming to the yellow, toad-like face beneath it.

She was speaking now to the restaurant attendant in a clear, courteous but completely autocratic tone.

'You will be sufficiently amiable to place in my compartment a bottle of mineral water and a large glass of orange juice. You will arrange that I shall have chicken cooked without sauces for dinner this evening – also some boiled fish.'

The attendant replied respectfully that it should be done.

She gave a slight gracious nod of the head and rose. Her glance caught Poirot's and swept over him with the nonchalance of the uninterested aristocrat.

'That is Princess Dragomiroff,' said M. Bouc in a low tone. 'She is a Russian. Her husband realized all this money before the Revolution and invested it abroad. She is extremely rich. A cosmopolitan.'

Poirot nodded. He had heard of Princess Dragomiroff.

'She is a personality,' said M. Bouc. 'Ugly as sin, but she makes herself felt. You agree?'

Poirot agreed.

At another of the large tables Mary Debenham was sitting with two other women. One of them was a tall middle-aged woman in a plaid blouse and tweed skirt. She had a mass of faded yellow hair unbecomingly arranged in a large bun, wore glasses, and had a long, mild, amiable face rather like a sheep. She was listening to the third woman, a stout, pleasant-faced, elderly woman who was talking in a slow clear monotone which showed no signs of pausing for breath or coming to a stop.

'. . . And so my daughter said, "Why," she said "you just

can't apply Amurrican methods in this country. It's just natural to the folks here to be indolent," she said. "They just haven't got any hustle in them." But all the same you'd be surprised to know what our college there is doing. They've gotten a fine staff of teachers. I guess there's nothing like education. We've got to apply our Western ideals and teach the East to recognize them. My daughter says –'

The train plunged into a tunnel. The calm monotonous voice was drowned.

At the next table, a small one, sat Colonel Arbuthnot – alone. His gaze was fixed upon the back of Mary Debenham's head. They were not sitting together. Yet it could easily have been managed. Why?

Perhaps, Poirot thought, Mary Debenham had demurred. A governess learns to be careful. Appearances are important. A girl with her living to get has to be discreet.

His glance shifted to the other side of the carriage. At the far end, against the wall, was a middle-aged woman dressed in black with a broad expressionless face. German or Scandinavian, he thought. Probably a German lady's-maid.

After her came a couple leaning forward and talking animatedly together. The man wore English clothes of loose tweed – but he was not English. Though only the back of his head was visible to Poirot, the shape of it and the set of the shoulders betrayed him. A big man, well made. He turned his head suddenly and Poirot saw his profile. A very handsome man of thirty odd with a big fair moustache.

The woman opposite him was a mere girl – twenty at a guess. A tight-fitting little black coat and skirt, white satin blouse, small chic black toque perched at the fashionable outrageous angle. She had a beautiful foreign-looking face, dead white skin, large brown eyes, jet-black hair. She was smoking a cigarette in a long holder. Her manicured hands had deep red nails. She wore one large emerald set in platinum. There was coquetry in her glance and voice.

'*Elle est jolie – et chic*,' murmured Poirot. 'Husband and wife – eh?'

M. Bouc nodded.

'Hungarian Embassy, I believe,' he said. 'A handsome couple.'

There were only two more lunchers – Poirot's fellow traveller MacQueen and his employer Mr Ratchett. The latter sat facing Poirot, and for the second time Poirot studied that unprepossessing face, noting the false benevolence of the brow and the small, cruel eyes.

Doubtless M. Bouc saw a change in his friend's expression.

'It is at your wild animal you look?' he asked.

Poirot nodded.

As his coffee was brought to him, M. Bouc rose to his feet. Having started before Poirot, he had finished some time ago.

'I return to my compartment,' he said. 'Come along presently and converse with me.'

'With pleasure.'

Poirot sipped his coffee and ordered a liqueur. The attendant was passing from table to table with his box of money, accepting payment for bills. The elderly American lady's voice rose shrill and plaintive.

'My daughter said, "Take a book of food tickets and you'll have no trouble – no trouble at all." Now, that isn't so. Seems they have to have a ten per cent. tip, and then there's that bottle of mineral water – and a queer sort of water too. They hadn't got any Evian or Vichy, which seems queer to me.'

'It is – they must – how you say – serve the water of the country,' explained the sheep-faced lady.

'Well, it seems queer to me.' She looked distastefully at the heap of small change on the table in front of her. 'Look at all this peculiar stuff he's given me. Dinars or something. Just a lot of rubbish, it looks. My daughter said –'

Mary Debenham pushed back her chair and left with a slight bow to the other two. Colonel Arbuthnot got up and followed her. Gathering up her despised money, the American lady followed suit, followed by the lady like a sheep. The Hungarians had already departed. The restaurant-car was empty save for Poirot and Ratchett and MacQueen.

Ratchett spoke to his companion, who got up and left the car. Then he rose himself, but instead of following MacQueen he dropped unexpectedly into the seat opposite Poirot.

'Can you oblige me with a light?' he said. His voice was soft – faintly nasal. 'My name is Ratchett.'

Poirot bowed slightly. He slipped his hand into his pocket and produced a matchbox which he handed to the other man, who took it but did not strike a light.

'I think,' he went on, 'that I have the pleasure of speaking to M. Hercule Poirot. Is that so?'

Poirot bowed again.

'You have been correctly informed, Monsieur.'

The detective was conscious of those strange shrewd eyes summing him up before the other spoke again.

'In my country,' he said, 'we come to the point quickly. Mr Poirot, I want you to take on a job for me.'

Hercule Poirot's eyebrows went up a trifle.

'My *clientèle*, Monsieur, is limited nowadays. I undertake very few cases.'

'Why, naturally, I understand that. But this, Mr Poirot, means big money.' He repeated again in his soft, persuasive voice, 'Big money.'

Hercule Poirot was silent a minute or two, then he said:

'What is it you wish me to do for you, M. – er – Ratchett?'

'Mr Poirot, I am a rich man – a very rich man. Men in that position have enemies. I have an enemy.'

'Only one enemy?'

'Just what do you mean by that question?' asked Ratchett sharply.

'Monsieur, in my experience when a man is in a position to have, as you say, enemies, then it does not usually resolve itself into one enemy only.'

Ratchett seemed relieved by Poirot's answer. He said quickly:

'Why, yes, I appreciate that point. Enemy or enemies – it doesn't matter. What does matter is my safety.'

'Safety?'

'My life has been threatened, Mr Poirot. Now, I'm a man who can take pretty good care of himself.' From the pocket of his coat his hand brought a small automatic into sight for a moment. He continued grimly. 'I don't think I'm the kind of man to be caught napping. But as I look at it I might as well make assurance doubly sure. I fancy you're the man for my money, Mr Poirot. And remember – *big* money.'

Poirot looked at him thoughtfully for some minutes. His face was completely expressionless. The other could have had no clue as to what thoughts were passing in that mind.

'I regret, Monsieur,' he said at length. 'I cannot oblige you.'

The other looked at him shrewdly.

'Name your figure, then,' he said.

Poirot shook his head.

'You do not understand, Monsieur. I have been very fortunate in my profession. I have made enough money to satisfy both my needs and my caprices. I take now only such cases as – interest me.'

'You've got a pretty good nerve,' said Ratchett. 'Will twenty thousand dollars tempt you?'

'It will not.'

'If you're holding out for more, you won't get it. I know what a thing's worth to me.'

'I also – M. Ratchett.'

'What's wrong with my proposition?'

Poirot rose.

'If you will forgive me for being personal – I do not like your face, M. Ratchett,' he said.

And with that he left the restaurant-car.

CHAPTER 4

A CRY IN THE NIGHT

The Simplon Orient Express arrived at Belgrade at a quarter to nine that evening. It was not due to depart again until 9.15, so Poirot descended to the platform. He did not, however, remain there long. The cold was bitter and though the platform itself was protected, heavy snow was falling outside. He returned to his compartment. The conductor, who was on the platform stamping his feet and waving his arms to keep warm, spoke to him.

'Your valises have been moved, Monsieur, to the compartment No. 1, the compartment of M. Bouc.'

'But where is M. Bouc, then?'

'He has moved into the coach from Athens which has just been put on.'

Poirot went in search of his friend. M. Bouc waved his protestations aside.

'It is nothing. It is nothing. It is more convenient like this. You are going through to England, so it is better that you should stay in the through coach to Calais. Me, I am very well here. It is most peaceful. This coach is empty save for myself and one little Greek doctor. Ah! my friend, what a night! They say there has not been so much snow for years. Let us hope we shall not be held up. I am not too happy about it, I can tell you.'

At 9.15 punctually the train pulled out of the station, and shortly afterwards Poirot got up, said good-night to his friend and made his way along the corridor back into his own coach which was in front next to the dining-car.

On this, the second day of the journey, barriers were breaking down. Colonel Arbuthnot was standing at the door of his compartment talking to MacQueen.

MacQueen broke off something he was saying when he saw Poirot. He looked very surprised.

'Why,' he cried, 'I thought you'd left us. You said you were getting off at Belgrade.'

'You misunderstood me,' said Poirot, smiling. 'I remember now, the train started from Stamboul just as we were talking about it.'

'But, man, your baggage – it's gone.'

'It has been moved into another compartment – that is all.'

'Oh, I see.'

He resumed his conversation with Arbuthnot and Poirot passed on down the corridor.

Two doors from his own compartment, the elderly American lady, Mrs Hubbard, was standing talking to the sheep-like lady who was a Swede. Mrs Hubbard was pressing a magazine on the other.

'No, do take it, my dear,' she said. 'I've got plenty other things to read. My, isn't the cold something frightful?' She nodded amicably to Poirot.

'You are most kind,' said the Swedish lady.

'Not at all. I hope you'll sleep well and that your head will be better in the morning.'

'It is the cold only. I make now myself a cup of tea.'

'Have you got some aspirin? Are you sure, now? I've got plenty. Well, good-night, my dear.'

She turned to Poirot conversationally as the other woman departed.

'Poor creature, she's a Swede. As far as I can make out, she's a kind of missionary – a teaching one. A nice creature, but doesn't talk much English. She was *most* interested in what I told her about my daughter.'

Poirot, by now, knew all about Mrs Hubbard's daughter. Everyone on the train who could understand English did! How she and her husband were on the staff of a big American college in Smyrna and how this was Mrs Hubbard's first journey to the East, and what she thought of the Turks and their slipshod ways and the condition of their roads.

The door next to them opened and the thin, pale manservant stepped out. Inside Poirot caught a glimpse of Mr Ratchett sitting up in bed. He saw Poirot and his face changed, darkening with anger. Then the door was shut.

Mrs Hubbard drew Poirot a little aside.

'You know, I'm dead scared of that man. Oh, not the valet – the other – his master. Master, indeed! There's something *wrong* about that man. My daughter always says I'm very intuitive. "When Momma gets a hunch, she's dead right," that's what my daughter says. And I've got a hunch about that man. He's next door to me, and I don't like it. I put my grips against the communicating door last night. I thought I heard him trying the handle. Do you know, I shouldn't be surprised if that man turns out to be a murderer – one of these train robbers you read about. I dare say I'm foolish, but there it is. I'm downright scared of the man! My daughter said I'd have an easy journey, but somehow I don't feel happy about it. It may be foolish, but I feel anything might happen. Anything at all. And how that nice young fellow can bear to be his secretary I can't think.'

Colonel Arbuthnot and MacQueen were coming towards them down the corridor.

'Come into my carriage,' MacQueen was saying. 'It isn't made up for the night yet. Now what I want to get right about your policy in India is this –'

The men passed and went on down the corridor to MacQueen's carriage.

Mrs Hubbard said good-night to Poirot.

'I guess I'll go right to bed and read,' she said. 'Good-night.'

'Good-night, Madame.'

Poirot passed into his own compartment, which was the next one beyond Ratchett's. He undressed and got into bed, read for about half an hour and then turned out the light.

He awoke some hours later, and awoke with a start. He knew what it was that had wakened him – a loud groan, almost a cry, somewhere close at hand. At the same moment the ting of a bell sounded sharply.

Poirot sat up and switched on the light. He noticed that the train was at a standstill – presumably at a station.

That cry had startled him. He remembered that it was Ratchett who had the next compartment. He got out of bed and opened the door just as the Wagon Lit conductor came hurrying along the corridor and knocked on Ratchett's door. Poirot kept his door open a crack and watched. The conductor tapped a second time. A bell rang and a light showed over another door farther down. The conductor glanced over his shoulder.

At the same moment a voice from within the next-door compartment called out:

'*Ce n'est rien. Je me suis trompé.*'

'*Bien, Monsieur.*' The conductor scurried off again, to knock at the door where the light was showing.

Poirot returned to bed, his mind relieved, and switched off the light. He glanced at his watch. It was just twenty-three minutes to one.

CHAPTER 5

THE CRIME

He found it difficult to go to sleep again at once. For one thing, he missed the motion of the train. If it *was* a station outside it was curiously quiet. By contrast, the noises on the train seemed unusually loud. He could hear Ratchett moving about next door – a click as he pulled down the washbasin, the sound of the tap running, a splashing noise, then another click as the basin shut to again. Footsteps passed up the corridor outside, the shuffling footsteps of someone in bedroom slippers.

Hercule Poirot lay awake staring at the ceiling. Why was the station outside so silent? His throat felt dry. He had forgotten to ask for his usual bottle of mineral water. He looked at his watch again. Just after a quarter-past one. He would ring for the conductor and ask him for some mineral water. His finger went out to the bell, but he paused as in the stillness he heard a ting. The man couldn't answer every bell at once.

Ting . . . ting . . . ting . . .

It sounded again and again. Where was the man? Somebody was getting impatient.

Ting . . .

Whoever it was was keeping their finger solidly on the push.

Suddenly with a rush, his footsteps echoing up the aisle, the man came. He knocked at a door not far from Poirot's own.

Then came voices – the conductor's, deferential, apologetic, and a woman's – insistent and voluble.

Mrs Hubbard.

Poirot smiled to himself.

The altercation – if it was one – went on for some time. Its proportions were ninety per cent. of Mrs Hubbard's to a soothing ten per cent. of the conductor's. Finally the matter seemed to be adjusted. Poirot heard distinctly:

'*Bonne nuit*, Madame,' and a closing door.

He pressed his own finger on the bell.

The conductor arrived promptly. He looked hot and worried.

'*De l'eau minérale, s'il vous plait.*'

'*Bien, Monsieur.*' Perhaps a twinkle in Poirot's eye led him to unburden himself.

'*La Dame Américaine* –'

'Yes?'

He wiped his forehead.

'Imagine to yourself the time I have had with her! She insists – but *insists* – that there is a man in her compartment! Figure to yourself, Monsieur. In a space of this size.' He swept a hand round. 'Where would he conceal himself? I argue with her. I point out that it is impossible. She insists. She woke up and there was a man there. And how, I ask, did he get out and leave the door bolted behind him? But she will not listen to reason. As though, there were not enough to worry us already. This snow –'

'Snow?'

'But yes, Monsieur. Monsieur has not noticed? The train has stopped. We have run into a snowdrift. Heaven knows how long we shall be here. I remember once being snowed up for seven days.'

'Where are we?'

'Between Vincovi and Brod.'

'*Là là*,' said Poirot vexedly.

The man withdrew and returned with the water.

'*Bon soir, Monsieur.*'

Poirot drank a glass of water and composed himself to sleep.

He was just dropping off when something again woke him. This time it was as though something heavy had fallen with a thud against the door.

He sprang up, opened it and looked out. Nothing. But to his right some way down the corridor a woman wrapped in a scarlet kimono was retreating from him. At the other end, sitting on his little seat, the conductor was entering up figures on large sheets of paper. Everything was deathly quiet.

'Decidedly I suffer from the nerves,' said Poirot and retired to bed again. This time he slept till morning.

When he awoke the train was still at a standstill. He raised a blind and looked out. Heavy banks of snow surrounded the train.

He glanced at his watch and saw that it was past nine o'clock.

At a quarter to ten, neat, spruce, and dandified as ever, he made his way to the restaurant-car, where a chorus of woe was going on.

Any barriers there might have been between the passengers had now quite broken down. All were united by a common misfortune. Mrs Hubbard was loudest in her lamentations.

'My daughter said it would be the easiest way in the world. Just sit in the train until I got to Parrus. And now we may be here for days and days,' she wailed. 'And my boat sails the day after tomorrow. How am I going to catch it now? Why,

I can't even wire to cancel my passage. I feel too mad to talk about it.'

The Italian said that he had urgent business himself in Milan. The large American said that that was 'too bad, Ma'am,' and soothingly expressed a hope that the train might make up time.

'My sister – her children wait me,' said the Swedish lady and wept. 'I get no word to them. What they think? They will say bad things have happen to me.'

'How long shall we be here?' demanded Mary Debenham. 'Doesn't anybody *know*?'

Her voice sounded impatient, but Poirot noted that there were no signs of that almost feverish anxiety which she had displayed during the check to the Taurus Express.

Mrs Hubbard was off again.

'There isn't anybody knows a thing on this train. And nobody's trying to do anything. Just a pack of useless foreigners. Why, if this were at home, there'd be someone at least *trying* to do something.'

Arbuthnot turned to Poirot and spoke in careful British French.

'*Vous êtes un directeur de la ligne, je crois, Monsieur. Vous pouvez nous dire –*'

Smiling Poirot corrected him.

'No, no,' he said in English. 'It is not I. You confound me with my friend M. Bouc.'

'Oh! I'm sorry.'

'Not at all. It is most natural. I am now in the compartment that he had formerly.'

M. Bouc was not present in the restaurant-car. Poirot looked about to notice who else was absent.

Princess Dragomiroff was missing and the Hungarian couple. Also Ratchett, his valet, and the German lady's-maid.

The Swedish lady wiped her eyes.

'I am foolish,' she said. 'I am baby to cry. All for the best, whatever happen.'

This Christian spirit, however, was far from being shared.

'That's all very well,' said MacQueen restlessly. 'We may be here for days.'

'What is this country anyway?' demanded Mrs Hubbard tearfully.

On being told it was Yugo-Slavia she said:

'Oh! one of these Balkan things. What can you expect?'

'You are the only patient one, Mademoiselle,' said Poirot to Miss Debenham.

She shrugged her shoulders slightly.

'What can one do?'

'You are a philosopher, Mademoiselle.'

'That implies a detached attitude. I think my attitude is more selfish. I have learned to save myself useless emotion.'

She was not even looking at him. Her gaze went past him, out of the window to where the snow lay in heavy masses.

'You are a strong character, Mademoiselle,' said Poirot gently. 'You are, I think, the strongest character amongst us.'

'Oh, no. No, indeed. I know one far far stronger than I am.'

'And that is –?'

She seemed suddenly to come to herself, to realize that she was talking to a stranger and a foreigner with whom, until this morning, she had only exchanged half a dozen sentences.

She laughed a polite but estranging laugh.

'Well – that old lady, for instance. You have probably noticed her. A very ugly old lady, but rather fascinating. She has only to lift a little finger and ask for something in a polite voice – and the whole train runs.'

'It runs also for my friend M. Bouc,' said Poirot. 'But that is because he is a director of the line, not because he has a masterful character.'

Mary Debenham smiled.

The morning wore away. Several people, Poirot amongst them, remained in the dining-car. The communal life was felt, at the moment, to pass the time better. He heard a good deal more about Mrs Hubbard's daughter and he heard the lifelong habits of Mr Hubbard, deceased, from his rising in the morning and commencing breakfast with a cereal to his final rest at night in the bed-socks that Mrs Hubbard herself had been in the habit of knitting for him.

It was when he was listening to a confused account of the missionary aims of the Swedish lady that one of the Wagon Lit conductors came into the car and stood at his elbow.

'*Pardon, Monsieur.*'

'Yes?'

'The compliments of M. Bouc, and he would be glad if you would be so kind as to come to him for a few minutes.'

Poirot rose, uttered excuses to the Swedish lady and followed the man out of the dining-car.

It was not his own conductor, but a big fair man.

He followed his guide down the corridor of his own carriage and along the corridor of the next one. The man tapped at a door, then stood aside to let Poirot enter.

The compartment was not M. Bouc's own. It was a second-class one – chosen presumably because of its slightly larger size. It certainly gave the impression of being crowded.

M. Bouc himself was sitting on the small seat in the opposite corner. In the corner next the window facing him was a small, dark man looking out at the snow. Standing up and quite preventing Poirot from advancing any farther was a big man in blue uniform (the *chef de train*) and his own Wagon Lit conductor.

'Ah, my good friend,' cried M. Bouc. 'Come in. We have need of you.'

The little man in the window shifted along the seat, Poirot squeezed past the other two men and sat down facing his friend.

The expression on M. Bouc's face gave him, as he would have expressed it, furiously to think. It was clear that something out of the common had happened.

'What has occurred?' he asked.

'You may well ask that. First this snow – this stoppage. And now –'

He paused – and a sort of strangled gasp came from the Wagon Lit conductor.

'And now what?'

'*And now a passenger lies dead in his berth – stabbed.*'

M. Bouc spoke with a kind of calm desperation.

'A passenger? Which passenger?'

'An American. A man called – called –' he consulted some notes in front of him. 'Ratchett – that is right – Ratchett?'

'Yes, Monsieur,' the Wagon Lit man gulped.

Poirot looked at him. He was as white as chalk.

'You had better let that man sit down,' he said. 'He may faint otherwise.'

The *chef de train* moved slightly and the Wagon Lit man sank down in the corner and buried his face in his hands.

'Brr!' said Poirot. 'This is serious!'

'Certainly it is serious. To begin with, a murder – that by itself is a calamity of the first water. But not only that, the circumstances are unusual. Here we are, brought to a standstill. We may be here for hours – and not only hours – days! Another circumstance. Passing through most countries we have the police of that country on the train. But in Yugo-Slavia – no. You comprehend?'

'It is a position of great difficulty,' said Poirot.

'There is worse to come. Dr Constantine – I forgot, I have not introduced you – Dr Constantine, M. Poirot.'

The little dark man bowed and Poirot returned it.

'Dr Constantine is of the opinion that death occurred at about 1 a.m.'

'It is difficult to say exactly in these matters,' said the doctor, 'but I think I can say definitely that death occurred between midnight and two in the morning.'

'When was this M. Ratchett last seen alive?' asked Poirot.

'He is known to have been alive at about twenty minutes to one, when he spoke to the conductor,' said M. Bouc.

'That is quite correct,' said Poirot. 'I myself heard what passed. That is the last thing known?'

'Yes.'

Poirot turned toward the doctor, who continued:

'The window of M. Ratchett's compartment was found wide open, leading one to suppose that the murderer escaped that way. But in my opinion that open window is a blind. Anyone departing that way would have left distinct traces in the snow. There were none.'

'The crime was discovered – when?' asked Poirot.

'Michel!'

The Wagon Lit conductor sat up. His face still looked pale and frightened.

'Tell this gentleman exactly what occurred,' ordered M. Bouc.

The man spoke somewhat jerkily.

'The valet of this M. Ratchett, he tapped several times at the door this morning. There was no answer. Then, half an hour ago, the restaurant-car attendant came. He wanted to know if Monsieur was taking *déjeuner*. It was eleven o'clock, you comprehend.

'I open the door for him with my key. But there is a chain, too, and that is fastened. There is no answer and it is very still in there, and cold – but cold. With the window open and snow drifting in. I thought the gentleman had had a fit, perhaps. I got the *chef de train*. We broke the chain and went in. He was – *Ah! c'était terrible*!'

He buried his face in his hands again.

'The door was locked and chained on the inside,' said Poirot thoughtfully. 'It was not suicide – eh?'

The Greek doctor gave a sardonic laugh.

'Does a man who commits suicide stab himself in ten – twelve – fifteen places?' he asked.

Poirot's eyes opened.

'That is great ferocity,' he said.

'It is a woman,' said the *chef de train*, speaking for the first time. 'Depend upon it, it was a woman. Only a woman would stab like that.'

Dr Constantine screwed up his face thoughtfully.

'She must have been a very strong woman,' he said. 'It is not my desire to speak technically – that is only confusing – but I can assure you that one or two of the blows were delivered with such force as to drive them through hard belts of bone and muscle.'

'It was not, clearly, a scientific crime,' said Poirot.

'It was most unscientific,' said Dr Constantine. 'The blows seem to have been delivered haphazard and at random. Some have glanced off, doing hardly any damage. It is as though somebody had shut their eyes and then in a frenzy struck blindly again and again.'

'*C'est une femme*,' said the *chef de train* again. 'Women are like that. When they are enraged they have great strength.' He nodded so sagely that everyone suspected a personal experience of his own.

'I have, perhaps, something to contribute to your store of knowledge,' said Poirot. 'M. Ratchett spoke to me yesterday. He told me, as far as I was able to understand him, that he was in danger of his life.'

'"Bumped off" – that is the American expression, is it not?'

said M. Bouc. 'Then it is not a woman. It is a "Gangster" or a "gunman".'

The *chef de train* looked pained at his theory having come to naught.

'If so,' said Poirot, 'it seems to have been done very amateurishly.'

His tone expressed professional disapproval.

'There is a large American on the train,' said M. Bouc, pursuing his idea – 'a common-looking man with terrible clothes. He chews the gum which I believe is not done in good circles. You know whom I mean?'

The Wagon Lit conductor to whom he had appealed nodded.

'*Oui*, Monsieur, the No. 16. But it cannot have been he. I should have seen him enter or leave the compartment.'

'You might not. You might not. But we will go into that presently. The question is, what to do?' He looked at Poirot.

Poirot looked back at him.

'Come, my friend,' said M. Bouc. 'You comprehend what I am about to ask of you. I know your powers. Take command of this investigation! No, no, do not refuse. See, to us it is serious – I speak for the Compagnie Internationale des Wagons Lits. By the time the Yugo-Slavian police arrive, how simple if we can present them with the solution! Otherwise delays, annoyances, a million and one inconveniences. Perhaps, who knows, serious annoyance to innocent persons. Instead – *you* solve the mystery! We say, "A murder has occurred – *this* is the criminal!"'

'And suppose I do not solve it?'

'Ah! *mon cher*.' M. Bouc's voice became positively caressing. 'I know your reputation. I know something of your methods. This is the ideal case for you. To look up the antecedents of all these people, to discover their *bona fides* – all that takes time and endless inconvenience. But have I not heard you say often that to solve a case a man has only to lie back in his chair and think? Do that. Interview the passengers on the train, view the body, examine what clues there are and then – well, I have faith in you! I am assured that it is no idle boast of yours. Lie back and think – use (as I have heard you say so often) the little grey cells of the mind – and you will *know*!'

He leaned forward, looking affectionately at his friend.

'Your faith touches me, my friend,' said Poirot emotionally. 'As you say, this cannot be a difficult case. I myself, last night – but we will not speak of that now. In truth, this problem intrigues me. I was reflecting, not half an hour ago, that many hours of boredom lay ahead whilst we are stuck here. And now – a problem lies ready to my hand.'

'You accept then?' said M. Bouc eagerly.

'*C'est entendu.* You place the matter in my hands.'

'Good – we are all at your service.'

'To begin with, I should like a plan of the Istanbul-Calais coach, with a note of the people who occupied the several compartments, and I should also like to see their passports and their tickets.'

'Michel will get you those.'

The Wagon Lit conductor left the compartment.

'What other passengers are there on the train?' asked Poirot.

'In this coach Dr Constantine and I are the only travellers. In the coach from Bucharest is an old gentleman with a lame leg. He is well known to the conductor. Beyond that are the ordinary carriages, but these do not concern us, since they were locked after dinner had been served last night. Forward of the Istanbul-Calais coach there is only the dining-car.'

'Then it seems,' said Poirot slowly, 'as though we must look for our murderer in the Istanbul-Calais coach.' He turned to the doctor. 'That is what you were hinting, I think?'

The Greek nodded.

'At half an hour after midnight we ran into the snowdrift. No one can have left the train since then.'

M. Bouc said solemnly.

'*The murderer is with us – on the train now . . .*'

CHAPTER 6

A WOMAN?

'First of all,' said Poirot, 'I should like a word or two with young M. MacQueen. He may be able to give us valuable information.'

'Certainly,' said M. Bouc.

He turned to the *chef de train.*

'Get M. MacQueen to come here.'

The *chef de train* left the carriage.

The conductor returned with a bundle of passports and tickets. M. Bouc took them from him.

'Thank you, Michel. It would be best now, I think, if you were to go back to your post. We will take your evidence formally later.'

'Very good, Monsieur.'

Michel in his turn left the carriage.

'After we have seen young MacQueen,' said Poirot, 'perhaps M. le docteur will come with me to the dead man's carriage.'

'Certainly.'

'After we have finished there –'

But at this moment the *chef de train* returned with Hector MacQueen.

M. Bouc rose.

'We are a little cramped here,' he said pleasantly. 'Take my seat, M. MacQueen. M. Poirot will sit opposite you – so.'

He turned to the *chef de train.*

'Clear all the people out of the restaurant-car,' he said, 'and let it be left free for M. Poirot. You will conduct your interviews there, *mon cher*?'

'It would be the most convenient, yes,' agreed Poirot.

MacQueen had stood looking from one to the other, not quite following the rapid flow of French.

'*Qu'est ce qu'il y a*?' he began laboriously. '*Pourquoi* –?'

With a vigorous gesture Poirot motioned him to the seat in the corner. He took it and began once more.

'*Pourquoi* –?' then, checking himself and relapsing into his own tongue, 'What's up on the train? Has anything happened?'

He looked from one man to another.

Poirot nodded.

'Exactly. Something has happened. Prepare yourself for a shock. *Your employer, M. Ratchett, is dead!*'

MacQueen's mouth pursed itself in a whistle. Except that his eyes grew a shade brighter, he showed no signs of shock or distress.

'So they got him after all,' he said.

'What exactly do you mean by that phrase, M. MacQueen?' MacQueen hesitated.

'You are assuming,' said Poirot, 'that M. Ratchett was murdered?'

'Wasn't he?' This time MacQueen did show surprise. 'Why, yes,' he said slowly. 'That's just what I did think. Do you mean he just died in his sleep? Why, the old man was as tough as – as tough –'

He stopped, at a loss for a simile.

'No, no,' said Poirot. 'Your assumption was quite right. Mr Ratchett was murdered. Stabbed. But I should like to know why you were so sure it *was* murder, and not just – death.'

MacQueen hesitated.

'I must get this clear,' he said. 'Who exactly are you? And where do you come in?'

'I represent the Compagnie Internationale des Wagons Lits.' He paused, then added, 'I am a detective. My name is Hercule Poirot.'

If he expected an effect he did not get one. MacQueen said merely, 'Oh, yes?' and waited for him to go on.

'You know the name, perhaps.'

'Why, it does seem kind of familiar – only I always thought it was a woman's dressmaker.'

Hercule Poirot looked at him with distaste.

'It is incredible!' he said.

'What's incredible?'

'Nothing. Let us advance with the matter in hand. I want you to tell me, M. MacQueen, all that you know about the dead man. You were not related to him?'

'No. I am – was – his secretary.'

'For how long have you held that post?'

'Just over a year.'

'Please give me all the information you can.'

'Well, I met Mr Ratchett just over a year ago when I was in Persia –'

Poirot interrupted.

'What were you doing there?'

'I had come over from New York to look into an oil concession. I don't suppose you want to hear all about that. My friends and I had been let in rather badly over it. Mr Ratchett was in the same hotel. He had just had a row with his secretary. He offered me the job and I took it. I was at a loose end, and glad to find a well-paid job ready made, as it were.'

'And since then?'

'We've travelled about. Mr Ratchett wanted to see the world. He was hampered by knowing no languages. I acted more as a courier than as a secretary. It was a pleasant life.'

'Now tell me as much as you can about your employer.'

The young man shrugged his shoulders. A perplexed expression passed over his face.

'That's not so easy.'

'What was his full name?'

'Samuel Edward Ratchett.'

'He was an American citizen?'

'Yes.'

'What part of America did he come from?'

'I don't know.'

'Well, tell me what you do know.'

'The actual truth is, Mr Poirot, that I know nothing at all! Mr Ratchett never spoke of himself, or of his life in America.'

'Why do you think that was?'

'I don't know. I imagined that he might have been ashamed of his beginnings. Some men are.'

'Does that strike you as a satisfactory solution?'

'Frankly, it doesn't.'

'Has he any relations?'

'He never mentioned any.'

Poirot pressed the point.

'You must have formed *some* theory, M. MacQueen.'

'Well, yes, I did. For one thing, I don't believe Ratchett was his real name. I think he left America definitely in order to escape someone or something. I think he was successful – until a few weeks ago.'

'And then?'

'He began to get letters – threatening letters.'

'Did you see them?'

'Yes. It was my business to attend to his correspondence. The first letter came a fortnight ago.'

'Were these letters destroyed?'

'No, I think I've got a couple still in my files – one I know Ratchett tore up in a rage. Shall I get them for you?'

'If you would be so good.'

MacQueen left the compartment. He returned a few minutes later and laid down two sheets of rather dirty notepaper before Poirot.

The first letter ran as follows:

'Thought you'd doublecross us and get away with it, did you? Not on your life. We're out to GET you, Ratchett, and we WILL get you!'

There was no signature.

With no comment beyond raised eyebrows, Poirot picked up the second letter.

'We're going to take you for a ride, Ratchett. Some time soon. We're going to GET you, see?'

Poirot laid the letter down.

'The style is monotonous!' he said. 'More so than the handwriting.'

MacQueen stared at him.

'You would not observe,' said Poirot pleasantly. 'It requires the eye of one used to such things. This letter was not written by one person, M. MacQueen. Two or more persons wrote it – each writing a letter of a word at a time. Also, the letters are printed. That makes the task of identifying the handwriting much more difficult.'

He paused, then said:

'Did you know that M. Ratchett had applied for help to me?'

'To *you*?'

MacQueen's astonished tone told Poirot quite certainly that the young man had not known of it. He nodded.

'Yes. He was alarmed. Tell me, how did he act when he received the first letter?'

MacQueen hesitated.

'It's difficult to say. He – he – passed it off with a laugh in that quiet way of his. But somehow' – he gave a slight shiver – 'I felt that there was a good deal going on underneath the quietness.'

Poirot nodded. Then he asked an unexpected question.

'Mr MacQueen, will you tell me, quite honestly, exactly how you regarded your employer? Did you like him?'

Hector MacQueen took a moment or two before replying.

'No,' he said at last. 'I did not.'

'Why?'

'I can't exactly say. He was always quite pleasant in his manner.' He paused, then said, 'I'll tell you the truth, Mr Poirot. I disliked and distrusted him. He was, I am sure, a cruel and a dangerous man. I must admit, though, that I have no reasons to advance for my opinion.'

'Thank you, M. MacQueen. One further question – when did you last see M. Ratchett alive?'

'Last evening about' – he thought for a minute – 'ten o'clock, I should say. I went into his compartment to take down some memoranda from him.'

'On what subject?'

'Some tiles and antique pottery that he bought in Persia. What was delivered was not what he had purchased. There has been a long, vexatious correspondence on the subject.'

'And that was the last time M. Ratchett was seen alive?'

'Yes, I suppose so.'

'Do you know when M. Ratchett received the last threatening letter?'

'On the morning of the day we left Constantinople.'

'There is one more question I must ask you, M. MacQueen: were you on good terms with your employer?'

The young man's eyes twinkled suddenly.

'This is where I'm supposed to go all gooseflеshy down the back. In the words of a best seller, "You've nothing on me." Ratchett and I were on perfectly good terms.'

'Perhaps, M. MacQueen, you will give me your full name and your address in America.'

MacQueen gave his name – Hector Willard MacQueen, and an address in New York.

Poirot leaned back against the cushions.

'That is all for the present, M. MacQueen,' he said. 'I should be obliged if you would keep the matter of M. Ratchett's death to yourself for a little time.'

'His valet, Masterman, will have to know.'

'He probably knows already,' said Poirot dryly. 'If so try to get him to hold his tongue.'

'That oughtn't to be difficult. He's a Britisher, and does what he calls "Keeps himself to himself." He's a low opinion of Americans and no opinion at all of any other nationality.'

'Thank you, M. MacQueen.'

The American left the carriage.

'Well?' demanded M. Bouc. 'You believe what he says, this young man?'

'He seems honest and straightforward. He did not pretend to any affection for his employer as he probably would have done had he been involved in any way. It is true M. Ratchett did not tell him that he had tried to enlist my services and failed, but I do not think that is really a suspicious circumstance. I fancy M. Ratchett was a gentleman who kept his own counsel on every possible occasion.'

'So you pronounce one person at least innocent of the crime,' said M. Bouc jovially.

Poirot cast on him a look of reproach.

'Me, I suspect everybody till the last minute,' he said. 'All the same, I must admit that I cannot see this sober, long-headed MacQueen losing his head and stabbing his victim twelve or fourteen times. It is not in accord with his psychology – not at all.'

'No,' said Mr Bouc thoughtfully. 'That is the act of a man driven almost crazy with a frenzied hate – it suggests more the Latin temperament. Or else it suggests, as our friend the *chef de train* insisted, a woman.'

CHAPTER 7

THE BODY

Followed by Dr Constantine, Poirot made his way to the next coach and the compartment occupied by the murdered man. The conductor came and unlocked the door for them with his key.

The two men passed inside. Poirot turned inquiringly to his companion.

'How much has been disarranged in this compartment?'

'Nothing has been touched. I was careful not to move the body in making my examination.'

Poirot nodded. He looked round him.

The first thing that struck the senses was the intense cold. The window was pushed down as far as it would go and the blind was drawn up.

'Brrr,' observed Poirot.

The other smiled appreciatively.

'I did not like to close it,' he said.

Poirot examined the window carefully.

'You are right,' he announced. 'Nobody left the carriage this way. Possibly the open window was intended to suggest the fact, but, if so, the snow has defeated the murderer's object.'

He examined the frame of the window carefully. Taking a small case from his pocket he blew a little powder over it.

'No fingerprints at all,' he said. 'That means it has been wiped. Well, if there had been fingerprints it would have told us very little. They would have been those of M. Ratchett or his valet or the conductor. Criminals do not make mistakes of that kind nowadays.

'And that being so,' he added cheerfully, 'we might as well shut the window. Positively it is the cold storage in here!'

He suited the action to the word and then turned his attention for the first time to the motionless figure lying in the bunk.

Ratchett lay on his back. His pyjama jacket, stained with rusty patches, had been unbuttoned and thrown back.

'I had to see the nature of the wounds, you see,' explained the doctor.

Poirot nodded. He bent over the body. Finally he straightened himself with a slight grimace.

'It is not pretty,' he said. 'Someone must have stood there and stabbed him again and again. How many wounds are there exactly?'

'I make it twelve. One or two are so slight as to be practically scratches. On the other hand, at least three would be capable of causing death.'

Something in the doctor's tone caught Poirot's attention. He looked at him sharply. The little Greek was standing staring down at the body with a puzzled frown.

'Something strikes you as odd, does it not?' he asked gently. 'Speak, my friend. There is something here that puzzles you?'

'You are right,' acknowledged the other.

'What is it?'

'You see, these two wounds – here and here,' – he pointed. 'They are deep, each cut must have severed blood-vessels – and yet – the edges do not gape. They have not bled as one would have expected.'

'Which suggests?'

'That the man was already dead – some little time dead – when they were delivered. But that is surely absurd.'

'It would seem so,' said Poirot thoughtfully. 'Unless our murderer figured to himself that he had not accomplished his job properly and came back to make quite sure; but that is manifestly absurd! Anything else?'

'Well, just one thing.'

'And that?'

'You see this wound here – under the right arm – near the right shoulder. Take this pencil of mine. Could you deliver such a blow?'

Poirot raised his hand.

'*Précisément*,' he said. 'I see. With the *right* hand it is exceedingly difficult – almost impossible. One would have to strike backhanded, as it were. But if the blow were struck with the *left* hand –'

'Exactly, M. Poirot. That blow was almost certainly struck with the *left* hand.'

'So that our murderer is left-handed? No, it is more difficult than that, is it not?'

'As you say, M. Poirot. Some of these other blows are just as obviously right-handed.'

'Two people. We are back at two people again,' murmured the detective. He asked abruptly:

'Was the electric light on?'

'It is difficult to say. You see it is turned off by the conductor every morning about ten o'clock.'

'The switches will tell us,' said Poirot.

He examined the switch of the top light and also the roll back bed-head light. The former was turned off. The latter was closed.

'*Eh bien*,' he said thoughtfully. 'We have here a hypothesis of the First and Second Murderer, as the great Shakespeare would put it. The First Murderer stabbed his victim and left the compartment, turning off the light. The Second Murderer came in in the dark, did not see that his or her work had been done and stabbed at least twice at a dead body. *Que pensez vous de ça?*'

'Magnificent,' said the little doctor with enthusiasm.

The other's eyes twinkled.

'You think so? I am glad. It sounded to me a little like the nonsense.'

'What other explanation can there be?'

'That is just what I am asking myself. Have we here a coincidence or what? Are there any other inconsistencies, such as would point to two people being concerned?'

'I think I can say yes. Some of these blows, as I have already said, point to a weakness – a lack of strength or a lack of determination. They are feeble glancing blows. But this one here – and this one –' Again he pointed. 'Great strength was needed for those blows. They have penetrated the muscle.'

'They were, in your opinion, delivered by a man?'

'Most certainly.'

'They could not have been delivered by a woman?'

'A young, vigorous, athletic woman might have struck them, especially if she were in the grip of a strong emotion, but it is in my opinion highly unlikely.'

Poirot was silent a moment or two.

The other said anxiously.

'You understand my point?'

'Perfectly,' said Poirot. 'The matter begins to clear itself up wonderfully! The murderer was a man of great strength, he was feeble, it was a woman, it was a right-handed person, it was a left-handed person – *Ah! c'est rigolo, tout ça*!'

He spoke with sudden anger.

'And the victim – what does he do in all this? Does he cry out? Does he struggle? Does he defend himself?'

He slipped his hand under the pillow and drew out the automatic pistol which Ratchett had shown him the day before.

'Fully loaded, you see,' he said.

They looked round them. Ratchett's day clothing was hanging from the hooks on the wall. On the small table formed by the lid of the washing basin were various objects – false teeth in a glass of water; another glass, empty; a bottle of mineral water, a large flask and an ash-tray containing the butt of a cigar and some charred fragments of paper; also two burnt matches.

The doctor picked up the empty glass and sniffed it.

'Here is the explanation of the victim's inertia,' he said quietly.

'Drugged?'

'Yes.'

Poirot nodded. He picked up the two matches and scrutinized them carefully.

'You have a clue then?' demanded the little doctor eagerly.

'Those two matches are of a different shape,' said Poirot. 'One is flatter than the other. You see?'

'It is the kind you get on a train,' said the doctor, 'in paper covers.'

Poirot was feeling in the pockets of Ratchett's clothing. Presently he pulled out a box of matches. He compared them carefully.

'The rounder one is a match struck by Mr Ratchett,' he said. 'Let us see if he had also the flatter kind.'

But a further search showed no other matches.

Poirot's eyes were darting about the compartment. They were bright and sharp like a bird's. One felt that nothing could escape their scrutiny.

With a little exclamation he bent and picked up something from the floor.

It was a small square of cambric, very dainty. 'Our friend the *chef de train* was right. There is a woman concerned in this.'

'And most conveniently she leaves her handkerchief behind!' said Poirot. 'Exactly as it happens in the books and on the films – and to make things even easier for us it is marked with an initial.'

'What a stroke of luck for us!' exclaimed the doctor.

'Is it not?' said Poirot.

Something in his tone surprised the doctor.

But before he could ask for elucidation, Poirot had made another dive on to the floor.

This time he held out on the palm of his hand – a pipe-cleaner.

'It is perhaps the property of M. Ratchett?' suggested the doctor.

'There was no pipe in any of his pockets, and no tobacco or tobacco pouch.'

'Then it is a clue.'

'Oh! decidedly. And again dropped most conveniently. A masculine clue this time, you note! One cannot complain of having no clues in this case. There are clues here in abundance. By the way, what have you done with the weapon?'

'There was no sign of any weapon. The murderer must have taken it away with him.'

'I wonder why,' mused Poirot.

'Ah!' The doctor had been delicately exploring the pyjama pockets of the dead man.

'I overlooked this,' he said. 'I unbuttoned the jacket and threw it straight back.'

From the breast pocket he brought out a gold watch. The case was dented savagely, and the hands pointed to a quarter-past one.

'You see?' cried Constantine eagerly. 'This gives us the hour of the crime. It agrees with my calculations. Between midnight and two in the morning is what I said, and probably about one o'clock, though it is difficult to be exact in these matters. *Eh bien*, here is confirmation. A quarter-past one. That was the hour of the crime.'

'It is possible, yes. It is certainly possible.'

The doctor looked at him curiously.

'You will pardon me, M. Poirot, but I do not quite understand you.'

'I do not understand myself,' said Poirot. 'I understand nothing at all, and, as you perceive, it worries me.'

He sighed and bent over the little table, examining the charred fragment of paper. He murmured to himself.

'What I need at this moment is an old-fashioned woman's hat-box.'

Dr Constantine was at a loss to know what to make of this singular remark. In any case, Poirot gave him no time for questions. Opening the door into the corridor, he called for the conductor.

The man arrived at a run.

'How many women are there in this coach?'

The conductor counted on his fingers.

'One, two, three – six, Monsieur. The old American lady, a Swedish lady, the young English lady, the Countess Andrenyi and Madame la Princess Dragomiroff and her maid.'

Poirot considered.

'They all have hat-boxes, yes?'

'Yes, Monsieur.'

'Then bring me – let me see – yes, the Swedish lady's and that of the lady's-maid. Those two are the only hope. You will tell them it is a customs regulation – something – anything that occurs to you.'

'That will be all right Monsieur. Neither lady is in her compartment at the moment.'

'Then be quick.'

The conductor departed. He returned with the two hat-boxes. Poirot opened that of the lady's-maid and tossed it aside. Then he opened the Swedish lady's and uttered an exclamation of satisfaction. Removing the hats carefully, he disclosed round humps of wire-netting.

'Ah, here is what we need. About fifteen years ago hat-boxes were made like this. You skewered through the hat with a hatpin on to this hump of wire-netting.'

As he spoke he was skilfully removing two of the attachments. Then he repacked the hat-box and told the conductor to return them both where they belonged.

When the door was shut once more he turned to his companion.

'See you, my dear doctor, me, I am not one to rely upon the expert procedure. It is the psychology I seek, not the fingerprint or the cigarette ash. But in this case I would welcome a little scientific assistance. This compartment is full of clues, but can I be sure that those clues are really what they seem to be?'

'I do not quite understand you, M. Poirot.'

'Well, to give you an example – we find a woman's handkerchief. Did a woman drop it? Or did a man, committing the crime, say to himself "I will make this look like a woman's crime. I will stab my enemy an unnecessary number of times, making some of the blows feeble and ineffective, and I will drop this handkerchief where no one can miss it." That is one possibility. Then there is another. Did a woman kill him and did she deliberately drop a pipe cleaner to make it look like a man's work? Or are we seriously to suppose that two people – a man and a woman – were separately concerned, and that each was so careless as to drop a clue to their identity? It is a little too much of a coincidence, that!'

'But where does the hat-box come in?' asked the doctor, still puzzled.

'Ah! I'm coming to that. As I say, these clues, the watch stopped at a quarter-past one, the handkerchief, the pipe-cleaner, they may be genuine, or they may be fake. As to that I cannot yet tell. But there is *one* clue here which I believe – though again I may be wrong – has *not* been faked. I mean this flat match, M. le docteur. I *believe that that match was used by the murderer, not by M. Ratchett.* It was used to burn an incriminating paper of some kind. Possibly a note. If so, there was something in that note, some mistake, some error, that left a possible clue to the assailant. I am going to endeavour to resurrect what that something was.'

He went out of the compartment and returned a few moments later with a small spirit stove and a pair of curling tongs.

'I use them for the moustaches,' he said, referring to the latter.

The doctor watched him with great interest. He flattened out the two humps of wire, and with great care wriggled the charred scrap of paper on to one of them. He clapped the other on top of it and then, holding both pieces together with the tongs, held the whole thing over the flame of the spirit lamp.

'It is a very makeshift affair, this,' he said over his shoulder. 'Let us hope that it will answer its purpose.'

The doctor watched the proceedings attentively. The metal began to glow. Suddenly he saw faint indications of letters. Words formed themselves slowly – words of fire.

It was a very tiny scrap. Only three words and a part of another showed.

'–member little Daisy Armstrong.'

'Ah!' Poirot gave a sharp exclamation.

'It tells you something?' asked the doctor.

Poirot's eyes were shining. He laid down the tongs carefully.

'Yes,' he said. '*I know the dead man's real name. I know why he had to leave America.*'

'What was his name?'

'Cassetti.'

'Cassetti.' Constantine knitted his brows. 'It brings back to me something. Some years ago. I cannot remember . . . It was a case in America, was it not?'

'Yes,' said Poirot. 'A case in America.'

Further than that Poirot was not disposed to be communicative. He looked round him as he went on:

'We will go into all that presently. Let us first make sure that we have seen all there is to be seen here.'

Quickly and deftly he went once more through the pockets of the dead man's clothes but found nothing there of interest. He tried the communicating door which led through to the next compartment, but it was bolted on the other side.

'There is one thing that I do not understand,' said Dr Constantine. 'If the murderer did not escape through the window, and if this communicating door was bolted on the other side, and if the door into the corridor was not only locked on the inside but chained, how then did the murderer leave the compartment?'

'That is what the audience says when a person bound hand and foot is shut into a cabinet – and disappears.'

'You mean –'

'I mean,' explained Poirot, 'that if the murderer intended us to believe that he had escaped by way of the window he would naturally make it appear that the other two exits were impossible. Like the "disappearing person" in the cabinet – it is a trick. It is our business to find out how the trick is done.'

He locked the communicating door on their side.

'In case,' he said, 'the excellent Mrs Hubbard should take it into her head to acquire first-hand details of the crime to write to her daughter.'

He looked round once more.

'There is nothing more to do here, I think. Let us rejoin M. Bouc.'

CHAPTER 8

THE ARMSTRONG KIDNAPPING CASE

They found M. Bouc finishing an omelette.

'I thought it best to have lunch served immediately in the restaurant-car,' he said. 'Afterwards it will be cleared and M. Poirot can conduct his examination of the passengers there. In the meantime I have ordered them to bring us three some food here.'

'An excellent idea,' said Poirot.

Neither of the other two men was hungry, and the meal was soon eaten, but not till they were sipping their coffee did M. Bouc mention the subject that was occupying all their minds.

'*Eh bien*?' he asked.

'*Eh bien*, I have discovered the identity of the victim. I know why it was imperative he should leave America.'

'Who was he?'

'Do you remember reading of the Armstrong baby? This is the man who murdered little Daisy Armstrong – Cassetti.'

'I recall it now. A shocking affair – though I cannot remember the details.'

'Colonel Armstrong was an Englishman – a V.C. He was half American, as his mother was a daughter of W.K. Van der Halt, the Wall Street millionaire. He married the daughter of Linda Arden, the most famous tragic American actress of her day. They lived in America and had one child – a girl – whom they idolized. When she was three years old she was kidnapped, and an impossibly high sum demanded as the price of her return. I will not weary you with all the intricacies that followed. I will come to the moment, when, after having paid over the enormous sum of two hundred thousand dollars, the child's dead body was discovered, it having been dead at least a fortnight. Public indignation rose to fever point. And there was worse to follow. Mrs Armstrong was expecting another child. Following the shock of the discovery, she gave birth to a dead child born prematurely, and herself died. Her broken-hearted husband shot himself.'

'*Mon Dieu*, what a tragedy. I remember now,' said M. Bouc. 'There was also another death, if I remember rightly?'

'Yes – an unfortunate French or Swiss nursemaid. The police were convinced that she had some knowledge of the crime. They refused to believe her hysterical denials. Finally, in a fit of despair, the poor girl threw herself from a window and was killed. It was proved afterwards that she was absolutely innocent of any complicity in the crime.'

'It is not good to think of,' said M. Bouc.

'About six months later, this man Cassetti was arrested as the head of the gang who had kidnapped the child. They had used the same methods in the past. If the police seemed likely to get on their trail, they had killed their prisoner, hidden the body, and continued to extract as much money as possible before the crime was discovered.

'Now, I will make clear to you this, my friend. Cassetti was the man! But by means of the enormous wealth he had piled up and by the secret hold he had over various persons, he was acquitted on some technical inaccuracy. Notwithstanding that, he would have been lynched by the populace had he not been clever enough to give them the slip. It is now clear to me what happened. He changed his name and left America. Since then he has been a gentleman of leisure, travelling abroad and living on his *rentes*.'

'*Ah! quel animal*!' M. Bouc's tone was redolent of heartfelt disgust. 'I cannot regret that he is dead – not at all!'

'I agree with you.'

'*Tout de même*, it is not necessary that he should be killed on the Orient Express. There are other places.'

Poirot smiled a little. He realized that M. Bouc was biased in the matter.

'The question we have now to ask ourselves is this,' he said. 'Is this murder the work of some rival gang whom Cassetti had double-crossed in the past, or is it an act of private vengeance?'

He explained his discovery of the few words on the charred fragment of paper.

'If I am right in my assumption, then the letter was burnt by the murderer. Why? Because it mentioned the word "Armstrong", which is the clue to the mystery.'

'Are there any members of the Armstrong family living?'

'That, unfortunately, I do not know. I think I remember reading of a younger sister of Mrs Armstrong's.'

Poirot went on to relate the joint conclusions of himself and Dr Constantine. M. Bouc brightened at the mention of the broken watch.

'That seems to give us the time of the crime very exactly.'

'Yes,' said Poirot. 'It is very convenient.'

There was an indescribable something in his tone that made both the other two look at him curiously.

'You say that you yourself heard Ratchett speak to the conductor at twenty minutes to one?'

Poirot related just what had occurred.

'Well,' said M. Bouc, 'that proves at least that Cassetti – or Ratchett, as I shall continue to call him – was certainly alive at twenty minutes to one.'

'Twenty-three minutes to one, to be precise.'

'Then at twelve thirty-seven, to put it formally, M. Ratchett was alive. That is *one* fact, at least.'

Poirot did not reply. He sat looking thoughtfully in front of him.

There was a tap on the door, and the restaurant attendant entered.

'The restaurant-car is free now, Monsieur,' he said.

'We will go there,' said M. Bouc, rising.

'I may accompany you?' asked Constantine.

'Certainly, my dear doctor. Unless M. Poirot has any objection?'

'Not at all. Not at all,' said Poirot.

After a little politeness in the matter of procedure, '*Après vous, Monsieur.*' '*Mais non, après vous,*' they left the compartment.

PART 2 • THE EVIDENCE

CHAPTER 1

THE EVIDENCE OF THE WAGON LIT CONDUCTOR

In the restaurant-car all was in readiness.

Poirot and M. Bouc sat together on one side of a table. The doctor sat across the aisle.

On the table in front of Poirot was a plan of the Istanbul-Calais coach with the names of the passengers marked in in red ink.

The passports and tickets were in a pile at one side. There was writing paper, ink, pen and pencils.

'Excellent,' said Poirot. 'We can open our Court of Inquiry without more ado. First, I think, we should take the evidence of the Wagon Lit conductor. You probably know something about the man. What character has he? Is he a man in whose word you would place reliance?'

'I should say so most assuredly. Pierre Michel has been employed by the company for over fifteen years. He is a Frenchman – lives near Calais. Thoroughly respectable and honest. Not, perhaps, remarkable for brains.'

Poirot nodded comprehendingly.

'Good,' he said. 'Let us see him.'

Pierre Michel had recovered some of his assurance, but he was still extremely nervous.

'I hope Monsieur will not think that there has been any negligence on my part,' he said anxiously, his eyes going from Poirot to M. Bouc. 'It is a terrible thing that has happened. I hope Monsieur does not think that it reflects on me in any way?'

Having soothed the man's fears, Poirot began his questions. He first elicited Michel's name and address, his length of service, and the length of time he had been on this particular route. These particulars he already knew, but the routine questions served to put the man at his ease.

'And now,' went on Poirot, 'let us come to the events of last night. M. Ratchett retired to bed – when?'

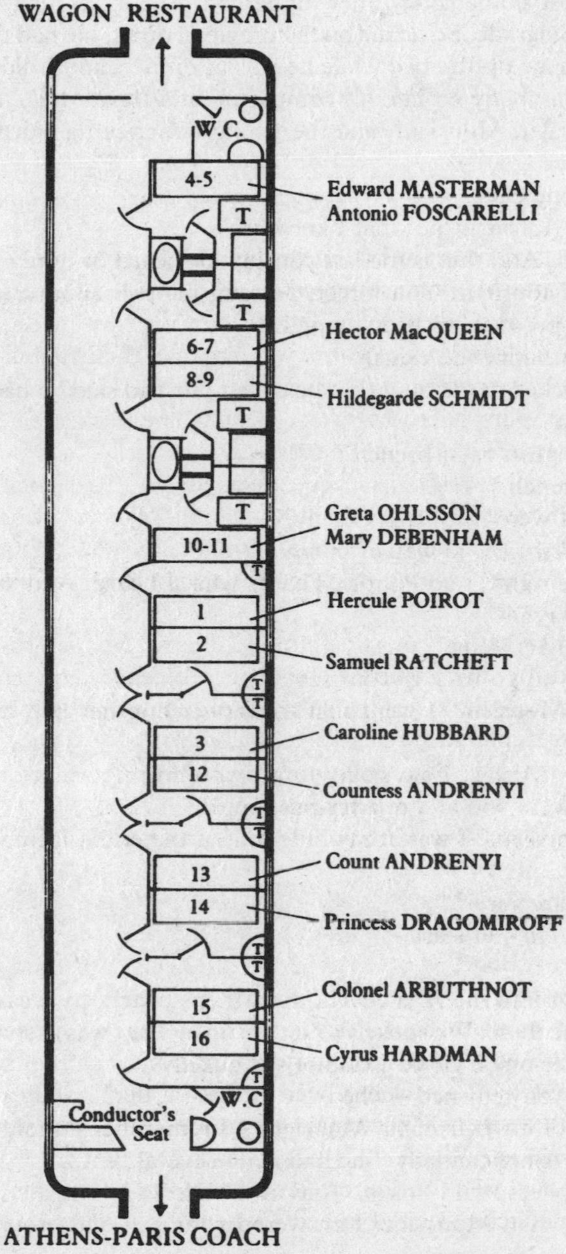
WAGON RESTAURANT
W.C.
4-5
Edward MASTERMAN
Antonio FOSCARELLI
T
T
Hector MacQUEEN
6-7
8-9
Hildegarde SCHMIDT
T
T
Greta OHLSSON
Mary DEBENHAM
10-11
T
1
Hercule POIROT
2
Samuel RATCHETT
T
T
3
Caroline HUBBARD
12
Countess ANDRENYI
T
T
13
Count ANDRENYI
14
Princess DRAGOMIROFF
T
T
15
Colonel ARBUTHNOT
16
Cyrus HARDMAN
T
W.C
Conductor's Seat
ATHENS-PARIS COACH

'Almost immediately after dinner, Monsieur. Actually before we left Belgrade. So he did on the previous night. He had directed me to make up the bed while he was at dinner, and I did so.'

'Did anybody go into his compartment afterwards?'

'His valet, Monsieur, and the young American gentleman his secretary.'

'Anyone else?'

'No, Monsieur, not that I know of.'

'Good. And that is the last you saw or heard of him?'

'No, Monsieur. You forget, he rang his bell about twenty to one – soon after we had stopped.'

'What happened exactly?'

'I knocked at the door, but he called out and said he had made a mistake.'

'In English or in French?'

'In French.'

'What were his words exactly?'

'*Ce n'est rien. Je me suis trompé.*'

'Quite right,' said Poirot. 'That is what I heard. And then you went away?'

'Yes, Monsieur.'

'Did you go back to your seat?'

'No, Monsieur, I went first to answer another bell that had just rung.'

'Now, Michel, I am going to ask you an important question. Where were you at a quarter-past one?'

'I, Monsieur? I was at my little seat at the end – facing up the corridor.'

'You are sure?'

'*Mais oui* – at least –'

'Yes?'

'I went into the next coach, the Athens coach, to speak to my colleague there. We spoke about the snow. That was at some time soon after one o'clock. I cannot say exactly.'

'And you returned – when?'

'One of my bells rang, Monsieur – I remember – I told you. It was the American lady. She had rung several times.'

'I recollect,' said Poirot. 'And after that?'

'After that, Monsieur? I answered your bell and brought you

some mineral water. Then, about half an hour later, I made up the bed in one of the other compartments – that of the young American gentleman, M. Ratchett's secretary.'

'Was M. MacQueen alone in his compartment when you went to make up his bed?'

'The English Colonel from No. 15 was with him. They had been sitting talking.'

'What did the Colonel do when he left M. MacQueen?'

'He went back to his own compartment.'

'No. 15 – that is quite close to your seat, is it not?'

'Yes, Monsieur, it is the second compartment from that end of the corridor.'

'His bed was already made up?'

'Yes, Monsieur. I had made it up while he was at dinner.'

'What time was all this?'

'I could not say exactly, Monsieur. Not later than two o'clock, certainly.'

'And after that?'

'After that, Monsieur, I sat in my seat till morning.'

'You did not go again into the Athens coach?'

'No, Monsieur.'

'Perhaps you slept?'

'I do not think so, Monsieur. The train being at a standstill prevented me from dozing off as I usually do.'

'Did you see any of the passengers moving up or down the corridor?'

The man reflected.

'One of the ladies went to the toilet at the far end, I think.'

'Which lady?'

'I do not know, Monsieur. It was far down the corridor, and she had her back to me. She had on a kimono of scarlet with dragons on it.'

Poirot nodded.

'And after that?'

'Nothing, Monsieur, until the morning.'

'You are sure?'

'Ah, pardon, you yourself, Monsieur, opened your door and looked out for a second.'

'Good, my friend,' said Poirot. 'I wondered whether you would remember that. By the way, I was awakened by what sounded like something heavy falling against my door. Have you any idea what that could have been?'

The man stared at him.

'There was nothing, Monsieur. Nothing, I am positive of it.'

'Then I must have had the *cauchemar*,' said Poirot philosophically.

'Unless,' said M. Bouc, 'it was something in the compartment next door that you heard.'

Poirot took no notice of the suggestion. Perhaps he did not wish to before the Wagon Lit conductor.

'Let us pass to another point,' he said. 'Supposing that last night an assassin joined the train. It is quite certain that he could not have left it after committing the crime?'

Pierre Michel shook his head.

'Nor that he can be concealed on it somewhere?'

'It has been well searched,' said M. Bouc. 'Abandon that idea, my friend.'

'Besides,' said Michel, 'no one could get on to the sleeping-car without my seeing them.'

'When was the last stop?'

'Vincovci.'

'What time was that?'

'We should have left there at 11.58. But owing to the weather we were twenty minutes late.'

'Someone might have come along from the ordinary part of the train?'

'No, Monsieur. After the service of dinner the door between the ordinary carriages and the sleeping-cars is locked.'

'Did you yourself descend from the train at Vincovci?'

'Yes, Monsieur. I got down on to the platform as usual and stood by the step up into the train. The other conductors did the same.'

'What about the forward door? The one near the restaurant-car?'

'It is always fastened on the inside.'

'It is not so fastened now.'

The man looked surprised, then his face cleared.

'Doubtless one of the passengers has opened it to look out on the snow.'

'Probably,' said Poirot.

He tapped thoughtfully on the table for a minute or two.

'Monsieur does not blame me?' said the man timidly.

Poirot smiled on him kindly.

'You have had the evil chance, my friend,' he said. 'Ah! One other point while I remember it. You said that another bell rang just as you were knocking at M. Ratchett's door. In fact, I heard it myself. Whose was it?'

'It was the bell of Madame la Princesse Dragomiroff. She desired me to summon her maid.'

'And you did so?'

'Yes, Monsieur.'

Poirot studied the plan in front of him thoughtfully. Then he inclined his head.

'That is all,' he said, 'for the moment.'

'Thank you, Monsieur.'

The man rose. He looked at M. Bouc.

'Do not distress yourself,' said the latter kindly. 'I cannot see that there has been any negligence on your part.'

Gratified, Pierre Michel left the compartment.

CHAPTER 2

THE EVIDENCE OF THE SECRETARY

For a minute or two Poirot remained lost in thought.

'I think,' he said at last, 'that it would be well to have a further word with M. MacQueen, in view of what we now know.'

The young American appeared promptly.

'Well,' he said, 'how are things going?'

'Not too badly. Since our last conversation I have learnt something – the identity of M. Ratchett.'

Hector MacQueen leaned forward interestedly.

'Yes?' he said.

'Ratchett, as you suspected, was merely an alias. Ratchett was Cassetti, the man who ran the celebrated kidnapping stunts – including the famous affair of little Daisy Armstrong.'

An expression of utter astonishment appeared on MacQueen's face; then it darkened.

'The damned skunk!' he exclaimed.

'You had no idea of this, M. MacQueen?'

'No, sir,' said the young American decidedly. 'If I had I'd have cut off my right hand before it had a chance to do secretarial work for him!'

'You feel strongly about the matter, M. MacQueen?'

'I have a particular reason for doing so. My father was the district attorney who handled the case, M. Poirot. I saw Mrs Armstrong more than once – she was a lovely woman. So gentle and heartbroken.' His face darkened. 'If ever a man deserved what he got, Ratchett or Cassetti is the man. I'm rejoiced at his end. Such a man wasn't fit to live!'

'You almost feel as though you would have been willing to do the good deed yourself?'

'I do. I –' He paused, then flushed rather guiltily. 'Seems I'm kind of incriminating myself.'

'I should be more inclined to suspect you, M. MacQueen, if you displayed an inordinate sorrow at your employer's decease.'

'I don't think I could do that, even to save myself from the chair,' said MacQueen grimly.

Then he added:

'If I'm not being unduly curious, just how did you figure this out? Cassetti's identity, I mean.'

'By a fragment of a letter found in his compartment.'

'But surely – I mean – that was rather careless of the old man?'

'That depends,' said Poirot, 'on the point of view.'

The young man seemed to find this remark rather baffling. He stared at Poirot as though trying to make him out.

'The task before me,' said Poirot, 'is to make sure of the movements of everyone on the train. No offence need be taken, you understand? It is only a matter of routine.'

'Sure. Get right on with it and let me clear my character if I can.'

'I need hardly ask you the number of your compartment,' said Poirot, smiling, 'since I shared it with you for a night. It is the second-class compartment Nos. 6 and 7, and after my departure you had it to yourself.'

'That's right.'

'Now, M. MacQueen, I want you to describe your movements last night from the time of leaving the dining-car.'

'That's quite easy. I went back to my compartment, read a bit, got out on the platform at Belgrade, decided it was too cold, and got in again. I talked for a while to a young English lady who is in the compartment next to mine. Then I fell into conversation with that Englishman, Colonel Arbuthnot – as a matter of fact I think you passed us as we were talking. Then I went in to Mr Ratchett and, as I told you, took down some memoranda of letters he wanted written. I said good-night to him and left him. Colonel Arbuthnot was still standing in the corridor. His compartment was already made up for the night, so I suggested that he should come along to mine. I ordered a couple of drinks and we got right down to it. Discussed world politics and the Government of India and our own troubles with the financial situation and the Wall Street crisis. I don't as a rule cotton to Britishers – they're a stiff-necked lot – but I liked this one.'

'Do you know what time it was when he left you?'

'Pretty late. Getting on for two o'clock, I should say.'

'You noticed that the train had stopped?'

'Oh, yes. We wondered a bit. Looked out and saw the snow lying very thick, but we didn't think it was serious.'

'What happened when Colonel Arbuthnot finally said good-night?'

'He went along to his compartment and I called to the conductor to make up my bed.'

'Where were you whilst he was making it?'

'Standing just outside the door in the corridor smoking a cigarette.'

'And then?'

'And then I went to bed and slept till morning.'

'During the evening did you leave the train at all?'

'Arbuthnot and I thought we'd get out at – what was the name of the place? – Vincovci to stretch our legs a bit. But it was bitterly cold – a blizzard on. We soon hopped back again.'

'By which door did you leave the train?'

'By the one nearest to our compartment.'

'The one next to the dining-car?'

'Yes.'

'Do you remember if it was bolted?'

MacQueen considered.

'Why, yes, I seem to remember it was. At least there was a kind of bar that fitted across the handle. Is that what you mean?'

'Yes. On getting back into the train did you replace that bar?'

'Why, no – I don't think I did. I got in last. No, I don't seem to remember doing so.'

He added suddenly:

'Is that an important point?'

'It may be. Now, I presume, Monsieur, that while you and Colonel Arbuthnot were sitting talking the door of your compartment into the corridor was open?'

Hector MacQueen nodded.

'I want you, if you can, to tell me if anyone passed along that corridor *after* the train left Vincovci until the time you parted company for the night.'

MacQueen drew his brows together.

'I think the conductor passed along once,' he said, 'coming from the direction of the dining-car. And a woman passed the other way, going towards it.'

'Which woman?'

'I couldn't say. I didn't really notice. You see, I was just arguing a point with Arbuthnot. I just seem to remember a glimpse of some scarlet silk affair passing the door. I didn't look, and anyway I wouldn't have seen the person's face. As you know, my carriage faces the dining-car end of the train, so a woman going along the corridor in that direction would have her back to me as soon as she passed.'

Poirot nodded.

'She was going to the toilet, I presume?'

'I suppose so.'

'And you saw her return?'

'Well, no, now that you mention it, I didn't notice her returning, but I suppose she must have done so.'

'One more question. Do you smoke a pipe, M. MacQueen?'

'No, sir, I do not.'

Poirot paused a moment.

'I think that is all at present. I should now like to see the valet of M. Ratchett. By the way, did both you and he always travel second-class?'

'He did. But I usually went first – if possible in the adjoining compartment to Mr Ratchett. Then he had most of his baggage put in my compartment and yet could get at both it and me easily whenever he chose. But on this occasion all the first-class berths were booked except the one which he took.'

'I comprehend. Thank you, M. MacQueen.'

CHAPTER 3

THE EVIDENCE OF THE VALET

The American was succeeded by the pale Englishman with the inexpressive face whom Poirot had already noticed on the day before. He stood waiting very correctly. Poirot motioned to him to sit down.

'You are, I understand, the valet of M. Ratchett?'

'Yes, sir.'

'Your name?'

'Edward Henry Masterman.'

'Your age?'

'Thirty-nine.'

'And your home address?'

'21 Friar Street, Clerkenwell.'

'You have heard that your master has been murdered?'

'Yes, sir. A very shocking occurrence.'

'Will you now tell me, please, at what hour you last saw M. Ratchett?'

The valet considered.

'It must have been about nine o'clock, sir, last night. That or a little after.'

'Tell me in your own words exactly what happened.'

'I went in to Mr Ratchett as usual, sir, and attended to his wants.'

'What were your duties exactly?'

'To fold or hang up his clothes, sir. Put his dental plate in water and see that he had everything he wanted for the night.'

'Was his manner much the same as usual?'

The valet considered a moment.

'Well, sir, I think he was upset.'

'In what way – upset?'

'Over a letter he'd been reading. He asked me if it was I who had put it in his compartment. Of course I told him I hadn't done any such thing, but he swore at me and found fault with everything I did.'

'Was that unusual?'

'Oh, no, sir, he lost his temper easily – as I say, it just depended what had happened to upset him.'

'Did your master ever take a sleeping draught?'

Dr Constantine leaned forward a little.

'Always when travelling by train, sir. He said he couldn't sleep otherwise.'

'Do you know what drug he was in the habit of taking?'

'I couldn't say, I'm sure, sir. There was no name on the bottle. Just "*The Sleeping Draught to be taken at bedtime.*"'

'Did he take it last night?'

'Yes, sir. I poured it into a glass and put it on top of the toilet table ready for him.'

'You didn't actually see him drink it?'

'No, sir.'

'What happened next?'

'I asked if there was anything further, and asked what time M. Ratchett would like to be called in the morning. He said he didn't want to be disturbed till he rang.'

'Was that usual?'

'Quite usual, sir. He used to ring the bell for the conductor and then send him for me when he was ready to get up.'

'Was he usually an early or a late riser?'

'It depended, sir, on his mood. Sometimes he'd get up for breakfast, sometimes he wouldn't get up till just on lunch time.'

'So that you weren't alarmed when the morning wore on and no summons came?'

'No, sir.'

'Did you know that your master had enemies?'

'Yes, sir.'

The man spoke quite unemotionally.

'How did you know?'

'I had heard him discussing some letters, sir, with Mr MacQueen.'

'Had you an affection for your employer, Masterman?'

Masterman's face became, if possible, even more inexpressive than it was normally.

'I should hardly like to say that, sir. He was a generous employer.'

'But you didn't like him?'

'Shall we put it that I don't care very much for Americans, sir.'

'Have you ever been in America?'

'No, sir.'

'Do you remember reading in the paper of the Armstrong kidnapping case?'

A little colour came into the man's cheeks.

'Yes, indeed, sir. A little baby girl, wasn't it? A very shocking affair.'

'Did you know that your employer, M. Ratchett, was the principal instigator in that affair?'

'No, indeed, sir.' The valet's tone held positive warmth and feeling for the first time. 'I can hardly believe it, sir.'

'Nevertheless, it is true. Now, to pass to your own movements last night. A matter of routine, you understand. What did you do after leaving your master?'

'I told Mr MacQueen, sir, that the master wanted him. Then I went to my own compartment and read.'

'Your compartment was –?'

'The end second-class one, sir. Next to the dining-car.'

Poirot was looking at his plan.

'I see – and you had which berth?'

'The lower one, sir.'

'That is No. 4?'

'Yes, sir.'

'Is there anyone in with you?'

'Yes, sir. A big Italian fellow.'

'Does he speak English?'

'Well, a kind of English, sir.' The valet's tone was deprecating. 'He's been in America – Chicago – I understand.'

'Do you and he talk together much?'

'No, sir. I prefer to read.'

Poirot smiled. He could visualize the scene – the large voluble

Italian, and the snub direct administered by the gentleman's gentleman.

'And what, may I ask, are you reading?' he inquired.

'At present, sir, I am reading *Love's Captive*, by Mrs Arabella Richardson.'

'A good story?'

'I find it highly enjoyable, sir.'

'Well, let us continue. You returned to your compartment and read *Love's Captive* till – when?'

'At about ten-thirty, sir, this Italian wanted to go to bed. So the conductor came and made the beds up.'

'And then you went to bed and to sleep?'

'I went to bed, sir, but I didn't sleep.'

'Why didn't you sleep?'

'I had the toothache, sir.'

'Oh, *là là* – that is painful.'

'Most painful, sir.'

'Did you do anything for it?'

'I applied a little oil of cloves, sir, which relieved the pain a little, but I was still not able to get to sleep. I turned the light on above my head and continued to read – to take my mind off it, as it were.'

'And did you not go to sleep at all?'

'Yes, sir, I dropped off about four in the morning.'

'And your companion?'

'The Italian fellow? Oh, he just snored.'

'He did not leave the compartment at all during the night?'

'No, sir.'

'Did you?'

'No, sir.'

'Did you hear anything during the night?'

'I don't think so, sir. Nothing unusual, I mean. The train being at a standstill made it all very quiet.'

Poirot was silent a moment or two, then he said:

'Well, I think there is very little more to be said. You cannot throw any light upon the tragedy?'

'I'm afraid not. I'm sorry, sir.'

'As far as you know, was there any quarrel or bad blood between your master and M. MacQueen?'

'Oh, no, sir. Mr MacQueen was a very pleasant gentleman.'

'Where were you in service before you came to M. Ratchett?'

'With Sir Henry Tomlinson, sir, in Grosvenor Square.'

'Why did you leave him?'

'He was going to East Africa, sir, and did not require my services any longer. But I am sure he will speak for me, sir. I was with him some years.'

'And you have been with M. Ratchett – how long?'

'Just over nine months, sir.'

'Thank you, Masterman. By the way, are you a pipe smoker?'

'No, sir. I only smoke cigarettes – gaspers, sir.'

'Thank you. That will do.'

The valet hesitated a moment.

'You'll excuse me, sir, but the elderly American lady is in what I might describe as a state, sir. She's saying she knows all about the murderer. She's in a very excitable condition, sir.'

'In that case,' said Poirot, smiling, 'we had better see her next.'

'Shall I tell her, sir? She's been demanding to see someone in authority for a long time. The conductor's been trying to pacify her.'

'Send her to us, my friend,' said Poirot. 'We will listen to her story now.'

CHAPTER 4

THE EVIDENCE OF THE AMERICAN LADY

Mrs Hubbard arrived in the dining-car in such a state of breathless excitement that she was hardly able to articulate her words.

'Now just tell me this. Who's in authority here? I've got some vurry important information, *vurry* important, indeed, and I just want to tell it to someone in authority as soon as may be. If you gentlemen –'

Her wavering glance fluctuated between the three men. Poirot leaned forward.

'Tell it to me, Madame,' he said. 'But, first, pray be seated.'

Mrs Hubbard plumped heavily down on to the seat opposite to him.

'What I've got to tell you is just this. There was a murder on the train last night, and the murderer was *right there in my compartment*!'

She paused to give dramatic emphasis to her words.

'You are sure of this, Madame?'

'Of course I'm sure! The idea! I know what I'm talking about. I'll tell you just everything there is to tell. I'd gotten into bed and gone to sleep, and suddenly I woke up – all in the dark, it was – and I knew there was a man in my compartment. I was just so scared I couldn't scream, if you know what I mean. I just lay there and thought, "Mercy, I'm going to be killed." I just can't describe to you how I felt. These nasty trains, I thought, and all the outrages I'd read of. And I thought, "Well, anyway, he won't get my jewellery." Because, you see, I'd put that in a stocking and hidden it under my pillow – which isn't so mighty comfortable, by the way, kinder bumpy, if you know what I mean. But that's neither here nor there. Where was I?'

'You realized, Madame, that there was a man in your compartment.'

'Yes, well, I just lay there with my eyes closed, and I thought whatever should I do, and I thought, "Well, I'm just thankful that my daughter doesn't know the plight I'm in." And then, somehow, I got my wits about me and I felt about with my hand and I pressed the bell for the conductor. I pressed it and I pressed it, but nothing happened, and I can tell you I thought my heart was going to stop beating. "Mercy," I said to myself, "maybe they've murdered every single soul on the train." It was at a standstill, anyhow, and a nasty quiet feel in the air. But I just went on pressing that bell, and oh! the relief when I heard footsteps coming running down the corridor and a knock on the door. "Come in," I screamed, and I switched on the lights at the same time. And, would you believe it, there wasn't a soul there.'

This seemed to Mrs Hubbard to be a dramatic climax rather than an anti-climax.

'And what happened next, Madame?'

'Why, I told the man what had happened, and he didn't seem to believe me. Seemed to imagine I'd dreamt the whole thing. I made him look under the seat, though he said there wasn't room for a man to squeeze himself in there. It was plain enough the man had got away, but there *had* been a man there and it just made me mad the way the conductor tried to soothe me down! I'm not one to imagine things, Mr – I don't think I know your name?'

'Poirot, Madame, and this is M. Bouc, a director of the company, and Dr Constantine.'

Mrs Hubbard murmured:

'Pleased to meet you, I'm sure,' to all three of them in an abstracted manner, and then plunged once more into her recital.

'Now I'm just not going to pretend I was as bright as I might have been. I got it into my head that it was the man from next door – the poor fellow who's been killed. I told the conductor to look at the door between the compartments, and sure enough it wasn't bolted. Well, I soon saw to that, I told him to bolt it then and there, and after he'd gone out I got up and put a suitcase against it to make sure.'

'What time was this, Mrs Hubbard?'

'Well, I'm sure I can't tell you. I never looked to see. I was so upset.'

'And what is your theory now?'

'Why, I should say it was just as plain as plain could be. The man in my compartment was the murderer. Who else could he be?'

'And you think he went back into the adjoining compartment?'

'How do I know where he went? I had my eyes tight shut.'

'He must have slipped out through the door into the corridor.'

'Well, I couldn't say. You see, I had my eyes tight shut.'

Mrs Hubbard sighed convulsively.

'Mercy, I was scared! If my daughter only knew –'

'You do not think, Madame, that what you heard was the noise of someone moving about next door – in the murdered man's compartment?'

'No, I do not, Mr – what is it? – Poirot. The man was *right there in the same compartment with me.* And, what's more, I've got proof of it.'

Triumphantly she hauled a large handbag into view and proceeded to burrow in its interior.

She took out in turn two large clean handkerchiefs, a pair of horn-rimmed glasses, a bottle of aspirin, a packet of Glauber's salts, a celluloid tube of bright green peppermints, a bunch of keys, a pair of scissors, a book of American Express cheques, a snapshot of an extraordinarily plain-looking child, some letters, five strings of pseudo Oriental beads and a small metal object – a button.

'You see this button? Well, it's not one of *my* buttons. It's not off anything I've got. I found it this morning when I got up.'

As she placed it on the table, M. Bouc leaned forward and gave an exclamation.

'But this is a button from the tunic of a Wagon Lit attendant!'

'There may be a natural explanation for that,' said Poirot.

He turned gently to the lady.

'This button, Madame, may have dropped from the conductor's uniform, either when he searched your cabin, or when he was making the bed up last night.'

'I just don't know what's the matter with all you people. Seems as though you don't do anything but make objections. Now listen here. I was reading a magazine last night before I went to sleep. Before I turned the light out I placed that magazine on a little case that was standing on the floor near the window. Have you got that?'

They assured her that they had.

'Very well, then. The conductor looked under the seat from near the door and then he came in and bolted the door between me and the next compartment, but he never went up near the window. Well, this morning that button was lying right on top of the magazine. What do you call that, I should like to know?'

'That, Madame, I call evidence,' said Poirot.

The answer seemed to appease the lady.

'It makes me madder than a hornet to be disbelieved,' she explained.

'You have given us most interesting and valuable evidence,' said Poirot soothingly. 'Now, may I ask you a few questions?'

'Why, willingly.'

'How was it, since you were nervous of this man Ratchett, that you hadn't already bolted the door between the compartments?'

'I had,' returned Mrs Hubbard promptly.

'Oh, you had?'

'Well, as a matter of fact, I asked that Swedish creature – a pleasant soul – if it was bolted, and she said it was.'

'How was it you couldn't see for yourself?'

'Because I was in bed and my sponge-bag was hanging on the door handle.'

'What time was it when you asked her to do this for you?'

'Now let me think. It must have been round about half-past ten or a quarter to eleven. She'd come along to see if I'd got an aspirin. I told her where to find it, and she got it out of my grip.'

'You yourself were in bed?'

'Yes.'

Suddenly she laughed.

'Poor soul – she was in quite a taking. You see, she'd opened the door of the next compartment by mistake.'

'M. Ratchett's?'

'Yes. You know how difficult it is as you come along the train and all the doors are shut. She opened his by mistake. She was very distressed about it. He'd laughed, it seemed, and I fancy he may have said something not quite nice. Poor thing, she was all in a flutter. "Oh! I make mistake," she said. "I ashamed make mistake. Not nice man," she said. "He say, 'You too old.'"'

Dr Constantine sniggered and Mrs Hubbard immediately froze him with a glance.

'He wasn't a nice kind of man,' she said, 'to say a thing like that to a lady. It's not right to laugh at such things.'

Dr Constantine hastily apologized.

'Did you hear any noise from M. Ratchett's compartment after that?' asked Poirot.

'Well – not exactly.'

'What do you mean by that, Madame?'

'Well –' she paused. 'He snored.'

'Ah! he snored, did he?'

'Terribly. The night before it quite kept me awake.'

'You didn't hear him snore after you had had the scare about a man being in your compartment?'

'Why, Mr Poirot, how could I? He was dead.'

'Ah, yes, truly,' said Poirot. He appeared confused.

'Do you remember the affair of the Armstrong kidnapping, Mrs Hubbard?' he asked.

'Yes, indeed I do. And how the wretch that did it escaped scot free! My, I'd have liked to get my hands on him.'

'He has not escaped. He is dead. He died last night.'

'You don't mean –?' Mrs Hubbard half rose from her chair in excitement.

'But yes, I do. Ratchett was the man.'

'*Well!* Well, to think of that! I must write and tell my daughter. Now, didn't I tell you last night that that man had an evil face? I was right, you see. My daughter always says: "When Momma's got a hunch, you can bet your bottom dollar it's O.K."'

'Were you acquainted with any of the Armstrong family, Mrs Hubbard?'

'No. They moved in a very exclusive circle. But I've always heard that Mrs Armstrong was a perfectly lovely woman and that her husband worshipped her.'

'Well, Mrs Hubbard, you have helped us very much – very much indeed. Perhaps you will give me your full name?'

'Why, certainly. Caroline Martha Hubbard.'

'Will you write your address down here?'

Mrs Hubbard did so, without ceasing to speak.

'I just can't get over it. Cassetti – on this train. I had a hunch about that man, didn't I, Mr Poirot?'

'Yes, indeed, Madame. By the way, have you a scarlet silk dressing-gown?'

'Mercy, what an odd question! Why, no. I've got two dressing-gowns with me – a pink flannel one that's kind of cosy for on board ship, and one my daughter gave me as a present – a kind of local affair in purple silk. But what in creation do you want to know about my dressing-gowns for?'

'Well, you see, Madame, someone in a scarlet kimono entered either your or Mr Ratchett's compartment last night. It is, as you said just now, very difficult when all the doors are shut to know which compartment is which.'

'Well, no one in a scarlet dressing-gown came into my compartment.'

'Then she must have gone into M. Ratchett's.'

Mrs Hubbard pursed her lips together and said grimly:

'That wouldn't surprise me any.'

Poirot leaned forward.

'So you heard a woman's voice next door?'

'I don't know how you guessed that, Mr Poirot. I don't really. But – well – as a matter of fact, I *did*.'

'But when I asked you just now if you heard anything next door, you only said you heard Mr Ratchett snoring.'

'Well that was true enough. He *did* snore part of the time. As for the other –' Mrs Hubbard got rather pink. 'It isn't a very nice thing to speak about.'

'What time was it when you heard a woman's voice?'

'I can't tell you. I just woke up for a minute and heard a woman talking, and it was plain enough where she was. So I just thought, "Well that's the kind of man he is. Well, I'm not surprised," and then I went to sleep again, and I'm sure I should never have mentioned anything of the kind to three strange gentlemen if you hadn't dragged it out of me.'

'Was it before the scare about the man in your compartment, or after?'

'Why, that's like what you said just now! He wouldn't have had a woman talking to him if he were dead, would he?'

'*Pardon*. You must think me very stupid, Madame.'

'I guess even you get kinder muddled now and then. I just can't get over it being that monster Cassetti. What my daughter will say –'

Poirot managed adroitly to help the good lady to restore the contents of her handbag and he then shepherded her towards the door.

At the last moment he said:

'You have dropped your handkerchief, Madame.'

Mrs Hubbard looked at the little scrap of cambric he held out to her.

'That's not mine, Mr Poirot. I've got mine right here.'

'*Pardon*. I thought as it had the initial H on it –'

'Well, now, that's curious, but it's certainly not mine. Mine are marked C.M.H., and they're sensible things – not expensive Paris fallals. What good is a handkerchief like that to anybody's nose?'

Neither of the three men seemed to have an answer to this question, and Mrs Hubbard sailed out triumphantly.

CHAPTER 5

THE EVIDENCE OF THE SWEDISH LADY

M. Bouc was handling the button Mrs Hubbard had left behind her.

'This button. I cannot understand it. Does it mean that, after all, Pierre Michel is involved in some way?' he said. He paused, then continued, as Poirot did not reply. 'What have you to say, my friend?'

'That button, it suggests possibilities,' said Poirot thoughtfully. 'Let us interview next the Swedish lady before we discuss the evidence we have heard.'

He sorted through the pile of passports in front of him.

'Ah! here we are. Greta Ohlsson, age forty-nine.'

M. Bouc gave directions to the restaurant attendant, and presently the lady with the yellowish-grey bun of hair and the long mild sheep-like face was ushered in. She peered short-sightedly at Poirot through her glasses, but was quite calm.

It transpired that she understood and spoke French, so that the conversation took place in that language. Poirot first asked her the questions to which he already knew the answers – her name, age, and address. He then asked her her occupation.

She was, she told him, matron in a missionary school near Stamboul. She was a trained nurse.

'You know, of course, of what took place last night, Mademoiselle?'

'Naturally. It is very dreadful. And the American lady tells me that the murderer was actually in her compartment.'

'I hear, Mademoiselle, that you were the last person to see the murdered man alive?'

'I do not know. It may be so. I opened the door of his compartment by mistake. I was much ashamed. It was a most awkward mistake.'

'You actually saw him?'

'Yes. He was reading a book. I apologized quickly and withdrew.'

'Did he say anything to you?'

A slight flush showed on the worthy lady's cheek.

'He laughed and said a few words. I – I did not quite catch them.'

'And what did you do after that, Mademoiselle?' asked Poirot, passing from the subject tactfully.

'I went in to the American lady, Mrs Hubbard. I asked her for some aspirin and she gave it to me.'

'Did she ask you whether the communicating door between her compartment and that of M. Ratchett was bolted?'

'Yes.'

'And was it?'

'Yes.'

'And after that?'

'After that I go back to my own compartment, I take the aspirin and lie down.'

'What time was all this?'

'When I got into bed it was five minutes to eleven, because I look at my watch before I wind it up.'

'Did you go to sleep quickly?'

'Not very quickly. My head got better, but I lay awake some time.'

'Had the train come to a stop before you went to sleep?'

'I do not think so. We stopped, I think, at a station, just as I was getting drowsy.'

'That would be Vincovci. Now your compartment, Mademoiselle, is this one?' he indicated it on the plan.

'That is so, yes.'

'You had the upper or the lower berth?'

'The lower berth, No. 10.'

'And you had a companion?'

'Yes, a young English lady. Very nice, very amiable. She had travelled from Baghdad.'

'After the train left Vincovci, did she leave the compartment?'

'No, I am sure she did not.'

'Why are you sure if you were asleep?'

'I sleep very lightly. I am used to waking at a sound. I am sure if she had come down from the berth above I would have awakened.'

'Did you yourself leave the compartment?'

'Not until this morning.'

'Have you a scarlet silk kimono, Mademoiselle?'

'No, indeed. I have a good comfortable dressing-gown of Jaeger material. A pale mauve abba such as you buy in the East.'

Poirot nodded. Then he said in a friendly tone:

'Why are you taking this journey? A holiday?'

'Yes, I am going home for a holiday. But first I go to Lausanne to stay with a sister for a week or so.'

'Perhaps you will be so amiable as to write me down the name and address of your sister?'

'With pleasure.'

She took the paper and pencil he gave her and wrote down the name and address as requested.

'Have you ever been in America, Mademoiselle?'

'No. Very nearly once. I was to go with an invalid lady, but it was cancelled at the last moment. I much regretted. They are very good, the Americans. They give much money to found schools and hospitals. They are very practical.'

'Do you remember hearing of the Armstrong kidnapping case?'

'No, what was that?'

Poirot explained.

Greta Ohlsson was indignant. Her yellow bun of hair quivered with her emotion.

'That there are in the world such evil men! It tries one's faith. The poor mother. My heart aches for her.'

The amiable Swede departed, her kindly face flushed, her eyes suffused with tears.

Poirot was writing busily on a sheet of paper.

'What is it you write there, my friend?' asked M. Bouc.

'*Mon cher*, it is my habit to be neat and orderly. I make here a little table of chronological events.'

He finished writing and passed the paper to M. Bouc.

9.15 Train leaves Belgrade.

about 9.40 Valet leaves Ratchett with sleeping draught beside him.

about 10.00 MacQueen leaves Ratchett.

about 10.40 Greta Ohlsson sees Ratchett (last seen alive). N.B. – He was awake reading a book.

0.10 Train leaves Vincovci (late).

0.30 Train runs into a snowdrift.
0.37 Ratchett's bell rings. Conductor answers it. Ratchett says, '*Ce n'est rien. Je me suis trompé.*'
about 1.17 Mrs Hubbard thinks man is in her carriage. Rings for conductor.

M. Bouc nodded approval.

'That is very clear,' he said.

'There is nothing there that strikes you as at all odd?'

'No, it seems all quite clear and above board. It seems quite plain that the crime was committed at 1.15. The evidence of the watch shows us that, and Mrs Hubbard's story fits in. For my mind, I will make a guess at the identity of the murderer. I say, my friend, that it is the big Italian. He comes from America – from Chicago – and remember an Italian's weapon is the knife, and he stabs not once but several times.'

'That is true.'

'Without a doubt, that is the solution of the mystery. Doubtless he and this Ratchett were in this kidnapping business together. Cassetti is an Italian name. In some way Ratchett did on him what they call the double-cross. The Italian tracks him down, sends him warning letters first, and finally revenges himself upon him in a brutal way. It is all quite simple.'

Poirot shook his head doubtfully.

'It is hardly as simple as that, I fear,' he murmured.

'Me, I am convinced it is the truth,' said M. Bouc, becoming more and more enamoured of his theory.

'And what about the valet with the toothache who swears that the Italian never left the compartment?'

'That is the difficulty.'

Poirot twinkled.

'Yes, it is annoying, that. Unlucky for your theory, and extremely lucky for our Italian friend that M. Ratchett's valet should have had the toothache.'

'It will be explained,' said M. Bouc with magnificent certainty.

Poirot shook his head again.

'No, it is hardly so simple as that,' he murmured again.

CHAPTER 6

THE EVIDENCE OF THE RUSSIAN PRINCESS

'Let us hear what Pierre Michel has to say about this button,' he said.

The Wagon Lit conductor was recalled. He looked at them inquiringly.

M. Bouc cleared his throat.

'Michel,' he said. 'Here is a button from your tunic. It was found in the American lady's compartment. What have you to say for yourself about it?'

The conductor's hand went automatically to his tunic.

'I have lost no button, Monsieur,' he said. 'There must be some mistake.'

'That is very odd.'

'I cannot account for it, Monsieur.'

The man seemed astonished, but not in any way guilty or confused.

M. Bouc said meaningly:

'Owing to the circumstances in which it was found, it seems fairly certain that this button was dropped by the man who was in Mrs Hubbard's compartment last night when she rang the bell.'

'But, Monsieur, there was no one there. The lady must have imagined it.'

'She did not imagine it, Michael. The assassin of M. Ratchett passed that way – *and dropped that button.*'

As the significance of M. Bouc's word became plain to him, Pierre Michel flew into a violent state of agitation.

'It is not true, Monsieur, it is not true!' he cried. 'You are accusing me of the crime. Me? I am innocent. I am absolutely innocent. Why should I want to kill a Monsieur whom I have never seen before?'

'Where were you when Mrs Hubbard's bell rang?'

'I told you, Monsieur, in the next coach, talking to my colleague.'

'We will send for him.'

'Do so, Monsieur, I implore you, do so.'

The conductor of the next coach was summoned. He immediately confirmed Pierre Michel's statement. He added that the conductor from the Bucharest coach had also been there. The three of them had been discussing the situation caused by the snow. They had been talking some ten minutes when Michel fancied he heard a bell. As he opened the doors connecting the two coaches, they had all heard it plainly. A bell ringing repeatedly. Michel had run post-haste to answer it.

'So you see, Monsieur, I am not guilty,' cried Michel anxiously.

'And this button from a Wagon Lit tunic – how do you explain it?'

'I cannot, Monsieur. It is a mystery to me. All my buttons are intact.'

Both of the other conductors also declared that they had not lost a button. Also that they had not been inside Mrs Hubbard's compartment at any time.

'Calm yourself, Michel,' said M. Bouc, 'and cast your mind back to the moment when you ran to answer Mrs Hubbard's bell. Did you meet anyone at all in the corridor?'

'No, Monsieur.'

'Did you see anyone going away from you down the corridor in the other direction?'

'Again, no. Monsieur.'

'Odd,' said M. Bouc.

'Not so very,' said Poirot. 'It is a question of time. Mrs Hubbard wakes to find someone in her compartment. For a minute or two she lies paralysed, her eyes shut. Probably it was then that the man slipped out into the corridor. Then she starts ringing the bell. But the conductor does not come at once. It is only the third or fourth peal that he hears. I should say myself that there was ample time –'

'For what? For what, *mon cher*? Remember that there are thick drifts of snow all round the train.'

'There are two courses open to our mysterious assassin,' said Poirot slowly. 'He could retreat into either of the toilets or he could disappear into one of the compartments.'

'But they were all occupied.'

'Yes.'

'You mean that he could retreat into his *own* compartment?'

Poirot nodded.

'It fits, it fits,' murmured M. Bouc. 'During that ten minutes' absence of the conductor, the murderer comes from his own compartment, goes into Ratchett's, kills him, locks and chains the door on the inside, goes out through Mrs Hubbard's compartment and is back safely in his own compartment by the time the conductor arrives.'

Poirot murmured:

'It is not quite so simple as that, my friend. Our friend the doctor here will tell you so.'

With a gesture M. Bouc signified that the three conductors might depart.

'We have still to see eight passengers,' said Poirot. 'Five first-class passengers – Princess Dragomiroff, Count and Countess Andrenyi, Colonel Arbuthnot and Mr Hardman. Three second-class passengers – Miss Debenham, Antonio Foscarelli and the lady's-maid, Fräulein Schmidt.'

'Who will you see first – the Italian?'

'How you harp on your Italian! No, we will start at the top of the tree. Perhaps Madame la Princesse will be so good as to spare us a few moments of her time. Convey that message to her, Michel.'

'*Oui, Monsieur,*' said the conductor, who was just leaving the car.

'Tell her we can wait on her in her compartment if she does not wish to put herself to the trouble of coming here,' called M. Bouc.

But Princess Dragomiroff declined to take this course. She appeared in the dining-car, inclined her head slightly and sat down opposite Poirot.

Her small toad-like face looked even yellower than the day before. She was certainly ugly, and yet, like the toad, she had eyes like jewels, dark and imperious, revealing latent energy and an intellectual force that could be felt at once.

Her voice was deep, very distinct, with a slight grating quality in it.

She cut short a flowery phrase of apology from M. Bouc.

'You need not offer apologies, Messieurs. I understand a murder has taken place. Naturally, you must interview all the passengers. I shall be glad to give all the assistance in my power.'

'You are most amiable, Madame,' said Poirot.

'Not at all. It is a duty. What do you wish to know?'

'Your full Christian names and address, Madame. Perhaps you would prefer to write them yourself?'

Poirot proffered a sheet of paper and pencil, but the Princess waved them aside.

'You can write it,' she said. 'There is nothing difficult – Natalia Dragomiroff, 17 Avenue Kleber, Paris.'

'You are travelling home from Constantinople, Madame?'

'Yes, I have been staying at the Austrian Embassy. My maid is with me.'

'Would you be so good as to give me a brief account of your movements last night from dinner onwards?'

'Willingly. I directed the conductor to make up my bed whilst I was in the dining-car. I retired to bed immediately after dinner. I read until the hour of eleven, when I turned out my light. I was unable to sleep owing to certain rheumatic pains from which I suffer. At about a quarter to one I rang for my maid. She massaged me and then read aloud till I felt sleepy. I cannot say exactly when she left me. It may have been half an hour, it may have been later.'

'The train had stopped then?'

'The train had stopped.'

'You heard nothing – nothing unusual during the time, Madame?'

'I heard nothing unusual.'

'What is your maid's name?'

'Hildegarde Schmidt.'

'She has been with you long?'

'Fifteen years.'

'You consider her trustworthy?'

'Absolutely. Her people come from an estate of my late husband's in Germany.'

'You have been in America, I presume, Madame?'

The abrupt change of subject made the old lady raise her eyebrows.

'Many times.'

'Were you at any time acquainted with a family of the name of Armstrong – a family in which a tragedy occurred?'

With some emotion in her voice the old lady said:

'You speak of friends of mine, Monsieur.'

'You knew Colonel Armstrong well, then?'

'I knew him slightly; but his wife, Sonia Armstrong, was my god-daughter. I was on terms of friendship with her mother, the actress, Linda Arden. Linda Arden was a great genius, one of the greatest tragic actresses in the world. As Lady Macbeth, as Magda, there was no one to touch her. I was not only an admirer of her art, I was a personal friend.'

'She is dead?'

'No, no, she is alive, but she lives in complete retirement. Her health is very delicate, she has to lie on a sofa most of the time.'

'There was, I think, a second daughter?'

'Yes, much younger than Mrs Armstrong.'

'And she is alive?'

'Certainly.'

'Where is she?'

The old woman bent an acute glance at him.

'I must ask you the reason of these questions. What have they to do with the matter in hand – the murder on this train?'

'They are connected in this way, Madame, the man who was murdered was the man responsible for the kidnapping and murder of Mrs Armstrong's child.'

'Ah!'

The straight brows drew together. Princess Dragomiroff drew herself a little more erect.

'In my view, then, this murder is an entirely admirable happening! You will pardon my slightly biased point of view.'

'It is most natural, Madame. And now to return to the question you did not answer. Where is the younger daughter of Linda Arden, the sister of Mrs Armstrong?'

'I honestly cannot tell you, Monsieur. I have lost touch with the younger generation. I believe she married an Englishman some years ago and went to England, but at the moment I cannot recollect the name.'

She paused a minute and then said:

'Is there anything further you want to ask me, gentlemen?'

'Only one thing, Madame, a somewhat personal question. The colour of your dressing-gown.'

She raised her eyebrows slightly.

'I must suppose you have a reason for such a question. My dressing-gown is of blue satin.'

'There is nothing more, Madame. I am much obliged to you for answering my questions so promptly.'

She made a slight gesture with her heavily-beringed hand.

Then, as she rose, and the others rose with her, she stopped.

'You will excuse me, Monsieur,' she said, 'but may I ask your name? Your face is somehow familiar to me.'

'My name, Madame, is Hercule Poirot – at your service.'

She was silent a minute, then:

'Hercule Poirot,' she said. 'Yes. I remember now. This is Destiny.'

She walked away, very erect, a little stiff in her movements.

'*Voilà une grande dame*,' said M. Bouc. 'What do you think of her, my friend?'

But Hercule Poirot merely shook his head.

'I am wondering,' he said, 'what she meant by Destiny.'

CHAPTER 7

THE EVIDENCE OF COUNT AND COUNTESS ANDRENYI

Count and Countess Andrenyi were next summoned. The Count, however, entered the dining-car alone.

There was no doubt that he was a fine-looking man seen face to face. He was at least six feet in height, with broad shoulders and slender hips. He was dressed in very well-cut English tweeds, and might have been taken for an Englishman had it not been for the length of his moustache and something in the line of the cheek-bone.

'Well, Messieurs,' he said, 'what can I do for you?'

'You understand, Monsieur,' said Poirot, 'that in view of what has occurred I am obliged to put certain questions to all the passengers.'

'Perfectly, perfectly,' said the Count easily. 'I quite understand your position. Not, I fear, that my wife and I can do much to assist you. We were asleep and heard nothing at all.'

'Are you aware of the identity of the deceased, Monsieur?'

'I understand it was the big American – a man with a decidedly unpleasant face. He sat at the table at meal times.'

He indicated with a nod of his head the table at which Ratchett and MacQueen had sat.

'Yes, yes, Monsieur, you are perfectly correct. I meant did you know the name of the man?'

'No.' The Count looked thoroughly puzzled by Poirot's queries.

'If you want to know his name,' he said, 'surely it is on his passport?'

'The name on his passport is Ratchett,' said Poirot. 'But that, Monsieur, is not his real name. He is the man Cassetti, who was responsible for a celebrated kidnapping outrage in America.'

He watched the Count closely as he spoke, but the latter seemed quite unaffected by the piece of news. He merely opened his eyes a little.

'Ah!' he said. 'That certainly should throw light upon the matter. An extraordinary country America.'

'You have been there, perhaps, Monsieur le Comte?'

'I was in Washington for a year.'

'You knew, perhaps, the Armstrong family?'

'Armstrong – Armstrong – it is difficult to recall – one met so many.'

He smiled, shrugged his shoulders.

'But to come back to the matter in hand, gentlemen,' he said. 'What more can I do to assist you?'

'You retired to rest – when, Monsieur le Comte?'

Hercule Poirot's eyes stole to his plan. Count and Countess Andrenyi occupied compartments No. 12 and 13 adjoining.

'We had one compartment made up for the night whilst we were in the dining-car. On returning we sat in the other for a while –'

'What number would that be?'

'No. 13. We played picquet together. About eleven o'clock my wife retired for the night. The conductor made up my compartment and I also went to bed. I slept soundly until morning.'

'Did you notice the stopping of the train?'

'I was not aware of it till this morning.'

'And your wife?'

The Count smiled.

'My wife always takes a sleeping draught when travelling by train. She took her usual dose of trional.'

He paused.

'I am sorry I am not able to assist you in any way.'

Poirot passed him a sheet of paper and a pen.

'Thank you, Monsieur le Comte. It is a formality, but will you just let me have your name and address?'

The Count wrote slowly and carefully.

'It is just as well I should write this for you,' he said pleasantly. 'The spelling of my country estate is a little difficult for those unacquainted with the language.'

He passed the paper across to Poirot and rose.

'It will be quite unnecessary for my wife to come here,' he said. 'She can tell you nothing more than I have.'

A little gleam came into Poirot's eye.

'Doubtless, doubtless,' he said. 'But all the same I think I should like to have just one little word with Madame la Comtesse.'

'I assure you it is quite unnecessary.'

His voice rang out authoritatively.

Poirot blinked gently at him.

'It will be a mere formality,' he said. 'But you understand, it is necessary for my report.'

'As you please.'

The Count gave way grudgingly. He made a short, foreign bow and left the dining-car.

Poirot reached out a hand to a passport. It set out the Count's name and titles. He passed on to the further information – *accompanied by wife.* Christian name Elena Maria; maiden name Goldenberg; age twenty. A spot of grease had been dropped some time by a careless official on it.

'A diplomatic passport,' said M. Bouc. 'We must be careful, my friend, to give no offence. These people can have nothing to do with the murder.'

'Be easy, *mon vieux*, I will be most tactful. A mere formality.'

His voice dropped as the Countess Andrenyi entered the dining-car. She looked timid and extremely charming.

'You wish to see me, Messieurs?'

'A mere formality, Madame la Comtesse.' Poirot rose gallantly, bowed her into the seat opposite him. 'It is only to ask you if you saw or heard anything last night that may throw light upon this matter.'

'Nothing at all, Monsieur. I was asleep.'

'You did not hear, for instance, a commotion going on in the compartment next to yours? The American lady who occupies it had quite an attack of hysterics and rang for the conductor.'

'I heard nothing, Monsieur. You see, I had taken a sleeping draught.'

'Ah! I comprehend. Well, I need not detain you further.' Then, as she rose swiftly, 'Just one little minute – these particulars, your maiden name, age and so on, they are correct?'

'Quite correct, Monsieur.'

'Perhaps you will sign this memorandum to that effect, then.'

She signed quickly, a graceful slanting handwriting.

Elena Andrenyi.

'Did you accompany your husband to America, Madame?'

'No, Monsieur.' She smiled, flushed a little. 'We were not married then; we have only been married a year.'

'Ah yes, thank you, Madame. By the way, does your husband smoke?'

She stared at him as she stood poised for departure.

'Yes.'

'A pipe?'

'No. Cigarettes and cigars.'

'Ah! Thank you.'

She lingered; her eyes watched him curiously. Lovely eyes they were, dark and almond shaped, with very long black lashes that swept the exquisite pallor of her cheeks. Her lips, very scarlet, in the foreign fashion, were parted just a little. She looked exotic and beautiful.

'Why did you ask me that?'

'Madame,' Poirot waved an airy hand, 'detectives have to ask all sorts of questions. For instance, perhaps you will tell me the colour of your dressing-gown?'

She stared at him. Then she laughed.

'It is corn-coloured chiffon. Is that really important?'

'Very important, Madame.'

She asked curiously:

'Are you really a detective, then?'

'At your service, Madame.'

'I thought there were no detectives on the train when it passed through Yugo-Slavia – not until one got to Italy.'

'I am not a Yugo-Slavian detective, Madame. I am an international detective.'

'You belong to the League of Nations?'

'I belong to the world, Madame,' said Poirot dramatically. He went on, 'I work mainly in London. You speak English?' he added in that language.

'I speak a leetle, yes.'

Her accent was charming.

Poirot bowed once more.

'We will not detain you further, Madame. You see, it was not so very terrible.'

She smiled, inclined her head and departed.

'*Elle est jolie femme*,' said M. Bouc appreciatively.

He sighed.

'Well, that did not advance us much.'

'No,' said Poirot. 'Two people who saw nothing and heard nothing.'

'Shall we now see the Italian?'

Poirot did not reply for a moment. He was studying a grease spot on a Hungarian diplomatic passport.

CHAPTER 8

THE EVIDENCE OF COLONEL ARBUTHNOT

Poirot roused himself with a slight start. His eyes twinkled a little as they met the eager ones of M. Bouc.

'Ah! my dear old friend,' he said. 'You see, I have become what they call the snob! The first-class, I feel it should be attended to before the second-class. Next, I think, we will interview the good-looking Colonel Arbuthnot.'

Finding the Colonel's French to be of a severely limited description, Poirot conducted his interrogation in English.

Arbuthnot's name, age, home address and exact military standing were all ascertained. Poirot proceeded:

'It is that you come home from India on what is called the leave – what we call *en permission?*'

Colonel Arbuthnot, uninterested in what a pack of foreigners called anything, replied with true British brevity:

'Yes.'

'But you do not come home on the P. & O. boat?'

'No.'

'Why not?'

'I chose to come by the overland route for reasons of my own.'

'And that,' his manner seemed to say, 'is one for you, you interfering little jackanapes.'

'You came straight through from India?'

The Colonel replied dryly:

'I stopped for one night to see Ur of the Chaldees and for three days in Baghdad with the A.O.C., who happens to be an old friend of mine.'

'You stopped three days in Baghdad. I understand that the young English lady, Miss Debenham, also comes from Baghdad. Perhaps you met her there?'

'No, I did not. I first met Miss Debenham when she and I shared the railway convoy car from Kirkuk to Nissibin.'

Poirot leaned forward. He became persuasive and a little more foreign than he need have been.

'Monsieur, I am about to appeal to you. You and Miss Debenham are the only two English people on the train. It is necessary that I should ask you each your opinion of the other.'

'Highly irregular,' said Colonel Arbuthnot coldly.

'Not so. You see, this crime, it was most probably committed by a woman. The man was stabbed no less than twelve times. Even the *chef de train* said at once, "It is a woman." Well, then, what is my first task? To give all the women travelling on the Stamboul-Calais coach what Americans call the "once over". But to judge of an Englishwoman is difficult. They are very reserved, the English. So I appeal to you, Monsieur, in the interests of justice. What sort of a person is this Miss Debenham? What do you know about her?'

'Miss Debenham,' said the Colonel with some warmth, 'is a lady.'

'Ah!' said Poirot with every appearance of being much gratified. 'So you do not think that she is likely to be implicated in this crime?'

'The idea is absurd,' said Arbuthnot. 'The man was a perfect stranger – she had never seen him before.'

'Did she tell you so?'

'She did. She commented at once upon his somewhat unpleasant appearance. If a woman *is* concerned, as you seem to think (to my mind without any evidence but mere assumption), I can assure you that Miss Debenham could not possibly be indicated.'

'You feel warmly in the matter,' said Poirot with a smile.

Colonel Arbuthnot gave him a cold stare.

'I really don't know what you mean,' he said.

The stare seemed to abash Poirot. He dropped his eyes and began fiddling with the papers in front of him.

'All this is by the way,' he said. 'Let us be practical and come to facts. This crime, we have reason to believe, took place at a quarter-past one last night. It is part of the necessary routine to ask everyone on the train what he or she was doing at that time.'

'Quite so. At a quarter-past one, to the best of my belief, I was talking to the young American fellow – secretary to the dead man.'

'Ah! Were you in his compartment, or was he in yours?'

'I was in his.'

'That is the young man of the name of MacQueen?'

'Yes.'

'He was a friend or acquaintance of yours?'

'No, I never saw him before this journey. We fell into casual conversation yesterday and both became interested. I don't as a rule like Americans – haven't any use for 'em –'

Poirot smiled, remembering MacQueen's strictures on 'Britishers.'

'– But I liked this young fellow. He'd got hold of some tomfool idiotic ideas about the situation in India; that's the worst of Americans – they're so sentimental and idealistic. Well, he was interested in what I had to tell him. I've had nearly thirty years experience of the country. And I was interested in what he had to tell me about the financial situation in America. Then we got down to world politics in general. I was quite surprised to look at my watch and find it was a quarter to two.'

'That is the time you broke up this conversation?'

'Yes.'

'What did you do then?'

'Walked along to my own compartment and turned in.'

'Your bed was made up ready?'

'Yes.'

'That is the compartment – let me see – No. 15 – the one next but one to the end away from the dining-car?'

'Yes.'

'Where was the conductor when you went to your compartment?'

'Sitting at the end at a little table. As a matter of fact, MacQueen called him just as I went to my own compartment.'

'Why did he call him?'

'To make up his bed, I suppose. The compartment hadn't been made up for the night.'

'Now, Colonel Arbuthnot, I want you to think carefully. During the time you were talking to Mr MacQueen did anyone pass along the corridor outside the door?'

'A good many people, I should think. I wasn't paying attention.'

'Ah! but I am referring to – let us say the last hour and a half of your conversation. You got out at Vincovci, didn't you?'

'Yes, but only for about a minute. There was a blizzard on. The cold was something frightful. Made one quite thankful to get back to the fug, though as a rule I think the way these trains are overheated is something scandalous.'

M. Bouc sighed.

'It is very difficult to please everybody,' he said. 'The English, they open everything – then others, they come along and shut everything. It is very difficult.'

Neither Poirot nor Colonel Arbuthnot paid any attention to him.

'Now, Monsieur, cast your mind back,' said Poirot encouragingly. 'It was cold outside. You have returned to the train.

You sit down again, you smoke – perhaps a cigarette, perhaps a pipe –'

He paused for the fraction of a second.

'A pipe for me. MacQueen smoked cigarettes.'

'The train starts again. You smoke your pipe. You discuss the state of Europe – of the world. It is late now. Most people have retired for the night. Does anyone pass the door – think?'

Arbuthnot frowned in the effort of remembrance.

'Difficult to say,' he said. 'You see, I wasn't paying any attention.'

'But you have the soldier's observation for detail. You notice without noticing, so to speak.'

The Colonel thought again, but shook his head.

'I couldn't say. I don't remember anyone passing except the conductor. Wait a minute – and there was a woman, I think.'

'You saw her? Was she old – young?'

'Didn't see her. Wasn't looking that way. Just a rustle and a sort of smell of scent.'

'Scent? A *good* scent?'

'Well, rather fruity, if you know what I mean. I mean you'd smell it a hundred yards away. But mind you,' the Colonel went on hastily, 'this may have been earlier in the evening. You see, as you said just now, it was just one of those things you notice without noticing, so to speak. Some time that evening I said to myself, "Woman – scent – got it on pretty thick." But *when* it was I can't be sure, except that – why, yes, it must have been after Vincovci.'

'Why?'

'Because I remember – sniffing, you know – just when I was talking about the utter washout Stalin's Five Year Plan was turning out. I know the idea – woman – brought the idea of the position of women in Russia into my mind. And I know we hadn't got on to Russia until pretty near the end of our talk.'

'You can't pin it down more definitely than that?'

'N-no. It must have been roughly within the last half-hour.'

'It was after the train had stopped?'

The other nodded.

'Yes, I'm almost sure it was.'

'Well, we will pass from that. Have you ever been in America, Colonel Arbuthnot?'

'Never. Don't want to go.'

'Did you ever know a Colonel Armstrong?'

'Armstrong – Armstrong – I've known two or three Armstrongs. There was Tommy Armstrong in the 60th – you don't mean him? And Selby Armstrong – he was killed on the Somme.'

'I mean the Colonel Armstrong who married an American wife and whose only child was kidnapped and killed.'

'Ah, yes, I remember reading about that – shocking affair. I don't think I actually ever came across the fellow, though, of course, I knew of him. Toby Armstrong. Nice fellow. Everybody liked him. He had a very distinguished career. Got the V.C.'

'The man who was killed last night was the man responsible for the murder of Colonel Armstrong's child.'

Arbuthnot's face grew rather grim.

'Then in my opinion the swine deserved what he got. Though I would have preferred to have seen him properly hanged – or electrocuted, I suppose, over there.'

'In fact, Colonel Arbuthnot, you prefer law and order to private vengeance?'

'Well, you can't go about having blood feuds and stabbing each other like Corsicans or the Mafia,' said the Colonel. 'Say what you like, trial by jury is a sound system.'

Poirot looked at him thoughtfully for a minute or two.

'Yes,' he said. 'I am sure that would be your view. Well, Colonel Arbuthnot, I do not think there is anything more I have to ask you. There is nothing you yourself can recall last night that in any way struck you – or shall we say strikes you now looking back – as suspicious?'

Arbuthnot considered for a moment or two.

'No,' he said. 'Nothing at all. Unless –' he hesitated.

'But yes, continue, I pray of you.'

'Well, it's nothing really,' said the Colonel slowly. 'But you said *anything*.'

'Yes, yes. Go on.'

'Oh, it's nothing. A mere detail. But as I got back to my compartment I noticed that the door of the one beyond mine – the end one, you know –'

'Yes, No. 16.'

'Well, the door of it was not quite closed. And the fellow inside peered out in a furtive sort of way. Then he pulled the door to quickly. Of course, I know there's nothing in that – but it just struck me as a bit odd. I mean, it's quite usual to open a door and stick your head out if you want to see anything. But it was the furtive way he did it that caught my attention.'

'Ye-es,' said Poirot doubtfully.

'I told you there was nothing to it,' said Arbuthnot apologetically. 'But you know what it is – early hours of the morning – everything very still – the thing had a sinister look – like a detective story. All nonsense, really.'

He rose.

'Well, if you don't want me any more –'

'Thank you, Colonel Arbuthnot, there is nothing else.'

The soldier hesitated for a minute. His first natural distaste for being questioned by 'foreigners' had evaporated.

'About Miss Debenham,' he said rather awkwardly. 'You can take it from me that she's all right. She's a *pukka sahib*.'

Flushing a little, he withdrew.

'What,' asked Dr Constantine with interest, 'does a *pukka sahib* mean?'

'It means,' said Poirot, 'that Miss Debenham's father and brothers were at the same kind of school as Colonel Arbuthnot.'

'Oh!' said Dr Constantine, disappointed. 'Then it has nothing to do with the crime at all.'

'Exactly,' said Poirot.

He fell into a reverie, beating a light tattoo on the table. Then he looked up.

'Colonel Arbuthnot smokes a pipe,' he said. 'In the compartment of M. Ratchett I found a pipe-cleaner. M. Ratchett smoked only cigars.'

'You think –?'

'He is the only man so far who admits to smoking a pipe. And he knew of Colonel Armstrong – perhaps actually did know him though he won't admit it.'

'So you think it possible –'

Poirot shook his head violently.

'That is just it – it is *im*possible – quite impossible – that an honourable, slightly stupid, upright Englishman should stab an enemy twelve times with a knife! Do you not feel, my friends, how impossible it is?'

'That is the psychology,' said M. Bouc.

'And one must respect the psychology. This crime has a signature and it is certainly not the signature of Colonel Arbuthnot. But now to our next interview.'

This time M. Bouc did not mention the Italian. But he thought of him.

CHAPTER 9

THE EVIDENCE OF MR HARDMAN

The last of the first-class passengers to be interviewed – Mr Hardman – was the big flamboyant American who had shared a table with the Italian and the valet.

He wore a somewhat loud check suit, a pink shirt, a flashy tiepin, and was rolling something round his tongue as he entered the dining-car. He had a big, fleshy, coarse-featured face, with a good-humoured expression.

'Morning, gentlemen,' he said. 'What can I do for you?'

'You have heard of this murder, Mr – er – Hardman?'

'Sure.'

He shifted the chewing gum deftly.

'We are of necessity interviewing all the passengers on the train.'

'That's all right by me. Guess that's the only way to tackle the job.'

Poirot consulted the passport lying in front of him.

'You are Cyrus Bethman Hardman, United States subject, forty-one years of age, travelling salesman for typewriting ribbons?'

'O.K., that's me.'

'You are travelling from Stamboul to Paris?'

'That's so.'

'Reason?'

'Business.'

'Do you always travel first-class, Mr Hardman?'

'Yes, sir. The firm pays my travelling expenses.'

He winked.

'Now, Mr Hardman, we come to the events of last night.'

The American nodded.

'What can you tell us about the matter?'

'Exactly nothing at all.'

'Ah, that is a pity. Perhaps, Mr Hardman, you will tell us exactly what you did last night, from dinner onwards?'

For the first time the American did not seem ready with his reply. At last he said:

'Excuse me, gentlemen, but just who are you? Put me wise.'

'This is M. Bouc, a director of the Compagnie des Wagons Lits. This gentleman is the doctor who examined the body.'

'And you yourself?'

'I am Hercule Poirot. I am engaged by the company to investigate this matter.'

'I've heard of you,' said Mr Hardman. He reflected a minute or two longer. 'Guess I'd better come clean.'

'It will certainly be advisable for you to tell us all you know,' said Poirot dryly.

'You'd have said a mouthful if there was anything I *did* know. But I don't. I know nothing at all – just as I said. But I *ought* to know something. That's what makes me sore. I *ought* to.'

'Please explain, Mr Hardman.'

Mr Hardman sighed, removed the chewing gum, and dived into a pocket. At the same time his whole personality seemed to undergo a change. He became less of a stage character and more of a real person. The resonant nasal tones of his voice became modified.

'That passport's a bit of bluff,' he said. 'That's who I really am.'

Poirot scrutinized the card flipped across to him. M. Bouc peered over his shoulder.

Mr Cyrus B. Hardman
McNeil's Detective Agency,
New York.

Poirot knew the name. It was one of the best known and most reputable private detective agencies in New York.

'Now, Mr Hardman,' he said. 'Let us hear the meaning of this.'

'Sure. Things came about this way. I'd come over to Europe trailing a couple of crooks – nothing to do with this business. The chase ended in Stamboul. I wired the Chief and got his instructions to return, and I would have been making my tracks back to little old New York when I got this.'

He pushed across a letter.

The heading at the top was the Tokatlian Hotel.

Dear Sir, – You have been pointed out to me as an operative of the McNeil Detective Agency. Kindly report to my suite at four o'clock this afternoon.

It was signed 'S.E. Ratchett.'

'*Eh bien?*'

'I reported at the time stated and Mr Ratchett put me wise to the situation. He showed me a couple of letters he'd got.'

'He was alarmed?'

'Pretended not to be, but he was rattled all right. He put up a proposition to me. I was to travel by the same train as he did to Parrus and see that nobody got him. Well, gentlemen, I *did* travel by the same train and, in spite of me, somebody *did* get him. I certainly feel sore about it. It doesn't look any too good for me.'

'Did he give you any indication of the line you were to take?'

'Sure. He had it all taped out. It was his idea that I should travel in the compartment alongside his – well, that was blown upon straight away. The only place I could get was berth No. 16, and I had a bit of a job getting that. I guess the conductor likes to keep that compartment up his sleeve. But that's neither here nor there. When I looked all round the situation, it seemed to me that No. 16 was a pretty good strategic position. There was only the dining-car in front of the Stamboul sleeping-car, the door on to the platform at the front end was barred at night. The only way a thug could come was through the rear end door to the platform or along the train from the rear – in either case he'd have to pass right by my compartment.'

'You had no idea, I suppose, of the identity of the possible assailant.'

'Well, I knew what he looked like. Mr Ratchett described him to me.'

'What?'

All three men leaned forward eagerly.

Hardman went on:

'A small man, dark, with a womanish kind of voice – that's what the old man said. Said, too, that he didn't think it would be the first night out. More likely the second or third.'

'He knew something,' said M. Bouc.

'He certainly knew more than he told his secretary,' said Poirot thoughtfully. 'Did he tell you anything about this enemy of his? Did he, for instance, say *why* his life was threatened?'

'No, he was kinder reticent about that part of it. Just said the fellow was out for his blood and meant to get it.'

'A small man – dark – with a womanish voice,' said Poirot thoughtfully.

Then, fixing a sharp glance on Hardman, he said:

'You knew who he really was, of course?'

'Which, mister?'

'Ratchett. You recognized him?'

'I don't get you.'

'Ratchett was Cassetti, the Armstrong murderer.'

Mr Hardman gave way to a prolonged whistle.

'That certainly is some surprise!' he said. 'Yes, *sir*! No, I didn't recognize him. I was away out West when that case came on. I suppose I saw photos of him in the papers, but I wouldn't recognize my own mother when a press photographer had done with her. Well, I don't doubt that a few people had it in for Cassetti all right.'

'Do you know of anyone connected with the Armstrong case who answers to that description – small, dark, womanish voice?'

Hardman reflected a minute or two.

'It's hard to say. Pretty nearly everyone to do with that case is dead.'

'There was the girl who threw herself out of the window, remember.'

'Sure. That's a good point, that. She was a foreigner of some kind. Maybe she had some wop relations. But you've got to remember that there were other cases besides the Armstrong case. Cassetti had been running this kidnapping stunt some time. You can't concentrate on that only.'

'Ah, but we have reason to believe that this crime is connected with the Armstrong case.'

Mr Hardman cocked an inquiring eye. Poirot did not respond. The American shook his head.

'I can't call to mind anybody answering that description in the Armstrong case,' he said slowly. 'But of course I wasn't in it and didn't know much about it.'

'Well, continue your narrative, M. Hardman.'

'There's very little to tell. I got my sleep in the daytime and stayed awake on the watch at night. Nothing suspicious happened the first night. Last night was the same, as far as I was concerned. I had my door a little ajar and watched. No stranger passed.'

'You are sure of that, M. Hardman?'

'I'm plumb certain. Nobody got on that train from outside and nobody came along the train from the rear carriages. I'll take my oath on that.'

'Could you see the conductor from your position?'

'Sure. He sits on that little seat almost flush with my door.'

'Did he leave that seat at all after the train stopped at Vincovci?'

'That was the last station? Why, yes, he answered a couple of bells – that would be just after the train came to a halt for good. Then, after that, he went past me into the rear coach – was there about a quarter of an hour. There was a bell ringing like mad and he came back running. I stepped out into the corridor to see what it was all about – felt a mite nervous, you understand – but it was only the American dame. She was raising hell about something or other. I grinned. Then he went on to another compartment and came back and got a bottle of mineral water for someone. After that he settled down in his seat till he went up to the far end to make somebody's bed up. I don't think he stirred after that until about five o'clock this morning.'

'Did he doze off at all?'

'That I can't say. He may have done.'

Poirot nodded. Automatically his hands straightened the papers on the table. He picked up the official card once more.

'Be so good as just to initial this,' he said.

The other complied.

'There is no one, I suppose, who can confirm your story of your identity, M. Hardman?'

'On this train? Well, not exactly. Unless it might be young MacQueen. I know him well enough – seen him in his father's office in New York – but that's not to say he'll remember me from a crowd of other operatives. No, Mr Poirot, you'll have to wait and cable New York when the snow lets up. But it's O.K. I'm not telling the tale. Well, so long, gentlemen. Pleased to have met you, Mr Poirot.'

Poirot proffered his cigarette case.

'But perhaps you prefer a pipe?'

'Not me.'

He helped himself, then strode briskly off.

The three men looked at each other.

'You think he is genuine?' asked Dr Constantine.

'Yes, yes. I know the type. Besides, it is a story that would be very easily disproved.'

'He has given us a piece of very interesting evidence,' said M. Bouc.

'Yes, indeed.'

'A small man, dark, with a high-pitched voice,' said M. Bouc thoughtfully.

'A description which applies to no one on the train,' said Poirot.

CHAPTER 10

THE EVIDENCE OF THE ITALIAN

'And now,' said Poirot with a twinkle in his eye, 'we will delight the heart of M. Bouc and see the Italian.'

Antonio Foscarelli came into the dining-car with a swift, cat-like tread. His face beamed. It was a typical Italian face, sunny looking and swarthy.

He spoke French well and fluently, with only a slight accent.

'Your name is Antonio Foscarelli?'

'Yes, Monsieur.'

'You are, I see, a naturalized American subject?'

The American grinned.

'Yes, Monsieur. It is better for my business.'

'You are an agent for Ford motor cars?'

'Yes, you see –'

A voluble exposition followed. At the end of it, anything that the three men did not know about Foscarelli's business methods, his journeys, his income, and his opinion of the United States and most European countries seemed a negligible factor. This was not a man who had to have information dragged from him. It gushed out.

His good-natured childish face beamed with satisfaction as with a last eloquent gesture, he paused and wiped his forehead with a handkerchief.

'So you see,' he said, 'I do big business. I am up to date. I understand salesmanship!'

'You have been in the United States, then, for the last ten years on and off?'

'Yes, Monsieur. Ah! well do I remember the day I first took the boat – to go to America, so far away! My mother, my little sister –'

Poirot cut short the flood of reminiscence.

'During your sojourn in the United States did you ever come across the deceased?'

'Never. But I know the type. Oh, yes.' He snapped his fingers expressively. 'It is very respectable, very well dressed, but underneath it is all wrong. Out of my experience, I should say he was the big crook. I give you my opinion for what it is worth.'

'Your opinion is quite right,' said Poirot dryly. 'Ratchett was Cassetti, the kidnapper.'

'What did I tell you? I have learned to be very acute – to read the face. It is necessary. Only in America do they teach you the proper way to sell.'

'You remember the Armstrong case?

'I do not quite remember. The name, yes? It was a little girl – a baby – was it not?'

'Yes, a very tragic affair.'

The Italian seemed the first person to demur to this view.

'Ah, well, these things they happen,' he said philosophically, 'in a great civilization such as America –'

Poirot cut him short.

'Did you ever come across any members of the Armstrong family?'

'No, I do not think so. It is difficult to say. I will give you some figures. Last year alone I sold –'

'Monsieur, pray confine yourself to the point.'

The Italian's hands flung themselves out in a gesture of apology.

'A thousand pardons.'

'Tell me, if you please, your exact movements last night from dinner onwards.'

'With pleasure. I stay here as long as I can. It is more amusing. I talk to the American gentleman at my table. He sells typewriter ribbons. Then I go back to my compartment. It is empty. The miserable John Bull who shares it with me is away attending to his master. At last he comes back – very long face as usual. He will not talk – says yes and no. A miserable race, the English – not sympathetic. He sits in the corner, very stiff, reading a book. Then the conductor comes and makes our beds.'

'Nos. 4 and 5,' murmured Poirot.

'Exactly – the end compartment. Mine is the upper berth. I get up there. I smoke and read. The little Englishman has, I think, the toothache. He gets out a little bottle of stuff that smells very strong. He lies in bed and groans. Presently I sleep. Whenever I wake I hear him groaning.'

'Do you know if he left the carriage at all during the night?'

'I do not think so. That, I should hear. The light from the corridor – one wakes up automatically thinking it is the Customs examination at some frontier.'

'Did he ever speak of his master? Ever express any animus against him?'

'I tell you he did not speak. He was not sympathetic. A fish.'

'You smoke, you say – a pipe, cigarettes, cigars?'

'Cigarettes only.'

Poirot proffered him one which he accepted.

'Have you ever been in Chicago?' inquired M. Bouc.

'Oh, yes – a fine city – but I know best New York, Washington, Detroit. You have been to the States? No? You should go, it –'

Poirot pushed a sheet of paper across to him.

'If you will sign this, and put your permanent address, please.'

The Italian wrote with a flourish. Then he rose – his smile was as engaging as ever.

'That is all? You do not require me further? Good-day to you, Messieurs. I wish we could get out of the snow. I have an appointment in Milan –' He shook his head sadly. 'I shall lose the business.'

He departed.

Poirot looked at his friend.

'He has been a long time in America,' said M. Bouc, 'and he is an Italian, and Italians use the knife! And they are great liars! I do not like Italians.'

'*Ça se voit*,' said Poirot with a smile. 'Well, it may be that you are right, but I will point out to you, my friend, that there is absolutely no evidence against the man.'

'And what about the psychology? Do not Italians stab?'

'Assuredly,' said Poirot. 'Especially in the heat of a quarrel. But this – this is a different kind of crime. I have the little idea, my friend, that this is a crime very carefully planned and staged. It is a far-sighted, long-headed crime. It is not – how shall I express it? – a *Latin* crime. It is a crime that shows traces of a cool, resourceful, deliberate brain – I think an Anglo-Saxon brain.'

He picked up the last two passports.

'Let us now,' he said, 'see Miss Mary Debenham.'

CHAPTER 11

THE EVIDENCE OF MISS DEBENHAM

When Mary Debenham entered the dining-car she confirmed Poirot's previous estimate of her.

Very neatly dressed in a little black suit with a French grey shirt, the smooth waves of her dark head were neat and unruffled. Her manner was as calm and unruffled as her hair.

She sat down opposite Poirot and M. Bouc and looked at them inquiringly.

'Your name is Mary Hermione Debenham, and you are twenty-six years of age?' began Poirot.

'Yes.'

'English?'

'Yes.'

'Will you be so kind, Mademoiselle, as to write down your permanent address on this piece of paper?'

She complied. Her writing was clear and legible.

'And now, Mademoiselle, what have you to tell us of the affair last night?'

'I am afraid I have nothing to tell you. I went to bed and slept.'

'Does it distress you very much, Mademoiselle, that a crime has been committed on this train?'

The question was clearly unexpected. Her grey eyes widened a little.

'I don't quite understand you.'

'It was a perfectly simple question that I asked you, Mademoiselle. I will repeat it. Are you very much distressed that a crime should have been committed on this train?'

'I have not really thought about it from that point of view. No, I cannot say that I am at all distressed.'

'A crime – it is all in the day's work to you, eh?'

'It is naturally an unpleasant thing to have happen,' said Mary Debenham quietly.

'You are very Anglo-Saxon. Mademoiselle. *Vous n'éprouvez pas d'émotion.*'

She smiled a little.

'I am afraid I cannot have hysterics to prove my sensibility. After all, people die every day.'

'They die, yes. But murder is a little more rare.'

'Oh, certainly.'

'You were not acquainted with the dead man?'

'I saw him for the first time when lunching here yesterday.'

'And how did he strike you?'

'I hardly noticed him.'

'He did not strike you as an evil personality.'

She shrugged her shoulders slightly.

'Really, I cannot say I thought about it.'

Poirot looked at her keenly.

'You are, I think, a little bit contemptuous of the way I prosecute my inquiries,' he said with a twinkle. 'Not so, you think, would an English inquiry be conducted. There everything would be cut and dried – it would be all kept to the facts – a well-ordered business. But I, Mademoiselle, have my little originalities. I look first at my witness, I sum up his or her character, and I frame my questions accordingly. Just a little minute ago I am asking questions of a gentleman who wants to tell me all his ideas on every subject. Well, him I keep strictly to the point. I want him to answer yes or no, this or that. And then you come. I see at once that you will be orderly and methodical. You will confine yourself to the matter in hand. Your answers will be brief and to the point. And because, Mademoiselle, human nature is perverse, I ask of you quite different questions. I ask what you *feel*, what you *thought*. It does not please you this method?'

'If you will forgive my saying so, it seems somewhat of a waste of time. Whether or not I liked Mr Ratchett's face does not seem likely to be helpful in finding out who killed him.'

'Do you know who the man Ratchett really was, Mademoiselle?'

She nodded.

'Mrs Hubbard has been telling everyone.'

'And what do you think of the Armstrong affair?'

'It was quite abominable,' said the girl crisply.

Poirot looked at her thoughtfully.

'You are travelling from Baghdad, I believe, Miss Debenham?'

'Yes.'

'To London?'

'Yes.'

'What have you been doing in Baghdad?'

'I have been acting as governess to two children.'

'Are you returning to your post after your holiday?'

'I am not sure.'

'Why is that?'

'Baghdad is rather out of things. I think I should prefer a post in London if I can hear of a suitable one.'

'I see. I thought, perhaps, you might be going to be married.'

Miss Debenham did not reply. She raised her eyes and looked Poirot full in the face. The glance said plainly, 'You are impertinent.'

'What is your opinion of the lady who shares your compartment – Miss Ohlsson?'

'She seems a pleasant, simple creature.'

'What colour is her dressing-gown?'

Mary Debenham stared.

'A kind of brownish colour – natural wool.'

'Ah! I may mention without indiscretion, I hope, that I noticed the colour of your dressing-gown on the way from Aleppo to Stamboul. A pale mauve, I believe.'

'Yes, that is right.'

'Have you any other dressing-gown, Mademoiselle? A scarlet dressing-gown, for example?'

'No, that is not mine.'

Poirot leaned forward. He was like a cat pouncing on a mouse.

'Whose, then?'

The girl drew back a little, startled.

'I don't know. What do you mean?'

'You do not say, "No, I have no such thing." You say, "That is not mine" – meaning that such a thing *does* belong to someone else.'

She nodded.

'Somebody else on this train?'

'Yes.'

'Whose is it?'

'I told you just now. I don't know. I woke up this morning about five o'clock with the feeling that the train had been standing still for a long time. I opened the door and looked out into the corridor, thinking we might be at a station. I saw someone in a scarlet kimono some way down the corridor.'

'And you don't know who it was? Was she fair or dark or grey-haired?'

'I can't say. She had on a shingle cap and I only saw the back of her head.'

'And in build?'

'Tallish and slim, I should judge, but it's difficult to say. The kimono was embroidered with dragons.'

'Yes, yes that is right, dragons.'

He was silent a minute. He murmured to himself:

'I cannot understand. I cannot understand. None of this makes sense.'

Then, looking up, he said:

'I need not keep you further, Mademoiselle.'

'Oh!' she seemed rather taken aback, but rose promptly. In the doorway, however, she hesitated a minute and then came back.

'The Swedish lady – Miss Ohlsson, is it? – seems rather worried. She says you told her she was the last person to see this man alive. She thinks, I believe, that you suspect her on that account. Can't I tell her that she has made a mistake? Really, you know, she is the kind of creature who wouldn't hurt a fly.'

She smiled a little as she spoke.

'What time was it that she went to fetch the aspirin from Mrs Hubbard?'

'Just after half-past ten.'

'She was away – how long?'

'About five minutes.'

'Did she leave the compartment again during the night?'

'No.'

Poirot turned to the doctor.

'Could Ratchett have been killed as early as that?'

The doctor shook his head.

'Then I think you can reassure your friend, Mademoiselle.'

'Thank you.' She smiled suddenly at him, a smile that invited sympathy. 'She's like a sheep, you know. She gets anxious and bleats.'

She turned and went out.

CHAPTER 12

THE EVIDENCE OF THE GERMAN LADY'S-MAID

M. Bouc was looking at his friend curiously.

'I do not quite understand you, *mon vieux*. You were trying to do – what?'

'I was searching for a flaw, my friend.'

'A flaw?'

'Yes – in the armour of a young lady's self-possession. I wished to shake her *sang-froid*. Did I succeed? I do not know. But I know this – she did not expect me to tackle the matter as I did.'

'You suspect her,' said M. Bouc slowly. 'But why? She seems a very charming young lady – the last person in the world to be mixed up in a crime of this kind.'

'I agree,' said Constantine. 'She is cold. She has not emotions. She would not stab a man; she would sue him in the law courts.'

Poirot sighed 'You must, both of you, get rid of your obsession that this is an unpremeditated and sudden crime. As for the reason why I suspect Miss Debenham, there are two. One is because of something that I overheard, and that you do not as yet know.'

He retailed to them the curious interchange of phrases he had overheard on the journey from Aleppo.

'That is curious, certainly,' said M. Bouc when he had finished. 'It needs explaining. If it means what you suspect it means, then they are both of them in it together – she and the stiff Englishman.'

Poirot nodded.

'And that is just what is not borne out by the facts,' he said. 'See you, if they were both in this together, what should we expect to find – that each of them would provide an alibi for the other. Is not that so? But no – that does not happen. Miss Debenham's alibi is provided by a Swedish woman whom she has never seen before, and Colonel Arbuthnot's alibi is vouched for by MacQueen, the dead man's secretary. No, that solution of the puzzle is too easy.'

'You said there was another reason for your suspicions of her,' M. Bouc reminded him.

Poirot smiled.

'Ah! but that is only psychological. I ask myself, is it possible for Miss Debenham to have planned this crime? Behind this business, I am convinced, there is a cool, intelligent, resourceful brain. Miss Debenham answers to that description.'

M. Bouc shook his head.

'I think you are wrong, my friend. I do not see that young English girl as a criminal.'

'Ah, well,' said Poirot, picking up the last passport, 'to the final name on our list. Hildegarde Schmidt, lady's-maid.'

Summoned by the attendant, Hildegarde Schmidt came into the restaurant-car and stood waiting respectfully.

Poirot motioned her to sit down.

She did so, folding her hands and waiting placidly till he questioned her. She seemed a placid creature altogether – eminently respectable – perhaps not over intelligent.

Poirot's methods with Hildegarde Schmidt were a complete contrast to his handling of Mary Debenham.

He was at his kindest and most genial, setting the woman at her ease. Then, having got her to write down her name and address, he slid gently into his questions.

The interview took place in German.

'We want to know as much as possible about what happened last night,' he said. 'We know that you cannot give us much information bearing on the crime itself, but you may have seen or heard something that, while conveying nothing to you, may be valuable to us. You understand?'

She did not seem to. Her broad, kindly face remained set in its expression of placid stupidity as she answered:

'I do not know anything, Monsieur.'

'Well, for instance, you know that your mistress sent for you last night?'

'That, yes.'

'Do you remember the time?'

'I do not, Monsieur. I was asleep, you see, when the attendant came and told me.'

'Yes, yes. Was it usual for you to be sent for in this way?'

'It was not unusual, Monsieur. The gracious lady often required attention at night. She did not sleep well.'

'*Eh bien*, then, you received the summons and you got up. Did you put on a dressing-gown?'

'No, Monsieur, I put on a few clothes. I would not like to go in to her Excellency in my dressing-gown.'

'And yet it is a very nice dressing-gown – scarlet, is it not?'

She stared at him.

'It is a dark-blue flannel dressing-gown, Monsieur.'

'Ah! continue. A little pleasantry on my part, that is all. So you went along to Madame la Princesse. And what did you do when you got there?'

'I gave her massage, Monsieur, and then I read aloud. I do not read aloud very well, but her Excellency says that is all the better. So it sends her better to sleep. When she became sleepy, Monsieur, she told me to go, so I closed the book and I returned to my own compartment.'

'Do you know what time that was?'

'No, Monsieur.'

'Well, how long had you been with Madame la Princesse?'

'About half an hour, Monsieur.'

'Good, continue.'

'First, I fetched her Excellency an extra rug from my compartment. It was very cold in spite of the heating. I arranged the rug over her and she wished me good-night. I poured her out some mineral water. Then I turned out the light and left her.'

'And then?'

'There is nothing more, Monsieur. I returned to my carriage and went to sleep.'

'And you met no one in the corridor?'

'No, Monsieur.'

'You did not, for instance, see a lady in a scarlet kimono with dragons on it?'

Her mild eyes bulged at him.

'No, indeed, Monsieur. There was nobody about except the attendant. Everyone was asleep.'

'But you did see the conductor?'

'Yes, Monsieur.'

'What was he doing?'

'He came out of one of the compartments, Monsieur.'

'What?' M. Bouc leaned forward. 'Which one?'

Hildegarde Schmidt looked frightened again and Poirot cast a reproachful glance at his friend.

'Naturally,' he said. 'The conductor often has to answer bells at night. Do you remember which compartment it was?'

'It was about the middle of the coach, Monsieur. Two or three doors from Madame la Princesse.'

'Ah! tell us, if you please, exactly where this was and what happened.'

'He nearly ran into me, Monsieur. It was when I was returning from my compartment to that of the Princess with the rug.'

'And he came out of a compartment and almost collided with you? In which direction was he going?'

'Towards me, Monsieur. He apologized and passed on down the corridor towards the dining-car. A bell began ringing, but I do not think he answered it.'

She paused and then said:

'I do not understand. How is it –?'

Poirot spoke reassuringly.

'It is just a question of times,' he said. 'All a matter of routine. This poor conductor, he seems to have had a busy night – first waking you and then answering bells.'

'It was not the same conductor who woke me, Monsieur. It was another one.'

'Ah, another one! Had you seen him before?'

'No. Monsieur.'

'Ah! Do you think you would recognize him if you saw him?'

'I think so, Monsieur.'

Poirot murmured something in M. Bouc's ear. The latter got up and went to the door to give an order.

Poirot was continuing his questions in an easy friendly manner.

'Have you ever been to America, Frau Schmidt?'

'Never, Monsieur. It must be a fine country.'

'You have heard, perhaps, of who this man who was killed really was – that he was responsible for the death of a little child.'

'Yes, I have heard, Monsieur. It was abominable – wicked. The good God should not allow such things. We are not so wicked as that in Germany.'

Tears had come into the woman's eyes. Her strong motherly soul was moved.

'It was an abominable crime,' said Poirot gravely.

He drew a scrap of cambric from his pocket and handed it to her.

'Is this your handkerchief, Frau Schmidt?'

There was a moment's silence as the woman examined it. She looked up after a minute. The colour had mounted a little in her face.

'Ah! no, indeed. It is not mine, Monsieur.'

'It has the initial H, you see. That is why I thought it was yours.'

'Ah! Monsieur, it is a lady's handkerchief, that. A very expensive handkerchief. Embroidered by hand. It comes from Paris, I should say.'

'It is not yours and you do not know whose it is?'

'I? Oh, no, Monsieur.'

Of the three listening, only Poirot caught the nuance of hesitation in the reply.

M. Bouc whispered in his ear. Poirot nodded and said to the woman:

'The three sleeping-car attendants are coming in. Will you be so kind as to tell me which is the one you met last night as you were going with the rug to the Princess?'

The three men entered. Pierre Michel, the big blond conductor of the Athens-Paris coach, and the stout burly conductor of the Bucharest one.

Hildegarde Schmidt looked at them and immediately shook her head.

'No, Monsieur,' she said. 'None of these is the man I saw last night.'

'But these are the only conductors on the train. You must be mistaken.'

'I am quite sure, Monsieur. These are all tall, big men. The one I saw was small and dark. He had a little moustache. His voice when he said "*Pardon*" was weak like a woman's. Indeed, I remember him very well, Monsieur.'

CHAPTER 13

SUMMARY OF THE PASSENGERS' EVIDENCE

'A small dark man with a womanish voice,' said M. Bouc.

The three conductors and Hildegarde Schmidt had been dismissed.

'But I understand nothing – but nothing of all this! The enemy that this Ratchett spoke of, he was then on the train after all? But where is he now? How can he have vanished into thin air? My head, it whirls. Say something, then, my friend, I implore you. Show me how the impossible can be possible!'

'It is a good phrase that,' said Poirot. 'The impossible cannot have happened, therefore the impossible must be possible in spite of appearances.'

'Explain to me then, quickly, what actually happened on the train last night.'

'I am not a magician, *mon cher*. I am, like you, a very puzzled man. This affair advances in a very strange manner.'

'It does not advance at all. It stays where it was.'

Poirot shook his head.

'No, that is not true. We are more advanced. We know certain things. We have heard the evidence of the passengers.'

'And what has that told us? Nothing at all.'

'I would not say that, my friend.'

'I exaggerate, perhaps. The American, Hardman, and the German maid – yes, they have added something to our knowledge. That is to say, they have made the whole business more unintelligible than it was.'

'No, no, no,' said Poirot soothingly.

M. Bouc turned upon him.

'Speak, then, let us hear the wisdom of Hercule Poirot.'

'Did I not tell you that I was, like you, a very puzzled man? But at least we can face our problem. We can arrange such facts as we have with order and method.'

'Pray continue, Monsieur,' said Dr Constantine.

Poirot cleared his throat and straightened a piece of blotting-paper.

'Let us review the case as it stands at this moment. First, there are certain indisputable facts. This man Ratchett, or Cassetti, was stabbed in twelve places and died last night. That is fact one.'

'I grant it to you – I grant it, *mon vieux*,' said M. Bouc with a gesture of irony.

Hercule Poirot was not at all put out. He continued calmly.

'I will pass over for the moment certain rather peculiar appearances which Dr Constantine and I have already discussed together. I will come to them presently. The next fact of importance, to my mind, is the *time* of the crime.'

'That, again, is one of the few things we do know,' said M.

Bouc. 'The crime was committed at a quarter-past one this morning. Everything goes to show that that was so.'

'Not *everything*. You exaggerate. There is, certainly, a fair amount of evidence to support that view.'

'I am glad you admit that at least.'

Poirot went on calmly, unperturbed by the interruption.

'We have before us three possibilities:

'One: That the crime was committed, as you say, at a quarter-past one. This is supported by the evidence of the German woman, Hildegarde Schmidt. It agrees with the evidence of Dr Constantine.

'Possibility two: The crime was committed later and the evidence of the watch was deliberately faked.

'Possibility three: The crime was committed earlier and the evidence faked for the same reason as above.

'Now, if we accept possibility one as the most likely to have occurred and the one supported by most evidence, we must also accept certain facts arising from it. To begin with, if the crime was committed at a quarter-past one, the murderer cannot have left the train, and the question arises: Where is he? And *who* is he?

'To begin with, let us examine the evidence carefully. We first hear of the existence of this man – the small dark man with a womanish voice – from the man Hardman. He says that Ratchett told him of this person and employed him to watch out for the man. There is no *evidence* to support this – we have only Hardman's word for it. Let us next examine the question: Is Hardman the person he pretends to be – an operative of a New York Detective Agency?

'What to my mind is so interesting in this case is that we have none of the facilities afforded to the police. We cannot investigate the bona fides of any of these people. We have to rely solely on deduction. That, to me, makes the matter very much more interesting. There is no routine work. It is a matter of the intellect. I ask myself, "Can we accept Hardman's account of himself?" I make my decision and I answer, "Yes." I am of the opinion that we *can* accept Hardman's account of himself.'

'You rely on the intuition – what the Americans call the hunch?' said Dr Constantine.

'Not at all. I regard the probabilities. Hardman is travelling with a false passport – that will at once make him an object of suspicion. The first thing that the police will do when they do arrive upon the scene is to detain Hardman and cable as to whether his account of himself is true. In the case of many of the passengers, to establish their bona fides will be difficult; in most cases it will probably not be attempted, especially since there seems nothing in the way of suspicion attaching to them. But in Hardman's case it is simple. Either he is the person he represents himself to be or he is not. Therefore I say that all will prove to be in order.'

'You acquit him of suspicion?'

'Not at all. You misunderstand me. For all I know, any American detective might have his own private reasons for wishing to murder Ratchett. No, what I am saying is that I think we *can* accept Hardman's own account of *himself*. This story, then, that he tells of Ratchett's seeking him out and employing him, is not unlikely and is most probably, though not of course certainly, true. If we are going to accept it as true, we must see if there is any confirmation of it. We find it in rather an unlikely place – in the evidence of Hildegarde Schmidt. Her description of the man she saw in Wagon Lit uniform tallies exactly. Is there any further confirmation of these two stories? There is. There is the button found in her compartment by Mrs Hubbard. And there is also another corroborating statement which you may not have noticed.'

'What is that?'

'The fact that both Colonel Arbuthnot and Hector MacQueen mention that the conductor passed their carriage. They attached no importance to the fact, but Messieurs, *Pierre Michel has declared that he did not leave his seat except on certain specified occasions*, none of which would take him down to the far end of the coach past the compartment in which Arbuthnot and MacQueen were sitting.

'Therefore this story, the story of a small dark man with a womanish voice dressed in Wagon Lit uniform, rests on the testimony – direct or indirect – of four witnesses.'

'One small point,' said Dr Constantine. 'If Hildegarde Schmidt's story is true, how is it that the real conductor did not mention having seen her when he came to answer Mrs Hubbard's bell?'

'That is explained, I think. When he arrived to answer Mrs

Hubbard, the maid was in with her mistress. When she finally returned to her own compartment, the conductor was in with Mrs Hubbard.'

M. Bouc had been waiting with difficulty until they had finished.

'Yes, yes, my friend,' he said impatiently to Poirot. 'But whilst I admire your caution, your method of advancing a step at a time, I submit that you have not yet touched the point at issue. We are all agreed that this person exists. The point is – *where did he go*?'

Poirot shook his head reprovingly.

'You are in error. You are inclined to put the cart before the horse. Before I ask myself, "*Where did this man vanish to*?" I ask myself, "*Did such a man really exist*?" Because, you see, if the man were an invention – a fabrication – how much easier to make him disappear! So I try to establish first that there really *is* such a flesh and blood person.'

'And having arrived at the fact that there is – *eh bien* – where is he now?'

'There are only two answers to that, *mon cher*. Either he is still hidden on the train in a place of such extraordinary ingenuity that we cannot even think of it, or else he is, as one might say, *two persons*. That is, he is both himself – the man feared by M. Ratchett – and a passenger on the train so well disguised that M. Ratchett did not recognize him.'

'It is an idea, that,' said M. Bouc, his face lighting up. Then it clouded over again. 'But there is one objection –'

Poirot took the words out of his mouth.

'The height of the man. It is that you would say? With the exception of M. Ratchett's valet, all the passengers are big men – the Italian, Colonel Arbuthnot, Hector MacQueen, Count Andrenyi. Well, that leaves us the valet – not a very likely supposition. But there is another possibility. Remember the "womanish" voice. That gives us a choice of alternatives. The man may be disguised as a woman, or, alternatively, he may actually *be* a woman. A tall woman dressed in men's clothes would look small.'

'But surely Ratchett would have known –'

'Perhaps he *did* know. Perhaps, already this woman had attempted his life wearing men's clothes the better to accomplish her purpose. Ratchett may have guessed that she would use the same trick again, so he tells Hardman to look for a man. But he mentions, however, a womanish voice.'

'It is a possibility,' said M. Bouc. 'But –'

'Listen, my friend, I think that I should now tell you of certain inconsistencies noticed by Dr Constantine.'

He retailed at length the conclusions that he and the doctor had arrived at together from the nature of the dead man's wounds. M. Bouc groaned and held his head again.

'I know,' said Poirot sympathetically. 'I know exactly how you feel. The head spins, does it not?'

'The whole thing is a fantasy,' cried M. Bouc.

'Exactly. It is absurd – improbable – it cannot be. So I myself have said. And yet, my friend, *there it is*! One cannot escape from the facts.'

'It is madness!'

'Is it not? It is so mad, my friend, that sometimes I am haunted by the sensation that really it must be very simple . . .

'But that is only one of my "little ideas" . . .'

'Two murderers,' groaned M. Bouc. 'And on the Orient Express.'

The thought almost made him weep.

'And now let us make the fantasy more fantastic,' said Poirot cheerfully. 'Last night on the train there are two mysterious strangers. There is the Wagon Lit attendant answering to the description given us by M. Hardman, and seen by Hildegarde Schmidt, Colonel Arbuthnot and M. MacQueen. There is also a woman in a red kimono – a tall, slim woman – seen by Pierre Michel, by Miss Debenham, by M. MacQueen and by myself – and smelt, I may say, by Colonel Arbuthnot! Who was she? No one on the train admits to having a scarlet kimono. She, too, has vanished. Was she one and the same with the spurious Wagon Lit attendant? Or was she some quite distinct personality? Where are they, these two? And, incidentally, where is the Wagon Lit uniform and the scarlet kimono?'

'Ah! that is something definite.' M. Bouc sprang up eagerly. 'We must search all the passengers' luggage. Yes, that will be something.'

Poirot rose also.

'I will make a prophecy,' he said.

'You know where they are?'

'I have a little idea.'

'Where, then?'

'You will find the scarlet kimono in the baggage of one of the men and you will find the uniform of the Wagon Lit conductor in the baggage of Hildegarde Schmidt.'

'Hildegarde Schmidt? You think –'

'Not what you are thinking. I will put it like this. If Hildegarde Schmidt is guilty, the uniform *might* be found in her baggage – but if she is innocent it *certainly* will be.'

'But how –' began M. Bouc and stopped.

'What is this noise that approaches?' he cried. 'It resembles a locomotive in motion.'

The noise drew nearer. It consisted of shrill cries and protests in a woman's voice. The door at the end of the dining-car flew open. Mrs Hubbard burst in.

'It's too horrible,' she cried. 'It's just too horrible. In my sponge-bag. My sponge-bag. A great knife – all over blood.'

And, suddenly toppling forward, she fainted heavily on M. Bouc's shoulder.

CHAPTER 14

THE EVIDENCE OF THE WEAPON

With more vigour than chivalry, M. Bouc deposited the fainting lady with her head on the table. Dr Constantine yelled for one of the restaurant attendants, who came at a run.

'Keep her head so,' said the doctor. 'If she revives give her a little cognac. You understand?'

Then he hurried off after the other two. His interest lay wholly in the crime – swooning middle-aged ladies did not interest him at all.

It is possible that Mrs Hubbard revived rather quicker with these methods than she might otherwise have done. A few minutes later she was sitting up, sipping cognac from a glass proffered by the attendant, and talking once more.

'I just can't say how terrible it was. I don't suppose anybody on this train can understand my feelings. I've always been vurry, vurry sensitive ever since a child. The mere sight of blood – ugh – why even now I come over queer when I think about it.'

The attendant proffered the glass again.

'*Encore un peu, Madame.*'

'D'you think I'd better? I'm a lifelong teetotaller. I just never touch spirits or wine at any time. All my family are abstainers. Still perhaps as this is only medical –'

She sipped once more.

In the meantime Poirot and M. Bouc, closely followed by Dr Constantine, had hurried out of the restaurant-car and along the corridor of the Stamboul coach towards Mrs Hubbard's compartment.

Every traveller on the train seemed to be congregated outside the door. The conductor, a harrassed look on his face, was keeping them back.

'*Mais il n'y a rien à voir*,' he said, and repeated the sentiment in several other languages.

'Let me pass, if you please,' said M. Bouc.

Squeezing his rotundity past the obstructing passengers, he entered the compartment, Poirot close behind him.

'I am glad you have come Monsieur,' said the conductor with a sigh of relief. 'Everyone has been trying to enter. The American lady – such screams as she gave – *ma foi*! I thought she too had been murdered! I came at a run and there she was screaming like a mad woman, and she cried out that she must fetch you and she departed, screeching at the top of her voice and telling everybody whose carriage she passed what had occurred.'

He added, with a gesture of the hand:

'*It* is in there, Monsieur. I have not touched it.'

Hanging on the handle of the door that gave access to the next compartment was a large-size checked rubber sponge-bag. Below it on the floor, just where it had fallen from Mrs Hubbard's hand, was a straight-bladed dagger – a cheap affair, sham Oriental, with an embossed hilt and a tapering blade. The blade was stained with patches of what looked like rust.

Poirot picked it up delicately.

'Yes,' he murmured. 'There is no mistake. Here is our missing weapon all right – eh, docteur?'

The doctor examined it.

'You need not be so careful,' said Poirot. 'There will be no fingerprints on it save those of Mrs Hubbard.'

Constantine's examination did not take long.

'It is the weapon all right,' he said. 'It would account for any of the wounds.'

'I implore you, my friend, do not say that.'

The doctor looked astonished.

'Already we are heavily overburdened by coincidence. Two people decide to stab M. Ratchett last night. It is too much of a good thing that each of them should select an identical weapon.'

'As to that, the coincidence is not, perhaps, so great as it seems,' said the doctor. 'Thousands of these sham Eastern daggers are made and shipped to the bazaars of Constantinople.'

'You console me a little, but only a little,' said Poirot. He looked thoughtfully at the door in front of him, then, lifting off the sponge-bag, he tried the handle. The door did not budge. About a foot above the handle was the door bolt, Poirot drew it back and tried again, but still the door remained fast.

'We locked it from the other side, you remember,' said the doctor.

'That is true,' said Poirot absently. He seemed to be thinking about something else. His brow was furrowed as though in perplexity.

'It agrees, does it not?' said M. Bouc. 'The man passes through this carriage. As he shuts the communicating door behind him he feels the sponge-bag. A thought comes to him and he quickly slips the bloodstained knife inside. Then, all unwitting that he has awakened Mrs Hubbard, he slips out through the other door into the corridor.'

'As you say,' murmured Poirot. 'That is how it must have happened.'

But the puzzled look did not leave his face.

'But what is it?' demanded M. Bouc. 'There is something, is there not, that does not satisfy you?'

Poirot darted a quick look at him.

'The same point does not strike you? No, evidently not. Well, it is a small matter.'

The conductor looked into the carriage.

'The American lady is coming back.'

Dr Constantine looked rather guilty. He had, he felt, treated Mrs Hubbard rather cavalierly. But she had no reproaches for him. Her energies were concentrated on another matter.

'I'm just going to say one thing right out,' she said breathlessly as she arrived in the doorway. 'I'm not going on any longer in this compartment! Why, I wouldn't sleep in it tonight if you paid me a million dollars.'

'But, Madame –'

'I know what you are going to say, and I'm telling you right now that I won't do any such thing! Why, I'd rather sit up all night in the corridor.'

She began to cry.

'Oh! if my daughter could only know – if she could see me now, why –'

Poirot interrupted firmly.

'You misunderstand, Madame. Your demand is most reasonable. Your baggage shall be changed at once to another compartment.'

Mrs Hubbard lowered her handkerchief.

'Is that so? Oh, I feel better right away. But surely it's all full up, unless one of the gentlemen –'

M. Bouc spoke.

'Your baggage, Madame, shall be moved out of this coach altogether. You shall have a compartment in the next coach which was put on at Belgrade.'

'Why, that's splendid. I'm not an out of the way nervous woman, but to sleep in that compartment next door to a dead man –' She shivered. 'It would drive me plumb crazy.'

'Michel,' called M. Bouc. 'Move this baggage into a vacant compartment in the Athens-Paris coach.'

'Yes, Monsieur – the same one as this – the No. 3?'

'No,' said Poirot before his friend could reply. 'I think it would be better for Madame to have a different number altogether. The No. 12, for instance.'

'*Bien*, Monsieur.'

The conductor seized the luggage. Mrs Hubbard turned gratefully to Poirot.

'That's vurry kind and delicate of you. I appreciate it, I assure you.'

'Do not mention it, Madame. We will come with you and see you comfortably installed.'

Mrs Hubbard was escorted by the three men to her new home. She looked round her happily.

'This is fine.'

'It suits you, Madame? It is, you see, exactly like the compartment you have left.'

'That's so – only it faces the other way. But that doesn't matter, for these trains go first one way and then the other. I said to my daughter, "I want a carriage facing the engine," and she said, "Why, Momma, that'll be no good to you, for if you go to sleep one way, when you wake up the train's going the other." And it was quite true what she said. Why, last evening we went into Belgrade one way and out the other.'

'At any rate, Madame, you are quite happy and contented now?'

'Well, no, I wouldn't say that. Here we are stuck in a snowdrift and nobody doing anything about it, and my boat sailing the day after tomorrow.'

'Madame,' said M. Bouc, 'we are all in the same case – every one of us.'

'Well, that's true,' admitted Mrs Hubbard. 'But nobody else has had a murderer walking right through their compartment in the middle of the night.'

'What still puzzles me, Madame,' said Poirot, 'is how the man got into your compartment if the communicating door was bolted as you say. You are sure that it *was* bolted?'

'Why, the Swedish lady tried it before my eyes.'

'Let us just reconstruct that little scene. You were lying in your bunk – so – and you could not see for yourself, you say?'

'No, because of the sponge-bag. Oh, my, I shall have to get a new sponge-bag. It makes me feel sick in my stomach to look at this one.'

Poirot picked up the sponge-bag and hung it on the handle of the communicating door into the next carriage.

'*Précisément* – I see,' he said. 'The bolt is just underneath the handle – the sponge-bag masks it. You could not see from where you were lying whether the bolt were turned or not.'

'Why, that's just what I've been telling you!'

'And the Swedish lady, Miss Ohlsson, stood so, between you and the door. She tried it and told you it was bolted.'

'That's so.'

'All the same, Madame, she may have made an error. You see what I mean.' Poirot seemed anxious to explain. 'The bolt is just a projection of metal – so. Turned to the right the door is locked, left straight, it is not. Possibly she merely tried the door, and as it was locked on the other side she may have assumed that it was locked on your side.'

'Well I guess that would be rather stupid of her.'

'Madame, the most kind, the most amiable are not always the cleverest.'

'That's so, of course.'

'By the way, Madame, did you travel out to Smyrna this way?'

'No. I sailed right to Stamboul, and a friend of my daughter's – Mr Johnson (a perfectly lovely man; I'd like to have you know him) – met me and showed me all round Stamboul, which I found a very disappointing city – all tumbling down. And as for those mosques and putting on those great shuffling things over your shoes – where was I?'

'You were saying that Mr Johnson met you.'

'That's so, and he saw me on board a French Messagerie boat for Smyrna, and my daughter's husband was waiting right on the quay. What he'll say when he hears about all this! My daughter said this would be just the safest, easiest way imaginable. "You just sit in your carriage," she said, "and you get right to Parrus and there the American Express will meet you." And, oh dear, what am I to do about cancelling my steamship passage? I ought to let them know. I can't possibly make it now. This is just too terrible –'

Mrs Hubbard showed signs of tears once more.

Poirot, who had been fidgeting slightly, seized his opportunity.

'You have had a shock, Madame. The restaurant attendant shall be instructed to bring you along some tea and some biscuits.'

'I don't know that I'm so set on tea,' said Mrs Hubbard tearfully. 'That's more an English habit.'

'Coffee, then, Madame. You need some stimulant.'

'That cognac's made my head feel mighty funny. I think I would like some coffee.'

'Excellent. You must revive your forces.'

'My, what a funny expression.'

'But first, Madame, a little matter of routine. You permit that I make a search of your baggage?'

'Whatever for?'

'We are about to commence a search of all the passengers' luggage. I do not want to remind you of an unpleasant experience, but your sponge-bag – remember.'

'Mercy! Perhaps you'd better! I just couldn't bear to get any more surprises of that kind.'

The examination was quickly over. Mrs Hubbard was travelling with the minimum of luggage – a hat-box, a cheap suitcase, and a well-burdened travelling bag. The contents of all three were simple and straightforward, and the examination would not have taken more than a couple of minutes had not Mrs Hubbard delayed matters by insisting on due attention being paid to photographs of 'My daughter' and two rather ugly children – 'My daughter's children. Aren't they cunning?'

CHAPTER 15

THE EVIDENCE OF THE PASSENGERS' LUGGAGE

Having delivered himself of various polite insincerities, and having told Mrs Hubbard that he would order coffee to be brought to her, Poirot was able to take his leave accompanied by his two friends.

'Well, we have made a start and drawn a blank,' observed M. Bouc. 'Whom shall we tackle next?'

'It would be simplest, I think, just to proceed along the train carriage by carriage. That means that we start with No. 16 – the amiable M. Hardman.'

Mr Hardman, who was smoking a cigar, welcomed them affably.

'Come right in, gentlemen – that is, if it's humanly possible. It's just a mite cramped in here for a party.'

M. Bouc explained the object of their visit, and the big detective nodded comprehendingly.

'That's O.K. To tell the truth, I've been wondering you didn't get down to it sooner. Here are my keys, gentlemen and if you like to search my pockets too, why, you're welcome. Shall I reach the grips down for you?'

'The conductor will do that. Michel!'

The contents of Mr Hardman's two 'grips' were soon examined

and passed. They contained perhaps an undue proportion of spirituous liquor. Mr Hardman winked.

'It's not often they search your grips at the frontiers – not if you fix the conductor. I handed out a wad of Turkish notes right away, and there's been no trouble so far.'

'And at Paris?'

Mr Hardman winked again.

'By the time I get to Paris,' he said, 'what's left over of this little lot will go into a bottle labelled hairwash.'

'You are not a believer in Prohibition, Monsieur Hardman,' said M. Bouc with a smile.

'Well,' said Hardman. 'I can't say Prohibition has ever worried me any.'

'Ah!' said M. Bouc. 'The speakeasy.' He pronounced the word with care, savouring it.

'Your American terms are so quaint, so expressive,' he said.

'Me, I would much like to go to America,' said Poirot.

'You'd learn a few go-ahead methods over there,' said Hardman. 'Europe wants waking up. She's half asleep.'

'It is true that America is the country of progress,' agreed Poirot. 'There is much that I admire about Americans. Only – I am perhaps old-fashioned – but me, I find the American woman less charming than my own countrywomen. The French or Belgian girl, coquettish, charming – I think there is no one to touch her.'

Hardman turned away to peer out at the snow for a minute.

'Perhaps you're right, M. Poirot,' he said. 'But I guess every nation likes its own girls best.'

He blinked as though the snow hurt his eyes.

'Kind of dazzling, isn't it?' he remarked. 'Say, gentlemen, this business is getting on my nerves. Murder and the snow and all, and nothing *doing*. Just hanging about and killing time. I'd like to get busy after someone or something.'

'The true Western spirit of hustle,' said Poirot with a smile.

The conductor replaced the bags and they moved on to the next compartment. Colonel Arbuthnot was sitting in a corner smoking a pipe and reading a magazine.

Poirot explained their errand. The Colonel made no demur. He had two heavy leather suitcases.

'The rest of my kit has gone by long sea,' he explained.

Like most Army men, the Colonel was a neat packer. The examination of his baggage took only a few minutes. Poirot noted a packet of pipe-cleaners.

'You always use the same kind?' he asked.

'Usually. If I can get 'em.'

'Ah!' Poirot nodded.

These pipe-cleaners were identical with the one he had found on the floor of the dead man's compartment.

Dr Constantine remarked as much when they were out in the corridor again.

'*Tout de même*,' murmured Poirot, 'I can hardly believe it. It is not *dans son caractère*, and when you have said that you have said everything.'

The door of the next compartment was closed. It was that occupied by Princess Dragomiroff. They knocked on the door and the Princess's deep voice called, '*Entrez*.'

M. Bouc was spokesman. He was very deferential and polite as he explained their errand.

The Princess listened to him in silence, her small toad-like face quite impassive.

'If it is necessary, Messieurs,' she said quietly when he had finished, 'that is all there is to it. My maid has the keys. She will attend to it with you.'

'Does your maid always carry your keys, Madame?' asked Poirot.

'Certainly, Monsieur.'

'And if during the night at one of the frontiers the Customs officials should require a piece of luggage to be opened?'

The old lady shrugged her shoulders.

'It is very unlikely. But in such a case this conductor would fetch her.'

'You trust her, then, implicitly, Madame?'

'I have told you so already,' said the Princess quietly. 'I do not employ people whom I do not trust.'

'Yes,' said Poirot thoughtfully. 'Trust is indeed something in these days. It is, perhaps, better to have a homely woman whom one can trust than a more *chic* maid – for example, some smart Parisienne.'

He saw the dark intelligent eyes come slowly round and fasten themselves upon his face.

'What exactly are you implying, M. Poirot?'

'Nothing, Madame. I? Nothing.'

'But yes. You think, do you not, that I should have a smart Frenchwoman to attend to my toilet?'

'It would be, perhaps, more usual, Madame.'

She shook her head.

'Schmidt is devoted to me.' Her voice dwelt lingeringly on the words. 'Devotion – *c'est impayable.*'

The German woman had arrived with the keys. The Princess spoke to her in her own language, telling her to open the valises and help the gentlemen in their search. She herself remained in the corridor looking out at the snow and Poirot remained with her, leaving M. Bouc to the task of searching the luggage.

She regarded him with a grim smile.

'Well, Monsieur, do you not wish to see what my valises contain?'

He shook his head.

'Madame, it is a formality, that is all.'

'Are you so sure?'

'In your case, yes.'

'And yet I knew and loved Sonia Armstrong. What do you think, then? That I would not soil my hands with killing such *canaille* as that man Cassetti? Well, perhaps you are right.'

She was silent a minute or two, then she said:

'With such a man as that, do you know what I should have liked to have done? I should have liked to call to my servants: "Flog this man to death and fling him out on the rubbish heap." That is the way things were done when I was young. Monsieur.'

Still he did not speak, just listened attentively.

She looked at him with a sudden impetuosity.

'You do not say anything, M. Poirot. What is it that you are thinking, I wonder?'

He looked at her with a very direct glance.

'I think, Madame, that your strength is in your will – not in your arm.'

She glanced down at her thin, black-clad arms ending in those claw-like yellow hands with the rings on the fingers.

'It is true,' she said. 'I have no strength in these – none. I do not know if I am sorry or glad.'

Then she turned abruptly back towards her carriage, where the maid was busily packing up the cases.

The Princess cut short M. Bouc's apologies.

'There is not need for you to apologize, Monsieur,' she said. 'A murder has been committed. Certain actions have to be performed. That is all there is to it.'

'*Vous êtes bien amiable, Madame.*'

She inclined her head slightly as they departed.

The doors of the next two carriages were shut. M. Bouc paused and scratched his head.

'Diable!' he said. 'This may be awkward. These are diplomatic passports. Their baggage is exempt.'

'From Customs examination, yes. But a murder is different.'

'I know. All the same – we do not want to have complications –'

'Do not distress yourself, my friend. The Count and Countess will be reasonable. See how amiable Princess Dragomiroff was about it.'

'She is truly *grande dame.* These two are also of the same position, but the Count impressed me as a man of somewhat truculent disposition. He was not pleased when you insisted on questioning his wife. And this will annoy him still further. Suppose – eh – we omit them. After all, they can have nothing to do with the matter. Why should I stir up needless trouble for myself.'

'I do not agree with you,' said Poirot. 'I feel sure that Count Andrenyi will be reasonable. At any rate, let us make the attempt.'

And, before M. Bouc could reply, he rapped sharply on the door of No. 13.

A voice from within cried, '*Entrez.*'

The Count was sitting in the corner near the door reading a newspaper. The Countess was curled up in the opposite corner near the window. There was a pillow behind her head, and she seemed to have been asleep.

'Pardon, Monsieur le Comte,' began Poirot. 'Pray forgive this intrusion. It is that we are making a search of all the baggage on the train. In most cases a mere formality. But it has to be done. M. Bouc suggests that, as you have a diplomatic passport, you might reasonably claim to be exempt from such a search.'

The Count considered for a moment.

'Thank you,' he said. 'But I do not think that I care for an exception to be made in my case. I should prefer that our baggage should be examined like that of the other passengers.'

He turned to his wife.

'You do not object, I hope, Elena?'

'Not at all,' said the Countess without hesitation.

A rapid and somewhat perfunctory search followed. Poirot seemed to be trying to mask an embarrassment in making various small pointless remarks, such as:

'Here is a label all wet on your suitcase, Madame,' as he lifted down a blue morocco case with initials on it and a coronet.

The Countess did not reply to this observation. She seemed, indeed, rather bored by the whole proceeding, remaining curled up in her corner, staring dreamily out through the window whilst the men searched her luggage in the compartment next door.

Poirot finished his search by opening the little cupboard above the washbasin and taking a rapid glance at its contents – a sponge, face cream, powder and a small bottle labelled trional.

Then, with polite remarks on either side, the search party withdrew.

Mrs Hubbard's compartment, that of the dead man, and Poirot's own came next.

They now came to the second-class carriages. The first one, Nos. 10, 11, was occupied by Mary Debenham, who was reading a book, and Greta Ohlsson, who was fast asleep but woke with a start at their entrance.

Poirot repeated his formula. The Swedish lady seemed agitated, Mary Debenham calmly indifferent.

Poirot addressed himself to the Swedish lady.

'If you permit, Mademoiselle, we will examine your baggage first, and then perhaps you would be so good as to see how the American lady is getting on. We have moved her into one of the carriages in the next coach, but she is still very upset as the result of her discovery. I have ordered coffee to be sent to her, but I think she is of those to whom someone to talk to is a necessity of the first water.'

The good lady was instantly sympathetic. She would go immediately. It must have been indeed a terrible shock to the nerves, and already the poor lady was upset by the journey and leaving her daugher. Ah, yes, certainly she would go at once – her case was not locked – and she would take with her some sal ammoniac.

She bustled off. Her possessions were soon examined. They were meagre in the extreme. She had evidently not noticed the missing wires from the hat-box.

Miss Debenham had put her book down. She was watching Poirot. When he asked her, she handed over her keys. Then, as he lifted down a case and opened it, she said:

'Why did you send her away, M. Poirot?'

'I, Mademoiselle? Why, to minister to the American lady.'

'An excellent pretext – but a pretext all the same.'

'I don't understand you, Mademoiselle.'

'I think you understand me very well.'

She smiled.

'You wanted to get me alone. Wasn't that it?'

'You are putting words into my mouth, Mademoiselle.'

'And ideas into your head? No, I don't think so. The ideas are already there. That is right, isn't it?'

'Mademoiselle, we have a proverb –'

'*Que s'excuse s'accuse*; is that what you were going to say? You must give me the credit for a certain amount of observation and common sense. For some reason or other you have got it into your head that I know something about this sordid business – this murder of a man I never saw before.'

'You are imagining things, Mademoiselle.'

'No, I am not imagining things at all. But it seems to me that a lot of time is wasted by not speaking the truth – by beating about the bush instead of coming straight out with things.'

'And you do not like the waste of time. No, you like to come straight to the point. You like the direct method. *Eh bien*, I will give it to you, the direct method. I will ask you the meaning of certain words that I overheard on the journey from Syria. I had got out of the train to do what the English call "stretch the legs" at the station of Konya. Your voice and the Colonel's, Mademoiselle, they came to me out of the night. You said to him, "*Not now. Not now. When it's all over. When it's behind us.*" What did you mean by those words. Mademoiselle?'

She said very quietly:

'Do you think I meant – murder?'

'It is I who am asking you, Mademoiselle.'

She sighed – was lost a minute in thought. Then, as though rousing herself, she said:

'Those words had a meaning, Monsieur, but not one that I can tell you. I can only give you my solemn word of honour that I had never set eyes on this man Ratchett in my life until I saw him on this train.'

'And – you refuse to explain those words?'

'Yes – if you like to put it that way – I refuse. They had to do with – with a task I had undertaken.'

'A task that is now ended?'

'What do you mean?'

'It is ended, is it not?'

'Why should you think so?'

'Listen, Mademoiselle, I will recall to you another incident. There was a delay to the train on the day we were to reach Stamboul. You were very agitated, Mademoiselle. You, so calm, so self-controlled. You lost that calm.'

'I did not want to miss my connection.'

'So you said. But, Mademoiselle, the Orient Express leaves Stamboul every day of the week. Even if you had missed the connection it would only have been a matter of twenty-four hours' delay.'

Miss Debenham for the first time showed signs of losing her temper.

'You do not seem to realize that one may have friends awaiting one's arrival in London, and that a day's delay upsets arrangements and causes a lot of annoyance.'

'Ah, it is like that? There are friends awaiting your arrival? You do not want to cause them inconvenience?'

'Naturally.'

'And yet – it is curious –'

'What is curious?'

'On this train – again we have a delay. And this time a more serious delay, since there is no possibility of sending a telegram to your friends or of getting them on the long – the long –'

'The long distance? The telephone, you mean.'

'Ah, yes, the portmanteau call, as you say in England.'

Mary Debenham smiled a little in spite of herself.

'Trunk call,' she corrected. 'Yes, as you say, it is extremely annoying not to be able to get any word through, either by telephone or telegraph.'

'And yet, Mademoiselle, *this* time your manner is quite different. You no longer betray the impatience. You are calm and philosophical.'

Mary Debenham flushed and bit her lip. She no longer felt inclined to smile.

'You do not answer, Mademoiselle?'

'I am sorry. I did not know that there was anything to answer.'

'The explanation of your change of attitude, Mademoiselle.'

'Don't you think that you are making rather a fuss about nothing, M. Poirot?'

Poirot spread out his hands in an apologetic gesture.

'It is perhaps a fault with us detectives. We expect the behaviour to be always consistent. We do not allow for changes of mood.'

Mary Debenham made no reply.

'You know Colonel Arbuthnot well, Mademoiselle?'

He fancied that she was relieved by the change of subject.

'I met him for the first time on this journey.'

'Have you any reason to suspect that he may have known this man Ratchett?'

She shook her head decisively.

'I am quite sure he didn't.'

'Why are you sure?'

'By the way he spoke.'

'And yet, Mademoiselle, we found a pipe-cleaner on the floor of the dead man's compartment. And Colonel Arbuthnot is the only man on the train who smokes a pipe?'

He watched her narrowly, but she displayed neither surprise nor emotion, merely said:

'Nonsense. It's absurd. Colonel Arbuthnot is the last man in the world to be mixed up in a crime – especially a theatrical kind of crime like this.'

It was so much what Poirot himself thought that he found himself on the point of agreeing with her. He said instead:

'I must remind you that you do not know him very well, Mademoiselle.'

She shrugged her shoulders.

'I know the type well enough.'

He said very gently:

'You still refuse to tell me the meaning of those words – "When it's behind us"?'

She said coldly:

'I have nothing more to say.'

'It does not matter,' said Hercule Poirot. 'I shall find out.'

He bowed and left the compartment, closing the door after him.

'Was that wise, my friend?' asked M. Bouc. 'You have put her on her guard – and through her you have put the Colonel on his guard also.'

'*Mon ami*, if you wish to catch a rabbit you put a ferret into the hole, and if the rabbit is there he runs. That is all I have done.'

They entered the compartment of Hildegarde Schmidt.

The woman was standing in readiness, her face respectful but unemotional.

Poirot took a quick glance through the contents of the small case on the seat. Then he motioned to the attendant to get down the bigger suitcase from the rack.

'The keys?' he said.

'It is not locked, Monsieur.'

Poirot undid the hasps and lifted the lid.

'Aha!' he said, and turning to M. Bouc, 'You remember what I said? Look here a little moment!'

On the top of the suitcase was a hastily rolled up brown Wagon Lit uniform.

The stolidity of the German woman underwent a sudden change.

'Ach!' she cried. 'That is not mine. I did not put it there. I have never looked in that case since we left Stamboul. Indeed, indeed, it is true.'

She looked from one to another pleadingly.

Poirot took her gently by the arm and soothed her.

'No, no all is well. We believe you. Do not be agitated. I am as sure you did not hide the uniform there as I am sure that you are a good cook. See. You are a good cook, are you not?'

Bewildered, the woman smiled in spite of herself.

'Yes, indeed, all my ladies have said so. I –'

She stopped, her mouth open, looking frightened again.

'No, no,' said Poirot. 'I assure you all is well. See, I will tell you how this happened. This man, the man you saw in Wagon Lit uniform, comes out of the dead man's compartment. He collides with you. That is bad luck for him. He has hoped that no one will see him. What to do next? He must get rid of his uniform. It is now not a safeguard, but a danger.'

His glance went to M. Bouc and Dr Constantine, who were listening attentively.

'There is the snow, you see. The snow which confuses all his plans. Where can he hide these clothes? All the compartments are full. No, he passes one where the door is open and shows it to be unoccupied. It must be the one belonging to the woman with whom he has just collided. He slips in, removes the uniform and jams it hurriedly into a suitcase on the rack. It may be some time before it is discovered.'

'And then?' said M. Bouc.

'That we must discuss,' said Poirot with a warning glance.

He held up the tunic. A button, the third down, was missing. Poirot slipped his hand into the pocket and took out a conductor's pass key, used to unlock the doors of the compartments.

'Here is the explanation of how our man was able to pass through locked doors,' said M. Bouc. 'Your questions to Mrs Hubbard were unnecessary. Locked or not locked, the man could easily get through the communicating door. After all, if a Wagon Lit uniform, why not a Wagon Lit key?'

'Why not, indeed,' said Poirot.

'We might have known it, really. You remember Michel said that the door into the corridor of Mrs Hubbard's compartment was locked when he came in answer to her bell.'

'That is so, Monsieur,' said the conductor. 'That is why I thought the lady must have been dreaming.'

'But now it is easy,' continued M. Bouc. 'Doubtless he meant to relock the communicating door also, but perhaps he heard some movement from the bed and it startled him.'

'We have now,' said Poirot, 'only to find the scarlet kimono.'

'True. And these last two compartments are occupied by men.'

'We will search all the same.'

'Oh! assuredly. Besides, I remember what you said.'

Hector MacQueen acquiesced willingly in the search.

'I'd just as soon you did,' he said with a rueful smile. 'I feel I'm just definitely the most suspicious character on the train. You've only got to find a will in which the old man left me all his money, and that'll just about fix things.'

M. Bouc bent a suspicious glance upon him.

'That's just my fun,' said MacQueen hastily. 'He'd never have left me a cent, really. I was just useful to him – languages and so on. You're apt to be done down, you know, if you don't speak anything but good American. I'm no linguist myself, but I know what I call shopping and hotel snappy bits in French and German and Italian.'

His voice was a little louder than usual. It was as though he was slightly uneasy at the search in spite of his willingness.

Poirot emerged.

'Nothing,' he said. 'Not even a compromising bequest!'

MacQueen sighed.

'Well, that's a load off my mind,' he said humorously.

They moved on to the last compartment. The examination of the luggage of the big Italian and of the valet yielded no result.

The three men stood at the end of the coach looking at each other.

'What next?' asked M. Bouc.

'We will go back to the dining-car,' said Poirot. 'We know now all that we can know. We have the evidence of the passengers, the evidence of their baggage, the evidence of our eyes. We can expect no further help. It must be our part now to use our brains.'

He felt in his pocket for his cigarette case. It was empty.

'I will join you in a moment,' he said. 'I shall need the cigarettes. This is a very difficult, a very curious affair. Who wore that scarlet kimono? Where is it now? I wish I knew. There is something in this case – some factor – that escapes me! It is difficult because it has been made difficult. But we will discuss it. Pardon me a moment.'

He went hurriedly along the corridor to his own compartment. He had, he knew, a further supply of cigarettes in one of his valises.

He got it down and snapped back the lock.

Then he sat back on his heels and stared.

Neatly folded on the top of the case was a thin scarlet silk kimono embroidered with dragons.

'So,' he murmured. 'It is like that. A defiance. Very well. I take it up.'

PART 3 • HERCULE POIROT SITS BACK AND THINKS

CHAPTER 1

WHICH OF THEM?

M. Bouc and Dr Constantine were talking together when Poirot entered the dining-car. M. Bouc was looking depressed.

'*Le voilà*,' said the latter when he saw Poirot.

Then he added as his friend sat down:

'If you solve this case, *mon cher*, I shall indeed believe in miracles!'

'It worries you, this case?'

'Naturally it worries me. I cannot make head or tail of it.'

'I agree,' said the doctor.

He looked at Poirot with interest.

'To be frank,' he said, 'I cannot see what you are going to do next.'

'No?' said Poirot thoughtfully.

He took out his cigarette case and lit one of his tiny cigarettes. His eyes were dreamy.

'That, to me, is the interest of this case,' he said. 'We are cut off from all the normal routes of procedure. Are these people whose evidence we have taken speaking the truth or lying? We have no means of finding out – except such means as we can devise ourselves. It is an exercise, this, of the brain.'

'That is all very fine,' said M. Bouc. 'But what have you to go upon?'

'I told you just now. We have the evidence of the passengers and the evidence of our own eyes.'

'Pretty evidence – that of the passengers! It told us just nothing at all.'

Poirot shook his head.

'I do not agree, my friend. The evidence of the passengers gave us several points of interest.'

'Indeed,' said M. Bouc sceptically. 'I did not observe it.'

'That is because you did not listen.'

'Well, tell me – what did I miss?'

'I will just take one instance – the first evidence we heard – that of the young MacQueen. He uttered, to my mind, one very significant phrase.'

'About the letters?'

'No, not about the letters. As far as I can remember, his words were: "*We travelled about. Mr Ratchett wanted to see the world. He was hampered by knowing no languages. I acted more as a courier than a secretary.*"'

He looked from the doctor's face to that of M. Bouc.

'What? You still do not see? That is inexcusable – for you had a second chance again just now when he said, "*You're apt to be done down if you speak nothing but good American.*"'

'You mean –?' M. Bouc still looked puzzled.

'Ah, it is that you want it given to you in words of one syllable. Well, here it is! *M. Ratchett spoke no French.* Yet, when the conductor came in answer to his bell last night, it was a voice speaking in *French* that told him that it was a mistake and that he was not wanted. It was, moreover, a perfectly idiomatic phrase that was used, not one that a man knowing only a few words of French would have selected. "*Ce n'est rien. Je me suis trompé.*"'

'It is true,' cried Constantine excitedly. 'We should have seen that! I remember your laying stress on the words when you repeated them to us. Now I understand your reluctance to rely upon the evidence of the dented watch. Already, at twenty-three minutes to one, Ratchett was dead –'

'And it was his murderer speaking!' finished M. Bouc impressively.

Poirot raised a deprecating hand.

'Let us not go too fast. And do not let us assume more than we actually know. It is safe, I think, to say that at that time, twenty-three minutes to one, *some other person* was in Ratchett's compartment and that that person was either French, or could speak the French language fluently.'

'You are very cautious, *mon vieux*.'

'One should advance only a step at a time. We have no actual *evidence* that Ratchett was dead at that time.'

'There is the cry that awakened you.'

'Yes, that is true.'

'In one way,' said M. Bouc thoughtfully, 'this discovery does not affect things very much. You heard someone moving about next door. That someone was not Ratchett, but the other man. Doubtless he is washing blood from his hands, clearing up after the crime, burning the incriminating letter. Then he waits till all is still, and when he thinks it is safe and the coast is clear he locks and chains Ratchett's door on the inside, unlocks the communicating door through into Mrs Hubbard's compartment and slips out that way. In fact it is exactly as we thought – *with the difference that Ratchett was killed about half an hour earlier*, and the watch put on to a quarter-past one to create an alibi.'

'Not such a famous alibi,' said Poirot. 'The hands of the watch pointed to 1.15 – the exact time when the intruder actually left the scene of the crime.'

'True,' said M. Bouc, a little confused. 'What, then, does the watch convey to you?'

'If the hands were altered – I say *if* – then the time at which they were set *must* have a significance. The natural reaction would be to suspect anyone who had a reliable alibi for the time indicated – in this case 1.15.'

'Yes, Yes,' said the doctor. 'That reasoning is good.'

'We must also pay a little attention to the time the intruder *entered* the compartment. When had he an opportunity of doing so? Unless we are to assume the complicity of the real conductor, there was only one time when he could have done so – during the time the train stopped at Vincovci. After the train left Vincovci the conductor was sitting facing the corridor and whereas any one of the passengers would pay little attention to a Wagon Lit attendant, the *one* person who would notice an imposter would be the real conductor. But during the halt at Vincovci the conductor is out on the platform. The coast is clear.'

'And, by our former reasoning, it *must* be one of the passengers,' said M. Bouc. 'We come back to where we were. Which of them?'

Poirot smiled.

'I have made a list,' he said, 'If you like to see it, it will, perhaps, refresh your memory.'

The doctor and M. Bouc pored over the list together. It was

written out neatly in a methodical manner in the order in which the passengers had been interviewed.

Hector MacQueen – American subject. Berth No. 6. Second Class.

Motive: Possibly arising out of association with dead man?

Alibi: From midnight to 2 a.m. (Midnight to 1.30 vouched for by Col. Arbuthnot and 1.15 to 2 vouched for by conductor.)

Evidence Against Him: None.

Suspicious Circumstances: None.

Conductor – Pierre Michel – French subject.

Motive: None.

Alibi: From midnight to 2 a.m. (Seen by H.P. in corridor at same time as voice spoke from Ratchett's compartment at 12.37. From 1 a.m. to 1.16 vouched for by other two conductors.)

Evidence Against Him: None.

Suspicious Circumstances: The Wagon Lit uniform found is a point in his favour since it seems to have been intended to throw suspicion on him.

Edward Masterman – English subject. Berth No. 4. Second Class

Motive: Possibly arising out of connection with deceased, whose valet he was.

Alibi: From midnight to 2 a.m. (Vouched for by Antonio Foscarelli.)

Evidence Against Him or Suspicious Circumstances: None, except that he is the only man the right height or size to have worn the Wagon Lit uniform. On the other hand, it is unlikely that he speaks French well.

Mrs Hubbard – American subject. Berth No. 3. First Class.

Motive: None.

Alibi: From midnight to 2 a.m. – None.

Evidence Against Her or Suspicious Circumstances: Story of man in her compartment is substantiated by the evidence of Hardman and that of the woman Schmidt.

Greta Ohlsson – Swedish subject. Berth No. 10. Second Class.

Motive: None.

Alibi: From midnight to 2 a.m. (Vouched for by Mary Debenham).
Note. – Was last to see Ratchett alive.

Princess Dragomiroff – Naturalized French subject. Berth No. 14. First Class.

Motive: Was intimately acquainted with Armstrong family, and godmother to Sonia Armstrong.

Alibi: From midnight to 2 a.m. (Vouched for by conductor and maid.)

Evidence Against Her or Suspicious Circumstances: None.

Count Andrenyi – Hungarian subject. Diplomatic passport. Berth No. 13. First Class.

Motive: None.

Alibi: Midnight to 2 a.m. (Vouched for by conductor – this does not cover period from 1 to 1.15.)

Countess Andrenyi – As above. Berth No. 12.

Motive: None.

Alibi: Midnight to 2 a.m. Took trional and slept. (Vouched for by husband. Trional bottle in her cupboard.)

Colonel Arbuthnot – British subject. Berth No. 15. First Class

Motive: None.

Alibi: Midnight to 2 a.m. Talked with MacQueen till 1.30. Went to own compartment and did not leave it. (Substantiated by MacQueen and conductor.)

Evidence Against Him or Suspicious Circumstances: Pipe-cleaner.

Cyrus Hardman – American subject. Berth No. 16. Second Class

Motive: None known.

Alibi: Midnight to 2 a.m. Did not leave compartment. (Substantiated by MacQueen and conductor.)

Evidence Against Him or Suspicious Circumstances: None.

Antonio Foscarelli – American subject. (Italian birth.) Berth No. 5. Second Class

Motive: None known.

Alibi: Midnight to 2 a.m. (Vouched for by Edward Masterman.)

Evidence Against Him or Suspicious Circumstances: None, except that weapon used might be said to suit his temperament. (Vide M. Bouc.)

Mary Debenham – British subject. Berth No. 11. Second Class

Motive: None.

Alibi: Midnight to 2 a.m. (Vouched for by Greta Ohlsson.)

Evidence Against Her or Suspicious Circumstances: and her refusal to explain same.

Hildegarde Schmidt – German subject. Berth No. 8. Second Class.

Motive: None.

Alibi: Midnight to 2 a.m. (Vouched for by conductor and her mistress.) Went to bed. Was aroused by conductor at 12.38 approx. and went to mistress.

Note: The evidence of the passengers is supported by the statement of the conductor that no one entered or left Mr Ratchett's compartment between the hours of midnight to 1 o'clock (when he himself went into the next coach) and from 1.15 to 2 o'clock.

'That document, you understand,' said Poirot, 'is a mere précis of the evidence we heard, arranged that way for convenience.'

With a grimace M. Bouc handed it back.

'It is not illuminating,' he said.

'Perhaps you may find this more to your taste,' said Poirot with a slight smile as he handed him a second sheet of paper.

CHAPTER 2

TEN QUESTIONS

On the paper was written:

Things needing explanation.

1. The handkerchief marked with the initial H. Whose is it?
2. The pipe-cleaner. Was it dropped by Colonel Arbuthnot? Or by someone else?
3. Who wore the scarlet kimono?
4. Who was the man or woman masquerading in Wagon Lit uniform?
5. Why do the hands of the watch point to 1.15?

6. Was the murder committed at that time?
7. Was it earlier?
8. Was it later?
9. Can we be sure that Ratchett was stabbed by more than one person?
10. What other explanation of his wounds can there be?

'Well, let us see what we can do,' said M. Bouc, brightening a little at this challenge to his wits. 'The handkerchief to begin with. Let us by all means be orderly and methodical.'

'Assuredly,' said Poirot, nodding his head in a satisfied fashion.

M. Bouc continued somewhat didactically.

'The initial H is connected with three people – Mrs Hubbard, Miss Debenham, whose second name is Hermione, and the maid Hildegarde Schmidt.'

'Ah! And of those three?'

'It is difficult to say. But I *think* I should vote for Miss Debenham. For all one knows, she may be called by her second name and not her first. Also there is already some suspicion attaching to her. That conversation you overheard, *mon cher*, was certainly a little curious, and so is her refusal to explain it.'

'As for me, I plump for the American,' said Dr Constantine. 'It is a very expensive handkerchief that, and Americans, as all the world knows, do not care what they pay.'

'So you both eliminate the maid?' asked Poirot.

'Yes. As she herself said, it is the handkerchief of a member of the upper classes.'

'And the second question – the pipe-cleaner. Did Colonel Arbuthnot drop it, or somebody else?'

'That is more difficult. The English, they do not stab. You are right there. I incline to the view that someone else dropped the pipe-cleaner – and did so to incriminate the long-legged Englishman.'

'As you said, M. Poirot,' put in the doctor, '*two* clues is too much carelessness. I agree with M. Bouc. The handkerchief was a genuine oversight – hence no one will admit that it is theirs. The pipe-cleaner is a faked clue. In support of that theory, you notice that Colonel Arbuthnot shows no embarrassment and admits freely to smoking a pipe and using that type of cleaner.'

'You reason well,' said Poirot.

'Question No. 3 – who wore the scarlet kimono?' went on M. Bouc. 'As to that I will confess I have not the slightest idea. Have you any views on the subject, Dr Constantine?'

'None.'

'Then we confess ourselves beaten there. The next question has, at any rate, possibilities. Who was the man or woman masquerading in Wagon Lit uniform? Well, one can say with certainty a number of people whom it could *not* be. Hardman, Colonel Arbuthnot, Foscarelli, Count Andrenyi and Hector MacQueen are all too tall. Mrs Hubbard, Hildegarde Schmidt and Greta Ohlsson are too broad. That leaves the valet, Miss Debenham, Princess Dragomiroff and Countess Andrenyi – and none of them sounds likely! Greta Ohlsson in one case and Antonio Foscarelli in the other both swear that Miss Debenham and the valet never left their compartments, Hildegarde Schmidt swears to the Princess being in hers, and Count Andrenyi has told us that his wife took a sleeping draught. Therefore it seems impossible that it can be anybody – which is absurd!'

'As our old friend Euclid says,' murmured Poirot.

'It must be one of those four,' said Dr Constantine. 'Unless it is someone from outside who has found a hiding place – and that, we agreed, was impossible.'

M. Bouc had passed on to the next question on the list.

'No. 5 – why do the hands of the broken watch point to 1.15? I can see two explanations of that. Either it was done by the murderer to establish an alibi and afterwards he was prevented from leaving the compartment when he meant to do so by hearing people moving about, or else – wait – I have an idea coming –'

The other two waited respectfully while M. Bouc struggled in mental agony.

'I have it,' he said at last. 'It was *not* the Wagon Lit murderer who tampered with the watch! It was the person we have called the Second Murderer – the left-handed person – in other words the woman in the scarlet kimono. She arrives later and moves back the hands of the watch in order to make an alibi for herself.'

'Bravo,' said Dr Constantine. 'It is well imagined, that.'

'In fact,' said Poirot, 'she stabbed him in the dark, not realizing that he was dead already, but somehow deduced that he had a watch in his pyjama pocket, took it out, put back the hands blindly and gave it the requisite dent.'

M. Bouc looked at him coldly.

'Have you anything better to suggest yourself?' he asked.

'At the moment – no,' admitted Poirot.

'All the same,' he went on, 'I do not think you have either of you appreciated the most interesting point about that watch.'

'Does question No. 6 deal with it?' asked the doctor. 'To that question – was the murder committed at that time – 1.15 – I answer, "*No.*"'

'I agree,' said M. Bouc. '"Was it earlier?" is the next question. I say yes. You, too, doctor?'

The doctor nodded.

'Yes, but the question "Was it later?" can also be answered in the affirmative. I agree with your theory, M. Bouc, and so, I think, does M. Poirot, although he does not wish to commit himself. The First Murderer came earlier than 1.15, the Second Murderer came *after* 1.15. And as regards the question of left-handedness, ought we not to take steps to ascertain which of the passengers is left-handed?'

'I have not completely neglected that point,' said Poirot. 'You may have noticed that I made each passenger write either a signature or an address. That is not conclusive, because some people do certain actions with the right hand and others with the left. Some write right-handed, but play golf left-handed. Still it is something. Every person questioned took the pen in their right hand – with the exception of Princess Dragomiroff, who refused to write.'

'Princess Dragomiroff, impossible,' said M. Bouc.

'I doubt if she would have had the strength to inflict that particular left-handed blow,' said Dr Constantine dubiously. 'That particular wound had been inflicted with considerable force.'

'More force than a woman could use?'

'No, I would not say that. But I think more force than an elderly woman could display, and Princess Dragomiroff's physique is particularly frail.'

'It might be a question of the influence of mind over body,' said

Poirot. 'Princess Dragomiroff has great personality and immense will power. But let us pass from that for the moment.'

'To questions Nos. 9 and 10. Can we be sure that Ratchett was stabbed by more than one person, and what other explanation of the wounds can there be? In my opinion, medically speaking, there can be *no other* explanation of those wounds. To suggest that one man struck first feebly and then with violence, first with the right hand and then with the left, and after an interval of perhaps half an hour inflicted fresh wounds on a dead body – well, it does not make sense.'

'No,' said Poirot. 'It does not make sense. And you think that two murderers do make sense?'

'As you yourself have said, what other explanation can there be?'

Poirot stared straight ahead of him.

'That is what I ask myself,' he said. 'That is what I never cease to ask myself.'

He leaned back in his seat.

'From now on, it is all here,' he tapped himself on the forehead. 'We have thrashed it all out. The facts are all in front of us – neatly arranged with order and method. The passengers have sat here, one by one, giving their evidence. We know all that can be known – *from outside* . . .'

He gave an affectionate smile at M. Bouc.

'It has been a little joke between us, has it not – this business of sitting back and *thinking* out the truth? Well, I am about to put my theory into practice – here before your eyes. You two must do the same. Let us all three close our eyes and *think* . . .'

'One or more of those passengers killed Ratchett. *Which of them?*'

CHAPTER 3

CERTAIN SUGGESTIVE POINTS

It was quite a quarter of an hour before anyone spoke.

M. Bouc and Dr Constantine had started by trying to obey Poirot's instructions. They had endeavoured to see through the maze of conflicting particulars to a clear and outstanding solution.

M. Bouc's thoughts had run something as follows:

'Assuredly I must think. But as far as that goes I have already thought . . . Poirot obviously thinks this English girl is mixed up in the matter. I cannot help feeling that that is most unlikely . . . The English are extremely cold. Probably it is because they have no figures . . . But that is not the point. It seems that the Italian could not have done it – a pity. I suppose the English valet is not lying when he said the other never left the compartment? But why should he? It is not easy to bribe the English, they are so unapproachable. The whole thing is most unfortunate. I wonder when we shall get out of this. There must be *some* rescue work in progress. They are so slow in these countries . . . it is hours before anyone thinks of doing anything. And the police of these countries, they will be most trying to deal with – puffed up with importance, touchy, on their dignity. They will make a grand affair of all this. It is not often that such a chance comes their way. It will be in all the newspapers . . .'

And from there on M. Bouc's thoughts went along a well-worn course which they had already traversed some hundred times.

Dr Constantine's thoughts ran thus:

'He is queer, this little man. A genius? Or a crank? Will he solve this mystery? Impossible. I can see no way out of it. It is all too confusing . . . Everyone is lying, perhaps . . . But even then that does not help one. If they are all lying it is just as confusing as if they were speaking the truth. Odd about those wounds. I cannot understand it . . . It would be easier to understand if he had been shot – after all, the term gunman must mean that they shoot with a gun. A curious country, America. I should like to go there. It is so progressive. When I get home I must get hold of Demetrius Zagone – he has been to America, he has all the modern ideas . . . I wonder what Zia is doing at this moment. If my wife ever finds out –'

His thoughts went on to entirely private matters.

Hercule Poirot sat very still.

One might have thought he was asleep.

And then, suddenly, after a quarter of an hour's complete immobility, his eyebrows began to move slowly up his forehead. A little sigh escaped him. He murmured beneath his breath:

'But, after all, why not? And if so – why, if so, that would explain everything.'

His eyes opened. They were green like a cat's. He said softly:

'*Eh bien*. I have thought. And you?'

Lost in their reflections, both men started violently.

'I have thought also,' said M. Bouc just a shade guilty. 'But I have arrived at no conclusion. The elucidation of crime is your *métier*, not mine, my friend.'

'I, too, have reflected with great earnestness,' said the doctor unblushingly, recalling his thoughts from certain pornographic details. 'I have thought of many possible theories, but not one that really satisfies me.'

Poirot nodded amiably. His nod seemed to say:

'Quite right. That is the proper thing to say. You have given me the cue I expected.'

He sat very upright, threw out his chest, caressed his moustache and spoke in the manner of a practised speaker addressing a public meeting.

'My friends, I have reviewed the facts in my mind, and have also gone over to myself the evidence of the passengers – with this result. I see, nebulously as yet, a certain explanation that would cover the facts as we know them. It is a very curious explanation, and I cannot be sure as yet that it is the true one. To find out definitely, I shall have to make certain experiments.

'I would like first to mention certain points which appear to me suggestive. Let us start with a remark made to me by M. Bouc in this very place on the occasion of our first lunch together on the train. He commented on the fact that we were surrounded by people of all classes, of all ages, of all nationalities. That is a fact somewhat rare at this time of year. The Athens-Paris and the Bucharest-Paris coaches, for instance, are almost empty. Remember also one passenger who failed to turn up. It is, I think, significant. Then there are some minor points that strike me as suggestive – for instance, the position of Mrs Hubbard's sponge-bag, the name of Mrs Armstrong's mother, the detective methods of M. Hardman, the suggestion of M. MacQueen that Ratchett himself destroyed the charred note we found, Princess Dragomiroff's Christian name, and a grease spot on a Hungarian passport.'

The two men stared at him.

'Do they suggest anything to you, those points?' asked Poirot.

'Not a thing,' said M. Bouc frankly.

'And M. le docteur?'

'I do not understand in the least of what you are talking.'

M. Bouc, meanwhile, seizing upon the one tangible thing his friend had mentioned, was sorting through the passports. With a grunt he picked up that of Count and Countess Andrenyi and opened it.

'Is this what you mean? This dirty mark?'

'Yes. It is a fairly fresh grease spot. You notice where it occurs?'

'At the beginning of the description of the Count's wife – her Christian name, to be exact. But I confess that I still do not see the point.'

'I am going to approach it from another angle. Let us go back to the handkerchief found at the scene of the crime. As we have stated not long ago – three people are associated with the letter H. Mrs Hubbard, Miss Debenham and the maid, Hildegarde Schmidt. Now let us regard that handkerchief from another point of view. It is, my friends, an extremely expensive handkerchief – an *objet de luxe*, hand made, embroidered in Paris. Which of the passengers, apart from the initial, was likely to own such a handkerchief? Not Mrs Hubbard, a worthy woman with no pretensions to reckless extravagance in dress. Not Miss Debenham; that class of Englishwoman has a dainty linen handkerchief, but not an expensive wisp of cambric costing perhaps two hundred francs. And certainly not the maid. But there *are* two women on the train who would be likely to own such a handkerchief. Let us see if we can connect them in any way with the letter H. The two women I refer to are Princess Dragomiroff –'

'Whose Christian name is Natalia,' put in M. Bouc ironically.

'Exactly. And her Christian name, as I said just now, is decidedly suggestive. The other woman is Countess Andrenyi. And at once something strikes us –'

'*You!*'

'*Me*, then. Her Christian name on her passport is disfigured by a blob of grease. Just an accident, anyone would say. But consider that Christian name. Elena. Suppose that, instead of Elena, it were

Helena. That capital H could be turned into a capital E and then run over the small e next to it quite easily – and then a spot of grease dropped to cover up the alteration.'

'Helena,' cried M. Bouc. 'It is an idea, that.'

'Certainly it is an idea! I look about for any confirmation, however slight, of my idea – and I find it. One of the luggage labels on the Countess's baggage is slightly damp. It is one that happens to run over the first initial on top of the case. That label has been soaked off and put on again in a different place.'

'You begin to convince me,' said M. Bouc, 'But the Countess Andrenyi – surely –'

'Ah, now, *mon vieux*, you must turn yourself round and approach an entirely different angle of the case. How was this murder intended to appear to everybody? Do not forget that the snow has upset all the murderer's original plan. Let us imagine, for a little minute, that there is no snow, that the train proceeded on its normal course. What, then, would have happened?

'The murder, let us say, would still have been discovered in all probability at the Italian frontier early this morning. Much of the same evidence would have been given to the Italian police. The threatening letters would have been produced by M. MacQueen, M. Hardman would have told his story, Mrs Hubbard would have been eager to tell how a man passed through her compartment, the button would have been found. I imagine that two things only would have been different. The man would have passed through Mrs Hubbard's compartment just before one o'clock – and the Wagon Lit uniform would have been found cast off in one of the toilets.'

'You mean?'

'I mean that the murder was *planned to look like an outside job.* The assassin would have been presumed to have left the train at Brod, where the train is timed to arrive at 00.58. Somebody would probably have passed a strange Wagon Lit conductor in the corridor. The uniform would be left in a conspicuous place so as to show clearly just how the trick had been played. No suspicion would have been attached to the passengers. That, my friends, was how the affair was intended to appear to the outside world.

'But the accident to the train changes everything. Doubtless we have here the reason why the man remained in the compartment with his victim so long. He was waiting for the train to go on. But at last he realized *that the train was not going on.* Different plans would have to be made. The murderer would now be *known* to be still on the train.'

'Yes, yes,' said M. Bouc impatiently. 'I see all that. But where does the handkerchief come in?'

'I am returning to it by a somewhat circuitous route. To begin with, you must realize that the threatening letters were in the nature of a blind. They might have been lifted bodily out of an indifferently written American crime novel. They are not *real.* They are, in fact, simply intended for the police. What we have to ask ourselves is, "Did they deceive Ratchett?" On the face of it, the answer seems to be, "No". His instructions to Hardman seem to point to a definite "private" enemy of the identity of whom he was well aware. That is if we accept Hardman's story as true. But Ratchett certainly received *one* letter of a very different character – the one containing a reference to the Armstrong baby, a fragment of which we found in his compartment. In case Ratchett had not realized it sooner, this was to make sure that he understood the reason of the threats against his life. That letter, as I have said all along, was *not* intended to be found. The murderer's first care was to destroy it. This, then, was the second hitch in his plans. The first was the snow, the second was our reconstruction of that fragment.

'That note being destroyed so carefully can only mean one thing. *There must be on the train someone so intimately connected with the Armstrong family that the finding of that note would immediately direct suspicion upon that person.*

'Now we come to the other two clues that we found. I pass over the pipe-cleaner. We have already said a good deal about that. Let us pass on to the handkerchief. Taken at its simplest, it is a clue which directly incriminates someone whose initial is H, and it was dropped there unwittingly by that person.'

'Exactly,' said Dr Constantine. 'She finds out that she has dropped the handkerchief and immediately takes steps to conceal her Christian name.'

'How fast you go. You arrive at a conclusion much sooner than I would permit myself to do.'

'Is there any other alternative?'

'Certainly there is. Suppose, for instance, that you have committed a crime and wish to cast suspicion for it on someone else. Well, there is on the train a certain person connected intimately with the Armstrong family – a woman. Suppose, then, that you leave there a handkerchief belonging to that woman. She will be questioned, her connection with the Armstrong family will be brought out – *et voilà*. Motive – *and* an incriminating article of evidence.'

'But in such a case,' objected the doctor, 'the person indicated being innocent, would not take steps to conceal her identity.'

'Ah, really? That is what you think? That is truly the opinion of the police court. But I know human nature, my friend, and I tell you that, suddenly confronted with the possibility of being tried for murder, the most innocent person will lose their head and do the most absurd things. No, no, the grease spot and the changed label do not prove guilt – they only prove that the Countess Andrenyi is anxious for some reason to conceal her identity.'

'What do you think her connection with the Armstrong family can be? She has never been in America, she says.'

'Exactly, and she speaks broken English, and she has a very foreign appearance which she exaggerates. But it should not be difficult to guess who she is. I mentioned just now the name of Mrs Armstrong's mother. It was Linda Arden, and she was a very celebrated actress – among other things a Shakespearean actress. Think of *As You Like It* – the Forest of Arden and Rosalind. It was there she got the inspiration for her acting name. Linda Arden, the name by which she was known all over the world, was not her real name. It may have been Goldenberg – she quite likely had central European blood in her veins – a strain of Jewish, perhaps. Many nationalities drift to America. I suggest to you, gentlemen, that that young sister of Mrs Armstrong's, little more than a child at the time of the tragedy, was Helena Goldenberg the younger daughter of Linda Arden, and that she married Count Andrenyi when he was an attaché in Washington.'

'But Princess Dragomiroff says that she married an Englishman.'

'Whose name she cannot remember! I ask you, my friends – is that really likely? Princess Dragomiroff loved Linda Arden as great ladies do love great artists. She was godmother to one of her daughters. Would she forget so quickly the married name of the other daughter? It is not likely. No, I think we can safely say that Princess Dragomiroff was lying. She knew Helena was on the train, she had seen her. She realized at once, as soon as she heard who Ratchett really was, that Helena would be suspected. And so, when we question her as to the sister she promptly lies – is vague, cannot remember, but "thinks Helena married an Englishman" – a suggestion as far away from the truth as possible.'

One of the restaurant attendants came through the door at the end and approached them. He addressed M. Bouc.

'The dinner, Monsieur, shall I serve it? It is ready some little time.'

M. Bouc looked at Poirot. The latter nodded.

'By all means, let dinner be served.'

The attendant vanished through the doors at the other end. His bell could be heard ringing and his voice upraised:

'*Premier Service. Le dîner est servi. Premier dîner* – First Service.'

CHAPTER 4

THE GREASE SPOT ON A HUNGARIAN PASSPORT

Poirot shared a table with M. Bouc and the doctor.

The company assembled in the restaurant-car was a very subdued one. They spoke little. Even the loquacious Mrs Hubbard was unnaturally quiet. She murmured as she sat:

'I don't feel as though I've got the heart to eat anything,' and then partook of everything offered her, encouraged by the Swedish lady, who seemed to regard her as a special charge.

Before the meal was served Poirot had caught the chief attendant by the sleeve and murmured something to him. Constantine had a pretty good guess what the instructions had been, as he noticed that the Count and Countess Andrenyi were always served last and that at the end of the meal there was a delay in making out their bill. It therefore came about that the Count and Countess were the last left in the restaurant-car.

When they rose at length and moved in the direction of the door, Poirot sprang up and followed them.

'Pardon, Madame, you have dropped your handkerchief.'

He was holding out to her the tiny monogrammed square.

She took it, glanced at it, then handed it back to him.

'You are mistaken, Monsieur, that is not my handkerchief.'

'Not your handkerchief? Are you sure?'

'Perfectly sure, Monsieur.'

'And yet, Madame, it has your initial – the initial H.'

The Count made a sudden movement. Poirot ignored him. His eyes were fixed on the Countess's face.

Looking steadily at him she replied:

'I do not understand, Monsieur. My initials are E.A.'

'I think not. Your name is Helena – not Elena. Helena Goldenberg, the younger daughter of Linda Arden – Helena Goldenberg, the sister of Mrs Armstrong.'

There was a dead silence for a minute or two. Both the Count and Countess had gone deadly white. Poirot said in a gentler tone:

'It is of no use denying. That is the truth, is it not?'

The Count burst out furiously:

'I demand, Monsieur, by what right you –'

She interrupted him, putting up a small hand towards his mouth.

'No, Rudolph. Let me speak. It is useless to deny what this gentleman says. We had better sit down and talk the matter out.'

Her voice had changed. It still had the southern richness of tone, but it had become suddenly more clear cut and incisive. It was, for the first time, a definitely American voice.

The Count was silenced. He obeyed the gesture of her hand they both sat down opposite Poirot.

'Your statement, Monsieur, is quite true,' said the Countess. 'I am Helena Goldenberg, the younger sister of Mrs Armstrong.'

'You did not acquaint me with that fact this morning, Madame la Comtesse.'

'No.'

'In fact, all that your husband and you told me was a tissue of lies.'

'Monsieur,' cried the Count angrily.

'Do not be angry, Rudolph. M. Poirot puts the fact rather brutally, but what he says is undeniable.'

'I am glad you admit the fact so freely, Madame. Will you now tell me your reasons for so doing and also for altering your Christian name on your passport.'

'That was my doing entirely,' put in the Count.

Helena said quietly:

'Surely, M. Poirot, you can guess my reason – our reason. This man who was killed is the man who murdered my baby niece, who killed my sister, who broke my brother-in-law's heart. Three of the people I loved best and who made up my home – my world!'

Her voice rang out passionately. She was a true daughter of that mother, the emotional force of whose acting had moved huge audiences to tears.

She went on more quietly.

'Of all the people on the train, I alone had probably the best motive for killing him.'

'And you did not kill him, Madame?'

'I swear to you, M. Poirot, and my husband knows and will swear also – that, much as I may have been tempted to do so, I never lifted a hand against that man.'

'I too, gentlemen,' said the Count. 'I give you my word of honour that last night Helena never left her compartment. She took a sleeping draught exactly as I said. She is utterly and entirely innocent.'

Poirot looked from one to the other of them.

'On my word of honour,' repeated the Count.

Poirot shook his head slightly.

'And yet you took it upon yourself to alter the name in the passport?'

'Monsieur Poirot,' the Count spoke earnestly and passionately. 'Consider my position. Do you think I could stand the thought of my wife dragged through a sordid police case. She was innocent, I knew it, but what she said was true – because of her connection with the Armstrong family she would have been immediately suspected. She would have been questioned – arrested, perhaps. Since some evil chance had taken us on the same train as this man Ratchett, there was, I felt sure, but one thing for it. I admit, Monsieur, that I lied to you – all, that is, save in one thing. My wife never left her compartment last night.'

He spoke with an earnestness that it was hard to gainsay.

'I do not say that I disbelieve you, Monsieur,' said Poirot slowly. 'Your family is, I know, a proud and ancient one. It would be bitter indeed for you to have your wife dragged into an unpleasant police case. With that I can sympathize. But how, then, do you explain the presence of your wife's handkerchief actually in the dead man's compartment?'

'That handkerchief is not mine, Monsieur,' said the Countess.

'In spite of the initial H?'

'In spite of the initial. I have handkerchiefs not unlike that, but not one that is exactly of that pattern. I know, of course that I cannot hope to make you believe me, but I assure you that it is so. That handkerchief is not mine.'

'It may have been placed there by someone in order to incriminate you?'

She smiled a little.

'You are enticing me to admit that, after all, it is mine? But indeed, M. Poirot, it isn't.'

She spoke with great earnestness.

'Then why, if the handkerchief was not yours, did you alter the name in the passport?'

The Count answered this.

'Because we heard that a handkerchief had been found with the initial H on it. We talked the matter over together before we came to be interviewed. I pointed out to Helena that if it were seen that her Christian name began with an H she would immediately be subjected to much more rigorous questioning. And the thing was so simple – to alter Helena to Elena was easily done.'

'You have, M. le Comte, the makings of a very fine criminal,' remarked Poirot dryly. 'A great natural ingenuity, and an apparently remorseless determination to mislead justice.'

'Oh, no, no,' the girl leaned forward. 'M. Poirot, he's explained to you how it was.' She broke from French into English. 'I was scared – absolutely dead scared, you understand. It had been so awful – that time – and to have it all raked up again. And to be suspected and perhaps thrown into prison. I was just scared stiff, M. Poirot. Can't you understand at all?'

Her voice was lovely – deep – rich – pleading, the voice of the daughter of Linda Arden the actress.

Poirot looked gravely at her.

'If I am to believe you, Madame – and I do not say that I will *not* believe you – then you must help me.'

'Help you?'

'Yes. The reason for the murder lies in the past – in that tragedy which broke up your home and saddened your young life. Take me back into the past, Mademoiselle, that I may find there the link that explains the whole thing.'

'What can there be to tell you? They are all dead.' She repeated mournfully. 'All dead – all dead – Robert, Sonia – darling, darling Daisy. She was so sweet – so happy – she had such lovely curls. We were all just crazy about her.'

'There was another victim, Madame. An indirect victim, you might say.'

'Poor Susanne? Yes, I had forgotten about her. The police questioned her. They were convinced she had something to do with it. Perhaps she had – but if so, only innocently. She had, I believe, chatted idly with someone, giving information as to the time of Daisy's outings. The poor thing got terribly wrought up – she thought she was being held responsible.' She shuddered. 'She threw herself out of the window. Oh it was horrible.'

She buried her face in her hands.

'What nationality was she, Madame?'

'She was French.'

'What was her last name?'

'It's absurd, but I can't remember – we all called her Susanne. A pretty laughing girl. She was devoted to Daisy.'

'She was the nursery-maid, was she not?'

'Yes.'

'Who was the nurse?'

'She was a trained hospital nurse. Stengelberg her name was. She, too, was devoted to Daisy – and to my sister.'

'Now, Madame, I want you to think carefully before you answer this question. Have you, since you were on this train, seen anyone that you recognized?'

She stared at him.

'I? No, no one at all.'

'What about Princess Dragomiroff?'

'Oh, her? I know her, of course. I thought you meant anyone – anyone from – from that time.'

'So I did, Madame. Now think carefully. Some years have passed, remember. The person might have altered their appearance.'

Helena pondered deeply. Then she said:

'No – I am sure – there is no one.'

'You yourself – you were a young girl at the time – did you have no one to superintend your studies or to look after you?'

'Oh, yes, I had a dragon – a sort of governess to me and secretary to Sonia combined. She was English or rather Scotch – a big, red-haired woman.'

'What was her name?'

'Miss Freebody.'

'Young or old?'

'She seemed frightfully old to me. I suppose she couldn't have been more than forty. Susanne, of course, used to look after my clothes and maid me.'

'And there were no other inmates of the house?'

'Only servants.'

'And you are certain – quite certain, Madame – that you have recognized no one on the train?'

She replied earnestly:

'No one, Monsieur. No one at all.'

CHAPTER 5

THE CHRISTIAN NAME OF PRINCESS DRAGOMIROFF

When the Count and Countess had departed, Poirot looked across at the other two.

'You see,' he said, 'we make progress.'

'Excellent work,' said M. Bouc cordially. 'For my part, I should never have dreamed of suspecting Count and Countess Andrenyi. I will admit I thought them quite *hors de combat*. I suppose there is no doubt that she committed the crime? It is rather sad. Still, they will not guillotine her. There are extenuating circumstances. A few years' imprisonment – that will be all.'

'In fact you are quite certain of her guilt.'

'My dear friend, surely there is no doubt of it? I thought your reassuring manner was only to smooth things over till we are dug out of the snow and the police take charge.'

'You do not believe the Count's positive assertion – on his word of honour – that his wife is innocent?'

'*Mon cher* – naturally – what else *could* he say? He adores his wife. He wants to save her! He tells his lie very well – quite in the grand Seigneur manner, but what else than a lie could it be?'

'Well, you know, I had the preposterous idea that it might be the truth.'

'No, no. The handkerchief, remember. The handkerchief clinches the matter.'

'Oh, I am not so sure about the handkerchief. You remember, I always told you that there were two possibilities as to the ownership of the handkerchief.'

'All the same –'

M. Bouc broke off. The door at the end had opened, and Princess Dragomiroff entered the dining-car. She came straight to them and all three men rose to their feet.

She spoke to Poirot, ignoring the others.

'I believe, Monsieur,' she said, 'that you have a handkerchief of mine.'

Poirot shot a glance of triumph at the other two.

'Is this it, Madame?'

He produced the little square of fine cambric.

'That is it. It has my initial in the corner.'

'But, Madame la Princesse, that is the letter H,' said M. Bouc. 'Your Christian name – pardon me – is Natalia.'

She gave him a cold stare.

'That is correct, Monsieur. My handkerchiefs are always initialled in the Russian characters. H is N in Russian.'

M. Bouc was somewhat taken aback. There was something about this indomitable old lady which made him feel flustered and uncomfortable.

'You did not tell us that this handkerchief was yours at the inquiry this morning.'

'You did not ask me,' said the Princess dryly.

'Pray be seated, Madame,' said Poirot.

She sighed.

'I may as well, I suppose.'

She sat down.

'You need not make a long business of this, Messieurs. Your next question will be – how did my handkerchief come to be lying by a murdered man's body? My reply to that is that I have no idea.'

'You have really no idea.'

'None whatever.'

'You will excuse me, Madame, but how much can we rely upon the truthfulness of your replies?'

Poirot said the words very softly. Princess Dragomiroff answered contemptuously.

'I suppose you mean because I did not tell you that Helena Andrenyi was Mrs Armstrong's sister?'

'In fact you deliberately lied to us in the matter.'

'Certainly. I would do the same again. Her mother was my friend. I believe, Messieurs, in loyalty – to one's friends and one's family and one's caste.'

'You do not believe in doing your utmost to further the ends of justice?'

'In this case I consider that justice – strict justice – has been done.'

Poirot leaned forward.

'You see my difficulty, Madame. In this matter of the handkerchief, even, am I to believe you? Or are you shielding your friend's daughter?'

'Oh! I see what you mean.' Her face broke into a grim smile. 'Well, Messieurs, this statement of mine can be easily proved. I will give you the address of the people in Paris who make my handkerchiefs. You have only to show them the one in question and they will inform you that it was made to my order over a year ago. The handkerchief is mine, Messieurs.'

She rose.

'Have you anything further you wish to ask me?'

'Your maid, Madame, did she recognize this handkerchief when we showed it to her this morning?'

'She must have done so. She saw it and said nothing? Ah, well, that shows that she too can be loyal.'

With a slight inclination of her head she passed out of the dining-car.

'So that was it,' murmured Poirot softly. 'I noticed just a trifling hesitation when I asked the maid if she knew to whom the handkerchief belonged. She was uncertain whether or not to admit that it was her mistress's. But how does that fit in with that strange central idea of mine? Yes, it might well be.'

'Ah!' said M. Bouc with a characteristic gesture – 'she is a terrible old lady, that!'

'Could she have murdered Ratchett?' asked Poirot of the doctor.

He shook his head.

'Those blows – the ones delivered with great force penetrating the muscle – never, never could anyone with so frail a physique inflict them.'

'But the feebler ones?'

'The feebler ones, yes.'

'I am thinking,' said Poirot, 'of the incident this morning when I said to her that the strength was in her will rather than in her arm. It was in the nature of a trap, that remark. I wanted to see if she would look down at her right or her left arm. She did neither. She looked at them both. But she made a strange reply. She said, "No, I have no strength in these. I do not know whether to be sorry or glad." A curious remark that. It confirms me in my belief about the crime.'

'It did not settle the point about the left-handedness.'

'No. By the way, did you notice that Count Andrenyi keeps his handkerchief in his right-hand breast pocket?'

M. Bouc shook his head. His mind reverted to the astonishing revelations of the last half-hour. He murmured:

'Lies – and again lies – it amazes me, the amount of lies we had told to us this morning.'

'There are more still to discover,' said Poirot cheerfully.

'You think so?'

'I shall be very disappointed if it is not so.'

'Such duplicity is terrible,' said M. Bouc. 'But it seems to please you,' he added reproachfully.

'It has this advantage,' said Poirot. 'If you confront anyone who has lied with the truth, they usually admit it – often out of sheer surprise. It is only necessary to guess *right* to produce your effect.

'That is the only way to conduct this case. I select each passenger in turn, consider their evidence and say to myself, "*If* so and so is lying, on what point are they lying and what is the *reason* for the lie?" And I answer *if* they are lying – *if*, you mark – it could only be for such a reason and on such a point. We have done that once very successfully with Countess Andrenyi. We shall now proceed to try the same method on several other persons.'

'And supposing, my friend, that your guess happens to be wrong?'

'Then one person, at any rate, will be completely freed from suspicion.'

'Ah! A process of elimination.'

'Exactly.'

'And who do we tackle next?'

'We are going to tackle that *pukka sahib*, Colonel Arbuthnot.'

CHAPTER 6

A SECOND INTERVIEW WITH COLONEL ARBUTHNOT

Colonel Arbuthnot was clearly annoyed at being summoned to the dining-car for a second interview. His face wore a most forbidding expression as he sat down and said:

'Well?'

'All my apologies for troubling you a second time,' said Poirot. 'But there is still some information that I think you might be able to give us.'

'Indeed? I hardly think so.'

'To begin with, you see this pipe-cleaner?'

'Yes.'

'Is it one of yours?'

'Don't know. I don't put a private mark on them, you know.'

'Are you aware, Colonel Arbuthnot, that you are the only man amongst the passengers in the Stamboul-Calais carriage who smokes a pipe?'

'In that case it probably is one of mine.'

'Do you know where it was found?'

'Not the least idea.'

'It was found by the body of the murdered man.'

Colonel Arbuthnot raised his eyebrows.

'Can you tell us, Colonel Arbuthnot, how it is likely to have got there?'

'If you mean did I drop it there myself, no, I didn't.'

'Did you go into Mr Ratchett's compartment at any time?'

'I never even spoke to the man.'

'You never spoke to him and you did not murder him?'

The Colonel's eyebrows went up again sardonically.

'If I had, I should hardly be likely to acquaint you with the fact. As a matter of fact I *didn't* murder the fellow.'

'Ah, well,' murmured Poirot. 'It is of no consequence.'

'I beg your pardon?'

'I said that it was of no consequence.'

'Oh!' Arbuthnot looked taken aback. He eyed Poirot uneasily.

'Because, you see,' continued the little man, 'the pipe-cleaner, it is of no importance. I can myself think of eleven other excellent explanations of its presence.'

Arbuthnot stared at him.

'What I really wished to see you about was quite another matter,' went on Poirot. 'Miss Debenham may have told you, perhaps, that I overheard some words spoken to you at the station of Konya?'

Arbuthnot did not reply.

'She said, "*Not now. When it's all over. When it's behind us.*" Do you know to what those words referred?'

'I am sorry, M. Poirot, but I must refuse to answer that question.'

'*Pourquoi?*'

The Colonel said stiffly:

'I suggest that you should ask Miss Debenham herself for the meaning of those words.'

'I have done so.'

'And she refused to tell you?'

'Yes.'

'Then I should think it would have been perfectly plain – even to you – that my lips are sealed.'

'You will not give away a lady's secret?'

'You can put it that way, if you like.'

'Miss Debenham told me that they referred to a private matter of her own.'

'Then why not accept her word for it?'

'Because, Colonel Arbuthnot, Miss Debenham is what one might call a highly suspicious character.'

'Nonsense,' said the Colonel with warmth.

'It is not nonsense.'

'You have nothing whatever against her.'

'Not the fact that Miss Debenham was companion governess in the Armstrong household at the time of the kidnapping of little Daisy Armstrong?'

There was a minute's dead silence.

Poirot nodded his head gently.

'You see,' he said, 'we know more than you think. If Miss Debenham is innocent, why did she conceal that fact? Why did she tell me that she had never been in America?'

The Colonel cleared his throat.

'Aren't you possibly making a mistake?'

'I am making no mistake. Why did Miss Debenham lie to me?'

Colonel Arbuthnot shrugged his shoulders.

'You had better ask her. I still think that you are wrong.'

Poirot raised his voice and called. One of the restaurant attendants came from the far end of the car.

'Go and ask the English lady in No. 11 if she will be good enough to come here.'

'*Bien, Monsieur.*'

The man departed. The four men sat in silence. Colonel Arbuthnot's face looked as though it were carved out of wood, it was rigid and impassive.

The man returned.

'Thank you.'

A minute or two later Mary Debenham entered the dining-car.

CHAPTER 7

THE IDENTITY OF MARY DEBENHAM

She wore no hat. Her head was thrown back as though in defiance. The sweep of her hair back from her face, the curve of her nostril suggested the figurehead of a ship plunging gallantly into a rough sea. In that moment she was beautiful.

Her eyes went to Arbuthnot for a minute – just a minute.

She said to Poirot?

'You wished to see me?'

'I wished to ask you, Mademoiselle, why you lied to us this morning?'

'Lied to you? I don't know what you mean.'

'You concealed the fact that at the time of the Armstrong tragedy you were actually living in the house. You told me that you had never been in America.'

He saw her flinch for a moment and then recover herself.

'Yes,' she said. 'That is true.'

'No, Mademoiselle, it was false.'

'You misunderstood me. I mean that it is true that I lied to you.'

'Ah, you admit it?'

Her lips curved into a smile.

'Certainly. Since you have found me out.'

'You are at least frank, Mademoiselle.'

'There does not seem anything else for me to be.'

'Well, of course, that is true. And now, Mademoiselle, may I ask you the reason for these evasions?'

'I should have thought the reason leapt to the eye, M. Poirot?'

'It does not leap to mine, Mademoiselle.'

She said in a quiet, even voice with a trace of hardness in it:

'I have my living to get.'

'You mean –?'

She raised her eyes and looked him full in the face.

'How much do you know, M. Poirot, of the fight to get and keep decent employment? Do you think that a girl who had been detained in connection with a murder case, whose name and perhaps photographs were reproduced in the English papers

– do you think that any nice ordinary middle-class Englishwoman would want to engage that girl as governess to her daughters?'

'I do not see why not – if no blame attached to you.'

'Oh, blame – it is not blame – it is publicity! So far, M. Poirot, I have succeeded in life. I have had well-paid, pleasant posts. I was not going to risk the position I had attained when no good end could have been served.'

'I will venture to suggest, Mademoiselle, that I would have been the best judge of that, not you.'

She shrugged her shoulders.

'For instance, you could have helped me in the matter of identification.'

'What do you mean?'

'Is it possible, Mademoiselle, that you did not recognize in the Countess Andrenyi Mrs Armstrong's young sister whom you taught in New York?'

'Countess Andrenyi? No.' She shook her head. 'It may seem extraordinary to you, but I did not recognize her. She was not grown up, you see, when I knew her. That was over three years ago. It is true that the Countess reminded me of someone – it puzzled me. But she looks so foreign – I never connected her with the little American schoolgirl. It is true that I only glanced at her casually when coming into the restaurant-car. I noticed her clothes more than her face –' she smiled faintly – 'women do! And then – well, I had my own preoccupations.'

'You will not tell me your secret, Mademoiselle?'

Poirot's voice was very gentle and persuasive.

She said in a low voice:

'I can't – I can't.'

And suddenly, without warning she broke down, dropping her face down upon her outstretched arms and crying as though her heart would break.

The Colonel sprang up and stood awkwardly beside her.

'I – look here –'

He stopped and, turning round, scowled fiercely at Poirot.

'I'll break every bone in your damned body, you dirty little whipper-snapper,' he said.

'Monsieur,' protested M. Bouc.

Arbuthnot had turned back to the girl.

'Mary – for God's sake –'

She sprang up.

'It's nothing. I'm all right. You don't need me any more, do you, M. Poirot? If you do, you must come and find me. Oh, what an idiot – what an idiot I'm making of myself!'

She hurried out of the car. Arbuthnot, before following her, turned once more on Poirot.

'Miss Debenham's got nothing to do with this business – nothing, do you hear? And if she's worried and interfered with, you'll have me to deal with.'

He strode out.

'I like to see an angry Englishman,' said Poirot. 'They are very amusing. The more emotional they feel the less command they have of language.'

But M. Bouc was not interested in the emotional reactions of Englishmen. He was overcome by admiration of his friend.

'*Mon cher, vous êtes épatant,*' he cried. 'Another miraculous guess. *C'est formidable.*'

'It is incredible how you think of these things,' said Dr Constantine admiringly.

'Oh, I claim no credit this time. It was not a guess. Countess Andrenyi practically told me.'

'*Comment?* Surely not?'

'You remember I asked her about her governess or companion? I had already decided in my mind that *if* Mary Debenham were mixed up in the matter, she must have figured in the household in some such capacity.'

'Yes, but the Countess Andrenyi described a totally different person.'

'Exactly. A tall, middle-aged woman with red hair – in fact, the exact opposite in every respect of Miss Debenham, so much so as to be quite remarkable. But then she had to invent a name quickly, and there it was that the unconscious association of ideas gave her away. She said Miss Freebody, you remember.'

'Yes?'

'*Eh bien*, you may not know it, but there is a shop in London that was called, until recently, Debenham & Freebody. With the name Debenham running in her head, the Countess clutches at another name quickly, and the first that comes is Freebody. Naturally I understood immediately.'

'That is yet another lie. Why did she do it?'

'Possibly more loyalty. It makes things a little difficult.'

'*Ma foi*,' said M. Bouc with violence. 'But does everybody on this train tell lies?'

'That,' said Poirot, 'is what we are about to find out.'

CHAPTER 8

FURTHER SURPRISING REVELATIONS

'Nothing would surprise me now,' said M. Bouc. 'Nothing! Even if everybody in the train proved to have been in the Armstrong household I should not express surprise.'

'That is a very profound remark,' said Poirot. 'Would you like to see what your favourite suspect, the Italian, has to say for himself?'

'You are going to make another of these famous guesses of yours?'

'Precisely.'

'It is really a *most* extraordinary case,' said Constantine.

'No, it is most natural.'

M. Bouc flung up his arms in comic despair.

'If this is what you call natural, *mon ami* –'

Words failed him.

Poirot had by this time requested the dining-car attendant to fetch Antonio Foscarelli.

The big Italian had a wary look in his eye as he came in. He shot nervous glances from side to side like a trapped animal.

'What do you want?' he said. 'I have nothing to tell you – nothing, do you hear! *Per Dio* –' He struck his hand on the table.

'Yes, you have something more to tell us,' said Poirot firmly. 'The truth!'

'The truth?' He shot an uneasy glance at Poirot. All the assurance and geniality had gone out of his manner.

'*Mais oui*. It may be that I know it already. But it will be a point in your favour if it comes from you spontaneously.'

'You talk like the American police. "Come clean", that is what they say – "come clean."'

'Ah! so you have had experience of the New York police?'

'No, no, never. They could not prove a thing against me – but it was not for want of trying.'

Poirot said quietly:

'That was in the Armstrong case, was it not? You were the chauffeur?'

His eyes met those of the Italian. The bluster went out of the big man. He was like a pricked balloon.

'Since you know – why ask me?'

'Why did you lie this morning?'

'Business reasons. Besides, I do not trust the Yugo-Slav police. They hate the Italians. They would not have given me justice.'

'Perhaps it is exactly justice that they *would* have given you!'

'No, no, I had nothing to do with this business last night. I never left my carriage. The long-faced Englishman, he can tell you so. It was not I who killed this pig – this Ratchett. You cannot prove anything against me.'

Poirot was writing something on a sheet of paper. He looked up and said quietly?

'Very good. You can go.'

Foscarelli lingered uneasily.

'You realize that it was not I – that I could have had nothing to do with it?'

'I said that you could go.'

'It is a conspiracy. You are going to frame me? All for a pig of a man who should have gone to the chair! It was an infamy that he did not. If it had been me – if I had been arrested –'

'But it was not you. You had nothing to do with the kidnapping of the child.'

'What is that you are saying? Why, that little one – she was the delight of the house. Tonio, she called me. And she would sit in the car and pretend to hold the wheel. All the household worshipped her! Even the police came to understand that. Ah, the beautiful little one.'

His voice had softened. The tears came into his eyes. Then he wheeled round abruptly on his heel and strode out of the dining-car.

'Pietro,' called Poirot.

The dining-car attendant came at a run.

'The No. 10 – the Swedish lady.'

'*Bien, Monsieur.*'

'Another?' cried M. Bouc. 'Ah, no – it is not possible. I tell you it is not possible.'

'*Mon cher*, we have to know. Even if in the end everybody on the train proves to have a motive for killing Ratchett, we have to know. Once we know, we can settle once for all where the guilt lies.'

'My head is spinning,' groaned M. Bouc.

Greta Ohlsson was ushered in sympathetically by the attendant. She was weeping bitterly.

She collapsed on the seat facing Poirot and wept steadily into a large handkerchief.

'Now do not distress yourself, Mademoiselle. Do not distress yourself.' Poirot patted her on the shoulder. 'Just a few little words of truth, that is all. You were the nurse who was in charge of little Daisy Armstrong?'

'It is true – it is true,' wept the wretched woman. 'Ah, she was an angel – a little sweet, trustful angel. She knew nothing but kindness and love – and she was taken away by that wicked man – cruelly treated – and her poor mother – and the other little one who never lived at all. You cannot understand – you cannot know – if you had been there as I was – if you had seen the whole terrible tragedy – I ought to have told you the truth about myself this morning. But I was afraid – afraid. I did so rejoice that that evil man was dead – that he could not any more kill or torture little children. Ah! I cannot speak – I have no words . . .'

She wept with more vehemence than ever.

Poirot continued to pat her gently on the shoulder.

'There – there – I comprehend – I comprehend everything – everything, I tell you. I will ask you no more questions. It is enough that you have admitted what I know to be the truth. I understand, I tell you.'

By now inarticulate with sobs, Greta Ohlsson rose and groped her way blindly towards the door. As she reached it she collided with a man coming in.

It was the valet – Masterman.

He came straight up to Poirot and spoke in his usual, quiet, unemotional voice.

'I hope I'm not intruding, sir. I thought it best to come along at once, sir, and tell you the truth. I was Colonel Armstrong's batman in the war, sir, and afterwards I was his valet in New York. I'm afraid I concealed that fact this morning. It was very wrong of me, sir, and I thought I'd better come and make a clean breast of it. But I hope, sir, that you're not suspecting Tonio in any way. Old Tonio, sir, wouldn't hurt a fly. And I can swear positively that he never left the carriage all last night. So, you see, sir, he couldn't have done it. Tonio may be a foreigner, sir, but he's a very gentle creature – not like those nasty murdering Italians one reads about.'

He stopped.

Poirot looked steadily at him.

'Is that all you have to say?'

'That is all, sir.'

He paused, then, as Poirot did not speak, he made an apologetic little bow, and after a momentary hesitation left the dining-car in the same quiet, unobtrusive fashion as he had come.

'This,' said Dr Constantine, 'is more wildly improbable than any *roman policier* I have ever read.'

'I agree,' said M. Bouc. 'Of the twelve passengers in that coach, nine have been proved to have had a connection with the Armstrong case. What next, I ask you? Or, should I say, who next?'

'I can almost give you the answer to your question,' said Poirot. 'Here comes our American sleuth, M. Hardman.'

'Is he, too, coming to confess?'

Before Poirot could reply, the American had reached their table. He cocked an alert eye at them and, sitting down, he drawled out:

'Just exactly what's up on this train? It seems bughouse to me.'

Poirot twinkled at him:

'Are you quite sure, Mr Hardman, that you yourself were not the gardener at the Armstrong home?'

'They didn't have a garden,' replied Mr Hardman literally.

'Or the butler?'

'Haven't got the fancy manner for a place like that. No, I never had any connection with the Armstrong house – but I'm beginning to believe I'm about the only one on this train who hadn't! Can you beat it – that's what I say? Can you beat it?'

'It is certainly a little surprising,' said Poirot mildly.

'*C'est rigolo,*' burst from M. Bouc.

'Have you any ideas of your own about the crime, M. Hardman?' inquired Poirot.

'No, sir. It's got me beat. I don't know how to figure it out. They can't all be in it; but which one is the guilty party is beyond me. How did you get wise to all this, that's what I want to know?'

'I just guessed.'

'Then, believe me, you're a pretty slick guesser. Yes, I'll tell the world you're a slick guesser.'

Mr Hardman leaned back and looked at Poirot admiringly.

'You'll excuse me,' he said, 'but no one would believe it to look at you. I take off my hat to you. I do, indeed.'

'You are too kind, M. Hardman.'

'Not at all. I've got to hand it to you.'

'All the same,' said Poirot, 'the problem is not yet quite solved. Can we say with authority that we know who killed M. Ratchett?'

'Count me out,' said Mr Hardman. 'I'm not saying anything at all. I'm just full of natural admiration. What about the other two you've not had a guess at yet? The old American dame and the lady's-maid? I suppose we can take it that they're the only innocent parties on the train?'

'Unless,' said Poirot, smiling, 'we can fit them into our little collection as – shall we say? – housekeeper and cook in the Armstrong household.'

'Well, nothing in the world would surprise me now,' said Mr Hardman with quiet resignation. 'Bughouse – that's what this business is – bughouse!'

'Ah, *mon cher*, that would be indeed stretching coincidence a little too far,' said M. Bouc. 'They cannot all be in it.'

Poirot looked at him.

'You do not understand,' he said. 'You do not understand at all. Tell me,' he said, 'do you know who killed Ratchett?'

'Do you?' countered M. Bouc.

Poirot nodded.

'Oh, yes,' he said. 'I have known for some time. It is so clear that

I wonder you have not seen it also.' He looked at Hardman and asked, 'And you?'

The detective shook his head. He stared at Poirot curiously.

'I don't know,' he said. 'I don't know at all. Which of them was it?'

Poirot was silent a minute. Then he said:

'If you will be so good, M. Hardman, assemble everyone here. There are two possible solutions of this case. I want to lay them both before you all.'

CHAPTER 9

POIROT PROPOUNDS TWO SOLUTIONS

The passengers came crowding into the restaurant-car and took their seats round the tables. They all bore more or less the same expression, one of expectancy mingled with apprehension. The Swedish lady was still weeping and Mrs Hubbard was comforting her.

'Now you must just take a hold on yourself, my dear. Everything's going to be perfectly all right. You mustn't lose your grip on yourself. If one of us is a nasty murderer we know quite well it isn't you. Why, anyone would be crazy even to think of such a thing. You sit here and I'll stay right by you; and don't you worry any.'

Her voice died away as Poirot stood up.

The Wagon Lit conductor was hovering in the doorway.

'You permit that I stay, Monsieur?'

'Certainly, Michel.'

Poirot cleared his throat.

'Messieurs et Mesdames, I will speak in English, since I think all of you know a little of that language. We are here to investigate the death of Samuel Edward Ratchett – alias Cassetti. There are two possible solutions of the crime. I shall put them both before you, and I shall ask M. Bouc and Dr Constantine here to judge which solution is the right one.

'Now you all know the facts of the case. Mr Ratchett was found stabbed this morning. He was last known to be alive at 12.37 last night, when he spoke to the Wagon Lit conductor through the door. A watch in his pyjama pocket was found to be badly dented and it had stopped at a quarter-past one. Dr Constantine, who examined the body when found, puts the time of death as having occurred between midnight and two in the morning. At half an hour after midnight, as you all know, the train ran into a snowdrift. After that time it *was impossible for anyone to leave the train.*

'The evidence of Mr Hardman, who is a member of a New York Detective Agency' (several heads turned to look at Mr Hardman) 'shows that no one could have passed his compartment (No. 16 at the extreme end) without being seen by him. We are therefore forced to the conclusion that the murderer is to be found among the occupants of one particular coach – the Stamboul-Calais coach.

'That, I will say, *was* our theory.'

'*Comment*?' ejaculated M. Bouc, startled.

'But I will put before you an alternative theory. It is very simple. Mr Ratchett had a certain enemy whom he feared. He gave Mr Hardman a description of this enemy and told him that the attempt, if made at all, would most probably be made on the second night out from Stamboul.

'Now I put it to you, ladies and gentlemen, that Mr Ratchett knew a good deal more than he told. The enemy as Mr Ratchett expected, joined the train at *Belgrade, or possibly at Vincovci*, by the door left open by Colonel Arbuthnot and Mr MacQueen who had just descended to the platform. He was provided with a suit of Wagon Lit uniform, which he wore over his ordinary clothes, and a pass key which enabled him to gain access to Mr Ratchett's compartment in spite of the door being locked. Mr Ratchett was under the influence of a sleeping draught. This man stabbed him with great ferocity and left the compartment through the communicating door leading to Mrs Hubbard's compartment –'

'That's so,' said Mrs Hubbard, nodding her head.

'He thrust the dagger he had used into Mrs Hubbard's sponge-bag in passing. Without knowing it, he lost a button of his uniform. Then he slipped out of the compartment and along the corridor. He hastily thrust the uniform into a suitcase in an empty compartment, and a few minutes later, dressed in ordinary clothes, he left the train just before it started off. Again using the same means of egress – the door near the dining-car.'

Everybody gasped.

'What about that watch?' demanded Mr Hardman.

'There you have the explanation of the whole thing. *Mr Ratchett had omitted to put his watch back an hour as he should have done* at Tzaribrod. His watch still registered Eastern European time, which is one hour *ahead* of Central European time. It was a quarter-past *twelve* when Mr Ratchett was stabbed – not a quarter-past one.'

'But it is absurd, that explanation,' cried M. Bouc. 'What of the voice that spoke from the compartment at twenty-three minutes to one. It was either the voice of Ratchett – or else of his murderer.'

'Not necessarily. It might have been – well – a third person. One who had gone in to speak to Ratchett and found him dead. He rang the bell to summon the conductor, then, as you express it, the wind rose in him – he was afraid of being accused of the crime and he spoke pretending to be Ratchett.'

'*C'est possible*,' admitted M. Bouc grudgingly.

Poirot looked at Mrs Hubbard.

'Yes, Madame, you were going to say –?'

'Well, I don't quite know what I was going to say. Do you think I forgot to put my watch back too?'

'No, Madame. I think you heard the man pass through – but unconsciously; later you had a nightmare of a man being in your compartment and woke up with a start and rang for the conductor.'

'Well, I suppose that's possible,' admitted Mrs Hubbard.

Princess Dragomiroff was looking at Poirot with a very direct glance.

'How do you explain the evidence of my maid, Monsieur?'

'Very simply, Madame. Your maid recognized the handkerchief I showed her as yours. She somewhat clumsily tried to shield you. She did encounter the man – but earlier – while the train was at Vincovci station. She pretended to have seen him at a later hour with a confused idea of giving you a watertight *alibi*.'

The Princess bowed her head.

'You have thought of everything, Monsieur. I – I admire you.'

There was a silence.

Then everyone jumped as Dr Constantine suddenly hit the table a blow with his fist.

'But no,' he said. 'No, no, and again no! That is an explanation that will not hold water. It is deficient in a dozen minor points. The crime was not committed so – M. Poirot must know that perfectly well.'

Poirot turned a curious glance on him.

'I see,' he said, 'that I shall have to give my second solution. But do not abandon this one too abruptly. You may agree with it later.'

He turned back again to face the others.

'There is another possible solution of the crime. This is how I arrived at it.

'When I had heard all the evidence, I leaned back and shut my eyes and began to *think*. Certain points presented themselves to me as worthy of attention. I enumerated these points to my two colleagues. Some I have already elucidated – such as a grease spot on a passport, etc. I will run over the points that remain. The first and most important is a remark made to me by M. Bouc in the restaurant-car at lunch on the first day after leaving Stamboul – to the effect that the company assembled was interesting because it was so varied – representing as it did all classes and nationalities.

'I agreed with him, but when this particular point came into my mind, I tried to imagine whether such an assembly were ever likely to be collected under any other conditions. And the answer I made to myself was – only in America. In America there might be a household composed of just such varied nationalities – an Italian chauffeur, and English governess, a Swedish nurse, a French lady's-maid and so on. That led me to my scheme of "guessing" – that is, casting each person for a certain part in the Armstrong drama much as a producer casts a play. Well, that gave me an extremely interesting and satisfactory result.

'I had also examined in my own mind each separate person's evidence with some curious results. Take first the evidence of Mr MacQueen. My first interview with him was entirely satisfactory. But in my second he made rather a curious remark. I had described to him the finding of a note mentioning the Armstrong case. He said, "But surely –" and then paused and went on, "I mean – that was rather careless of the old man."

'Now I could feel that that was not what he had started out to say. *Supposing what he had meant to say was, "But surely that was burnt!*" In which case, *MacQueen knew of the note and of its destruction* – in other words, he was either the murderer or an accomplice of the murderer. Very good.

'Then the valet. He said his master was in the habit of taking a sleeping draught when travelling by train. That might be true, but *would Ratchett have taken one last night*? The automatic under his pillow gave the lie to that statement. Ratchett intended to be on the alert last night. Whatever narcotic was administered to him must have been done so without his knowledge. By whom? Obviously by MacQueen or the valet.

'Now we come to the evidence of Mr Hardman. I believed all that he told me about his own identity, but when it came to the actual methods he had employed to guard Mr Ratchett, his story was neither more nor less than absurd. The only way effectively to have protected Ratchett was to have passed the night actually in his compartment or in some spot where he could watch the door. The only thing that his evidence *did* show plainly was that no one *in any other part of the train could possibly have murdered Ratchett.* It drew a clear circle round the Stamboul-Calais carriage. That seemed to me a rather curious and inexplicable fact, and I put it aside to think over.

'You probably have all heard by now of the few words I overheard between Miss Debenham and Colonel Arbuthnot. The interesting thing to my mind was the fact that Colonel Arbuthnot called her *Mary* and was clearly on terms of intimacy with her. But the Colonel was only supposed to have met her a few days previously – and I know Englishmen of the Colonel's type. Even if he had fallen in love with the young lady at first sight, he would have advanced slowly and with decorum – not rushing things. Therefore I concluded that Colonel Arbuthnot and Miss Debenham were in reality well acquainted, and were for some reason pretending to be strangers. Another small point was Miss Debenham's easy familiarity with the term "long distance" for a telephone call. Yet Miss Debenham had told me that she had never been in the States.

'To pass to another witness. Mrs Hubbard had told us that lying in bed she was unable to see whether the communicating door was bolted or not, and so asked Miss Ohlsson to see for her. Now, though her statement would have been perfectly true if she had been occupying compartments Nos. 2, 4, 12, or any *even* number – where the bolt is directly under the handle of the door – in the *uneven* numbers, such as compartment No. 3, the bolt is well *above* the handle and could not therefore be masked by the sponge-bag in the least. I was forced to the conclusion that Mrs Hubbard was inventing an incident that had never occurred.

'And here let me say just a word or two about *times*. To my mind, the really interesting point about the dented watch was the place where it was found – in Ratchett's pyjama pocket, a singularly uncomfortable and unlikely place to keep one's watch, especially as there is a watch "hook" provided just by the head of the bed. I felt sure, therefore, that the watch had been deliberately placed in the pocket and faked. The crime, then, was not committed at a quarter-past one.

'Was it, then, committed earlier? To be exact, at twenty-three minutes to one? My friend M. Bouc advanced as an argument in favour of it the loud cry which awoke me from sleep. But if Ratchett were heavily drugged *he could not have cried out*. If he had been capable of crying out he would have been capable of making some kind of a struggle to defend himself, and there were no signs of any such struggle.

'I remembered that MacQueen had called attention, not once but twice (and the second time in a very blatant manner), to the fact that Ratchett could speak no French. I came to the conclusion that the whole business at twenty-three minutes to one was a comedy played for my benefit! Anyone might see through the watch business – it is a common enough device in detective stories. They assumed that I *should* see through it and that, pluming myself on my own cleverness, I would go on to assume that since Ratchett spoke no French the voice I heard at twenty-three minutes to one could not be his, and that Ratchett must be already dead. But I am convinced that at twenty-three minutes to one Ratchett was still lying in his drugged sleep.

'But the device has succeeded! I have opened my door and looked out. I have actually heard the French phrase used. If I am so unbelievably dense as not to realize the significance of that phrase, it must be brought to my attention. If necessary MacQueen can come right out in the open. He can say, "Excuse me, M. Poirot, *that can't have been Mr Ratchett speaking*. He can't speak French."

'Now when was the real time of the crime? And who killed him?

'In my opinion, and this is only an opinion, Ratchett was killed at some time very close upon two o'clock, the latest hour the doctor gives us as possible.

'As to who killed him –'

He paused, looking at his audience. He could not complain of any lack of attention. Every eye was fixed upon him. In the stillness you could have heard a pin drop.

He went on slowly:

'I was particularly struck by the extraordinary difficulty of proving a case against any one person on the train and on the rather curious coincidence that in each case the testimony giving an alibi came from what I might describe as an "unlikely" person. Thus Mr MacQueen and Colonel Arbuthnot provided alibis for each other – two persons between whom it seemed most unlikely there should be any prior acquaintanceship. The same thing happened with the English valet and the Italian, with the Swedish lady and the English girl. I said to myself, "This is extraordinary – they cannot *all* be in it!"

'And then, Messieurs, I saw light. They were *all* in it. For so many people connected with the Armstrong case to be travelling by the same train by a coincidence was not only unlikely, it was *impossible*. It must be not chance, but *design*. I remembered a remark of Colonel Arbuthnot's about trial by jury. A jury is composed of twelve people – there were twelve passengers – Ratchett was stabbed twelve times. And the thing that had worried me all along – the extraordinary crowd travelling in the Stamboul-Calais coach at a slack time of year was explained.

'Ratchett had escaped justice in America. There was no question as to his guilt. I visualized a self-appointed jury of twelve people who condemned him to death and were forced by exigencies of the case to be their own executioners. And immediately, on that assumption, the whole case fell into beautiful shining order.

'I saw it as a perfect mosaic, each person playing his or her allotted part. It was so arranged that if suspicion should fall on any one person, the evidence of one or more of the others would clear the accused person and confuse the issue. Hardman's evidence was necessary in case some outsider should be suspected of the crime and be unable to prove an alibi. The passengers in the Stamboul carriage were in no danger. Every minute detail of their evidence was worked out beforehand. The whole thing was a very cleverly-planned jig-saw puzzle, so arranged that every fresh piece of knowledge that came to light made the solution of the whole more difficult. As my friend M. Bouc remarked, the case seemed fantastically impossible! That was exactly the impression intended to be conveyed.

'Did this solution explain everything? Yes, it did. The nature of the wounds – each inflicted by a different person. The artificial threatening letters – artificial since they were unreal, written only to be produced as evidence. (Doubtless there were real letters, warning Ratchett of his fate, which MacQueen destroyed, substituting for them these others.) Then Hardman's story of being called in by Ratchett – a lie, of course, from beginning to end – the description of the mythical "small dark man with a womanish voice", a convenient description, since it had the merit of not incriminating any of the actual Wagon Lit conductors and would apply equally well to a man or a woman.

'The idea of stabbing is at first sight a curious one, but on reflection nothing would fit the circumstances so well. A dagger was a weapon that could be used by everyone – strong or weak – and it made no noise. I fancy, though I may be wrong, that each person in turn entered Ratchett's darkened compartment through that of Mrs Hubbard – and struck! They themselves would never know which blow actually killed him.

'The final letter which Ratchett had probably found on his pillow was carefully burnt. With no clue pointing to the Armstrong case, there would be absolutely no reason for suspecting any of the passengers on the train. It would be put down as an outside job, and the "small dark man with the womanish voice" would actually have been seen by one or more of the passengers leaving the train at Brod.

'I do not know exactly what happened when the conspirators discovered that that part of their plan was impossible owing to the accident to the train. There was, I imagine, a hasty consultation, and then they decided to go through with it. It was true that now one and all of the passengers were bound to come under suspicion, but that possibility had already been foreseen and provided for.

The only additional thing to be done was to confuse the issue even further. Two so-called "clues" were dropped in the dead man's compartment – one incriminating Colonel Arbuthnot (who had the strongest alibi and whose connection with the Armstrong family was probably the hardest to prove) and the second clue, the handkerchief, incriminating Princess Dragomiroff, who by virtue of her social position, her particularly frail physique and the alibi given her by her maid and the conductor, was practically in an unassailable position. Further to confuse the issue, a "red herring" was drawn across the trail – the mythical woman in the red kimono. Again I am to bear witness to this woman's existence. There is a heavy bang at my door. I get up and look out – and see the scarlet kimono disappearing in the distance. A judicious selection of people – the conductor, Miss Debenham and MacQueen – will also have seen her. It was, I think, someone with a sense of humour who thoughtfully placed the scarlet kimono on the top of my suitcase whilst I was interviewing people in the dining-car. Where the garment came from in the first place I do not know. I suspect it is the property of Countess Andrenyi, since her luggage contained only a chiffon negligée so elaborate as to be more a tea gown than a dressing-gown.

'When MacQueen first learned that the letter which had been so carefully burnt had in part escaped destruction, and that the word Armstrong was exactly the word remaining, he must at once have communicated his news to the others. It was at this minute that the position of Countess Andrenyi became acute and her husband immediately took steps to alter the passport. It was their second piece of bad luck!

'They one and all agreed to deny utterly any connection with the Armstrong family. They knew I had no immediate means of finding out the truth, and they did not believe that I should go into the matter unless my suspicions were aroused against one particular person.

'Now there was one further point to consider. Allowing that my theory of the crime was the correct one, and I believe that it *must* be the correct one, then obviously the Wagon Lit conductor himself must be privy to the plot. But if so, that gave us thirteen persons, not twelve. Instead of the usual formula, "Of so many people one is guilty", I was faced with the problem that of thirteen persons one and one only was innocent. Which was that person?

'I came to a very odd conclusion. I came to the conclusion that the person who had taken no part in the crime was the person who would be considered the most likely to do so. I refer to Countess Andrenyi. I was impressed by the earnestness of her husband when he swore to me solemnly on his honour that his wife never left her compartment that night. I decided that Count Andrenyi took, so to speak, his wife's place.

'If so, then Pierre Michel was definitely one of the twelve. But how could one explain his complicity? He was a decent man who had been many years in the employ of the Company – not the kind of man who could be bribed to assist in a crime. Then Pierre Michel must be involved in the Armstrong case. But that seemed very improbable. Then I remembered that the dead nursery-maid was French. Supposing that that unfortunate girl had been Pierre Michel's daughter. That would explain everything – it would also explain the place chosen for the staging of the crime. Were there any others whose part in the drama was not clear? Colonel Arbuthnot I put down as a friend of the Armstrongs. They had probably been through the war together. The maid, Hildegarde Schmidt, I could guess her place in the Armstrong household. I am, perhaps, overgreedy, but I sense a good cook instinctively. I laid a trap for her – she fell into it. I said I knew she was a good cook. She answered, "Yes, indeed, all my ladies have said so." But if you are employed as a *lady's-maid* your employers seldom have a chance of learning whether or not you are a good cook.

'Then there was Hardman. He seemed quite definitely not to belong to the Armstrong household. I could only imagine that he had been in love with the French girl. I spoke to him of the charm of foreign women – and again I obtained the reaction I was looking for. Sudden tears came into his eyes, which he pretended were dazzled by the snow.

'There remains Mrs Hubbard. Now Mrs Hubbard, let me say, played the most important part in the drama. By occupying the compartment communicating with that of Ratchett she was more open to suspicion than anyone else. In the nature of things she could not have an alibi to fall back upon. To play the part she played – the perfectly natural, slightly ridiculous American fond mother – an artist was needed. But there *was* an artist connected with the Armstrong family – Mrs Armstrong's mother – Linda Arden, the actress . . .'

He stopped.

Then, in a soft rich dreamy voice, quite unlike the one she had used all the journey, Mrs Hubbard said:

'I always fancied myself in comedy parts.'

She went on still dreamily:

'That slip about the sponge-bag was silly. It shows you should always rehearse properly. We tried it on the way out – I was in an even number compartment then, I suppose. I never thought of the bolts being in different places.'

She shifted her position a little and looked straight at Poirot.

'You know all about it, M. Poirot. You're a very wonderful man. But even you can't quite imagine what it was like – that awful day in New York. I was just crazy with grief – so were the servants – and Colonel Arbuthnot was there, too. He was John Armstrong's best friend.'

'He saved my life in the war,' said Arbuthnot.

'We decided then and there – perhaps we were mad – I don't know – that the sentence of death that Cassetti had escaped had got to be carried out. There were twelve of us – or rather eleven – Susanne's father was over in France, of course. First we thought we'd draw lots as to who should do it, but in the end we decided on this way. It was the chauffeur, Antonio, who suggested it. Mary worked out all the details later with Hector MacQueen. He'd always adored Sonia – my daughter – and it was he who explained to us exactly how Cassetti's money had managed to get him off.

'It took a long time to perfect our plan. We had first to track Ratchett down. Hardman managed that in the end. Then we had to try to get Masterman and Hector into his employment – or at any rate one of them. Well, we managed that. Then we had a consultation with Susanne's father. Colonel Arbuthnot was very keen on having twelve of us. He seemed to think it made it more in order. He didn't like the stabbing idea much, but he agreed that it did solve most of our difficulties. Well, Susanne's father was willing. Susanne was his only child. We knew from Hector that Ratchett would be coming back from the East sooner or later by the Orient Express. With Pierre Michel actually working on that train, the chance was too good to be missed. Besides, it would be a good way of not incriminating any outsiders.

'My daughter's husband had to know, of course, and he insisted on coming on the train with her. Hector wangled it so that Ratchett selected the right day for travelling when Michel would be on duty. We meant to engage every carriage in the Stamboul-Calais coach, but unfortunately there was one carriage we couldn't get. It was reserved long beforehand for a director of the company. Mr Harris, of course, was a myth. But it would have been awkward to have any stranger in Hector's compartment. And then, at the last minute, *you* came . . .'

She stopped.

'Well,' she said. 'You know everything now, M. Poirot. What are you going to do about it? If it must all come out, can't you lay the blame upon me and me only? I would have stabbed that man twelve times willingly. It wasn't only that he was responsible for my daughter's death and her child's, and that of the other child who might have been alive and happy now. It was more than that. There had been other children before Daisy – there might be others in the future. Society had condemned him; we were only carrying out the sentence. But it's unnecessary to bring all these others into it. All these good faithful souls – and poor Michel – and Mary and Colonel Arbuthnot – they love each other . . .'

Her voice was wonderful echoing through the crowded space – that deep, emotional, heart-stirring voice that had thrilled many a New York audience.

Poirot looked at his friend.

'You are a director of the company, M. Bouc,' he said, 'What do you say?'

M. Bouc cleared his throat.

'In my opinion, M. Poirot,' he said, 'the first theory you put forward was the correct one – decidedly so. I suggest that that is the solution we offer to the Yugo-Slavian police when they arrive. You agree, Doctor?'

'Certainly I agree,' said Dr Constantine. 'As regards the medical evidence, I think – er – that I made one or two fantastic suggestions.'

'Then,' said Poirot, 'having placed my solution before you, I have the honour to retire from the case . . .'

MURDER IN THE MEWS

To My Old Friend
Sybil Heeley
With affection

CHAPTER 1

I

'Penny for the guy, sir?'

A small boy with a grimy face grinned ingratiatingly.

'Certainly not!' said Chief Inspector Japp. 'And, look here, my lad –'

A short homily followed. The dismayed urchin beat a precipitate retreat, remarking briefly and succinctly to his youthful friends:

'Blimey, if it ain't a cop all togged up!'

The band took to its heels, chanting the incantation:

Remember, remember
The fifth of November
Gunpowder treason and plot.
We see no reason
Why gunpowder treason
Should ever be forgot.

The chief inspector's companion, a small, elderly man with an egg-shaped head and large, military-looking moustaches, was smiling to himself.

'*Très bien*, Japp,' he observed. 'You preach the sermon very well! I congratulate you!'

'Rank excuse for begging, that's what Guy Fawkes' Day is!' said Japp.

'An interesting survival,' mused Hercule Poirot. 'The fireworks go up – crack – crack – long after the man they commemorate and his deed are forgotten.'

The Scotland Yard man agreed.

'Don't suppose many of those kids really know who Guy Fawkes was.'

'And soon, doubtless, there will be confusion of thought. Is it in honour or in execration that on the fifth of November the *feux d'artifice* are sent up? To blow up an English Parliament, was it a sin or a noble deed?'

Japp chuckled.

'Some people would say undoubtedly the latter.'

Turning off the main road, the two men passed into the comparative quiet of a mews. They had been dining together and were now taking a short cut to Hercule Poirot's flat.

As they walked along the sound of squibs was still heard periodically. An occasional shower of golden rain illuminated the sky.

'Good night for a murder,' remarked Japp with professional interest. 'Nobody would hear a shot, for instance, on a night like this.'

'It has always seemed odd to me that more criminals do not take advantage of the fact,' said Hercule Poirot.

'Do you know, Poirot, I almost wish sometimes that *you* would commit a murder.'

'*Mon cher!*'

'Yes, I'd like to see just how you'd set about it.'

'My dear Japp, *if* I committed a murder you would not have the least chance of seeing – how I set about it! You would not even be aware, probably, that a murder had been committed.'

Japp laughed good-humouredly and affectionately.

'Cocky little devil, aren't you?' he said indulgently.

II

At half-past eleven the following morning, Hercule Poirot's telephone rang.

''Allo? 'Allo?'

'Hallo, that you, Poirot?'

'*Oui, c'est moi.*'

'Japp speaking here. Remember we came home last night through Bardsley Gardens Mews?'

'Yes?'

'And that we talked about how easy it would be to shoot a person with all those squibs and crackers and the rest of it going off?'

'Certainly.'

'Well, there was a suicide in that mews. No. 14. A young widow – Mrs Allen. I'm going round there now. Like to come?'

'Excuse me, but does someone of your eminence, my dear friend, usually get sent to a case of suicide?'

'Sharp fellow. No – he doesn't. As a matter of fact our doctor seems to think there's something funny about this. Will you come? I kind of feel you ought to be in on it.'

'Certainly I will come. No. 14, you say?'

'That's right.'

III

Poirot arrived at No. 14 Bardsley Gardens Mews almost at the same moment as a car drew up containing Japp and three other men.

No. 14 was clearly marked out as the centre of interest. A big circle of people, chauffeurs, their wives, errand boys, loafers, well-dressed passers-by and innumerable children were drawn up all staring at No. 14 with open mouths and a fascinated stare.

A police constable in uniform stood on the step and did his best to keep back the curious. Alert-looking young men with cameras were busy and surged forward as Japp alighted.

'Nothing for you now,' said Japp, brushing them aside. He nodded to Poirot. 'So here you are. Let's get inside.'

They passed in quickly, the door shut behind them and they found themselves squeezed together at the foot of a ladder-like flight of stairs.

A man came to the top of the staircase, recognized Japp and said:

'Up here, sir.'

Japp and Poirot mounted the stairs.

The man at the stairhead opened a door on the left and they found themselves in a small bedroom.

'Thought you'd like me to run over the chief points, sir.'

'Quite right, Jameson,' said Japp. 'What about it?'

Divisional Inspector Jameson took up the tale.

'Deceased's a Mrs Allen, sir. Lived here with a friend – a Miss Plenderleith. Miss Plenderleith was away staying in the country and returned this morning. She let herself in with her key, was surprised to find no one about. A woman usually comes in at nine o'clock to do for them. She went upstairs first into her own room (that's this room) then across the landing to her friend's room. Door was locked on the inside. She rattled the handle, knocked and called, but couldn't get any answer. In the end getting alarmed she rang up the police station. That was at ten forty-five. We came along at once and forced the door open. Mrs Allen was lying in a heap on the ground shot through the head. There was an automatic in her hand – a Webley .25 – and it looked a clear case of suicide.'

'Where is Miss Plenderleith now?'

'She's downstairs in the sitting-room, sir. A very cool, efficient young lady, I should say. Got a head on her.'

'I'll talk to her presently. I'd better see Brett now.'

Accompanied by Poirot he crossed the landing and entered the opposite room. A tall, elderly man looked up and nodded.

'Hallo, Japp, glad you've got here. Funny business, this.'

Japp advanced towards him. Hercule Poirot sent a quick searching glance round the room.

It was much larger than the room they had just quitted. It had a built-out bay window, and whereas the other room had been a bedroom pure and simple, this was emphatically a bedroom disguised as a sitting-room.

The walls were silver and the ceiling emerald green. There were curtains of a modernistic pattern in silver and green. There was a divan covered with a shimmering emerald green silk quilt and numbers of gold and silver cushions. There was a tall antique walnut bureau, a walnut tallboy, and several modern chairs of gleaming chromium. On a low glass table there was a big ashtray full of cigarette stubs.

Delicately Hercule Poirot sniffed the air. Then he joined Japp where the latter stood looking down at the body.

In a heap on the floor, lying as she had fallen from one of the chromium chairs, was the body of a young woman of perhaps twenty-seven. She had fair hair and delicate features. There was very little make-up on the face. It was a pretty, wistful, perhaps slightly stupid face. On the left side of the head was a mass of congealed blood. The fingers of the right hand were clasped round a small pistol. The woman was dressed in a simple frock of dark green high to the neck.

'Well, Brett, what's the trouble?'

Japp was looking down also at the huddled figure.

'Position's all right,' said the doctor. 'If she shot herself she'd probably have slipped from the chair into just that position. The door was locked and the window was fastened on the inside.'

'That's all right, you say. Then what's wrong?'

'Take a look at the pistol. I haven't handled it – waiting for the fingerprint men. But you can see quite well what I mean.'

Together Poirot and Japp knelt down and examined the pistol closely.

'I see what you mean,' said Japp rising. 'It's in the curve of her hand. It *looks* as though she's holding it – but as a matter of fact she *isn't* holding it. Anything else?'

'Plenty. She's got the pistol in her *right* hand. Now take a look at the wound. The pistol was held close to the head just above the left ear – the *left* ear, mark you.'

'H'm,' said Japp. 'That does seem to settle it. She couldn't hold a pistol and fire it in that position with her right hand?'

'Plumb impossible, I should say. You might get your arm round but I doubt if you could fire the shot.'

'That seems pretty obvious then. Someone else shot her and tried to make it look like suicide. What about the locked door and window, though?'

Inspector Jameson answered this.

'Window was closed and bolted, sir, but although the door was locked *we haven't been able to find the key.*'

Japp nodded.

'Yes, that was a bad break. Whoever did it locked the door when he left and hoped the absence of the key wouldn't be noticed.'

Poirot murmured:

'*C'est bête, ça!*'

'Oh, come now, Poirot, old man, you mustn't judge everybody else by the light of your shining intellect! As a matter of fact that's the sort of little detail that's quite apt to be overlooked. Door's locked. People break in. Woman found dead – pistol in her hand – clear case of suicide – she locked herself in to do it. They don't go hunting about for keys. As a matter of fact, Miss Plenderleith's sending for the police was lucky. She might have got one or two of the chauffeurs to come and burst in the door – and then the key question would have been overlooked altogether.'

'Yes, I suppose that is true,' said Hercule Poirot. 'It would have been many people's natural reaction. The police, they are the last resource, are they not?'

He was still staring down at the body.

'Anything strike you?' Japp asked.

The question was careless but his eyes were keen and attentive.

Hercule Poirot shook his head slowly.

'I was looking at her wrist-watch.'

He bent over and just touched it with a finger-tip. It was a dainty jewelled affair on a black moiré strap on the wrist of the hand that held the pistol.

'Rather a swell piece that,' observed Japp. 'Must have cost money!' He cocked his head inquiringly at Poirot. 'Something in that maybe?'

'It is possible – yes.'

Poirot strayed across to the writing-bureau. It was the kind that has a front flap that lets down. This was daintily set out to match the general colour scheme.

There was a somewhat massive silver inkstand in the centre, in front of it a handsome green lacquer blotter. To the left of the blotter was an emerald glass pen tray containing a silver penholder – a stick of green sealing-wax, a pencil and two stamps. On the right of the blotter was a movable calendar giving the day of the week, date and month. There was also a little glass jar of shot and standing in it a flamboyant green quill pen. Poirot seemed interested in the pen. He took it out and looked at it but the quill was innocent of ink. It was clearly a decoration – nothing more. The silver penholder with the ink-stained nib was the one in use. His eyes strayed to the calendar.

'Tuesday, November fifth,' said Japp. 'Yesterday. That's all correct.'

He turned to Brett.

'How long has she been dead?'

'She was killed at eleven thirty-three yesterday evening,' said Brett promptly.

Then he grinned as he saw Japp's surprised face.

'Sorry, old boy,' he said. 'Had to do the super doctor of fiction! As a matter of fact eleven is about as near as I can put it – with a margin of about an hour either way.'

'Oh, I thought the wrist-watch might have stopped – or something.'

'It's stopped all right, but it's stopped at a quarter past four.'

'And I suppose she couldn't have been killed possibly at a quarter past four.'

'You can put that right out of your mind.'

Poirot had turned back the cover of the blotter.

'Good idea,' said Japp. 'But no luck.'

The blotter showed an innocent white sheet of blotting-paper. Poirot turned over the leaves but they were all the same.

He turned his attention to the waste-paper basket.

It contained two or three torn-up letters and circulars. They were only torn once and were easily reconstructed. An appeal for money from some society for assisting ex-service men, an invitation to a cocktail party on November 3rd, an appointment with a dressmaker. The circulars were an announcement of a furrier's sale and a catalogue from a department store.

'Nothing there,' said Japp.

'No, it is odd . . .' said Poirot.

'You mean they usually leave a letter when it's suicide?'

'Exactly.'

'In fact, one more proof that it *isn't* suicide.'

He moved away.

'I'll have my men get to work now. We'd better go down and interview this Miss Plenderleith. Coming, Poirot?'

Poirot still seemed fascinated by the writing-bureau and its appointments.

He left the room, but at the door his eyes went back once more to the flaunting emerald quill pen.

CHAPTER 2

At the foot of the narrow flight of stairs a door gave admission to a large-sized living-room – actually the converted stable. In this room, the walls of which were finished in a roughened plaster effect and on which hung etchings and woodcuts, two people were sitting.

One, in a chair near the fireplace, her hand stretched out to the blaze, was a dark efficient-looking young woman of twenty-seven or eight. The other, an elderly woman of ample proportions who carried a string bag, was panting and talking when the two men entered the room.

'– and as I said, Miss, such a turn it gave me I nearly dropped down where I stood. And to think that this morning of all mornings –'

The other cut her short.

'That will do, Mrs Pierce. These gentlemen are police officers, I think.'

'Miss Plenderleith?' asked Japp, advancing.

The girl nodded.

'That is my name. This is Mrs Pierce who comes in to work for us every day.'

The irrepressible Mrs Pierce broke out again.

'And as I was saying to Miss Plenderleith, to think that this morning of all mornings, my sister's Louisa Maud should have been took with a fit and me the only one handy and as I say flesh and blood is flesh and blood, and I didn't think Mrs Allen would mind, though I never likes to disappoint my ladies –'

Japp broke in with some dexterity.

'Quite so, Mrs Pierce. Now perhaps you would take Inspector Jameson into the kitchen and give him a brief statement.'

Having then got rid of the voluble Mrs Pierce, who departed with Jameson talking thirteen to the dozen, Japp turned his attention once more to the girl.

'I am Chief Inspector Japp. Now, Miss Plenderleith, I should like to know all you can tell me about this business.'

'Certainly. Where shall I begin?'

Her self-possession was admirable. There were no signs of

grief or shock save for an almost unnatural rigidity of manner.

'You arrived this morning at what time?'

'I think it was just before half-past ten. Mrs Pierce, the old liar, wasn't here, I found –'

'Is that a frequent occurrence?'

Jane Plenderleith shrugged her shoulders.

'About twice a week she turns up at twelve – or not at all. She's supposed to come at nine. Actually, as I say, twice a week she either "comes over queer", or else some member of her family is overtaken by sickness. All these daily women are like that – fail you now and again. She's not bad as they go.'

'You've had her long?'

'Just over a month. Our last one pinched things.'

'Please go on, Miss Plenderleith.'

'I paid off the taxi, carried in my suitcase, looked round for Mrs P., couldn't see her and went upstairs to my room. I tidied up a bit then I went across to Barbara – Mrs Allen – and found the door locked. I rattled the handle and knocked but could get no reply. I came downstairs and rang up the police station.'

'*Pardon!*' Poirot interposed a quick, deft question. 'It did not occur to you to try and break down the door – with the help of one of the chauffeurs in the mews, say?'

Her eyes turned to him – cool, grey-green eyes. Her glance seemed to sweep over him quickly and appraisingly.

'No, I don't think I thought of that. If anything was wrong, it seemed to me that the police were the people to send for.'

'Then you thought – *pardon, mademoiselle* – that there *was* something wrong?'

'Naturally.'

'Because you could not get a reply to your knocks? But possibly your friend might have taken a sleeping draught or something of that kind –'

'She didn't take sleeping draughts.'

The reply came sharply.

'Or she might have gone away and locked her door before going?'

'Why should she lock it? In any case she would have left a note for me.'

'And she did not – leave a note for you? You are quite sure of that?'

'Of course I am sure of it. I should have seen it at once.'

The sharpness of her tone was accentuated.

Japp said:

'You didn't try and look through the keyhole, Miss Plenderleith?'

'No,' said Jane Plenderleith thoughtfully. 'I never thought of that. But I couldn't have seen anything, could I? Because the key would have been in it?'

Her inquiring gaze, innocent, wide-eyed, met Japp's. Poirot smiled suddenly to himself.

'You did quite right, of course, Miss Plenderleith,' said Japp. 'I suppose you'd no reason to believe that your friend was likely to commit suicide?'

'Oh, no.'

'She hadn't seemed worried – or distressed in any way?'

There was a pause – an appreciable pause before the girl answered.

'No.'

'Did you know she had a pistol?'

Jane Plenderleith nodded.

'Yes, she had it out in India. She always kept it in a drawer in her room.'

'H'm. Got a licence for it?'

'I imagine so. I don't know for certain.'

'Now, Miss Plenderleith, will you tell me all you can about Mrs Allen, how long you've known her, where her relations are – everything in fact.'

Jane Plenderleith nodded.

'I've known Barbara about five years. I met her first travelling abroad – in Egypt to be exact. She was on her way home from India. I'd been at the British School in Athens for a bit and was having a few weeks in Egypt before going home. We were on a Nile cruise together. We made friends, decided we liked each other. I was looking at the time for someone to share a flat or a tiny house with me. Barbara was alone in the world. We thought we'd get on well together.'

'And you did get on well together?' asked Poirot.

'Very well. We each had our own friends – Barbara was more social in her likings – my friends were more of the artistic kind. It probably worked better that way.'

Poirot nodded. Japp went on:

'What do you know about Mrs Allen's family and her life before she met you?'

Jane Plenderleith shrugged her shoulders.

'Not very much really. Her maiden name was Armitage, I believe.'

'Her husband?'

'I don't fancy that he was anything to write home about. He drank, I think. I gather he died a year or two after the marriage. There was one child, a little girl, which died when it was three years old. Barbara didn't talk much about her husband. I believe she married him in India when she was about seventeen. Then they went off to Borneo or one of the God-forsaken spots you send ne'er-do-wells to – but as it was obviously a painful subject I didn't refer to it.'

'Do you know if Mrs Allen was in any financial difficulties?'

'No, I'm sure she wasn't.'

'Not in debt – anything of that kind?'

'Oh, no! I'm sure she wasn't in that kind of a jam.'

'Now there's another question I must ask – and I hope you won't be upset about it, Miss Plenderleith. Had Mrs Allen any particular man friend or men friends?'

Jane Plenderleith answered coolly:

'Well, she was engaged to be married if that answers your question.'

'What is the name of the man she was engaged to?'

'Charles Laverton-West. He's M.P. for some place in Hampshire.'

'Had she known him long?'

'A little over a year.'

'And she has been engaged to him – how long?'

'Two – no – nearer three months.'

'As far as you know there has not been any quarrel?'

Miss Plenderleith shook her head.

'No. I should have been surprised if there had been anything of that sort. Barbara wasn't the quarrelling kind.'

'How long is it since you last saw Mrs Allen?'

'Friday last, just before I went away for the weekend.'

'Mrs Allen was remaining in town?'

'Yes. She was going out with her fiancé on the Sunday, I believe.'

'And you yourself, where did you spend the weekend?'

'At Laidells Hall, Laidells, Essex.'

'And the name of the people with whom you were staying?'

'Mr and Mrs Bentinck.'

'You only left them this morning?'

'Yes.'

'You must have left very early?'

'Mr Bentinck motored me up. He starts early because he has to get to the city by ten.'

'I see.'

Japp nodded comprehendingly. Miss Plenderleith's replies had all been crisp and convincing.

Poirot in his turn put a question.

'What is your own opinion of Mr Laverton-West?'

The girl shrugged her shoulders.

'Does that matter?'

'No, it does not matter, perhaps, but I should like to have your opinion.'

'I don't know that I've thought about him one way or the other. He's young – not more than thirty-one or two – ambitious – a good public speaker – means to get on in the world.'

'That is on the credit side – and on the debit?'

'Well,' Miss Plenderleith considered for a moment or two. 'In my opinion he's commonplace – his ideas are not particularly original – and he's slightly pompous.'

'Those are not very serious faults, mademoiselle,' said Poirot, smiling.

'Don't you think so?'

Her tone was slightly ironic.

'They might be to you.'

He was watching her, saw her look a little disconcerted. He pursued his advantage.

'But to Mrs Allen – no, she would not notice them.'

'You're perfectly right. Barbara thought he was wonderful – took him entirely at his own valuation.'

Poirot said gently:

'You were fond of your friend?'

He saw the hand clench on her knee, the tightening of the line of the jaw, yet the answer came in a matter-of-fact voice free from emotion.

'You are quite right. I was.'

Japp said:

'Just one other thing, Miss Plenderleith. You and she didn't have a quarrel? There was no upset between you?'

'None whatever.'

'Not over this engagement business?'

'Certainly not. I was glad she was able to be so happy about it.'

There was a momentary pause, then Japp said:

'As far as you know, did Mrs Allen have any enemies?'

This time there was a definite interval before Jane Plenderleith replied. When she did so, her tone had altered very slightly.

'I don't know quite what you mean by enemies?'

'Anyone, for instance, who would profit by her death?'

'Oh, no, that would be ridiculous. She had a very small income anyway.'

'And who inherits that income?'

Jane Plenderleith's voice sounded mildly surprised as she said:

'Do you know, I really don't know. I shouldn't be surprised if I did. That is, if she ever made a will.'

'And no enemies in any other sense?' Japp slid off to another aspect quickly. 'People with a grudge against her?'

'I don't think anyone had a grudge against her. She was a very gentle creature, always anxious to please. She had a really sweet, lovable nature.'

For the first time that hard, matter-of-fact voice broke a little. Poirot nodded gently.

Japp said:

'So it amounts to this – Mrs Allen has been in good spirits lately, she wasn't in any financial difficulty, she was engaged to be married and was happy in her engagement. There was nothing in the world to make her commit suicide. That's right, isn't it?'

There was a momentary silence before Jane said:

'Yes.'

Japp rose.

'Excuse me, I must have a word with Inspector Jameson.'

He left the room.

Hercule Poirot remained *tête-à-tête* with Jane Plenderleith.

CHAPTER 3

For a few minutes there was silence.

Jane Plenderleith shot a swift appraising glance at the little man, but after that she stared in front of her and did not speak. Yet a consciousness of his presence showed itself in a certain nervous tension. Her body was still but not relaxed. When at last Poirot did break the silence the mere sound of his voice seemed to give her a certain relief. In an agreeable everyday voice he asked a question.

'When did you light the fire, mademoiselle?'

'The fire?' Her voice sounded vague and rather absent-minded. 'Oh, as soon as I arrived this morning.'

'Before you went upstairs or afterwards?'

'Before.'

'I see. Yes, naturally . . . And it was already laid – or did you have to lay it?'

'It was laid. I only had to put a match to it.'

There was a slight impatience in her voice. Clearly she suspected him of making conversation. Possibly that was what he was doing. At any rate he went on in quiet conversational tones.

'But your friend – in her room I noticed there was a gas fire only?'

Jane Plenderleith answered mechanically.

'This is the only coal fire we have – the others are all gas fires.'

'And you cook with gas, too?'

'I think everyone does nowadays.'

'True. It is much labour saving.'

The little interchange died down. Jane Plenderleith tapped on the ground with her shoe. Then she said abruptly:

'That man – Chief Inspector Japp – is he considered clever?'

'He is very sound. Yes, he is well thought of. He works hard and painstakingly and very little escapes him.'

'I wonder –' muttered the girl.

Poirot watched her. His eyes looked very green in the firelight. He asked quietly:

'It was a great shock to you, your friend's death?'

'Terrible.'

She spoke with abrupt sincerity.

'You did not expect it – no?'

'Of course not.'

'So that it seemed to you at first, perhaps, that it was impossible – that it could not be?'

The quiet sympathy of his tone seemed to break down Jane Plenderleith's defences. She replied eagerly, naturally, without stiffness.

'That's just it. Even if Barbara *did* kill herself, I can't imagine her *killing herself that way*.'

'Yet she had a pistol?'

Jane Plenderleith made an impatient gesture.

'Yes, but that pistol was a – oh! a hang over. She'd been in out-of-the-way places. She kept it out of habit – not with any other idea. I'm sure of that.'

'Ah! and why are you sure of that?'

'Oh, because of the things she said.'

'Such as –?'

His voice was very gentle and friendly. It led her on subtly.

'Well, for instance, we were discussing suicide once and she said much the easiest way would be to turn the gas on and stuff up all the cracks and just go to bed. I said I thought that would be impossible – to lie there waiting. I said I'd far rather shoot myself. And she said no, she could never shoot herself. She'd be too frightened in case it didn't come off and anyway she said she'd hate the bang.'

'I see,' said Poirot. 'As you say, it is odd . . . Because, as you have just told me, *there was a gas fire in her room*.'

Jane Plenderleith looked at him, slightly startled.

'Yes, there was . . . I can't understand – no, I can't understand why she didn't do it that way.'

Poirot shook his head.

'Yes, it seems – odd – not natural somehow.'

'The whole thing doesn't seem natural. I still can't believe she killed herself. I suppose it *must* be suicide?'

'Well, there is one other possibility.'

'What do you mean?'

Poirot looked straight at her.

'It might be – murder.'

'Oh, no?' Jane Plenderleith shrank back. 'Oh no! What a horrible suggestion.'

'Horrible, perhaps, but does it strike you as an impossible one?'

'But the door was locked on the inside. So was the window.'

'The door was locked – yes. But there is nothing to show if it were locked from the inside or the outside. You see, *the key was missing*.'

'But then – if it is missing . . .' She took a minute or two. 'Then it must have been locked from the *outside*. Otherwise it would be somewhere in the room.'

'Ah, but it may be. The room has not been thoroughly searched yet, remember. Or it may have been thrown out of the window and somebody may have picked it up.'

'Murder!' said Jane Plenderleith. She turned over the possibility, her dark clever face eager on the scent. 'I believe you're right.'

'But if it were murder there would have been a motive. Do you know of a motive, mademoiselle?'

Slowly she shook her head. And yet, in spite of the denial, Poirot again got the impression that Jane Plenderleith was deliberately keeping something back. The door opened and Japp came in.

Poirot rose.

'I have been suggesting to Miss Plenderleith,' he said, 'that her friend's death was not suicide.'

Japp looked momentarily put out. He cast a glance of reproach at Poirot.

'It's a bit early to say anything definite,' he remarked. 'We've always got to take all possibilities into account, you understand. That's all there is to it at the moment.'

Jane Plenderleith replied quietly.

'I see.'

Japp came towards her.

'Now then, Miss Plenderleith, have you ever seen this before?'

On the palm of his hand he held out a small oval of dark blue enamel.

Jane Plenderleith shook her head.

'No, never.'

'It's not yours nor Mrs Allen's?'

'No. It's not the kind of thing usually worn by our sex, is it?'

'Oh! so you recognize it.'

'Well, it's pretty obvious, isn't it? That's half of a man's cuff link.'

CHAPTER 4

'That young woman's too cocky by half,' Japp complained.

The two men were once more in Mrs Allen's bedroom. The body had been photographed and removed and the fingerprint man had done his work and departed.

'It would be unadvisable to treat her as a fool,' agreed Poirot. 'She most emphatically is *not* a fool. She is, in fact, a particularly clever and competent young woman.'

'Think she did it?' asked Japp with a momentary ray of hope. 'She might have, you know. We'll have to get her alibi looked into. Some quarrel over this young man – this budding M.P. She's rather *too* scathing about him, I think! Sounds fishy. Rather as though she were sweet on him herself and he'd turned her down. She's the kind that would bump anyone off if she felt like it, and keep her head while she was doing it, too. Yes, we'll have to look into that alibi. She had it very pat and after all Essex isn't very far away. Plenty of trains. Or a fast car. It's worth while finding out if she went to bed with a headache for instance last night.'

'You are right,' agreed Poirot.

'In any case,' continued Japp, 'she's holding out on us. Eh? Didn't you feel that too? That young woman knows something.'

Poirot nodded thoughtfully.

'Yes, that could be clearly seen.'

'That's always a difficulty in these cases,' Japp complained. 'People *will* hold their tongues – sometimes out of the most honourable motives.'

'For which one can hardly blame them, my friend.'

'No, but it makes it much harder for *us*,' Japp grumbled.

'It merely displays to its full advantage your ingenuity,' Poirot consoled him. 'What about fingerprints, by the way?'

'Well, it's murder all right. No prints whatever on the pistol.

Wiped clean before being placed in her hand. Even if she managed to wind her arm round her head in some marvellous acrobatic fashion she could hardly fire off a pistol without hanging on to it and she couldn't wipe it after she was dead.'

'No, no, an outside agency is clearly indicated.'

'Otherwise the prints are disappointing. None on the door-handle. None on the window. Suggestive, eh? Plenty of Mrs Allen's all over the place.'

'Did Jameson get anything?'

'Out of the daily woman? No. She talked a lot but she didn't really know much. Confirmed the fact that Allen and Plenderleith were on good terms. I've sent Jameson out to make inquiries in the mews. We'll have to have a word with Mr Laverton-West too. Find out where he was and what he was doing last night. In the meantime we'll have a look through her papers.'

He set to without more ado. Occasionally he grunted and tossed something over to Poirot. The search did not take long. There were not many papers in the desk and what there were were neatly arranged and docketed.

Finally Japp leant back and uttered a sigh.

'Not very much, is there?'

'As you say.'

'Most of it quite straightforward – receipted bills, a few bills as yet unpaid – nothing particularly outstanding. Social stuff – invitations. Notes from friends. These –' he laid his hand on a pile of seven or eight letters – 'and her cheque book and passbook. Anything strike you there?'

'Yes, she was overdrawn.'

'Anything else?'

Poirot smiled.

'Is it an examination that you put me through? But yes, I noticed what you are thinking of. Two hundred pounds drawn to self three months ago – and two hundred pounds drawn out yesterday –'

'And nothing on the counterfoil of the cheque book. No other cheques to self except small sums – fifteen pounds the highest. And I'll tell you this – there's no such sum of money in the house. Four pounds ten in a handbag and an odd shilling or two in another bag. That's pretty clear, I think.'

'Meaning that she paid that sum away yesterday.'

'Yes. Now who did she pay it to?'

The door opened and Inspector Jameson entered.

'Well, Jameson, get anything?'

'Yes, sir, several things. To begin with, nobody actually heard the shot. Two or three women say they did because they want to think they did – but that's all there is to it. With all those fireworks going off there isn't a dog's chance.'

Japp grunted.

'Don't suppose there is. Go on.'

'Mrs Allen was at home most of yesterday afternoon and evening. Came in about five o'clock. Then she went out again about six but only to the post box at the end of the mews. At about nine-thirty a car drove up – Standard Swallow saloon – and a man got out. Description about forty-five, well set up military-looking gent, dark blue overcoat, bowler hat, toothbrush moustache. James Hogg, chauffeur from No. 18 says he's seen him calling on Mrs Allen before.'

'Forty-five,' said Japp. 'Can't very well be Laverton-West.'

'This man, whoever he was, stayed here for just under an hour. Left at about ten-twenty. Stopped in the doorway to speak to Mrs Allen. Small boy, Frederick Hogg, was hanging about quite near and heard what he said.'

'And what did he say?'

'"*Well, think it over and let me know.*" And then she said something and he answered: "*All right. So long.*" After that he got in his car and drove away.'

'That was at ten-twenty,' said Poirot thoughtfully.

Japp rubbed his nose.

'Then at ten-twenty Mrs Allen was still alive,' he said. 'What next?'

'Nothing more, sir, as far as I can learn. The chauffeur at No. 22 got in at half-past ten and he'd promised his kids to let off some fireworks for them. They'd been waiting for him – and all the other kids in the mews too. He let 'em off and everybody around about was busy watching them. After that everyone went to bed.'

'And nobody else was seen to enter No. 14?'

'No – but that's not to say they didn't. Nobody would have noticed.'

'H'm,' said Japp. 'That's true. Well, we'll have to get hold of this "military gentleman with the toothbrush moustache". It's pretty clear that he was the last person to see her alive. I wonder who he was?'

'Miss Plenderleith might tell us,' suggested Poirot.

'She might,' said Japp gloomily. 'On the other hand she might not. I've no doubt she could tell us a good deal if she liked. What about you, Poirot, old boy? You were alone with her for a bit. Didn't you trot out that Father Confessor manner of yours that sometimes makes such a hit?'

Poirot spread out his hands.

'Alas, we talked only of gas fires.'

'Gas fires – gas fires.' Japp sounded disgusted. 'What's the matter with you, old cock? Ever since you've been here the only things you've taken an interest in are quill pens and waste-paper baskets. Oh, yes, I saw you having a quiet look into the one downstairs. Anything in it?'

Poirot sighed.

'A catalogue of bulbs and an old magazine.'

'What's the idea, anyway? If anyone wants to throw away an incriminating document or whatever it is you have in mind they're not likely just to pitch it into a waste-paper basket.'

'That is very true what you say there. Only something quite unimportant would be thrown away like that.'

Poirot spoke meekly. Nevertheless Japp looked at him suspiciously.

'Well,' he said. 'I know what I'm going to do next. What about you?'

'*Eh bien*,' said Poirot. 'I shall complete my search for the unimportant. There is still the dustbin.'

He skipped nimbly out of the room. Japp looked after him with an air of disgust.

'Potty,' he said. 'Absolutely potty.'

Inspector Jameson preserved a respectful silence. His face said with British superiority: 'Foreigners!'

Aloud he said:

'So that's Mr Hercule Poirot! I've heard of him.'

'Old friend of mine,' explained Japp. 'Not half as balmy as he looks, mind you. All the same he's getting on now.'

'Gone a bit gaga as they say, sir,' suggested Inspector Jameson. 'Ah well, age will tell.'

'All the same,' said Japp, 'I wish I knew what he was up to.'

He walked over to the writing-table and stared uneasily at an emerald green quill pen.

CHAPTER 5

Japp was just engaging his third chauffeur's wife in conversation when Poirot, walking noiselessly as a cat, suddenly appeared at his elbow.

'Whew, you made me jump,' said Japp. 'Got anything?'

'Not what I was looking for.'

Japp turned back to Mrs James Hogg.

'And you say you've seen this gentleman before?'

'Oh, yes sir. And my husband too. We knew him at once.'

'Now look here, Mrs Hogg, you're a shrewd woman, I can see. I've no doubt that you know all about everyone in the mews. And you're a woman of judgment – unusually good judgment, I can tell that –' Unblushingly he repeated this remark for the third time. Mrs Hogg bridled slightly and assumed an expression of superhuman intelligence. 'Give me a line on those two young women – Mrs Allen and Miss Plenderleith. What were they like? Gay? Lots of parties? That sort of thing?'

'Oh, no sir, nothing of the kind. They went out a good bit – Mrs Allen especially – but they're *class*, if you know what I mean. Not like some as I could name down the other end. I'm sure the way that Mrs Stevens goes on – if she *is* a Mrs at all which I doubt – well I shouldn't like to tell you what goes on there – I . . .'

'Quite so,' said Japp, dexterously stopping the flow. 'Now that's very important what you've told me. Mrs Allen and Miss Plenderleith were well liked, then?'

'Oh yes, sir, very nice ladies, both of them – especially Mrs Allen. Always spoke a nice word to the children, she did. Lost her own little girl, I believe, poor dear. Ah well, I've buried three myself. And what I say is . . .'

'Yes, yes, very sad. And Miss Plenderleith?'

'Well, of course she was a nice lady too, but much more abrupt if you know what I mean. Just go by with a nod, she would, and not stop to pass the time of day. But I've nothing against her – nothing at all.'

'She and Mrs Allen got on well together?'

'Oh, yes sir. No quarrelling – nothing like that. Very happy and contented they were – I'm sure Mrs Pierce will bear me out.'

'Yes, we've talked to her. Do you know Mrs Allen's fiancé by sight?'

'The gentleman she's going to marry? Oh, yes. He's been here quite a bit off and on. Member of Parliament, they do say.'

'It wasn't he who came last night?'

'No, sir, it was *not*.' Mrs Hogg drew herself up. A note of excitement disguised beneath intense primness came into her voice. 'And if you ask me, sir, what you are thinking is all *wrong*. Mrs Allen wasn't *that* kind of lady, I'm sure. It's true there *was* no one in the house, but I do *not* believe anything of the kind – I said so to Hogg only this morning. "No, Hogg," I said, "Mrs Allen was a lady – a real lady – so don't go suggesting things" – knowing what a man's mind is, if you'll excuse my mentioning it. Always coarse in their ideas.'

Passing this insult by, Japp proceeded:

'You saw him arrive and you saw him leave – that's so, isn't it?'

'That's so, sir.'

'And you didn't hear anything else? Any sounds of a quarrel?'

'No, sir, nor likely to. Not, that is to say, that such things couldn't be heard – because the contrary to that is well known – and down the other end the way Mrs Stevens goes for that poor frightened maid of hers is common talk – and one and all we've advised her not to stand it, but there, the wages is good – temper of the devil she may have but pays for it – thirty shillings a week . . .'

Japp said quickly:

'But you didn't hear anything of the kind at No. 14?'

'No, sir. Nor likely to with fireworks popping off here, there and everywhere and my Eddie with his eyebrows singed off as near as nothing.'

'This man left at ten-twenty – that's right, is it?'

'It might be, sir. I couldn't say myself. But Hogg says so and he's a very reliable, steady man.'

'You actually saw him leave. Did you hear what he said?'

'No, sir. I wasn't near enough for that. Just saw him from my windows, standing in the doorway talking to Mrs Allen.'

'See her too?'

'Yes, sir, she was standing just inside the doorway.'

'Notice what she was wearing?'

'Now really, sir, I couldn't say. Not noticing particularly as it were.'

Poirot said:

'You did not even notice if she was wearing day dress or evening dress?'

'No, sir, I can't say I did.'

Poirot looked thoughtfully up at the window above and then across to No. 14. He smiled and for a moment his eye caught Japp's.

'And the gentleman?'

'He was in a dark blue overcoat and a bowler hat. Very smart and well set up.'

Japp asked a few more questions and then proceeded to his next interview. This was with Master Frederick Hogg, an impish-faced, bright-eyed lad, considerably swollen with self-importance.

'Yes, sir. I heard them talking. "*Think it over and let me know*," the gent said. Pleasant like, you know. And then she said something and he answered, "*All right. So long.*" And he got into the car – I was holding the door open but he didn't give me nothing,' said Master Hogg with a slight tinge of depression in his tone. 'And he drove away.'

'You didn't hear what Mrs Allen said?'

'No, sir, can't say I did.'

'Can you tell me what she was wearing? What colour, for instance?'

'Couldn't say, sir. You see, I didn't really see her. She must have been round behind the door.'

'Just so,' said Japp. 'Now look here, my boy, I want you to think and answer my next question very carefully. If you don't know and can't remember, say so. Is that clear?'

'Yes, sir.'

Master Hogg looked at him eagerly.

'Which of 'em closed the door, Mrs Allen or the gentleman?'

'The front door?'

'The front door, naturally.'

The child reflected. His eyes screwed themselves up in an effort of remembrance.

'Think the lady probably did – No, she didn't. He did. Pulled it to with a bit of a bang and jumped into the car quick. Looked as though he had a date somewhere.'

'Right. Well, young man, you seem a bright kind of shaver. Here's sixpence for you.'

Dismissing Master Hogg, Japp turned to his friend. Slowly with one accord they nodded.

'Could be!' said Japp.

'There are possibilities,' agreed Poirot.

His eyes shone with a green light. They looked like a cat's.

CHAPTER 6

On re-entering the sitting-room of No. 14, Japp wasted no time in beating about the bush. He came straight to the point.

'Now look here, Miss Plenderleith, don't you think it's better to spill the beans here and now. It's going to come to that in the end.'

Jane Plenderleith raised her eyebrows. She was standing by the mantelpiece, gently warming one foot at the fire.

'I really don't know what you mean.'

'Is that quite true, Miss Plenderleith?'

She shrugged her shoulders.

'I've answered all your questions. I don't see what more I can do.'

'Well, it's my opinion you could do a lot more – if you chose.'

'That's only an opinion, though, isn't it, Chief Inspector?'

Japp grew rather red in the face.

'I think,' said Poirot, 'that mademoiselle would appreciate better the reason for your questions if you told her just how the case stands.'

'That's very simple. Now then, Miss Plenderleith, the facts are as follows. Your friend was found shot through the head with a pistol in her hand and the door and the window fastened. That looked like a plain case of suicide. *But it wasn't suicide.* The medical evidence alone proves that.'

'How?'

All her ironic coolness had disappeared. She leaned forward – intent – watching his face.

'The pistol was in her hand – *but the fingers weren't grasping it.* Moreover there were *no fingerprints at all* on the pistol. And the angle of the wound makes it impossible that the wound should have been self-inflicted. Then again, she left no letter – rather an unusual thing for a suicide. And though the door was locked the key has not been found.'

Jane Plenderleith turned slowly and sat down in a chair facing them.

'So that's it!' she said. 'All along I've felt it was *impossible* that she should have killed herself! I was right! She *didn't* kill herself. Someone else killed her.'

For a moment or two she remained lost in thought. Then she raised her head brusquely.

'Ask me any questions you like,' she said. 'I will answer them to the best of my ability.'

Japp began:

'Last night Mrs Allen had a visitor. He is described as a man of forty-five, military bearing, toothbrush moustache, smartly dressed and driving a Standard Swallow saloon car. Do you know who that is?'

'I can't be sure, of course, but it sounds like Major Eustace.'

'Who is Major Eustace? Tell me all you can about him?'

'He was a man Barbara had known abroad – in India. He turned up about a year ago, and we've seen him on and off since.'

'He was a friend of Mrs Allen's?'

'He behaved like one,' said Jane dryly.

'What was her attitude to him?'

'I don't think she really liked him – in fact, I'm sure she didn't.'

'But she treated him with outward friendliness?'

'Yes.'

'Did she ever seem – think carefully, Miss Plenderleith – afraid of him?'

Jane Plenderleith considered this thoughtfully for a minute or two. Then she said:

'Yes – I think she was. She was always nervous when he was about.'

'Did he and Mr Laverton-West meet at all?'

'Only once, I think. They didn't take to each other much. That is to say, Major Eustace made himself as agreeable as he could to Charles, but Charles wasn't having any. Charles has got a very good nose for anybody who isn't well – quite – quite.'

'And Major Eustace was not – what you call – quite – quite?' asked Poirot.

The girl said dryly:

'No, he wasn't. Bit hairy at the heel. Definitely not out of the top drawer.'

'Alas – I do not know those two expressions. You mean to say he was not the *pukka sahib*?'

A fleeting smile passed across Jane Plenderleith's face, but she replied gravely, 'No.'

'Would it come as a great surprise to you, Miss Plenderleith, if I suggested that this man was blackmailing Mrs Allen?'

Japp sat forward to observe the result of his suggestion.

He was well satisfied. The girl started forward, the colour rose in her cheeks, she brought down her hand sharply on the arm of her chair.

'So that was it! What a fool I was not to have guessed. Of course!'

'You think the suggestion feasible, mademoiselle?' asked Poirot.

'I was a fool not to have thought of it! Barbara's borrowed small sums off me several times during the last six months. And I've seen her sitting poring over her passbook. I knew she was living well within her income, so I didn't bother, but, of course, if she was paying out sums of money –'

'And it would accord with her general demeanour – yes?' asked Poirot.

'Absolutely. She was nervous. Quite jumpy sometimes. Altogether different from what she used to be.'

Poirot said gently:

'Excuse me, but that is not just what you told us before.'

'That was different,' Jane Plenderleith waved an impatient hand. 'She wasn't depressed. I mean she wasn't feeling suicidal or anything like that. But blackmail – yes. I wish she'd told *me*. I'd have sent him to the devil.'

'But he might have gone – not to the devil, but to Mr Charles Laverton-West?' observed Poirot.

'Yes,' said Jane Plenderleith slowly. 'Yes . . . that's true . . .'

'You've no idea of what this man's hold over her may have been?' asked Japp.

The girl shook her head.

'I haven't the faintest idea. I can't believe, knowing Barbara, that it could have been anything really serious. On the other hand–' she paused, then went on. 'What I mean is, Barbara was a bit of a simpleton in some ways. She'd be very easily frightened. In fact, she was the kind of girl who would be a positive gift to a blackmailer! The nasty brute!'

She snapped out the last three words with real venom.

'Unfortunately,' said Poirot, 'the crime seems to have taken place the wrong way round. It is the victim who should kill the blackmailer, not the blackmailer his victim.'

Jane Plenderleith frowned a little.

'No – that is true – but I can imagine circumstances –'

'Such as?'

'Supposing Barbara got desperate. She may have threatened him with that silly little pistol of hers. He tries to wrench it away from her and in the struggle he fires it and kills her. Then he's horrified at what he's done and tries to pretend it was suicide.'

'Might be,' said Japp. 'But there's a difficulty.'

She looked at him inquiringly.

'Major Eustace (if it was him) left here last night at ten-twenty and said goodbye to Mrs Allen on the doorstep.'

'Oh,' the girl's face fell. 'I see.' She paused a minute or two. 'But he might have come back later,' she said slowly.

'Yes, that is possible,' said Poirot.

Japp continued:

'Tell me, Miss Plenderleith, where was Mrs Allen in the habit of receiving guests, here or in the room upstairs?'

'Both. But this room was used for more communal parties or for my own special friends. You see, the arrangement was that Barbara had the big bedroom and used it as a sitting-room as well, and I had the little bedroom and used this room.'

'If Major Eustace came by appointment last night, in which room do you think Mrs Allen would have received him?'

'I think she would probably bring him in here.' The girl sounded a little doubtful. 'It would be less intimate. On the other hand, if she wanted to write a cheque or anything of that kind, she would probably take him upstairs. There are no writing materials down here.'

Japp shook his head.

'There was no question of a cheque. Mrs Allen drew out two hundred pounds in cash yesterday. And so far we've not been able to find any trace of it in the house.'

'And she gave it to that brute? Oh, poor Barbara! Poor, poor Barbara!'

Poirot coughed.

'Unless, as you suggest, it was more or less an accident, it still seems a remarkable fact that he should kill an apparently regular source of income.'

'Accident? It wasn't an accident. He lost his temper and saw red and shot her.'

'That is how you think it happened?'

'Yes.' She added vehemently, 'It was murder – *murder*!'

Poirot said gravely:

'I will not say that you are wrong, mademoiselle.'

Japp said:

'What cigarettes did Mrs Allen smoke?'

'Gaspers. There are some in that box.'

Japp opened the box, took out a cigarette and nodded. He slipped the cigarette into his pocket.

'And you, mademoiselle?' asked Poirot.

'The same.'

'You do not smoke Turkish?'

'Never.'

'Nor Mrs Allen?'

'No. She didn't like them.'

Poirot asked:

'And Mr Laverton-West. What did he smoke?'

She stared hard at him.

'Charles? What does it matter what he smoked? You're not going to pretend that *he* killed her?'

Poirot shrugged his shoulders.

'A man has killed the woman he loved before now, mademoiselle.'

Jane shook her head impatiently.

'Charles wouldn't kill anybody. He's a very careful man.'

'All the same, mademoiselle, it is the careful men who commit the cleverest murders.'

She stared at him.

'But not for the motive you have just advanced, M. Poirot.'

He bowed his head.

'No, that is true.'

Japp rose.

'Well, I don't think that there's much more I can do here. I'd like to have one more look round.'

'In case that money should be tucked away somewhere? Certainly. Look anywhere you like. And in my room too – although it isn't likely Barbara would hide it there.'

Japp's search was quick but efficient. The living-room had given up all its secrets in a very few minutes. Then he went upstairs. Jane Plenderleith sat on the arm of a chair, smoking a cigarette and frowning at the fire. Poirot watched her.

After some minutes, he said quietly:

'Do you know if Mr Laverton-West is in London at present?'

'I don't know at all. I rather fancy he's in Hampshire with his people. I suppose I ought to have wired him. How dreadful. I forgot.'

'It is not easy to remember everything, mademoiselle, when a catastrophe occurs. And after all, the bad news, it will keep. One hears it only too soon.'

'Yes, that's true,' the girl said absently.

Japp's footsteps were heard descending the stairs. Jane went out to meet him.

'Well?'

Japp shook his head.

'Nothing helpful, I'm afraid, Miss Plenderleith. I've been over the whole house now. Oh, I suppose I'd better just have a look in this cupboard under the stairs.'

He caught hold of the handle as he spoke, and pulled.

Jane Plenderleith said:

'It's locked.'

Something in her voice made both men look at her sharply.

'Yes,' said Japp pleasantly. 'I can see it's locked. Perhaps you'll get the key.'

The girl was standing as though carved in stone.

'I – I'm not sure where it is.'

Japp shot a quick glance at her. His voice continued resolutely pleasant and off-hand.

'Dear me, that's too bad. Don't want to splinter the wood, opening it by force. I'll send Jameson out to get an assortment of keys.'

She moved forward stiffly.

'Oh,' she said. 'One minute. It might be –'

She went back into the living-room and reappeared a moment later holding a fair-sized key in her hand.

'We keep it locked,' she explained, 'because one's umbrellas and things have a habit of getting pinched.'

'Very wise precaution,' said Japp, cheerfully accepting the key.

He turned it in the lock and threw the door open. It was dark inside the cupboard. Japp took out his pocket flashlight and let it play round the inside.

Poirot felt the girl at his side stiffen and stop breathing for a second. His eyes followed the sweep of Japp's torch.

There was not very much in the cupboard. Three umbrellas – one broken, four walking sticks, a set of golf clubs, two tennis racquets, a neatly-folded rug and several sofa cushions in various stages of dilapidation. On the top of these last reposed a small, smart-looking attaché-case.

As Japp stretched out a hand towards it, Jane Plenderleith said quickly:

'That's mine. I – it came back with me this morning. So there can't be anything there.'

'Just as well to make quite sure,' said Japp, his cheery friendliness increasing slightly.

The case was unlocked. Inside it was fitted with shagreen brushes and toilet bottles. There were two magazines in it but nothing else.

Japp examined the whole outfit with meticulous attention.

When at last he shut the lid and began a cursory examination of the cushions, the girl gave an audible sigh of relief.

There was nothing else in the cupboard beyond what was plainly to be seen. Japp's examination was soon finished.

He relocked the door and handed the key to Jane Plenderleith.

'Well,' he said, 'that concludes matters. Can you give me Mr Laverton-West's address?'

'Farlescombe Hall, Little Ledbury, Hampshire.'

'Thank you, Miss Plenderleith. That's all for the present. I may be round again later. By the way, mum's the word. Leave it at suicide as far as the general public's concerned.'

'Of course, I quite understand.'

She shook hands with them both.

As they walked away down the mews, Japp exploded:

'What the – the hell was there in that cupboard? There was *something*.'

'Yes, there was something.'

'And I'll bet ten to one it was something to do with the attaché-case! But like the double-dyed mutt I must be, I couldn't find anything. Looked in all the bottles – felt the lining – what the devil could it be?'

Poirot shook his head thoughtfully.

'That girl's in it somehow,' Japp went on. 'Brought that case back this morning? Not on your life, she didn't! Notice that there were two magazines in it?'

'Yes.'

'Well, one of them was for *last July*!'

CHAPTER 7

I

It was the following day when Japp walked into Poirot's flat, flung his hat on the table in deep disgust and dropped into a chair.

'Well,' he growled. '*She's* out of it!'

'Who is out of it?'

'Plenderleith. Was playing bridge up to midnight. Host, hostess, naval-commander guest and two servants can all swear to that. No doubt about it, we've got to give up any idea of her being concerned in the business. All the same, I'd like to know *why* she went all hot and bothered about that little attaché-case under the stairs. That's something in *your* line, Poirot. You like solving the kind of triviality that leads nowhere. The Mystery of the Small Attaché-Case. Sounds quite promising!'

'I will give you yet another suggestion for a title. The Mystery of the Smell of Cigarette Smoke.'

'A bit clumsy for a title. Smell – eh? Was *that* why you were sniffing so when we first examined the body? I saw you – *and* heard you! Sniff – sniff – sniff. Thought you had a cold in your head.'

'You were entirely in error.'

Japp sighed.

'I always thought it was the little grey cells of the brain. Don't tell me the cells of your nose are equally superior to anyone else's.'

'No, no, calm yourself.'

'*I* didn't smell any cigarette smoke,' went on Japp suspiciously.

'No more did I, my friend.'

Japp looked at him doubtfully. Then he extracted a cigarette from his pocket.

'That's the kind Mrs Allen smoked – gaspers. Six of those stubs were hers. *The other three were Turkish.*'

'Exactly.'

'Your wonderful nose knew that without looking at them, I suppose!'

'I assure you my nose does not enter into the matter. My nose registered nothing.'

'But the brain cells registered a lot?'

'Well – there were certain indications – do you not think so?'

Japp looked at him sideways.

'Such as?'

'*Eh bien*, there was very definitely something missing from the room. Also something added, I think . . . And then, on the writing-bureau . . .'

'I knew it! We're coming to that damned quill pen!'

'*Du tout*. The quill pen plays a purely negative rôle.'

Japp retreated to safer ground.

'I've got Charles Laverton-West coming to see me at Scotland Yard in half an hour. I thought you might like to be there.'

'I should very much.'

'And you'll be glad to hear we've tracked down Major Eustace. Got a service flat in the Cromwell Road.'

'Excellent.'

'And we've got a little to go on there. Not at all a nice person, Major Eustace. After I've seen Laverton-West, we'll go and see him. That suit you?'

'Perfectly.'

'Well, come along then.'

II

At half-past eleven, Charles Laverton-West was ushered into Chief Inspector Japp's room. Japp rose and shook hands.

The M.P. was a man of medium height with a very definite personality. He was clean-shaven, with the mobile mouth of an actor, and the slightly prominent eyes that so often go with the gift of oratory. He was good-looking in a quiet, well-bred way.

Though looking pale and somewhat distressed, his manner was perfectly formal and composed.

He took a seat, laid his gloves and hat on the table and looked towards Japp.

'I'd like to say, first of all, Mr Laverton-West, that I fully appreciate how distressing this must be to you.'

Laverton-West waved this aside.

'Do not let us discuss my feelings. Tell me, Chief Inspector, have you any idea what caused my – Mrs Allen to take her own life?'

'You yourself cannot help us in any way?'

'No, indeed.'

'There was no quarrel? No estrangement of any kind between you?'

'Nothing of the kind. It has been the greatest shock to me.'

'Perhaps it will be more understandable, sir, if I tell you that it was not suicide – but murder!'

'Murder?' Charles Laverton-West's eyes popped nearly out of his head. 'You say *murder*?'

'Quite correct. Now, Mr Laverton-West, have you any idea who might be likely to make away with Mrs Allen?'

Laverton-West fairly spluttered out his answer.

'No – no, indeed – nothing of the sort! The mere idea is – is *unimaginable*!'

'She never mentioned any enemies? Anyone who might have a grudge against her?'

'Never.'

'Did you know that she had a pistol?'

'I was not aware of the fact.'

He looked a little startled.

'Miss Plenderleith says that Mrs Allen brought this pistol back from abroad with her some years ago.'

'Really?'

'Of course, we have only Miss Plenderleith's word for that. It is quite possible that Mrs Allen felt herself to be in danger from some source and kept the pistol handy for reasons of her own.'

Charles Laverton-West shook his head doubtfully. He seemed quite bewildered and dazed.

'What is your opinion of Miss Plenderleith, Mr Laverton-West? I mean, does she strike you as a reliable, truthful person?'

The other pondered a minute.

'I think so – yes, I should say so.'

'You don't like her?' suggested Japp, who had been watching him closely.

'I wouldn't say that. She is not the type of young woman I admire. That sarcastic, independent type is not attractive to me, but I should say she was quite truthful.'

'H'm,' said Japp. 'Do you know a Major Eustace?'

'Eustace? Eustace? Ah, yes, I remember the name. I met him once at Barbara's – Mrs Allen's. Rather a doubtful customer in my opinion. I said as much to my – to Mrs Allen. He wasn't the type of man I should have encouraged to come to the house after we were married.'

'And what did Mrs Allen say?'

'Oh! she quite agreed. She trusted my judgment implicitly. A man knows other men better than a woman can do. She explained that she couldn't very well be rude to a man whom she had not seen for some time – I think she felt especially a horror of being *snobbish*! Naturally, as my wife, she would find a good many of her old associates well – unsuitable, shall we say?'

'Meaning that in marrying you she was bettering her position?' Japp asked bluntly.

Laverton-West held up a well-manicured hand.

'No, no, not quite that. As a matter of fact, Mrs Allen's mother was a distant relation of my own family. She was fully my equal in birth. But of course, in my position, I have to be especially careful in choosing my friends – and my wife in choosing hers. One is to a certain extent in the limelight.'

'Oh, quite,' said Japp dryly. He went on, 'So you can't help us in any way?'

'No indeed. I am utterly at sea. Barbara! Murdered! It seems incredible.'

'Now, Mr Laverton-West, can you tell me what your own movements were on the night of November fifth?'

'My movements? *My* movements?'

Laverton-West's voice rose in shrill protest.

'Purely a matter of routine,' explained Japp. 'We – er – have to ask everybody.'

Charles Laverton-West looked at him with dignity.

'I should hope that a man in my position might be exempt.'

Japp merely waited.

'I was – now let me see . . . Ah, yes. I was at the House. Left at half-past ten. Went for a walk along the Embankment. Watched some of the fireworks.'

'Nice to think there aren't any plots of that kind nowadays,' said Japp cheerily.

Laverton-West gave him a fish-like stare.

'Then I – er – walked home.'

'Reaching home – your London address is Onslow Square, I think – at what time?'

'I hardly know exactly.'

'Eleven? Half-past?'

'Somewhere about then.'

'Perhaps someone let you in.'

'No, I have my key.'

'Meet anybody whilst you were walking?'

'No – er – really, Chief Inspector, I *resent* these questions very much!'

'I assure you, it's just a matter of routine, Mr Laverton-West. They aren't personal, you know.'

The reply seemed to soothe the irate M.P.

'If that is all –'

'That is all for the present, Mr Laverton-West.'

'You will keep me informed –'

'Naturally, sir. By the way, let me introduce M. Hercule Poirot. You may have heard of him.'

Mr Laverton-West's eye fastened itself interestedly on the little Belgian.

'Yes – yes – I have heard the name.'

'Monsieur,' said Poirot, his manner suddenly very foreign. 'Believe me, my heart bleeds for you. Such a loss! Such agony as you must be enduring! Ah, but I will say no more. How magnificently the English hide their emotions.' He whipped out his cigarette case. 'Permit me – Ah, it is empty. Japp?'

Japp slapped his pockets and shook his head.

Laverton-West produced his own cigarette case, murmured, 'Er – have one of mine, M. Poirot.'

'Thank you – thank you.' The little man helped himself.

'As you say, M. Poirot,' resumed the other, 'we English do not parade our emotions. A stiff upper lip – that is our motto.'

He bowed to the two men and went out.

'Bit of a stuffed fish,' said Japp disgustedly. '*And* a boiled owl! The Plenderleith girl was quite right about him. Yet he's a good-looking sort of chap – might go down well with some woman who had no sense of humour. What about that cigarette?'

Poirot handed it over, shaking his head.

'Egyptian. An expensive variety.'

'No, that's no good. A pity, for I've never heard a weaker alibi! In fact, it wasn't an alibi at all . . . You know, Poirot, it's a pity the boot wasn't on the other leg. If *she'd* been blackmailing him . . . He's a lovely type for blackmail – would pay out like a lamb! Anything to avoid a scandal.'

'My friend, it is very pretty to reconstruct the case as you would like it to be, but that is not strictly our affair.'

'No, Eustace is our affair. I've got a few lines on him. Definitely a nasty fellow.'

'By the way, did you do as I suggested about Miss Plenderleith?'

'Yes. Wait a sec, I'll ring through and get the latest.'

He picked up the telephone receiver and spoke through it.

After a brief interchange he replaced it and looked up at Poirot.

'Pretty heartless piece of goods. Gone off to play golf. That's a nice thing to do when your friend's been murdered only the day before.'

Poirot uttered an exclamation.

'What's the matter now?' asked Japp.

But Poirot was murmuring to himself.

'Of course . . . of course . . . but naturally . . . What an imbecile I am – why, it leapt to the eye!'

Japp said rudely:

'Stop jabbering to yourself and let's go and tackle Eustace.'

He was amazed to see the radiant smile that spread over Poirot's face.

'But – yes – most certainly let us tackle him. For now, see you, I know everything – but everything!'

CHAPTER 8

Major Eustace received the two men with the easy assurance of a man of the world.

His flat was small, a mere *pied-à-terre*, as he explained. He offered the two men a drink and when that was refused he took out his cigarette case.

Both Japp and Poirot accepted a cigarette. A quick glance passed between them.

'You smoke Turkish, I see,' said Japp as he twirled the cigarette between his fingers.

'Yes. I'm sorry, do you prefer a gasper? I've got one somewhere about.'

'No, no, this will do me very well.' Then he leaned forward – his tone changed. 'Perhaps you can guess, Major Eustace, what it was I came to see you about?'

The other shook his head. His manner was nonchalant. Major Eustace was a tall man, good-looking in a somewhat coarse fashion. There was a puffiness round the eyes – small, crafty eyes that belied the good-humoured geniality of his manner.

He said:

'No – I've no idea what brings such a big gun as a chief inspector to see me. Anything to do with my car?'

'No, it is not your car. I think you knew a Mrs Barbara Allen, Major Eustace?'

The major leant back, puffed out a cloud of smoke, and said in an enlightened voice:

'Oh, so that's it! Of course, I might have guessed. Very sad business.'

'You know about it?'

'Saw it in the paper last night. Too bad.'

'You knew Mrs Allen out in India, I think.'

'Yes, that's some years ago now.'

'Did you also know her husband?'

There was a pause – a mere fraction of a second – but during that fraction the little pig eyes flashed a quick look at the faces of the two men. Then he answered:

'No, as a matter of fact, I never came across Allen.'

'But you know something about him?'

'Heard he was by way of being a bad hat. Of course, that was only rumour.'

'Mrs Allen did not say anything?'

'Never talked about him.'

'You were on intimate terms with her?'

Major Eustace shrugged his shoulders.

'We were old friends, you know, old friends. But we didn't see each other very often.'

'But you did see her that last evening? The evening of November fifth?'

'Yes, as a matter of fact, I did.'

'You called at her house, I think.'

Major Eustace nodded. His voice took on a gentle, regretful note.

'Yes, she asked me to advise her about some investments. Of course, I can see what you're driving at – her state of mind – all that sort of thing. Well, really, it's very difficult to say. Her manner seemed normal enough and yet she *was* a bit jumpy, come to think of it.'

'But she gave you no hint as to what she contemplated doing?'

'Not the least in the world. As a matter of fact, when I said goodbye I said I'd ring her up soon and we'd do a show together.'

'You said you'd ring her up. Those were your last words?'

'Yes.'

'Curious. I have information that you said something quite different.'

Eustace changed colour.

'Well, of course, I can't remember the exact words.'

'My information is that what you actually said was, "*Well, think it over and let me know.*"'

'Let me see, yes I believe you're right. Not exactly that. I think I was suggesting she should let me know when she was free.'

'Not quite the same thing, is it?' said Japp.

Major Eustace shrugged his shoulders.

'My dear fellow, you can't expect a man to remember word for word what he said on any given occasion.'

'And what did Mrs Allen reply?'

'She said she'd give me a ring. That is, as near as I can remember.'

'And then you said, "*All right. So long.*"'

'Probably. Something of the kind anyway.'

Japp said quietly:

'You say that Mrs Allen asked you to advise her about her investments. *Did she, by any chance, entrust you with the sum of two hundred pounds in cash to invest for her?*'

Eustace's face flushed a dark purple. He leaned forward and growled out:

'What the devil do you mean by that?'

'Did she or did she not?'

'That's my business, Mr Chief Inspector.'

Japp said quietly:

'Mrs Allen drew out the sum of two hundred pounds in cash from her bank. Some of the money was in five-pound notes. The numbers of these can, of course, be traced.'

'What if she did?'

'*Was* the money for investment – or was it – blackmail, Major Eustace?'

'That's a preposterous idea. What next will you suggest?'

Japp said in his most official manner:

'I think, Major Eustace, that at this point I must ask you if you are willing to come to Scotland Yard and make a statement. There is, of course, no compulsion and you can, if you prefer it, have your solicitor present.'

'Solicitor? What the devil should I want with a solicitor? And what are you cautioning me for?'

'I am inquiring into the circumstances of the death of Mrs Allen.'

'Good God, man, you don't suppose – Why, that's nonsense! Look here, what happened was this. I called round to see Barbara by appointment . . .'

'That was at what time?'

'At about half-past nine, I should say. We sat and talked . . .'

'And smoked?'

'Yes, and smoked. Anything damaging in that?' demanded the major belligerently.

'Where did this conversation take place?'

'In the sitting-room. Left of the door as you go in. We talked together quite amicably, as I say. I left a little before half-past ten. I stayed for a minute on the doorstep for a few last words . . .'

'Last words – precisely,' murmured Poirot.

'Who are *you*, I'd like to know?' Eustace turned and spart the words at him. 'Some kind of damned dago! What are *you* butting in for?'

'I am Hercule Poirot,' said the little man with dignity.

'I don't care if you are the Achilles statue. As I say, Barbara and I parted quite amicably. I drove straight to the Far East Club. Got there at five and twenty to eleven and went straight up to the card-room. Stayed there playing bridge until one-thirty. Now then, put that in your pipe and smoke it.'

'I do not smoke the pipe,' said Poirot. 'It is a pretty *alibi* you have there.'

'It should be a pretty cast iron one anyway! Now then, sir,' he looked at Japp. 'Are you satisfied?'

'You remained in the sitting-room throughout your visit?'

'Yes.'

'You did not go upstairs to Mrs Allen's own boudoir?'

'No, I tell you. We stayed in the one room and didn't leave it.'

Japp looked at him thoughtfully for a minute or two. Then he said:

'How many sets of cuff links have you?'

'Cuff links? Cuff links? What's that got to do with it?'

'You are not bound to answer the question, of course.'

'Answer it? I don't mind answering it. I've got nothing to hide. And I shall demand an apology. There are these . . .' he stretched out his arms.

Japp noted the gold and platinum with a nod.

'And I've got these.'

He rose, opened a drawer and taking out a case, he opened it and shoved it rudely almost under Japp's nose.

'Very nice design,' said the chief inspector. 'I see one is broken – bit of enamel chipped off.'

'What of it?'

'You don't remember when that happened, I suppose?'

'A day or two ago, not longer.'

'Would you be surprised to hear that it happened *when you were visiting Mrs Allen*?'

'Why shouldn't it? I've not denied that I was there.' The major spoke haughtily. He continued to bluster, to act the part of the justly indignant man, but his hands were trembling.

Japp leaned forward and said with emphasis:

'Yes, but that bit of cuff link *wasn't found in the sitting-room*. It was found *upstairs* in Mrs Allen's boudoir – there in the room where she was killed, and where a man sat smoking *the same kind of cigarettes as you smoke*.'

The shot told. Eustace fell back into his chair. His eyes went from side to side. The collapse of the bully and the appearance of the craven was not a pretty sight.

'You've got nothing on me.' His voice was almost a whine. 'You're trying to frame me . . . But you can't do it. I've got an alibi . . . I never came near the house again that night . . .'

Poirot in his turn, spoke.

'No, you did not come near the house again . . . *You did not need to* . . . For perhaps Mrs Allen *was already dead when you left it*.'

'That's impossible – impossible – She was just inside the door – she spoke to me – People must have heard her – seen her . . .'

Poirot said softly:

'They heard *you* speaking to her . . . and pretending to wait for her answer and then speaking again . . . It is an old trick that . . . People may have *assumed* she was there, but they did not *see* her, because *they could not even say whether she was wearing evening dress or not – not even mention what colour she was wearing* . . .'

'My God – it isn't true – it isn't true –'

He was shaking now – collapsed . . .

Japp looked at him with disgust. He spoke crisply.

'I'll have to ask you, sir, to come with me.'

'You're arresting me?'

'Detained for inquiry – we'll put it that way.'

The silence was broken with a long, shuddering sigh. The despairing voice of the erstwhile blustering Major Eustace said:

'I'm sunk . . .'

Hercule Poirot rubbed his hands together and smiled cheerfully. He seemed to be enjoying himself.

CHAPTER 9

'Pretty the way he went all to pieces,' said Japp with professional appreciation, later that day.

He and Poirot were driving in a car along the Brompton Road.

'He knew the game was up,' said Poirot absently.

'We've got plenty on him,' said Japp. 'Two or three different aliases, a tricky business over a cheque, and a very nice affair when he stayed at the Ritz and called himself Colonel de Bathe. Swindled half a dozen Piccadilly tradesmen. We're holding him on that charge for the moment – until we get this affair finally squared up. What's the idea of this rush to the country, old man?'

'My friend, an affair must be rounded off properly. Everything must be explained. I am on the quest of the mystery you suggested. The Mystery of the Missing Attaché-Case.'

'The Mystery of the Small Attaché-Case – that's what I called it – It isn't missing that I know of.'

'Wait, *mon ami*.'

The car turned into the mews. At the door of No. 14, Jane Plenderleith was just alighting from a small Austin Seven. She was in golfing clothes.

She looked from one to the other of the two men, then produced a key and opened the door.

'Come in, won't you?'

She led the way. Japp followed her into the sitting-room. Poirot remained for a minute or two in the hall, muttering something about:

'*C'est embêtant* – how difficult to get out of these sleeves.'

In a moment or two he also entered the sitting-room minus his overcoat but Japp's lips twitched under his moustache. He had heard the very faint squeak of an opening cupboard door.

Japp threw Poirot an inquiring glance and the other gave a hardly perceptible nod.

'We won't detain you, Miss Plenderleith,' said Japp briskly.

'Only came to ask if you could tell us the name of Mrs Allen's solicitor.'

'Her solicitor?' The girl shook her head. 'I don't even know that she had one.'

'Well, when she rented this house with you, someone must have drawn up the agreement?'

'No, I don't think so. You see, I took the house, the lease is in my name. Barbara paid me half the rent. It was quite informal.'

'I see. Oh! well, I suppose there's nothing doing then.'

'I'm sorry I can't help you,' said Jane politely.

'It doesn't really matter very much.' Japp turned towards the door. 'Been playing golf?'

'Yes.' She flushed. 'I suppose it seems rather heartless to you. But as a matter of fact it got me down rather, being here in this house. I felt I must go out and *do* something – tire myself – or I'd choke!'

She spoke with intensity.

Poirot said quickly:

'I comprehend, mademoiselle. It is most understandable – most natural. To sit in this house and think – no, it would not be pleasant.'

'So long as you understand,' said Jane shortly.

'You belong to a club?'

'Yes, I play at Wentworth.'

'It has been a pleasant day,' said Poirot.

'Alas, there are few leaves left on the trees now! A week ago the woods were magnificent.'

'It was quite lovely today.'

'Good afternoon, Miss Plenderleith,' said Japp formally. 'I'll let you know when there's anything definite. As a matter of fact we have got a man detained on suspicion.'

'What man?'

She looked at them eagerly.

'Major Eustace.'

She nodded and turned away, stooping down to put a match to the fire.

'Well?' said Japp as the car turned the corner of the mews.

Poirot grinned.

'It was quite simple. The key was in the door this time.'

'And –?'

Poirot smiled.

'*Eh, bien*, the golf clubs had gone –'

'Naturally. The girl isn't a fool, whatever else she is. *Anything else gone*?'

Poirot nodded his head.

'Yes, my friend – *the little attaché-case*!'

The accelerator leaped under Japp's foot.

'Damnation!' he said. 'I knew there was *something*. But what the devil is it? I searched that case pretty thoroughly.'

'My poor Japp – but it is – how do you say, "obvious, my dear Watson"?'

Japp threw him an exasperated look.

'Where are we going?' he asked.

Poirot consulted his watch.

'It is not yet four o'clock. We could get to Wentworth, I think, before it is dark.'

'Do you think she really went there?'

'I think so – yes. She would know that we might make inquiries. Oh, yes, I think we will find that she has been there.'

Japp grunted.

'Oh well, come on.' He threaded his way dexterously through the traffic. 'Though what this attaché-case business has to do with the crime I can't imagine. I can't see that it's got anything at all to do with it.'

'Precisely, my friend, I agree with you – it has nothing to do with it.'

'Then why – No, don't tell me! Order and method and everything nicely rounded off! Oh, well, it's a fine day.'

The car was a fast one. They arrived at Wentworth Golf Club a little after half-past four. There was no great congestion there on a week day.

Poirot went straight to the caddie-master and asked for Miss Plenderleith's clubs. She would be playing on a different course tomorrow, he explained.

The caddie-master raised his voice and a boy sorted through some golf clubs standing in a corner. He finally produced a bag bearing the initials, J.P.

'Thank you,' said Poirot. He moved away, then turned carelessly and asked, 'She did not leave with you a small attaché-case also, did she?'

'Not today, sir. May have left it in the clubhouse.'

'She was down here today?'

'Oh, yes, I saw her.'

'Which caddie did she have, do you know? She's mislaid an attaché-case and can't remember where she had it last.'

'She didn't take a caddie. She came in here and bought a couple of balls. Just took out a couple of irons. I rather fancy she had a little case in her hand then.'

Poirot turned away with a word of thanks. The two men walked round the clubhouse. Poirot stood a moment admiring the view.

'It is beautiful, is it not, the dark pine trees – and then the lake. Yes, the lake –'

Japp gave him a quick glance.

'That's the idea, is it?'

Poirot smiled.

'I think it possible that someone may have seen something. I should set the inquiries in motion if I were you.'

CHAPTER 10

I

Poirot stepped back, his head a little on one side as he surveyed the arrangement of the room. A chair here – another chair there. Yes, that was very nice. And now a ring at the bell – that would be Japp.

The Scotland Yard man came in alertly.

'Quite right, old cock! Straight from the horse's mouth. A young woman was seen to throw something into the lake at Wentworth yesterday. Description of her answers to Jane Plenderleith. We managed to fish it up without much difficulty. A lot of reeds just there.'

'And it was?'

'It was the attaché-case all right! But *why*, in heaven's name? Well, it beats me! Nothing inside it – not even the magazines. Why a presumably sane young woman should want to fling an expensively-fitted dressing-case into a lake – d'you know, I worried all night because I couldn't get the hang of it.'

'*Mon pauvre Japp!* But you need worry no longer. Here is the answer coming. The bell has just rung.'

George, Poirot's immaculate man-servant, opened the door and announced:

'Miss Plenderleith.'

The girl came into the room with her usual air of complete self-assurance. She greeted the two men.

'I asked you to come here –' explained Poirot. 'Sit here, will you not, and you here, Japp – because I have certain news to give you.'

The girl sat down. She looked from one to the other, pushing aside her hat. She took it off and laid it aside impatiently.

'Well,' she said. 'Major Eustace has been arrested.'

'You saw that, I expect, in the morning paper?'

'Yes.'

'He is at the moment charged with a minor offence,' went on

Poirot. 'In the meantime we are gathering evidence in connection with the murder.'

'It *was* murder, then?'

The girl asked it eagerly.

Poirot nodded his head.

'Yes,' he said. 'It was murder. The wilful destruction of one human being by another human being.'

She shivered a little.

'Don't,' she murmured. 'It sounds horrible when you say it like that.'

'Yes – but it is horrible!'

He paused – then he said:

'Now, Miss Plenderleith, I am going to tell you just how I arrived at the truth in this matter.'

She looked from Poirot to Japp. The latter was smiling.

'He has his methods, Miss Plenderleith,' he said. 'I humour him, you know. I think we'll listen to what he has to say.'

Poirot began:

'As you know, mademoiselle, I arrived with my friend at the scene of the crime on the morning of November the sixth. We went into the room where the body of Mrs Allen had been found and I was struck at once by several significant details. There were things, you see, in that room that were decidedly odd.'

'Go on,' said the girl.

'To begin with,' said Poirot, 'there was the smell of cigarette smoke.'

'I think you're exaggerating there, Poirot,' said Japp. '*I* didn't smell anything.'

Poirot turned on him in a flash.

'Precisely. *You did not smell any stale smoke. No more did I.* And that was very, very strange – for the door and the window were both closed and on an ashtray there were the stubs of no fewer than ten cigarettes. It was odd, very odd, that the room should smell – as it did, perfectly fresh.'

'So that's what you were getting at!' Japp sighed. 'Always have to get at things in such a tortuous way.'

'Your Sherlock Holmes did the same. He drew attention, remember, to the curious incident of the dog in the night-time – and the answer to that was there was no curious incident. The dog did nothing in the night-time. To proceed:

'The next thing that attracted my attention was a wrist-watch worn by the dead woman.'

'What about it?'

'Nothing particular about it, but it was worn on the *right* wrist. Now in my experience it is more usual for a watch to be worn on the left wrist.'

Japp shrugged his shoulders. Before he could speak, Poirot hurried on:

'But as you say, there is nothing very definite about *that*. Some people *prefer* to wear one on the right hand. And now I come to something really interesting – I come, my friends, to the writing-bureau.'

'Yes, I guessed that,' said Japp.

'That was really *very* odd – *very* remarkable! For two reasons. The first reason was that something was missing from that writing-table.'

Jane Plenderleith spoke.

'What was missing?'

Poirot turned to her.

'*A sheet of blotting-paper, mademoiselle*. The blotting-book had on top a clean, untouched piece of blotting-paper.'

Jane shrugged her shoulders.

'Really, M. Poirot. People do occasionally tear off a very much used sheet!'

'Yes, but what do they do with it? Throw it into the waste-paper basket, do they not? *But it was not in the waste-paper basket*. I looked.'

Jane Plenderleith seemed impatient.

'Because it had probably been already thrown away the day before. The sheet was clean because Barbara hadn't written any letters that day.'

'That could hardly be the case, mademoiselle. *For Mrs Allen was seen going to the post box that evening. Therefore she must have been writing letters*. She could not write downstairs – there were no writing materials. She would be hardly likely to go to *your* room to write. So, then, what had happened to the sheet of paper on which she had blotted her letters? It is true that people sometimes throw things in the fire instead of the waste-paper basket, but there was only a gas fire in the room. *And the fire downstairs had not been alight the previous day, since you told me it was all laid ready when you put a match to it.*'

He paused.

'A curious little problem. I looked everywhere, in the waste-paper baskets, in the dustbin, but I could not find a sheet of used blotting-paper – and that seemed to me very important. It looked as though someone had deliberately taken that sheet of blotting-paper away. Why? Because there was writing on it that could easily have been read by holding it up to a mirror.

'But there was a second curious point about the writing-table. Perhaps, Japp, you remember roughly the arrangement of it? Blotter and inkstand in the centre, pen tray to the left, calendar and quill pen to the right. *Eh bien*? You do not see? The quill pen, remember, I examined, it was for show only – it had not been used. Ah! *still* you do not see? I will say it again. Blotter in the centre, pen tray to the left – to the *left*, Japp. But is it not usual to find a pen tray *on the right*, convenient to *the right hand*?

'Ah, now it comes to you, does it not? The pen tray on the *left* – the wrist-watch on the *right* wrist – the blotting-paper removed – and something else brought *into* the room – the ashtray with the cigarette ends!

'That room was fresh and pure smelling, Japp, a room in which the window had been *open*, not closed all night . . . And I made myself a picture.'

He spun round and faced Jane.

'A picture of you, mademoiselle, driving up in your taxi, paying it off, running up the stairs, calling perhaps, "Barbara" – and you open the door and you find your friend there lying dead with the pistol clasped in her hand – the left hand, naturally, *since she is left-handed* and therefore, too, the bullet has entered on the *left side of the head*. There is a note there addressed to you. It tells you what it is that has driven her to take her own life. It was, I fancy, a very moving letter . . . A young, gentle, unhappy woman driven by blackmail to take her life . . .

'I think that, almost at once, the idea flashed into your head. This was a certain man's doing. Let him be punished – fully and adequately punished! You take the pistol, wipe it and place it in the *right* hand. You take the note and you tear off the top sheet of the blotting-paper on which the note has been blotted. You go down, light the fire and put them both on the flames. Then you carry up the ashtray – to further the illusion that two people sat there talking – and you also take up a fragment of enamel cuff link that is on the floor. That is a lucky find and you expect it to clinch matters. Then you close the window and lock the door. There must be no suspicion that you have tampered with the room. The police must see it exactly as it is – so you do not seek help in the mews but ring up the police straightaway.

'And so it goes on. You play your chosen rôle with judgment and coolness. You refuse at first to say anything but cleverly you suggest doubts of suicide. Later you are quite ready to set us on the trail of Major Eustace . . .

'Yes, mademoiselle, it was clever – a very clever murder – for that is what it is. The attempted murder of Major Eustace.'

Jane Plenderleith sprang to her feet.

'It wasn't murder – it was justice. That man *hounded* poor Barbara to her death! She was so sweet and helpless. You see, poor kid, she got involved with a man in India when she first went out. She was only seventeen and he was a married man years older than her. Then she had a baby. She could have put it in a home but she wouldn't hear of that. She went off to some out of the way spot and came back calling herself Mrs Allen. Later the child died. She came back here and she fell in love with Charles – that pompous, stuffed owl; she adored him – and he took her adoration very complacently. If he had been a different kind of man I'd have advised her to tell him everything. But as it was, I urged her to hold her tongue. After all, nobody knew anything about that business except me.

'And then that devil Eustace turned up! You know the rest. He began to bleed her systematically, but it wasn't till that last evening that she realised that she was exposing Charles too, to the risk of scandal. Once married to Charles, Eustace had got her where he wanted her – married to a rich man with a horror of any scandal! When Eustace had gone with the money she had got for him she sat thinking it over. Then she came up and wrote a letter to me. She said she loved Charles and couldn't live without him, but that for his own sake she mustn't marry him. She was taking the best way out, she said.'

Jane flung her head back.

'Do you wonder I did what I did? And you stand there calling it *murder*!'

'Because it is murder,' Poirot's voice was stern. 'Murder can sometimes seem justified, *but it is murder all the same*. You are truthful and clear-minded – face the truth, mademoiselle! Your friend died, in the last resort, *because she had not the courage to live*. We may sympathize with her. We may pity her. But the fact remains – the act was *hers* – not another.'

He paused.

'And you? That man is now in prison, he will serve a long sentence for other matters. Do you really wish, of your own volition, to destroy the life – the *life*, mind – of *any* human being?'

She stared at him. Her eyes darkened. Suddenly she muttered:

'No. You're right. I don't.'

Then, turning on her heel, she went swiftly from the room. The outer door banged . . .

II

Japp gave a long – a very prolonged – whistle.

'Well, I'm damned!' he said.

Poirot sat down and smiled at him amiably. It was quite a long time before the silence was broken. Then Japp said:

'Not murder disguised as suicide, but suicide made to look like murder!'

'Yes, and very cleverly done, too. Nothing over-emphasized.'

Japp said suddenly:

'But the attaché-case? Where did that come in?'

'But, my dear, my very dear friend, I have already told you that *it did not come in*.'

'Then why –'

'The golf clubs. The golf clubs, Japp. *They were the golf clubs of a left-handed person*. Jane Plenderleith kept her clubs at Wentworth. Those were Barbara Allen's clubs. No wonder the girl got, as you say, the wind up when we opened that cupboard. Her whole plan might have been ruined. But she is quick, she realized that she had, for one short moment, given herself away. *She* saw that *we* saw. So she does the best thing she can think of on the spur of the moment.

She tries to focus our attention on the *wrong object*. She says of the attaché-case "That's mine. I – it came back with me this morning. So there can't be anything there." And, as she hoped, away you go on the false trail. For the same reason, when she sets out the following day to get rid of the golf clubs, she continues to use the attaché-case as a – what is it – kippered herring?'

'Red herring. Do you mean that her real object was –?'

'Consider, my friend. Where is the best place to get rid of a bag of golf clubs? One cannot burn them or put them in a dustbin. If one leaves them somewhere they may be returned to you. Miss Plenderleith took them to a golf course. She leaves them in the clubhouse while she gets a couple of irons from her own bag, and then she goes round without a caddy. Doubtless at judicious intervals she breaks a club in half and throws it into some deep undergrowth, and ends by throwing the empty bag away. If anyone should find a broken golf club here and there it will not create surprise. People have been known to break and throw away *all* their clubs in a mood of intense exasperation over the game! It is, in fact, that kind of game!

'But since she realizes that her actions may still be a matter of interest, she throws that useful red herring – the attaché-case – in a somewhat spectacular manner into the lake – and that, my friend, is the truth of "The Mystery of the Attaché-Case."'

Japp looked at his friend for some moments in silence. Then he rose, clapped him on the shoulder, and burst out laughing.

'Not so bad for an old dog! Upon my word, you take the cake! Come out and have a spot of lunch?'

'With pleasure, my friend, but we will not have the cake. Indeed, an Omelette aux Champignons, Blanquette de Veau, Petits pois à la Française, and – to follow – a Baba au Rhum.'

'Lead me to it,' said Japp.

HERCULE POIROT'S CHRISTMAS

My dear James

You have always been one of the most faithful and kindly of my readers, and I was therefore seriously perturbed when I received from you a word of criticism.

You complained that my murders were getting too refined – anaemic, in fact. You yearned for a 'good violent murder with lots of blood'. A murder where there was no doubt about its being murder!

So this is your special story – written for you. I hope it may please.

Your affectionate sister-in-law

Agatha

CONTENTS

PART I

DECEMBER 22ND

I

Stephen pulled up the collar of his coat as he walked briskly along the platform. Overhead a dim fog clouded the station. Large engines hissed superbly, throwing off clouds of steam into the cold raw air. Everything was dirty and smoke-grimed.

Stephen thought with revulsion:

'What a foul country – what a foul city!'

His first excited reaction to London, its shops, its restaurants, its well-dressed, attractive women, had faded. He saw it now as a glittering rhinestone set in a dingy setting.

Supposing he were back in South Africa now . . . He felt a quick pang of homesickness. Sunshine – blue skies – gardens of flowers – cool blue flowers – hedges of plumbago – blue convolvulus clinging to every little shanty.

And here – dirt, grime, and endless, incessant crowds – moving, hurrying – jostling. Busy ants running industriously about their ant-hill.

For a moment he thought, 'I wish I hadn't come . . .'

Then he remembered his purpose and his lips set back in a grim line. No, by hell, he'd go on with it! He'd planned this for years. He'd always meant to do – what he was going to do. Yes, he'd go on with it!

That momentary reluctance, that sudden questioning of himself: 'Why? Is it worth it? Why dwell on the past? Why not wipe out the whole thing?' – all that was only weakness. He was not a boy – to be turned this way and that by the whim of the moment. He was a man of forty, assured, purposeful. He would go on with it. He would do what he had come to England to do.

He got on the train and passed along the corridor looking for a place. He had waved aside a porter and was carrying his own raw-hide suitcase. He looked into carriage after carriage. The train was full. It was only three days before Christmas. Stephen Farr looked distastefully at the crowded carriages.

People! Incessant, innumerable people! And all so – so – what was the word – so *drab*-looking! So alike, so horribly alike! Those that hadn't got faces like sheep had faces like rabbits, he thought. Some of them chattered and fussed. Some, heavily middle-aged men, grunted. More like pigs, those. Even the girls, slender, egg-faced, scarlet-lipped, were of a depressing uniformity.

He thought with a sudden longing of open veldt, sun-baked and lonely . . .

And then, suddenly, he caught his breath, looking into a carriage. This girl was different. Black hair, rich creamy pallor – eyes with the depth and darkness of night in them. The sad proud eyes of the South . . . It was all wrong that this girl should be sitting in this train among these dull, drab-looking people – all wrong that she should be going into the dreary midlands of England. She should have been on a balcony, a rose between her lips, a piece of black lace draping her proud head, and there should have been dust and heat and the smell of blood – the smell of the bull-ring – in the air . . . She should be somewhere splendid, not squeezed into the corner of a third-class carriage.

He was an observant man. He did not fail to note the shabbiness of her little black coat and skirt, the cheap quality of her fabric gloves, the flimsy shoes and the defiant note of a flame-red handbag. Nevertheless splendour was the quality he associated with her. She *was* splendid, fine, exotic . . .

What the hell was she doing in this country of fogs and chills and hurrying industrious ants?

He thought, 'I've got to know who she is and what she's doing here . . . I've got to know . . .'

II

Pilar sat squeezed up against the window and thought how very odd the English smelt . . . It was what had struck her so far most forcibly about England – the difference of smell. There was no garlic and no dust and very little perfume. In this carriage now there was a smell of cold stuffiness – the sulphur smell of the trains – the smell of soap and another very unpleasant smell – it came, she thought, from the fur collar of the stout woman sitting beside her. Pilar sniffed delicately, imbibing the odour of mothballs reluctantly. It was a funny scent to choose to put on yourself, she thought.

A whistle blew, a stentorian voice cried out something and the train jerked slowly out of the station. They had started. She was on her way . . .

Her heart beat a little faster. Would it be all right? Would she be able to accomplish what she had set out to do? Surely – surely – she had thought it all out so carefully . . . She was prepared for every eventuality. Oh, yes, she would succeed – she must succeed . . .

The curve of Pilar's red mouth curved upwards. It was suddenly cruel, that mouth. Cruel and greedy – like the mouth of a child or a kitten – a mouth that knew only its own desires and that was as yet unaware of pity.

She looked round her with the frank curiosity of a child. All these people, seven of them – how funny they were, the English! They all seemed so rich, so prosperous – their clothes – their boots – Oh! undoubtedly England was a very rich country as she had always heard. But they were not at all gay – no, decidedly not gay.

That was a handsome man standing in the corridor . . . Pilar thought he was very handsome. She liked his deeply bronzed face and his high-bridged nose and his square shoulders. More quickly than any English girl, Pilar had seen that the man admired her. She had not looked at him once directly, but she knew perfectly how often he had looked at her and exactly how he had looked.

She registered the facts without much interest or emotion. She came from a country where men looked at women as a matter of course and did not disguise the fact unduly. She wondered if he was an Englishman and decided that he was not.

'He is too alive, too real, to be English,' Pilar decided. 'And yet he is fair. He may be perhaps Americano.' He was, she thought, rather like the actors she had seen in Wild West films.

An attendant pushed his way along the corridor.

'First lunch, please. First lunch. Take your seats for first lunch.'

The seven occupants of Pilar's carriage all held tickets for the first lunch. They rose in a body and the carriage was suddenly deserted and peaceful.

Pilar quickly pulled up the window which had been let down a couple of inches at the top by a militant-looking, grey-haired lady in the opposite corner. Then she sprawled comfortably back on her seat and peered out of the window at the northern suburbs of London. She did not turn her head at the sound of the door sliding back. It was the man from the corridor, and Pilar knew, of course, that he had entered the carriage on purpose to talk to her.

She continued to look pensively out of the window.

Stephen Farr said:

'Would you like the window down at all?'

Pilar replied demurely:

'On the contrary. I have just shut it.'

She spoke English perfectly, but with a slight accent.

During the pause that ensued, Stephen thought:

'A delicious voice. It has the sun in it . . . It is warm like a summer night . . .'

Pilar thought:

'I like his voice. It is big and strong. He is attractive – yes, he is attractive.'

Stephen said: 'The train is very full.'

'Oh, yes, indeed. The people go away from London, I suppose, because it is so black there.'

Pilar had not been brought up to believe that it was a crime to talk to strange men in trains. She could take care of herself as well as any girl, but she had no rigid taboos.

If Stephen had been brought up in England he might have felt ill at ease at entering into conversation with a young girl. But Stephen was a friendly soul who found it perfectly natural to talk to anyone if he felt like it.

He smiled without any self-consciousness and said:

'London's rather a terrible place, isn't it?'

'Oh, yes. I do not like it at all.'

'No more do I.'

Pilar said: 'You are not English, no?'

'I'm British, but I come from South Africa.'

'Oh, I see, that explains it.'

'Have you just come from abroad?'

Pilar nodded. 'I come from Spain.'

Stephen was interested.

'From Spain, do you? You're Spanish, then?'

'I am half Spanish. My mother was English. That is why I talk English so well.'

'What about this war business?' asked Stephen.

'It is very terrible, yes – very sad. There has been damage done, quite a lot – yes.'

'Which side are you on?'

Pilar's politics seemed to be rather vague. In the village where she came from, she explained, nobody had paid very much attention to the war. 'It has not been near us, you understand. The Mayor, he is, of course, an officer of the Government, so he is for the Government, and the priest is for General Franco – but most of the people are busy with the vines and the land, they have not time to go into these questions.'

'So there wasn't any fighting round you?'

Pilar said that there had not been. 'But then I drove in a car,' she explained, 'all across the country and there was much destruction. And I saw a bomb drop and it blew up a car – yes, and another destroyed a house. It was very exciting!'

Stephen Farr smiled a faintly twisted smile.

'So that's how it seemed to you?'

'It was a nuisance, too,' explained Pilar. 'Because I wanted to get on, and the driver of my car, he was killed.'

Stephen said, watching her:

'That didn't upset you?'

Pilar's great dark eyes opened very wide.

'Everyone must die! That is so, is it not? If it comes quickly from the sky – bouff – like that, it is as well as any other way. One is alive for a time – yes, and then one is dead. That is what happens in this world.'

Stephen Farr laughed.

'I don't think you are a pacifist.'

'You do not think I am what?' Pilar seemed puzzled by a word which had not previously entered her vocabulary.

'Do you forgive your enemies, señorita?'

Pilar shook her head.

'I have no enemies. But if I had –'

'Well?'

He was watching her, fascinated anew by the sweet, cruel upward-curving mouth.

Pilar said gravely:

'If I had an enemy – if anyone hated me and I hated them – then I would cut my enemy's throat like *this* . . .'

She made a graphic gesture.

It was so swift and so crude that Stephen Farr was momentarily taken aback. He said:

'You are a bloodthirsty young woman!'

Pilar asked in a matter-of-fact tone:

'What would you do to your enemy?'

He started – stared at her, then laughed aloud.

'I wonder –' he said. 'I wonder!'

Pilar said disapprovingly:

'But surely – you know.'

He checked his laughter, drew in his breath and said in a low voice:

'Yes. I know . . .'

Then with a rapid change of manner, he asked:

'What made you come to England?'

Pilar replied with a certain demureness.

'I am going to stay with my relations – with my English relations.'

'I see.'

He leaned back in his seat, studying her – wondering what these English relations of whom she spoke were like – wondering what they would make of this Spanish stranger . . . trying to picture her in the midst of some sober British family at Christmas time.

Pilar asked: 'Is it nice, South Africa, yes?'

He began to talk to her about South Africa. She listened with the pleased attention of a child hearing a story. He enjoyed her naïve but shrewd questions and amused himself by making a kind of exaggerated fairy story of it all.

The return of the proper occupants of the carriage put an end to this diversion. He rose, smiled into her eyes, and made his way out again into the corridor.

As he stood back for a minute in the doorway, to allow an elderly lady to come in, his eyes fell on the label of Pilar's obviously foreign straw case. He read the name with interest

– *Miss Pilar Estravados* – then as his eye caught the address it widened to incredulity and some other feeling – *Gorston Hall, Longdale, Addlesfield.*

He half turned, staring at the girl with a new expression – puzzled, resentful, suspicious . . . He went out into the corridor and stood there smoking a cigarette and frowning to himself . . .

III

In the big blue and gold drawing-room at Gorston Hall Alfred Lee and Lydia, his wife, sat discussing their plans for Christmas. Alfred was a squarely built man of middle age with a gentle face and mild brown eyes. His voice when he spoke was quiet and precise with a very clear enunciation. His head was sunk into his shoulders and he gave a curious impression of inertia. Lydia, his wife, was an energetic, lean greyhound of a woman. She was amazingly thin, but all her movements had a swift, startled grace about them.

There was no beauty in her careless, haggard face, but it had distinction. Her voice was charming.

Alfred said:

'Father insists! There's nothing else to it.'

Lydia controlled a sudden impatient movement. She said:

'Must you always give in to him?'

'He's a very old man, my dear –'

'Oh, I know – I know!'

'He expects to have his own way.'

Lydia said dryly:

'Naturally, since he has always had it! But some time or other, Alfred, you will have to make a stand.'

'What do you mean, Lydia?'

He stared at her, so palpably upset and startled, that for a moment she bit her lip and seemed doubtful whether to go on.

Alfred Lee repeated:

'What do you mean, Lydia?'

She shrugged her thin, graceful shoulders.

She said, trying to choose her words cautiously:

'Your father is – inclined to be – tyrannical –'

'He's old.'

'And will grow older. And consequently more tyrannical. Where will it end? Already he dictates our lives to us completely. We can't make a plan of our own! If we do, it is always liable to be upset.'

Alfred said:

'Father expects to come first. He is very good to us, remember.'

'Oh! good to us!'

'*Very* good to us.'

Alfred spoke with a trace of sternness.

'Lydia said calmly:

'You mean financially?'

'Yes. His own wants are very simple. But he never grudges us money. You can spend what you like on dress and on this house, and the bills are paid without a murmur. He gave us a new car only last week.'

'As far as money goes, your father is very generous, I admit,' said Lydia. 'But in return he expects us to behave like slaves.'

'Slaves?'

'That's the word I used. You *are* his slave, Alfred. If we have planned to go away and Father suddenly wishes us not to go, you cancel your arrangements and remain without a murmur! If the whim takes him to send us away, we go . . . We have no lives of our own – no independence.'

Her husband said distressfully:

'I wish you wouldn't talk like this, Lydia. It is very ungrateful. My father has done everything for us . . .'

She bit off a retort that was on her lips. She shrugged those thin, graceful shoulders once more.

Alfred said:

'You know, Lydia, the old man is very fond of you –'

His wife said clearly and distinctly:

'I am not at all fond of him.'

'Lydia, it distresses me to hear you say things like that. It is so unkind –'

'Perhaps. But sometimes a compulsion comes over one to speak the truth.'

'If Father guessed –'

'Your father knows perfectly well that I do not like him! It amuses him, I think.'

'Really, Lydia, I am sure you are wrong there. He has often told me how charming your manner to him is.'

'Naturally I've always been polite. I always shall be. I'm just letting you know what my real feelings are. I dislike your father, Alfred. I think he is a malicious and tyrannical old man. He bullies you and presumes on your affection for him. You ought to have stood up to him years ago.'

Alfred said sharply:

'That will do, Lydia. Please don't say any more.'

She sighed.

'I'm sorry. Perhaps I was wrong . . . Let's talk of our Christmas arrangements. Do you think your brother David will really come?'

'Why not?'

She shook her head doubtfully.

'David is – queer. He's not been inside the house for years, remember. He was so devoted to your mother – he's got some feeling about this place.'

'David always got on Father's nerves,' said Alfred, 'with his music and his dreamy ways. Father was, perhaps, a bit hard on him sometimes. But I think David and Hilda will come all right. Christmas time, you know.'

'Peace and goodwill,' said Lydia. Her delicate mouth curved ironically. 'I wonder! George and Magdalene are coming. They said they would probably arrive tomorrow. I'm afraid Magdalene will be frightfully bored.'

Alfred said with some slight annoyance:

'Why my brother George ever married a girl twenty years younger than himself I can't think! George was always a fool!'

'He's very successful in his career,' said Lydia. 'His constituents like him. I believe Magdalene works quite hard politically for him.'

Alfred said slowly:

'I don't think I like her very much. She is very good-looking – but I sometimes think she is like one of those beautiful pears one gets – they have a rosy flush and a rather waxen appearance –' He shook his head.

'And they're bad inside?' said Lydia. 'How funny you should say that, Alfred!'

'Why funny?'

She answered:

'Because – usually – you are such a gentle soul. You hardly ever say an unkind thing about anyone. I get annoyed with you sometimes because you're not sufficiently – oh, what shall I say? – sufficiently suspicious – not worldly enough!'

Her husband smiled.

'The world, I always think, is as you yourself make it.'

Lydia said sharply:

'No! Evil is not only in one's mind. Evil exists! *You* seem to have no consciousness of the evil in the world. I have. I can feel it. I've always felt it – here in this house –' She bit her lip and turned away.

Alfred said, 'Lydia –'

But she raised a quick admonitory hand, her eyes looking past him at something over his shoulder. Alfred turned.

A dark man with a smooth face was standing there deferentially.

Lydia said sharply:

'What is it, Horbury?'

Horbury's voice was low, a mere deferential murmur.

'It's Mr Lee, madam. He asked me to tell you that there would be two more guests arriving for Christmas, and would you have rooms prepared for them.'

Lydia said, 'Two more guests?'

Horbury said smoothly, 'Yes, madam, another gentleman and a young lady.'

Alfred said wonderingly: 'A young lady?'

'That's what Mr Lee said, sir.'

Lydia said quickly:

'I will go up and see him –'

Horbury made one little step, it was a mere ghost of a movement but it stopped Lydia's rapid progress automatically.

'Excuse me, madam, but Mr Lee is having his afternoon sleep. He asked specifically that he should not be disturbed.'

'I see,' said Alfred. 'Of course we won't disturb him.'

'Thank you, sir.' Horbury withdrew.

Lydia said vehemently:

'How I dislike that man! He creeps about the house like a cat! One never hears him going or coming.'

'I don't like him very much either. But he knows his job. It's not so easy to get a good male nurse attendant. And Father likes him, that's the main thing.'

'Yes, that's the main thing, as you say. Alfred, what is this about a young lady? What young lady?'

Her husband shook his head.

'I can't imagine. I can't even think of anyone it might be likely to be.'

They stared at each other. Then Lydia said, with a sudden twist of her expressive mouth:

'Do you know what I think, Alfred?'

'What?'

'I think your father has been bored lately. I think he is planning a little Christmas diversion for himself.'

'By introducing two strangers into a family gathering?'

'Oh! I don't know what the details are – but I do fancy that your father is preparing to – amuse himself.'

'I hope he *will* get some pleasure out of it,' said Alfred gravely. 'Poor old chap, tied by the leg, an invalid – after the adventurous life he has led.'

Lydia said slowly:

'After the – adventurous life he has led.'

The pause she made before the adjective gave it some special though obscure significance. Alfred seemed to feel it. He flushed and looked unhappy.

She cried out suddenly:

'How he ever had a son like you, I can't imagine! You two are poles apart. And he fascinates you – you simply worship him!'

Alfred said with a trace of vexation:

'Aren't you going a little far, Lydia? It's natural, I should say, for a son to love his father. It would be very unnatural not to do so.'

Lydia said:

'In that case, most of the members of this family are – unnatural! Oh, don't let's argue! I apologize. I've hurt your feelings, I know. Believe me, Alfred, I really didn't mean to do that. I admire you enormously for your – your – *fidelity*. Loyalty is such a rare virtue in these days. Let us say, shall we, that I am jealous? Women are supposed to be jealous of their mothers-in-law – why not, then, of their fathers-in-law?'

He put a gentle arm round her.

'Your tongue runs away with you, Lydia. There's no reason for you to be jealous.'

She gave him a quick remorseful kiss, a delicate caress on the tip of his ear.

'I know. All the same, Alfred, I don't believe I should have been in the least jealous of your mother. I wish I'd known her.'

'She was a poor creature,' he said.

His wife looked at him interestedly.

'So that's how she struck you . . . as a poor creature . . . That's interesting.'

He said dreamily:

'I remember her as nearly always ill . . . Often in tears . . .' He shook his head. 'She had no spirit.'

Still staring at him, she murmured very softly:

'How odd . . .'

But as he turned a questioning glance on her, she shook her head quickly and changed the subject.

'Since we are not allowed to know who our mysterious guests are I shall go out and finish my garden.'

'It's very cold, my dear, a biting wind.'

'I'll wrap up warmly.'

She left the room. Alfred Lee, left alone, stood for some minutes motionless, frowning a little to himself, then he walked over to the big window at the end of the room. Outside was a terrace running the whole length of the house. Here, after a minute or two, he saw Lydia emerge, carrying a flat basket. She was wearing a big blanket coat. She set down the basket and began to work at a square stone sink slightly raised above ground level.

Her husband watched for some time. At last he went out of the room, fetched himself a coat and muffler, and emerged on to the terrace by a side door. As he walked along he passed various other stone sinks arranged as miniature gardens, all the products of Lydia's agile fingers.

One represented a desert scene with smooth yellow sand, a little clump of green palm trees in coloured tin, and a procession of camels with one or two little Arab figures. Some primitive mud houses had been constructed of plasticine. There was an Italian garden with terraces and formal beds with flowers in coloured sealing-wax. There was an Arctic one, too, with clumps of green glass for icebergs, and a little cluster of penguins. Next came a Japanese garden with a couple of beautiful little stunted trees, looking-glass arranged for water, and bridges modelled out of plasticine.

He came at last to stand beside her where she was at work. She had laid down blue paper and covered it over with glass. Round this were lumps of rock piled up. At the moment she was pouring out coarse pebbles from a little bag and forming them into a beach. Between the rocks were some small cactuses.

Lydia was murmuring to herself:

'Yes, that's exactly right – exactly what I want.'

Alfred said:

'What's this latest work of art?'

She started, for she had not heard him come up.

'This? Oh, it's the Dead Sea, Alfred. Do you like it?'

He said, 'It's rather arid, isn't it? Oughtn't there to be more vegetation?'

She shook her head.

'It's my idea of the Dead Sea. It *is* dead, you see –'

'It's not so attractive as some of the others.'

'It's not meant to be specially attractive.'

Footsteps sounded on the terrace. An elderly butler, white-haired and slightly bowed, was coming towards them.

'Mrs George Lee on the telephone, madam. She says will it be convenient if she and Mr George arrive by the five-twenty tomorrow?'

'Yes, tell her that will be quite all right.'

'Thank you, madam.'

The butler hurried away. Lydia looked after him with a softened expression on her face.

'Dear old Tressilian. What a standby he is! I can't imagine what we should do without him.'

Alfred agreed.

'He's one of the old school. He's been with us nearly forty years. He's devoted to us all.'

Lydia nodded.

'Yes. He's like the faithful old retainers of fiction. I believe he'd lie himself blue in the face if it was necessary to protect one of the family!'

Alfred said:

'I believe he would . . . Yes, I believe he would.'

Lydia smoothed over the last bit of her shingle.

'There,' she said. 'That's ready.'

'Ready?' Alfred looked puzzled.

She laughed.

'For Christmas, silly! For this sentimental family Christmas we're going to have.'

IV

David was reading the letter. Once he screwed it up into a ball and thrust it away from him. Then, reaching for it, he smoothed it out and read it again.

Quietly, without saying anything, his wife, Hilda, watched him. She noted the jerking muscle (or was it a nerve?) in his temple, the slight tremor of the long delicate hands, the nervous spasmodic movements of his whole body. When he pushed aside the lock of fair hair that always tended to stray down over his forehead and looked across at her with appealing blue eyes she was ready.

'Hilda, what shall we do about it?'

Hilda hesitated a minute before speaking. She had heard the appeal in his voice. She knew how dependent he was upon her – had always been ever since their marriage – knew that she could probably influence his decision finally and decisively. But for just that reason she was chary of pronouncing anything too final.

She said, and her voice had the calm, soothing quality that can be heard in the voice of an experienced nannie in a nursery:

'It depends on how you feel about it, David.'

A broad woman, Hilda, not beautiful, but with a certain magnetic quality. Something about her like a Dutch picture. Something warming and endearing in the sound of her voice. Something strong about her – the vital hidden strength that appeals to weakness. An over-stout dumpy middle-aged woman – not clever – not brilliant – but with *something* about her that you couldn't pass over. Force! Hilda Lee had force!

David got up and began pacing up and down. His hair was practically untouched by grey. He was strangely boyish-looking.

His face had the mild quality of a Burne-Jones knight. It was, somehow, not vcry real . . .

He said, and his voice was wistful:

'You know how I feel about it, Hilda. You must.'

'I'm not sure.'

'But I've told you – I've told you again and again! How I hate it all – the house and the country round and everything! It brings back nothing but misery. I hated every moment that I spent there! When I think of it – of all that *she* suffered – my mother . . .'

His wife nodded sympathetically.

'She was so sweet, Hilda, and so patient. Lying there, often in pain, but bearing it – enduring everything. And when I think of my father' – his face darkened – 'bringing all that misery into her life – humiliating her – boasting of his love affairs – constantly unfaithful to her and never troubling to conceal it.'

Hilda Lee said:

'She should not have put up with it. She should have left him.'

He said with a touch of reproof:

'She was too good to do that. She thought it was her duty to remain. Besides, it was her home – where else should she go?'

'She could have made a life of her own.'

David said fretfully:

'Not in those days! You don't understand. Women didn't behave like that. They put up with things. They endured patiently. She had us to consider. Even if she divorced my father, what would have happened? He would probably have married again. There might have been a second family. *Our* interests might have gone to the wall. She had to think of all those considerations.'

Hilda did not answer.

David went on:

'No, she did right. She was a saint! She endured to the end – uncomplainingly.'

Hilda said, 'Not quite uncomplainingly or you would not know so much, David!'

He said softly, his face lighting up:

'Yes – she told me things – She knew how I loved her. When she died –'

He stopped. He ran his hands through his hair.

'Hilda, it was awful – horrible! The desolation! She was quite young still, she *needn't* have died. *He* killed her – my father! He was responsible for her dying. He broke her heart. I decided then that I'd not go on living under his roof. I broke away – got away from it all.'

Hilda nodded.

'You were very wise,' she said. 'It was the right thing to do.'

David said:

'Father wanted me to go into the works. That would have meant living at home. I couldn't have stood that. I can't think how Alfred stands it – how he has stood it all these years.'

'Did he never rebel against it?' asked Hilda with some interest. 'I thought you told me something about his having given up some other career.'

David nodded.

'Alfred was going into the army. Father arranged it all. Alfred, the eldest, was to go into some cavalry regiment, Harry was to go into the works, so was I. George was to enter politics.'

'And it didn't work out like that?'

David shook his head.

'Harry broke all that up! He was always frightfully wild. Got into debt – and all sorts of other troubles. Finally he went off one day with several hundred pounds that didn't belong to him, leaving a note behind him saying an office stool didn't suit him and he was going to see the world.'

'And you never heard any more of him?'

'Oh, yes, we did!' David laughed. 'We heard quite often! He was always cabling for money from all over the world. He usually got it too!'

'And Alfred?'

'Father made him chuck up the army and come back and go into the works.'

'Did he mind?'

'Very much to begin with. He hated it. But Father could always twist Alfred round his little finger. He's absolutely under Father's thumb still, I believe.'

'And you – escaped!' said Hilda.

'Yes. I went to London and studied painting. Father told me plainly that if I went off on a fool's errand like that I'd get a small allowance from him during his lifetime and nothing when he died. I said I didn't care. He called me a young fool, and that was that! I've never seen him since.'

Hilda said gently:

'And you haven't regretted it?'

'No, indeed. I realize I shan't ever get anywhere with my art. I shall never be a great artist – but we're happy enough in this cottage – we've got everything we want – all the essentials. And if I die, well, my life's insured for you.'

He paused and then said:

'And now – *this*!'

He struck the letter with his open hand.

'I am sorry your father ever wrote that letter, if it upsets you so much,' said Hilda.

David went on as though he had not heard her.

'Asking me to bring my wife for Christmas, expressing a hope that we may be all together for Christmas; a united family! What can it mean?'

Hilda said:

'Need it mean anything more than it says?'

He looked at her questioningly.

'I mean,' she said, smiling, 'that your father is growing old. He's beginning to feel sentimental about family ties. That does happen, you know.'

'I suppose it does,' said David slowly.

'He's an old man and he's lonely.'

He gave her a quick look.

'You want me to go, don't you, Hilda?'

She said slowly:

'It seems a pity – not to answer an appeal. I'm old-fashioned, I dare say, but why not have peace and goodwill at Christmas time?'

'After all I've told you?'

'I know, dear, I know. But all that's in the *past*. It's all done and finished with.'

'Not for me.'

'No, *because you won't let it die*. You keep the past alive in your own mind.'

'I can't forget.'

'You *won't* forget – that's what you mean, David.'

His mouth set in a firm line.

'We're like that, we Lees. We remember things for years – brood about them, keep memory green.'

Hilda said with a touch of impatience:

'Is that anything to be proud of? I do not think so!'

He looked thoughtfully at her, a touch of reserve in his manner.

He said: 'You don't attach much value to loyalty, then – loyalty to a memory?'

Hilda said:

'I believe the *present* matters – not the past! The past must go. If we seek to keep the past alive, we end, I think, by *distorting* it. We see it in exaggerated terms – a false perspective.'

'I can remember every word and every incident of those days perfectly,' said David passionately.

'Yes, but you *shouldn't*, my dear! It isn't natural to do so! You're applying the judgment of a boy to those days instead of looking back on them with the more temperate outlook of a man.'

'What difference would that make?' demanded David.

Hilda hesitated. She was aware of unwisdom in going on, and yet there were things she badly wanted to say.

'I think,' she said, 'that you're seeing your father as a *bogy*! Probably, if you were to see him now, you would realize that he was only a very ordinary man; a man, perhaps, whose passions ran away with him, a man whose life was far from blameless, but nevertheless merely a *man* – not a kind of inhuman monster!'

'You don't understand! His treatment of my mother –'

Hilda said gravely:

'There is a certain kind of meekness – of submission – brings out the worst in a man – whereas that same man, faced by spirit and determination, might be a different creature!'

'So you say it was her fault –'

Hilda interrupted him.

'No, of course I don't! I've no doubt your father treated your mother very badly indeed, but marriage is an extraordinary thing – and I doubt if any outsider – even a child of the marriage – has the right to judge. Besides, all this resentment on your part now cannot help your mother. It is all *gone* – it is behind you! What is left now is an old man, in feeble health, asking his son to come home for Christmas.'

'And you want me to go?'

Hilda hesitated, then she suddenly made up her mind. 'Yes,' she said. 'I do. I want you to go and lay the bogy once and for all.'

V

George Lee, M.P. for Westeringham, was a somewhat corpulent gentleman of forty-one. His eyes were pale blue and slightly prominent with a suspicious expression, he had a heavy jowl, and a slow pedantic utterance.

He said now in a weighty manner:

'I have told you, Magdalene, that I think it my *duty* to go.'

His wife shrugged her shoulders impatiently.

She was a slender creature, a platinum blonde with plucked eyebrows and a smooth egg-like face. It could, on occasions, look quite blank and devoid of any expression whatever. She was looking like that now.

'Darling,' she said, 'it will be perfectly grim, I am sure of it.'

'Moreover,' said George Lee, and his face lit up as an attractive idea occurred to him, 'it will enable us to save considerably. Christmas is always an expensive time. We can put the servants on board wages.'

'Oh, well!' said Magdalene. 'After all, Christmas is pretty grim anywhere!'

'I suppose,' said George, pursuing his own line of thought, 'they will expect to have a Christmas dinner? A nice piece of beef, perhaps, instead of a turkey.'

'Who?' The servants? Oh, George, don't fuss so. You're always worrying about money.'

'Somebody has to worry,' said George.

'Yes, but it's absurd to pinch and scrape in all these little ways. Why don't you make your father give you some more money?'

'He already gives me a very handsome allowance.'

'It's awful to be completely dependent on your father, as you are! He ought to settle some money on you outright.'

'That's not his way of doing things.'

Magdalene looked at him. Her hazel eyes were suddenly sharp

and keen. The expressionless egg-like face showed sudden meaning.

'He's frightfully rich, isn't he, George? A kind of millionaire, isn't he?'

'A millionaire twice over, I believe.'

Magdalene gave an envious sigh.

'How did he make it all? South Africa, wasn't it?'

'Yes, he made a big fortune there in his early days. Mainly diamonds.'

'Thrilling!' said Magdalene.

'Then he came to England and started in business and his fortune has actually doubled or trebled itself, I believe.'

'What will happen when he dies?' asked Magdalene.

'Father's never said much on the subject. Of course one can't exactly *ask*. I should imagine that the bulk of his money will go to Alfred and myself. Alfred, of course, will get the larger share.'

'You've got other brothers, haven't you?'

'Yes, there's my brother David. I don't fancy *he* will get much. He went off to do art or some tomfoolery of that kind. I believe Father warned him that he would cut him out of his will and David said he didn't care.'

'How silly!' said Magdalene with scorn.

'There was my sister Jennifer too. She went off with a foreigner – a Spanish artist – one of David's friends. But she died just over a year ago. She left a daughter, I believe. Father might leave a little money to her, but nothing much. And of course there's Harry –'

He stopped, slightly embarrassed.

'Harry?' said Magdalene, surprised. 'Who is Harry?'

'Ah – er – my brother.'

'I never knew you had another brother.'

'My dear, he wasn't a great – er – credit – to us. We don't mention him. His behaviour was disgraceful. We haven't heard anything of him for some years now. He's probably dead.'

Magdalene laughed suddenly.

'What is it? What are you laughing at?'

Magdalene said:

'I was only thinking how funny it was that you – *you*, George, should have a disreputable brother! You're so very respectable.'

'I should hope so,' said George coldly.

Her eyes narrowed.

'Your father isn't – very respectable, George.'

'Really, Magdalene!'

'Sometimes the things he says make me feel quite uncomfortable.'

George said:

'Really, Magdalene, you surprise me. Does – er – does Lydia feel the same?'

'He doesn't say the same kind of things to Lydia,' said Magdalene. She added angrily, '*No*, he never says them to *her*. I can't think why not.'

George glanced at her quickly and then glanced away.

'Oh, well,' he said vaguely. 'One must make allowances. At Father's age – and with his health being so bad –'

He paused. His wife asked:

'Is he really – pretty ill?'

'Oh, I wouldn't say *that*. He's remarkably tough. All the same, since he wants to have his family round him at Christmas, I think we are quite right to go. It may be his last Christmas.'

She said sharply:

'You *say* that, George, but really, I suppose, he may live for years?'

Slightly taken aback, her husband stammered:

'Yes – yes, of course he may.'

Magdalene turned away.

'Oh, well,' she said, 'I suppose we're doing the right thing by going.'

'I have no doubt about it.'

'But I hate it! Alfred's so dull, and Lydia snubs me.'

'Nonsense.'

'She does. And I hate that beastly manservant.'

'Old Tressilian?'

'No, Horbury. Sneaking round like a cat and smirking.'

'Really, Magdalene, I can't see that Horbury can affect you in any way!'

'He just gets on my nerves, that's all. But don't let's bother. We've got to go, I can see that. Won't do to offend the old man.'

'No – no, that's just the point. About the servants' Christmas dinner –'

'Not now, George, some other time. I'll just ring up Lydia and tell her that we'll come by the five-twenty tomorrow.'

Magdalene left the room precipitately. After telephoning she went up to her own room and sat down in front of the desk. She let down the flap and rummaged in its various pigeon-holes. Cascades of bills came tumbling out. Magdalene sorted through them, trying to arrange them in some kind of order. Finally, with an impatient sigh, she bundled them up and thrust them back whence they had come. She passed a hand over her smooth platinum head.

'What on earth am I to do?' she murmured.

VI

On the first floor of Gorston Hall a long passage led to a big room overlooking the front drive. It was a room furnished in the more flamboyant of old-fashioned styles. It had heavy brocaded wallpaper, rich leather armchairs, large vases embossed with dragons, sculptures in bronze . . . Everything in it was magnificent, costly and solid.

In a big grandfather armchair, the biggest and most imposing of all the chairs, sat the thin, shrivelled figure of an old man. His long clawlike hands rested on the arms of the chair. A gold-mounted stick was by his side. He wore an old shabby blue dressing-gown. On his feet were carpet slippers. His hair was white and the skin of his face was yellow.

A shabby, insignificant figure, one might have thought. But the nose, aquiline and proud, and the eyes, dark and intensely alive, might cause an observer to alter his opinion. Here was fire and life and vigour.

Old Simeon Lee cackled to himself, a sudden, high cackle of amusement.

He said:

'You gave my message to Mrs Alfred, hey?'

Horbury was standing beside his chair. He replied in his soft deferential voice:

'Yes, sir.'

'Exactly in the words I told you? Exactly, mind?'

'Yes, sir. I didn't make a mistake, sir.'

'No – you don't make mistakes. You'd better not make mistakes either – or you'll regret it! And what did she say, Horbury? What did Mr Alfred say?'

Quietly, unemotionally, Horbury repeated what had passed. The old man cackled again and rubbed his hands together.

'Splendid . . . First rate . . . They'll have been thinking and wondering – all the afternoon! Splendid! I'll have 'em up now. Go and get them.'

'Yes, sir.'

Horbury walked noiselessly across the room and went out.

'And, Horbury –'

The old man looked round, then cursed to himself.

'Fellow moves like a cat. Never know where he is.'

He sat quite still in his chair, his fingers caressing his chin till there was a tap on the door, and Alfred and Lydia came in.

'Ah, there you are, there you are. Sit here, Lydia, my dear, by me. What a nice colour you've got.'

'I've been out in the cold. It makes one's cheeks burn afterwards.'

Alfred said:

'How are you, Father, did you have a good rest this afternoon?'

'First rate – first rate. Dreamt about the old days! That was before I settled down and became a pillar of society.'

He cackled with sudden laughter.

His daughter-in-law sat silently smiling with polite attention.

Alfred said:

'What's this, Father, about two extra being expected for Christmas?'

'Ah, that! Yes, I must tell you about that. It's going to be a grand Christmas for me this year – a grand Christmas. Let me see, George is coming and Magdalene –'

Lydia said:

'Yes, they are arriving tomorrow by the five-twenty.'

Old Simeon said:

'Poor stick, George! Nothing but a gasbag! Still, he *is* my son.'

Alfred said:

'His constituents like him.'

Simeon cackled again.

'They probably think he's honest. Honest! There never was a Lee who was honest yet.'

'Oh, come now, Father.'

'I except you, my boy. I except you.'

'And David?' asked Lydia.

'David now. I'm curious to see the boy after all these years. He was a namby-pamby youngster. Wonder what his wife is like? At any rate *he* hasn't married a girl twenty years younger than himself, like that fool George!'

'Hilda wrote a very nice letter,' said Lydia. 'I've just had a wire from her confirming it and saying they are definitely arriving tomorrow.'

Her father-in-law looked at her, a keen, penetrating glance.

He laughed.

'I never get any change out of Lydia,' he said. 'I'll say this for you, Lydia, you're a well-bred woman. Breeding tells. I know that well enough. A funny thing, though, heredity. There's only one of you that's taken after me – only one out of all the litter.'

His eyes danced.

'Now guess who's coming for Christmas. I'll give you three guesses and I'll bet you a fiver you won't get the answer.'

He looked from one face to the other. Alfred said frowning:

'Horbury said you expected a young lady.'

'That intrigued you – yes, I dare say it did. Pilar will be arriving any minute now. I gave orders for the car to go and meet her.'

Alfred said sharply:

'*Pilar?*'

Simeon said:

'Pilar Estravados. Jennifer's girl. My granddaughter. I wonder what she'll be like.'

Alfred cried out:

'Good heavens, Father, you never told me . . .'

The old man was grinning.

'No, I thought I'd keep it a secret! Got Charlton to write out and fix things.'

Alfred repeated, his tone hurt and reproachful:

'You never told me . . .'

His father said, still grinning wickedly:

'It would have spoilt the surprise! Wonder what it will be like to have young blood under this roof again? I never saw Estravados. Wonder which the girl takes after – her mother or her father?'

'Do you really think it's wise, Father,' began Alfred. 'Taking everything into consideration –'

The old man interrupted him.

'Safety – safety – you play for safety too much, Alfred! Always have! That hasn't been my way! Do what you want and be damned to it! That's what I say! The girl's my granddaughter – the only grandchild in the family! I don't care what her father was or what he did! She's my flesh and blood! And she's coming to live here in my house.'

Lydia said sharply: 'She's coming to *live* here?'

He darted a quick look at her. 'Do you object?'

She shook her head. She said smiling:

'I couldn't very well object to your asking someone to your own house, could I? No, I was wondering about – her.'

'About her – what d'you mean?'

'Whether she would be happy here.'

Old Simeon flung up his head.

'She's not got a penny in the world. She ought to be thankful!'

Lydia shrugged her shoulders.

Simeon turned to Alfred:

'You see? It's going to be a grand Christmas! All my children round me. *All* my children! There, Alfred, there's your clue. Now guess who the other visitor is.'

Alfred stared at him.

'All my children! Guess, boy! *Harry*, of course! Your brother Harry!'

Alfred had gone very pale. He stammered:

'Harry – not Harry –'

'Harry himself!'

'But we thought he was dead!'

'Not he!'

'You – you are having him back here? After everything?'

'The prodigal son, eh? You're right. The fatted calf! We must kill the fatted calf, Alfred. We must give him a grand welcome.'

Alfred said:

'He treated you – all of us – disgracefully. He –'

'No need to recite his crimes! It's a long list. But Christmas, you'll remember, is the season of forgiveness! We'll welcome the prodigal home.'

Alfred rose. He murmured:

'This has been – rather a shock. I never dreamt that Harry would ever come inside these walls again.'

Simeon leaned forward.

'You never liked Harry, did you?' he said softly.

'After the way he behaved to you –'

Simeon cackled. He said:

'Ah, but bygones must be bygones. That's the spirit for Christmas, isn't it, Lydia?'

Lydia, too, had gone pale. She said dryly:

'I see that you have thought a good deal about Christmas this year.'

'I want my family round me. Peace and goodwill. I'm an old man. Are you going, my dear?'

Alfred had hurried out. Lydia paused a moment before following him.

Simeon nodded his head after the retreating figure.

'It's upset him. He and Harry never got on. Harry used to jeer at Alfred. Called him old Slow and Sure.'

Lydia's lips parted. She was about to speak, then, as she saw the old man's eager expression, she checked herself. Her self-control, she saw, disappointed him. The perception of that fact enabled her to say:

'The hare and the tortoise. Ah, well, the tortoise wins the race.'

'Not always,' said Simeon. 'Not always, my dear Lydia.'

She said, still smiling:

'Excuse me, I must go after Alfred. Sudden excitements always upset him.'

Simeon cackled.

'Yes, Alfred doesn't like changes. He always was a regular sobersides.'

Lydia said:

'Alfred is very devoted to *you*.'

'That seems odd to you, doesn't it?'

'Sometimes,' said Lydia, 'it does.'

She left the room. Simeon looked after her.

He chuckled softly and rubbed his palms together. 'Lots of fun,' he said. 'Lots of fun still. I'm going to enjoy this Christmas.'

With an effort he pulled himself upright, and with the help of his stick, shuffled across the room.

He went to a big safe that stood at the corner of the room. He twirled the handle of the combination. The door came open and, with shaking fingers, he felt inside.

He lifted out a small wash-leather bag, and opening it, let a stream of uncut diamonds pass through his fingers.

'Well, my beauties, well . . . Still the same – still my old friends. Those were good days – good days . . . They shan't carve you and cut you about, my friends. *You* shan't hang round the necks of women or sit on their fingers or hang on their ears. You're *mine*! My old friends! We know a thing or two, you and I. I'm old, they say, and ill, but I'm not done for! Lots of life in the old dog yet. And there's still some fun to be got out of life. Still some fun –'

PART 2

DECEMBER 23RD

I

Tressilian went to answer the doorbell. It had been an unusually aggressive peal, and now, before he could make his slow way across the hall, it pealed out again.

Tressilian flushed. An ill-mannered, impatient way of ringing the bell at a gentleman's house! If it was a fresh lot of those carol singers he'd give them a piece of his mind.

Through the frosted glass of the upper half of the door he saw a silhouette – a big man in a slouch hat. He opened the door. As he had thought – a cheap, flashy stranger – nasty pattern of suit he was wearing – loud! Some impudent begging fellow!

'Blessed if it isn't Tressilian,' said the stranger. 'How are you, Tressilian?'

Tressilian stared – took a deep breath – stared again. That bold arrogant jaw, the high-bridged nose, the rollicking eye. Yes, they had all been there three years ago. More subdued then . . .

He said with a gasp:

'Mr Harry!'

Harry Lee laughed.

'Looks as though I'd given you quite a shock. Why? I'm expected, aren't I?'

'Yes, indeed, sir. Certainly, sir.'

'Then why the surprise act?' Harry stepped back a foot or two and looked up at the house – a good solid mass of red brick, unimaginative but solid.

'Just the same ugly old mansion,' he remarked. 'Still standing, though, that's the main thing. How's my father, Tressilian?'

'He's somewhat of an invalid, sir. Keeps his room, and can't get about much. But he's wonderfully well, considering.'

'The old sinner!'

Harry Lee came inside, let Tressilian remove his scarf and take the somewhat theatrical hat.

'How's my dear brother Alfred, Tressilian?'

'He's very well, sir.'

Harry grinned.

'Looking forward to seeing me? Eh?'

'I expect so, sir.'

'I don't! Quite the contrary. I bet it's given him a nasty jolt, my turning up! Alfred and I never did get on. Ever read your Bible, Tressilian?'

'Why, yes, sir, sometimes, sir.'

'Remember the tale of the prodigal's return? The good brother didn't like it, remember? Didn't like it at all! Good old stay-at-home Alfred doesn't like it either, I bet.'

Tressilian remained silent looking down his nose. His stiffened back expressed protest. Harry clapped him on the shoulder.

'Lead on, old son,' he said. 'The fatted calf awaits me! Lead me right to it.'

Tressilian murmured:

'If you will come this way into the drawing-room, sir. I am not quite sure where everyone is . . . They were unable to send to meet you, sir, not knowing the time of your arrival.'

Harry nodded. He followed Tressilian along the hall, turning his head to look about him as he went.

'All the old exhibits in their place, I see,' he remarked. 'I don't believe anything has changed since I went away twenty years ago.'

He followed Tressilian into the drawing-room. The old man murmured:

'I will see if I can find Mr or Mrs Alfred,' and hurried out.

Harry Lee had marched into the room and had then stopped, staring at the figure who was seated on one of the window-sills. His eyes roamed incredulously over the black hair and the creamy exotic pallor.

'Good Lord!' he said. 'Are you my father's seventh and most beautiful wife?'

Pilar slipped down and came towards him.

'I am Pilar Estravados,' she announced. 'And you must be my Uncle Harry, my mother's brother.'

Harry said, staring:

'So that's who you are! Jenny's daughter.'

Pilar said: 'Why did you ask me if I was your father's seventh wife? Has he really had six wives?'

Harry laughed.

'No, I believe he's only had one official one. Well – Pil – what's your name?'

'Pilar, yes.'

'Well, Pilar, it really gives me quite a turn to see something like you blooming in this mausoleum.'

'This – maus – please?'

'This museum of stuffed dummies! I always thought this house was lousy! Now I see it again I think it's lousier than ever!'

Pilar said in a shocked voice:

'Oh, no, it is very handsome here! The furniture is good and the carpets – thick carpets everywhere – and there are lots of ornaments. Everything is very good quality and very, very rich!'

'You're right there,' said Harry, grinning. He looked at her with amusement. 'You know, I can't help getting a kick out of seeing you in the midst –'

He broke off as Lydia came rapidly into the room.

She came straight to him.

'How d'you do, Harry? I'm Lydia – Alfred's wife.'

'How de do, Lydia.' He shook hands, examining her intelligent mobile face in a swift glance and approving mentally of the way she walked – very few women moved well.

Lydia in her turn took quick stock of him.

She thought: 'He looks a frightful tough – attractive though. I wouldn't trust him an inch . . .'

She said smiling:

'How does it look after all these years? Quite different, or very much the same?'

'Pretty much the same.' He looked round him. 'This room's been done over.'

'Oh, many times.'

He said:

'I meant by you. You've made it – different.'

'Yes, I expect so . . .'

He grinned at her, a sudden impish grin that reminded her with a start of the old man upstairs.

'It's got more class about it now! I remember hearing that old Alfred had married a girl whose people came over with the Conqueror.'

Lydia smiled. She said:

'I believe they did. But they've rather run to seed since those days.'

Harry said:

'How's old Alfred? Just the same blessed old stick-in-the-mud as ever?'

'I've no idea whether you will find him changed or not.'

'How are the others? Scattered all over England?'

'No – they're all here for Christmas, you know.'

Harry's eyes opened.

'Regular Christmas family reunion? What's the matter with the old man? He used not to give a damn for sentiment. Don't remember his caring much for his family, either. He must have changed!'

'Perhaps.' Lydia's voice was dry.

Pilar was staring, her big eyes wide and interested.

Harry said:

'How's old George? Still the same skinflint? How he used to howl if he had to part with a halfpenny of his pocket-money!'

Lydia said:

'George is in Parliament. He's member for Westeringham.'

'What? Popeye in Parliament? Lord, that's good.'

Harry threw back his head and laughed.

It was rich stentorian laughter – it sounded uncontrolled and brutal in the confined space of the room. Pilar drew in her breath with a gasp. Lydia flinched a little.

Then, at a movement behind him, Harry broke off his laugh and turned sharply. He had not heard anyone coming in, but Alfred was standing there quietly. He was looking at Harry with an odd expression on his face.

Harry stood a minute, then a slow smile crept to his lips. He advanced a step.

'Why,' he said, 'it's Alfred!'

Alfred nodded.

'Hallo, Harry,' he said.

They stood staring at each other. Lydia caught her breath. She thought:

'How absurd! Like two dogs – looking at each other . . .'

Pilar's gaze widened even further. She thought to herself:

'How silly they look standing there . . . Why do they not embrace? No, of course the English do not do that. But they might *say* something. Why do they just *look*?'

Harry said at last:

'Well, well. Feels funny to be here again!'

'I expect so – yes. A good many years since you – got out.'

Harry threw up his head. He drew his finger along the line of his jaw. It was a gesture that was habitual with him. It expressed belligerence.

'Yes,' he said. 'I'm glad I have come' – he paused to bring out the word with greater significance – '*home* . . .'

II

'I've been, I suppose, a very wicked man,' said Simeon Lee.

He was leaning back in his chair. His chin was raised and with one finger he was stroking his jaw reflectively. In front of him a big fire glowed and danced. Beside it sat Pilar, a little screen of papier-mâché held in her hand. With it she shielded her face from the blaze. Occasionally she fanned herself with it, using her wrist in a supple gesture. Simeon looked at her with satisfaction.

He went on talking, perhaps more to himself than to the girl, and stimulated by the fact of her presence.

'Yes,' he said. 'I've been a wicked man. What do you say to that, Pilar?'

Pilar shrugged her shoulders. She said:

'All men are wicked. The nuns say so. That is why one has to pray for them.'

'Ah, but I've been more wicked than most.' Simeon laughed. 'I don't regret it, you know. No, I don't regret anything. I've enjoyed myself . . . every minute! They say you repent when you get old. That's bunkum. I don't repent. And as I tell you, I've done most things . . . all the good old sins! I've cheated and stolen and lied . . . lord, yes! And women – always women! Someone told me the other day of an Arab chief who had a bodyguard of forty of his sons – all roughly the same age! Aha! Forty! I don't know about forty, but I bet I could produce a very fair bodyguard if I went about looking for the brats! Hey, Pilar, what do you think of that? Shocked?'

Pilar stared.

'No, why should I be shocked? Men always desire women. My father, too. That is why wives are so often unhappy and why they go to church and pray.'

Old Simeon was frowning.

'I made Adelaide unhappy,' he said. He spoke almost under his breath, to himself. 'Lord, what a woman! Pink and white and pretty as they make 'em when I married her! And afterwards? Always wailing and weeping. It rouses the devil in a man when his wife is always crying . . . She'd no guts, that's what was the matter with Adelaide. If she'd stood up to me! But she never did – not once. I believed when I married her that I was going to be able to settle down, raise a family – cut loose from the old life . . .'

His voice died away. He stared – stared into the glowing heart of the fire.

'Raise a family . . . God, what a family!' He gave a sudden shrill pipe of angry laughter. 'Look at 'em – look at 'em! Not a child among them – to carry on! What's the matter with them? Haven't they got any of my blood in their veins? Not a son among 'em, legitimate or illegitimate. Alfred, for instance – heavens above, how bored I get with Alfred! Looking at me with his dog's eyes. Ready to do anything I ask. Lord, what a fool! His wife, now – Lydia – I like Lydia. She's got spirit. She doesn't like me, though. No, she doesn't like me. But she has to put up with me for that nincompoop Alfred's sake.' He looked over at the girl by the fire. 'Pilar – remember – nothing is so boring as devotion.'

She smiled at him. He went on, warmed by the presence of her youth and strong femininity.

'George? What's George? A stick! A stuffed codfish! a pompous windbag with no brains and no guts – and mean about money as well! David? David always was a fool – a fool and a dreamer. His mother's boy, that was always David. Only sensible thing he ever did was to marry that solid comfortable-looking woman.' He brought down his hand with a bang on the edge of his chair. 'Harry's the best of 'em! Poor old Harry, the wrong 'un! But at any rate he's *alive*!'

Pilar agreed.

'Yes, he is nice. He laughs – laughs out loud – and throws his head back. Oh, yes, I like him very much.'

The old man looked at her.

'You do, do you, Pilar? Harry always had a way with the girls. Takes after me there.' He began to laugh, a slow wheezy chuckle. 'I've had a good life – a very good life. Plenty of everything.'

Pilar said:

'In Spain we have a proverb. It is like this:

'*Take what you like and pay for it, says God.*'

Simeon beat an appreciative hand on the arm of his chair.

'That's good. That's the stuff. Take what you like . . . I've done that – all my life – taken what I wanted . . .'

Pilar said, her voice high and clear, and suddenly arresting:

'And you have paid for it?'

Simeon stopped laughing to himself. He sat up and stared at her. He said, 'What's that you say?'

'I said, have you paid for it, Grandfather?'

Simeon Lee said slowly:

'I – don't know . . .'

Then, beating his fist on the arm of the chair, he cried out with sudden anger:

'What makes you say that, girl? What makes you say that?'

Pilar said:

'I – wondered.'

Her hand, holding the screen, was arrested. Her eyes were dark and mysterious. She sat, her head thrown back, conscious of herself, of her womanhood.

Simeon said:

'You devil's brat . . .'

She said softly:

'But you like me, Grandfather. You like me to sit here with you.'

Simeon said: 'Yes, I like it. It's a long time since I've seen anything so young and beautiful . . . It does me good, warms my old bones . . . And you're my own flesh and blood . . . Good for Jennifer, she turned out to be the best of the bunch after all!'

Pilar sat there smiling.

'Mind you, you don't fool me,' said Simeon. 'I know why you sit here so patiently and listen to me droning on. It's money – it's all money . . . Or do you pretend you love your old grandfather?'

Pilar said: 'No, I do not love you. But I like you. I like you very much. You must believe that, for it is true. I think you have been wicked, but I like that too. You are more real than the other people in this house. And you have interesting things to say. You have travelled and you have led a life of adventure. If I were a man I would be like that, too.'

Simeon nodded.

'Yes, I believe you would . . . We've gipsy blood in us, so it's always been said. It hasn't shown much in my children – except Harry – but I think it's come out in you. I can be patient, mind you, when it's necessary. I waited once fifteen years to get even with a man who'd done me an injury. That's another characteristic of the Lees – they don't forget! They'll avenge a wrong if they have to wait years to do it. A man swindled me. I waited fifteen years till I saw my chance – and then I struck. I ruined him. Cleaned him right out!'

He laughed softly.

Pilar said:

'That was in South Africa?'

'Yes. A grand country.'

'You have been back there, yes?'

'I went back last five years after I married. That was the last time.'

'But before that? You were there for many years?'

'Yes.'

'Tell me about it.'

He began to talk. Pilar, shielding her face, listened.

His voice slowed, wearied. He said:

'Wait, I'll show you something.'

He pulled himself carefully to his feet. Then, with his stick, he limped slowly across the room. He opened the big safe. Turning, he beckoned her to him.

'There, look at these. Feel them, let them run through your fingers.'

He looked into her wondering face and laughed.

'Do you know what they are? Diamonds, child, diamonds.'

Pilar's eyes opened. She said as she bent over:

'But they are little pebbles, that is all.'

Simeon laughed.

'They are uncut diamonds. That is how they are found – like this.'

Pilar asked incredulously:

'And if they were cut they would be real diamonds?'

'Certainly.'

'They would flash and sparkle?'

'Flash and sparkle.'

Pilar said childishly:

'O-o-o, I cannot believe it!'

He was amused.

'It's quite true.'

'They are valuable?'

'Fairly valuable. Difficult to say before they are cut. Anyway, this little lot is worth several thousands of pounds.'

Pilar said with a space between each word:

'Several – thousands – of – pounds?'

'Say nine or ten thousands – they're biggish stones, you see.'

Pilar asked, her eyes opening:

'But why do you not sell them, then?'

'Because I like to have them here.'

'But all that money?'

'I don't need the money.'

'Oh – I see,' Pilar looked impressed.

She said:

'But why do you not have them cut and made beautiful?'

'Because I prefer them like this.' His face was set in a grim line. He turned away and began speaking to himself. 'They take me back – the touch of them, the feel of them through my fingers . . . It all comes back to me, the sunshine, and the smell of the veldt, the oxen – old Eb – all the boys – the evenings . . .'

There was a soft tap on the door.

Simeon said: 'Put 'em back in the safe and bang it to.'

Then he called: 'Come in.'

Horbury came in, soft and deferential.

He said: 'Tea is ready downstairs.'

III

Hilda said: 'So there you are, David. I've been looking for you everywhere. Don't let's stay in this room, it's so frightfully cold.'

David did not answer for a minute. He was standing looking at a chair, a low chair with faded satin upholstery. He said abruptly:

'That's her chair . . . the chair she always sat in . . . just the same – it's just the same. Only faded, of course.'

A little frown creased Hilda's forehead. She said:

'I see. Do let's come out of here, David. It's frightfully cold.'

David took no notice. Looking round, he said:

'She sat in here mostly. I remember sitting on that stool there while she read to me. *Jack the Giant Killer* – that was it – *Jack the Giant Killer*. I must have been six years old then.'

Hilda put a firm hand through his arm.

'Come back to the drawing-room, dear. There's no heating in this room.'

He turned obediently, but she felt a little shiver go through him.

'Just the same,' he murmured. 'Just the same. As though time had stood still.'

Hilda looked worried. She said in a cheerful determined voice:

'I wonder where the others are? It must be nearly tea-time.'

David disengaged his arm and opened another door.

'There used to be a piano in here . . . Oh, yes, here it is! I wonder if it's in tune.'

He sat down and opened the lid, running his hands lightly over the keys.

'Yes, it's evidently kept tuned.'

He began to play. His touch was good, the melody flowed out from under his fingers.

Hilda asked: 'What is that? I seem to know it, and I can't quite remember.'

He said: 'I haven't played it for years. *She* used to play it. One of Mendelssohn's Songs Without Words.'

The sweet, over-sweet, melody filled the room. Hilda said:

'Play some Mozart, do.'

David shook his head. He began another Mendelssohn.

Then suddenly he brought his hands down upon the keys in a harsh discord. He got up. He was trembling all over. Hilda went to him.

She said: 'David – David.'

He said: 'It's nothing – it's nothing . . .'

IV

The bell pealed aggressively. Tressilian rose from his seat in the pantry and went slowly out and along to the door.

The bell pealed again. Tressilian frowned. Through the frosted glass of the door he saw the silhouette of a man wearing a slouch hat.

Tressilian passed a hand over his forehead. Something worried him. It was as though everything was happening twice.

Surely this had happened before. Surely –

He drew back the latch and opened the door.

Then the spell broke. The man standing there said:

'Is this where Mr Simeon Lee lives?'

'Yes, sir.'

'I'd like to see him, please.'

A faint echo of memory awoke in Tressilian. It was an intonation of voice that he remembered from the old days when Mr Lee was first in England.

Tressilian shook his head dubiously.

'Mr Lee is an invalid, sir. He doesn't see many people now. If you –'

The stranger interrupted.

He drew out an envelope and handed it to the butler.

'Please give this to Mr Lee.'

'Yes, sir.'

V

Simeon Lee took the envelope. He drew out the single sheet of paper it held. He looked surprised. His eyebrows rose, but he smiled.

'By all that's wonderful!' he said.

Then to the butler: 'Show Mr Farr up here, Tressilian.'

'Yes, sir.'

Simeon said: 'I was just thinking of old Ebenezer Farr. He

was my partner out there in Kimberley. Now here's his son come along!'

Tressilian reappeared. He announced: 'Mr Farr.'

Stephen Farr came in with a trace of nervousness. He disguised it by putting on a little extra swagger. He said – and just for the moment his South African accent was more marked than usual: 'Mr Lee?'

'I'm glad to see you. So you're Eb's boy?'

Stephen Farr grinned rather sheepishly.

He said: 'My first visit to the old country. Father always told me to look you up if I did come.'

'Quite right.' The old man looked round. 'This is my granddaughter, Pilar Estravados.'

'How do you do?' said Pilar demurely.

Stephen Farr thought with a touch of admiration:

'Cool little devil. She was surprised to see me, but it only showed for a flash.'

He said, rather heavily: 'I'm very pleased to make your acquaintance, Miss Estravados.'

'Thank you,' said Pilar.

Simeon Lee said: 'Sit down and tell me all about yourself. Are you in England for long?'

'Oh, I shan't hurry myself now I've really got here!'

He laughed, throwing his head back.

Simeon Lee said: 'Quite right. You must stay here with us for a while.'

'Oh, look here, sir. I can't butt in like that. It's only two days to Christmas.'

'You must spend Christmas with us – unless you've got other plans?'

'Well, no, I haven't, but I don't like –'

Simeon said: 'That's settled.' He turned his head. 'Pilar?'

'Yes, Grandfather.'

'Go and tell Lydia we shall have another guest. Ask her to come up here.'

Pilar left the room. Stephen's eyes followed her. Simeon noted the fact with amusement.

He said: 'You've come straight here from South Africa?'

'Pretty well.'

They began to talk of that country.

Lydia entered a few minutes later.

Simeon said: 'This is Stephen Farr, son of my old friend and partner, Ebenezer Farr. He's going to be with us for Christmas if you can find room for him.'

Lydia smiled.

'Of course.' Her eyes took in the stranger's appearance. His bronzed face and blue eyes and the easy backward tilt of his head.

'My daughter-in-law,' said Simeon.

Stephen said: 'I feel rather embarrassed – butting in on a family party like this.'

'You're one of the family, my boy,' said Simeon. 'Think of yourself as that.'

'You're too kind, sir.'

Pilar re-entered the room. She sat down quietly by the fire and picked up the hand screen. She used it as a fan, slowly tilting her wrist to and fro. Her eyes were demure and downcast.

PART 3

DECEMBER 24TH

I

'Do you really want me to stay on here, Father?' asked Harry. He tilted his head back. 'I'm stirring up rather a hornet's nest, you know.'

'What do you mean?' asked Simeon sharply.

'Brother Alfred,' said Harry. 'Good brother Alfred! He, if I may say so, resents my presence here.'

'The devil he does!' snapped Simeon. 'I'm master in this house.'

'All the same, sir, I expect you're pretty dependent on Alfred. I don't want to upset –'

'You'll do as I tell you,' snapped his father.

Harry yawned.

'Don't know that I shall be able to stick a stay-at-home life. Pretty stifling to a fellow who's knocked about the world.'

His father said: 'You'd better marry and settle down.'

Harry said: 'Who shall I marry? Pity one can't marry one's niece. Young Pilar is devilish attractive.'

'You've noticed that?'

'Talking of settling down, fat George has done well for himself as far as looks go. Who was she?'

Simeon shrugged his shoulders.

'How should I know? George picked her up at a mannequin parade, I believe. She says her father was a retired naval officer.'

Harry said:

'Probably a second mate of a coasting steamer. George will have a bit of trouble with her if he's not careful.'

'George,' said Simeon Lee, 'is a fool.'

Harry said: 'What did she marry him for – his money?'

Simeon shrugged his shoulders.

Harry said: 'Well, you think that you can square Alfred all right?'

'We'll soon settle that,' said Simeon grimly.

He touched a bell that stood on a table near him.

Horbury appeared promptly. Simeon said:

'Ask Mr Alfred to come here.'

Horbury went out and Harry drawled:

'That fellow listens at doors!'

Simeon shrugged his shoulders.

'Probably.'

Alfred hurried in. His face twitched when he saw his brother. Ignoring Harry, he said pointedly:

'You wanted me, Father?'

'Yes, sit down. I was just thinking we must reorganize things a bit now that we have two more people living in the house.'

'*Two?*'

'Pilar will make her home here, naturally. And Harry is home for good.'

Alfred said: 'Harry is coming to live here?'

'Why not, old boy?' said Harry.

Alfred turned sharply to him.

'I should think that you yourself would see that!'

'Well, sorry – but I don't.'

'After everything that has happened? The disgraceful way you behaved. The scandal –'

Harry waved an easy hand.

'All that's in the past, old boy.'

'You behaved abominably to Father, after all he's done for you.'

'Look here, Alfred, it strikes me that's Father's business, not yours. If he's willing to forgive and forget –'

'I'm willing,' said Simeon. 'Harry's my son, after all, you know, Alfred.'

'Yes, but – I resent it – for Father's sake.'

Simeon said: 'Harry's coming here! I wish it.' He laid a hand gently on the latter's shoulder. 'I'm very fond of Harry.'

Alfred got up and left the room. His face was white. Harry rose too and went after him, laughing.

Simeon sat chuckling to himself. Then he started and looked

round. 'Who the devil's that? Oh, it's you, Horbury. Don't creep about that way.'

'I beg your pardon, sir.'

'Never mind. Listen, I've got some orders for you. I want everybody to come up here after lunch – *everybody*.'

'Yes, sir.'

'There's something else. When they come, you come with them. And when you get half-way along the passage *raise your voice so that I can hear*. Any pretext will do. Understand?'

'Yes, sir.'

Horbury went downstairs. He said to Tressilian:

'If you ask me, we *are* going to have a Merry Christmas.'

Tressilian said sharply: 'What d'you mean?'

'You wait and see, Mr Tressilian. It's Christmas Eve today, and a nice Christmas spirit abroad – I don't think!'

II

They came into the room and paused at the doorway.

Simeon was speaking into the telephone. He waved a hand to them.

'Sit down, all of you. I shan't be a minute.'

He went on speaking into the telephone.

'Is that Charlton, Hodgkins & Bruce? Is that you, Charlton? Simeon Lee speaking. Yes, isn't it? . . . Yes . . . No, I wanted you to make a new will for me . . . Yes, it's some time since I made the other . . . Circumstances have altered . . . Oh no, no hurry. Don't want you to spoil your Christmas. Say Boxing Day or the day after. Come along, and I'll tell you what I want done. No, that's quite all right. I shan't be dying just yet.'

He replaced the receiver, then looked round at the eight members of his family. He cackled and said:

'You're all looking very glum. What is the matter?'

Alfred said: 'You sent for us . . .'

Simeon said quickly: 'Oh, sorry – nothing portentous about it. Did you think it was a family council? No, I'm just rather tired today, that's all. None of you need come up after dinner. I shall go to bed. I want to be fresh for Christmas Day.'

He grinned at them. George said earnestly:

'Of course . . . of course . . .'

Simeon said: 'Grand old institution, Christmas. Promotes solidarity of family feeling. What do *you* think, Magdalene, my dear?'

Magdalene Lee jumped. Her rather silly little mouth flew open and then shut itself. She said: 'Oh – oh, *yes*!'

Simeon said: 'Let me see, you lived with a retired naval officer' – he paused – 'your *father*. Don't suppose you made much of Christmas. It needs a big family for that!'

'Well – well – yes, perhaps it does.'

Simeon's eyes slid past her.

'Don't want to talk of anything unpleasant at this time of year, but you know, George, I'm afraid I'll have to cut down your allowance a bit. My establishment here is going to cost me a bit more to run in future.'

George got very red.

'But look here, Father, you can't do that!'

Simeon said softly: 'Oh, can't I!'

'My expenses are very heavy already. Very heavy. As it is, I don't know how I make both ends meet. It needs the most rigorous economy.'

'Let your wife do a bit more of it,' said Simeon. 'Women are good at that sort of thing. They often think of economies where a man would never have dreamt of them. And a clever woman can make her own clothes. My wife, I remember, was clever with her needle. About all she *was* clever with – a good woman, but deadly dull –'

David sprang up. His father said:

'Sit down, boy, you'll knock something over –'

David said: 'My mother –'

Simeon said: 'Your mother had the brains of a louse! And it seems to me she's transmitted those brains to her children.' He raised himself up suddenly. A red spot appeared on each cheek. His voice came high and shrill. 'You're not worth a penny piece, any of you! I'm sick of you all! You're not *men*! You're weaklings – a set of namby-pamby weaklings. Pilar's worth any two of you put together! I'll swear to heaven I've got a better son somewhere in the world than any of you, even if you are born the right side of the blanket!'

'Here, Father, hold hard,' cried Harry.

He had jumped up and stood there, a frown on his usually good-humoured face. Simeon snapped:

'The same goes for *you*! What have *you* ever done? Whined to me for money from all over the world! I tell you I'm sick of the sight of you all! Get out!'

He leaned back in his chair, panting a little.

Slowly, one by one, his family went out. George was red and indignant. Magdalene looked frightened. David was pale and quivering. Harry blustered out of the room. Alfred went like a man in a dream. Lydia followed him with her head held high. Only Hilda paused in the doorway and came slowly back.

She stood over him, and he started when he opened his eyes and found her standing there. There was something menacing in the solid way she stood there quite immovably.

He said irritably: 'What is it?'

Hilda said: 'When your letter came I believed what you said – that you wanted your family round you for Christmas, I persuaded David to come.'

Simeon said: 'Well, what of it?'

Hilda said slowly: 'You *did* want your family round you – but not for the purpose you said! You wanted them there, didn't you, in order to set them all by the ears? God help you, it's your idea of *fun*!'

Simeon chuckled. He said: 'I always had rather a specialized sense of humour. I don't expect anyone else to appreciate the joke. *I'm* enjoying it!'

She said nothing. A vague feeling of apprehension came over Simeon Lee. He said sharply:

'What are you thinking about?'

Hilda Lee said slowly: 'I'm afraid . . .'

Simeon said: 'You're afraid – of me?'

Hilda said: 'Not *of* you. I'm afraid – *for* you!'

Like a judge who has delivered sentence, she turned away. She marched, slowly and heavily, out of the room . . .

Simeon sat staring at the door.

Then he got to his feet and made his way over to the safe. He murmured: 'Let's have a look at my beauties.'

III

The doorbell rang about a quarter to eight.

Tressilian went to answer it. He returned to his pantry to find Horbury there, picking up the coffee-cups off the tray and looking at the mark on them.

'Who was it?' said Horbury.

'Superintendent of Police – Mr Sugden – mind what you're doing!'

Horbury had dropped one of the cups with a crash.

'Look at that now,' lamented Tressilian. 'Eleven years I've had the washing up of those and never one broken, and now you come along touching things you've no business to touch, and look what happens!'

'I'm sorry, Mr Tressilian. I am indeed,' the other apologized. His face was covered with perspiration. 'I don't know how it happened. Did you say a Superintendent of Police had called?'

'Yes – Mr Sugden.'

The valet passed a tongue over pale lips.

'What – what did he want?'

'Collecting for the Police Orphanage.'

'Oh!' The valet straightened his shoulders. In a more natural voice he said:

'Did he get anything?'

'I took up the book to old Mr Lee, and he told me to fetch the superintendent up and to put the sherry on the table.'

'Nothing but begging, this time of year,' said Horbury. 'The old devil's generous, I will say that for him, in spite of his other failings.'

Tressilian said with dignity:

'Mr Lee has always been an open-handed gentleman.'

Horbury nodded.

'It's the best thing about him! Well, I'll be off now.'

'Going to the pictures?'

'I expect so. Ta-ta, Mr Tressilian.'

He went through the door that led to the servants' hall.

Tressilian looked up at the clock hanging on the wall.

He went into the dining-room and laid the rolls in the napkins.

Then, after assuring himself that everything was as it should be, he sounded the gong in the hall.

As the last note died away the police superintendent came down the stairs. Superintendent Sugden was a large handsome man. He wore a tightly buttoned blue suit and moved with a sense of his own importance.

He said affably: 'I rather think we shall have a frost tonight. Good thing: the weather's been very unseasonable lately.'

Tressilian said, shaking his head:

'The damp affects my rheumatism.'

The superintendent said that the rheumatism was a painful complaint, and Tressilian let him out by the front door.

The old butler refastened the door and came back slowly into the hall. He passed his hand over his eyes and sighed. Then he straightened his back as he saw Lydia pass into the drawing-room. George Lee was just coming down the stairs.

Tressilian hovered ready. When the last guest, Magdalene, had entered the drawing-room, he made his own appearance, murmuring:

'Dinner is served.'

In his way Tressilian was a connoisseur of ladies' dress. He always noted and criticized the gowns of the ladies as he circled round the table, decanter in hand.

Mrs Alfred, he noted, had got on her new flowered black and white taffeta. A bold design, very striking, but she could carry it off, though many ladies couldn't. The dress Mrs George had on was a model, he was pretty sure of that. Must have cost a pretty penny. He wondered how Mr George would like paying for it! Mr George didn't like spending money – he never had. Mrs David now: a nice lady, but didn't have any idea of how to dress. For her figure, plain black velvet would have been the best. Figured velvet, and crimson at that, was a bad choice. Miss Pilar, now, it didn't matter what she wore, with her figure and her hair she looked well in anything. A flimsy cheap little white gown it was, though. Still, Mr Lee would soon see to that! Taken to her wonderful, he had. Always was the same way when a gentleman was elderly. A young face could do anything with him!

'Hock or claret?' murmured Tressilian in a deferential whisper in Mrs George's ear. Out of the tail of his eye he noted that Walter, the footman, was handing the vegetables before the gravy again – after all he had been told!

Tressilian went round with the soufflé. It struck him, now that his interest in the ladies' toilettes and his misgivings over Walter's deficiencies were a thing of the past, that everyone was very silent tonight. At least, not exactly *silent*: Mr Harry was talking enough for twenty – no, not Mr Harry, the South African gentleman. And the others were talking too, but only, as it were, in spasms. There was something a little – queer about them.

Mr Alfred, for instance, he looked downright ill. As though he had had a shock or something. Quite dazed he looked and just turning over the food on his plate without eating it. The mistress, she was worried about him. Tressilian could see that. Kept looking down the table towards him – not noticeably, of course, just quietly. Mr George was very red in the face – gobbling his food, he was, without tasting it. He'd get a stroke one day if he wasn't careful. Mrs George wasn't eating. Slimming, as likely as not. Miss Pilar seemed to be enjoying her food all right and talking and laughing up at the South African gentleman. Properly taken with her, he was. Didn't seem to be anything on *their* minds!

Mr David? Tressilian felt worried about Mr David. Just like his mother, he was, to look at. And remarkably young-looking still. But nervy; there, he'd knocked over his glass.

Tressilian whisked it away, mopped up the stream deftly. It was all over. Mr David hardly seemed to notice what he had done, just sat staring in front of him with a white face.

Thinking of white faces, funny the way Horbury had looked in the pantry just now when he'd heard a police officer had come to the house . . . almost as though –

Tressilian's mind stopped with a jerk. Walter had dropped a pear off the dish he was handing. Footmen were no good nowadays! They might be stable-boys, the way they went on!

He went round with the port. Mr Harry seemed a bit distrait tonight. Kept looking at Mr Alfred. Never had been any love lost between those two, not even as boys. Mr Harry, of course, had always been his father's favourite, and that had rankled with Mr Alfred. Mr Lee had never cared for Mr Alfred much. A pity, when Mr Alfred always seemed so devoted to his father.

There, Mrs Alfred was getting up now. She swept round the

table. Very nice that design on the taffeta; that cape suited her. A very graceful lady.

He went out to the pantry, closing the dining-room door on the gentlemen with their port.

He took the coffee tray into the drawing-room. The four ladies were sitting there rather uncomfortably, he thought. They were not talking. He handed round the coffee in silence.

He went out again. As he went into his pantry he heard the dining-room door open. David Lee came out and went along the hall to the drawing-room.

Tressilian went back into his pantry. He read the riot act to Walter. Walter was nearly, if not quite, impertinent!

Tressilian, alone in his pantry, sat down rather wearily.

He had a feeling of depression. Christmas Eve, and all this strain and tension . . . He didn't like it!

With an effort he roused himself. He went to the drawing-room and collected the coffee-cups. The room was empty except for Lydia, who was standing half concealed by the window curtain at the far end of the room. She was standing there looking out into the night.

From next door the piano sounded.

Mr David was playing. But why, Tressilian asked himself, did Mr David play the 'Dead March'? For that's what it was. Oh, indeed things were very wrong.

He went slowly along the hall and back into his pantry.

It was then he first heard the noise from overhead: a crashing of china, the overthrowing of furniture, a series of cracks and bumps.

'Good gracious!' thought Tressilian. 'Whatever is the master doing? What's happening up there?'

And then, clear and high, came a scream – a horrible high wailing scream that died away in a choke or gurgle.

Tressilian stood there a moment paralysed, then he ran out into the hall and up the broad staircase. Others were with him. That scream had been heard all over the house.

They raced up the stairs and round the bend, past a recess with statues gleaming white and eerie, and along the straight passage to Simeon Lee's door. Mr Farr was there already and Mrs David. She was leaning back against the wall and he was twisting at the door handle.

'The door's locked,' he was saying. 'The door's locked!'

Harry Lee pushed past and wrested it from him. He, too, turned and twisted at the handle.

'Father,' he shouted. 'Father, let us in.'

He held up his hand and in the silence they all listened. There was no answer. No sound from inside the room.

The front door bell rang, but no one paid any attention to it.

Stephen Farr said:

'We've got to break the door down. It's the only way.'

Harry said: 'That's going to be a tough job. These doors are good solid stuff. Come on, Alfred.'

They heaved and strained. Finally they went and got an oak bench and used it as a battering-ram. The door gave at last. Its hinges splintered and the door sank shuddering from its frame.

For a minute they stood there huddled together looking in. What they saw was a sight that no one of them ever forgot . . .

There had clearly been a terrific struggle. Heavy furniture was overturned. China vases lay splintered on the floor. In the middle of the hearthrug in front of the blazing fire lay Simeon Lee in a great pool of blood . . . Blood was splashed all round. The place was like a shambles.

There was a long shuddering sigh, and then two voices spoke in turn. Strangely enough, the words they uttered were both quotations.

David Lee said:

'*The mills of God grind slowly . . .*'

Lydia's voice came like a fluttering whisper:

'*Who would have thought the old man to have had so much blood in him? . . .*'

IV

Superintendent Sugden had rung the bell three times. Finally, in desperation, he pounded on the knocker.

A scared Walter at length opened the door.

'Oo-er,' he said. A look of relief came over his face. 'I was just ringing up the police.'

'What for?' said Superintendent Sugden sharply. 'What's going on here?'

Walter whispered:

'It's old Mr Lee. *He's been done in . . .*'

The superintendent pushed past him and ran up the stairs. He came into the room without anyone being aware of his entrance. As he entered he saw Pilar bend forward and pick up something from the floor. He saw David Lee standing with his hands over his eyes.

He saw the others huddled into a little group. Alfred Lee alone had stepped near his father's body. He stood now quite close, looking down. His face was blank.

George Lee was saying importantly:

'Nothing must be touched – remember that – *nothing* – till the police arrive. That is *most* important!'

'Excuse me,' said Sugden.

He pushed his way forward, gently thrusting the ladies aside.

Alfred Lee recognized him.

'Ah,' he said. 'It's you, Superintendent Sugden. You've got here very quickly.'

'Yes, Mr Lee.' Superintendent Sugden did not waste time on explanations. 'What's all this?'

'My father,' said Alfred Lee, 'has been killed – *murdered* . . .'

His voice broke.

Magdalene began suddenly to sob hysterically.

Superintendent Sugden held up a large official hand. He said authoritatively:

'Will everybody kindly leave the room except Mr Lee and – er – Mr George Lee? . . .'

They moved slowly towards the door, reluctantly, like sheep. Superintendent Sugden intercepted Pilar suddenly.

'Excuse me, miss,' he said pleasantly. 'Nothing must be touched or disturbed.'

She stared at him. Stephen Farr said impatiently:

'Of course not. She understands that.'

Superintendent Sugden said, still in the same pleasant manner: 'You picked up something from the floor just now?'

Pilar's eyes opened. She stared and said incredulously: '*I* did?'

Superintendent Sugden was still pleasant. His voice was just a little firmer.

'Yes, I saw you . . .'

'Oh!'

'So please give it to me. It's in your hand now.'

Slowly Pilar unclosed her hand. There lay in it a wisp of rubber and a small object made of wood. Superintendent Sugden took them, enclosed them in an envelope and put them away in his breast pocket. He said: 'Thank you.'

He turned away. Just for a minute Stephen Farr's eyes showed a startled respect. It was as though he had underestimated the large handsome superintendent.

They went slowly out of the room. Behind them they heard the superintendent's voice saying officially:

'And now, if you please . . .'

V

'Nothing like a wood fire,' said Colonel Johnson as he threw on an additional log and then drew his chair nearer to the blaze. 'Help yourself,' he added, hospitably calling attention to the tantalus and siphon that stood near his guest's elbow.

The guest raised a polite hand in negation. Cautiously he edged his own chair nearer to the blazing logs, though he was of the opinion that the opportunity for roasting the soles of one's feet (like some mediaeval torture) did not offset the cold draught that swirled round the back of the shoulders.

Colonel Johnson, Chief Constable of Middleshire, might be of the opinion that nothing could beat a wood fire, but Hercule Poirot was of the opinion that central heating could and did every time!

'Amazing business that Cartwright case,' remarked the host reminiscently. 'Amazing man! Enormous charm of manner. Why, when he came here with you, he had us all eating out of his hand.'

He shook his head.

'We'll never have anything like that case!' he said. 'Nicotine poisoning is rare, fortunately.'

'There was a time when you would have considered all poisoning unEnglish,' suggested Hercule Poirot. 'A device of foreigners! Unsportsmanlike!'

'I hardly think we could say that,' said the chief constable. 'Plenty of poisoning by arsenic – probably a good deal more than has ever been suspected.'

'Possibly, yes.'

'Always an awkward business, a poisoning case,' said Johnson. 'Conflicting testimony of the experts – then doctors are usually so extremely cautious in what they say. Always a difficult case to take to a jury. No, if one *must* have murder (which heaven forbid!) give me a straightforward case. Something where there's no ambiguity about the cause of death.'

Poirot nodded.

'The bullet wound, the cut throat, the crushed-in skull? It is there your preference lies?'

'Oh, don't call it a preference, my dear fellow. Don't harbour the idea that I *like* murder cases! Hope I never have another. Anyway, we ought to be safe enough during your visit.'

Poirot began modestly:

'My reputation –'

But Johnson had gone on.

'Christmas time,' he said. 'Peace, goodwill – and all that kind of thing. Goodwill all round.'

Hercule Poirot leaned back in his chair. He joined his fingertips. He studied his host thoughtfully.

He murmured: 'It is, then, your opinion that Christmas time is an unlikely season for crime?'

'That's what I said.'

'Why?'

'Why?' Johnson was thrown slightly out of his stride. 'Well, as I've just said – season of good cheer, and all that!'

Hercule Poirot murmured:

'The British, they are so sentimental!'

Johnson said stoutly: 'What if we are? What if we do like the old ways, the old traditional festivities? What's the harm?'

'There is no harm. It is all most charming! But let us for a moment examine *facts*. You have said that Christmas is a season of good cheer. That means, does it not, a lot of eating and drinking? It means, in fact, the *over*eating! And with the overeating there comes the indigestion! And with the indigestion there comes the irritability!'

'Crimes,' said Colonel Johnson, 'are not committed from irritability.'

'I am not so sure! Take another point. There is, at Christmas, a spirit of goodwill. It is, as you say, "the thing to do". Old quarrels are patched up, those who have disagreed consent to agree once more, even if it is only temporarily.'

Johnson nodded.

'Bury the hatchet, that's right.'

Poirot pursued his theme:

'And families now, families who have been separated throughout the year, assemble once more together. Now under these conditions, my friend, you must admit that there will occur a great amount of *strain*. People who do not *feel* amiable are putting great pressure on themselves to *appear* amiable! There is at Christmas time a great deal of *hypocrisy*, honourable hypocrisy, hypocrisy undertaken *pour le bon motif, c'est entendu*, but nevertheless hypocrisy!'

'Well, I shouldn't put it quite like that myself,' said Colonel Johnson doubtfully.

Poirot beamed upon him.

'No, no. It is *I* who am putting it like that, not *you*. I am pointing out to you that under these conditions – mental strain, physical *malaise* – it is highly probable that dislikes that were before merely mild and disagreements that were trivial might suddenly assume a more serious character. The result of pretending to be a more amiable, a more forgiving, a more high-minded person than one really is, has sooner or later the effect of causing one to behave as a more disagreeable, a more ruthless and an altogether more unpleasant person than is actually the case! If you dam the stream of natural behaviour, *mon ami*, sooner or later the dam bursts and a cataclysm occurs!'

Colonel Johnson looked at him doubtfully.

'Never know when you're serious and when you're pulling my leg,' he grumbled.

Poirot smiled at him.

'I am not serious! Not in the least am I serious! But all the same, it is true what I say – artificial conditions bring about their natural reaction.'

Colonel Johnson's manservant entered the room.

'Superintendent Sugden on the phone, sir.'

'Right. I'll come.'

With a word of apology the chief constable left the room.

He returned some three minutes later. His face was grave and perturbed.

'Damn it all!' he said. 'Case of murder! On Christmas Eve, too!'

Poirot's eyebrows rose.

'It is that definitely – murder, I mean?'

'Eh? Oh, no other solution possible! Perfectly clear case. Murder – and a brutal murder at that!'

'Who is the victim?'

'Old Simeon Lee. One of the richest men we've got! Made his money in South Africa originally. Gold – no, diamonds, I believe. He sunk an immense fortune in manufacturing some particular gadget of mining machinery. His own invention, I believe. Anyway, it's paid him hand over fist! They say he's a millionaire twice over.'

Poirot said: 'He was well liked, yes?'

Johnson said slowly:

'Don't think anyone liked him. Queer sort of chap. He's been an invalid for some years now. I don't know very much about him myself. But of course he is one of the big figures of the county.'

'So this case, it will make a big stir?'

'Yes. I must get over to Longdale as fast as I can.'

He hesitated, looking at his guest. Poirot answered the unspoken question:

'You would like that I should accompany you?'

Johnson said awkwardly:

'Seems a shame to ask you. But, well, you know how it is! Superintendent Sugden is a good man, none better, painstaking, careful, thoroughly sound – but – well, he's not an *imaginative* chap in any way. Should like very much, as you are here, benefit of your advice.'

He halted a little over the end part of his speech, making it somewhat telegraphic in style. Poirot responded quickly.

'I shall be delighted. You can count on me to assist you in any way I can. We must not hurt the feelings of the good superintendent. It will be his case – not mine. I am only the unofficial consultant.'

Colonel Johnson said warmly:

'You're a good fellow, Poirot.'

With those words of commendation, the two men started out.

VI

It was a constable who opened the front door to them and saluted. Behind him, Superintendent Sugden advanced down the hall and said:

'Glad you've got here, sir. Shall we come into this room here on the left – Mr Lee's study? I'd like to run over the main outlines. The whole thing's a rum business.'

He ushered them into a small room on the left of the hall. There was a telephone there and a big desk covered with papers. The walls were lined with bookcases.

The chief constable said: 'Sugden, this is M. Hercule Poirot. You may have heard of him. Just happened to be staying with me. Superintendent Sugden.'

Poirot made a little bow and looked the other man over. He saw a tall man with square shoulders and a military bearing who had an aquiline nose, a pugnacious jaw and a large flourishing chestnut-coloured moustache. Sugden stared hard at Hercule Poirot after acknowledging the introduction. Hercule Poirot stared hard at Superintendent Sugden's moustache. Its luxuriance seemed to fascinate him.

The superintendent said:

'Of course I have heard of you, Mr Poirot. You were in this part of the world some years ago, if I remember rightly. Death of Sir Bartholomew Strange. Poisoning case. Nicotine. Not my district, but of course I heard all about it.'

Colonel Johnson said impatiently:

'Now, then, Sugden, let's have the facts. A clear case, you said.'

'Yes, sir, it's murder right enough – not a doubt of that. Mr Lee's throat was cut – jugular vein severed, I understand from the doctor. But there's something very odd about the whole matter.'

'You mean –?'

'I'd like you to hear my story first, sir. These are the circumstances: This afternoon, about five o'clock, I was rung up by Mr Lee at Addlesfield police station. He sounded a bit odd over the phone – asked me to come and see him at eight o'clock this evening – made a special point of the time. Moreover, he instructed me to say to the butler that I was collecting subscriptions for some police charity.'

The chief constable looked up sharply.

'Wanted some plausible pretext to get you into the house?'

'That's right, sir. Well, naturally, Mr Lee is an important person, and I acceded to his request. I got here a little before eight o'clock, and represented myself as seeking subscriptions for the Police Orphanage. The butler went away and returned to tell me that Mr Lee would see me. Thereupon he showed me up to Mr Lee's room, which is situated on the first floor, immediately over the dining-room.'

Superintendent Sugden paused, drew a breath and then proceeded in a somewhat official manner with his report.

'Mr Lee was seated in a chair by the fireplace. He was wearing a dressing-gown. When the butler had left the room and closed the door, Mr Lee asked me to sit near him. He then said rather hesitatingly that he wanted to give me particulars of a robbery. I asked him what had been taken. He replied that he had reason to believe that diamonds (uncut diamonds, I think he said) to the value of several thousand pounds had been stolen from his safe.'

'Diamonds, eh?' said the chief constable.

'Yes, sir. I asked him various routine questions, but his manner was very uncertain and his replies were somewhat vague in character. At last he said, "You must understand, Superintendent, that I may be mistaken in this matter." I said, "I do not quite understand, sir. Either the diamonds are missing or they are not missing – one or the other." He replied, "The diamonds are certainly missing, but it is just possible, Superintendent, that their disappearance may be simply a rather foolish kind of practical joke." Well, that seemed odd to me, but I said nothing. He went on: "It is difficult for me to explain in detail, but what it amounts to is this: So far as I can see, only two persons can possibly have the stones. One of those persons might have done it as a joke. If the other person took them, then they have definitely been stolen." I said, "What exactly do you want me to do, sir?" He said quickly, "I want you, Superintendent, to return here in about an hour – no, make it a little more than that – say nine-fifteen. At that time I shall be able to tell you definitely whether I have been robbed or not." I was a little mystified, but I agreed and went away.'

Colonel Johnson commented:

'Curious – very curious. What do you say, Poirot?'

Hercule Poirot said:

'May I ask, Superintendent, what conclusions you yourself drew?'

The superintendent stroked his jaw as he replied carefully:

'Well, various ideas occurred to me, but on the whole, I figured it out this way. There was no question of any practical joke. The diamonds had been stolen all right. But the old gentleman wasn't sure who'd done it. It's my opinion that he was speaking the truth when he said that it might have been one of two people – and of those two people one was a servant and the other was a *member of the family*.'

Poirot nodded appreciatively.

'*Très bien*. Yes, that explains his attitude very well.'

'Hence his desire that I should return later. In the interval he meant to have an interview with the person in question. He would tell them that he had already spoken of the matter to the police but that, if restitution were promptly made, he could hush the matter up.'

Colonel Johnson said:

'And if the suspect didn't respond?'

'In that case, he meant to place the investigation in our hands.'

Colonel Johnson frowned and twisted his moustache. He demurred.

'Why not take that course *before* calling you in?'

'No, no, sir.' The superintendent shook his head. 'Don't you see, if he had done that, it might have been bluff. It wouldn't have been half so convincing. The person might say to himself, "The old man won't call the police in, no matter what he suspects!" But if the old gentleman says to him, "I've *already spoken to the police*, the superintendent has only just left." Then the thief asks the butler, say, and the butler confirms that. He says, "Yes, the superintendent was here just before dinner." Then the chief is convinced the old gentleman means business and it's up to him to cough up the stones.'

'H'm, yes, I see that,' said Colonel Johnson. 'Any idea, Sugden, who this "member of the family" might be?'

'No, sir.'

'No indication whatsoever?'

'None.'

Johnson shook his head. Then he said:

'Well, let's get on with it.'

Superintendent Sugden resumed his official manner.

'I returned to the house, sir, at nine-fifteen precisely. Just as I was about to ring the front door bell, I heard a scream from inside the house, and then a confused sound of shouts and a general commotion. I rang several times and also used the knocker. It was three or four minutes before the door was answered. When the footman at last opened it I could see that something momentous had occurred. He was shaking all over and looked as though he was about to faint. He gasped out that Mr Lee had been murdered. I ran hastily upstairs. I found Mr Lee's room in a state of wild confusion. There had evidently been a severe struggle. Mr Lee himself was lying in front of the fire with his throat cut in a pool of blood.'

The chief constable said sharply:

'He couldn't have done it himself?'

Sugden shook his head.

'Impossible, sir. For one thing, there were the chairs and tables overturned, and the broken crockery and ornaments, and then there was no sign of the razor or knife with which the crime had been committed.'

The chief constable said thoughtfully:

'Yes, that seems conclusive. Anyone in the room?'

'Most of the family were there, sir. Just standing round.'

Colonel Johnson said sharply:

'Any ideas, Sugden?'

The superintendent said slowly:

'It's a bad business, sir. It looks to me as though one of them must have done it. I don't see how anyone from outside could have done it and got away in time.'

'What about the window? Closed or open?'

'There are two windows in the room, sir. One was closed and locked. The other was open a few inches at the bottom – but it was fixed in that position by a burglar screw, and moreover, I've tried it and it's stuck fast – hasn't been opened for years, I should say. Also the wall outside is quite smooth and unbroken – no ivy or creepers. I don't see how anyone could have left that way.'

'How many doors in the room?'

'Just one. The room is at the end of a passage. That door was locked on the inside. When they heard the noise of the struggle and the old man's dying scream, and rushed upstairs, they had to break down the door to get in.'

Johnson said sharply:

'And who was in the room?'

Superintendent Sugden replied gravely:

'Nobody was in the room, sir, except the old man who had been killed not more than a few minutes previously.'

VII

Colonel Johnson stared at Sugden for some minutes before he spluttered:

'Do you mean to tell me, Superintendent, that this is one of those damned cases you get in detective stories where a man is killed in a locked room by some apparently supernatural agency?'

A very faint smile agitated the superintendent's moustache as he replied gravely:

'I do not think it's quite as bad as that, sir.'

Colonel Johnson said:

'Suicide. It must be suicide!'

'Where's the weapon, if so? No, sir, suicide won't do.'

'Then how did the murderer escape? By the window?' Sugden shook his head.

'I'll take my oath he didn't do that.'

'But the door was locked, you say, on the inside.'

The superintendent nodded. He drew a key from his pocket and laid it on the table.

'No fingerprints,' he announced. 'But just look at that key, sir. Take a look at it with that magnifying glass there.'

Poirot bent forward. He and Johnson examined the key together. The chief constable uttered an exclamation.

'By Jove, I get you. Those faint scratches on the end of the barrel. You see 'em, Poirot?'

'But yes, I see. That means, does it not, that the key was turned from outside the door – turned by means of a special implement that went through the keyhole and gripped the barrel – possibly an ordinary pair of pliers would do it.'

The superintendent nodded.

'It can be done all right.'

Poirot said: 'The idea being, then, that the death would be thought to be suicide, since the door was locked and no one was in the room?'

'That was the idea, M. Poirot, not a doubt of it, I should say.'

Poirot shook his head doubtfully.

'But the disorder in the room! As you say, that by itself wiped out the idea of suicide. Surely the murderer would first of all have set the room to rights.'

Superintendent Sugden said: 'But he hadn't *time*, Mr Poirot. That's the whole point. He hadn't time. Let's say he counted on catching the old gentleman unawares. Well, that didn't come off. There was a struggle – a struggle heard plainly in the room underneath; and, what's more, the old gentleman called out for help. Everyone came rushing up. The murderer's only got time to nip out of the room and turn the key from the outside.'

'That is true,' Poirot admitted. 'Your murderer, he may have made the bungle. But why, oh why, did he not at least leave the weapon? For naturally, if there is no weapon, it cannot be suicide! That was an error most grave.'

Superintendent Sugden said stolidly:

'Criminals usually make mistakes. That's our experience.'

Poirot gave a light sigh. He murmured:

'But all the same, in spite of his mistakes, he has escaped this criminal.'

'I don't think he has exactly *escaped*.'

'You mean he is in the house still?'

'I don't see where else he can be. It was an inside job.'

'But, *tout de même*,' Poirot pointed out gently, 'he has escaped to this extent: *You do not know who he is*.'

Superintendent Sugden said gently bur firmly:

'I rather fancy that we soon shall. We haven't done any questioning of the household yet.'

Colonel Johnson cut in:

'Look here, Sugden, one thing strikes me. Whoever turned that key from the outside must have had some knowledge of the job. That's to say, he probably has had criminal experience. These sort of tools aren't easy to manage.'

'You mean it was a professional job, sir?'

'That's what I mean.'

'It does seem like it,' the other admitted. 'Following that up, it looks as though there were a professional thief among the servants. That would explain the diamonds being taken and the murder would follow on logically from that.'

'Well, anything wrong with that theory?'

'It's what I thought myself to begin with. But it's difficult. There are eight servants in the house; six of them are women, and of those six, five have been here for four years and more. Then there's the butler and the footman. The butler has been here for close on forty years – bit of a record that, I should say. The footman's local, son of the gardener, and brought up here. Don't see very well how he can be a professional. The only other person is Mr Lee's valet attendant. He's comparatively new, but he was out of the house – still is – went out just before eight o'clock.'

Colonel Johnson said:

'Have you got a list of just who exactly was in the house?'

'Yes, sir. I got it from the butler.' He took out his note-book. 'Shall I read it to you?'

'Please, Sugden.'

'Mr and Mrs Alfred Lee. Mr George Lee, M.P., and his wife, Mr Henry Lee, Mr and Mrs David Lee. Miss' – the superintendent paused a little, taking the words carefully – 'Pilar' – he pronounced it like a piece of architecture – 'Estravados. Mr Stephen Farr. Then for the servants: Edward Tressilian, butler. Walter Champion, footman. Emily Reeves, cook. Queenie Jones, kitchenmaid. Gladys Spent, head housemaid. Grace Best, second housemaid. Beatrice Moscombe, third housemaid. Joan Kench, betweenmaid. Sydney Horbury, valet attendant.'

'That's the lot, eh?'

'That's the lot, sir.'

'Any idea where everybody was at the time of the murder?'

'Only roughly. As I told you, I haven't questioned anybody yet. According to Tressilian, the gentlemen were in the dining-room still. The ladies had gone to the drawing-room. Tressilian had served coffee. According to his statement, he had just got back to his pantry when he heard a noise upstairs. It was followed by a scream. He ran out into the hall and upstairs in the wake of the others.'

Colonel Johnson said:

'How many of the family live in the house, and who are just staying here?'

'Mr and Mrs Alfred Lee live here. The others are just visiting.'

Johnson nodded.

'Where are they all?'

'I asked them to stay in the drawing-room until I was ready to take their statements.'

'I see. Well, we'd better go upstairs and take a look at the doings.'

The superintendent led the way up the broad stairs and along the passage.

As he entered the room where the crime had taken place, Johnson drew a deep breath.

'Pretty horrible,' he commented.

He stood for a minute studying the overturned chairs, the smashed china, and the blood-bespattered débris.

A thin elderly man stood up from where he had been kneeling by the body and gave a nod.

'Evening, Johnson,' he said. 'Bit of a shambles, eh?'

'I should say it was. Got anything for us, doctor?'

The doctor shrugged his shoulders. He grinned.

'I'll let you have the scientific language at the inquest! Nothing complicated about it. Throat cut like a pig. He bled to death in less than a minute. No sign of the weapon.'

Poirot went across the room to the windows. As the superintendent had said, one was shut and bolted. The other was open about four inches at the bottom. A thick patent screw of the kind known many years ago as an anti-burglar screw secured it in that position.

Sugden said: 'According to the butler, that window was never shut wet or fine. There's a linoleum mat underneath it in case rain beat in, but it didn't much, as the overhanging roof protects it.'

Poirot nodded.

He came back to the body and stared down at the old man.

The lips were drawn back from the bloodless gums in something that looked like a snarl. The fingers were curved like claws.

Poirot said:

'He does not seem a strong man, no.'

The doctor said:

'He was pretty tough, I believe. He'd survived several pretty bad illnesses that would have killed most men.'

Poirot said: 'I do not mean that. I mean, he was not big, not strong physically.'

'No, he's frail enough.'

Poirot turned from the dead man. He bent to examine an overturned chair, a big chair of mahogany. Beside it was a round mahogany table and the fragments of a big china lamp. Two other smaller chairs lay nearby, also the smashed fragments of a decanter and two glasses, a heavy glass paperweight was unbroken, some miscellaneous books, a big Japanese vase smashed in pieces, and a bronze statuette of a naked girl completed the débris.

Poirot bent over all these exhibits, studying them gravely, but without touching them. He frowned to himself as though perplexed.

The chief constable said:

'Anything strike you, Poirot?'

Hercule Poirot sighed. He murmured:

'Such a frail shrunken old man – and yet – all this.'

Johnson looked puzzled. He turned away and said to the sergeant, who was busy at his work:

'What about prints?'

'Plenty of them, sir, all over the room.'

'What about the safe?'

'No good. Only prints on that are those of the old gentleman himself.'

Johnson turned to the doctor.

'What about bloodstains?' he asked. 'Surely whoever killed him must have got blood on him.'

The doctor said doubtfully:

'Not necessarily. Bleeding was almost entirely from the jugular vein. That wouldn't spout like an artery.'

'No, no. Still, there seems a lot of blood about.'

Poirot said:

'Yes, there is a lot of blood – it strikes one, that. A lot of blood.'

Superintendent Sugden said respectfully:

'Do you – er – does that suggest anything to you, Mr Poirot?'

Poirot looked about him. He shook his head perplexedly.

He said:

'There is something here – some violence . . .' He stopped a minute, then went on: 'Yes, that is it – *violence* . . . And blood – an insistence on *blood* . . . There is – how shall I put it? – there is *too much blood*. Blood on the chairs, on the tables, on the carpet . . . The blood ritual? Sacrificial blood? Is that it? Perhaps. Such a frail old man, so thin, so shrivelled, so dried up – and yet – in his death – *so much blood* . . .'

His voice died away. Superintendent Sugden, staring at him with round, startled eyes, said in an awed voice:

'Funny – that's what she said – the lady . . .'

Poirot said sharply:

'What lady? What was it she said?'

Sugden answered: 'Mrs Lee – Mrs Alfred. Stood over there by the door and half whispered it. It didn't make sense to me.'

'What did she say?'

'Something about who would have thought the old gentleman had so much blood in him . . .'

Poirot said softly:

'"*Who would have thought the old man to have had so much blood in him?*" The words of Lady Macbeth. She said that . . . Ah, that is interesting . . .'

VIII

Alfred Lee and his wife came into the small study where Poirot, Sugden and the chief constable were standing waiting. Colonel Johnson came forward.

'How do you do, Mr Lee? We've never actually met, but as you know, I'm chief constable of the county. Johnson's my name. I can't tell you how distressed I am by this.'

Alfred, his brown eyes like those of a suffering dog, said hoarsely:

'Thank you. It's terrible – quite terrible. I – this is my wife.'

Lydia said in her quiet voice:

'It has been a frightful shock to my husband – to all of us – but particularly to him.'

Her hand was on her husband's shoulder.

Colonel Johnson said:

'Won't you sit down, Mrs Lee? Let me introduce M. Hercule Poirot.'

Hercule Poirot bowed. His eyes went interestedly from husband to wife.

Lydia's hands pressed gently on Alfred's shoulder.

'Sit down, Alfred.'

Alfred sat. He murmured:

'Hercule Poirot. Now, who – who –?'

He passed his hand in a dazed fashion over his forehead.

Lydia Lee said:

'Colonel Johnson will want to ask you a lot of questions, Alfred.'

The chief constable looked at her with approval. He was thankful that Mrs Alfred Lee was turning out to be such a sensible and competent woman.

Alfred said:

'Of course. Of course . . .'

Johnson said to himself:

'Shock seems to have knocked him out completely. Hope he can pull himself together a bit.'

Aloud he said:

'I've got a list here of everybody who was in the house tonight. Perhaps you'll tell me, Mr Lee, if it is correct.'

He made a slight gesture to Sugden and the latter pulled out his note-book and once more recited the list of names.

The businesslike procedure seemed to restore Alfred Lee to something more like his normal self. He had regained command of himself, his eyes no longer looked dazed and staring. When Sugden finished, he nodded in agreement.

'That's quite right,' he said.

'Do you mind telling me a little more about your guests? Mr and Mrs George Lee and Mr and Mrs David Lee are, I gather, relatives?'

'They are my two younger brothers and their wives.'

'They are staying here only?'

'Yes, they came to us for Christmas.'

'Mr Henry Lee is also a brother?'

'Yes.'

'And your two other guests? Miss Estravados and Mr Farr?'

'Miss Estravados is my niece. Mr Farr is the son of my father's one-time partner in South Africa.'

'Ah, an old friend.'

Lydia intervened.

'No, actually we have never seen him before.'

'I see. But you invited him to stay with you for Christmas?'

Alfred hesitated, then looked towards his wife. She said clearly:

'Mr Farr turned up quite unexpectedly yesterday. He happened to be in the neighbourhood and came to call upon my father-in-law. When my father-in-law found he was the son of his old friend and partner, he insisted on his remaining with us for Christmas.'

Colonel Johnson said:

'I see. That explains the household. As regards the servants, Mrs Lee, do you consider them all trustworthy?'

Lydia considered for a moment before replying. Then she said:

'Yes. I am quite sure they are all thoroughly reliable. They have mostly been with us for many years. Tressilian, the butler, has been here since my husband was a young child. The only newcomers are the betweenmaid, Joan, and the nurse-valet who attended on my father-in-law.'

'What about them?'

'Joan is rather a silly little thing. That is the worst that can be said of her. I know very little about Horbury. He has been here just over a year. He was quite competent at his job and my father-in-law seemed satisfied with him.'

Poirot said acutely:

'But you, madame, were not so satisfied?'

Lydia shrugged her shoulders slightly.

'It was nothing to do with me.'

'But you are the mistress of the house, madame. The servants are your concern?'

'Oh yes, of course. But Horbury was my father-in-law's personal attendant. He did not come under my jurisdiction.'

'I see.'

Colonel Johnson said:

'We come now to the events of tonight. I'm afraid this will be painful for you, Mr Lee, but I would like your account of what happened.'

Alfred said in a low voice: 'Of course.'

Colonel Johnson said, prompting him:

'When, for instance, did you last see your father?'

A slight spasm of pain crossed Alfred's face as he replied in a low voice:

'It was after tea. I was with him for a short time. Finally I said goodnight to him and left him at – let me see – about a quarter to six.'

Poirot observed: 'You said goodnight to him? You did not then expect to see him again that evening?'

'No. My father's supper, a light meal, was always brought to him at seven. After that he sometimes went to bed early or sometimes sat up in his chair, but he did not expect to see any members of the family again unless he specially sent for them.'

'Did he often send for them?'

'Sometimes. If he felt like it.'

'But it was not the ordinary procedure?'

'No.'

'Go on, please, Mr Lee.'

Alfred continued:

'We had our dinner at eight o'clock. Dinner was over and my wife and the other ladies had gone into the drawing-room.' His voice faltered. His eyes began to stare again. 'We were sitting there – at the table . . . Suddenly there was the most astounding noise overheard. Chairs overturning, furniture crashing, breaking glass and china, and then – Oh, God' – he shuddered – 'I can hear it still – my father screamed – a horrible, long-drawn scream – the scream of a man in mortal agony . . .'

He raised shaking hands to cover his face. Lydia stretched out her hand and touched his sleeve. Colonel Johnson said gently: 'And then?'

Alfred said in a broken voice:

'I think – just for a moment we were *stunned*. Then we sprang up and went out of the door and up the stairs to my father's room. The door was locked. We couldn't get in. It had to be broken open. Then, when we did get in, we saw –'

His voice died away.

Johnson said quickly:

'There's no need to go into that part of it, Mr Lee. To go back a little, to the time you were in the dining-room. Who was there with you when you heard the cry?'

'Who was there? Why, we were all – No, let me see. My brother was there – my brother Harry.'

'Nobody else?'

'No one else.'

'Where were the other gentlemen?'

Alfred sighed and frowned in an effort of remembrance.

'Let me see – it seems so long ago – yes, like years – what did happen? Oh, of course, George had gone to telephone. Then we began to talk of family matters, and Stephen Farr said something about seeing we wanted to discuss things, and he took himself off. He did it very nicely and tactfully.'

'And your brother David?'

Alfred frowned.

'David? Wasn't he there? No, of course, he wasn't. I don't quite know when he slipped away.'

Poirot said gently:

'So you had the family matters to discuss?'

'Er – yes.'

'That is to say, you had matters to discuss with *one* member of your family?'

Lydia said:

'What do you mean, M. Poirot?'

He turned quickly to her.

'Madame, your husband says that Mr Farr left them because he saw they had affairs of the family to discuss. But it was not a *conseil de famille*, since M. David was not there and M. George was not there. It was, then, a discussion between two members of the family only.'

Lydia said:

'My brother-in-law, Harry, had been abroad for a great number of years. It was natural that he and my husband should have things to talk over.'

'Ah! I see. It was like that.'

She shot him a quick glance, then turned her eyes away.

Johnson said:

'Well, that seems clear enough. Did you notice anyone else as you ran upstairs to your father's room?'

'I – really I don't know. I think so. We all came from different directions. But I'm afraid I didn't notice – I was so alarmed. That terrible cry . . .'

Colonel Johnson passed quickly to another subject.

'Thank you, Mr Lee. Now, there is another point. I understand that your father had some valuable diamonds in his possession.'

Alfred looked rather surprised.

'Yes,' he said. 'That is so.'

'Where did he keep them?'

'In the safe in his room.'

'Can you describe them at all?'

'They were rough diamonds – that is, uncut stones.'

'Why did your father have them there?'

'It was a whim of his. They were stones he had brought with him from South Africa. He never had them cut. He just liked keeping them in his possession. As I say, it was a whim of his.'

'I see,' said the chief constable.

From his tone it was plain that he did not see. He went on: 'Were they of much value?'

'My father estimated their value at about ten thousand pounds.'

'In fact, they were very valuable stones?'

'Yes.'

'It seems a curious idea to keep such stones in a bedroom safe.'

Lydia interposed.

'My father-in-law, Colonel Johnson, was a somewhat curious man. His ideas were not the conventional ones. It definitely gave him pleasure to handle those stones.'

'They recalled, perhaps, the past to him,' said Poirot.

She gave him a quick appreciative look.

'Yes,' she said. 'I think they did.'

'Were they insured?' asked the chief constable.

'I think not.'

Johnson leaned forward. He asked quietly:

'Did you know, Mr Lee, that those stones had been stolen?'

'What?' Alfred Lee stared at him.

'Your father said nothing to you of their disappearance?'

'Not a word.'

'You did not know that he had sent for Superintendent Sugden here and had reported the loss to him?'

'I hadn't the faintest idea of such a thing!'

The chief constable transferred his gaze.

'What about you, Mrs Lee?'

Lydia shook her head.

'I heard nothing about it.'

'As far as you knew, the stones were still in the safe?'

'Yes.'

She hesitated and then asked:

'Is that why he was killed? For the sake of those stones?'

Colonel Johnson said:

'That is what we arc going to find out!'

He went on:

'Have you any idea, Mrs Lee, who could have engineered such a theft?'

She shook her head.

'No, indeed. I am sure the servants are all honest. In any case, it would be very difficult for them to get at the safe. My father-in-law was always in his room. He never came downstairs.'

'Who attended to the room?'

'Horbury. He made the bed and dusted. The second housemaid

went in to do the grate and lay the fire every morning, otherwise Horbury did everything.'

Poirot said:

'So Horbury would be the person with the best opportunity?'

'Yes.'

'Do you think that it was he who stole the diamonds, then?'

'It is possible. I suppose . . . He had the best opportunity. Oh! I don't know what to think.'

Colonel Johnson said:

'Your husband has given us his account of the evening. Will you do the same, Mrs Lee? When did you last see your father-in-law?'

'We were all up in his room this afternoon – before tea. That was the last time I saw him.'

'You did not see him later to bid him goodnight?'

'No.'

Poirot said:

'Do you usually go and say goodnight to him?'

Lydia said sharply:

'No.'

The chief constable went on:

'Where were you when the crime took place?'

'In the drawing-room.'

'You heard the noise of the struggle?'

'I think I heard something heavy fall. Of course my father-in-law's room is over the dining-room, not the drawing-room, so I shouldn't hear so much.'

'But you heard the cry?'

Lydia shuddered.

'Yes, I heard that . . . It was horrible – like – like a soul in hell. I knew at once something dreadful had happened. I hurried out and followed my husband and Harry up the stairs.'

'Who else was in the drawing-room at the time?'

Lydia frowned.

'Really – I can't remember. David was next door in the music-room, playing Mendelssohn. I think Hilda had gone to join him.'

'And the other two ladies?'

Lydia said slowly:

'Magdalene went to telephone. I can't remember whether she had come back or not. I don't know where Pilar was.'

Poirot said gently:

'In fact, you may have been quite alone in the drawing-room?'

'Yes – yes – as a matter of fact, I believe I was.'

Colonel Johnson said:

'About these diamonds. We ought, I think, to make quite sure about them. Do you know the combination of your father's safe, Mr Lee? I see it is of a somewhat old-fashioned pattern.'

'You will find it written down in a small note-book he carried in the pocket of his dressing-gown.'

'Good. We will go and look presently. It will be better, perhaps, if we interview the other members of the house-party first. The ladies may want to get to bed.'

Lydia stood up.

'Come, Alfred.' She turned to them. 'Shall I send them in to you?'

'One by one, if you wouldn't mind, Mrs Lee.'

'Certainly.'

She moved towards the door. Alfred followed her.

Suddenly, at the last moment, he swung round.

'Of course,' he said. He came quickly back to Poirot. 'You are Hercule Poirot! I don't know where my wits have been. I should have realized at once.'

He spoke quickly, in a low, excited voice.

'It's an absolute godsend your being here! You must find out the truth, M. Poirot. Spare no expense! I will be responsible for any expense. *But find out . . .* My poor father – killed by someone – killed with the utmost brutality! You *must* find out, M. Poirot. My father has got to be avenged.'

Poirot answered quietly:

'I can assure you, M. Lee, that I am prepared to do my utmost to assist Colonel Johnson and Superintendent Sugden.'

Alfred Lee said:

'I want you to work for *me*. My father has got to be avenged.'

He began to tremble violently. Lydia had come back. She went up to him and drew his arm through hers.

'Come, Alfred,' she said. 'We must get the others.'

Her eyes met Poirot's. They were eyes that kept their own secrets. They did not waver.

Poirot said softly:

'*Who would have thought the old man –*'

She interrupted him:

'Stop! Don't say that!'

Poirot murmured:

'*You* said it, madame.'

She breathed softly:

'I know . . . I remember . . . It was – so horrible.'

Then she went abruptly out of the room, her husband beside her.

IX

George Lee was solemn and correct.

'A terrible business,' he said, shaking his head. 'A terrible, terrible business. I can only believe that it must – er – have been the work of a *lunatic*!'

Colonel Johnson said politely:

'That is your theory?'

'Yes. Yes, indeed. A homicidal maniac. Escaped, perhaps, from some mental home in the vicinity.'

Superintendent Sugden put in:

'And how do you suggest this – er – lunatic gained admittance to the house, Mr Lee? And how did he leave it?'

George shook his head.

'That,' he said firmly, 'is for the police to discover.'

Sugden said:

'We made the round of the house at once. All windows were closed and barred. The side door was locked, so was the front door. Nobody could have left by the kitchen premises without being seen by the kitchen staff.'

George Lee cried:

'But that's absurd! You'll be saying next that my father was never murdered at all!'

'He was murdered all right,' said Superintendent Sugden. 'There's no doubt about that.'

The chief constable cleared his throat and took up the questioning.

'Just where were you, Mr Lee, at the time of the crime?'

'I was in the dining-room. It was just after dinner. No, I was, I think, in this room. I had just finished telephoning.'

'You had been telephoning?'

'Yes. I had put a call through to the Conservative agent in Westeringham – my constituency. Some urgent matters.'

'And it was after that that you heard the scream?'

George Lee gave a slight shiver.

'Yes, very unpleasant. It – er – froze my marrow. It died away in a kind of choke or gurgle.'

He took out a handkerchief and wiped his forehead where the perspiration had broken out.

'Terrible business,' he muttered.

'And then you hurried upstairs?'

'Yes.'

'Did you see your brothers, Mr Alfred and Mr Harry Lee?'

'No, they must have gone up just ahead of me, I think.'

'When did you last see your father, Mr Lee?'

'This afternoon. We were all up there.'

'You did not see him after that?'

'No.'

The chief constable paused, then he said:

'Were you aware that your father kept a quantity of valuable uncut diamonds in the safe in his bedroom?'

George Lee nodded.

'A most unwise procedure,' he said pompously. 'I often told him so. He might have been murdered for them – I mean – that is to say –'

Colonel Johnson cut in: 'Are you aware that these stones have disappeared?'

George's jaw dropped. His protuberant eyes stared.

'Then he *was* murdered for them?'

The chief constable said slowly:

'He was aware of their loss and reported it to the police some hours before his death.'

George said:

'But, then – I don't understand – I – . . .'

Hercule Poirot said gently:

'We, too, do not understand . . .'

X

Harry Lee came into the room with a swagger. For a moment Poirot stared at him, frowning. He had a feeling that somewhere he had seen this man before. He noted the features: the high-bridged nose, the arrogant poise of the head, the line of the jaw; and he realized that though Harry was a big man and his father had been a man of merely middle height, yet there had been a good deal of resemblance between them.

He noted something else, too. For all his swagger, Harry Lee was nervous. He was carrying it off with a swing, but the anxiety underneath was real enough.

'Well, gentlemen,' he said. 'What can I tell you?'

Colonel Johnson said:

'We shall be glad of any light you can throw on the events of this evening.'

Harry Lee shook his head.

'I don't know anything at all. It's all pretty horrible and utterly unexpected.'

Poirot said:

'You have recently returned from abroad, I think, Mr Lee?'

Harry turned to him quickly.

'Yes. Landed in England a week ago.'

Poirot said:

'You had been away a long time?'

Harry Lee lifted up his chin and laughed.

'You might as well hear straight away – someone will soon tell you! I'm the prodigal son, gentlemen! It's nearly twenty years since I last set foot in this house.'

'But you returned – now. Will you tell us why?' asked Poirot.

With the same appearance of frankness Harry answered readily enough.

'It's the good old parable still. I got tired of the husks that the swine do eat – or don't eat, I forget which. I thought to myself that the fatted calf would be a welcome exchange. I had a letter from my father suggesting that I come home. I obeyed the summons and came. That's all.'

Poirot said:

'You came for a short visit – or a long one?'

Harry said: 'I came home – for good!'

'Your father was willing?'

'The old man was delighted.' He laughed again. The corners of his eyes crinkled engagingly. 'Pretty boring for the old man living here with Alfred! Alfred's a dull stick – very worthy and all that, but poor company. My father had been a bit of a rip in his time. He was looking forward to my company.'

'And your brother and his wife, were they pleased that you were to live here?'

Poirot asked the question with a slight lifting of his eyebrows.

'Alfred? Alfred was livid with rage. Don't know about Lydia. She was probably annoyed on Alfred's behalf. But I've no doubt she'd be quite pleased in the end. I like Lydia. She's a delightful woman. I should have got on with Lydia. But Alfred was quite another pair of shoes.' He laughed again. 'Alfred's always been as jealous as hell of me. He's always been the good dutiful stay-at-home stick-in-the-mud son. And what was he going to get for it in the end? – what the good boy of the family always gets – a kick in the pants. Take it from me, gentlemen, virtue doesn't pay.' He looked from one face to another.

'Hope you're not shocked by my frankness. But after all, it's the truth you're after. You'll drag out all the family dirty linen into the light of day in the end. I might as well display mine straight away. I'm not particularly broken-hearted by my father's death – after all, I hadn't seen the old devil since I was a boy – but nevertheless he was my father and he was murdered. I'm all out for revenge on the murderer.' He stroked his jawbone, watching them. 'We're rather hot on revenge in our family. None of the Lees forget easily. I mean to make sure that my father's murderer is caught and hanged.'

'I think you can trust us to do our best in that line, Mr Lee,' said Sugden.

'If you don't I shall take the law into my own hands,' said Harry Lee.

The chief constable said sharply:

'Have you any ideas on the subject of the murderer's identity, then, Mr Lee?'

Harry shook his head.

'No,' he said slowly. 'No – I haven't. You know it's rather a jolt. Because I've been thinking about it – and I don't see that it can have been an outside job . . .'

'Ah,' said Sugden, nodding his head.

'And if so,' said Harry Lee, 'then someone here in the house killed him . . . But who the devil could have done it? Can't suspect the servants. Tressilian has been here since the year one. The half-witted footman? Not on your life. Horbury, now, he's a cool customer, but Tressilian tells me he was out at the pictures. So what do you come to? Passing over Stephen Farr (and why the devil should Stephen Farr come all the way from South Africa and murder a total stranger?) there's only the family. And for the life of me I can't see one of us doing it. Alfred? He adored Father. George? He hasn't got the guts. David? David's always been a moon dreamer. He'd faint if he saw his own finger bleed. The wives? Women don't go and slit a man's throat in cold blood. So who did? Blessed if I know. But it's damned disturbing.'

Colonel Johnson cleared his throat – an official habit of his – and said:

'When did you last see your father this evening?'

'After tea. He'd just had a row with Alfred – about your humble servant. The old man was no end bucked with himself. He always liked stirring up trouble. In my opinion, that's why he kept my arrival dark from the others. Wanted to see the fur fly when I blew in unexpectedly! That's why he talked about altering his will, too.'

Poirot stirred softly. He murmured:

'So your father mentioned his will?'

'Yes – in front of the whole lot of us, watching us like a cat to see how we reacted. Just told the lawyer chap to come over and see him about it after Christmas.'

Poirot asked:

'What changes did he contemplate making?'

Harry Lee grinned:

'He didn't tell us that! Trust the old fox! I imagine – or shall we say I hoped – that the change was to the advantage of your humble servant! I should imagine I'd been cut out of any former wills. Now, I rather fancy, I was to go back. Nasty blow for the others. Pilar, too – he'd taken a fancy to her. She was in for something good, I should imagine. You haven't seen her yet?

My Spanish niece. She's a beautiful creature, Pilar – with the lovely warmth of the South – and its cruelty. Wish I wasn't a mere uncle!'

'You say your father took to her?'

Harry nodded.

'She knew how to get round the old man. Sat up there with him a good deal. I bet she knew just what she was after! Well, he's dead now. No wills can be altered in Pilar's favour – nor mine either, worse luck.'

He frowned, paused a minute, and then went on with a change of tone.

'But I'm wandering from the point. You wanted to know what was the last time I saw my father? As I've told you, it was after tea – might have been a little past six. The old man was in good spirits then – a bit tired, perhaps. I went away and left him with Horbury. I never saw him again.'

'Where were you at the time of his death?'

'In the dining-room with brother Alfred. Not a very harmonious after-dinner session. We were in the middle of a pretty sharp argument when we heard the noise overhead. Sounded as though ten men were wrestling up there. And then poor old Father screamed. It was like killing a pig. The sound of it paralysed Alfred. He just sat there with his jaw dropping. I fairly shook him back to life, and we started off upstairs. The door was locked. Had to break it open. Took some doing, too. How the devil that door came to be locked, I can't imagine! There was no one in the room but Father, and I'm damned if anyone could have got away through the windows.'

Superintendent Sugden said:

'The door was locked from the outside.'

'What?' Harry stared. 'But I'll swear the key was on the *inside*.'

Poirot murmured:

'So you noticed that?'

Harry Lee said sharply:

'I do notice things. It's a habit of mine.'

He looked sharply from one face to the other.

'Is there anything more you want to know, gentlemen?'

Johnson shook his head.

'Thank you, Mr Lee, not for the moment. Perhaps you will ask the next member of the family to come along?'

'Certainly I will.'

He walked to the door and went out without looking back.

The three men looked at each other.

Colonel Johnson said:

'What about it, Sugden?'

The superintendent shook his head doubtfully. He said:

'He's afraid of something. I wonder why? . . .'

XI

Magdalene Lee paused effectively in the doorway. One long slender hand touched the burnished platinum sheen of her hair. The leaf-green velvet frock she wore clung to the delicate lines of her figure. She looked very young and a little frightened.

The three men were arrested for a moment looking at her. Johnson's eyes showed a sudden surprised admiration. Superintendent Sugden's showed no animation, merely the impatience of a man anxious to get on with his job. Hercule Poirot's eyes were deeply appreciative (as she saw) but the appreciation was not for her beauty, but for the effective use she made of it. She did not know that he was thinking to himself:

'*Jolie mannequin, la petite. Mais elle a les yeux durs.*'

Colonel Johnson was thinking:

'Damned good-looking girl. George Lee will have trouble with her if he doesn't look out. Got an eye for a man all right.'

Superintendent Sugden was thinking:

'Empty-headed vain piece of goods. Hope we get through with her quickly.'

'Will you sit down, Mrs Lee? Let me see, you are –?'

'Mrs George Lee.'

She accepted the chair with a warm smile of thanks. 'After all,' the glance seemed to say, 'although you *are* a man and a policeman, you are not so dreadful after all.'

The tail-end of the smile included Poirot. Foreigners were so susceptible where women were concerned. About Superintendent Sugden she did not bother.

She murmured, twisting her hands together in a pretty distress:

'It's all so terrible. I feel so frightened.'

'Come, come, Mrs Lee,' said Colonel Johnson kindly but briskly. 'It's been a shock, I know, but it's all over now. We just want an account from you of what happened this evening.'

She cried out:

'But I don't know anything about it – I don't indeed.'

For a moment the chief constable's eyes narrowed. He said gently: 'No, of course not.'

'We only arrived here yesterday. George *would* make me come here for Christmas! I wish we hadn't. I'm sure I shall never feel the same again!'

'Very upsetting – yes.'

'I hardly know George's family, you see. I've only seen Mr Lee once or twice – at our wedding and once since. Of course I've seen Alfred and Lydia more often, but they're really all quite strangers to me.'

Again the wide-eyed frightened-child look. Again Hercule Poirot's eyes were appreciative – and again he thought to himself:

Elle joue très bien la comédie, cette petite . . .'

'Yes, yes,' said Colonel Johnson. 'Now just tell me about the last time you saw your father-in-law – Mr Lee – alive.'

'Oh, *that*! That was this afternoon. It was dreadful!'

Johnson said quickly:

'Dreadful? Why?'

'They were so angry!'

'Who was angry?'

'Oh, all of them . . . I don't mean George. His father didn't say anything to him. But all the others.'

'What happened exactly?'

'Well, when we got there – he asked for all of us – he was speaking into the telephone – to his lawyers about his will. And then he told Alfred he was looking very glum. I think that was because of Harry coming home to live. Alfred was very upset about that, I believe. You see, Harry did something quite dreadful. And then he said something about his wife – she's dead long ago – but she had the brains of a louse, he said, and David sprang up and looked as though he'd like to murder him – Oh!' She stopped suddenly, her eyes alarmed. 'I didn't *mean* that – I didn't mean it at all!'

Colonel Johnson said soothingly:

'Quite – quite, figure of speech, that was all.'

'Hilda, that's David's wife, quieted him down and – well, I think that's all. Mr Lee said he didn't want to see anyone again that evening. So we all went away.'

'And that was the last time you saw him?'

'Yes. Until – until –'

She shivered.

Colonel Johnson said:

'Yes, quite so. Now, where were you at the time of the crime?'

'Oh – let me see, I think I was in the drawing-room.'

'Aren't you sure?'

Magdalene's eyes flickered a little, the lids drooped over them. She said:

'Of course! How stupid of me . . . I'd gone to telephone. One gets so mixed up.'

'You were telephoning, you say. In this room?'

'Yes, that's the only telephone except the one upstairs in my father-in-law's room.'

Superintendent Sugden said:

'Was anybody else in the room with you?'

Her eyes widened.

'Oh, no, I was quite alone.'

'Had you been here long?'

'Well – a little time. It takes some time to put a call through in the evening.'

'It was a trunk call, then?'

'Yes – to Westeringham.'

'I see.'

'And then?'

'And then there was that awful scream – and everybody running – and the door being locked and having to break it down. Oh! It was like a *nightmare*! I shall always remember it!'

'No, no,' Colonel Johnson's tone was mechanically kind. He went on:

'Did you know that your father-in-law kept a quantity of valuable diamonds in his safe?'

'No, did he?' Her tone was quite frankly thrilled. 'Real diamonds?'

Hercule Poirot said:

'Diamonds worth about ten thousand pounds.'

'Oh!' It was a soft gasping sound – holding in it the essence of feminine cupidity.

'Well,' said Colonel Johnson, 'I think that's all for the present. We needn't bother you any further, Mrs Lee.'

'Oh, thank you.'

She stood up – smiled from Johnson to Poirot – the smile of a grateful little girl, then she went out walking with her head held high and her palms a little turned outwards.

Colonel Johnson called:

'Will you ask your brother-in-law, Mr David Lee, to come here?' Closing the door after her, he came back to the table.

'Well,' he said, 'what do you think? We're getting at some of it now! You notice one thing: George Lee was telephoning when he heard the scream! His wife was telephoning when she heard it! That doesn't fit – it doesn't fit at all.'

He added:

'What do you think, Sugden?'

The superintendent said slowly:

'I don't want to speak offensively of the lady, but I should say that though she's the kind who would be first class at getting money out a gentleman, I don't think she's the kind who'd cut a gentleman's throat. That wouldn't be her line at all.'

'Ah, but one never knows, *mon vieux*,' murmured Poirot.

The chief constable turned round on him.

'And you, Poirot, what do you think?'

Hercule Poirot leaned forward. He straightened the blotter in front of him and flicked a minute speck of dust from a candlestick. He answered:

'I would say that the character of the late Mr Simeon Lee begins to emerge for us. It is there, I think, that the whole importance of the case lies . . . in the character of the dead man.'

Superintendent Sugden turned a puzzled face to him.

'I don't quite get you, Mr Poirot,' he said. 'What exactly has the character of the deceased got to do with his murder?'

Poirot said dreamily:

'The character of the victim has always something to do with his or her murder. The frank and unsuspicious mind of Desdemona was the direct cause of her death. A more suspicious woman would have seen Iago's machinations and circumvented them much earlier. The uncleanness of Marat directly invited his end in a bath. From the temper of Mercutio's mind came his death at the sword's point.'

Colonel Johnson pulled his moustache.

'What exactly are you getting at, Poirot?'

'I am telling you that because Simeon Lee was a certain kind of man, he set in motion certain forces, which forces in the end brought about his death.'

'You don't think the diamonds had anything to do with it, then?'

Poirot smiled at the honest perplexity in Johnson's face.

'*Mon cher*,' he said. 'It was because of Simeon Lee's peculiar character that he kept ten thousand pounds worth of uncut diamonds in his safe! You have not there the action of every man.'

'That's very true, Mr Poirot,' said Superintendent Sugden, nodding his head with the air of a man who at last sees what a fellow-conversationalist is driving at. 'He was a queer one, Mr Lee was. He kept those stones there so he could take them out and handle them and get the feeling of the past back. Depend upon it, that's why he never had them cut.'

Poirot nodded energetically.

'Precisely – precisely. I see you have great acumen, Superintendent.'

The superintendent looked a little doubtful at the compliment, but Colonel Johnson cut in:

'There's something else, Poirot. I don't know whether it has struck you –'

'*Mais oui*,' said Poirot. 'I know what you mean. Mrs George Lee, she let the cat out of the bag more than she knew! She gave us a pretty impression of that last family meeting. She indicates – oh! so naïvely – that Alfred was angry with his father – and that David looked as "though he could murder him". Both those statements I think were true. But from them we can draw our own reconstruction. What did Simeon Lee assemble his family for? Why should they have arrived in time to hear him telephoning to his lawyer? *Parbleu*, it was no error, that. He *wanted* them to hear it! The poor old one, he sits in his chair and he has lost the diversions of his younger days. So he invents a new diversion for himself. He amuses himself by playing upon the cupidity and the greed of human nature – yes, and on its emotions and its passions, too! But from that arises one further deduction. In his game of rousing the greed and emotion of his children, he would not omit anyone. He must, logically and necessarily, have had his dig at Mr George Lee as well as at the others! His wife is carefully silent about that. At her, too, he may have shot a poisoned arrow or two. We shall find out, I think, from others, what Simeon Lee had to say to George Lee and George Lee's wife –'

He broke off. The door opened and David Lee came in.

XII

David Lee had himself well in hand. His demeanour was calm – almost unnaturally so. He came up to them, drew a chair forward and sat down, looking with grave interrogation at Colonel Johnson.

The electric light touched the fair peak of hair that grew on his forehead and showed up the sensitive modelling of the cheek bones. He looked absurdly young to be the son of that shrivelled old man who lay dead upstairs.

'Yes, gentlemen,' he said, 'what can I tell you?'

Colonel Johnson said:

'I understand, Mr Lee, that there was a kind of family meeting held in your father's room this afternoon?'

'There was. But it was quite informal. I mean, it was not a family council or anything of that kind.'

'What took place there?'

David Lee answered calmly:

'My father was in a difficult mood. He was an old man and an invalid, of course, one had to make allowances for him. He seemed to have assembled us there in order to – well – vent his spite upon us.'

'Can you remember what he said?'

David said quietly:

'It was really all rather foolish. He said we were no use – any of us – that there wasn't a single man in the family! He said Pilar (that is my Spanish niece) was worth two of any of us. He said –' David stopped.

Poirot said:

'Please, Mr Lee, the exact words, if you can.'

David said reluctantly:

'He spoke rather coarsely – said he hoped that somewhere in the world he had better sons – even if they were born the wrong side of the blanket . . .'

His sensitive face showed distaste for the words he was repeating. Superintendent Sugden looked up, suddenly alert. Leaning forward, he said:

'Did your father say anything in particular to your brother, Mr George Lee?'

'To George? I don't remember. Oh, yes, I believe he told him he would have to cut down expenses in future; he'd have to reduce his allowance. George was very upset, got as red as a turkey cock. He spluttered and said he couldn't possibly manage with less. My father said quite coolly that he'd have to. He said he'd better get his wife to help him economize. Rather a nasty dig, that – George has always been the economical one – saves and stints on every penny. Magdalene, I fancy, is a bit of a spender – she has extravagant tastes.'

Poirot said:

'So that she, too, was annoyed?'

'Yes. Besides, my father worded something else rather crudely – mentioned her as having lived with a naval officer. Of course he really meant her father, but it sounded rather dubious. Magdalene went scarlet. I don't blame her.'

Poirot said:

'Did your father mention his late wife, your mother?'

The red blood ran in waves up David's temples. His hands clenched themselves on the table in front of him, trembling slightly.

He said in a low choked voice:

'Yes, he did. He insulted her.'

Colonel Johnson said:

'What did he say?'

David said abruptly:

'I don't remember. Just some slighting reference.'

Poirot said softly:

'Your mother has been dead some years?'

David said shortly:

'She died when I was a boy.'

'She was not – perhaps – very happy in her life here?'

David gave a scornful laugh:

'Who could be happy with a man like my father? My mother was a saint. She died a broken-hearted woman.'

Poirot went on:

'Your father was, perhaps, distressed by her death?'

David said abruptly:

'I don't know. I left home.'

He paused and then said:

'Perhaps you may not be aware of the fact that when I came on this visit I had not seen my father for nearly twenty years. So you see I can't tell you very much about his habits or his enemies or what went on here.'

Colonel Johnson asked:

'Did you know that your father kept a lot of valuable diamonds in the safe in his bedroom?'

David said indifferently:

'Did he? Seems a foolish sort of thing to do.'

Johnson said:

'Will you describe briefly your own movements last night?'

'Mine? Oh, I went away from the dinner-table fairly quickly. It bores me, this sitting round over port. Besides, I could see that Alfred and Harry were working up for a quarrel. I hate rows. I slipped away and went to the music-room and played the piano.'

Poirot asked:

'The music-room, it is next to the drawing-room, is it not?'

'Yes. I played there for some time – till – till the thing happened.'

'What did you hear exactly?'

'Oh! A far-off noise of furniture being overturned somewhere upstairs. And then a pretty ghastly cry.' He clenched his hands again. 'Like a soul in hell. God, it was awful!'

Johnson said:

'Were you alone in the music-room?'

'Eh? No, my wife, Hilda, was there. She'd come in from the drawing-room. We – we went up with the others.'

He added quickly and nervously:

'You don't want me, do you, to describe what – what I saw there?'

Colonel Johnson said:

'No, quite unnecessary. Thank you, Mr Lee, there's nothing more. You can't imagine, I suppose, who would be likely to want to murder your father?'

David Lee said recklessly:

'I should think – quite a lot of people! I don't know of anyone definite.'

He went out rapidly, shutting the door loudly behind him.

XIII

Colonel Johnson had had no time to do more than clear his throat when the door opened again and Hilda Lee came in.

Hercule Poirot looked at her with interest. He had to admit to himself that the wives these Lees had married were an interesting study. The swift intelligence and greyhound grace of Lydia, the meretricious airs and graces of Magdalene, and now, the solid comfortable strength of Hilda. She was, he saw, younger than her rather dowdy style of hair-dressing and unfashionable clothes made her appear. Her mouse-brown hair was unflecked with grey and her steady hazel eyes set in the rather podgy face shone out like beacons of kindliness. She was, he thought, a nice woman.

Colonel Johnson was talking in his kindliest tone.

'. . . A great strain on all of you,' he was saying. 'I gather from your husband, Mrs Lee, that this is the first time you have been to Gorston Hall?'

She bowed her head.

'Were you previously acquainted with your father-in-law, Mr Lee?'

Hilda replied in her pleasant voice:

'No. We were married soon after David left home. He always wanted to have nothing to do with his family. Until now we have not seen any of them.'

'How, then, did this visit come about?'

'My father-in-law wrote to David. He stressed his age and his desire that all his children should be with him this Christmas.'

'And your husband responded to this appeal?'

Hilda said:

'His acceptance was, I am afraid, all my doing – I misunderstood the situation.'

Poirot interposed. He said:

'Will you be so kind as to explain yourself a little more clearly, madame? I think what you can tell us may be of value.'

She turned to him immediately.

She said:

'At that time I had never seen my father-in-law. I had no idea what his real motive was. I assumed that he was old and lonely and that he really wanted to be reconciled to all his children.'

'And what was his real motive, in your opinion, madame?'

Hilda hesitated a moment. Then she said slowly:

'I have no doubt – no doubt at all – that what my father-in-law really wanted was not to promote peace but to stir up strife.'

'In what way?'

Hilda said in a low voice:

'It amused him to – to appeal to the worst instincts in human nature. There was – how can I put it? – a kind of diabolical impishness about him. He wished to set every member of the family at loggerheads with one another.'

Johnson said sharply: 'And did he succeed?'

'Oh, yes,' said Hilda Lee. 'He succeeded.'

Poirot said:

'We have been told, madame, of a scene that took place this afternoon. It was, I think, rather a violent scene.'

She bowed her head.

'Will you describe it to us – as truthfully as possible, if you please.'

She reflected a minute.

'When we went in my father-in-law was telephoning.'

'To his lawyer, I understand?'

'Yes, he was suggesting that Mr – was it Charlton? – I don't quite remember the name – should come over as he, my father-in-law, wanted to make a new will. His old one, he said, was quite out of date.'

Poirot said:

'Think carefully, madame; in your opinion did your father-in-law deliberately ensure that you should all overhear this conversation, or was it just by *chance* that you overheard it?'

Hilda Lee said:

'I am almost sure that he meant us to overhear.'

'With the object of fomenting doubt and suspicions among you?'

'Yes.'

'So that, really, he may not have meant to alter his will at all?'

She demurred.

'No, I think that part of it was quite genuine. He probably did wish to make a new will – but he enjoyed underlining the fact.'

'Madame,' said Poirot, 'I have no official standing and my questions, you understand, are not perhaps those that an English officer of the law would ask. But I have a great desire to know what form you think that new will would have taken. I am asking, you perceive, not for your knowledge, but simply for your opinion. *Les femmes*, they are never slow to form an opinion, *Dieu merci*.'

Hilda Lee smiled a little.

'I don't mind saying what I think. My husband's sister Jennifer married a Spaniard, Juan Estravados. Her daughter, Pilar, has just arrived here. She is a very lovely girl – and she is, of course, the only grandchild in the family. Old Mr Lee was delighted with her. He took a tremendous fancy to her. In my opinion, he wished to leave her a considerable sum in his new will. Probably he had only left her a small portion or even nothing at all in an old one.'

'Did you know your sister-in-law at all?'

'No, I never met her. Her Spanish husband died in tragic circumstances, I believe, soon after the marriage. Jennifer herself died a year ago. Pilar was left an orphan. This is why Mr Lee sent for her to come and live with him in England.'

'And the other members of the family, did they welcome her coming?'

Hilda said quietly:

'I think they all liked her. It was very pleasant to have someone young and alive in the house.'

'And she, did she seem to like being here?'

Hilda said slowly:

'I don't know. It must seem cold and strange to a girl brought up in the South – in Spain.'

Johnson said:

'Can't be very pleasant being in Spain just at present. Now, Mrs Lee, we'd like to hear your account of the conversation this afternoon.'

Poirot murmured:

'I apologize. I have made the digressions.'

Hilda Lee said:

'After my father-in-law finished telephoning, he looked round at us and laughed, and said we all looked very glum. Then he said he was tired and should go to bed early. Nobody was to come up and see him this evening. He said he wanted to be in good form for Christmas Day. Something like that.'

'Then –' Her brows knit in an effort of remembrance. 'I think he said something about its being necessary to be one of a large family to appreciate Christmas, and then he went on to speak of money. He said it would cost him more to run this house in future. He told George and Magdalene they would have to economize. Told her she ought to make her own clothes. Rather an old-fashioned idea, I'm afraid. I don't wonder it annoyed her. He said his own wife had been clever with her needle.'

Poirot said gently:

'Is that all that he said about her?'

Hilda flushed.

'He made a slighting reference to her brains. My husband was very devoted to his mother, and that upset him very much. And then, suddenly Mr Lee began shouting at us all. He worked himself up about it. I can understand, of course, how he felt –'

Poirot said gently, interrupting her:

'How did he feel?'

She turned her tranquil eyes upon him.

'He was disappointed, of course,' she said. 'Because there are no grandchildren – no boys, I mean – no Lees to carry on. I can see that that must have festered for a long time. And suddenly he couldn't keep it in any longer and vented his rage against his sons – saying they were a lot of namby-pamby old women – something like that. I felt sorry for him, then, because I realized how his pride was hurt by it.'

'And then?'

'And then,' said Hilda slowly, 'we all went away.'

'That was the last you saw of him?'

She bowed her head.

'Where were you at the time the crime occurred?'

'I was with my husband in the music-room. He was playing to me.'

'And then?'

'We heard tables and chairs overturned upstairs, and china being broken – some terrible struggle. And then that awful scream as his throat was cut . . .'

Poirot said:

'Was it such an awful scream? Was it' – he paused – '*like a soul in hell?*'

Hilda Lee said:

'It was worse than that!'

'What do you mean, madame?'

'It was like someone *who had no soul* . . . It was inhuman like a beast . . .'

Poirot said gravely:

'So – you have judged him, madame?'

She raised a hand in sudden distress. Her eyes fell and she stared down at the floor.

XIV

Pilar came into the room with the wariness of an animal who suspects a trap. Her eyes went quickly from side to side. She looked not so much afraid as deeply suspicious.

Colonel Johnson rose and put a chair for her. Then he said:

'You understand English, I suppose, Miss Estravados?'

Pilar's eyes opened wide. She said:

'Of course. My mother was English. I am really very English indeed.'

A faint smile came to Colonel Johnson's lips, as his eyes took in the black gloss of her hair, the proud dark eyes, and the curling red lips. Very English! An incongruous term to apply to Pilar Estravados.

He said:

'Mr Lee was your grandfather. He sent for you to come from Spain. And you arrived a few days ago. Is that right?'

Pilar nodded.

'That is right. I had – oh! a lot of adventures getting out of Spain – there was a bomb from the air and the chauffeur he was killed – where his head had been there was all blood. And I could not drive a car, so for a long way I had to walk – and I do not like walking. I never walk. My feet were sore – but sore –'

Colonel Johnson smiled. He said:

'At any rate you arrived here. Had your mother spoken to you of your grandfather much?'

Pilar nodded cheerfully.

'Oh, yes, she said he was an old devil.'

Hercule Poirot smiled. He said:

'And what did you think of him when you arrived, mademoiselle?'

Pilar said:

'Of course he was very, very old. He had to sit in a chair – and his face was all dried up. But I liked him all the same. I think that when he was a young man, he must have been handsome – very handsome, like you,' said Pilar to Superintendent Sugden. Her eyes dwelt with naïve pleasure on his handsome face, which had turned brick-red at the compliment.

Colonel Johnson stifled a chuckle. It was one of the few occasions when he had seen the stolid superintendent taken aback.

'But of course,' Pilar continued regretfully, 'he could never have been so big as you.'

Hercule Poirot sighed.

'You like, then, big men, señorita?' he inquired.

Pilar agreed enthusiastically.

'Oh, yes, I like a man to be very big, tall, and the shoulders broad, and very, very strong.'

Colonel Johnson said sharply:

'Did you see much of your grandfather when you arrived here?'

Pilar said:

'Oh, yes. I went to sit with him. He told me things – that he had been a very wicked man, and all the things he did in South Africa.'

'Did he ever tell you that he had diamonds in the safe in his room?'

'Yes, he showed them to me. But they were not like diamonds – they were just like pebbles – very ugly – very ugly indeed.'

Superintendent Sugden said shortly:

'So he showed them to you, did he?'

'Yes.'

'He didn't give you any of them?'

Pilar shook her head.

'No, he did not. I thought that perhaps one day he would – if I were very nice to him and came often to sit with him. Because old gentlemen they like very much young girls.'

Colonel Johnson said:

'Do you know that those diamonds have been stolen?'

Pilar opened her eyes very wide.

'Stolen?'

'Yes, have you any idea who might have taken them?'

Pilar nodded her head.

'Oh, yes,' she said. 'It would be Horbury.'

'Horbury? You mean the valet?'

'Yes.'

'Why do you think that?'

'Because he has the face of a thief. His eyes go so, from side to side, he walks softly and listens at doors. He is like a cat. And all cats are thieves.'

'H'm,' said Colonel Johnson. 'We'll leave it at that. Now I understand that all the family were up in your grandfather's room this afternoon, and that some – er – angry words passed.'

Pilar nodded and smiled.

'Yes,' she said. 'It was great fun. Grandfather made them oh! so angry!'

'Oh, you enjoyed it, did you?'

'Yes. I like to see people get angry. I like it very much. But here in England they do not get angry like they do in Spain. In Spain they take out their knives and they curse and shout. In England they do nothing, just get very red in the face and shut up their mouths tight.'

'Do you remember what was said?'

Pilar seemed rather doubtful.

'I am not sure. Grandfather said they were no good – that they had not got any children. He said I was better than any of them. He liked me, very much.'

'Did he say anything about money or a will?'

'A will – no, I don't think so. I don't remember.'

'What happened?'

'They all went away – except Hilda – the fat one, David's wife, she stayed behind.'

'Oh, she did, did she?'

'Yes. David looked very funny. He was all shaking and oh! so white. He looked as though he might be sick.'

'And what then?'

'Then I went and found Stephen. We danced to the gramophone.'

'Stephen Farr?'

'Yes. He is from South Africa – he is the son of Grandfather's partner. He is very handsome too. Very brown and big, and he has nice eyes.'

Johnson asked:

'Where were you when the crime occurred?'

'You ask where I was?'

'Yes.'

'I had gone into the drawing-room with Lydia. And then I went up to my room and did my face. I was going to dance again with Stephen. And then, far away, I heard a scream and everyone was running, so I went too. And they were trying to break down Grandfather's door. Harry did it with Stephen, they are both big strong men.'

'Yes?'

'And then – crash – down it went – and we all looked in. Oh, such a sight – everything smashed and knocked over, and Grandfather lying in a lot of blood, and his throat was cut like *this*' – she made a vivid dramatic gesture at her own neck – 'right up under his ear.'

She paused, having obviously enjoyed her narrative.

Johnson said:

'The blood didn't make you feel ill?'

She stared.

'No, why should it? There is usually blood when people are killed. There was, oh! so much blood everywhere!'

Poirot said: 'Did anyone say anything?'

Pilar said:

'David said such a funny thing – what was it? Oh, yes. The mills of God – that is what he said' – she repeated it with emphasis on each word – '*The mills – of – God* – What does that mean? Mills are what make flour, are they not?'

Colonel Johnson said:

'Well, I don't think there is anything more just now, Miss Estravados.'

Pilar got up obediently. She flashed a quick charming smile at each man in turn.

'I will go now, then.' She went out.

Colonel Johnson said:

'*The mills of God grind slowly, but they grind exceeding small.* And David Lee said that!'

XV

As the door opened once more, Colonel Johnson looked up. For a moment he took the entering figure to be that of Harry Lee, but as Stephen Farr advanced into the room he saw his error.

'Sit down, Mr Farr,' he said.

Stephen sat. His eyes, cool, intelligent eyes, went from one to the other of the three men. He said:

'I'm afraid I shan't be much use to you. But please ask me anything that you think may help. Perhaps I'd better explain, to start with, who I am. My father, Ebenezer Farr, was Simeon Lee's partner in South Africa in the old days. I'm talking of over forty years ago.'

He paused.

'My dad talked to me a lot about Simeon Lee – what a personality he was. He and Dad cleaned up a good bit together. Simeon Lee went home with a fortune and my father didn't do badly either. My father always told me that when I came to this country I was to look up Mr Lee. I said once that it was a long time ago and that he'd probably not know who I was, but Dad scoffed at the idea. He said, "When two men have been through what

Simeon and I went through, they don't forget." Well, my father died a couple of years ago. This year I came over to England for the first time, and I thought I'd act on Dad's advice and look up Mr Lee.'

With a slight smile he went on:

'I was just a little nervous when I came along here, but I needn't have been. Mr Lee gave me a warm welcome and absolutely insisted that I should stay with the family over Christmas. I was afraid I was butting in, but he wouldn't hear of a refusal.'

He added rather shyly:

'They were all very nice to me – Mr and Mrs Alfred Lee couldn't have been nicer. I'm terribly sorry for them that all this should come upon them.'

'How long have you been here, Mr Farr?'

'Since yesterday.'

'Did you see Mr Lee today at all?'

'Yes, I had a chat with him this morning. He was in good spirits then and anxious to hear about a lot of people and places.'

'That was the last time you saw him?'

'Yes.'

'Did he mention to you that he kept a quantity of uncut diamonds in his safe?'

'No.'

He added before the other could speak:

'Do you mean that this business was murder and robbery?'

'We're not sure yet,' said Johnson. 'Now to come to the events of this evening, will you tell me, in your own words, what you were doing?'

'Certainly. After the ladies left the dining-room I stayed and had a glass of port. Then I realized that the Lees had family business they wanted to discuss and that my being there was hampering them so I excused myself and left them.'

'And what did you do then?'

Stephen Farr leaned back in his chair. His forefinger caressed his jaw. He said rather woodenly:

'I – er – went along to a big room with a parquet floor – a kind of ballroom, I fancy. There's a gramophone there and dance records. I put some records on.'

Poirot said:

'It was possible, perhaps, that someone might join you there?'

A very faint smile curved Stephen Farr's lips. He answered:

'It was possible, yes. One always hopes.'

And he grinned outright.

Poirot said:

'Señorita Estravados is very beautiful.'

Stephen answered:

'She's easily the best thing to look at that I've seen since I came to England.'

'Did Miss Estravados join you?' asked Colonel Johnson.

Stephen shook his head.

'I was still there when I heard the rumpus. I came out into the hall and ran hell for leather to see what was the matter. I helped Harry Lee to break the door down.'

'And that's all you have to tell us?'

'Absolutely all, I'm afraid.'

Hercule Poirot leaned forward. He said softly:

'But I think, Monsieur Farr, that you could tell us a good deal if you liked.'

Farr said sharply:

'What d'you mean?'

'You can tell us something that is very important in this case – the character of Mr Lee. You say that your father talked much of him to you. What manner of a man was it that he described to you?'

Stephen Farr said slowly:

'I think I see what you're driving at. What was Simeon Lee like in his young days? Well – you want me to be frank, I suppose?'

'If you please.'

'Well, to begin with, I don't think that Simeon Lee was a highly moral member of society. I don't mean that he was exactly a crook, but he sailed pretty near the wind. His morals were nothing to boast about anyway. He had charm, though, a good deal of it. And he was fantastically generous. No one with a hard-luck story ever appealed to him in vain. He drank a bit, but not over-much, was attractive to women, and had a sense of humour. All the same, he had a queer revengeful streak in him. Talk of the elephant never forgets and you talk of Simeon Lee.

My father told me of several cases where Lee waited years to get even with someone who'd done him a nasty turn.'

Superintendent Sugden said:

'Two might play at that game. You've no knowledge, I suppose, Mr Farr, of anyone who Simeon Lee had done a bad turn to out there? Nothing out of the past that could explain the crime committed here this evening?'

Stephen Farr shook his head.

'He had enemies, of course, must have had, being the man he was. But I know of no specific case. Besides,' his eyes narrowed, 'I understand (as a matter of fact, I've been questioning Tressilian) there have been no strangers in or near the house this evening.'

Hercule Poirot said:

'*With the exception of yourself, M. Farr.*'

Stephen Farr swung round upon him.

'Oh, so that's it? Suspicious stranger within the gates! Well, you won't find anything of that kind. No back history of Simeon Lee doing Ebenezer Farr down, and Eb's son coming over to revenge his dad! No,' he shook his head. 'Simeon and Ebenezer had nothing against each other. I came here, as I've told you, out of sheer curiosity. And moreover, I should imagine a gramophone is as good an alibi as anything else. I never stopped putting on records – somebody must have heard them. One record wouldn't give me time to race away upstairs – these passages are a mile long, anyway – slit an old man's throat, wash off the blood, and get back again before the others came rushing up. The idea's farcical!'

Colonel Johnson said:

'We're not making any insinuations against you, Mr Farr.'

Stephen Farr said:

'I didn't care much for the tone of Mr Hercule Poirot's voice.'

'That,' said Hercule Poirot, 'is unfortunate!'

He smiled benignly at the other.

Stephen Farr looked angrily at him.

Colonel Johnson interposed quickly:

'Thank you, Mr Farr. That will be all for the present. You will, of course, not leave this house.'

Stephen Farr nodded. He got up and left the room, walking with a freely swinging stride.

As the door closed behind him, Johnson said:

'There goes X, the unknown quantity. His story seems straightforward enough. All the same, he's the dark horse. He *might* have pinched those diamonds – might have come here with a bogus story just to gain admittance. You'd better get his fingerprints, Sugden, and see if he's known.'

'I've already got them,' said the superintendent with a dry smile.

'Good man. You don't overlook much. I suppose you're on to all the obvious lines?'

Superintendent Sugden checked off on his fingers.

'Check up on those telephone calls – times, etc. Check up on Horbury. What time he left, who saw him go. Check up all entrances and exits. Check up on staff generally. Check up financial position of members of family. Get on to the lawyers and check up on will. Search house for the weapon and for bloodstains on clothing – also possibly diamonds hidden somewhere.'

'That covers everything, I think,' said Colonel Johnson approvingly. 'Can you suggest anything, M. Poirot?'

Poirot shook his head. He said:

'I find the superintendent admirably thorough.'

Sugden said gloomily:

'It won't be any joke looking through this house for the missing diamonds. Never saw so many ornaments and knick-knacks in my life.'

'The hiding-places are certainly abundant,' Poirot agreed.

'And there's really nothing you would suggest, Poirot?'

The chief constable looked a little disappointed – rather like a man whose dog has refused to do its trick.

Poirot said:

'You will permit that I take a line of my own?'

'Certainly – certainly,' said Johnson at the same moment as Superintendent Sugden said rather suspiciously:

'What line?'

'I would like,' said Hercule Poirot, 'to converse – very often – very frequently – with members of the family.'

'You mean you'd like to have another shot at questioning

them?' asked the colonel, a little puzzled.

'No, no, not to question – to converse!'

'Why?' asked Sugden.

Hercule Poirot waved an emphatic hand.

'In conversation, points arise! If a human being converses much, it is impossible for him to avoid the truth!'

Sugden said:

'Then you think someone is lying?'

Poirot sighed.

'*Mon cher*, everyone lies – in parts like the egg of the English curate. It is profitable to separate the harmless lies from the vital ones.'

Colonel Johnson said sharply:

'All the same, it's incredible, you know. Here's a particularly crude and brutal murder – and whom have we as suspects? Alfred Lee and his wife – both charming, well-bred, quiet people. George Lee, who's a Member of Parliament and the essence of respectability. His wife? She's just an ordinary modern lovely. David Lee seems a gentle creature and we've got his brother Harry's word for it that he can't stand the sight of blood. His wife seems a nice sensible woman – quite commonplace. Remains the Spanish niece and the man from South Africa. Spanish beauties have hot tempers, but I don't see that attractive creature slitting the old man's neck in cold blood, especially as from what has come out she had every reason to keep him alive – at any rate until he had signed a new will. Stephen Farr's a possibility – that is to say, he may be a professional crook and have come here after the diamonds. The old man discovered the loss and Farr slit his throat to keep him quiet. That could have been so – that gramophone alibi isn't too good.'

Poirot shook his head.

'My dear friend,' he said. 'Compare the physique of M. Stephen Farr and old Simeon Lee. If Farr decided to kill the old man he could have done it in a minute – Simeon Lee couldn't possibly have put up that fight against him. Can one believe that that frail old man and that magnificent specimen of humanity struggled for some minutes overturning chairs and breaking china? To imagine such a thing is fantastic!'

Colonel Johnson's eyes narrowed.

'You mean,' he said, 'that it was a *weak* man who killed Simeon Lee?'

'Or a woman!' said the superintendent.

XVI

Colonel Johnson looked at his watch.

'Nothing much more that I can do here. You've got things well in hand, Sugden. Oh, just one thing. We ought to see the butler fellow. I know you've questioned him, but we know a bit more about things now. It's important to get confirmation of just where everybody says he was at the time of the murder.'

Tressilian came in slowly. The chief constable told him to sit down.

'Thank you, sir. I will, if you don't mind. I've been feeling very queer – very queer indeed. My legs, sir, and my head.'

Poirot said gently: 'You have had the shock, yes.'

The butler shuddered. 'Such – such a violent thing to happen. In this house! Where everything has always gone on so quietly.'

Poirot said:

'It was a well-ordered house, yes? But not a happy one?'

'I wouldn't like to say that, sir.'

'In the old days when all the family was at home, it was happy then?'

Tressilian said slowly:

'It wasn't perhaps what one would call very harmonious, sir.'

'The late Mrs Lee was somewhat of an invalid, was she not?'

'Yes, sir, very poorly she was.'

'Were her children fond of her?'

'Mr David, he was devoted to her. More like a daughter than a son. And after she died he broke away, couldn't face living here any longer.'

Poirot said: 'And Mr Harry? What was he like?'

'Always rather a wild young gentleman, sir, but good-hearted. Oh, dear, gave me quite a turn, it did, when the bell rang – and then again, so impatient like, and I opened the door and there was a strange man, and then Mr Harry's voice said, "Hallo, Tressilian. Still here, eh?" Just the same as ever.'

Poirot said sympathetically:

'It must have been the strange feeling, yes, indeed.'

Tressilian said, a little pink flush showing in his cheek:

'It seems sometimes, sir, as though the past isn't the past! I believe there's been a play on in London about something like that. There's something in it, sir – there really is. There's a feeling comes over you – as though you'd done everything before. It just seems to me as though the bell rings and I go to answer it and there's Mr Harry – even if it should be Mr Farr or some other person – I'm just saying to myself – *but I've done this before . . .*'

Poirot said:

'That is very interesting – very interesting.'

Tressilian looked at him gratefully.

Johnson, somewhat impatient, cleared his throat and took charge of the conversation.

'Just want to get various times checked correctly,' he said. 'Now, when the noise upstairs started, I understand that only Mr Alfred Lee and Mr Harry Lee were in the dining-room. Is that so?'

'I really couldn't tell you, sir. All the gentlemen were there when I served coffee to them – but that would be about a quarter of an hour earlier.'

'Mr George Lee was telephoning. Can you confirm that?'

'I think somebody did telephone, sir. The bell rings in my pantry, and when anybody takes off the receiver to call a number, there's just a faint noise on the bell. I do remember hearing that, but I didn't pay attention to it.'

'You don't know exactly when it was?'

'I couldn't say, sir. It was after I had taken coffee to the gentlemen, that is all I can say.'

'Do you know where any of the ladies were at the time I mentioned?'

'Mrs Alfred was in the drawing-room, sir, when I went for the coffee tray. That was just a minute or two before I heard the cry upstairs.'

Poirot asked:

'What was she doing?'

'She was standing by the far window, sir. She was holding the curtain a little back and looking out.'

'And none of the other ladies were in the room?'

'No, sir.'

'Do you know where they were?'

'I couldn't say at all, sir.'

'You don't know where anyone else was?'

'Mr David, I think, was playing in the music-room next door to the drawing-room.'

'You heard him playing?'

'Yes, sir.' Again the old man shivered. 'It was like a sign, sir, so I felt afterwards. It was the "Dead March" he was playing. Even at the time, I remember, it gave me the creeps.'

'It is curious, yes,' said Poirot.

'Now, about this fellow, Horbury, the valet,' said the chief constable. 'Are you definitely prepared to swear that he was out of the house by eight o'clock?'

'Oh yes, sir. It was just after Mr Sugden here arrived. I remember particular because he broke a coffee-cup.'

Poirot said:

'Horbury broke a coffee-cup?'

'Yes, sir – one of the old Worcester ones. Eleven years I've washed them up and never one broken till this evening.'

Poirot said:

'What was Horbury doing with the coffee-cups?'

'Well, of course, sir, he'd no business to have been handling them at all. He was just holding one up, admiring it like, and I happened to mention that Mr Sugden had called, and he dropped it.'

Poirot said:

'Did you say "Mr Sugden" or did you mention the word police?'

Tressilian looked a little startled.

'Now I come to think of it, sir, I mentioned that the police superintendent had called.'

'And Horbury dropped the coffee-cup,' said Poirot.

'Seems suggestive, that,' said the chief constable. 'Did Horbury ask any questions about the superintendent's visit?'

'Yes, sir, asked what he wanted here. I said he'd come collecting for the Police Orphanage and had gone up to Mr Lee.'

'Did Horbury seemed relieved when you said that?'

'Do you know, sir, now you mention it, he certainly did. His manner changed at once. Said Mr Lee was a good old chap and free with his money – rather disrespectfully he spoke – and then he went off.'

'Which way?'

'Out through the door to the servants' hall.'

Sugden interposed:

'All that's O.K., sir. He passed through the kitchen, where the cook and the kitchenmaid saw him, and out through the back door.'

'Now listen, Tressilian, and think carefully. Is there any means by which Horbury could return to the house without anyone seeing him?'

The old man shook his head.

'I don't see how he could have done so, sir. All the doors are locked on the inside.'

'Supposing he had had a key?'

'The doors are bolted as well.'

'How does he get in when he comes?'

'He has a key of the back door, sir. All the servants come in that way.'

'He *could* have returned that way, then?'

'Not without passing through the kitchen, sir. And the kitchen would be occupied till well after half-past nine or a quarter to ten.'

Colonel Johnson said:

'That seems conclusive. Thank you, Tressilian.'

The old man got up and with a bow left the room. He returned, however, a minute or two later.

'Horbury has just returned, sir. Would you like to see him now?'

'Yes, please, send him in at once.'

XVII

Sydney Horbury did not present a very prepossessing appearance. He came into the room and stood rubbing his hands together and darting quick looks from one person to another. His manner was unctuous.

Johnson said:

'You're Sydney Horbury?'

'Yes, sir.'

'Valet attendant to the late Mr Lee?'

'Yes, sir. It's terrible, isn't it? You could have knocked me down with a feather when I heard from Gladys. Poor old gentleman –'

Johnson cut him short.

'Just answer my questions, please.'

'Yes, sir, certainly, sir.'

'What time did you go out tonight, and where have you been?'

'I left the house just before eight, sir. I went to the Superb, sir, just five minutes' walk away. *Love in Old Seville* was the picture, sir.'

'Anyone who saw you there?'

'The young lady in the box office, sir, she knows me. And the commissionaire at the door, he knows me too. And – er – as a matter of fact, I was with a young lady, sir. I met her there by appointment.'

'Oh, you did, did you? What's her name?'

'Doris Buckle, sir. She works in the Combined Dairies, sir, 23, Markham Road.'

'Good. We'll look into that. Did you come straight home?'

'I saw my young lady home first, sir. Then I came straight back. You'll find it's quite all right, sir. I didn't have anything to do with this. I was –'

Colonel Johnson said curtly:

'Nobody's accusing you of having anything to do with it.'

'No, sir, of course not, sir. But it's not very pleasant when a murder happens in a house.'

'Nobody said it was. Now, then, how long had you been in Mr Lee's service?'

'Just over a year, sir.'

'Did you like your place here?'

'Yes, sir. I was quite satisfied. The pay was good. Mr Lee was rather difficult sometimes, but of course I'm used to attending on invalids.'

'You've had previous experience?'

'Oh, yes, sir. I was with Major West and with the Honourable Jasper Finch –'

'You can give all those particulars to Sugden later. What I want to know is this: At what time did you last see Mr Lee this evening?'

'It was about half-past seven, sir. Mr Lee had a light supper brought to him every evening at seven o'clock. I then prepared him for bed. After that he would sit in front of the fire in his dressing-gown till he felt like going to bed.'

'What time was that usually?'

'It varied, sir. Sometimes hc would go to bed as early as eight o'clock – that's if he felt tired. Sometimes he would sit up till eleven or after.'

'What did he do when he did want to go to bed?'

'Usually he rang for me, sir.'

'And you assisted him to bed?'

'Yes, sir.'

'But this was your evening out. Did you always have Fridays?'

'Yes, sir. Friday was my regular day.'

'What happened then when Mr Lee wanted to go to bed?'

'He would ring his bell and either Tressilian or Walter would see to him.'

'He was not helpless? He could move about?'

'Yes, sir, but not very easily. Rheumatoid arthritis was what he suffered from, sir. He was worse some days than others.'

'Did he never go into another room in the daytime?'

'No, sir. He preferred to be in just the one room. Mr Lee wasn't luxurious in his tastes. It was a big room with plenty of air and light in it.'

'Mr Lee had his supper at seven, you say?'

'Yes, sir. I took the tray away and put out the sherry and two glasses on the bureau.'

'Why did you do that?'

'Mr Lee's orders.'

'Was that usual?'

'Sometimes. It was the rule that none of the family came to see Mr Lee in the evening unless he invited them. Some evenings he liked to be alone. Other evenings he'd send down and ask Mr Alfred, or Mrs Alfred, or both of them, to come up after dinner.'

'But, as far as you know, he had not done so on this occasion? That is, he had not sent a message to any member of the family requesting their presence?'

'He hadn't sent any message by *me*, sir.'

'So that he wasn't expecting any of the family?'

'He might have asked one of them personally, sir.'

'Of course.'

Horbury continued:

'I saw that everything was in order, wished Mr Lee goodnight and left the room.'

Poirot asked:

'Did you make up the fire before you left the room?'

The valet hesitated.

'It wasn't necessary, sir. It was well built up.'

'Could Mr Lee have done that himself?'

'Oh no, sir. I expect Mr Harry Lee had done it.'

'Mr Harry Lee was with him when you came in before supper?'

'Yes, sir. He went away when I came.'

'What was the relationship between the two as far as you could judge?'

'Mr Harry Lee seemed in very good spirits, sir. Throwing back his head and laughing a good deal.'

'And Mr Lee?'

'He was quiet and rather thoughtful.'

'I see. Now, there's something more I want to know, Horbury: What can you tell us about the diamonds Mr Lee kept in his safe?'

'Diamonds, sir? I never saw any diamonds.'

'Mr Lee kept a quantity of uncut stones there. You must have seen him handling them.'

'Those funny little pebbles, sir? Yes, I did see him with them once or twice. But I didn't know they were diamonds. He was showing them to the foreign young lady only yesterday – or was it the day before?'

Colonel Johnson said abruptly:

'These stones have been stolen.'

Horbury cried out:

'I hope you don't think, sir, that *I* had anything to do with it!'

'I'm not making any accusations,' said Johnson. 'Now then, is there anything you can tell us that has any bearing on this matter?'

'The diamonds, sir? Or the murder?'

'Both.'

'Horbury considered. He passed his tongue over his pale lips. At last he looked up with eyes that were a shade furtive.

'I don't think there's anything, sir.'

Poirot said softly:

'Nothing you've overheard, say, in the course of your duties, which might be helpful?'

The valet's eyelids flickered a little.

'No, sir, I don't think so, sir. There was a little awkwardness between Mr Lee and – and some members of his family.'

'Which members?'

'I gathered there was a little trouble over Mr Harry Lee's return. Mr Alfred Lee resented it. I understand he and his father had a few words about it – but that was all there was to it. Mr Lee didn't accuse him for a minute of having taken any diamonds. And I'm sure Mr Alfred wouldn't do such a thing.'

Poirot said quickly:

'His interview with Mr Alfred was *after* he had discovered the loss of the diamonds, was it not, though?'

'Yes, sir.'

Poirot leaned forward.

'I thought, Horbury,' he said softly, '*that you did not know of the theft of the diamonds until we informed you of it just now*. How, then, do you know that Mr Lee had discovered his loss *before* he had this conversation with his son?'

Horbury turned brick-red.

'No use lying. Out with it,' said Sugden. 'When did you know?'

Horbury said sullenly:

'I heard him telephoning to someone about it.'

'You weren't in the room?'

'No, outside the door. Couldn't hear much – only a word or two.'

'What did you hear exactly?' asked Poirot sweetly.

'I heard the words robbery and diamonds, and I heard him say, "I don't know who to suspect" – and I heard him say something about this evening at eight o'clock.'

Superintendent Sugden nodded.

'That was to me he was speaking, my lad. About five-ten, was it?'

'That's right, sir.'

'And when you went into his room afterwards, did he look upset?'

'Just a bit, sir. Seemed absent-minded and worried.'

'So much so that you got the wind up – eh?'

'Look here, Mr Sugden, I won't have you saying things like that. Never touched any diamonds, I didn't, and you can't prove I did. I'm not a thief.'

Superintendent Sugden, unimpressed, said:

'That remains to be seen.' He glanced questioningly at the chief constable, received a nod, and went on: 'That'll do for you, my lad. Shan't want you again tonight.'

Horbury went out gratefully in haste.

Sugden said appreciatively:

'Pretty bit of work, M. Poirot. You trapped him as neatly as I've ever seen it done. He may be a thief or he may not, but he's certainly a first-class liar!'

'An unprepossessing person,' said Poirot.

'Nasty bit of goods,' agreed Johnson. 'Question is, what do we think of his evidence?'

Sugden summarized the position neatly.

'Seems to me there are three possibilities: (1) Horbury's a thief *and* a murderer. (2) Horbury's a thief, but *not* a murderer. (3) Horbury's an innocent man. Certain amount of evidence for (1). He overheard telephone call and knew the theft had been discovered. Gathered from old man's manner that he was suspected. Made his plans accordingly. Went out ostentatiously at eight o'clock and cooked up an alibi. Easy enough to slip out of a cinema and return there unnoticed. He'd have to be pretty sure of the girl, though, that she wouldn't give him away. I'll see what I can get out of her tomorrow.'

'How, then, did he manage to re-enter the house?' asked Poirot.

'That's more difficult,' Sugden admitted. 'But there might be ways. Say one of the women servants unlocked a side door for him.'

Poirot raised his eyebrows quizzically.

'He places, then, his life at the mercy of two women? With *one* woman it would be taking a big risk; with *two* – *eh bien*, I find the risk fantastic!'

Sugden said:

'Some criminals think they can get away with anything!'

He went on:

'Let's take (2). Horbury pinched those diamonds. He took 'em out of the house tonight and has possibly passed them on to some accomplice. That's quite easy going and highly probable. Now we've got to admit that somebody else chose this night to murder Mr Lee. That somebody being quite unaware of the diamond complication. It's possible, of course, but it's a bit of a coincidence.

'Possibility (3) – Horbury's innocent. Somebody else both took the diamonds and murdered the old gentleman. There it is; it's up to us to get at the truth.'

Colonel Johnson yawned. He looked again at his watch and got up.

'Well,' he said, 'I think we'll call it a night, eh? Better just have a look in the safe before we go. Odd thing if those wretched diamonds were there all the time.'

But the diamonds were not in the safe. They found the combination where Alfred Lee had told them, in the small note-book taken from the dressing-gown pocket of the dead man. In the safe they found an empty chamois-leather bag. Among the papers the safe contained only one was of interest.

It was a will dated some fifteen years previously. After various legacies and bequests, the provisions were simple enough. Half Simeon Lee's fortune went to Alfred Lee. The other half was to be divided in equal shares between his remaining children: Harry, George, David and Jennifer.

PART 4

DECEMBER 25TH

I

In the bright sun of Christmas noon, Poirot walked in the gardens of Gorston Hall. The Hall itself was a large solidly built house with no special architectural pretensions.

Here, on the south side, was a broad terrace flanked with a hedge of clipped yew. Little plants grew in the interstices of the stone flags and at intervals along the terrace there were stone sinks arranged as miniature gardens.

Poirot surveyed them with benign approval. He murmured to himself:

'*C'est bien imaginé, ça!*'

In the distance he caught sight of two figures going towards an ornamental sheet of water some three hundred yards away. Pilar was easily recognizable as one of the figures, and he thought at first the other was Stephen Farr, then he saw that the man with Pilar was Harry Lee. Harry seemed very attentive to his attractive niece. At intervals he flung his head back and laughed, then bent once more attentively towards her.

'Assuredly, there is one who does not mourn,' Poirot murmured to himself.

A soft sound behind him made him turn. Magdalene Lee was standing there. She, too, was looking at the retreating figures of the man and girl. She turned her head and smiled enchantingly at Poirot. She said:

'It's such a glorious sunny day! One can hardly believe in all the horrors of last night, can one, M. Poirot?'

'It is difficult, truly, madame.'

Magdalene sighed.

'I've never been mixed up in tragedy before. I've – I've really only just grown up. I stayed a child too long, I think – That's not a good thing to do.'

Again she sighed. She said:

'Pilar, now, seems so extraordinarily self-possessed – I suppose it's the Spanish blood. It's all very odd, isn't it?'

'What is odd, madame?'

'The way she turned up here, out of the blue!'

Poirot said:

'I have learned that Mr Lee had been searching for her for some time. He had been in correspondence with the Consulate in Madrid and with the vice-consul at Aliquara, where her mother died.'

'He was very secretive about it all,' said Magdalene. 'Alfred knew nothing about it. No more did Lydia.'

'Ah!' said Poirot.

Magdalene came a little nearer to him. He could smell the delicate perfume she used.

'You know, M. Poirot, there's some story connected with Jennifer's husband, Estravados. He died quite soon after the marriage, and there's some mystery about it. Alfred and Lydia know. I believe it was something – rather disgraceful . . .'

'That,' said Poirot, 'is indeed sad.'

Magdalene said:

'My husband feels – and I agree with him – that the family ought to have been told more about the girl's antecedents. After all, if her father was a *criminal* –'

She paused, but Hercule Poirot said nothing. He seemed to be admiring such beauties of nature as could be seen in the winter season in the grounds of Gorston Hall.

Magdalene said:

'I can't help feeling that the manner of my father-in-law's death was somehow *significant*. It – it was so very *unEnglish*.'

Hercule Poirot turned slowly. His grave eyes met hers in innocent inquiry.

'Ah,' he said. 'The Spanish touch, you think?'

'Well, they *are* cruel, aren't they?' Magdalene spoke with an effect of childish appeal. 'All those bull fights and things!'

Hercule Poirot said pleasantly:

'You are saying that in your opinion Señorita Estravados cut her grandfather's throat?'

'Oh no, M. Poirot!' Magdalene was vehement. She was

shocked. 'I never said anything of the kind! Indeed I didn't!'

'Well,' said Poirot. 'Perhaps you did not.'

'But I *do* think that she is – well, a suspicious person. The furtive way she picked up something from the floor of that room last night, for instance.'

A different note crept into Hercule Poirot's voice. He said sharply:

'She picked up something from the floor last night?'

Magdalene nodded. Her childish mouth curved spitefully.

'Yes, as soon as we got into the room. She gave a quick glance round to see if anyone was looking, and then pounced on it. But the superintendent man saw her, I'm glad to say, and made her give it up.'

'What was it that she picked up, do you know, madame?'

'No. I wasn't near enough to see.' Magdalene's voice held regret. 'It was something quite small.'

Poirot frowned to himself.

'It is interesting, that,' he murmured to himself.

Magdalene said quickly:

'Yes, I thought you ought to know about it. After all, we don't know *anything* about Pilar's upbringing and what her life has been like. Alfred is always so suspicious and dear Lydia is so casual.' Then she murmured: 'Perhaps I'd better go and see if I can help Lydia in any way. There may be letters to write.'

She left him with a smile of satisfied malice on her lips.

Poirot remained lost in thought on the terrace.

II

To him there came Superintendent Sugden. The police superintendent looked gloomy. He said:

'Good morning, Mr Poirot. Doesn't seem quite the right thing to say Merry Christmas, does it?'

'*Mon cher collègue*, I certainly do not observe any traces of merriment on your countenance. If you had said Merry Christmas I should not have replied "Many of them!"'

'I don't want another one like this one, and that's a fact,' said Sugden.

'You have made the progress, yes?'

'I've checked up on a good many points. Horbury's alibi is

holding water all right. The commissionaire at the cinema saw him go in with the girl, and saw him come out with her at the end of the performance, and seems pretty positive he didn't leave, and couldn't have left and returned during the performance. The girl swears quite definitely he was with her in the cinema all the time.'

Poirot's eyebrows rose.

'I hardly see, then, what more there is to say.'

The cynical Sugden said:

'Well, one never knows with girls! Lie themselves black in the face for the sake of a man.'

'That does credit to their hearts,' said Hercule Poirot.

Sugden growled.

'That's a foreign way of looking at it. It's defeating the ends of justice.'

Hercule Poirot said:

'Justice is a very strange thing. Have you ever reflected on it?'

Sugden stared at him. He said:

'You're a queer one, Mr Poirot.'

'Not at all. I follow a logical train of thought. But we will not enter into a dispute on the question. It is your belief, then, that this demoiselle from the milk shop is not speaking the truth?'

Sugden shook his head.

'No,' he said, 'it's not like that at all. As a matter of fact, I think she *is* telling the truth. She's a simple kind of girl, and I think if she was telling me a pack of lies I'd spot it.'

Poirot said:

'You have the experience, yes?'

'That's just it, Mr Poirot. One does know, more or less, after a lifetime of taking down statements, when a person's lying and when they're not. No, I think the girl's evidence is genuine, and if so, Horbury *couldn't* have murdered old Mr Lee, and that brings us right back to the people in the house.'

He drew a deep breath.

'One of 'em did it, Mr Poirot. One of 'em did it. But *which*?'

'You have no new data?'

'Yes, I've had a certain amount of luck over the telephone calls. Mr George Lee put through a call to Westeringham at two minutes to nine. That call lasted under six minutes.'

'Aha!'

'As you say! Moreover, *no other call* was put through – to Westeringham or anywhere else.'

'Very interesting,' said Poirot, with approval. 'M. George Lee says he has just finished telephoning when he hears the noise overhead – but actually he had finished telephoning nearly *ten minutes before that.* Where was he in those ten minutes? Mrs George Lee says that *she* was telephoning – but actually she never put through a call at all. Where was *she*?'

Sugden said:

'I saw you talking to her, M. Poirot?'

His voice held a question, but Poirot replied:

'You are in error!'

'Eh?'

'*I* was not talking to *her* – she was talking to *me*!'

'Oh –' Sugden seemed to be about to brush the distinction aside impatiently; then, as its significance sank in, he said:

'*She* was talking to *you*, you say?'

'Most definitely. She came out here for that purpose.'

'What did she have to say?'

'She wished to stress certain points: the unEnglish character of the crime – the possibly undesirable antecedents of Miss Estravados on the paternal side – the fact that Miss Estravados had furtively picked up something from the floor last night.'

'She told you that, did she?' said Sugden with interest.

'Yes. What was it that the señorita picked up?'

Sugden sighed.

'I could give you three hundred guesses! I'll show it to you. It's the sort of thing that solves the whole mystery in detective stories! If you can make anything out of it, I'll retire from the police force!'

'Show it me.'

Sugden took an envelope from his pocket and tilted its contents on to the palm of his hand. A faint grin showed on his face.

'There you are. What do you make of it?'

On the superintendent's broad palm lay a little triangular piece of pink rubber and a small wooden peg.

His grin broadened as Poirot picked up the articles and frowned over them.

'Make anything of them, Mr Poirot?'

'This little piece of stuff might have been cut from a spongebag?'

'It was. It comes from a spongebag in Mr Lee's room. Somebody with sharp scissors just cut a small triangular piece out of it. Mr Lee may have done it himself, for all I know. But it beats me *why* he should do it. Horbury can't throw any light on the matter. As for the peg, it's about the size of a cribbage peg, but they're usually made of ivory. This is just rough wood – whittled out of a bit of deal, I should say.'

'Most remarkable,' murmured Poirot.

'Keep 'em if you like,' said Sugden kindly. '*I* don't want them.'

'*Mon ami*, I would not deprive you of them!'

'They don't mean anything at all to you?'

'I must confess – nothing whatever!'

'Splendid!' said Sugden with heavy sarcasm, returning them to his pocket. 'We *are* getting on!'

Poirot said:

'Mrs George Lee, she recounts that the young lady stooped and picked these bagatelles up in a furtive manner. Should you say that that was true?'

Sugden considered the point.

'N-o,' he said hesitatingly. 'I shouldn't quite go as far as that. She didn't look guilty – nothing of that kind – but she did set about it rather – well, quickly and quietly – if you know what I mean. *And she didn't know I'd seen her do it!* That I'm sure of. She jumped when I rounded on her.'

Poirot said thoughtfully:

'Then there *was* a reason? But what conceivable reason could there have been? That little piece of rubber is quite fresh. It has not been used for anything. It can have no meaning whatsoever; and yet –'

Sugden said impatiently:

'Well, you can worry about it if you like, Mr Poirot. I've got other things to think about.'

Poirot asked:

'The case stands – where, in your opinion?'

Sugden took out his note-book.

'Let's get down to *facts*. To begin with, there are the people who *couldn't* have done it. Let's get them out of the way first –'

'They are –?'

'Alfred and Harry Lee. They've got a definite alibi. Also Mrs Alfred Lee, since Tressilian saw her in the drawing-room only about a minute before the row started upstairs. Those three are clear. Now for the others. Here's a list. I've put it this way for clearness.'

He handed the book to Poirot.

	At the time of the crime
George Lee	?
Mrs George Lee	?
David Lee	playing piano in music-room (confirmed by his wife)
Mrs David Lee	in music-room (confirmed by husband)
Miss Estravados	in her bedroom (no confirmation)
Stephen Farr	in ballroom playing gramophone (confirmed by three of staff who could hear the music in servants' hall).

Poirot said, handing back the list:

'And therefore?'

'And therefore,' said Sugden, 'George Lee could have killed the old man. Mrs George Lee could have killed him. Pilar Estravados could have killed him; and *either Mr or Mrs David Lee could have killed him*, but not *both*.'

'You do not, then, accept that alibi?'

Superintendent Sugden shook his head emphatically.

'Not on your life! Husband and wife – devoted to each other! They may be in it together, or if one of them did it, the other is ready to swear to an alibi. I look at it this way: *Someone* was in the music-room playing the piano. It *may* have been David Lee. It probably *was*, since he was an acknowledged musician, but there's nothing to say his wife was there too *except her word and his*. In the same way, it *may* have been Hilda who was playing that piano while David Lee crept upstairs and killed his father!

No, it's an absolutely different case from the two brothers in the dining-room. Alfred Lee and Harry Lee don't love each other. Neither of them would perjure himself for the other's sake.'

'What about Stephen Farr?'

'He's a possible suspect because that gramophone alibi is a bit thin. On the other hand, it's the sort of alibi that's really sounder than a good cast-iron dyed-in-the-wool alibi which, ten to one, has been faked up beforehand!'

Poirot bowed his head thoughtfully.

'I know what you mean. It is the alibi of a man *who did not know that he would be called upon to provide such a thing.*'

'Exactly! And anyway, somehow, I don't believe a stranger was mixed up in this thing.'

Poirot said quickly:

'I agree with you. It is here a *family* affair. It is a poison that works in the blood – it is intimate – it is deep-seated. There is here, I think, *hate* and *knowledge* . . .'

He waved his hands.

'I do not know – it is difficult!'

Superintendent Sugden had waited respectfully, but without being much impressed. He said:

'Quite so, Mr Poirot. But we'll get at it, never fear, with elimination and logic. We've got the *possibilities* now – the people with *opportunity*. George Lee, Magdalene Lee, David Lee, Hilda Lee, Pilar Estravados, and I'll add, Stephen Farr. Now we come to *motive*. Who had a *motive* for putting old Mr Lee out of the way? There again we can wash out certain people. Miss Estravados, for one. I gather that as the will stands now, she doesn't get anything at all. If Simeon Lee had died before her mother, her mother's share would have come down to her (unless her mother willed it otherwise), but as Jennifer Estravados predeceased Simeon Lee, that particular legacy reverts to the other members of the family. So it was definitely to Miss Estravados' interests to keep the old man alive. He'd taken a fancy to her; it's pretty certain he'd have left her a good slice of money when he made a new will. She had everything to lose and nothing to gain by his murder. You agree to that?'

'Perfectly.'

'There remains, of course, the possibility that she cut his throat in the heat of a quarrel, but that seems extremely unlikely to me. To begin with, they were on the best of terms, and she hadn't been here long enough to bear him a grudge about anything. It therefore seems highly unlikely that Miss Estravados has anything to do with the crime – except that you might argue that to cut a man's throat is an unEnglish sort of thing to do, as your friend Mrs George put it?'

'Do not call her *my* friend,' said Poirot hastily. 'Or I shall speak of *your* friend Miss Estravados, who finds you such a handsome man!'

He had the pleasure of seeing the superintendent's official poise upset again. The police officer turned crimson. Poirot looked at him with malicious amusement.

He said, and there was a wistful note in his voice:

'It is true that your moustache is superb . . . Tell me, do you use for it a special *pomade*?'

'Pomade? Good lord, no!'

'What do you use?'

'Use? Nothing at all. It – it just *grows*.'

Poirot sighed.

'You are favoured by nature.' He caressed his own luxuriant black moustache, then sighed. 'However expensive the preparation,' he murmured, 'to restore the natural colour does somewhat impoverish the quality of the hair.'

Superintendent Sugden, uninterested in hair-dressing problems, was continuing in a stolid manner:

'Considering the *motive* for the crime, I should say that we can probably wash out Mr Stephen Farr. It's just possible that there was some hanky-panky between his father and Mr Lee and the former suffered, but I doubt it. Farr's manner was too easy and assured when he mentioned that subject. He was quite confident – and I don't think he was acting. No, I don't think we'll find anything there.'

'I do not think you will,' said Poirot.

'And there's one other person with a motive for keeping old Mr Lee alive – his son Harry. It's true that he benefits under the will, but I don't believe *he was aware of the fact*. Certainly couldn't have been *sure* of it! The general impression seemed to be that Harry had been definitely cut out of his share of the inheritance at the time he cut loose. But now he was on the point of coming back into favour! It was all to his advantage that his father should make a new will. He wouldn't be such a fool as to kill him now. Actually, as we know, he *couldn't* have done it. You see, we're getting on; we're clearing quite a lot of people out of the way.'

'How true. Very soon there will be nobody left!'

Sugden grinned.

'We're not going as fast as that! We've got George Lee and his wife, and David Lee and Mrs David. They all benefit by the death, and George Lee, from all I can make out, is grasping about money. Moreover, his father was threatening to cut down supplies. So we've got George Lee with motive and opportunity!'

'Continue,' said Poirot.

'And we've got Mrs George! As fond of money as a cat is fond of cream; and I'd be prepared to bet she's heavily in debt at the minute! She was jealous of the Spanish girl. She was quick to spot that the other was gaining an ascendancy over the old man. She'd heard him say that he was sending for the lawyer. So she struck quickly. You could make out a case.'

'Possibly.'

'Then there's David Lee and his wife. They inherit under the present will, but I don't believe, somehow, that the money motive would be particularly strong in their case.'

'No?'

'No. David Lee seems to be a bit of a dreamer – not a mercenary type. But he's – well, he's *odd*. As I see it, there are three possible motives for this murder: There's the diamond complication, there's the will, and there's – well – just plain *hate*.'

'Ah, you see that, do you?'

Sugden said:

'Naturally. It's been present in my mind all along. *If* David Lee killed his father, I don't think it was for money. And if he was the criminal it might explain the – well, the blood-letting!'

Poirot looked at him appreciatively.

'Yes, I wondered when you would take that into consideration. *So much blood* – that is what Mrs Alfred said. It takes one back to ancient rituals – to blood sacrifice, to the anointing with the blood of the sacrifice . . .'

Sugden said, frowning:

'You mean whoever did it was mad?'

'*Mon cher* – there are all sorts of deep instincts in man of which he himself is unaware. The craving for blood – the demand for sacrifice!'

Sugden said doubtfully:

'David Lee looks a quiet, harmless fellow.'

Poirot said:

'You do not understand the psychology. David Lee is a man who lives in the past – a man in whom the memory of his mother is still very much alive. He kept away from his father for many years because he could not forgive his father's treatment of his mother. He came here, let us suppose, to forgive. *But he may not have been able to forgive* . . . We do know one thing – that when David Lee stood by his father's dead body, some part of him was appeased and satisfied. "*The mills of God grind slowly, yet they grind exceeding small.*" Retribution! Payment! The wrong wiped out by expiation!'

Sugden gave a sudden shudder. He said:

'Don't talk like that, Mr Poirot. You give me quite a turn. It may be that it's as you say. If so, Mrs David knows – and means to shield him all she knows how. I can imagine her doing that. On the other hand, I can't imagine her being a murderess. She's such a comfortable commonplace sort of woman.'

Poirot looked at him curiously.

'So she strikes you like that?' he murmured.

'Well, yes – a homely body, if you know what I mean!'

'Oh, I know what you mean perfectly!'

Sugden looked at him.

'Come, now, Mr Poirot, you've got ideas about the case. Let's have them.'

Poirot said slowly: 'I have ideas, yes, but they are rather nebulous. Let me first hear your summing-up of the case.'

'Well, it's as I said – three possible motives: hate, gain, and this diamond complication. Take the facts chronologically.

'3.30. Family gathering. Telephone conversation to lawyer overheard by all the family. Then the old man lets loose on his family, tells them where they all get off. They slink out like a lot of scared rabbits.'

'Hilda Lee remained behind,' said Poirot.

'So she did. But not for long. Then about six Alfred has an interview with his father – unpleasant interview. Harry is to be reinstated. Alfred isn't pleased. Alfred, of course, *ought* to be our principal suspect. He had by far the strongest motive. However, to get on, Harry comes along next. Is in boisterous spirits. Has got the old man just where he wants him. But *before* those two interviews Simeon Lee has discovered the loss of the diamonds and has telephoned to me. He doesn't mention his loss to either of his two sons. Why? In my opinion because he was quite sure neither of them had anything to do with it. Neither of them were under suspicion. I believe, as I've said all along, that the old man suspected Horbury and *one other person.* And I'm pretty sure of what he meant to do. Remember, he said definitely he didn't want anyone to come and sit with him that evening. Why? Because he was preparing the way for two things: First, my visit; and second, *the visit of that other suspected person.* He did ask *someone* to come and see him immediately after dinner. Now who was that person likely to be? Might have been George Lee. Much more likely to have been his wife. And there's another person who comes back into the picture here – Pilar Estravados. He's shown her the diamonds. He'd told her their value. How do we know that girl isn't a thief? Remember these mysterious hints about the disgraceful behaviour of her father. Perhaps *he* was a professional thief and finally went to prison for it.'

Poirot said slowly:

'And so, as you say, Pilar Estravados comes back into the picture . . .'

'Yes – as a *thief.* No other way. She *may* have lost her head when she was found out. She *may* have flown at her grandfather and attacked him.'

Poirot said slowly:

'It is possible – yes . . .'

Superintendent Sugden looked at him keenly.

'But that's not *your* idea? Come, Mr Poirot, what *is* your idea?'

Poirot said:

'I go back always to the same thing: *the character of the dead man.* What manner of a man was Simeon Lee?'

'There isn't much mystery about that,' said Sugden, staring.

'Tell me, then. That is to say, tell me from the local point of view what was known of the man.'

Superintendent Sugden drew a doubtful finger along his jawbone. He looked perplexed. He said:

'I'm not a local man myself. I come from Reeveshire, over the border – next county. But of course old Mr Lee was a well-known figure in these parts. I know all about him by hearsay.'

'Yes? And that hearsay was – what?'

Sugden said:

'Well, he was a sharp customer; there weren't many who could get the better of him. But he was generous with his money. Open-handed as they make 'em. Beats me how Mr George Lee can be the exact opposite, and be his father's son.'

'Ah! But there are two distinct strains in the family. Alfred, George, and David resemble – superficially at least – their mother's side of the family. I have been looking at some portraits in the gallery this morning.'

'He was hot-tempered,' continued Superintendent Sugden, 'and of course he had a bad reputation with women – that was in his younger days. He's been an invalid for many years now. But even there he always behaved generously. If there was trouble, he always paid up handsomely and got the girl married off as often as not. He may have been a bad lot, but he wasn't mean. He treated his wife badly, ran after other women, and neglected her. She died of a broken heart, so they say. It's a convenient term, but I believe she was really very unhappy, poor lady. She was always sickly and never went about much. There's no doubt that Mr Lee was an odd character. Had a revengeful streak in him, too. If anyone did him a nasty turn he always paid it back, so they say, and didn't mind how long he had to wait to do it.'

'The mills of God grind slowly, yet they grind exceeding small,' murmured Poirot.

Superintendent Sugden said heavily:

'Mills of the devil, more likely! Nothing saintly about Simeon Lee. The kind of man you might say had sold his soul to the devil and enjoyed the bargain! And he was proud, too, proud as Lucifer.'

'Proud as Lucifer!' said Poirot. 'It is suggestive, what you say there.'

Superintendent Sugden said, looking puzzled:

'You don't mean that he was murdered because he was proud?'

'I mean,' said Poirot, 'that there is such a thing as inheritance. Simeon Lee transmitted that pride to his sons –'

He broke off. Hilda Lee had come out of the house and was standing looking along the terrace.

III

'I wanted to find you, M. Poirot.'

Superintendent Sugden had excused himself and gone back into the house. Looking after him, Hilda said:

'I didn't know he was with you. I thought he was with Pilar. He seems a nice man, quite considerate.'

Her voice was pleasant, a low, soothing cadence to it.

Poirot asked:

'You wanted to see me, you say?'

She inclined her head.

'Yes. I think you can help me.'

'I shall be delighted to do so, madame.'

She said:

'You are a very intelligent man, M. Poirot. I saw that last night. There are things which you will, I think, find out quite easily. I want you to understand my husband.'

'Yes, madame?'

'I shouldn't talk like this to Superintendent Sugden. He wouldn't understand. But you will.'

Poirot bowed. 'You honour me, madame.'

Hilda went calmly on:

'My husband, for many years, ever since I married him, has been what I can only describe as a mental cripple.'

'Ah!'

'When one suffers some great hurt physically, it causes shock and pain, but slowly it mends, the flesh heals, the bone knits. There may be, perhaps, a little weakness, a slight scar, but nothing more. My husband, M. Poirot, suffered a great hurt *mentally* at his most susceptible age. He adored his mother and he saw her die. He believed that his father was morally responsible for that death. From that shock he has never quite recovered. His resentment against his father never died down. It was I who persuaded David to come here this Christmas, to be reconciled to his father. I wanted it – for *his* sake – I wanted that mental wound to heal. I realize now that coming here was a mistake. Simeon Lee amused himself by probing into that old wound. It was – a very dangerous thing to do . . .'

Poirot said: 'Are you telling me, madame, that your husband killed his father?'

'I am telling you, M. Poirot, that he easily *might* have done so . . . And I will also tell you this – that he did *not*! When Simeon Lee was killed, his son was playing the "Dead March". The wish to kill was in his heart. It passed out through his fingers and died in waves of sound – that is the truth.'

Poirot was silent for a minute or two, then he said:

'And you, madame, what is your verdict on that past drama?'

'You mean the death of Simeon Lee's wife?'

'Yes.'

Hilda said slowly:

'I know enough of life to know that you can never judge any case on its outside merits. To all seeming, Simeon Lee was entirely to blame and his wife was abominably treated. At the same time, I honestly believe that there is a kind of meekness, a predisposition to martyrdom which does arouse the worst instincts in men of a certain type. Simeon Lee would have admired, I think, spirit and force of character. He was merely irritated by patience and tears.'

Poirot nodded. He said:

'Your husband said last night: "My mother never complained." Is that true?'

Hilda Lee said impatiently:

'Of course it isn't! She complained the whole time to David! She laid the whole burden of her unhappiness on his shoulders. He was too young – far too young to bear all she gave him to bear!'

Poirot looked thoughtfully at her. She flushed under his gaze and bit her lip.

He said:

'I see.'

She said sharply:

'What do you see?'

He answered:

'I see that you have had to be a mother to your husband when you would have preferred to be a wife.'

She turned away.

At that moment David Lee came out of the house and along the terrace towards them. He said, and his voice had a clear joyful note in it:

'Hilda, isn't it a glorious day? Almost like spring instead of winter.'

He came nearer. His head was thrown back, a lock of fair hair fell across his forehead, his blue eyes shone. He looked amazingly young and boyish. There was about him a youthful eagerness, a carefree radiance. Hercule Poirot caught his breath . . .

David said: 'Let's go down to the lake, Hilda.'

She smiled, put her arm through his, and they moved off together.

As Poirot watched them go, he saw her turn and give him a rapid glance. He caught a momentary glimpse of swift anxiety – or was it, he wondered, fear?

Slowly Hercule Poirot walked to the other end of the terrace. He murmured to himself:

'As I have always said, me, I am the father confessor! And since women come to confession more frequently than men, it is women who have come to me this morning. Will there, I wonder, be another very shortly?'

As he turned at the end of the terrace and paced back again, he knew that his question was answered. Lydia Lee was coming towards him.

IV

Lydia said:

'Good morning, M. Poirot. Tressilian told me I should find you out here with Harry; but I am glad to find you alone. My husband has been speaking about you. I know he is very anxious to talk to you.'

'Ah! Yes? Shall I go and see him now?'

'Not just yet. He got hardly any sleep last night. In the end I gave him a strong sleeping draught. He is still asleep, and I don't want to disturb him.'

'I quite understand. That was very wise. I could see last night that the shock had been very great.'

She said seriously:

'You see, M. Poirot, he really *cared* – much more than the others.'

'I understand.'

She asked:

'Have you – has the superintendent – any idea of who can have done this awful thing?'

Poirot said deliberately:

'We have certain ideas, madame, as to who did *not* do it.'

Lydia said, almost impatiently:

'It's like a nightmare – so fantastic – I can't believe it's *real*!'

She added:

'What about Horbury? Was he really at the cinema, as he said?'

'Yes, madame, his story has been checked. He was speaking the truth.'

Lydia stopped and plucked at a bit of yew. Her face went a little paler. She said:

'But that's *awful*! It only leaves – the family!'

'Exactly.'

'M. Poirot, I *can't* believe it!'

'Madame, you *can* and you *do* believe it!'

She seemed about to protest. Then suddenly she smiled ruefully.

She said:

'What a hypocrite one is!'

He nodded.

'If you were to be frank with me, madame,' he said, 'you would admit that to you it seems quite natural that one of his family should murder your father-in-law.'

Lydia said sharply:

'That's really a fantastic thing to say, M. Poirot!'

'Yes, it is. But your father-in-law was a fantastic person!'

Lydia said:

'Poor old man. I can feel sorry for him now. When he was alive, he just annoyed me unspeakably!'

Poirot said:

'So I should imagine!'

He bent over one of the stone sinks.

'They are very ingenious, these. Very pleasing.'

'I'm glad you like them. It's one of my hobbies. Do you like this Arctic one with the penguins and the ice?'

'Charming. And this – what is this?'

'Oh, that's the Dead Sea – or going to be. It isn't finished yet. You mustn't look at it. Now this one is supposed to be Piana in Corsica. The rocks there, you know, are quite pink and too lovely where they go down into the blue sea. This desert scene is rather fun, don't you think?'

She led him along. When they had reached the farther end she glanced at her wrist-watch.

'I must go and see if Alfred is awake.'

When she had gone Poirot went slowly back again to the garden representing the Dead Sea. He looked at it with a good deal of interest. Then he scooped up a few of the pebbles and let them run through his fingers.

Suddenly his face changed. He held up the pebbles close to his face.

'*Sapristi*!' he said. 'This is a surprise! Now what exactly does this mean?'

PART 5

DECEMBER 26TH

I

The chief constable and Superintendent Sugden stared at Poirot incredulously. The latter returned a stream of small pebbles carefully into a small cardboard box and pushed it across to the chief constable.

'Oh, yes,' he said. 'It is the diamonds all right.'

'And you found them where, did you say? In the garden?'

'In one of the small gardens constructed by Madame Alfred Lee.'

'Mrs Alfred?' Sugden shook his head. 'Doesn't seem likely.'

Poirot said:

'You mean, I suppose, that you do not consider it likely that Mrs Alfred cut her father-in-law's throat?'

Sugden said quickly:

'We know she didn't do that. I meant it seemed unlikely that she pinched these diamonds.'

Poirot said:

'One would not easily believe her a thief – no.'

Sugden said:

'Anybody could have hidden them there.'

'That is true. It was convenient that in that particular garden – the Dead Sea as it represents – there happened to be pebbles very similar in shape and appearance.'

Sugden said:

'You mean she fixed it like that beforehand? Ready?'

Colonel Johnson said warmly:

'I don't believe it for a moment. Not for a moment. Why should she take the diamonds in the first place?'

'Well, as to that –' Sugden said slowly.

Poirot nipped in quickly:

'There is a possible answer to that. She took the diamonds to suggest a motive for the murder. That is to say she knew that murder was going to be done though she herself took no active part in it.'

Johnson frowned.

'That won't hold water for a minute. You're making her out to be an accomplice – but whose accomplice would she be likely to be? Only her husband's. But as we know that he, too, had nothing to do with the murder, the whole theory falls to the ground.'

Sugden stroked his jaw reflectively.

'Yes,' he said, 'that's so. No, if Mrs Lee took the diamonds – and it's a big if – it was just plain robbery, and it's true she might have prepared that garden specially as a hiding-place for them till the hue and cry had died down. Another possibility is that of *coincidence.* That garden, with its similarity of pebbles, struck the thief, whoever he or she was, as an ideal hiding-place.'

Poirot said:

'That is quite possible. I am always prepared to admit *one* coincidence.'

Superintendent Sugden shook his head dubiously.

Poirot said:

'What is your opinion, Superintendent?'

The superintendent said cautiously:

'Mrs Lee's a very nice lady. Doesn't seem likely that she'd be mixed up in any business that was fishy. But, of course, one never knows.'

Colonel Johnson said testily:

'In any case, whatever the truth is about the diamonds, her being mixed up in the murder is out of the question. The butler saw her in the drawing-room at the actual time of the crime. You remember that, Poirot?'

Poirot said:

'I had not forgotten that.'

The chief constable turned to his subordinate.

'We'd better get on. What have you to report? Anything fresh?'

'Yes, sir. I've got hold of some new information. To start with – Horbury. There's a reason why he might be scared of the police.'

'Robbery? Eh?'

'No, sir. Extorting money under threats. Modified blackmail.

The case couldn't be proved so he got off, but I rather fancy he's got away with a thing or two in that line. Having a guilty conscience, he probably thought we were on to something of that kind when Tressilian mentioned a police officer last night and it made him get the wind up.'

The chief constable said:

'H'm! So much for Horbury. What else?'

The superintendent coughed.

'Er – Mrs George Lee, sir. We've got a line on her before her marriage. Was living with a Commander Jones. Passed as his daughter – but she *wasn't his daughter* . . . I think from what we've been told, that old Mr Lee summed her up pretty correctly – he was smart where women were concerned, knew a bad lot when he saw one – and was just amusing himself by taking a shot in the dark. *And* he got her on the raw!'

Colonel Johnson said thoughtfully:

'That gives her another possible motive – apart from the money angle. She may have thought he knew something definite and was going to give her away to her husband. That telephone story of hers is pretty fishy. She *didn't* telephone.'

Sugden suggested:

'Why not have them in together, sir, and get at that telephone business straight? See what we get.'

Colonel Johnson said:

'Good idea.'

He rang the bell. Tressilian answered it.

'Ask Mr and Mrs George Lee to come here.'

'Very good, sir.'

As the old man turned away, Poirot said:

'The date on that wall calendar, has it remained like it is since the murder?'

Tressilian turned back.

'Which calendar, sir?'

'The one on the wall over there.'

The three men were sitting once more in Alfred Lee's small sitting-room. The calendar in question was a large one with tear-off leaves, a bold date on each leaf.

Tressilian peered across the room, then shuffled slowly across till he was a foot or two away.

He said:

'Excuse me, sir, it has been torn off. It's the twenty-sixth today.'

'Ah, pardon. Who would have been the person to tear it off?'

'Mr Lee does, sir, every morning. Mr Alfred, he's a very methodical gentleman.'

'I see. Thank you.'

Tressilian went out. Sugden said, puzzled:

'Is there anything fishy about that calendar, Mr Poirot? Have I missed something there?'

With a shrug of his shoulders Poirot said:

'The calendar is of no importance. It was just a little experiment I was making.'

Colonel Johnson said:

'Inquest tomorrow. There'll be an adjournment, of course.'

Sugden said:

'Yes, sir, I've seen the Coroner and it's all arranged for.'

II

George Lee came into the room, accompanied by his wife.

Colonel Johnson said:

'Good morning. Sit down, will you? There are a few questions I want to ask both of you. Something I'm not quite clear about.'

'I shall be glad to give you any assistance I can,' said George, somewhat pompously.

Magdalene said faintly:

'Of course!'

The chief constable gave a slight nod to Sugden. The latter said:

'About those telephone calls on the night of the crime. You put through a call to Westeringham, I think you said, Mr Lee?'

George said coldly:

'Yes, I did. To my agent in the constituency. I can refer you to him and –'

Superintendent Sugden held up his hand to stem the flow.

'Quite so – quite so, Mr Lee. We're not disputing that point. Your call went through at 8.59 exactly.'

'Well – I – er – couldn't say as to the exact time.'

'Ah,' said Sugden. 'But we can! We always check up on these

things very carefully. Very carefully indeed. The call was put through at 8.59 and it was terminated at 9.04. Your father, Mr Lee, was killed about 9.15. I must ask you once more for an account of your movements.'

'I've told you – I was telephoning!'

'No, Mr Lee, you weren't.'

'Nonsense – you must have made a mistake! Well, I may, perhaps, have just finished telephoning – I think I debated making another call – was just considering whether it was – er – worth – the expense – when I heard the noise upstairs.'

'You would hardly debate whether or not to make a telephone call for ten minutes.'

George went purple. He began to splutter.

'What do you mean? What the devil do you mean? Damned impudence! Are you doubting my word? Doubting the word of a man of my position? I – er – why should I have to account for every minute of my time?'

Superintendent Sugden said with a stolidness that Poirot admired:

'It's usual.'

George turned angrily on the chief constable.

'Colonel Johnson. Do you countenance this – this unprecedented attitude?'

The chief constable said crisply: 'In a murder case, Mr Lee, then questions must be asked – *and answered*.'

'I have answered them! I had finished telephoning and was – er – debating a further call.'

'You were in this room when the alarm was raised upstairs?'

'I was – yes, I was.'

Johnson turned to Magdalene.

'I think, Mrs Lee,' he said, 'that you stated that *you* were telephoning when the alarm broke out, and that at the time you were alone in this room?'

Magdalene was flustered. She caught her breath, looked sideways at George – at Sugden, then appealingly at Colonel Johnson. She said:

'Oh, really – I don't know – I don't remember what I said . . . I was so *upset* . . .'

Sugden said:

'We've got it all written down, you know.'

She turned her batteries on him – wide appealing eyes – quivering mouth. But she met in return the rigid aloofness of a man of stern respectability who didn't approve of her type.

She said uncertainly:

'I – I – of course I telephoned. I can't be quite sure just *when* –'

She stopped.

George said:

'What's all this? Where did you telephone from? Not in here.'

Superintendent Sugden said:

'I suggest, Mrs Lee, that *you didn't telephone at all*. In that case, where were you and what were you doing?'

Magdalene glanced distractedly about her and burst into tears. She sobbed:

'George, don't let them bully me! You know that if anyone frightens me and thunders questions at me, I can't remember anything *at all*! I – I don't know *what* I was saying that night – it was all so horrible – and I was so upset – and they're being so beastly to me . . .'

She jumped up and ran sobbing out of the room.

Springing up, George Lee blustered:

'What d'you mean? I won't have my wife bullied and frightened out of her life! She's very sensitive. It's disgraceful! I shall have a question asked in the House about the disgraceful bullying methods of the police. It's absolutely disgraceful!'

He strode out of the room and banged the door.

Superintendent Sugden threw his head back and laughed.

He said:

'We've got them going properly! Now we'll see!'

Johnson said frowning:

'Extraordinary business! Looks fishy. We must get a further statement out of her.'

Sugden said easily:

'Oh! She'll be back in a minute or two. When she's decided what to say. Eh, Mr Poirot?'

Poirot, who had been sitting in a dream, gave a start.

'*Pardon!*'

'I said she'll be back.'

'Probably – yes, possibly – oh, yes!'

Sugden said, staring at him:

'What's the matter, Mr Poirot? Seen a ghost?'

Poirot said slowly:

'You know – I am not sure that I have not done *just exactly that.*'

Colonel Johnson said impatiently:

'Well, Sugden, anything else?'

Sugden said:

'I've been trying to check up on the order in which everyone arrived on the scene of the murder. It's quite clear what must have happened. After the murder when the victim's dying cry had given the alarm, the murderer slipped out, locked the door with pliers, or something of that kind, and a moment or two later became one of the people hurrying *to* the scene of the crime. Unfortunately it's not easy to check exactly whom everyone has seen because people's memories aren't very accurate on a point like that. Tressilian says he saw Harry and Alfred Lee cross the hall from the dining-room and race upstairs. That lets them out, but we don't suspect them anyway. As far as I can make out, Miss Estravados got there late – one of the last. The general idea seems to be that Farr, Mrs George, and Mrs David were the first. Each of those three says one of the others was just ahead of them. That's what's so difficult, you can't distinguish between a deliberate lie and a genuine haziness of recollection. Everybody ran there – that's agreed, but in what order they ran isn't so easy to get at.'

Poirot said slowly:

'You think that important?'

Sugden said:

'It's the time element. The time, remember, was incredibly short.'

Poirot said:

'I agree with you that the time element is very important in this case.'

Sugden went on:

'What makes it more difficult is that there are two staircases. There's the main one in the hall here about equidistant from the dining-room and the drawing-room doors. Then there's one the other end of the house. Stephen Farr came up by the latter. Miss Estravados came along the upper landing from that end of the house (her room is right the other end). The others say they went up by this one.'

Poirot said:

'It is a confusion, yes.'

The door opened and Magdalene came quickly in. She was breathing fast and had a bright spot of colour in each cheek. She came up to the table and said quietly:

'My husband thinks I'm lying down. I slipped out of my room quietly. Colonel Johnson,' she appealed to him with wide, distressed eyes, 'if I tell you the truth you *will* keep quiet about it, won't you? I mean you don't have to make *everything* public?'

Colonel Johnson said:

'You mean, I take it, Mrs Lee, something that has no connection with the crime?'

'Yes, no connection at all. Just something in my – my private life.'

The chief constable said:

'You'd better make a clean breast of it, Mrs Lee, and leave us to judge.'

Magdalene said, her eyes swimming:

'Yes, I will trust you. I know I can. You look so kind. You see, it's like this. There's somebody –' She stopped.

'Yes, Mrs Lee?'

'I wanted to telephone to somebody last night – a man – a friend of mine, and I didn't want George to know about it. I know it was very wrong of me – but well, it was like that. So I went to telephone after dinner when I thought George would be safely in the dining-room. But when I got here I heard him telephoning, so I waited.'

'Where did you wait, madame?' asked Poirot.

'There's a place for coats and things behind the stairs. It's dark there. I slipped back there, where I could see George come out from this room. But he didn't come out, and then all the noise happened and Mr Lee screamed, and I ran upstairs.'

'So your husband did not leave this room until the moment of the murder?'

'No.'

The chief constable said:

'And you yourself from nine o'clock to nine-fifteen were waiting in the recess behind the stairs?'

'Yes, but I couldn't *say* so, you see! They'd want to know what I was doing there. It's been very, very awkward for me, you *do* see that, *don't* you?'

Johnson said dryly:

'It was certainly awkward.'

She smiled at him sweetly.

'I'm *so* relieved to have told you the truth. And you *won't* tell my husband, will you? No, I'm sure you won't! I can trust you, all of you.'

She included them all in her final pleading look, then she slipped quickly out of the room.

Colonel Johnson drew a deep breath.

'Well,' he said. 'It *might* be like that! It's a perfectly plausible story. On the other hand –'

'It might not,' finished Sugden. 'That's just it. We don't know.'

III

Lydia Lee stood by the far window of the drawing-room looking out. Her figure was half hidden by the heavy window curtains. A sound in the room made her turn with a start to see Hercule Poirot standing by the door.

She said:

'You startled me, M. Poirot.'

'I apologize, madame. I walk softly.'

She said:

'I thought it was Horbury.'

Hercule Poirot nodded.

'It is true, he steps softly, that one – like a cat – or a *thief*.'

He paused a minute, watching her.

Her face showed nothing, but she made a slight grimace of distaste as she said:

'I have never cared for that man. I shall be glad to get rid of him.'

'I think you will be wise to do so, madame.'

She looked at him quickly. She said:

'What do you mean? Do you know anything against him?'

Poirot said:

'He is a man who collects secrets – and uses them to his advantage.'

She said sharply:

'Do you think he knows anything – about the murder?'

Poirot shrugged his shoulders. He said:

'He has quiet feet and long ears. He may have overheard something that he is keeping to himself.'

Lydia said clearly:

'Do you mean that he may try to blackmail one of us?'

'It is within the bounds of possibility. But that is not what I came here to say.'

'What did you come to say?'

Poirot said slowly:

'I have been talking with M. Alfred Lee. He has made me a proposition, and I wished to discuss it with you before accepting or declining it. But I was so struck by the picture you made – the charming pattern of your jumper against the deep red of the curtains, that I paused to admire.'

Lydia said sharply:

'Really, M. Poirot, must we waste time in compliments?'

'I beg your pardon, madame. So few English ladies understand *la toilette.* The dress you were wearing the first night I saw you, its bold but simple pattern, it had grace – distinction.'

Lydia said impatiently:

'What was it you wanted to see me about?'

Poirot became grave.

'Just this, madame. Your husband, he wishes me to take up the investigation very seriously. He demands that I stay here, in the house, and do my utmost to get to the bottom of the matter.'

Lydia said sharply:

'Well?'

Poirot said slowly:

'I should not wish to accept an invitation that was not endorsed by the lady of the house.'

She said coldly:

'Naturally I endorse my husband's invitation.'

'Yes, madame, but I need more than that. Do you really *want* me to come here?'

'Why not?'

'Let us be more frank. What I ask you is this: do you want the truth to come out, or not?'

'Naturally.'

Poirot sighed.

'Must you return me these conventional replies?'

Lydia said:

'I am a conventional woman.'

Then she bit her lip, hesitated, and said:

'Perhaps it is better to speak frankly. Of course I understand you! The position is not a pleasant one. My father-in-law has been brutally murdered, and unless a case can be made out against the most likely suspect – Horbury – for robbery and murder – and it seems that it cannot – then it comes to this – *one of his own family killed him*. To bring that person to justice will mean bringing shame and disgrace on us all . . . If I am to speak honestly I must say that I do *not* want this to happen.'

Poirot said:

'You are content for the murderer to escape unpunished?'

'There are probably several undiscovered murderers at large in the world.'

'That, I grant you.'

'Does one more matter, then?'

Poirot said:

'And what about the other members of the family? The innocent?'

She stared.

'What about them?'

'Do you realize that if it turns out as you hope, *no one will ever know*. The shadow will remain on all alike . . .'

She said uncertainly:

'I hadn't thought of that.'

Poirot said:

'*No one will ever know who the guilty person is* . . .'

He added softly:

'Unless *you* already know, madame?'

She cried out:

'You have no business to say that! It's not true! Oh! If only it could be a stranger – not a member of the family.'

Poirot said:

'It might be both.'

She stared at him.

'What do you mean?'

'It might be a member of the family – and, at the same time, a stranger . . . You do not see what I mean? *Eh bien*, it is an idea that has occurred to the mind of Hercule Poirot.'

He looked at her.

'Well, madame, what am I to say to Mr Lee?'

Lydia raised her hands and let them fall in a sudden helpless gesture.

She said:

'Of course – you must accept.'

IV

Pilar stood in the centre of the music-room. She stood very straight, her eyes darting from side to side like an animal who fears an attack.

She said:

'I want to get away from here!'

Stephen Farr said gently:

'You're not the only one who feels like that. But they won't let us go, my dear.'

'You mean – the police?'

'Yes.'

Pilar said very seriously:

'It is not nice to be mixed up with the police. It is a thing that should not happen to respectable people.'

Stephen said with a faint smile:

'Meaning yourself?'

Pilar said:

'No, I mean Alfred and Lydia and David and George and Hilda and – yes – Magdalene too.'

Stephen lit a cigarette. He puffed at it for a moment or two before saying:

'Why the exception?'

'What is that, please?'

Stephen said:

'Why leave out brother Harry?'

Pilar laughed, her teeth showing white and even.

'Oh, Harry is different! I think he knows very well what it is to be mixed up with the police.'

'Perhaps you are right. He certainly is a little too picturesque to blend well into the domestic picture.'

He went on:

'Do you like your English relations, Pilar?'

Pilar said doubtfully:

'They are kind – they are all very kind. But they do not laugh much, they are not gay.'

'My dear girl, there's just been a murder in the house!'

'Y-es,' said Pilar doubtfully.

'A murder,' said Stephen instructively, 'is not such an everyday occurrence as your nonchalance seems to imply. In England they take their murders seriously whatever they may do in Spain.'

Pilar said:

'You are laughing at me . . .'

Stephen said:

'You're wrong. I'm not in a laughing mood.'

Pilar looked at him and said:

'Because you, too, wish to get away from here?'

'Yes.'

'And the big, handsome policeman will not let you go?'

'I haven't asked him. But if I did, I've no doubt he'd say no. I've got to watch my step, Pilar, and be very very careful.'

'That is tiresome,' said Pilar, nodding her head.

'It's just a little bit more than tiresome, my dear. Then there's that lunatic foreigner prowling about. I don't suppose he's any good but he makes me feel jumpy.'

Pilar was frowning. She said:

'My grandfather was very, very rich, was he not?'

'I should imagine so.'

'Where does his money go to now? To Alfred and the others?'

'Depends on his will.'

Pilar said thoughtfully: 'He might have left me some money, but I am afraid that perhaps he did not.'

Stephen said kindly:

'You'll be all right. After all, you're one of the family. You belong here. They'll have to look after you.'

Pilar said with a sigh: 'I – belong here. It is very funny, that. And yet it is not funny at all.'

'I can see that you mightn't find it very humorous.'

Pilar sighed again. She said:

'Do you think if we put on the gramophone, we could dance?'

Stephen said dubiously:

'It wouldn't look any too good. This is a house of mourning, you callous Spanish baggage.'

Pilar said, her big eyes opening very wide:

'But I do not feel sad at all. Because I did not really know my grandfather, and though I liked to talk to him, I do not want to cry and be unhappy because he is dead. It is very silly to pretend.'

Stephen said: 'You're adorable!'

Pilar said coaxingly:

'We could put some stockings and some gloves in the gramophone, and then it would not make much noise, and no one would hear.'

'Come along then, temptress.'

She laughed happily and ran out of the room, going along towards the ballroom at the far end of the house.

Then, as she reached the side passage which led to the garden door, she stopped dead. Stephen caught up with her and stopped also.

Hercule Poirot had unhooked a portrait from the wall and was studying it by the light from the terrace. He looked up and saw them.

'Aha!' he said. 'You arrive at an opportune moment.'

Pilar said: 'What are you doing?'

She came and stood beside him.

Poirot said gravely:

'I am studying something very important, the face of Simeon Lee when he was a young man.'

'Oh, is that my grandfather?'

'Yes, mademoiselle.'

She stared at the painted face. She said slowly:

'How different – how very different . . . He was so old, so

shrivelled up. Here he is like Harry, like Harry might have been ten years ago.'

Hercule Poirot nodded.

'Yes, mademoiselle. Harry Lee is very much the son of his father. Now here –' He led her a little way along the gallery. 'Here is madame, your grandmother – a long gentle face, very blonde hair, mild blue eyes.'

Pilar said:

'Like David.'

Stephen said:

'Just a look of Alfred too.'

Poirot said:

'The heredity, it is very interesting. Mr Lee and his wife were diametrically opposite types. On the whole, the children of the marriage took after the mother. See here, mademoiselle.'

He pointed to a picture of a girl of nineteen or so, with hair like spun gold and wide, laughing blue eyes. The colouring was that of Simeon Lee's wife, but there was a spirit, a vivacity that those mild blue eyes and placid features had never known.

'Oh!' said Pilar.

The colour came up in her face.

Her hand went to her neck. She drew out a locket on a long gold chain. She pressed the catch and it flew open. The same laughing face looked up at Poirot.

'My mother,' said Pilar.

Poirot nodded. On the opposite side of the locket was the portrait of a man. He was young and handsome, with black hair and dark blue eyes.

Poirot said: 'Your father?'

Pilar said:

'Yes, my father. He is very beautiful, is he not?'

'Yes, indeed. Few Spaniards have blue eyes, have they, señorita?'

'Sometimes, in the North. Besides, my father's mother was Irish.'

Poirot said thoughtfully:

'So you have Spanish blood, and Irish and English, and a touch of gipsy too. Do you know what I think, mademoiselle? With that inheritance, you should make a bad enemy.'

Stephen said, laughing:

'Remember what you said in the train, Pilar? That your way of dealing with your enemies would be to cut their throats. Oh!'

He stopped – suddenly realizing the import of his words.

Hercule Poirot was quick to lead the conversation away. He said:

'Ah, yes, there was something, señorita, I had to ask you. Your passport. It is needed by my friend the superintendent. There are, you know, police regulations – very stupid, very tiresome, but necessary – for a foreigner in this country. And of course, by law, you are a foreigner.'

Pilar's eyebrows rose.

'My passport? Yes, I will get it. It is in my room.'

Poirot said apologetically as he walked by her side:

'I am most sorry to trouble you. I am indeed.'

They had reached the end of the long gallery. Here was a flight of stairs. Pilar ran up and Poirot followed. Stephen came too. Pilar's bedroom was just at the head of the stairs.

She said as she reached the door: 'I will get it for you.'

She went in. Poirot and Stephen Farr remained waiting outside.

Stephen said remorsefully:

'Damn' silly of me to say a thing like that. I don't think she noticed, though, do you?'

Poirot did not answer. He held his head a little on one side as though listening.

He said:

'The English are extraordinarily fond of fresh air. Miss Estravados must have inherited that characteristic.'

Stephen said staring:

'Why?'

Poirot said softly:

'Because though it is today extremely cold – the black frost you call it (not like yesterday so mild and sunny) Miss Estravados has just flung up her lower window-sash. Amazing to love so much the fresh air.'

Suddenly there was an exclamation in Spanish from inside the room and Pilar reappeared laughingly dismayed.

'Ah!' she cried. 'But I am stupid – and clumsy. My little case it was on the window-sill, and I was sorting through it so quickly and very stupidly I knock my passport out of the window. It is down on the flower-bed below. I will get it.'

'I'll get it,' said Stephen, but Pilar had flown past him and cried back over her shoulder:

'No, it was my stupidity. You go to the drawing-room with M. Poirot and I will bring it to you there.'

Stephen Farr seemed inclined to go after her, but Poirot's hand fell gently on his arm and Poirot's voice said:

'Let us go this way.'

They went along the first-floor corridor towards the other end of the house until they got to the head of the main staircase. Here Poirot said:

'Let us not go down for a minute. If you will come with me to the room of the crime there is something I want to ask you.'

They went along the corridor which led to Simeon Lee's room. On their left they passed an alcove which contained two marble statues, stalwart nymphs clasping their draperies in an agony of Victorian propriety.

Stephen Farr glanced at them and murmured:

'Pretty frightful by daylight. I thought there were three of them when I came along the other night, but thank goodness there are only two!'

'They are not what is admired nowadays,' admitted Poirot. 'But no doubt they cost much money in their time. They look better by night, I think.'

'Yes, one sees only a white glimmering figure.'

Poirot murmured:

'All cats are grey in the dark!'

They found Superintendent Sugden in the room. He was kneeling by the safe and examining it with a magnifying glass. He looked up as they entered.

'This was opened with the key all right,' he said. 'By someone who knew the combination. No sign of anything else.'

Poirot went up to him, drew him aside, and whispered something. The superintendent nodded and left the room.

Poirot turned to Stephen Farr, who was standing staring at the armchair in which Simeon Lee always sat. His brows were drawn together and the veins showed in his forehead. Poirot looked at him for a minute or two in silence, then he said:

'You have the memories – yes?'

Stephen said slowly:

'Two days ago he sat there alive – and now . . .'

Then, shaking off his absorption, he said: 'Yes, M. Poirot, you brought me here to ask me something?'

'Ah, yes. You were, I think, the first person to arrive on the scene that night?'

'Was I? I don't remember. No, I think one of the ladies was here before me.'

'Which lady?'

'One of the wives – George's wife or David's – I know they were both here pretty soon.'

'You did not hear the scream, I think you said?'

'I don't think I did. I can't quite remember. Somebody did cry out but that may have been someone downstairs.'

Poirot said:

'You did not hear a noise like this?'

He threw his head back and suddenly gave vent to a piercing yell.

It was so unexpected that Stephen started backwards and nearly fell over. He said angrily:

'For the Lord's sake, do you want to scare the whole house? No, I didn't hear anything in the least like that! You'll have the whole place by the ears again! They'll think another murder has happened!'

Poirot looked crestfallen. He murmured:

'True . . . it was foolish . . . We must go at once.'

He hurried out of the room. Lydia and Alfred were at the foot of the stairs peering up – George came out of the library to join them, and Pilar came running, a passport held in her hand.

Poirot cried:

'It is nothing – nothing. Do not be alarmed. A little experiment that I make. That was all.'

Alfred looked annoyed and George indignant. Poirot left Stephen to explain and he hurriedly slipped away along the passage to the other end of the house.

At the end of the passage Superintendent Sugden came quietly out of Pilar's door and met Poirot.

'*Eh bien*?' asked Poirot.

The superintendent shook his head.

'Not a sound.'

His eyes met Poirot's appreciatively and he nodded.

V

Alfred Lee said: 'Then you accept, M. Poirot?'

His hand, as it went to his mouth, shook slightly. His mild brown eyes were alight with a new and feverish expression. He stammered slightly in his speech. Lydia, standing silently by, looked at him with some anxiety.

Alfred said:

'You don't know – you c-c-can't imagine – what it m-m-means to me . . . My father's murderer *must* be f-f-found.'

Poirot said:

'Since you have assured me that you have reflected long and carefully – yes, I accept. But you comprehend, Mr Lee, there can be no drawing back. I am not the dog one sets on to hunt and then recalls because you do not like the game he puts up!'

'Of course . . . of course . . . Everything is ready. Your bedroom is prepared. Stay as long as you like –'

Poirot said gravely: 'It will not be long.'

'Eh? What's that?'

'I said it will not be long. There is in this crime such a restricted circle that it cannot possibly take long to arrive at the truth. Already, I think, the end draws near.'

Alfred stared at him, 'Impossible!' he said.

'Not at all. The facts all point more or less clearly in one direction. There is just some irrelevant matter to be cleared out of the way. When this is done the truth will appear.'

Alfred said incredulously:

'You mean you *know*?'

Poirot smiled. 'Oh, yes,' he said. 'I know.'

Alfred said:

'My father – my father –' He turned away.

Poirot said briskly:

'There are, M. Lee, two requests that I have to make.'

Alfred said in a muffled voice:

'Anything – anything.'

'Then, in the first place, I would like the portrait of M. Lee as a young man placed in the bedroom you are good enough to allot to me.'

Alfred and Lydia stared at him.

The former said: 'My father's portrait – but why?'

Poirot said with a wave of the hand:

'It will – how shall I say – inspire me.'

Lydia said sharply:

'Do you propose, M. Poirot, to solve a crime by clairvoyance?'

'Let us say, madame, that I intend to use not only the eyes of the body, but the eyes of the mind.'

She shrugged her shoulders.

Poirot continued:

'Next, M. Lee, I should like to know of the true circumstances attending the death of your sister's husband, Juan Estravados.'

Lydia said: 'Is that necessary?'

'I want all the facts, madame.'

Alfred said:

'Juan Estravados, as the result of a quarrel about a woman, killed another man in a café.'

'How did he kill him?'

Alfred looked appealingly at Lydia. She said evenly:

'He stabbed him. Juan Estravados was not condemned to death, as there had been provocation. He was sentenced to a term of imprisonment and died in prison.'

'Does his daughter know about her father?'

'I think not.'

Alfred said:

'No, Jennifer never told her.'

'Thank you.'

Lydia said:

'You don't think that Pilar – Oh, it's absurd!'

Poirot said:

'Now, M. Lee, will you give me some facts about your brother, M. Harry Lee?'

'What do you want to know?'

'I understand that he was considered somewhat of a disgrace to the family. Why?'

Lydia said:

'It is so long ago . . .'

Alfred said, the colour coming up in his face:

'If you want to know, M. Poirot, he stole a large sum of money by forging my father's name to a cheque. Naturally my father didn't prosecute. Harry's always been crooked. He's been in trouble all over the world. Always cabling for money to get out of a scrape. He's been in and out of gaol here, there and everywhere.'

Lydia said:

'You don't really *know* all this, Alfred.'

Alfred said angrily, his hands shaking:

'Harry's no good – no good whatever! He never has been!'

Poirot said:

'There is, I see, no love lost between you?'

Alfred said:

'He victimized my father – victimized him shamefully!'

Lydia sighed – a quick, impatient sigh. Poirot heard it and gave her a sharp glance.

She said:

'If only those diamonds could be found. I'm sure the solution lies there.'

Poirot said:

'*They have been found*, madame.'

'What?'

Poirot said gently:

'They were found in your little garden of the Dead Sea . . .'

Lydia cried:

'In my garden? How – how extraordinary!'

Poirot said softly:

'Is it not, madame?'

PART 6

DECEMBER 27TH

I

Alfred Lee said with a sigh:

'That was better than I feared!'

They had just returned from the inquest.

Mr Charlton, an old-fashioned type of solicitor with a cautious blue eye, had been present and had returned with them. He said:

'Ah – I told you the proceedings would be purely formal – purely formal – there was bound to be an adjournment – to enable the police to gather up additional evidence.'

George Lee said vexedly:

'It is all most unpleasant – really *most* unpleasant – a terrible position in which to be placed! I myself am quite convinced that this crime was done by a maniac who somehow or other gained admittance to the house. That man Sugden is as obstinate as a mule. Colonel Johnson should enlist the aid of Scotland Yard. These local police are no good. Thick-headed. What about this man Horbury, for instance? I hear his past is definitely unsatisfactory but the police do nothing whatever about it.'

Mr Charlton said:

'Ah – I believe the man Horbury has a satisfactory alibi covering the period of time in question. The police have accepted it.'

'Why should they?' George fumed. 'If I were they, I should accept such an alibi with reserve – with great reserve. Naturally, a criminal always provides himself with an alibi! It is the duty of the police to break down the alibi – that is, if they know their job.'

'Well, well,' said Mr Charlton. 'I don't think it's quite our business to teach the police their jobs, eh? Pretty competent body of men on the whole.'

George shook his head darkly.

'Scotland Yard should be called in. I'm not at all satisfied with Superintendent Sugden – he may be painstaking – but he is certainly far from brilliant.'

Mr Charlton said:

'I don't agree with you, you know. Sugden's a good man. Doesn't throw his weight about, but he gets there.'

Lydia said:

'I'm sure the police are doing their best. Mr Charlton, will you have a glass of sherry?'

Mr Charlton thanked her politely, but declined. Then, clearing his throat, he proceeded to the reading of the will, all members of the family being assembled.

He read it with a certain relish, lingering over its more obscure phraseology, and savouring its legal technicalities.

He came to the end, took off his glasses, wiped them, and looked round on the assembled company inquiringly.

Harry Lee said:

'All this legal stuff's a bit hard to follow. Give us the bare bones of it, will you?'

'Really,' said Mr Charlton. 'It's a perfectly simple will.'

Harry said:

'My God, what's a difficult will like then?'

Mr Charlton rebuked him with a cold glance. He said:

'The main provisions of the will are quite simple. Half Mr Lee's property goes to his son, Mr Alfred Lee, the remainder is divided between his other children.'

Harry laughed unpleasantly. He said:

'As usual, Alfred's struck lucky! Half my father's fortune! Lucky dog, aren't you, Alfred?'

Alfred flushed. Lydia said sharply:

'Alfred was a loyal and devoted son to his father. He's managed the works for years and has had all the responsibility.'

Harry said: 'Oh, yes, Alfred was always the good boy.'

Alfred said sharply:

'You may consider *yourself* lucky, I think, Harry, that my father left you anything at all!'

Harry laughed, throwing his head back. He said:

'You'd have liked it better if he'd cut me right out, wouldn't you? You've always disliked me.'

Mr Charlton coughed. He was used – only too well used – to

the painful scenes that succeeded the reading of a will. He was anxious to get away before the usual family quarrel got too well under way.

He murmured:

'I think – er – that that is all that I need – er –'

Harry said sharply: 'What about Pilar?'

Mr Charlton coughed again, this time apologetically.

'Er – Miss Estravados is not mentioned in the will.'

Harry said: Doesn't she get her mother's share?'

Mr Charlton explained.

'Señora Estravados, if she had lived, would of course have received an equal share with the rest of you, but as she is dead, the portion that would have been hers goes back into the estate to be shared out between you.'

Pilar said slowly in her rich Southern voice:

'Then – I have – nothing?'

Lydia said quickly:

'My dear, the family will see to that, of course.'

George Lee said:

'You will be able to make your home here with Alfred – eh, Alfred? We – er – you are our niece – it is our duty to look after you.'

Hilda said: 'We shall always be glad to have Pilar with us.'

Harry said:

'She ought to have her proper share. She ought to have Jennifer's whack.'

Mr Charlton murmured:

'Must really – er – be going. Goodbye, Mrs Lee – anything I can do – er – consult me at any time . . .'

He escaped quickly. His experience enabled him to predict that all the ingredients for a family row were present.

As the door shut behind him Lydia said in her clear voice:

'I agree with Harry. I think Pilar is entitled to a definite share. This will was made many years before Jennifer's death.'

'Nonsense,' said George. 'Very slipshod and illegal way of thinking, Lydia. The law's the law. We must abide by it.'

Magdalene said:

'It's hard luck, of course, and we're all very sorry for Pilar, but George is right. As he says, the law is the law.'

Lydia got up. She took Pilar by the hand.

'My dear,' she said. 'This must be very unpleasant for you. Will you please leave us while we discuss the question?'

She led the girl to the door.

'Don't worry, Pilar, dear,' she said. 'Leave it to me.'

Pilar went slowly out of the room. Lydia shut the door behind her and turned back.

There was a moment's pause while everyone drew breath and in another moment the battle was in full swing.

Harry said:

'You've always been a damned skinflint, George.'

George retorted:

'At any rate, I've not been a sponge and a rotter!'

'You've been just as much of a sponge as I have! You've battened on Father all these years.'

'You seem to forget that I hold a responsible and arduous position which –'

Harry said:

'Responsible and arduous my foot! You're only an inflated gasbag!'

Magdalene screamed: 'How dare you?'

Hilda's calm voice, slightly raised, said:

'Couldn't we just discuss this *quietly*?'

Lydia threw her a grateful glance.

David said with sudden violence:

'Must we have all this disgraceful fuss over *money*!'

Magdalene said venomously to him:

'It's all very well to be so high-minded. You're not going to refuse your legacy, are you? *You* want money just as much as the rest of us do! All this unworldliness is just a pose!'

David said in a strangled voice:

'You think I ought to refuse it? I wonder –'

Hilda said sharply:

'Of course you oughtn't. Must we all behave like children? Alfred, you're the head of the family –'

Alfred seemed to wake out of a dream. He said:

'I beg your pardon. All of you shouting at once. It – it confuses me.'

Lydia said:

'As Hilda has just pointed out, why must we behave like greedy children? Let us discuss this thing quietly and sanely and' – she added this quickly – 'one thing at a time. Alfred shall speak first because he is the eldest. What do you think, Alfred, we should do about Pilar?'

He said slowly:

'She must make her home here, certainly. And we should make her an allowance. I do not see she has any legal claim to the money which would have gone to her mother. She's not a Lee, remember. She's a Spanish subject.'

'No legal claim, no,' said Lydia. 'But I think she has a *moral* claim. As I see it, your father, although his daughter had married a Spaniard against his wishes, recognized her to have an equal claim upon him. George, Harry, David, and Jennifer were to share equally. Jennifer only died last year. I am sure that when he sent for Mr Charlton, he meant to make ample provision for Pilar in a new will. He would have allotted her at least her mother's share. It is possible that he might have done much more than that. She was the only grandchild, remember. I think the least *we* can do is to endeavour to remedy any injustice that your father himself was preparing to remedy.'

Alfred said warmly:

'Well put, Lydia! I was wrong. I agree with you that Pilar must be given Jennifer's share of my father's fortune.'

Lydia said: 'Your turn, Harry.'

Harry said:

'As you know, I agree. I think Lydia has put the case very well, and I'd like to say I admire her for it.'

Lydia said:

'George?'

George was red in the face. He spluttered:

'Certainly not! Whole thing's preposterous! Give her a home and a decent dress allowance. Quite enough for her!'

'Then you refuse to co-operate?' asked Alfred.

'Yes, I do.'

'And he's quite right,' said Magdalene. 'It's disgraceful to suggest he should do anything of the kind! Considering that George is the *only* member of the family who has done *anything* in the world, I think it's a shame his father left him so little!'

Lydia said: 'David?'

David said vaguely:

'Oh, I think you're right. It's a pity there's got to be so much ugliness and disputing about it all.'

Hilda said:

'You're quite right, Lydia. It's only justice!'

Harry looked round. He said:

'Well, that's clear. Of the family, Alfred, myself and David are in favour of the motion. George is against it. The ayes have it.'

George said sharply:

'There is no question of ayes and noes. My share of my father's estate is mine absolutely. I shall not part with a penny of it.'

'No, indeed,' said Magdalene.

Lydia said sharply:

'If you like to stand out, that is your business. The rest of us will make up your share of the total.'

She looked round for assent and the others nodded.

Harry said: 'Alfred's got the lion's share. He ought to stand most of the racket.'

Alfred said: 'I see that your original disinterested suggestion will soon break down.'

Hilda said firmly:

'Don't let's start again! Lydia shall tell Pilar what we've decided. We can settle details later.' She added in the hope of making a diversion, 'I wonder where Mr Farr is, and M. Poirot?'

Alfred said:

'We dropped Poirot in the village on our way to the inquest. He said he had an important purchase to make.'

Harry said: 'Why didn't *he* go to the inquest? Surely he ought to have done!'

Lydia said:

'Perhaps he knew it was not going to be important. Who's that out there in the garden? Superintendent Sugden, or Mr Farr?'

The efforts of the two women were successful. The family conclave broke up.

Lydia said to Hilda privately:

'Thank you, Hilda. It was nice of you to back me up. You know, you really *have* been a comfort in all this.'

Hilda said thoughtfully: 'Queer how money upsets people.'

The others had all left the room. The two women were alone.

Lydia said:

'Yes – even Harry – although it was his suggestion! And my poor Alfred – he is so British – he doesn't really like Lee money going to a Spanish subject.'

Hilda said, smiling:

'Do you think we women are more unworldly?'

Lydia said with a shrug of her graceful shoulders:

'Well, you know, it isn't really our money – not our *own*! That may make a difference.'

Hilda said thoughtfully:

'She is a strange child – Pilar, I mean. I wonder what will become of her?'

Lydia sighed.

'I'm glad that she will be independent. To live here, to be given a home and a dress allowance, would not, I think, be very satisfactory to her. She's too proud and, I think, too – too alien.'

She added musingly:

'I once brought some beautiful blue lapis home from Egypt. Out there, against the sun and the sand, it was a glorious colour – a brilliant warm blue. But when I got it home, the blue of it hardly showed any more. It was just a dull, darkish string of beads.'

Hilda said:

'Yes, I see . . .'

Lydia said gently:

'I am so glad to come to know you and David at last. I'm glad you both came here.'

Hilda sighed:

'How often I've wished in the last few days that we hadn't!'

'I know. You must have done . . . But you know, Hilda, the shock hasn't affected David nearly as badly as it might have done. I mean, he is so sensitive that it might have upset him completely. Actually, since the murder, he's seemed ever so much better –'

Hilda looked slightly disturbed. She said:

'So you've noticed that? It's rather dreadful in a way . . . But oh! Lydia, it's undoubtedly so!'

She was silent a minute recollecting words that her husband

had spoken only the night before. He had said to her, eagerly, his fair hair tossed back from his forehead:

'Hilda, you remember in *Tosca* – when Scarpia is dead and Tosca lights the candles at his head and feet? Do you remember what she says: '*Now* I can forgive him . . .' That is what I feel – about Father. I see now that all these years I couldn't forgive him, and yet I really wanted to . . . But no – *now* there's no rancour any more. It's all wiped away. And I feel – oh, I feel as though a great load had been lifted from my back.'

She had said, striving to fight back a sudden fear:

'Because he's dead?'

He had answered quickly, stammering in his eagerness:

'No, no, you don't understand. Not because *he* is dead, but because my childish stupid hate of him is dead . . .'

Hilda thought of those words now.

She would have liked to repeat them to the woman at her side, but she felt instinctively that it was wiser not.

She followed Lydia out of the drawing-room into the hall.

Magdalene was there, standing by the hall table with a little parcel in her hand. She jumped when she saw them. She said:

'Oh, this must be M Poirot's important purchase. I saw him put it down here just now. I wonder what it is.'

She looked from one to the other of them, giggling a little, but her eyes were sharp and anxious, belying the affected gaiety of her words.

Lydia's eyebrows rose. She said:

'I must go and wash before lunch.'

Magdalene said, still with that affectation of childishness, but unable to keep the desperate note out of her voice:

'I must just *peep*!'

She unrolled the piece of paper and gave a sharp exclamation. She stared at the thing in her hand.

Lydia stopped and Hilda too. Both women stared.

Magdalene said in a puzzled voice:

'It's a false moustache. But – but – why?'

Hilda said doubtfully:

'Disguise? But –'

Lydia finished the sentence for her.

'But M. Poirot has a very fine moustache of his own!'

Magdalene was wrapping the parcel up again. She said:

'I don't understand. It's – it's *mad. Why* does M. Poirot buy a false moustache?'

II

When Pilar left the drawing-room she walked slowly along the hall. Stephen Farr was coming in through the garden door. He said:

'Well? Is the family conclave over? Has the will been read?'

Pilar said, her breath coming fast:

'I have got nothing – nothing at all! It was a will made many years ago. My grandfather left money to my mother, but because she is dead it does not go to me but goes back to *them*.'

Stephen said:

'That seems rather hard lines.'

Pilar said:

'If that old man had lived, he would have made another will. He would have left money to *me* – a lot of money! Perhaps in time he would have left me *all* the money!'

Stephen said, smiling:

'That wouldn't have been very fair either, would it?'

'Why not? He would have liked me best, that is all.'

Stephen said:

'What a greedy child you are. A real little gold-digger.'

Pilar said soberly:

'The world is very cruel to women. They must do what they can for themselves – while they are young. When they are old and ugly no one will help them.'

Stephen said slowly:

'That's more true than I like to think. But it isn't *quite* true. Alfred Lee, for instance, was genuinely fond of his father in spite of the old man being thoroughly trying and exacting.'

Pilar's chin went up.

'Alfred,' she said, 'is rather a fool.'

Stephen laughed.

Then he said:

'Well, don't worry, lovely Pilar. The Lees are bound to look after you, you know.'

Pilar said disconsolately:

'It will not be very amusing, that.'

Stephen said slowly:

'No, I'm afraid it won't. I can't see you living here, Pilar. Would you like to come to South Africa?'

Pilar nodded.

Stephen said:

'There's sun there, and space. There's hard work too. Are you good at work, Pilar?'

Pilar said doubtfully:

'I do not know.'

He said:

'You'd rather sit on a balcony and eat sweets all day long? And grow enormously fat and have three double chins?'

Pilar laughed and Stephen said:

'That's better. I've made you laugh.'

Pilar said:

'I thought I should laugh this Christmas! In books I have read that an English Christmas is very gay, that one eats burning raisins and there is a plum pudding all in flames, and something that is called a Yule log.'

Stephen said:

'Ah, but you must have a Christmas uncomplicated by murder. Come in here a minute. Lydia took me in here yesterday. It's her store-room.'

He led her into a small room little bigger than a cupboard.

'Look, Pilar, boxes and boxes of crackers, and preserved fruits and oranges and dates and nuts. And here –'

'Oh!' Pilar clasped her hands. 'They are pretty, these gold and silver balls.'

'Those were to hang on a tree, with presents for the servants. And here are little snowmen all glittering with frost to put on the dinner table. And here are balloons of every colour all ready to blow up!'

'Oh!' Pilar's eyes shone. 'Oh! can we blow one up? Lydia would not mind. I do love balloons.'

Stephen said: 'Baby! Here, which will you have?'

Pilar said: 'I will have a red one.'

They selected their balloons and blew, their cheeks distended. Pilar stopped blowing to laugh, and her balloon went down again.

She said:

'You look so funny – blowing – with your cheeks puffed out.'

Her laugh rang out. Then she fell to, blowing industriously. They tied up their balloons carefully and began to play with them, patting them upwards, sending them to and fro.

Pilar said:

'Out in the hall there would be more room.'

They were sending the balloons to each other, and laughing, when Poirot came along the hall. He regarded them indulgently.

'So you play *les jeux d'enfants*? It is pretty, that!'

Pilar said breathlessly:

'Mine is the red one. It is bigger than his. Much bigger. If we took it outside it would go right up in the sky.'

'Let's send them up and wish,' said Stephen.

'Oh, yes, that is a good idea.'

Pilar ran to the garden door, Stephen followed. Poirot came behind, still looking indulgent.

'I will wish for a great deal of money,' announced Pilar.

She stood on tiptoe, holding the string of the balloon. It tugged gently as a puff of wind came. Pilar let go and it floated along, taken by the breeze.

Stephen laughed.

'You mustn't tell your wish.'

'No? Why not?'

'Because it doesn't come true. Now, I'm going to wish.'

He released his balloon. But he was not so lucky. It floated sideways, caught on a holly bush and expired with a bang.

Pilar ran to it.

She announced tragically:

'It is gone . . .'

Then, as she stirred the little limp wisp of rubber with her toe, she said:

'So that was what I picked up in Grandfather's room. He, too, had had a balloon, only his was a pink one.'

Poirot gave a sharp exclamation. Pilar turned inquiringly.

Poirot said:

'It is nothing. I stabbed – no stubbed – the toe.'

He wheeled round and looked at the house.

He said:

'So many windows! A house, mademoiselle, has its eyes – and its ears. It is indeed regrettable that the English are so fond of open windows.'

Lydia came out on the terrace. She said:

'Lunch is just ready. Pilar, my dear, everything has been settled quite satisfactorily. Alfred will explain the exact details to you after lunch. Shall we come in?'

They went into the house. Poirot came last. He was looking grave.

III

Lunch was over.

As they came out of the dining-room, Alfred said to Pilar:

'Will you come into my room? There is something I want to talk over with you.'

He led her across the hall and into his study, shutting the door after him. The others went on into the drawing-room. Only Hercule Poirot remained in the hall looking thoughtfully at the closed study door.

He was aware suddenly of the old butler hovering uneasily near him.

Poirot said: 'Yes, Tressilian, what is it?'

The old man seemed troubled. He said:

'I wanted to speak to Mr Lee. But I don't like to disturb him now.'

Poirot said: 'Something has occurred?'

Tressilian said slowly:

'It's such a queer thing. It doesn't make sense.'

'Tell me,' said Hercule Poirot.

Tressilian hesitated. Then he said:

'Well, it's this, sir. You may have noticed that each side of the front door there was a cannon ball. Big heavy stone things. Well, sir, *one of them's gone.*'

Hercule Poirot's eyebrows rose. He said; 'Since when?'

'They were both there this morning, sir. I'll take my oath on that.'

'Let me see.'

Together they went outside the front door. Poirot bent and

examined the remaining cannon ball. When he straightened himself, his face was very grave.

Tressilian quavered:

'Who'd want to steal a thing like that, sir? It doesn't make *sense.*'

Poirot said: 'I do not like it. I do not like it at all . . .'

Tressilian was watching him anxiously. He said slowly:

'What's come to the house, sir? Ever since the master was murdered it doesn't seem like the same place. I feel the whole time as though I was going about in a dream. I mix things up, and I sometimes feel I can't trust my own eyes.'

Hercule Poirot shook his head. He said:

'You are wrong. Your own eyes are just what you must trust.'

Tressilian said, shaking his head:

'My sight's bad – I can't see like I used to do. I get things mixed up – and people. I'm getting too old for my work.'

Hercule Poirot clapped him on the shoulder and said:

'Courage.'

'Thank you, sir. You mean it kindly, I know. But there it is, I am too old. I'm always going back to the old days and the old faces. Miss Jenny and Master David and Master Alfred. I'm always seeing them as young gentlemen and ladies. Ever since that night when Mr Harry came home –'

Poirot nodded.

'Yes,' he said, 'that is what I thought. You said just now "Ever since the master was murdered" – but it began before that. *It is ever since Mr Harry came home*, is it not, that things have altered and seemed unreal?'

The butler said:

'You're quite right, sir. It was then. Mr Harry always brought trouble into the house, even in the old days.'

His eyes wandered back to the empty stone base.

'Who can have taken it, sir?' he whispered. 'And why? It's – it's like a madhouse.'

Hercule Poirot said:

'It is not madness I am afraid of. It is sanity! Somebody, Tressilian, is in great danger.'

He turned and re-entered the house.

At that moment Pilar came out from the study. A red spot

shone on either cheek. She held her head high and her eyes glittered.

As Poirot came up to her, she suddenly stamped her foot and said: 'I will not take it.'

Poirot raised his eyebrows. He said:

'What is it that you will not take, mademoiselle?'

Pilar said:

'Alfred has just told me that I am to have my mother's share of the money my grandfather left.'

'Well?'

'I could not get it by law, he said. But he and Lydia and the others consider it should be mine. They say it is a matter of justice. And so they will hand it over to me.'

Poirot said again:

'Well?'

Pilar stamped once more with her foot.

'Do you not understand? They are giving it to me – *giving* it to me.'

'Need that hurt your pride? Since what they say is true – that it should in justice be yours?'

Pilar said:

'You do not understand . . .'

Poirot said:

'On the contrary – I understand very well.'

'Oh! . . .' She turned away pettishly.

There was a ring at the bell. Poirot glanced over his shoulder. He saw the silhouette of Superintendent Sugden outside the door. He said hurriedly to Pilar:

'Where are you going?'

She said sulkily:

'To the drawing-room. To the others.'

Poirot said quickly:

'Good. Stay with them there. Do not wander about the house alone, especially after dark. Be on your guard. You are in great danger, mademoiselle. You will never be in greater danger than you are today.'

He turned away from her and went to meet Sugden.

The latter waited till Tressilian had gone back into his pantry. Then he shoved a cable form under Poirot's nose.

'Now we've got it!' he said. 'Read that. It's from the South African Police.'

The cable said:

'*Ebenezer Farr's only son died two years ago.*'

Sugden said:

'So now we know! Funny – I was on a different tack altogether . . .'

IV

Pilar marched into the drawing-room, her head held high.

She went straight up to Lydia, who was sitting in the window with some knitting.

Pilar said:

'Lydia, I have come to tell you that I will not take that money. I am going away – at once . . .'

Lydia looked astonished. She laid down her knitting. She said:

'My dear child, Alfred must have explained very badly! It is not in the least a matter of charity, if that is what you feel. Really, it is not a question of kindness or generosity on our part. It is a plain matter of right and wrong. In the ordinary course of events your mother would have inherited this money, and you would have come into it from her. It is your right – your blood right. It is a matter, not of charity, but of *justice*!'

Pilar said fiercely:

'And that is why I cannot do it – not when you speak like that – not when you are like that! I enjoyed coming here. It was fun! It was an adventure, but now you have spoilt it all! I am going away now, at once – you will never be bothered by me again . . .'

Tears choked her voice. She turned and ran blindly out of thc room.

Lydia stared. She said helplessly:

'I'd no idea she would take it like that!'

Hilda said:

'The child seems quite upset.'

George cleared his throat and said portentously:

'Er – as I pointed out this morning – the principle involved is wrong. Pilar has the wit to see that for herself. She refuses to accept charity –'

Lydia said sharply:

'It is *not* charity. It is her right!'

George said:

'She does not seem to think so!'

Superintendent Sugden and Hercule Poirot came in. The former looked round and asked:

'Where's Mr Farr? I want a word with him.'

Before anyone had time to answer, Hercule Poirot said sharply:

'Where is the Señorita Estravados?'

George Lee said with a trace of malicious satisfaction:

'Going to clear out, so she says. Apparently she has had enough of her English relations.'

Poirot wheeled round.

He said to Sugden:

'Come!'

As the two men emerged into the hall, there was the sound of a heavy crash and a far-away shriek.

Poirot cried:

'Quick . . . Come . . .'

They raced along the hall and up the far staircase. The door of Pilar's room was open and a man stood in the doorway. He turned his head as they ran up. It was Stephen Farr.

He said:

'She's alive . . .'

Pilar stood crouched against the wall of her room. She was staring at the floor where a big stone cannon ball was lying.

She said breathlessly:

'It was on top of my door, balanced there. It would have crashed down on my head when I came in, but my skirt caught on a nail and jerked me back just as I was coming in.'

Poirot knelt down and examined the nail. On it was a thread of purple tweed. He looked up and nodded gravely.

'That nail, mademoiselle,' he said, 'saved your life.'

The superintendent said, bewildered:

'Look here, what's the meaning of all this?'

Pilar said:

'Someone tried to kill me!'

She nodded her head several times.

Superintendent Sugden glanced up at the door.

'Booby trap,' he said. 'An old-fashioned booby trap – and its purpose was murder! That's the second murder planned in this house. But this time it didn't come off!'

Stephen Farr said huskily:

'Thank God you're safe.'

Pilar flung out her hands in a wide, appealing gesture.

'*Madre de Dios*,' she cried. 'Why should anyone wish to kill *me*? What have I done?'

Hercule Poirot said slowly:

'You should rather ask, mademoiselle, *what do I know*?'

She stared.

'Know? I do not know anything.'

Hercule Poirot said:

'That is where you are wrong. Tell me, Mademoiselle Pilar, where were you at the time of the murder? You were not in this room.'

'I was. I have told you so!'

Superintendent Sugden said with deceptive mildness:

'Yes, but you weren't speaking the truth when you said that, you know. You told us you heard your grandfather scream – you couldn't have heard that if you were in here – Mr Poirot and I tested that yesterday.'

'Oh!' Pilar caught her breath.

Poirot said:

'You were somewhere very much nearer his room. I will tell you where I think you were, mademoiselle. You were in the recess with the statues quite close to your grandfather's door.'

Pilar said, startled:

'Oh . . . How did you know?'

Poirot said with a faint smile:

'Mr Farr saw you there.'

Stephen said sharply:

'I did not. That's an absolute lie!'

Poirot said:

'I ask your pardon, Mr Farr, but you *did* see her. Remember your impression that there were *three* statues in that recess, not *two*. Only one person wore a white dress that night, Mademoiselle Estravados. *She* was the third white figure you saw. That is so, is it not, mademoiselle?'

Pilar said, after a moment's hesitation: 'Yes, it is true.'

Poirot said gently: 'Now tell us, mademoiselle, the whole truth. *Why* were you there?'

Pilar said:

'I left the drawing-room after dinner and I thought I would go and see my grandfather. I thought he would be pleased. But when I turned into the passage I saw someone else was there at his door. I did not want to be seen because I knew my grandfather had said he did not want to see anyone that night. I slipped into the recess in case the person at the door turned round.'

'Then, all at once, I heard the most horrible sounds, tables – chairs' – she waved her hands – 'everything falling and crashing. I did not move. I do not know why. I was frightened. And then there was a terrible scream' – she crossed herself – 'and my heart it stopped beating, and I said, "*Someone is dead . . .*"'

'And then?'

'And then people began coming running along the passage and I came out at the end and joined them.'

Superintendent Sugden said sharply:

'You said nothing of all this when we first questioned you. Why not?'

Pilar shook her head. She said, with an air of wisdom:

'It is not good to tell too much to the police. I thought, you see, that if I said I was near there you might think that *I* had killed him. So I said I was in my room.'

Sugden said sharply:

'If you tell deliberate lies all that it ends in is that you're bound to come under suspicion.'

Stephen Farr said: 'Pilar?'

'Yes?'

'*Who did you see standing at the door* when you turned into the passage? Tell us.'

Sugden said: 'Yes, tell us.'

For a moment the girl hesitated. Her eyes opened, then narrowed. She said slowly:

'I don't know who it was. It was too dimly lit to see. *But it was a woman . . .*'

V

Superintendent Sugden looked round at the circle of faces. He said, with something as near irritation as he had yet shown:

'This is very irregular, Mr Poirot.'

Poirot said:

'It is a little idea of mine. I wish to share with everyone the knowledge that I have acquired. I shall then invite their co-operation, and so we shall get at the truth.'

Sugden murmured under his breath: 'Monkey tricks.'

He leaned back in his chair. Poirot said:

'To begin with, you have, I think, an explanation to ask of Mr Farr.'

Sugden's mouth tightened.

'I should have chosen a less public moment,' he said. 'However, I've no objection.' He handed the cable to Stephen Farr. 'Now, Mr *Farr*, as you call yourself, perhaps you can explain *this*?'

Stephen Farr took it. Raising his eyebrows, he read it slowly out loud. Then, with a bow, he handed it back to the superintendent.

'Yes,' he said. 'It's pretty damning, isn't it?'

Sugden said:

'Is that all you've got to say about it? You quite understand there is no obligation on you to make a statement –'

Stephen Farr interrupted. He said:

'You needn't caution me, Superintendent. I can see it trembling on your tongue! Yes, I'll give you an explanation. It's not a very good one, but it's the truth.'

He paused. Then he began:

'I'm not Ebenezer Farr's son. But I knew both father and son quite well. Now try and put yourself in my place. (My name is Stephen Grant, by the way.) I arrived in this country for the first time in my life. I was disappointed. Everything and everybody seemed drab and lifeless. Then I was travelling by train and I saw a girl. I've got to say it straight out: I fell for that girl! She was the loveliest and most unlikely creature in the world! I talked to her for a while in the train and I made up my mind then and there not to lose sight of her. As I was leaving the compartment I caught sight of the label on her suitcase. Her name meant nothing to me, but the address to which she was travelling did. I'd heard of Gorston Hall, and I knew all about its owner. He was Ebenezer Farr's one-time partner and old Eb often talked about him and said what a personality he was.

'Well, the idea came to me to go to Gorston Hall and pretend I was Eb's son. He had died, as this cable says, two years ago, but I remembered old Eb saying that he had not heard from Simeon Lee now for many years, and I judged that Lee would not know of the death of Eb's son. Anyway, I felt it was worth trying.'

Sugden said: 'You didn't try it on at once, though. You stayed in the King's Arms at Addlesfield for two days.'

Stephen said:

'I was thinking it over – whether to try it or not. At last I made up my mind I would. It appealed to me as a bit of an adventure. Well, it worked like a charm! The old man greeted me in the friendliest manner and at once asked me to come and stay in the house. I accepted. There you are, Superintendent, there's my explanation. If you don't fancy it, cast your mind back to your courting days and see if you don't remember some bit of foolishness you indulged in then. As for my real name, as I say, it's Stephen Grant. You can cable to South Africa and check up on me, but I'll tell you this: you'll find I'm a perfectly respectable citizen. I'm not a crook or a jewel thief.'

Poirot said softly: 'I never believed you were.'

Superintendent Sugden stroked his jaw cautiously. He said:

'I'll have to check up on that story. What I'd like to know is this: Why didn't you come clean after the murder instead of telling us a pack of lies?'

Stephen said disarmingly:

'Because I was a fool! I thought I could get away with it! I thought it would look fishy if I admitted to being here under a false name. If I hadn't been a complete idiot I would have realized you were bound to cable to Jo'burg.'

Sugden said:

'Well, Mr Farr – er – Grant – I'm not saying I disbelieve your story. It will be proved or disproved soon enough.'

He looked across inquiringly at Poirot. The latter said:

'I think Miss Estravados has something to say.'

Pilar had gone very white. She said, in a breathless voice:

'It is true. I would never have told you, but for Lydia and the money. To come here and pretend and cheat and act – that was fun, but when Lydia said the money was mine and that it was only justice, that was different; it was not fun any longer.'

Alfred Lee said with a puzzled face:

'I do not understand, my dear, what you are talking about.'

Pilar said:

'You think I am your niece, Pilar Estravados? But that is not so! Pilar was killed when I was travelling with her in a car in Spain. A bomb came and it hit the car and she was killed, but I was not touched. I did not know her very well, but she had told me all about herself and how her grandfather had sent for her to go to England and that he was very rich. And I had no money at all and I did not know where to go or what to do. And I thought suddenly: "Why should not I take Pilar's passport and go to England and become very rich?"' Her face lit up with its sudden wide smile. 'Oh, it was fun wondering if I could get away with it! Our faces on the photograph were not unlike. But when they wanted my passport here I opened the window and threw it out and ran down to get it, and then I rubbed some earth just over the face a little because at a barrier travelling they do not look very closely, but here they might –'

Alfred Lee said angrily:

'Do you mean to say that you represented yourself to my father as his granddaughter, and played on his affection for you?'

Pilar nodded. She said complacently:

'Yes, I saw at once I could make him like me very much.'

George Lee broke out:

'Preposterous!' he spluttered. 'Criminal! Attempting to get money by false pretences.'

Harry Lee said:

'She didn't get any from *you*, old boy! Pilar, I'm on your side! I've got a profound admiration for your daring. And, thank goodness, I'm not your uncle any more! That gives me a much freer hand.'

Pilar said to Poirot: '*You* knew? When did you know?'

Poirot smiled:

'Mademoiselle, if you have studied the laws of Mendel you would know that two blue-eyed people are not likely to have a brown-eyed child. Your mother was, I was sure, a most chaste and respectable lady. It followed, then, that you were not Pilar Estravados at all. When you did your trick with the passport, I was quite sure of it. It was ingenious, but not, you understand, quite ingenious enough.'

Superintendent Sugden said unpleasantly:

'The whole thing's not quite ingenious enough.'

Pilar stared at him. She said:

'I don't understand . . .'

Sugden said: 'You've told us a story – but I think there's a good deal more you haven't told.'

Stephen said: 'You leave her alone!'

Superintendent Sugden took no notice. He went on:

'You've told us that you went up to your grandfather's room after dinner. You said it was an impulse on your part. I'm going to suggest something else. It was you who stole those diamonds. You'd handled them. On occasion, perhaps, you'd put them away in the safe and the old man hadn't watched you do it! When he found the stones were missing, he saw at once that only two people could have taken them. One was Horbury, who might have got to know the combination and have crept in and stolen them during the night. The other person was *you*.

'Well, Mr Lee at once took measures. He rang me up and had me come to see him. Then he sent word to you to come and see him immediately after dinner. You did so and he accused you of the theft. You denied it; he pressed the charge. I don't know what happened next – perhaps he tumbled to the fact that you weren't his granddaughter, but a very clever little professional thief. Anyway, the game was up, exposure loomed over you, and you slashed at him with a knife. There was a struggle and he screamed. You were properly up against it then. You hurried out of the room, turned the key from the outside and then, knowing you could not get away, before the others came, *you slipped into the recess by the statues*.'

Pilar cried shrilly:

'It is not true! It is not true! I did not steal the diamonds! I did not kill him. I swear it by the Blessed Virgin.'

Sugden said sharply:

'*Then who did?* You say you saw a figure standing outside Mr

Lee's door. According to your story, *that person must have been the murderer. No one else* passed the recess! But we've only *your* word for it *that there was a figure there at all.* In other words, *you made that up* to exculpate yourself!'

George Lee said sharply:

'Of course she's guilty! It's all clear enough! I always *said* an outsider killed my father! Preposterous nonsense to pretend one of his family would do a thing like that! It – it wouldn't be natural!'

Poirot stirred in his seat. He said:

'I disagree with you. Taking into consideration the character of Simeon Lee, it would be a very natural thing to happen.'

'Eh?' George's jaw dropped. He stared at Poirot.

Poirot went on:

'And, in my opinion, that very thing *did* happen. Simeon Lee was killed by his own flesh and blood, for what seemed to the murderer a very good and sufficient reason.'

George cried: 'One of us? I deny –'

Poirot's voice broke in hard as steel.

'There is a case against every person here. We will, Mr George Lee, begin with the case against *you. You* had no love for your father! You kept on good terms with him for the sake of money. On the day of his death *he threatened to cut down your allowance.* You knew that on his death you would probably inherit a very substantial sum. There is the motive. After dinner you went, as you say, to telephone. You *did* telephone – but the call lasted only *five minutes.* After that you could easily have gone to your father's room, chatted with him, and then attacked him and killed him. You left the room and turned the key from outside, for you hoped the affair would be put down to a burglar. You omitted, in your panic, to make sure that the window was fully open so as to support the burglar theory. That was stupid; but you are, if you will pardon my saying so, rather a stupid man!

'However,' said Poirot, after a brief pause during which George tried to speak and failed, 'many stupid men have been criminals!'

He turned his eyes on Magdalene.

'Madame, too, she also had a motive. She is, I think, in debt, and the tone of certain of your father's remarks may – have caused her uneasiness. She, too, has no alibi. She went to telephone, but she did *not* telephone, and we have *only her word* for what she did do . . .

'Then,' he paused, 'there is Mr David Lee. We have heard, not once but many times, of the revengeful tempers and long memories that went with the Lee blood. Mr David Lee did not forget or forgive the way his father had treated his mother. A final jibe directed at the dead lady may have been the last straw. David Lee is said to have been playing the piano at the time of the murder. By a coincidence he was playing the "Dead March". But suppose *somebody else* was playing that "Dead March", somebody who knew what he was going to do, and who approved his action?'

Hilda Lee said quietly:

'That is an infamous suggestion.'

Poirot turned to her. 'I will offer you another, madame. It was *your* hand that did the deed. It was *you* who crept upstairs to execute judgment on a man you considered beyond human forgiveness. You are of those, madame, who can be terrible in anger . . .'

Hilda said: 'I did not kill him.'

Superintendent Sugden said brusquely:

'Mr Poirot's quite right. There is a possible case against everyone except Mr Alfred Lee, Mr Harry Lee, and Mrs Alfred Lee.'

Poirot said gently:

'I should not even except those three . . .'

The superintendent protested: 'Oh, come now, Mr Poirot!'

Lydia Lee said:

'And what is the case against me, M. Poirot?'

She smiled a little as she spoke, her brows raised ironically.

Poirot bowed. He said:

'Your motive, madame, I pass over. It is sufficiently obvious. As to the rest, you were wearing last night a flowered taffeta dress of a very distinctive pattern with a cape. I will remind you of the fact that Tressilian, the butler, is shortsighted. Objects at a distance are dim and vague to him. I will also point out that your drawing-room is big and lighted by heavily shaded lamps. On that night, a minute or two before the cries were heard, Tressilian came into the drawing-room to take away the coffee-cups. He saw you, *as he thought*, in a familiar attitude by the far window half concealed by the heavy curtains.'

Lydia Lee said: 'He did see me.'

Poirot went on:

'I suggest that it is possible that *what Tressilian saw was the cape of your dress*, arranged to show by the window curtain, as though you yourself were standing there.'

Lydia said: 'I was standing there . . .'

Alfred said: 'How dare you suggest –?'

Harry interrupted him.

'Let him go on, Alfred. It's our turn next. How do you suggest that dear Alfred killed his beloved father since we were both together in the dining-room at the time?'

Poirot beamed at him.

'That,' he said, 'is very simple. An alibi gains in force accordingly as it is unwillingly given. You and your brother are on bad terms. It is well known. *You* jibe at *him* in public. *He* has not a good word to say for *you*! But, *supposing that were all part of a very clever plot*. Supposing that Alfred Lee is tired of dancing attendance upon an exacting taskmaster. Supposing that you and he have got together some time ago. Your plan is laid. You come home. Alfred appears to resent your presence. He shows jealousy and dislike of you. You show contempt for him. And then comes the night of the murder you have so cleverly planned together. One of you remains in the dining-room, talking and perhaps quarrelling aloud as though two people were there. *The other goes upstairs and commits the crime . . .*'

Alfred sprang to his feet.

'You devil!' he said. His voice was inarticulate.

Sugden was staring at Poirot. He said:

'Do you really mean –?'

Poirot said, with a sudden ring of authority in his voice:

'I have had to show you the *possibilities*! These are the things that *might* have happened! Which of them actually *did* happen we can only tell by passing from the outside appearance to the inside reality . . .'

He paused and then said slowly:

'We must come back, as I said before, to the character of Simeon Lee himself . . .'

VI

There was a momentary pause. Strangely enough, all indignation and all rancour had died down. Hercule Poirot held his audience under the spell of his personality. They watched him, fascinated, as he began slowly to speak.

'It is all there, you see. The dead man is the focus and centre of the mystery! We must probe deep into the heart and mind of Simeon Lee and see what we find there. For a man does not live and die to himself alone. That which he has, he hands on – to those who come after him . . .

'What had Simeon Lee to bequeath to his sons and daughter? Pride, to begin with – a pride which, in the old man, was frustrated in his disappointment over his children. Then there was the quality of patience. We have been told that Simeon Lee waited patiently for years in order to revenge himself upon someone who had done him an injury. We see that that aspect of his temperament was inherited by the son who resembled him least in face. David Lee also could remember and continue to harbour resentment through long years. In *face*, Harry Lee was the only one of his children who closely resembled him. That resemblance is quite striking when we examine the portrait of Simeon Lee as a young man. There is the same high-bridged aquiline nose, the long sharp line of the jaw, the backward poise of the head. I think, too, that Harry inherited many of his father's mannerisms – that habit, for instance, of throwing back his head and laughing, and another habit of drawing his finger along the line of his jaw.

'Bearing all these things in mind, and being convinced that the murder was committed by a person closely connected with the dead man, I studied the family from the psychological standpoint. That is, I tried to decide which of them were *psychologically possible criminals*. And, in my judgment, only two persons qualified in that respect. They were Alfred Lee and Hilda Lee, David's wife. David himself I rejected as a possible murderer. I do not think a person of his delicate susceptibilities could have faced the actual bloodshed of a cut throat. George Lee and his wife I likewise rejected. Whatever their desires, I did not think they had the temperament to take a *risk*. They were both essentially cautious. Mrs Alfred Lee I felt sure was quite incapable of an act of violence. She has too much irony in her nature. About Harry Lee I hesitated. He had a certain coarse truculence of aspect, but I was nearly sure that Harry Lee, in spite of his bluff and his bluster, was essentially a weakling. That, I now know, was also his father's opinion. Harry, he said, was worth no more than the rest. That left me with two people I have already mentioned. Alfred Lee was a person capable of a great deal of selfless devotion. He was a man who had controlled and subordinated himself to the will of another for many years. It was always possible under these conditions for something to snap. Moreover, he might quite possibly have harboured a secret grudge against his father which might gradually have grown in force through never being expressed in any way. It is the quietest and meekest people who are often capable of the most sudden and unexpected violence for the reason that when their control does snap, it does so entirely! The other person I considered was capable of the crime was Hilda Lee. She is the kind of individual who is capable, on occasions, of taking the law into her own hands – though never through selfish motives. Such people judge and also execute. Many Old Testament characters are of this type. Jael and Judith, for example.

'And now having got so far I examined the circumstances of the crime itself. And the first thing that arises – that strikes one in the face, as it were – is the extraordinary conditions under which that crime took place! Take your minds back to that room where Simeon Lee lay dead. If you remember, there was both a heavy table and a heavy chair overturned, a lamp, crockery, glasses, etc. But the chair and the table were especially surprising. They were of solid mahogany. It was hard to see how *any* struggle between that frail old man and his opponent could result in so much solid furniture being overturned and knocked down. The whole thing seemed *unreal*. And yet surely no one in their senses would stage such an effect if it had not really occurred – unless possibly Simeon Lee had been killed by a powerful man and the idea was to suggest that the assailant was a woman or somebody of weak physique.

'But such an idea was unconvincing in the extreme, since the noise of the furniture would give the alarm and the murderer would thereby have very little time to make his exit. It would surely be to *anyone's* advantage to cut Simeon Lee's throat as *quietly* as possible.

'Another extraordinary point was the turning of the key in the lock from the outside. Again, there seemed no *reason* for such a proceeding. It could not suggest suicide, since nothing in the death itself accorded with suicide. It was not to suggest escape through the windows – for those windows were so arranged that escape that way was impossible! Moreover, once again, it involved *time*. Time which *must* be precious to the murderer!

'There was one other incomprehensible thing – a piece of rubber cut from Simeon Lee's spongebag and a small wooden peg shown to me by Superintendent Sugden. These had been picked up from the floor by one of the persons who first entered the room. There again – *these things did not make sense*! They meant exactly nothing at all! Yet they had been there.

'The crime, you perceive, is becoming increasingly incomprehensible. It has no order, no method – *enfin*, it is not *reasonable*.

'And now we come to a further difficulty. Superintendent Sugden was sent for by the dead man; a robbery was reported to him, and he was asked to return an hour and a half later. *Why?* If it is because Simeon Lee suspected his granddaughter or some other member of the family, why does he not ask Superintendent Sugden to wait downstairs while he has his interview straight away with the suspected party? With the superintendent actually in the house, his lever over the guilty person would have been much stronger.

'So now we arrive at the point where not only the behaviour of the murderer is extraordinary, but the behaviour of Simeon Lee also is extraordinary!

'And I say to myself: "This thing is all wrong!" Why? Because we are looking at it *from the wrong angle*. We are looking at it *from the angle that the murderer wants us to look at it . . .*

'We have three things that do not make sense: the struggle, the turned key, and the snip of rubber. But there *must* be some way of looking at those three things which *would* make sense! And I empty my mind blank and forget the circumstances of the crime and take these things *on their own merits*. I say – a *struggle*. What does *that* suggest? Violence – breakage – noise . . . The *key*? *Why* does one turn a key? So that no one shall enter? But the key did not prevent that, since the door was broken down almost immediately. To keep someone *in*? To keep someone *out*? A snip of rubber? I say to myself: "A little piece of a spongebag is a little piece of a spongebag, and that is all!"

'So you would say there is nothing there – and yet that is not strictly true, for three impressions remain: noise – seclusion – blankness . . .

'Do they fit with either of my two possibles? No, they do not. To both Alfred Lee and Hilda Lee a *quiet* murder would have been infinitely preferable, to have wasted time in locking the door from the outside is absurd, and the little piece of spongebag means yet once more – nothing at all!

'And yet I have very strongly the feeling that there is nothing absurd about this crime – that it is on the contrary, very well planned and admirably executed. That is has, in fact, *succeeded*! Therefore that everything that has happened was *meant* . . .

'And then, going over it again, I got my first glimmer of light . . .

'Blood – *so much blood* – blood everywhere . . . An insistence on blood – fresh, wet, gleaming blood . . . So much blood – *too much blood* . . .

'And a second thought comes with that. This is a crime of *blood* – it is *in* the blood. *It is Simeon Lee's own blood that rises up against him . . .*'

Hercule Poirot leaned forward.

'The two most valuable clues in this case were uttered quite unconsciously by two different people. The first was when Mrs Alfred Lee quoted a line from *Macbeth*: "*Who would have thought the old man to have had so much blood in him?*" The other was a phrase uttered by Tressilian, the butler. He described how he felt dazed and things seemed to be happening that had happened before. It was a very simple occurrence that gave him that strange feeling. He heard a ring at the bell and went to open the door to Harry Lee, and the next day he did the same thing to Stephen Farr.

'Now *why* did he have that feeling? Look at Harry Lee and Stephen Farr *and you will see why*. They are astoundingly alike! *That* was why *opening the door to Stephen Farr was just like opening the door to Harry Lee.* It might almost have been the same man standing there. And then, only today, Tressilian mentioned that he was always getting muddled between people. No wonder! Stephen Farr has a high-bridged nose, a habit of throwing his head back when he laughs, and a trick of stroking his jaw with his forefinger. Look long and earnestly at the portrait of Simeon Lee as a young man and you see *not only Harry Lee, but Stephen Farr . . .*'

Stephen moved. His chair creaked. Poirot said:

'Remember that outburst of Simeon Lee, his tirade against his family. He said, you remember it, that he would swear he had better sons *born the wrong side of the blanket.* We are back again at the character of Simeon Lee. Simeon Lee, who was successful with women and who broke his wife's heart! Simeon Lee, who boasted to Pilar that he might have a bodyguard of sons almost the same age! So I came to this conclusion: Simeon Lee had not only his legitimate family in the house, *but an unacknowledged and unrecognized son of his own blood.*'

Stephen got to his feet. Poirot said:

'That was your real reason, wasn't it? Not that pretty romance of the girl you met in the train! You were coming here *before you met her.* Coming to see *what kind of a man your father was . . .*'

Stephen had gone dead white. He said, and his voice was broken and husky:

'Yes, I've always wondered . . . Mother spoke about him sometimes. It grew into a kind of obsession with me – to see what he was like! I made a bit of money and I came to England. I wasn't going to let him know who I was. I pretended to be old Eb's son. I came here for one reason only – to see the man who was my father . . .'

Superintendent Sugden said in almost a whisper:

'Lord, I've been blind . . . I can see it now. Twice I've taken you for Mr Harry Lee and then seen my mistake, and yet I never guessed!'

He turned on Pilar.

'That was it, wasn't it? It was Stephen Farr you saw standing outside that door? You hesitated, I remember, and looked at him before you said it was a woman. It was Farr you saw, *and you weren't going to give him away.*'

There was a gentle rustle. Hilda Lee's deep voice spoke:

'No,' she said. 'You're wrong. It was *I* whom Pilar saw . . .'

Poirot said:

'You, madame? Yes, I thought so . . .'

Hilda said quietly:

'Self-preservation is a curious thing. I wouldn't believe I could be such a coward. To keep silence just because I was afraid!'

Poirot said:

'You will tell us now?'

She nodded.

'I was with David in the music-room. He was playing. He was in a very queer mood. I was a little frightened and I felt my responsibility very keenly because it was I who had insisted on coming here. David began to play the "Dead March", and suddenly I made up my mind. However odd it might seem, I determined that we would both leave at once – that night. I went quietly out of the music-room and upstairs. I meant to go to old Mr Lee and tell him quite plainly why we were going. I went along the corridor to his room and knocked on the door. There was no answer. I knocked again a little louder. There was still no answer. Then I tried the door handle. The door was locked. And then, as I stood hesitating, *I heard a sound inside the room* –'

She stopped.

'You won't believe me, but it's true! *Someone was in there* – assaulting Mr Lee. I heard tables and chairs overturned and the crash of glass and china, and then I heard that one last horrible cry that died away to nothing – and then silence.

'I stood there paralysed! I couldn't move! And then Mr Farr came running along and Magdalene and all the others and Mr Farr and Harry began to batter on the door. It went down and we saw the room, *and there was no one in it* – except Mr Lee lying dead in all that blood.'

Her quiet voice rose higher. She cried:

'*There was no one else there* – *no one*, you understand! And *no one had come out of the room . . .*'

VII

Superintendent Sugden drew a deep breath. He said:

'Either I'm going mad or everybody else is! What you've said, Mrs Lee, is just plumb impossible. It's crazy!'

Hilda Lee cried:

'I tell you I heard them fighting in there, and I heard the old man scream when his throat was cut – and no one came out and no one was in the room!'

Hercule Poirot said:

'And all this time you have said nothing.'

Hilda Lee's face was white, but she said steadily:

'No, because if I told you what had happened, there's only one thing you could say or think – that it was *I* who killed him . . .'

Poirot shook his head.

'No,' he said. 'You did not kill him. His son killed him.'

Stephen Farr said:

'I swear before God I never touched him!'

'Not you,' said Poirot. 'He had other sons!'

Harry said:

'What the hell –'

George stared. David drew his hand across his eyes. Alfred blinked twice.

Poirot said:

'The very first night I was here – the night of the murder – I saw a ghost. *It was the ghost of the dead man.* When I first saw Harry Lee I was puzzled. I felt I had seen him before. Then I noted his features carefully and I realized how like his father he was, and I told myself that that was what caused the feeling of familiarity.

'But yesterday a man sitting opposite me threw back his head and laughed – *and I knew who it was Harry Lee reminded me of.* And I traced again, in another face, the features of the dead man.

'No wonder poor old Tressilian felt confused when he had answered the door not to two, but to *three* men who resembled each other closely. No wonder he confessed to getting muddled about people when there were three men in the house who, at a little distance, could pass for each other! The same build, the same gestures (one in particular, a trick of stroking the jaw), the same habit of laughing with the head thrown back, the same distinctive high-bridged nose. Yet the similarity was not always easy to see – *for the third man had a moustache*.'

He leaned forward.

'One forgets sometimes that police officers are men, that they have wives and children, mothers' – he paused – 'and *fathers* . . . Remember Simeon Lee's local reputation: a man who broke his wife's heart because of his affairs with women. A son born the wrong side of the blanket may inherit many things. He may inherit his father's features and even his gestures. He may inherit his pride and his patience and his revengeful spirit!'

His voice rose.

'All your life, Sugden, you've resented the wrong your father did you. I think you determined long ago to kill him. You come from the next county, not very far away. Doubtless your mother, with the money Simeon Lee so generously gave her, was able to find a husband who would stand father to her child. Easy for you to enter the Middleshire Police Force and wait your opportunity. A police superintendent has a grand opportunity of committing a murder and getting away with it.'

Sugden's face had gone white as paper.

He said:

'You're mad! I was outside the house when he was killed.'

Poirot shook his head.

'No, you killed him before you left the house the first time. No one saw him alive after you left. It was all so easy for you. Simeon Lee expected you, yes, *but he never sent for you*. It was *you* who rang him up and spoke vaguely about an attempt at robbery. You said you would call upon him just before eight that night and would pretend to be collecting for a police charity. Simeon Lee had no suspicions. He did not know you were his son. You came and told him a tale of substituted diamonds. He opened the safe to show you that the real diamonds were safe in his possession. You apologized, came back to the hearth with him and, catching him unawares, you cut his throat, holding your hand over his mouth so that he shouldn't cry out. Child's play to a man of your powerful physique.

'Then you set the scene. You took the diamonds. You piled up tables and chairs, lamps and glasses, and twined a very thin rope or cord which you had brought in coiled round your body, in and out between them. You had with you a bottle of some freshly killed animal's blood to which you had added a quantity of sodium citrate. You sprinkled this about freely and added more sodium citrate to the pool of blood which flowed from Simeon Lee's wound. You made up up the fire so that the body should keep its warmth. Then you passed the two ends of the cord out through the narrow slit at the bottom of the window and let them hang down the wall. You left the room and turned the key from the outside. That was vital, *since no one must, by any chance, enter that room.*

'Then you went out and hid the diamonds in the stone sink garden. If, sooner or later, they were discovered there, they would only focus suspicion more strongly where you wanted it: on the members of Simeon Lee's legitimate family. A little before nine-fifteen you returned and, going up to the wall underneath the window, you pulled on the cord. That dislodged the carefully piled-up structure you had arranged. Furniture and china fell with a crash. You pulled on one end of the cord and re-wound it round your body under your coat and waistcoat.

'You had one further device!'

He turned to the others.

'Do you remember, all of you, how each of you described the dying scream of Mr Lee in a different way? You, Mr Lee, described it as the cry of a man in mortal agony. Your wife and David Lee both used the expression: a soul in hell. Mrs David Lee, on the contrary, said it was the cry of someone who had *no* soul. She said it was inhuman, like a beast. It was Harry Lee who came nearest to the truth. He said it sounded like killing a pig.

'Do you know those long pink bladders that are sold at fairs with faces painted on them called "Dying Pigs"? As the air rushes out they give forth an inhuman wail. That, Sugden, was your final touch. You arranged one of those in the room. The mouth of it was stopped up with a peg, but that peg was connected to the cord. When you pulled on the cord the peg came out and the pig began to deflate. On top of the falling furniture came the scream of the "Dying Pig".'

He turned once more to the others.

'You see now what it was that Pilar Estravados picked up? The superintendent had hoped to get there in time to retrieve that little wisp of rubber before anyone noticed it. However, he took it from Pilar quickly enough in his most official manner. But remember *he never mentioned that incident to anyone.* In itself, that was a singularly suspicious fact. I heard of it from Magdalene Lee and tackled him about it. He was prepared for that eventuality. He had snipped a piece from Mr Lee's rubber spongebag and produced that, together with a wooden peg. Superficially it answered to the same description – a fragment of rubber and a piece of wood. It meant, as I realized at the time, absolutely nothing! But, fool that I was, I did not at once say; "This means nothing, *so it cannot have been there, and Superintendent Sugden is lying . . .*" No, I foolishly went on trying to find an explanation for it. It was not until Mademoiselle Estravados was playing with a balloon that burst, and she cried out that it must have been a burst balloon she picked up in Simeon Lee's room, that I saw the truth.

'You see now how everything fits in? The improbable struggle, *which is necessary to establish a false time of death*; the locked door – so that nobody shall find the body too soon; the dying man's scream. The crime is now logical and reasonable.

'But from the moment that Pilar Estravados cried aloud her discovery about the balloon, she was a source of danger to the murderer. And if that remark had been heard by him from the house (which it well might, for her voice was high and clear and the windows were open), she herself was in considerable danger. Already she had given the murderer one very nasty moment. She had said, speaking of old Mr Lee, "He must have been very good-looking when he was young." And had added, speaking directly to Sugden: "*Like you.*" She meant that literally, and Sugden knew it. No wonder Sugden went purple in the face and nearly choked. It was so unexpected and so deadly dangerous. He hoped, after that, to fix the guilt on her, but it proved unexpectedly difficult, since, as the old man's portionless granddaughter, she had obviously no motive for the crime. Later, when he overheard from the house her clear, high voice calling out its remark about the balloon, he decided on desperate measures. He set that booby trap when we were at lunch. Luckily, almost by a miracle, it failed . . .'

There was dead silence. Then Sugden said quietly:

'When were you sure?'

Poirot said:

'I was not quite sure till I brought home a false moustache and tried it on Simeon Lee's picture. Then – the face that looked at me was yours.'

Sugden said:

'God rot his soul in hell! I'm glad I did it!'

PART 7

DECEMBER 28TH

I

Lydia Lee said:

'Pilar, I think you had better stay with us until we can arrange something definite for you.'

Pilar said meekly:

'You are very good, Lydia. You are nice. You forgive people quite easily without making a fuss about it.'

Lydia said, smiling:

'I still call you Pilar, though I suppose your name is something else.'

'Yes, I am really Conchita Lopez.'

'Conchita is a pretty name too.'

'You are really almost too nice, Lydia. But you don't need to be bothered by me. I am going to marry Stephen, and we are going to South Africa.'

Lydia said, smiling:

'Well, that rounds off things very nicely.'

Pilar said timidly:

'Since you have been so kind, do you think, Lydia, that one day we might come back and stay with you – perhaps for Christmas – and then we could have the crackers and the burning raisins and those shiny things on a tree and the little snowmen?'

'Certainly, you shall come and have a real English Christmas.'

'That will be lovely. You see, Lydia, I feel that this year it was not a nice Christmas at all.'

Lydia caught her breath. She said:

'No, it was not a nice Christmas . . .'

II

Harry said:

'Well, goodbye, Alfred. Don't suppose you'll be troubled by seeing much of me. I'm off to Hawaii. Always meant to live there if I had a bit of money.'

Alfred said:

'Goodbye, Harry. I expect you'll enjoy yourself. I hope so.'

Harry said rather awkwardly:

'Sorry I riled you so much, old man. Rotten sense of humour I've got. Can't help trying to pull a fellow's leg.'

Alfred said with an effort:

'Suppose I must learn to take a joke.'

Harry said with relief:

'Well – so-long.'

III

Alfred said:

'David, Lydia and I have decided to sell up this place. I thought perhaps you'd like some of the things that were our mother's – her chair and that footstool. You were always her favourite.'

David hesitated a minute. Then he said slowly:

'Thanks for the thought, Alfred, but do you know, I don't think I will. I don't want anything out of the house. I feel it's better to break with the past altogether.'

Alfred said:

'Yes, I understand. Maybe you're right.'

IV

George said:

'Well, goodbye, Alfred. Goodbye, Lydia. What a terrible time we have been through. There's the trial coming on, too. I suppose the whole disgraceful story is bound to come out – Sugden being – er – my father's son. One couldn't arrange for it to be put to him, I suppose, that it would be better if he pleaded advanced Communist views and dislike of my father as a capitalist – something of that kind?'

Lydia said:

'My dear George, do you really imagine that a man like Sugden would tell lies to soothe *our* feelings?'

George said:

'Er – perhaps not. No, I see your point. All the same, the man must be mad. Well, goodbye again.'

Magdalene said:

'*Good*bye. Next year do let's all go to the Riviera or somewhere for Christmas and be really gay.'

George said:

'Depends on the Exchange.'

Magdalene said:

'Darling, don't be *mean*.'

V

Alfred came out on the terrace. Lydia was bending over a stone sink. She straightened up when she saw him.

He said with a sigh:

'Well – they've all gone.'

Lydia said:

'Yes – what a blessing.'

'It is, rather.'

Alfred said:

'You'll be glad to leave here.'

She asked:

'Will you mind very much?'

'No, I shall be glad. There are so many interesting things we can do together. To live on here would be to be constantly reminded of that nightmare. Thank God it's all over!'

Lydia said:

'Thanks to Hercule Poirot.'

'Yes. You know, it was really amazing the way everything fell into place when he explained it.'

'I know. Like when you finish a jig-saw puzzle and all the queer-shaped bits you swear won't fit in anywhere find their places quite naturally.'

Alfred said:

'There's one little thing that never fitted in. What *was* George doing *after* he telephoned? Why wouldn't he say?'

'Don't you know? I knew all the time. He was having a look

through your papers on your desk.'

'Oh! No, Lydia, no one would do a thing like that!'

'George would. He's frightfully curious about money matters. But of course he couldn't say so. He'd have had to be actually in the dock before he'd have owned up to that.'

Alfred said:

'Are you making another garden?'

'Yes.'

'What is it this time?'

'I think,' said Lydia, 'it's an attempt at the Garden of Eden. A new version – without any serpent – and Adam and Eve are definitely middle-aged.'

Alfred said gently:

'Dear Lydia, how patient you have been all these years. You have been very good to me.'

Lydia said:

'But, you see, Alfred, I love you . . .'

VI

Colonel Johnson said:

'God bless my soul!' Then he said:

'Upon my word!' And finally, once more: 'God bless my soul!'

He leaned back in his chair and stared at Poirot. He said plaintively:

'My best man! What's the police coming to?'

Poirot said:

'Even policemen have private lives! Sugden was a very proud man.'

Colonel Johnson shook his head.

To relieve his feelings he kicked at the logs in the grate. He said jerkily:

'I always say – nothing like a wood fire.'

Hercule Poirot, conscious of the draughts round his neck, thought to himself:

'*Pour moi*, every time the central heating . . .'